of love & life

ISBN 978-0-276-44448-7

www.readersdigest.co.uk

Published in the United Kingdom by Vivat Direct Limited (t/a Reader's Digest),
157 Edgware Road, London W2 2HR

and in Canada
www.rd.ca

The Reader's Digest Association (Canada) ULC, 1100 René-Lévesque Blvd. West, Montréal,
Québec, H3B 5H5 Canada

Three novels selected and condensed
by Reader's Digest

The Reader's Digest Association Inc., London, Montreal

CONTENTS

ERICA JAMES
The Queen of New Beginnings
9

SARAH ADDISON ALLEN
The Girl Who Chased the Moon
185

LINDA HOLEMAN
The Saffron Gate
305

The Queen of New Beginnings
ERICA JAMES

I've always enjoyed writing from a male perspective and it was the character of Clayton Miller that was the catalyst for this particular story. He became established in my head and I could hear his voice clearly long before I started to write. I imagined him as a misunderstood man, lost and adrift, a man who at times is his own worst enemy. But, above all, I saw him as quirkily likable with his heart in the right place.

'The Queen of New Beginnings' is one of those novels that came together so easily it seemingly wrote itself. Often the process is slow and painful, but this book was a joy from start to finish. I hope readers will feel the same.

Erica

Chapter One

CLAYTON MILLER had a new hobby. Some might argue it was more of an obsession than a hobby and certainly he knew Stacey wouldn't hesitate to use the word 'obsession'. She would probably say that it was yet another example of his rampant self-absorption.

Maybe she was right. Either way, he didn't care. So what if he now spent what Stacey would describe as an unnatural amount of time writing his obituary? It served the purpose of keeping his mind active while distracting it at the same time.

The obituary page was often what he read first in a newspaper; he enjoyed peering in through the gap in the curtains of a stranger's life. Frequently, though, he found himself speculating just how accurate the descriptions were. The question he was facing with his own obituary was just how truthful he should be. The lure to embellish his life with a flourish of colour here and there was proving strong.

> Clayton Miller, aged only forty-four and undoubtedly one of the most prolific and best comedy scriptwriters this country has produced, tragically died on his way home to his weekend retreat in the country from an award ceremony, during which he'd been given a much-deserved lifetime achievement award for his contribution to the world of comedy; the standing ovation he received went on for a record twelve minutes and fifty-two seconds. His Bentley Continental GTC Convertible was involved in a head-on collision with a Vauxhall Astra driven by an unknown man. The unknown man survived the crash, but will spend the rest of his life with the death of a truly exceptional writer on his conscience.

In a bizarre twist of fate it would later be revealed that the unknown man was none other than Barry Osborne, Clayton's one-time best friend and writing partner.

He was not a vindictive man by nature, but circumstances had altered Clayton's thinking when it came to Barry—or Lucky Bazza as he thought of him. He couldn't go so far as to kill him off in his imagination or wish a gruesome life-threatening illness on him, but he did think it appropriate that if Clayton should be unfortunate enough to meet an untimely end, Lucky Bazza should suffer for it. If only with a guilty conscience. A fair exchange in Clayton's opinion, given that Bazza had robbed Clayton not only of his writing career, but his long-term partner as well.

But so much for embellishment. A truthful obituary would sadly fall well short of this glowing tribute. All that would stand up to a lie detector would be Clayton's age. By no stretch of the imagination could he now be described as prolific. Nor did he own a Bentley. Or a house in the country. And since he hadn't written anything more coherent than a shopping list or his obituary in the past three years, there would be some people who would call him a has-been. A failure.

If it hadn't been for recent events—he squeezed his eyes shut at the memory—he would be lucky to get more than a couple of lines in the papers: **Clayton Miller, co-writer and creator of the hit series *Joking Aside*, died today aged forty-four. Separated from his long-term girlfriend six months ago, he lived alone with only his writer's block for company.**

But if he were to die right now, as a consequence of recent events he would garner quite a few column inches. Probably they would point the finger at his mental balance and say he'd been off his rocker. They might even hint that his death was not from natural causes, that he had engineered it.

He opened his eyes. Another five minutes trapped in this taxi and engineering his suicide would look remarkably appealing. The car's lurching motion was causing his stomach to pitch and heave. He was sure that his face was as green as the toxic, pine tree-shaped air freshener dangling from the rearview mirror.

Clayton blamed his current predicament on Glen, his agent.

It had been Glen's idea for him to hide out in some off-the-beaten-track place where the press wouldn't find him. And whatever hellish place he was destined to take refuge in, he hoped the driver knew the way. There was no sign of any satnav equipment on the dashboard, which Clayton took to be a good sign. It ruled out the possibility of a bossy-voiced woman misdirecting them down a one-way track to a ravine and their certain death.

Death. It kept popping into his thoughts. Was he suicidal?

Murderous, more like. He could happily take out all those journalists who had written about him lately and never experience a moment's regret. It wouldn't solve a damned thing, but since when had revenge been about solving anything?

He wiped at the steamed-up window and looked out. Nothing. Just miles of empty fields and dry-stone walls. With the light fading, it looked suspiciously like the end of the world. He closed his eyes.

It was dark when the taxi finally came to a stop. The sound of the handbrake being yanked up woke Clayton. He stepped out of the car and stretched. Weary and dishevelled, he was in need of a hot shower.

He looked up at the house and didn't like what he saw. It was huge. Huge and unwelcoming. It made him want to run and hide.

'It's some place you've got yourself here,' the driver said as he hauled Clayton's luggage out of the boot.

'It's not mine,' Clayton answered him.

'Just visiting, then?'

Eager not to part with any information about himself—Glen had warned him to keep his mouth shut—he shrugged and nodded evasively. He paid the man and watched the taillights of the Nissan disappear down the lengthy, straight drive and into the night.

He let himself in and at once experienced a pang of longing for the toxic warmth of the taxi. The house was icy-cold. Was this his punishment? To freeze in hell? How Stacey and Lucky Bazza would love that.

'**O**K, Alice, we're all done here. That last bit works perfectly now. Thanks for doing it again. You're a star.'

Alice looked through the glass to where Josie and the sound engineer were sitting; she nodded at the thumbs-up sign they were giving her. She took off her headphones and stretched. It had been a tiring day. Eight hours of speaking like a chipmunk would wear anyone out.

Alice first discovered she had a talent for mimicry when she was eleven years old. Her mother had been away in London and her father, in a frenzy of creativity, had locked himself in his darkroom at the top of the house. Which meant Alice was left to her own devices, a state of affairs she was more than used to. On this particular Monday morning, being between au pairs, she had knocked on her father's door to ask him to drive her to school. Getting no response, and being a resourceful child, she had taken matters into her own hands. She had gone back downstairs and dialled the number for the school secretary's office. She could have walked to school but it would have taken for ever, and it would also have drawn attention to her father's somewhat casual attitude to parenting. And anyway, Alice hadn't felt like school that day. 'I'm very sorry,' she had said in her mother's low velvet-smooth voice—the voice that millions were familiar with both on radio and television—'This is Mrs Barrett and I'm calling to say that Alice is suffering from a horrible stomach bug and will be staying at home today.'

She had spent most of the day lying on the sofa watching corny old movies, happily dreaming one day of being an actress herself. Her father appeared in the middle of the afternoon and didn't bat an eyelid at the sight of her. 'You're home early,' he had remarked.

From mimicking her mother, she moved on to impersonating her teachers. This raised her stock among her peers—if not her teachers—and further fuelled her ambition to be an actress.

Five years ago she might have believed that there was still a chance of that dream coming true. But now, at the age of thirty-one, she had accepted that things hadn't turned out quite as she'd hoped; stardom had passed her by on the other side of the road.

Instead she did voiceovers, along with reading for audio books. She was doing rather well with children's books right now and the author James Montgomery—be still her beating heart—was, as her agent told her, her number one fan and would have no one else read his books. His sales were growing but experience told Alice this was a double-edged sword. If his books became massively successful, a big-name actor would be brought in to take her place. Some years back she had been the original voice of This Little Piggy—a porcine version of My Little Pony. Her voice, so she had been told, was perfect when the television advertisement was first aired but, six months later, when sales for This Little Piggy had gone through the roof, her agent telephoned with the bad news that Zoë Wanamaker had been signed up in her place.

So yes, Alice was pragmatic enough to know that James Montgomery might well be her number one fan now, but things had a nasty habit of changing. Whatever the future held, she was quite used to taking disappointment on the chin and convincing herself that something better—a new beginning—was just round the corner.

She left the recording studio thirty minutes later and drove home. Whenever she told people what she did for a living, they always assumed that she was up and down to London to some kind of glamorous Media

Land studio, mixing with the rich and famous. When she explained that the bulk of her work was done in a converted coach house on the outskirts of Nottingham, her work suddenly didn't seem so thrilling. And nor was it: it could be painstaking and exhausting. But at least the work her agent found her was plentiful and varied. She could be in a studio in Manchester one day doing an advert for a radio station, the next she could be down in London providing the voice for a major bank and its telephone-operated accounts.

It took her longer than usual to complete the journey home to Stonebridge and before she had got the key in the door of her cottage, she heard footsteps behind her. She turned, hoping it wasn't who she thought it might be. She really wasn't in the mood.

Sure enough it was Bob the Body Builder. 'Hello, Bob,' she said. 'What are you doing there, lurking like a mugger in the shadows?'

'Hey, no one who looks as good as this lurks in the shadows.' To prove his point, he flexed his biceps and thrust out his colossal chest.

Despite the cold November weather, he was dressed in his customary bursting-at-the-seams T-shirt and baggy track-suit bottoms. Goodness only knew how many hours of weightlifting he was doing now or what quantity of steroids he was consuming. His exposed flesh was sunbed-tanned and as hairless as a baby's bottom.

'So what can I do for you?'

'Mum needs a favour. She said to ask you to come round the moment you got home.' Suddenly Bob the Body Builder sounded like a six-year-old boy. Sweet.

'Tell her I'll be there in five minutes.'

He puffed out his chest again. 'How about that drink you're just dying to have with me tonight?'

Ah, not so sweet. 'Sorry, Bob, it's been a long day.'

He shrugged. 'Your loss.'

'I'll do my best to try and get over it,' she said. She turned the key in the lock of her door and stepped inside.

Ever since Bob and his mother had moved in next door last year, Ronnetta Tanner had been trying to fix Alice up with her beloved son. 'He'd be perfect for you,' Ronnetta had said. In what way exactly, Alice wasn't entirely sure. The only thing they had in common was their age.

'What'll it be, then?' Ronnetta asked Alice in her gravelly voice.

'I'll have my usual, but make it a small one, please, Ronnetta. Go easy on the gin. What was it you wanted to ask me?'

Ronnetta handed Alice her tumbler and settled herself in the chair opposite.

'I've been let down by one of my girls, and I was wondering if you could help me out. I need someone tomorrow.'

'What kind of a job is it this time?'

'Cleaner, possibly a bit of housekeeping thrown in.'

'And how many times a week would I be needed?'

'That's up to the client really. I said to the chap who's organised it all on behalf of the client that we'd play it by ear, see how things go. You'll have to do the man's shopping, though. He doesn't drive.'

'What about cooking?'

'I don't think you'll be expected to do that.'

Alice considered Ronnetta's request. Since Ronnetta had started her cleaning agency, Alice had often helped her neighbour out when she'd been let down. It wasn't that she needed the money; it was more a matter of enjoying the opportunity to poke about in someone else's life. 'How long will you need me for?' she asked.

'Only for the next week or two. By then I'll have found a replacement for the girl who's messed me about. Usual wages apply.'

'Go on then, why not?' Alice gave in. 'It looks like I'm in for a quiet fortnight anyway. What time do I have to be on parade tomorrow?'

'Eleven o'clock.'

'Is it here in the village?'

'On the outskirts, on the Matlock road. It's vast, and very remote. Real back-of-beyond stuff, half a mile from the main road. Not a single neighbour on the doorstep. I'll get the address for you.'

While Ronnetta was out of the room, Alice took a long, thoughtful sip of her drink. Huge place, outskirts of Stonebridge. On the Matlock road. What were the chances? A huge place with not a single neighbour? It sounded very like Cuckoo House.

'Here you are,' Ronnetta said when she returned and handed over a slip of paper to Alice. 'The client is a Mr Shannon and he's staying at Cuckoo House. Have you heard of it?'

'It certainly rings a bell.'

Out of a choice of seven bedrooms, Clayton had picked one that wasn't the largest, but it had an interesting windowed turret in the farthest corner of the room. It also had a panoramic view of the garden and a more extensive view of a whole lot of nothing. The nothingness was green, hilly and rain-sodden. Wet and depressingly dreary, it was pure hillbilly country. He could understand why Glen had said it would be the perfect place to lie low.

Glen had phoned him late last night, just as Clayton had given up ever figuring out how to switch on the boiler and inject some warmth into the place. 'Everything all right?' Glen had said.

'No! Everything is not all right! The boiler doesn't work, I'm dying of cold and there's nothing to eat.'

'Don't complain, Clay. With only twenty-four hours' notice I've found you a house with furniture, electricity, water, even the Internet. So yes, feel free to go ahead and call me Mr Wonderful. Just don't expect me to throw in room service as well.'

'Tell me again about these friends of yours. What kind of people are they that want to live in this place? I swear my nearest neighbour must be at least ten miles away.'

'Craig and Anthea moved up there for a change of lifestyle. They spend the winter months in the Caribbean. Remember, they're letting you stay there as a favour to me. Don't let me down. You've trashed your career; please don't trash their home in a fit of pique as well. Oh, and don't forget, the cleaning agency is sending someone round in the morning. About eleven, I think. Be nice to whoever it is. You'll be totally dependent on the person they send.'

'So that's two things I have to remember. One: I must not trash the house, and two: I must be nice to the cleaner. Anything else?'

'Yes. Sort your head out. And when you've done that, try doing some writing. After all, what else are you going to do up there?'

Good bloody question, Clayton had thought.

At twenty minutes past eleven, Clayton gave up waiting for the sound of the doorbell and decided to make himself a cup of coffee. He turned on the tap and water immediately bounced off the rim of the kettle and shot up into his face and down his front.

That was when he heard the doorbell. He banged the kettle down and traversed the mile to the front door.

'You're late,' he said, wiping his face with his scarf. 'Timekeeping not your speciality, I take it?'

For a moment the girl, swamped in a thick padded jacket, didn't say anything. She just stood there in the porch, sheltering from the rain. Her eyes, though, were darting about, looking beyond and round him, as if she were casing the joint.

'I sorry for late,' she said eventually. 'I lose myself. You going to keep me here on doorstep all day, mister? Why you covered in water?'

He frowned at the foreign accent. That was all he needed, a lippy Polish cleaner. There again, she didn't look Polish. Romanian or Bulgarian perhaps. Now that she'd pushed back the hood of her jacket, he could see her hair was long and wavy and dark brown. As dark as her eyes, which, now they had stopped darting about, were assessing him. Her stare was disconcertingly direct.

She shrugged and, armed with a plethora of cleaning equipment, she stepped inside. 'Thank you. A cup of coffee before I start working very hard for you. Thank you, mister.'

He closed the door. 'Are you Polish?' he asked.

The dark assessing eyes leaped to his. 'How many languages you speak?'

He silently groaned. Great. Her English wasn't up to much. 'I asked if you were Polish,' he said, this time more loudly.

'And I said, how many languages you speak?'

'Just English.'

'Oh, so mister who no speak anything but English thinks I am speaking Polish. Well, clean out ears, mister.'

Stunned at her rudeness, his jaw dropped. The cheeky little strumpet! He said, 'I didn't say that. All I meant was that you *sound* Polish.'

'Well, I not Polish. You insult me. This way to kitchen?'

He chased after her down the stone-flagged corridor. He wasn't going to stand for this sort of behaviour. 'I think there's been a mistake,' he tried. 'The agency must have sent you to the wrong house.'

'No mistake, mister. This is Cuckoo House. I am Katya. All is correct.'

He searched again for a way out. 'And you're here in the UK legally? I don't want any trouble.'

She skewered him with a look. 'You read too much newspaper shit.'

He scoffed. 'I assure you I do no such thing. I wouldn't wipe my arse with a single one of those rags.'

'And don't get no funny ideas about me doing that for you, mister.' She wagged a finger at him. 'You go to toilet on your own.'

She turned her back on him, shook off her coat and began sorting noisily through her collection of cloths and cleaning products.

He walked round to the other side of the table, using it as a barrier. 'So if you're not from Poland, where are you from?'

'Does it matter where I from?'

'I'm just trying to be polite.'

'Well, you not polite. You rude. You very rude man.'

'You think it's an insult for someone to enquire about your cultural background? And if you don't mind me saying, your reaction to me thinking you were Polish smacks of racism.'

She looked up sharply. 'What's that you say? You want to smack me? Let me tell you, mister. One smack from you and I report you to police!'

He put his hands up. '*Whoa!* That's not what I said.' Choosing his words with extra care, he added, 'I think it might be better if the agency sends someone who can speak English properly.'

'Now you accuse me of being stupid. Mister, I plenty smart enough. My brain goes whir, whir, all day long.'

Clayton could believe it. Her tongue, too. 'Tell me,' he said, no longer caring whether he offended her, 'does your yapper ever stop?'

She looked at him blankly. She had a quirky face, he decided, wide cheekbones and a small pointy chin. Almost pixie-like. 'Do you ever stop talking, is what I asked,' he said.

Her lips curved into a faint smile. 'I know. I proving you wrong.'

'How so?'

'Mister, you really are as stupid as you look. I was proving I can stop my yapper any time I choose. And I like my coffee with no sugar.'

Clayton gave up. *Stupid!* She had actually called him stupid. Didn't she know who was paying her wages? He went over to the kettle. 'And when does the mothership come back for you?' he muttered.

'Nothing wrong with my hearing, mister. I no alien. And if you want the truth, I am from Latvia. You even hear of my country?'

It was his appalling rudeness that had set Alice off. That and her apprehension about being back at Cuckoo House. She had come close to telling Ronnetta she had changed her mind about taking on the job, but curiosity had got the better of her. Undoubtedly, however, she had messed up in grand style. She had given the client every reason to complain and demand someone else take her place.

It wasn't the first time she had adopted a different persona when she helped Ronnetta out—not that Ronnetta knew that. It was the actress in her. Sometimes she wore a blonde wig and pretended she was Astrid from Dusseldorf. But Katya was new. She had been devised very much on the spur of the moment. It had been fun putting such a rude man in his place and she would make no apology for that. She had watched him clatter ineptly about the kitchen making the coffee. Tall and thin, he seemed all angles. She wondered if he always looked so crumpled and angry. Interestingly, his eyes looked younger than the rest of him.

The coffee finally made, he had taken himself off, leaving her, he'd said pointedly, to get on with her work.

It was difficult to pin an exact age on him; he could be mid-forties or early fifties. Oddly, there was something familiar about him. He'd look a lot better if he tidied himself up, though. A shave and a brush through his thick unruly hair would be a good start. The tatty old pullover he was wearing was fraying at the cuffs and the scarf round his neck was distinctly moth-eaten. Overall he cut an eccentric and shambolic figure. She could almost feel sorry for him. Almost.

She took a sip of the coffee he'd made and dismissed him from her mind. She had more important things to think of. Like having a good snoop round. To establish, after all this time, exactly how she really felt being back where she had grown up.

And where better to start than upstairs in her bedroom?

But first, how about some heat? The house was bone-numbingly cold. She went over to the nearest radiator and touched it. Hmm . . .

As he warmed his hands on his mug of coffee, Clayton considered his latest attempt at his obituary on his laptop. This time it revolved round being found frozen to death by a crazy Latvian housekeeper.

The room he had retreated to was directly beneath the bedroom he had chosen and he was sitting at an antique writing desk in the window of the turret. He gazed disconsolately out of the window. It was still raining. The sky was still grey. It still depressed the hell out of him.

Somewhere in the faraway distance, he could hear Katya moving about upstairs. He had made up his mind. Just as soon as she had stocked the cupboards and fridge with food, he'd call Glen and insist he speak to the agency and demand someone else to shop and clean for him.

A scratching noise behind him had him spinning round in his chair.

Mice? He cocked his head and listened hard. There it was again. Not mice, he concluded.

Seconds passed. Tick . . . tick . . . gurgle . . . tick.

Was it possible?

He went over to one of the two radiators in the room. *Yes!* Heat. Glorious heat. The girl was a miracle worker.

Of all the bedrooms he could have picked, Mr Shannon had chosen Alice's old bedroom. But, like the kitchen downstairs, which was sleek and showroom-smart, it bore very little resemblance to the room of

Alice's childhood. When it had been Alice's bedroom, it had contained an eclectic mix of rugs and cumbersome furniture, including her great-aunt Eliza's rocking chair. Alice had spent hours rocking in it, either lost in a book or simply daydreaming while gazing out of the windows.

As an only child she had learned to lose herself in her imagination and would often write, direct and star in her own one-woman shows. At the end of her bed there had been a large wooden trunk that had travelled the world with Great-Aunt Eliza. It had ended its life as Alice's dressing-up box and most of its contents—suits, evening dresses, scarves, beads, brooches, hats, shoes and handbags—had belonged to a woman that Alice remembered only from photographs.

As well as a dressing-up box, Alice also had an intriguing store of props to use in her shows. This was mostly down to her father, who had an obsessive eye for anything of a fanciful or theatrical nature. 'I came across this the other day and thought you might like it, Alice,' he would say. One day he presented her with an ornate birdcage with a stuffed mynah bird inside. Other 'finds' had included a top hat, a false beard, an old-fashioned telephone, a battered dinner gong and a scruffy pair of red tap shoes, which her father soon regretted giving her.

To Alice's disappointment the tap shoes fitted her for only a few months. But during those months she drove her parents to distraction by endlessly tap-tap-tapping her way round the house. If her parents were away she would dance until her legs ached. But if her father was home, he would crash into her room after only a few minutes, throw her over his shoulder and threaten to chuck her down the stairs if she made any more noise. She never actually thought he would, but on one occasion the au pair thought he was serious. At the sight of Alice being dangled over the banisters, she burst into tears with fright. She packed her bags and left that very evening in a taxi, saying she couldn't stay in such a madhouse a moment longer.

Thalia from Athens had been one of many young au pairs who came to Cuckoo House. They rarely stayed long. Some said they couldn't cope with the isolation, or the unconventional way the household was run. Others, the prettier ones, had a different reason for leaving.

Untidiness was a sign of a creative mind, so Alice's mother maintained. Which seemed to be the family excuse for the chaotic state of the house, a chaos that guaranteed nothing could ever be found when it was needed. Her parents would frequently drive themselves wild looking for their car keys or a pen. Shrieking at the top of their voices, they would accuse each other of moving whatever it was they couldn't find.

Invariably it was Alice who would find what they were looking for.

So much for Cuckoo House when she was growing up, when it had been a casual, messy and informal environment.

Under its current ownership, it looked and felt very different. Her old bedroom reeked of good taste and sophistication, and of order. Most striking of all was the enormous bed with its intricately carved headboard. Not so striking was that Mr Shannon hadn't bothered to cover the duvet or pillows.

After a brief search, she found fresh bed linen and began making up the bed, allowing herself once again to explore her memories.

One of her earliest memories was when her father had returned home from one of his many trips abroad. He had tiptoed into her room and woken her with a scratchy kiss. He'd given her a toy koala.

As a naturalist photographer of some repute, Bruce Barrett was frequently away for months at a time. His work was always being featured in the *National Geographic* magazine. When he was home he was more often than not at the top of the house in his darkroom. There was no guessing what kind of mood he'd be in when he emerged blinking mole-like into the light. He could be sulky and withdrawn, or waging war on anything or anyone who was unfortunate enough to get in his way. At other times he had a ridiculous sense of the dramatic and would dress up as a pirate, complete with wooden peg leg and eye patch. Waving a fake cutlass he would chase Alice round the house until her giddy excitement tipped over into high-pitched squealing terror. There were other times, though, when he would sit for hours at a time quietly reading to her. She often fell asleep in his arms.

Alice's mother, Dr Barbara Barrett, was a psychiatrist who became a media family and relationship expert. By the time Alice was ten, Dr Barbara Barrett was writing a weekly column for a national newspaper and appeared regularly on the television and radio. Yet for all her so-called professional expertise, Barbara Barrett had no handle on her own domestic situation. She regularly forgot Alice's birthday and left most of her care to whichever au pair was currently employed. Her husband was beyond her comprehension, or control. These two larger-than-life characters had a volatile love-hate relationship; they couldn't cope with each other on a full-time basis, nor could they live without each other. Any agony aunt worth her salt would have told them to take greater care of each other. Had they done so, who knows how differently life would have been at Cuckoo House in the years that followed?

Chapter Two

CLAYTON HAD EATEN WELL last night, he'd slept, he was warm, it had stopped raining and the coffee was made. The only dilemma to the day was whether to have two fried eggs with his sausages and bacon, or one. What the hell, he'd have two. Ooh, yeah, life was good.

He switched off the gas, tipped the frying pan with well-practised precision and slid his breakfast onto a warmed plate. 'There, the perfect breakfast.' Clayton often held conversations with himself. He used to quip that it was the only way he could participate in an intelligent discussion. He tucked in with relish. 'My compliments to the chef. And to lippy Katya for doing my shopping.'

For all their getting off on the wrong foot yesterday, he was grateful for what Katya had done for him. She had shown him how the heating system worked and had bought him everything he'd put on his shopping list, plus other things he hadn't given a thought to, such as toilet paper and tissues. He had given her a wad of cash and, convinced that she would try to con him, he'd checked all the items off against the till receipts when she'd left. But everything was just as it should be.

He had decided not to call Glen. For now, the girl could stay. Her next scheduled visit was for the day after tomorrow. She had offered to cook for him, but he'd said he was quite capable of cooking for himself.

Stacey would have sneered at that. 'You, cook?' she would have said. 'Don't make me laugh.'

How he had ever got sucked into Stacey's gravitational force field, he didn't know. He used to say that they were such opposites that they'd met at their polar parts coming in the opposite direction.

Actually, he knew exactly how they had been drawn together and who was responsible: Lucky Bazza. Bazza had got himself a new date lined up and had suggested Clayton and the date's best friend join them at the pub to make a foursome. This was back in 1994, in the days when they were sharing a flat in Clapham and struggling to make ends meet. They were both twenty-nine and beginning to think they had hit a dead end, when suddenly their script had been accepted by the BBC.

They had been writing together since their days at university, mostly gags and sketches for up-and-coming comedians. Their goal was to write situation comedy, but not just any old sitcom; they wanted to claim the crown of Best-Ever Sitcom. Which they did. They racked up record ratings and made stars of the actors. The fourth and final series of *Joking Aside* had been broadcast five years ago, yet only last year it had come out top again in a poll to establish the best-ever sitcom.

Bazza hadn't been able to attend the award ceremony at the Grosvenor Hotel in London; he'd been over in Los Angeles, but doubtless he would have made a far more eloquent and self-effacing acceptance speech. But then, had Bazza been around to accept the award, Clayton wouldn't have gone within a mile of the place. He and Bazza hadn't spoken for more than two years. Their relationship, as Bazza repeatedly referred to their writing partnership in the countless interviews he gave, had lost its creative spark. That wasn't all it had lost.

Normally only too quick to attend a lavish do, Stacey hadn't accompanied Clayton to the Grosvenor; she had stayed at home, saying she didn't want to be seen in public with him when, once again, he would make an idiot of himself. But Glen had been there. Through thick and thin, his agent had always been there for Clayton.

It had meant a lot to him that when Bazza made the unilateral decision to end their writing partnership—claiming he felt stifled—Glen, who had represented them both, stuck with Clayton. It was a decision he must have regretted. Had he chosen Bazza, he would have earned much more than he did with Clayton. Not that Clayton was hard up. Far from it. The royalties from *Joking Aside* showed no sign of drying up. Even if he never wrote another successful script again, he would be comfortable for the rest of his life.

But he missed the buzz that writing used to give him. His life felt meaningless without a script in front of him. It was his identity. And it was thanks to Bazza that he couldn't write. He had been gutted when Bazza had ended the partnership. To his eternal shame, he had resorted to begging Bazza to reconsider.

'No, I want to write on my own. It's something I've wanted to do for some time. I'm sorry, Clayton, it's over. We've gone as far as we can.'

In the days, weeks and months that followed, Clayton swung from high optimism that he was free to write the best stuff he'd ever written to feeling incapable of writing a single line of dialogue.

Then his parents died. One minute they were both alive and nagging him to visit, the next his father died of a heart attack and two months later his mother suffered a massive stroke and died a week later. It was then that he discovered that while they had both been supremely proud of what he had achieved, they hadn't trusted it. After his mother's funeral, he had found a building society book. It had over £450,000 in it. It was the exact amount Clayton had sent his parents month by month to provide them with a bit of luxury. But they hadn't spent a penny of his success. There had been a handwritten note in the pages—and it said that when they died, the money they had saved was for Clayton, just in case things hadn't worked out for him.

If there had been any uncertainty before that he was experiencing a phase of writer's block, losing his parents and squaring up to his own mortality ensured there was not a shred of doubt from then on.

Meanwhile, Lucky Bazza's writing career went from strength to strength. While Clayton was deeply mired in a state of inertia, Bazza had written a film script for a major box-office hit. Clayton had tried hard to pretend that Lucky Bazza's success didn't bother him, but the truth was it hurt like hell. He had believed it to be the bitterest pill of all to swallow. But then Stacey left him for Bazza.

Throughout this dark, depressing period of his life, and presumably in an effort to raise his flagging spirits, Stacey had kept up a steady onslaught of derogatory comments. 'You're not funny at all,' she complained. 'I can't remember the last time you made me laugh.'

He couldn't remember ever telling her that he was funny. Why would he? Comedy doesn't work that way. Everyone knows that. Everyone except for Stacey, maybe.

When it became obvious that Clayton was not going to earn his agent any money from fresh writing, Glen began getting him appearances on panel shows for TV and radio. He rapidly made a name for himself as the grumpy, dry-witted, mordant guest. Then one week when he was appearing on a topical news show, he let rip with a vociferous attack on the guest host, a sickening man with a squeaky-clean image. Clayton couldn't abide him. Off camera, the squeaky-clean image was anything but squeaky-clean. 'Let me stop you right there, Baby Doll,' Clayton had said when the host had started to describe Clayton as a one-hit wonder who couldn't write without Barry Osborne.

Clayton's diatribe made the headlines the next day and, ever since, when an example of a truly excruciating onscreen moment was called for, the clip of him outing the host as a cokehead with a penchant for dressing up in baby-doll nightdresses while indulging in sex with men twenty years his junior was shown. The man's proclivities were well known in certain showbiz circles, and Clayton didn't regret his outburst, or the man's subsequent downfall from prime-time television.

For weeks afterwards Clayton was hot property. Every newspaper and chat-show host wanted to interview him, probably in the hope that he would let rip with some other salacious exposé. He was glad when the circus left town and the telephone stopped ringing.

Stacey wasn't so happy. He had never been interested in being Mr Showbiz, but Stacey had loved the razzmatazz of an opening night or the chance of being snapped by the paparazzi. He'd played along initially, knowing that it pleased her, but when they'd reached the sniping stage of their relationship, he told her he would sooner stay at home playing Scrabble. Stacey's response was to accuse him of being small-minded. Later, when she announced that she was leaving him for Bazza, she said his small-mindedness wasn't his only area of deficiency. Small in the trouser department? That was news to him.

Gravitational force fields were odd things. He had been sucked into Bazza's life, then Stacey's, and now here he was holed up miles from anywhere pretending his name was Shannon, and with only a cheeky Latvian housekeeper for intermittent company. Once again he was hot property, but this time it was because he'd made a spectacularly stupid mistake. The press was baying for his blood. He was a hated man.

'You're not cross with me, then?'

Ronnetta laughed. 'Cross with you? I wish I'd been there to witness your performance! As well as all your previous ones.'

'But what if Mr Shannon complains to you?' Alice pressed. 'He was a bit weird, but he can't have failed to notice I was breathtakingly rude to him.'

'Stop beating yourself up. If he was going to complain, don't you think he would have done so by now?'

It was a good point. Twenty-four hours had passed since Alice's encounter with Mr Shannon, so maybe he'd decided not to make a fuss. He had seemed happy enough yesterday when she'd left him. She'd known, however, that the first thing he would have done after she'd driven off was to check the till receipts she had given him.

The mobile on Ronnetta's desk rang; she picked it up to take the call. Alice took it as her cue to leave. They both had work to do. A manuscript had arrived in the post that morning and Alice was eager to make a start on reading it.

She let herself in at the back door, put the kettle on and opened the Jiffy bag that contained the manuscript for a new children's book. The title of it was *Liar, Liar, Pants on Fire*. It made her think of the conversation she'd just had with Ronnetta.

Alice hadn't actually lied to her neighbour, but at no stage had she mentioned that she knew Cuckoo House, let alone admitted that she had grown up there. If, for some reason, that was now to come out, it would be rather embarrassing, to say the least.

The trouble with telling lies, even small ones, or lies by omission, is that once you start, there seems no way to stop. One way or another, Alice had been telling lies nearly all her adult life. She wasn't a crazy fantasist, it was more a matter of creating edited versions of the truth, of constructing separate universes within her own world in order to compartmentalise her life. The untruths she told were not designed to hurt anyone, merely to keep people out.

She had learned the art of crafting slight truths at the feet of two of the greatest technicians: her parents. Typical untruths for Alice's mother had been to lie about her age or to give the public the impression that her home life was other than it really was. As for Alice's father, a man who had never seemed to have a real grasp on reality, anything went for truth as far as he was concerned.

As a child Alice had lost herself in colourful landscapes of make-believe where anything was possible, so what could be more natural than to do the same as an adult? This wasn't as bad as it sounded; she did it only as a means of reinventing herself. Even then, not to the point that she was unrecognisable to herself.

Really, it was extraordinary how easy it was to make people think what you wanted them to think merely by glossing over the bits you didn't want them to know. Another trick was to deflect any unwanted questions by inviting people to talk about themselves. Yes, she would say if she was pushed to explain herself, she had spent her childhood living in the area . . . no, no brothers or sisters. . . and sadly both parents now dead . . . but tell me about you; where did you grow up?

Keeping people at arm's length was the easiest thing in the world to do. Allowing herself to be close to anyone was not so easy for Alice. Of course, she could have saved herself a lot of bother by not coming back to the area. But what did they say about criminals always returning to the scene of the crime?

Two and a half years ago, when she was approaching her twenty-eighth birthday and yet another relationship had unravelled, she had felt alone and aimless. Sitting in her London flat in Earls Court, she began to dream of the scenery of her childhood, the wide open spaces, the vast empty skies, the undulating hills and the sweeping stretches of moorland. She almost succeeded in resisting the beckoning call, and then she had learned that her father was dead. That he had been dead for some years. The beckoning call became a screaming siren.

There was nothing else for it. She had packed an overnight bag and headed north. Her plan was simple. She would visit Stonebridge safe in the knowledge that one look at it would be enough to convince her that it was the last place on earth she should move back to. She also believed that the visit would help resolve her feelings for her father.

It was a silly plan; there was only ever going to be one outcome. Sure enough, nine weeks later she moved into Dragonfly Cottage just five miles away from Cuckoo House. Her agent, Hazel, said that Alice couldn't have made a smarter move as a new recording studio had just started operating on the outskirts of Nottingham.

Ha, ha! The Queen of New Beginnings triumphs again!

Clayton had been busy. In readiness for Katya's visit he had been swotting up. She had accused him of knowing nothing about her country; well, today he'd gone online and read all he could about Latvia. He'd also looked up a few key words of vocabulary and had been practising his pronunciation. Nobody got away with making out he was a jackass by implying he was ignorant. No siree!

Perversely he was now looking forward to Katya's arrival. His hands clasped behind his head, he leaned back in the chair and stared out of the window. The windows looked directly out onto the front garden and, in the distance at the end of the drive, the white-painted metal gate and the thick impenetrable hedge. Laurel? Rhododendron? He racked his brain to think what else it could be. It didn't look coniferous. Holly? Beech? No, beech was deciduous. Any fool knew that. He scratched his chin and once again surprised himself at the feel of it. Two weeks without shaving and he had developed quite a beard.

It was raining again. Perhaps that was how it was going to be; whenever it was a Katya day it would rain. Certainly there was something of the storm cloud about her.

So far he hadn't put a foot outside of his prison walls. Instead, he had explored the house, starting from the ridiculously oversized entrance hall. Opposite was a dining room; beyond were two sitting rooms. At the back of the house was the kitchen and a collection of associated rooms—laundry, pantry and larder. A wide staircase led up to four bedrooms and three bathrooms on the first floor, and a smaller staircase gave access to a further three bedrooms and two more bathrooms.

At the end of the drive, he saw what looked like a red toy car stop at the gate. He checked his watch. Eleven o'clock. Katya was on time today. He drew a piece of paper towards him and quickly read through the vocabulary he'd been learning. No worries, he was word perfect.

'*Sveiki!*' he greeted her at the door. '*Ka jums klajas?*'

From the expression on her face, he could see she really was amazed. Who wouldn't be? He'd said hi, and enquired after her health. He let her in. '*Paldies par palidzibu*,' he continued. He was showing off now, thanking her for coming.

She still had the same look on her face.

'I've been learning Latvian,' he said. 'Aren't you impressed?' Of course she was. He could see it in her eyes, and by the way she had put a finger to her top lip and her face was reddening. But then her expression changed. She began to smile. Next thing she was giggling, a hand covering her mouth. 'What?' he said. 'What's so funny?'

'Sorry, mister. Sorry for rude. But you just say big funny thing. You say you have sexy goat in bath.'

His jaw dropped.

She laughed some more. 'I tell you, I no clean bath if goat in it.'

'But I've . . . I've been practising.' He felt embarrassed at the admission. Far from impressing her he'd just made a fool of himself. *No change there, then*, he heard the irritating voice of Captain Sensible mutter inside his head. *That's what you get for showing off*.

'Is good for you to learn new language but bad for me. I here to learn English. I no want to speak Latvian.'

'Oh,' he said, feeling flattened.

'Now I roll up sleeves and start work.' She sped off towards the kitchen. 'Ooh,' she let out, 'look at big mess mister has made here.'

Clayton left her to it.

That, Alice told herself, had been a close-run thing. She hadn't seen that coming. Fancy him trying to learn Latvian. Given that she knew next to nothing about her supposed country of birth, she had to hope that his next step wasn't to start badgering her about it. If he did that she would have to read up on the subject; the last thing she wanted to do was to let Ronnetta down. After discussing the matter, they had both decided that it would be better for Alice to continue as Katya.

When she had finished cleaning the kitchen, Alice went upstairs to see how big a mess Mr Shannon had made up there. It wasn't too bad.

She wondered what he did to pass the time. Was he lonely? Bored? Was that why he had been teaching himself a few choice Latvian expressions? The fact that he had, amused her and, to a degree, raised him in her estimation. Had she really been Latvian, she would have been pleased that he'd gone to so much trouble.

She finished cleaning his bathroom, then went downstairs for the vacuum cleaner. Passing his door, she knocked on it, waited politely for him to respond then went inside. 'Sorry to disturb, mister,' she said. 'You make list for shopping?'

'Not yet,' he said, not bothering to turn round and look at her. His attention was focused on his laptop in front of him. She was reminded of all the occasions her mother had sat in the very same spot. Clattering away on her typewriter, she would barely notice if anyone came into the room. Alice once timed how long it took for her mother to stop what she was doing and to answer Alice's question: ten whole minutes. She had been a patient and determined child.

'I make busy with vacuum,' Alice said, 'and then I go shopping for you. You want me to clean in here?' She stepped farther into the room, peered to see what was of such interest to him on his laptop. She made out just one word—'OBITUARY'.

As if sensing what she was doing, he snapped the lid shut and turned to face her. He then looked about the room. 'It doesn't look like it needs cleaning to me. Does it to you?'

She shrugged. 'Perhaps no. You very tidy in here.'

He raised an eyebrow. 'Unlike the kitchen?'

'Much grease everywhere in kitchen. You fry too much. Try grill or oven. Healthier for you. Maybe you like me to cook you one day.'

He cracked a smile. 'Trust me; I've been well and truly cooked.'

'Well, mister, I leave you to write list.' She closed the door after her. Interesting, she thought. What exactly did he mean by being cooked?

She lugged the vacuum cleaner upstairs. When she reached the landing, instead of turning right to go to her old bedroom, which Mr Shannon was using, she turned left and pushed open the door of her parents' old bedroom. It was like all the other rooms in the house, beautifully furnished and tastefully decorated. Alice went over to the window seat, sat down and closed her eyes. In her mind's eye she could see the room as it had once been. Clothes strewn everywhere, rugs rucked up, dusty lampshades and teetering piles of books.

Alice had been twelve when her mother died. Dr Barbara Barrett's sudden death had been perfectly in keeping with the way her parents lived their lives. Why go quietly when you could go with a bang? Her mother had died with a bang. She had managed to electrocute herself while watching television in the bath.

The coroner's verdict was that Dr Barbara Barrett must have slipped while getting into the bath and had accidentally knocked the portable TV set in with her. She wasn't found for two days, not until Alice's father returned from a trip photographing Emperor penguins. Alice was bluntly informed of her death at school by the headmistress.

Her father came to fetch her home from the boarding school she had recently started attending and the only words he uttered while driving her back to Cuckoo House were, 'Thank God I was out of the country when it happened. At least no one can accuse me of finishing her off!' The day of the funeral, with tears in his eyes, he admitted to Alice that they'd had a terrible row before he'd left for Antarctica and he just wished they'd had a chance to make up before she'd died.

Less than a year later, the same headmistress who had informed Alice that her mother was dead informed her that she now had a stepmother. Her father had by now established a habit of delivering good and bad news by proxy.

At first, Clayton thought it was his mobile. However, the ringtone wasn't coming from his phone, but from the one on the kitchen table next to Katya's bag. He took the mobile and went to look for her.

By the time he'd tracked her down to his bedroom the mobile had stopped ringing. 'Sorry I wasn't fast enough,' he said.

He watched her check to see who had called and saw her trying but failing to suppress a smile. It was a smile of undisguised delight. The mobile started to ring again. He left her to answer it.

It was wrong what he did next. Wholly wrong. But he was curious. He wanted to know what or who had made her smile in the way she had. He crept back and listened at the door. Initially he couldn't make sense of what he was hearing. Katya was speaking perfect English. *Proper* English. Queen's English. Holy hell, she was no more Latvian that he was! What the devil was she up to?

Alice switched off her mobile. She punched the air and danced a little jig. James Montgomery had called to invite her to have lunch with him. Oh, yes! The girl was hot. Hot, hot, *hot*!

Agitated, Clayton paced the length of the room. Why would Katya pretend to be foreign, go to such lengths to conceal her true identity?

Then it hit him. And the thought chilled him to the bone. She was a journalist! She was pretending to be a Latvian cleaner just so she could get some kind of a scoop on him.

He called Glen. But Glen wasn't answering his mobile.

What should he do? If he got the police involved, it would come out who he was and then he'd have other journalists banging on the door. Whatever he did he was screwed. Either way—whether he challenged the girl or continued to play along—she was going to write a humiliating piece about him. He had to get rid of her.

A knock at the door made him jump. He steadied himself with a deep breath, went to the door and opened it.

There she was staring back at him. As cool as you like. 'I go for shopping now,' she said, hitching her bag onto her shoulder. 'You have list?'

The sound of her fake bad English was too much. 'No,' he said, 'I don't have a list for you. I want you to go.'

'I sorry,' she said, a startled look on her face. 'I no understand.'

'I think you understand all too well,' he replied, 'so do us both a favour and drop the act. I know you're no more from Latvia than I am.'

Her face blushed crimson and her gaze wavered.

'Let me help you,' he said. 'I know exactly what you're really doing here. How about you just get your things and go? I'm sure you're disappointed you haven't got the story you hoped for. For the record, which newspaper are you from?'

'Newspaper?' she repeated, her gaze back on his face again. 'Why do you say that?' But at least she had dropped the fake accent.

'You know what? I'm surprising myself here at just how calm I'm being, but please don't test my patience any further. I'll ask you again: which newspaper do you write for?'

She shook her head. 'I'm sorry, I don't have any idea what you're talking about. I don't write for a newspaper. Do you think we could sit down so I can apologise and try and explain why I did what I did?'

'An apology from a journalist? That's a first.'

'You think I'm a journalist?'

'I think you're a lot of things, but the word "journalist" will suffice for now.' He stepped away from the door. 'Be my guest. Come on in and make yourself at home. You'll have to excuse me if I don't sit down; I may need to rush to the nearest loo to be violently sick if your apology is too much to take.'

She went to the fireplace. Perched on the worn green leather of the club fender, she looked up at him. 'What gave me away?'

'I heard you talking on your mobile.'

'You eavesdropped on me? That's outrageous.'

'Hey, you're in no position to try and take the moral high ground.'

She sighed. 'You're right. The thing is, I used to be an actress, now I do voiceover work, and sometimes I can't help myself. I hadn't intended to do it when I turned up here but it was . . .' she hesitated. 'Well, can we just say extenuating circumstances made me do it?'

'No, we cannot!' he snapped. 'And frankly, you're going to have to do a lot better than that load of bull before I accept your apology.'

'I'm telling you the truth. And if you hadn't been so rude to me when you opened the door I might not have got myself into this mess.'

'Now it's my fault!' He laughed. 'Where have I heard that before?'

'You're not a very happy man, are you?'

'My happiness has got nothing to do with you.'

She shrugged. 'Just making conversation.'

'No, you weren't. You were looking for a way to make me open up to you. Well, forget it. I'm not that stupid. Confide in a journalist? I'd sooner stick a wasp up my arse!'

'Why do you think I'm a journalist?'

'Because what else could you be? Certainly not an actress.'

She sat up straight. 'Don't you go disparaging my acting skills. Not when I convinced you every step of the way that I was Katya from Latvia. But the question I keep asking myself is why you think a journalist would be so interested in you. Who are you? What have you done that makes you so incredibly newsworthy?'

'Who said anything about me being newsworthy?'

'You with your paranoia, thinking I was a journalist. Which I'm not.'

'You expect me to believe that you're telling the truth when you've done nothing but lie since you showed up here? Don't make me laugh. And you were extremely rude to me.'

'Yes, I was. Sorry about that. But once I got into the character of Katya, I couldn't stop myself. She just seemed naturally bossy.'

'Does that mean in the real world you're nothing like her?'

She smiled. 'I spend as little time in the real world as I possibly can.'

'Meaning what exactly? That you're crazy?'

'Aren't we all from time to time?'

'What's your real name?' he asked. 'In the *real* world?'

'Alice,' she replied. 'Alice Shoemaker.'

'Yeah, right, and I'm Michael Schumacher. I've never heard a more made-up name.'

She rooted in her bag, pulled out a wallet, opened it and crossed the room to him. 'See, there's my driving licence. It clearly states my name.'

It did. And her address. 'You're local? You're not from London?'

'I'm as local as it's possible to be. In fact . . .' She broke off.

'In fact what?'

'I was born in this house. I grew up here.'

Clayton raked a hand through his hair. It was all becoming too much for him. 'You're an actress. So why, then, are you keeping house for me? Are times that hard that you clean while you're "resting"?'

'Sorry to correct you, but as I said earlier, it's voiceover work that I do, not acting per se. And not that it's any of your business, but times are far from hard for me; I'm doing this job as a favour for my neighbour who runs the cleaning agency.'

'Can you prove it?'

'You really are paranoid, aren't you?' Once more she rooted round inside her bag, pulled out her wallet again. 'There,' she said, 'my equity card. Satisfied now? Or would you like to speak to Ronnetta who runs the cleaning agency? She'll corroborate everything I've told you. Well, except the bit about me having grown up here. She doesn't know that.'

'And the reason why not?'

'It's complicated and nothing to do with you,' she said.

Shoulders squared, they glared at each other.

Then Clayton lost it. For no real reason he could think of, he began to laugh. He laughed and laughed.

Unnerved, Alice didn't know what to make of this strange man. 'Are you all right?' she asked when his manic laughter finally subsided. *All right?* What was she saying? The man was deranged! 'Look,' she said, inching away from him and towards the door. 'I'd better be going.'

'No,' he said, 'don't go.'

'You were very clear about wanting me to go a short while ago.'

'I've changed my mind.' He wiped his eyes. 'I'm sorry,' he said. 'I lost it there for a moment. I've . . . I've been under a lot of stress recently. I think I need a drink. Have one with me.'

This was insane! How had she got herself into a situation whereby she was being held hostage by a madman insisting that she have coffee with him? She had to be glad that it hadn't been an alcoholic drink he'd had in mind. At least she was spared the prospect of having to fend off a drunken madman. As she sat apprehensively at the kitchen table, Alice waited for him to finish fossicking around with the coffee machine.

Eventually he brought two goldfish bowl-sized cups of frothy coffee to the table. Once he was settled, she started the process of negotiating her freedom by engaging him in conversation. 'Um . . . you mentioned something about being under a lot of stress. Problems at work?'

'Problems with everything would be a more accurate description,' he said glumly. 'My life's hit the skids and there doesn't seem to be a damn thing I can do about it. I'm a cliché in my own lifetime.'

'Oh, we've all been there,' she said airily.

'But did you have your every misfortune, failure and cock-up written about in the newspapers? Did you have journalists door-stepping you at all hours of the day and night?'

Alice thought of her mother's death and then of the events that took place some years later. There had been a brief flurry of press interest and speculation, but not on the level he appeared to be talking about. 'No,' she said, 'I can't say that I have.'

'Then count yourself lucky.'

His tone was morose and it made her wonder. There was something going on here. She had been right to think there was more to him than met the eye. Feeling that she was now the one in control of the situation, she said, 'Having established *my* true identity, how about we do the same with you?'

'I don't know what you're talking about.'

She smiled her best winsomely enticing smile, the same smile she would be putting to good use during lunch with James Montgomery.

He looked at her strangely. 'You've got . . .' he flapped his hand vaguely across his top lip, 'coffee froth on your . . .'

She wiped her mouth. So much for winsome and enticing. 'What did you find so hysterically funny earlier?' she asked.

He shifted awkwardly in his seat. He said, 'I think it was the absurdity of it all. That and remembering something Beckett once said, that there's nothing funnier than unhappiness.'

A profoundly unhappy guy, she thought. 'Shall I tell Ronnetta that she needs to find a replacement for me?'

A silence fell between them.

'I'd rather not have anyone else,' he said after a lengthy pause.

'Will you be able to manage on your own?' she asked, surprised. 'What about your shopping? How will you do that without a car? You could walk, but it's over three miles to the nearest shops.'

He picked up his coffee cup and looked at her uneasily over its rim. 'I thought maybe you could keep coming.'

'Even though I lied to you and you think I'm untrustworthy?'

'Who's to say the next person won't lie to me? But at least I know you.'

'Now that's where you're wrong. You know my name, my profession, that I grew up here, and that I live locally. But you don't know *me*.'

'Wrong. I know that you take your coffee without sugar. I know that a certain man called James makes you smile and turns you pink at the edges, and that you're probably unhappy with your life the way it is. Maybe you never have been happy with it. Oh, and I also know that you're thirty-one years old.'

'That's nothing but a load of supposition and guesswork.'

'You think so? How old are you, then?'

She frowned. 'OK, you got that right. But how?'

'Your driving licence.'

'Mmm . . . you're sharper than you look.'

'I certainly hope so.'

'The beard—it's a new thing for you, isn't it?'

'It could be.'

'I think you probably look better without it. Maybe even younger. Are you hiding behind it? Just as you're hiding here at Cuckoo House?'

'Have another biscuit and be quiet.'

'You are, aren't you?'

He didn't say anything.

'I won't tell anyone. I'm very good with secrets. Just as long as I'm in on them.' She gave him what she hoped was a deep, penetrating look.

'That sounds suspiciously like a threat.'

'In the nicest possible way.' She leaned across the table and smiled. 'Tell me who you are. Please.' Back to being winsome and enticing.

'And if I don't?'

'You'll have to manage on your own.'

His face twitched with something that could have very nearly passed for a smile. 'I think I preferred it when you were Katya.'

'You saw only the good side of her.'

'And which side of you am I currently seeing?'

'Oh, definitely my good side. Believe me, you don't want to see my bad side. Why did you say you thought I was unhappy with my life?'

'It's obvious: why else would you choose, and I quote, *to spend as little time in the real world as I possibly can*, if you were happy with it?'

Ouch, thought Alice. 'And what about you? Are you happy with your lot as you sit here in a strange house wearing a strange beard?'

'I've been happier,' he admitted.

It would be difficult not to have been, she thought. 'Well,' she said, 'this has been fun but I really ought to be going.' She stood up.

'What about my shopping?' he asked.

She looked at him. There was a mystery here and by hook or by crook she wanted to get to the bottom of it. 'You know deal, mister. You tell Katya the truth, then she shop for you.'

He let out a short laugh. 'Not even in the game, kid. I'll walk.'

'Well, if there isn't anything else I can do for you, I'll be going. Enjoy your stay here.' She pulled on her coat.

From the window of the room he'd claimed as his den, Clayton watched the small red car drive away. Well, he thought. That's that, then. He retraced his steps to the kitchen. He needed something to eat. He opened the bread bin and found a solitary crust.

Chapter Three

IT WASN'T OFTEN that an author came into the studio, but James Montgomery always came for the first day of recording; he said he liked to be a part of the process.

As a child Alice would have loved James's books and his spirited protagonist Matilda; she would have read and reread them. She enjoyed them as an adult, too. But then she was biased. She would love anything James wrote.

It was seriously uncool to have a crush on someone at her age, but Alice couldn't help herself. Nor was she alone in her adoration. Josie always came over all of a dither whenever James came to the studio, and she was *way* older than Alice. And it wasn't just the females at the studio who batted their eyelashes at him. In his own words, Chris, the sound engineer, considered him as majorly droolworthy.

This morning James was indeed looking majorly droolworthy. His trademark lopsided fringe of dark brown hair was flopping sexily across his wide intelligent forehead and brushing his sapphire-blue eyes. He was sinfully good-looking.

He was chatting with Josie on the other side of the glass. They were taking a break while Chris twiddled the knobs—the noise of an aeroplane flying overhead had been picked up and they would have to redo the last page. Alice took a long, thirsty swig of water from her bottle on the desk, got up and stretched. Her shoulders ached from sitting still for so long. She imagined James offering to rub her neck and shoulders and instantly felt the tension drain out of her.

She had once read that the greater part of any relationship was carried out inside one's head. The hopes, the longing, the erotic fantasy of desire, in short, the best of a relationship, was all acted out in the mind. Alice couldn't disagree with the theory. In her own head (putting aside all the great sex they'd had—it went without saying that they were a perfect match in bed) she had been on countless dates with James.

The life she led inside her head was far more interesting that the one she really lived. The most excitement she'd had this last week was to clean for a strange man while fooling him she was Latvian.

Following her last visit to Cuckoo House, Alice had told Ronnetta what had happened, that her Katya act had been rumbled, and in her typical come-what-may fashion Ronnetta had told Alice not to lose any sleep over it. She had said she would ring the contact number she had and see if the agency's services were still required.

Alice had to concede that as strange as Laughing Boy clearly was, he was not unobservant. He had sussed her feelings for James with disturbing alacrity. Was is possible that others had picked up on the effect James had on her? Had James himself? Was that why he had invited her out for lunch today? To put her gently right, to explain that while he was enormously flattered, there could never be anything other than a working relationship between them?

She might have known that she had got the wrong end of the stick. Lunch was not the cosy intimate affair Alice had imagined, or hoped for. Instead, James had invited Josie and Chris as well. What on earth had made her think that James would single her out for lunch? A stonking great dose of wishful thinking, that's what!

They were sitting at a corner table in the Fox and Barrel, a drab pub within walking distance of the studio. The middle of Alice's pizza was stone cold—judging from its rubbery outer ring, it probably hadn't spent long enough in the microwave—and she was struggling to rally any enthusiasm to eat it.

'Aren't you going to eat that?'

Alice looked up. Josie's fork was pointing at her barely touched pizza. 'I'm not really hungry,' Alice responded.

'Waste not, want not!' Josie gave a cheerful laugh. 'Eu-ew!' she said, after she'd taken a mouthful. 'That's disgusting. It's barely cooked.'

'Really?' asked James. The perfect gentleman, he was up on his feet, the offending plate of pizza in his hands. 'Come on, Alice, let's go and order you something that's edible.'

Alice didn't need asking twice. Hurrah, alone with him at last!

The young girl behind the bar was working solo and had her hands full. 'Looks like we could be here for a while,' Alice said, adding, but not meaning it, 'You'd better go back and eat your lunch.'

James smiled. 'No rush. My Caesar salad won't spoil. In fact, I'm pleased that we've got this chance to be alone. There's something I want to talk to you about.'

Oh God, was this going to be the I'm-flattered-but-there-can-never-be-anything-between-us talk?

'The thing is . . .' His words hung in the air, his attention diverted by a messily folded newspaper to the left of him. He reached for it, opened it and smoothed out the pages. 'What do you make of this story?'

'What story's that?' she asked, moving closer to James.

'I was at school with him. Well, we were at the same school; he was in the sixth form when I joined aged eleven.'

'Who?'

James laughed and pointed at one of the photographs. 'Only one of the greatest comedy writers this country's ever produced.'

'Really? What's he known for?'

'Latterly for all the wrong reasons. But you must have heard of him. His name's Clayton Miller and he and his writing partner, Barry Osborne, wrote *Joking Aside*—'

'*Joking Aside*?' Alice interrupted. 'I loved that. It was brilliant.'

'It still is. Which is more than can be said for Clayton Miller. He's disappeared. Gone crackers maracas if the papers are to be believed.'

Alice looked at the double-page spread. There was a small photo of a man wearing a tuxedo minus the bow tie and holding up an award. He had a wide grin on his face; he looked nothing short of ecstatic, like a man on top of the world. Below it was another picture of a very different-looking man, dishevelled, shoulders hunched, and a hand partially covering a scowling face. On the opposite page was a picture of a man and a woman sitting on a sofa; they were holding hands and looking adoringly into each other's eyes. They looked very staged, like one of those couples who'd just undergone a makeover.

'Sorry to keep you waiting. What can I get you?'

Alice looked up to see the young girl behind the bar wilting beneath the strength of James's devastating smile. 'I think your chef must be having an off day,' he said good-naturedly while handing her the plate.

'My pizza wasn't cooked properly,' explained Alice.

'No problem,' the girl said brightly. 'Shall I put it back in the oven for you? Or would you prefer to choose something else?'

Her gaze was fixed on James; Alice was as good as invisible. James turned to Alice. 'I'll have a sandwich,' she said. 'Cheese and pickle.'

'No problem. I'll bring it over to your table.'

Alice turned to go. James put a hand on her arm. 'Alice,' he said, 'before we join the others, can I just—' But he got no further. He pulled out his ringing mobile. 'Sorry,' he said.

Alice stayed where she was, fighting the urge to snatch the mobile and tell whoever was calling him to call back later. She pretended to be fascinated by the newspaper article they'd been looking at.

James's call seemed set to go on and on. The sensible thing to do would be to leave him to it and go back to Chris and Josie, but by now she was reading the newspaper article properly. Halfway through it she began to get a funny feeling. She stared at the photographs closely. Not the large one of the couple whose names were Barry Osborne and Stacey Cook, but the two smaller pictures; the ones of the two very different-looking men. She now knew that it was the same man in the photographs, a classic comparison of before and after pictures. There was something distinctly familiar about the 'after' shot.

But did you have your every misfortune, failure and cock-up written about in the newspapers? Did you have journalists door-stepping you at all hours of the day and night?

If this particular newspaper was to be believed, Alice knew the exact whereabouts of a dangerously vindictive man who, according to Stacey Cook, was sick in the head and in urgent need of medical help.

Clayton was not going to be beaten. Well, no more beaten than he already was. If food was required, then he would go in search of it.

For his intrepid expedition he had helped himself to a selection of outdoor clothing from a room off the kitchen—boots, thick socks, a full-length green raincoat and a hat with a wide brim so large a family of four could take shelter beneath it. He looked and felt ridiculous. But at least there wasn't a chance of anyone recognising him in this get-up. He didn't recognise himself, come to that.

He had been walking for what felt like several days, but was in actual fact only three-quarters of an hour, and still there was no sign of any shops. Had that wretched girl Alice deliberately lied to him? Were the shops farther away than she'd made out?

The weather was dreadful. It had rained solidly all day. He'd been tempted to go online and arrange for a supermarket to deliver the things he needed, but after nearly a week of being cooped up, cabin fever had kicked in. He needed a change of scene.

He'd also acquired a fixation for peanut butter. He hadn't eaten it for years but suddenly it was all he could think of. He had to get his hands on a jar to satisfy his craving.

As a young child he used to eat masses of it, usually in front of the television on a Sunday evening while waiting for his hair to dry before going to bed. His mother had been a belt and braces kind of mother, the sort who believed he would catch pneumonia if he went to bed with so much as a single strand of hair that was damp. He had been eight years old when he'd finally convinced her that he didn't need to take a spare pair of underpants to school with him every day.

When *Joking Aside* took off and he and Bazza were regularly pitching up at award ceremonies, Clayton's mother was constantly on the phone warning him of the perils of not having an extra pair of trousers to hand for such a special occasion. 'What if you trip on the way and rip your trousers? Everyone will *see*. What will they *think* of you?'

God only knew how his mother would have coped with the shame of the past few weeks. Death had at least spared her the ignominy of having to face the neighbours.

He stomped through a puddle and hoped he wasn't making the mistake of reliving his childhood to avoid the here and now. He had never been in favour of staring up his backside in search of an answer to the meaning of life. He'd had enough of that with Stacey.

In the last year of their relationship she had taken to sitting up in bed preaching to him from the latest book of life-enhancing flim-flam she was currently swallowing whole. 'You need to hug and touch more,' she had informed him one night.

'I tried that earlier and you said you weren't interested.'

'That was sex, Clayton. I'm talking about embracing your inner child and inviting others to touch that child. Hugging a stranger might just make you less of a stranger to yourself.'

It was all part of the You-know-what's-wrong-with-you-don't-you? catalogue. Would hugging people he didn't know have saved his career or his relationship with Stacey? Was that what Lucky Bazza was so good at?

He felt his mobile vibrating in his jeans pocket. Glen. About time too!

'So how's it going?' Glen asked.

'Glad you could find the time to ask,' Clayton replied. 'Two words: bloody and awful.'

'That's three.'

'Your perspicacity astounds me at times.' Clayton then recounted his discovery, regarding Alice pretending to be Katya.

He'd just got as far as saying how she'd admitted that she'd grown up at Cuckoo House when Glen said, 'Yes, I got a call from the cleaning agency this morning. I must say, that girl sounds nearly as off-kilter as you. Do you think she knows who you are?'

'I'm pretty sure she doesn't. She even tried to blackmail me about it.'

'*What?*'

'She said she would continue to shop and clean for me if I told her who I really was.'

'I don't like the sound of that. You be careful. Have you seen a newspaper recently?'

'I've seen zilch. I'm not even looking at the stuff online. Why?'

'You're back in a few of the red tops today. Stacey and Bazza are whoring themselves around the neighbourhood again. I heard they're making another television appearance in the coming week.'

'What do you think they're trying to gain by it?'

'Sympathy? Higher profile? You tell me.'

'At this rate I'll never be able to come home.'

'We need an angle, Clay. Something with which to fight back. Got any ideas?'

'I could try committing suicide.'

'Mmm . . . you know, that might just work.'

'I was joking!'

'Oh, right. It's good you haven't lost your sense of humour. No chance that you've had a creative urge and written anything, have you?'

'St Glen the Patron Saint of the Bottom Line. You're all heart, Glen.'

'It's just a thought. Besides, what else have you got to do up there? Now what do you want me to tell that woman at the cleaning agency? Do you want someone else?'

'I'll manage on my own,' Clayton cut in impatiently.

'It'll probably be safer that way. Just don't make a mess of the house.'

Clayton rang off and trudged on in the rain. Having slogged to the crest of a hill, he was now peering through the rain and misty gloom at a stretch of long and winding tarmac road; it was completely deserted, not a car or person in sight. Had he missed a vital turning? What should he do? Retrace his steps?

No. He had to have that peanut butter. The answer was to press on and hope for the—

He froze.

Gunfire? What was this, bandit country? Another gunshot going off had him looking round for something to take cover behind. Then through the gloom, coming from the direction he'd just walked, he saw what was causing the noise: it was a car. Deliverance!

He stepped into the middle of the road as the car slowly approached. It was an ancient Morris Minor, with . . . with no one at the wheel. How was that possible?

Whatever was driving it, the car appeared to have no intention of stopping. He held his ground. It was almost upon him when through the windscreen he saw a small, beaky face peering over the steering wheel. A hand was waving furiously at him to get out of the way. Clayton held his breath and stayed where he was. He wanted that jar of peanut butter and nothing on this earth was going to stop him.

Just inches from the toes of his borrowed boots, the car backfired to a stop. His heart banging with fear and relief inside his chest, Clayton swallowed. He went round to the driver's side of the car. The small, beaky face belonged to a hobgoblin wearing a plastic rain-hood.

On closer inspection the hobgoblin was in actual fact a wizened old woman. She was staring implacably at him through the steamed-up side window. The ferocious hostility in her face made him take a step back. But he would not be denied his peanut butter. He leaned down and tapped on the window.

'I seem to have lost my way,' he said loudly. 'Can you help me?' Very slowly, the window was lowered and a grudging three-inch gap appeared at the top.

Through which the barrel of a handgun appeared.

'OK, sonny, I'm warning you now, any funny business and I'll blow your head off.'

Rooted to the spot, Clayton knew that he should be backing away, and fast. But he couldn't move. He was rigid with mind-numbing terror. The only part of him that appeared to have any ability to move was the bit that Glen maintained he'd never been able to control: his mouth. 'And a good day to you, madam,' he heard himself say.

'Oh, fancy yourself a smart aleck, do you? Well, let's see how smart you are with half your ugly mug missing!'

Clayton Miller, aged just forty-four and the nation's favourite comedy writer, was brutally murdered by a madwoman.

'Are you listening to me?'

'I'm sorry,' he said, 'I'd drifted off there for a moment.'

Her beady eyes looked at him incredulously. 'Are you on drugs?'

'Never touch the stuff. So don't try to sell me any.'

She pursed her thin lips. 'You've escaped from somewhere, haven't you?' she said. 'You're not the full shilling.'

'Do you suppose we could hold this delightful conversation without that gun being pointed at me?'

'Not until I'm sure about you. What do you want?'

'Directions. I'm trying to get to the nearest shops.'

The bright eyes tightened their grip on him. 'You're obviously not local. Where are you staying? Come on, out with it.' She had the sort of voice that had been born to boss people about.

'Cuckoo House,' he said obediently.

'Oh, there. You're a friend of the Armstrongs, then?'

'Yes,' he lied. 'They're letting me stay there until I've got myself sorted.'

'If you'd said that at the outset, it would have saved us both a lot of bother.' She withdrew the gun. 'Get in. I'm on my way to the shops; I'll give you a lift. I'll give you a lift back if you behave yourself.'

At about ten miles an hour the Morris Minor rattled, juddered and backfired its way along the winding road. Its driver seemed happily oblivious to the deafening racket of the car. 'Sorry about the gun,' she shouted. 'But one can never be too careful. What's your name?'

'Ralph Shannon,' Clayton said.

'Well, Shannon, you can call me George.'

'Is that Miss, Ms or Mrs?'

'Just George. And that's Percy in the back.'

Percy? Clayton spun round. On the back seat was a large, murderous-looking rooster. His head was tilted and his eyes were as beady as those of the madwoman driving the car. The rooster glared threateningly at Clayton, then began scratching at the tattered seat. 'Stop that at once, Percy!' the woman roared, making Clayton jump. She turned to

Clayton. 'I had to bring him with me. He's turned into a frightful sex pest and won't leave the poor hens alone.'

'Right,' said Clayton as though they were having a perfectly normal conversation.

'So where's home?' she demanded. 'London, I'm guessing. You have that worn-down manner only Londoners have. Had some kind of a breakdown, have you?'

'Why do you ask that?'

'You're as jumpy as hell.'

'So would you be if you'd just had a gun shoved in your face.'

She thumped the steering wheel with both hands and laughed out loud as though he'd said the funniest thing. He had to find a way to stop the old biddy asking so many questions. A thought occurred to him. 'Do you know a girl called Alice Shoemaker? I believe she grew up here.'

'Shoemaker, you say. No, that name doesn't ring a bell. I knew an Alice Barrett. The Barretts owned Cuckoo House years ago.'

'How many years ago was that?'

With a bloodcurdling scream of resistance from the engine, she changed gear and shot him a look. 'Why do you want to know?'

'I . . . . I met a girl at Cuckoo House the other day called Alice Shoemaker and she said she grew up there.'

'Really? How old was she?'

'Thirty-one.'

'In that case I'd say you met Alice Barrett, as was. Well, I never. Alice back at Cuckoo House. Mind you, I thought she'd show up one day.' After another gear change and a thunderous explosion from the rear of the car, they juddered to an abrupt stop. 'Right, Shannon, here we are. There's a Co-op over there. A butcher's next door, a grocer's shop across the road and a baker's right here where we're parked.'

'Is there a bank?'

'In between the outdoor-clothing shop and the Penny-Farthing café. Be back here in an hour. Any later and I'll be gone.'

It was mid-afternoon and the light was fading; illuminated shop windows shone invitingly. His first port of call was the bank. He needed some cash. This he acquired from a hole in the wall. He then progressed to the butcher's for sausages. He could use the freezer back at Cuckoo House to store a fortnight's worth of them. He did the same with bacon. And since the butcher also sold eggs, he bought a dozen of those.

Next it was on to the Co-op. *Peanut butter, peanut butter*, he silently chanted to himself. He stripped the shelf of its entire stock, all three jars. He then worked methodically round the store. He was at the check-out when he noticed the depleted racks of newspapers. He couldn't stop himself. He added three tabloids to the basket.

It took an age to pay and, heavily laden with six bags of shopping, he hurried outside. He crossed the street to where he'd been instructed to meet the old woman. But there was no sign of her. Or of the Morris Minor. He checked his watch. He was two minutes late.

Alice's headlights picked out the lumbering figure ahead of her. Even before he turned round, she knew who it was and what she was going to do and say. After all, this was no accidental meeting; curiosity in all its grubby glory had drawn her here.

She slowed the car, pulled alongside him and lowered her window. 'You're lucky it's stopped raining,' she said. 'Want a lift?'

A grimace of tired relief passed across his face. 'I'll give you anything you want, just so long as you get me back to Cuckoo House.'

She got out of the car, went round to the boot and opened it. She helped him to load the shopping inside.

He slumped in the passenger seat next to her. 'What brings you to this neck of the woods? The desire to gloat?'

'Oh, don't be like that. Would "thank you" be so very difficult for you to say?'

'Thank you.'

She smiled to herself and drove the rest of the journey in silence. When they reached the gate at Cuckoo House, she said, 'You left it open; I wouldn't have thought a man in your position would do that.'

He said nothing.

She drove through the gate, then stopped. She turned and looked at him. 'Yes, that's right, I'm waiting for you to get out and close it.'

Scowling, he did as she instructed.

When he was back in the car, he said, 'What did you mean, *a man in my position?*'

'You tell me.' She saw a flicker of unease darken his eyes.

Up at the house, she helped him carry his shopping inside and noticed the newspapers protruding from one of the carrier bags. 'Since I'm here, is there anything you'd like me to do for you?'

'I've dispensed with the agency.'

'I know. I was offering my services for free.'

'Free? There's no such thing.'

'Not in your world maybe, but in mine there is.' She reached into a bag and pulled out the newspapers. The one she'd read at lunchtime was on the top. 'Would you mind if I checked the television programmes for tonight, please?' Without waiting for him to respond, she opened the paper, but seeing the undisguised alarm in his face, she stopped what she was doing. It was unnecessarily cruel to tease him this way. She had no idea how much truth had been written about him in the papers, if any, but one thing she knew with unquestionable certainty, from first-hand experience, was that things were rarely as they first appeared.

'I have a confession to make,' she said, deciding to come clean. 'I found out earlier today who you really are. You're Clayton Miller.'

He could not have looked more shocked.

'I read about you in the paper,' she explained, experiencing a rush of compassion for him. Seeing him like this, she couldn't believe the worst of what she'd read. It just didn't square up. He seemed no madder or more malicious than her. 'It took me a while to make the connection,' she said, 'but I eventually recognised you from the pictures.'

He came over to her, held out his hand for the newspaper. 'May I?'

She gave it to him, then watched him sink into the nearest chair. He flicked through the pages until he found what he was looking for. His hand flat on the table as if steadying himself, he began reading. Not knowing what else to do, Alice made herself useful brewing the tea and toasting crumpets. She slid one in front of the man whose spirit she appeared to have broken. 'How do you like your tea?' she asked.

'Milk, no sugar,' he murmured.

She poured out two mugs, gave him one. Her hand resting on the back of a chair opposite, she said, 'May I?'

He nodded.

'Is *any* of it true?' she asked, inclining her head towards the paper.

'They've got my name right and the fact that I haven't managed to write anything since Barry ended our partnership.'

'And the bit about you being responsible for them losing their baby?'

He raked his hands through his hair. 'Stacey and Bazza say I'm responsible, so I must be.'

'But if you're not, you're just going to take what's been written about you?'

'What would you do?'

She sighed. 'I'd run away and hide, just like you.'

'You don't strike me as the run-and-hide sort. Far from it.'

'My track record says otherwise. The circumstances weren't entirely the same, but years ago, I ran and hid from . . .' she hesitated, searching for the right words. 'Let's just call it a difficult situation.'

'Was it something to do with living here?'

She took a bite of crumpet and chewed on it slowly and thoughtfully. 'What makes you think that?' she said at length.

'While you were putting two and two together about me today, I found out your surname used to be Barrett.'

'How did you come across that?'

'I met a crazy old woman called George this afternoon.'

'Good God! She's not still alive is she?'

'She was very much alive. I stopped her car to ask for directions to the shops and she pulled a gun on me.'

Alice laughed. 'A small handgun?'

'It didn't look that small to me.'

'It's a fake. She always used to ride around with it. She wasn't by any chance still driving her beloved Morris Minor?'

'She was certainly driving a clapped-out Morris Minor. Whether it was beloved I couldn't say.'

'How extraordinary.' Alice pondered. 'Georgina Harrington-Smythe still alive and kicking. Who'd have thought it.'

'Is that her real name?'

'Yes. But she used to use it only with people she didn't like. If she introduced herself as George it means she took a shine to you.'

'I'm not sure she took that much of a shine to me. She didn't hang around to give me a lift back.'

'I wouldn't take that personally. How did she seem to you?'

'One word covers it: indomitable. Not unlike the friend she had with her. A sex pest of a rooster who goes by the name of Percy.'

Again Alice laughed. 'Exactly the kind of friend George would have.'

'They did seem ideally suited,' he agreed. 'Can I ask you what you're going to do now that you know who I am?' he added.

'What would you like me to do?'

'To keep quiet. To tell no one that I'm here.'

'Then that's exactly what I shall do. You have my word on it.'

A shadow of wary doubt covered his face. 'I haven't cut any corners to get to this level of neurosis,' he said, 'so I have to tell you that I'm obliged to ask why you would do that for me?'

'What can I say? You seem in need of a break in life. Plus, there's something about you I like.' She felt her cheeks redden at the admission.

'You have a weakness for failures?'

'Now you're just fishing for sympathy. You're not a failure. You created one of the best sitcoms ever. One of my absolute favourites.'

He didn't look especially flattered.

'I give you my word,' she said. 'I won't tell a soul. Who else knows you're here?'

'Only my agent.'

'And his connection with the house?'

'He knows the Armstrongs, the current owners. He asked them if a friend of his could stay here for a while. Is the house very different from how you remembered it?'

'Yes,' she said simply. 'You can't imagine how different.' Or how it makes me feel being back here, she thought. So many memories. So many emotions. It was almost too much to take in, as if she couldn't bring herself to acknowledge that she was really here. But then she had always been good at blocking out anything that was too painful to deal with. When her mother had died, she had hardly cried at all.

'Will you tell me how it happened?' she asked Clayton.

'How what happened?'

'What the papers are calling your "spectacular fall from grace".'

'Maybe. But first, I want to know more about you. Tell me about those circumstances that made you run and hide.'

She licked her finger. 'It's a very long story.'

'I've got time,' he said. 'How about you?'

Alice thought of what was waiting for her back at Dragonfly Cottage. Probably only another irresistible offer from Bob to turn down. But there was the slimmest of chances that James might call. He never had got round to saying whatever it was he'd wanted to share with her, and his parting words were that he'd give her a ring. He hadn't said when.

'No,' she said, 'I'm not busy this evening.'

'Then let's have another cup of tea and you can tell me your story. If nothing else, it'll take my mind off my predicament.'

Alice took charge of the crumpets again and he poured the tea. And although all the while she kidded herself that what she was about to tell Clayton was for his benefit, deep down she knew that what she was about to embark upon was for her own good. Being back at Cuckoo House had done exactly what she had known it would. It had crystallised the past and awakened an ache deep inside her.

'It was the cherry liqueurs that did it,' she said quietly, surprising herself that this should be her starting point.

Chapter Four

ALICE'S STEPMOTHER, Julia Raphael-Barrett, had a vague, spacey manner. She drifted aimlessly about Cuckoo House as if she were lost. With hindsight, she probably was.

When her father brought his new bride to live at Cuckoo House, it was the first sighting Alice had had of the woman who had replaced her mother. The wedding had taken place in London at Kensington Register Office while Alice was at school. Julia didn't arrive alone. With her came her two children—Rufus and Natasha.

It soon became apparent that, not unlike her predecessor, Julia had no interest in anything of a domestic nature and encouraged Alice, along with her own children, to do whatever they wanted rather than bother her. She didn't mind if they left their clothes strewn on the floor, or played music so loud the windows rattled, or made bonfires that got out of hand. In many ways, Alice had always had a free rein but sharing that freedom with Natasha and Rufus made it all the more enjoyable. Tasha, as she insisted Alice call her, was the same age as Alice—thirteen—and Rufus, whom Tasha idolised, was three years older. Whereas Tasha was open and direct, Rufus was quiet and withdrawn. He scowled a lot and was often astonishingly rude. Alice developed an instant crush on him.

It was her first real crush and she kept it hidden; he was her step-brother, after all. He was the best-looking boy she had ever set eyes on. He was tall, broad-shouldered and he had the most amazing blue eyes. His skin had an olive hue, as did Tasha's, and his hair was very dark. His hand was constantly pushing his dangly fringe out of his eyes. He excelled at whatever he put his mind to, particularly sport.

Alice had no idea why her father had married Julia, or how they'd met, but she was glad he had because for the first time in her life, she had a proper best friend and a sister all rolled into one. 'We'll be like twins,' Tasha announced one day. 'We'll even pretend we are.'

'But we don't look anything alike. We might both have dark hair,' Alice had conceded, 'but I'm pale and freckly and you're beautiful.'

There was no denying the disparity. According to Julia, who was a redhead with skin paler than Alice's, Tasha and Rufus had inherited their looks from their father, who had been half-French and had died two years before in a skiing accident in Switzerland.

That summer was one of the happiest times for Alice. There were no arguments between her father and Julia; it was only later that Alice realised this was more to do with her father being on his best behaviour for his new wife than Julia having an easy-going temperament.

At Julia's insistence they acquired a cook. Mrs Randall came in five days a week and the delicious meals she produced transformed Alice's eating habits. Alice enjoyed watching Mrs Randall at work. She found it comforting to watch the magical process happen before her eyes, breathing in the tantalising smells, enjoying the warm steamy environment. She would sit in rapt attention as Mrs Randall weighed ingredients, chopped, mixed and rolled. Tasha, who didn't know what all the fuss was about, left Alice to it.

The summer passed and in September Tasha switched schools to the boarding school that Alice attended. Rufus had refused point-blank to consider moving schools and with ten grade-A GCSEs under his belt, he stayed at his boarding school in Somerset and moved up into the lower sixth. His subjects were all science-based; he was going to be a doctor.

Once Julia was sure that all responsibility for the house and the children lay securely in the hands of others—an au pair would materialise during the school holidays—she washed her hands of them. She picked out a room for her own private use upstairs and turned it into what she called her sanctuary. She read in there, took naps late in the afternoon and listened to music.

'I'm never going to be like her when I grow up,' Tasha would say. 'She's so pathetically useless. I'm going to do something with my life. I don't want to be just a wife and mother.' Rufus, on the other hand, had a much closer relationship with their mother and if he ever heard his sister criticising Julia, he would rebuke her severely.

It was following one of Tasha's declarations that she was going to do something worthwhile with her life, that Alice shared with her her dream to be an actress. 'An actress,' repeated Tasha, her eyes wide. 'What a brilliant idea! Why don't we both be actresses?'

So it was agreed, she and Tasha would both be big stars. They rushed to tell Rufus the news. He scoffed at their excitement. But even so, the following term he accompanied Julia to see them both in their school production of *A Midsummer Night's Dream*. Alice's father couldn't make it; he was away on a photographic trip.

Rufus's appearance at their school caused a massive stir. For weeks afterwards, Tasha and Alice were pestered by girls wanting to know all about the heart-achingly good-looking Rufus Raphael-Barrett. Alice felt a faint stirring of jealousy.

Exactly a year after they'd come to live at Cuckoo House, Tasha confided in Alice that Rufus hadn't approved of his mother marrying Alice's father. In his opinion, Bruce Barrett wasn't good enough for his mother. What's more, he believed Bruce wasn't right in the head. Ever quick to defend her father, Alice had said, 'But he's a brilliant photographer,' as if this explained everything. But Tasha sided with her brother and said that surely Alice had to admit that he wasn't normal.

From then on, Alice observed her father through new eyes. She was so used to his wildness and unpredictable ways that she had never thought anything of it. Now she began to cringe whenever he stamped about the house and yelled uncontrollably at the top of his voice, or when Julia was out and he offered to show the au pair his darkroom. Obviously the honeymoon period of her father's good behaviour had passed. It was mortifying to discover that your father wasn't normal.

Nothing could have proved Rufus and Natasha's point more than when Alice's father woke them early one morning during the Christmas holiday and announced that he was taking them on a mystery outing.

'I'm not going anywhere,' Rufus muttered crossly. 'I've got revision to do for my mocks.'

'Please come,' Alice begged. 'You know how silly my father can be. He'll behave himself if you're with us.'

Rufus paused. 'You're right, Alice. Who knows what danger he'll put you both in without a responsible adult around?'

Alice was shocked that she'd resorted to such a tactic, reinforcing Rufus's view that her father was a dangerous lunatic, but at the same time she was delighted that Rufus would be joining them.

Julia declined to come, claiming she wasn't feeling well; a headache. She suffered from a lot of headaches these days.

Alice had been on many mystery outings with her father. Two stuck in her mind. The day after her sixth birthday he had driven her to London. Except, of course, she hadn't had a clue where they were going because that was all part of the game. They had driven round and round. She saw Buckingham Palace, the Royal Albert Hall, Trafalgar Square, Nelson's Column, Downing Street and a man peeing in the gutter. That was her abiding memory. It was what she rushed to tell her mother when, gone midnight, they arrived home. 'Mummy, Mummy,' she blurted out, 'I saw a man doing a number one in the street!'

'It wasn't your father, was it?' her mother had asked. Then in a hissy voice that immediately took the shine off the day, her mother had said to her father, 'Why the hell didn't you tell me you were taking off for the day? I didn't have a clue where you were. I was worried.'

A long time later, her father had taken her to Scotland. They didn't once get out of the car, they just cruised round, leaning out of the window whenever there was something of interest to look at. Her father said the point of the outing had nothing to do with their final destination; it was all about the journey.

In the car now, on a bitterly cold December morning, Rufus in the front with her father and Alice and Tasha in the back with a picnic hamper, Alice was feeling nauseous with anxiety. What if Tasha and Rufus didn't enjoy the outing? What if they didn't understand?

Then a worse thought occurred to her. What if *she* didn't understand any more? What if it would prove to be just a boring long drive somewhere? She realised then that it could never be like it used to be. She wasn't a young child any more; she and Tasha were fourteen and Rufus was seventeen. Why hadn't she tried to stop her father? It was all going to go horribly wrong. The day would turn out to be a disaster.

It started when Rufus's Nirvana cassette jammed in the tape player. He tried to eject it, only to end up with the cassette in his hand and the tape unwinding inside the machine. He swore loudly and kicked at the dashboard. Not once, but twice.

'Hey, watch the car!' The Jaguar, like the one Inspector Morse drove round in, was her father's pride and joy.

'Why should I?' retaliated Rufus. 'It's a bloody wreck, this car. My father wouldn't have been seen dead in a heap like this.'

'Then it's a good thing he's been spared the ignominy by dying.'

'You bastard!'

Alice's father laughed nastily. 'Takes one to know one.' He then wound down his window and chucked out Rufus's cassette. But, of course, it was still attached to the tape machine and wasn't going anywhere far. It clattered noisily against the outside of the car.

'You mad crazy bastard!' yelled Rufus. He gave the dashboard another vicious kick and the glove compartment popped open. Out fell a magazine. Rufus leaned forward to pick it up. From the back, Alice saw what kind of magazine it was. Her face turned beetroot.

Quick as a flash, her father snatched the magazine out of Rufus's hands and threw that the way of the cassette.

Rufus smirked. 'Anything else you want to throw out of the window, my pervy stepdad?'

'Yeah, you!'

'You realise, don't you, that my silence will cost you?'

'Oh, go to hell!'

Fraught with the need to intervene, to make the awful atmosphere go away, Alice leaned forward. 'Dad, can we stop please?'

'Why?' he snapped.

'Rufus's cassette will ruin the paintwork on your car.'

Her father looked at her in the rearview mirror. 'Good thought, Alice. At least someone cares about my car.'

Luckily Tasha had missed the entire exchange—she was listening to Take That on her Walkman with her eyes closed.

They had been driving for an hour when they ground to a halt in a deserted country lane. Five minutes later the reason for the breakdown became clear: they were out of petrol.

'And naturally you've got an emergency can of petrol in the boot?' Rufus enquired. He managed to make his question sound both helpful and mockingly sceptical.

Wiping his oily hands on the front of his jeans, her father smiled. 'As a matter of fact, Rufus, I do have an emergency supply. Yeah, I thought that would wipe the smirk off your pretty-boy face.'

Bowled over with surprise, Alice felt like hugging her father. She stepped out of the car and went round to the boot with him.

Under a tatty, oil-stained tartan blanket, there was a red metal can. 'Thank goodness for that,' she said.

'Don't tell me you doubted me, Alice?'

'Of course not, Dad.'

He grinned and unscrewed the black cap. He peered inside the can, then shook it. 'Oh, shit!' he said. 'It's empty. Sorry, Alice.'

She swallowed back something that felt like tearful anger. 'Couldn't you walk to the nearest garage and get it filled?'

He looked about him vaguely. 'I could, I suppose.' Frowning and surveying the deserted road to his right and to his left, he scratched his head. 'Can you cover for me?'

'How do you mean?'

'Tell smart-arse Rufus that there was a dead mouse in the can and we couldn't use it. You're good with stories; you'll easily convince him.'

'He's not a smart arse, Dad.' Her tone was tight and defensive.

Her father looked at her doubtfully and shrugged. 'If you say so. Right, I'll be off. Toodle-pip!'

Alice watched him saunter off, the empty can swinging from his arm. She then got back into the relative warmth of the Jag.

'So,' Rufus said with weighty emphasis. 'Just as I suspected, we have a zero fuel situation.'

'There was a dead mouse in the can,' Alice replied without hesitation. 'It would have been dangerous to use the petrol when it was contaminated. It would have ruined the engine.'

Rufus slowly turned round to face her. His face was dark and hopelessly handsome. 'And just how did the mouse get into the can in the first place?' he asked. 'Was the lid not screwed on properly?'

Stop it! Stop it! Stop it! She wanted to shout at him. *Stop making me choose between you and my father!* To her horror she burst into tears.

'Now see what you've done!' Tasha said. She put her arm round Alice. 'How about something to eat from the picnic? That'll make you feel better, won't it?'

Calmer now, Alice managed a small nod.

Rufus smiled. 'Alice, come and sit in the front with me. Tasha can act as waitress and serve us from the back, which is, of course, just where she belongs.'

Alice slipped into the driver's seat. Just as Tasha had done moments before, Rufus put his arm round her. 'There, that's better, isn't it?'

She didn't know what he was really referring to, but everything did indeed now feel better. 'I'm sorry about your cassette,' she said. 'And I'm sorry about my father. He doesn't mean half the things he says.'

'I'm not so sure about that. But you have to admit, his behaviour is not that of a normal, sane man, is it? But none of that's your fault, Alice, so no more apologising.' He put a finger to her chin and turned her face towards him. He stared intently at her. 'OK?'

Lost in the depths of his blue eyes, and thinking that she could never love anyone else as much as she loved Rufus, she whispered, 'OK.'

He smiled and she felt something well up inside her. Then her heart exploded. She had never seen him smile at her quite that way before. Was she imagining it, or was it possible that he could love her?

Money was a peculiar thing. Some people never referred to it, while others, like Tasha, were always going on about it.

George gave the impression of not having a bean to her name but the rumour was she was loaded. She had lived at Well House since time began and whenever something went wrong with the place, she fixed the problem herself. It was patched up like a ragged patchwork cushion and inside it was even untidier than Cuckoo House.

She grew most of what she ate, and occasionally kept pigs and sheep. For as long as Alice could remember, George had supplied her family with eggs and when she was home from school it had been Alice's job to fetch them.

Tasha didn't always go with Alice to fetch the eggs; she said she didn't like the smell of George's house. The chickens the old woman kept were given free rein to roam wherever they pleased and that included the house. It seemed perfectly normal to Alice to share a chair with a fluffy bantam but Tasha thought it was anything but normal. She also doubted that George had any money. 'If she really was sitting on a pile of money, don't you think she'd use it to do something about the hovel she lives in?' she argued.

'Her priorities aren't the same as other people's,' Alice tried to explain. She rather liked the way George lived. The woman didn't seem to give a damn about anything. She just quietly got on with enjoying her life.

In contrast, Tasha had always given the impression that there was plenty of money in her family—there were aunts, uncles and grandparents who, in Tasha's own words, were all amazingly well off. Alice had met a number of these relatives in the three years since her father had married Julia, and their lives did indeed appear quite glamorous compared to theirs; they regularly jetted off on exotic holidays to the Caribbean and the ski slopes of France and Switzerland.

When Alice's mother had been alive, family holidays had been non-existent. Her parents were perfectly happy to stay at home—they already spent enough time away from Cuckoo House. It was a way of life Alice had never once questioned. Tasha said she was too easy-going for her own good. Maybe she was. Maybe that was why she hadn't questioned Tasha's assertion that her mother was as wealthy as the rest of her family.

But when Alice had overheard a conversation between Rufus and his mother, that assertion was proved wrong.

Home from university for the Easter holidays—he was now studying medicine in London—Rufus had been asking his mother for money to buy a car now that he'd passed his driving test. Alice hadn't intended to listen in on the conversation but there was something in

Julia's tone that made her hover behind the slightly open door.

'I can't, Rufus,' Alice had heard his mother say. 'I simply don't have the money to buy you a car.'

'What do you mean? What about Dad's money?'

'It really wasn't that much, and what there was has gone.'

'Gone where?'

'Please don't badger me. Just leave things be.'

'No! No, I won't! Tell me exactly where the money has gone. Oh my God, you're not saying that fool of a man you married has taken it from you, are you? Because I'll bloody well—'

'Calm down, Rufus. Bruce hasn't done anything. But darling, these things are complicated.'

'Please don't patronise me, Mum. Just tell me the truth.'

There was a sigh, a rustle, and then, 'Rufus, the truth of the matter is, your father left us barely any money at all. I'm sorry, but he just wasn't the successful businessman you thought he was.'

'Why didn't you tell me this before?'

'Because I didn't want you to think badly of him.'

There was a long pause and then Rufus said, 'Why did you marry Bruce?'

'Why do you think? I wanted a secure future for you and Natasha.'

'But your family . . . Dad's family, they would have helped us—'

'I didn't want them to know the truth,' Julia interrupted. 'I don't want them treating us as the poor branch of the family.'

'So you married a raving lunatic to save face?'

'Yes.'

'In that case, I'll ask Bruce to buy me a car.' Rufus's voice was flat.

At the sound of a long silence and then crying—Julia crying—Alice had crept silently away to her bedroom. She had lain on her bed, her hands clasped behind her head as she stared up at the ceiling. Had her father any inkling of what he'd got himself into?

It was the first warm and sunny day of April, and Alice and Tasha were walking to Well House to fetch some eggs. Having kept what she knew to herself for two whole days, Alice was bursting with the need to tell Tasha what she'd overheard. But on a sudden whim to accompany her, Tasha was talking nineteen to the dozen and there wasn't a hope of getting a word in edgeways. Perhaps it was just as well. Besides, they had more important things to think about.

When she and Natasha returned to school after Easter they would take their GCSEs. If all went to plan, they were planning on taking the same A-level subjects and then going on to university together to study English Literature. After they graduated they would then get a place at drama school in London—Guildhall was their first choice.

Tasha had been all for skipping university and going straight to drama school, but Rufus had stepped in and advised against it. 'What if you don't make it in the acting world?' he'd asked. 'What then? A degree will be a great fall-back option.'

Alice suspected that the reason Tasha had suggested what she had was because exams didn't come easily to her. 'I'm not like you,' she often grumbled to Alice. 'You have a photographic memory.'

This wasn't strictly true. Yes, Alice had a good memory, but the way she learned things was by reading them to herself in a voice inside her head other than her own. For maths she had her father's megaphone voice booming inside her head; for biology and chemistry it was Rufus's, and for all the remaining subjects she mimicked her teachers.

Her skill for mimicry was better than ever and Rufus loved her impersonations. She had once phoned him when he was away at university and pretended to be his mother. She had totally fooled him. He'd seen the funny side of it, thank goodness.

She loved being able to make him laugh. When that happened, for that brief moment, it was as if she was at the centre of his world.

Alice had no idea if Rufus knew how she felt about him, but she was determined not to reveal her feelings until she was at least eighteen. If she did it now, he'd accuse her of childish infatuation.

It was a two-mile walk across the fields to Well House. When they reached their destination they found George at the front of the house at the top of a ladder painting a window frame. 'Be with you in a tick,' she shouted down to them. 'Why don't you go inside and make yourself at home. Oh, and put the kettle on while you're about it.'

Standing in the kitchen, Tasha wrinkled her nose. 'How does she put up with the stink? It can't be healthy.'

'It's not that bad,' Alice said absently from the sink where she was filling the kettle. A hen poked its head in through the open window. 'Hello,' Alice said. 'And what's your name?'

Tasha tutted. 'You're as crazy as she is.'

'Crazy as who?' asked George, coming into the kitchen.

'As nuts as a girl in our class at school,' Alice ad-libbed.

George put the paintbrush she'd been using into a jam jar of murky-coloured liquid on the kitchen table. 'You're the least crazy person I know, Alice,' she said. 'I'd go so far as to say you're the sanest person I know. How's that father of yours? Home or away?'

'Just back from a trip to Iceland.'

'Be sure to give him my regards. Now, who's for a cup of coffee?'

'We can't really stop for long,' Tasha said. 'We just came for the eggs.'

George swivelled round to look at Tasha. 'In that case, don't let me keep you. The eggs are in the box in the usual place.'

'I'm sure we could stay for a few minutes,' Alice placated.

'All right,' Tasha conceded grudgingly and threw Alice one of her looks—the look that said, *What on earth were you thinking?* 'But we can't stay too long; we've got revision to do.'

Tasha was still in a tetchy mood when they left to go home. 'There's no excuse for that woman allowing herself to live in such squalor. I could understand it if she really was poor, but you said yourself, she's got money. Lots of it.'

'What? Like your family?'

Tasha turned her head sharply. 'What's up with you?'

'Nothing's up with me. I just don't like you criticising George. What harm has she ever done to you?'

'Well, if that's how you feel, I shan't bother to come with you again. Mum's never been happy about me going inside that house. She reckons it has more germs than a public lavatory.'

'But she's happy enough to eat George's eggs,' Alice muttered.

'What's got into you? You're being a right bitch!'

On the verge of saying something she knew she would regret, Alice clamped her lips tightly shut and walked on fast. Until now she hadn't realised just how angry Julia and Rufus's conversation had made her feel. Her father was being used. Stomping across the fields, Alice experienced a sudden longing for her mother. Her parents may have fought like mad, but there had been a predictable and honest madness to their relationship. Neither one of them had pretended to be anything other than the person they were.

Alice wasn't the only one to be in a bad mood. Back at Cuckoo House, Rufus was in a furious temper and was refusing to say why. What was more, he was leaving. He was in his room, packing.

Alice climbed the stairs to the top of the house and knocked on the door of her father's darkroom. She asked him if he knew what had upset Rufus.

He laughed. 'Cheeky sod demanded I buy him a car. He even tried to blackmail me. I told him to get lost and buy himself a bike.'

'What did he try to blackmail you about?'

'Nothing you need to concern yourself with.' Scrutinising the photographs that were pegged above his head, he said, 'What do you think of these, Alice? Am I a genius, or what?'

She forced herself to smile. 'You're a genius, Dad.'

'Right, that's enough flattery. Now bugger off and let me get on.'

Tasha was upset her brother was leaving so suddenly and she kept asking him why he was going. He wouldn't say.

When it was almost time for Rufus to go, he knocked on Alice's door. She let him in, but couldn't look him in the eye. She was angry with her father for being the cause of Rufus's departure, but she was also angry with Rufus for behaving like a spoilt child.

'I know why you're going,' she said. 'Dad told me.'

He stood in the window in front of her. Sunlight poured in making his black hair shine. 'I know he's your father and you'll always take his side, but have you ever thought how difficult it is for me? He hates me.'

'Don't exaggerate. He doesn't hate you. He doesn't hate anyone.'

'You're wrong. He hates me because . . . because he knows how I really feel about you.'

Alice held her breath. 'What do you mean?'

He took her face in his hands. 'Your father doesn't think I'm good enough for his only daughter. It's possible he could be right.' Brushing the hair from her face, Rufus closed the gap between them and kissed her. Alice kept her eyes open, not wanting to miss a second of the single most important moment of her life.

He pulled away. 'I promised myself I wouldn't do that.'

She breathed out. 'Why?'

'I didn't want to risk ruining things between us. Have I?'

Mesmerised, her head spinning, her heart bursting, she shook her head. She had got her wish, at long last.

'I have to go now,' he whispered in her ear. 'Don't tell anyone about us. Especially not your father. Promise me that.'

'I'm sorry, I must be boring you to death with my rambling on.'

Clayton shook his head. 'Not at all.'

'Even so, I had no idea it was so late,' she said, rising from her chair.

Clayton was disappointed she was leaving. He was fascinated by her story. 'You can't leave me on such a cliffhanger,' he said. 'You have to tell me what happened next. I insist.'

She smiled faintly. 'Got any theories on how it works out?'

'I have the feeling there's not going to be a happy ending.'

'Not even close.' She hooked her bag over her shoulder. 'I'll be seeing you, then.'

'When exactly?'

Clayton woke several times in the night. Something was nagging away at him. It was a sensation he hadn't experienced in a long, long time. He almost didn't recognise it. But when he did, he sat up and switched on the bedside lamp. He was breathing hard. The nagging turned to a flutter of exhilaration that caused a low, resonating buzz in his head.

He smiled.

But then the smile slipped from his face.

Too soon, the voice of Captain Sensible warned him. *You've been here before. And on more than one occasion.*

He lay down. He closed his eyes. The buzzing receded.

There, Captain Sensible said smugly. *I told you it wasn't to be trusted.*

An hour later Clayton stirred. 'Cherry liqueurs,' he mumbled sleepily. 'What about the cherry liqueurs?'

The next morning, Alice made mistake after mistake, misreading lines, stumbling over words.

'Anything wrong?' Josie asked her.

'I'm sorry,' Alice said, 'I didn't sleep very well last night.'

She tried to focus her thoughts. But she couldn't. Her mind was elsewhere, with Rufus and Tasha, her father and Julia. And Isabel. After all, it was all down to Isabel what had happened in the end.

Last night for hour after hour she had lain awake in bed haunted by painful memories of those she had once loved. What little sleep she had finally snatched had been disrupted with myriad dreams. Most of them had revolved round Rufus. She had loved him so very much. She had believed that he was the only man she would ever love and to her shame, so far that had been true. All of her relationships had come undone for the same reason—she couldn't commit herself enough. Rufus had ensured she had never been able to trust anyone again.

She hadn't intended to tell Clayton her story in such detail last night, but once she had started she had become totally caught up in reliving those past events. In exchange for him cooking her supper this evening—heaven only knew what he would give her—she had promised to conclude her story. She could have offered him the no-frills version last night, but she had chosen not to. She had wanted to try to get to know him better. Well, it wasn't every day you stumbled across a man like Clayton Miller. She had loved *Joking Aside*, so naturally she was keen to know more about one of the show's creators.

Then, of course, there was all that stuff written about him in the newspapers. Could any of it be believed? The question they were all obsessed with was whether Clayton Miller was mad or just plain malicious, desperate to get back at his ex-partner and ex-girlfriend? He struck Alice as being neither mad nor malicious.

Mad was how she would describe her behaviour last night. After she had left Cuckoo House, she had tried ringing James. She simply *had* to know what it was he had wanted to say to her. When she'd got no reply—his mobile must have been switched off—she had been relieved. Any sane person would have accepted that if James had had anything of importance to say, such as 'Alice, I can't live without you!', he could have called her by now.

Work, she reminded herself.

Clayton was pulling out all the stops. He was cooking. Not just frying or grilling, but the real thing. Drum roll if you please. *Ta-daar!*

He had the CD player on; Leonard Cohen was singing 'First We Take Manhattan'. Accompanying the great man, Clayton shimmied his way across the kitchen, juggling eggs. Oh, yeah, look at him go! He had taught himself to juggle during the early stages of his writer's block. He had read somewhere that it could unblock and free the mind. Just went to show that you couldn't believe a damn word you read.

He placed the eggs carefully on the worktop beside the bag of flour he'd found in one of the cupboards and rolled up his sleeves. 'Right,' he said, flattening the pages of the cookery book. 'Toad-in-the-hole. First catch your toad. Ha, ha! Nothing like an old gag.' A loud rapping at the window made him jump. 'What the hell!' he exclaimed.

'Shannon!' yelled a voice. 'What are you playing at in there? Hurry up and let me in. I'm getting soaked to the skin out here.'

He recognised the haughty voice as belonging to the gun-toting old crone from yesterday. He went to let her in.

'You'd best put that near the boiler to dry,' she said, stripping off her dripping wet coat and shoving it at him.

He did as she said then found that she'd disappeared. He went through to the kitchen and found her poking about inside a cupboard.

'Bingo! I've found the glasses,' she said. 'Come on, sit yourself down and have a sip of this.' She brandished a bottle. 'It'll put the colour back in your cheeks.' She cocked an eye at the open cookery book. 'What are you cooking?'

'Roast neighbour. I reckon she'll just about fit in the oven.'

She laughed throatily and passed him a shot glass. 'Here's mud in your eye!' She chinked her glass against his.

He took a cautious sip. It seemed innocuous enough. Nothing too . . . *Whoa!* He opened his mouth, half expecting flames to leap out. He caught his breath. 'What the hell is that?'

'Just a little something I like to throw together. Top up?'

'You've got to be kidding!' He slammed a hand over his glass.

'Get on with you.' She downed her glass in one then poured herself another shot.

'I hope you're not planning to get drunk and take advantage of me.'

She roared with laughter. 'What a splendid idea! Bottoms up!'

He watched in amazement as she downed yet more of her evil brew. 'Why didn't you wait for me yesterday?' he asked.

'I told you to be there on time.'

'I was two minutes late.'

She shrugged. 'You may have time to squander but at my age I don't.' She cupped a hand behind her ear. 'Who's the crooner? A man in your state shouldn't be listening to something as grim as this.'

'What do you mean, a man in my *state*?'

'Your breakdown. So what caused it?'

'How can I say this in terms that you'll actually understand?' he said. 'I. Have. Not. Had. A. Breakdown.'

'Really? You do surprise me. Never mind. What time's supper?'

He shook his head. 'Sorry, but I have someone coming.'

'Oh? Is there love in the air?' she asked. 'And would it have anything to do with Alice Barrett?'

'Shoemaker,' he corrected her. He immediately regretted opening his mouth. He'd as good as admitted he and Alice had something going.

'So how's Alice these days? What is she up to? I remember she wanted to become an actress.'

'From what she's told me, the actress thing didn't come off. She does voiceovers.' He gingerly sipped his drink. 'When was the last time you saw her?' he asked.

George topped up her glass. 'She must have been about eighteen. I was sad to see her go. But I quite understood why she had to. If she'd stayed, she would have been the focus of an endless stream of tittle-tattle. Worse, they would have poured sympathy on her.' She paused, then once more tossed back the contents of her glass. 'Well, Shannon,' she said, pushing the empty shot glass away from her, 'this fancy dinner of yours won't cook itself.' She rose from her chair.

Clayton felt perversely cheated she was leaving. He wanted to know more. What had gone on here all those years ago? Could he rely on Alice to tell him the whole story?

'I'll see myself out,' George said when Clayton made no attempt to move from his seat.

'No chance,' he said. 'I want to make sure you've really gone.'

'And they say chivalry is dead.'

He helped her into her coat, then opened the back door. He pulled a face. 'It's a foul night.'

'I've seen worse.' She buttoned her coat up to her chin. 'Give Alice my best wishes. Tell her to call in on me. Tell her that I'm furious she hasn't done so before now. And . . .' She put a hand on his arm.

'And what?' he asked, nervous at what might be coming next.

'I've decided you need keeping an eye on, young fella m'lad. I'll call in again soon. Take care.'

Clayton had never cooked toad-in-the-hole before. How difficult could it be? The batter was just eggs, flour, milk and water. Nothing tricky. And surely, doubling the quantities involved so he could make a really big toad-in-the-hole couldn't have affected anything, could it? The trouble had started the moment an electric whisk was called for. He had never used one before. Had the juglike container not been the right bit of kit to use? Whatever it was, it was an instrument of the devil and had just sent the mixture flying at supersonic speed, splattering everything within range, including him. Now, as he tried to mop his face clean, two things occurred to him: should he have put a lid on the instrument of the devil before switching it on, and what had possessed him to say he'd cook for Alice? Middle-aged man trying to impress young girl? Was that what this was about? Pitiable. He groaned and checked the time. Forty-five minutes and Alice would be here. OK. He would dispense with any complicated machinery. Clearly he and electrical kitchen appliances of a whirring nature weren't compatible. He'd weigh yet more ingredients out and do things the old-fashioned way. His mother had used a handheld whisk. He rummaged round in the drawers and came up with just the thing.

'Right. Six ounces of flour.' No, that wasn't right. He had to double the amount. 'OK. Twelve ounces of flour.' He tipped the bag and poured. It seemed a hell of a lot. Well, all the more for him to eat.

He found a larger mixing bowl, transferred the flour to it, added the eggs, then some milk. He began whisking. The mixture was too stiff. He added more milk. Whisked again. Oh, what the hell. He added all the milk. And the water. 'Right,' he said with determined resolve. 'Here we go.' A puff of flour flew up into his face.

He lost track of how long he'd been trying to whisk some sense into the bowl of lumpy gloop when he heard the doorbell.

Here already? He looked at his watch. She was bang on time. Why couldn't she be more like Stacey? Stacey had turned being late into an art form. It used to drive him mad. On one occasion she'd taken two hours and thirty-seven minutes to get ready to go out.

It wasn't often that he was greeted with such a wide smile. 'What happened to you?' his guest asked when he opened the door.

He caught sight of himself in the mirror on the wall. Oh, smooth, he thought. His hair, face and beard were covered in a powdery, patchy white coating. He looked like he'd had his head in a trough of cocaine. Or he'd been Artexed. 'I was trying out a new face pack,' he said.

'Hmm . . . I think you may have overdone it.'

'Come through to the kitchen. But I have to warn you, there's been a hitch with supper. Basically, I'm wearing it.'

She laughed and carried on laughing as her eyes homed in on the instrument of the devil on the draining board. 'Oh, don't tell me,' she said. 'You forgot to put the lid on?'

'Don't be ridiculous,' he said, 'of course I put the lid on. Only a blithering fool would forget to do that.'

Her eyes then took in the table. 'Holy moley! Is that what I think it is? A bottle of George's grog? Tell me you didn't drink any.'

'I stopped after four,' he said, deadpan.

She raised an eyebrow. 'And you're still on your feet?'

He shrugged and spread out his hands. 'Oh, all right, I admit it, I'm nothing but a big wuss; I managed one solitary, pathetic sip.'

'If it's as bad as I remember, you did the right thing in avoiding it. She used to give us a bottle every year for Christmas. It's probably what's preserved her all these years.'

'Pickled on the inside and creosoted on the outside,' he agreed. 'Before I forget, I'm charged with passing on her best wishes to you and to instruct you to call in and see her. She was adamant on that point.'

'Did she . . . did she say anything about my family?'

Clayton noted the hesitancy. 'Nothing specific,' he said, 'only that had you not left Cuckoo House when you did you would have been on the receiving end of a certain amount of tittle-tattle.'

'How very discreet of her,' Alice murmured. Then looking about her again, she said, 'Would you like me to straighten things out here while you see to . . .' she turned and looked directly at him, 'your face pack? What exactly is it that you're covered in?'

'Batter mix. I was trying to make toad-in-the-hole. But the toad was a wriggly swine and wouldn't hold still.'

'I'd recommend you wash it off before it sets like concrete.'

'But I can't leave you down here tidying this lot up on your own.'

'I honestly don't mind.'

Left alone, Alice took a moment to take stock. What was it with men? They couldn't manage the simplest of things in the kitchen. Her father had once done exactly the same thing. The damage had been worse in his case since he'd been attempting to make carrot soup; nothing had ever shifted the stains. Or her father's unshakeable conviction that of course he'd screwed the lid on firmly—what did people take him for, a raving imbecile?

When she had everything in order, she made a fresh batch of batter. Next she found the sausages in the fridge, put them into the oven. After a search, she found a bag of peas in the freezer and some stock cubes in the cupboard. Toad-in-the-hole with peas and gravy: perfect.

She was opening a stock cube when her mobile rang. It was her agent and Hazel had bad news to deliver.

'I'm sorry, Alice, and I can't tell you how angry this makes me, but James Montgomery has just signed a new contract to write another five books and because his popularity is growing, his publishers want—'

'—someone else to read his books. A name. A *big* name.'

'You and I know all too well how this industry works.'

So that's what James had wanted to discuss with her. That's what he didn't have the nerve to go through with. What a fool she had been! A bloody stupid fool. Would she never learn to read the signs?

'Alice? Are you still there?'

'Yes,' she said tiredly. 'I'm still here. Thanks for letting me know.'

'I'll be chasing the next big thing for you, Alice. Trust me on that.'

Alice ended the call as cheerfully as she could manage. *The next big thing*. When it came down to it, that's what it was all about. From one day to the next, it was living in hope of the next big job. The next big relationship. The next big moment of happiness. The next new beginning. James must have known for some time that she wouldn't be reading any more of his books. He had waited for her to finish work on the last ones, then he had skedaddled. Yet, in fairness, he had very nearly plucked up the courage to talk to her. The mistake she had made was to read too much into his charming manner. He had never once given her cause to think that they had anything more than a professional relationship. It was her overactive imagination that had got the better of her. Everything was fantasy for her. It always had been.

'Mmm . . . something smells good.'

She turned at the sound of Clayton's voice. Except it wasn't Clayton. He was a clean-shaven stranger. His hair was neatly combed into place and his shirt and jeans were less rumpled.

He smiled ruefully and rubbed his smooth chin. 'You were right about that stuff setting like concrete. I gave up trying to wash it out of my beard; it was easier to hack the lot off.'

Alice had to fight the urge to gawp at him from all angles. The transformation was really quite something. 'Aren't you worried about someone recognising you?' she asked.

'Round here? I don't think so. Paranoia had me kidding myself that I had made that big an impression on the world. Better to believe in one's smallness than one's greatness, don't you think?'

'Funny you should say that. I've just received a call from my agent that's made me realise how insignificant I am. I've been replaced by a bigger name. It often happens in my line of work. If the product I've been helping to get off the ground hits the big time, the money men step in and demand a well-known actor be used.'

'And what's the product in this particular instance?'

'A series of children's books by James Montgomery.' She could see him thinking. 'Yes, he was the one who phoned me here the other day. The one you said made me go pink at the edges.'

'That wasn't very gallant of me. I'm sorry. Does it muddy the waters, then, as far as your relationship goes, that this guy's ditched you, professionally speaking, in favour of a big name?'

Without answering him, she went over to the oven. She pulled out the roasting tin of cooked sausages, poured the batter mix over them and returned the tin to the oven. 'Thirty-five minutes and we'll be ready,' she said. She removed the oven gloves and found that she was being stared at. She suddenly felt irritated. 'Are you going to keep staring at me until I've answered you, is that it?'

He took a moment to reply. 'Actually, I was just thinking how annoyed I was with myself for upsetting you. Especially when you've gone to so much trouble to salvage the evening. I'm sorry.'

'You've done a lot of apologising this evening.'

'What can I say? It's new to me. I'm trying to get the hang of it.'

She smiled. 'I'd say you've almost got it licked. And the answer to your question is that I had nothing but a work relationship with James. Typically, I misread the situation and thought there was more to it.'

'Ah, I see. Well, I'm doubly sorry in that case. Does that mean we get to spend part of the evening bitching about chummy-boy to make you feel better? We could go online and write some creatively cruel reviews about his books if you like.'

She laughed. 'That won't be necessary. I feel better already. By the way, it was him who pointed you out to me in the newspaper. In case you're wondering, I didn't let on that you were staying here.'

'Thank you for that. Right then, what can I do to help?'

'How about if you open the wine?'

Clayton sat back in his chair. He raised his glass to his dining companion. 'Alice, I can honestly say that was the best toad-in-the-hole I've ever eaten. Thank you. Can I hire you to come and cook for me every day?'

She wagged a finger at him. 'You had your opportunity when I was Katya.'

'Oh, how I miss Katya!'

'Liar. You hated her.'

'No, I didn't. I was terrified of her!'

Alice laughed.

Clayton tipped his head back and closed his eyes. He had forgotten how much he enjoyed making someone laugh. He'd also forgotten how infectious laughter could be. He hadn't felt this relaxed in someone else's company in a very long while. He couldn't remember the last time when he'd found anything remotely amusing or experienced an emotion other than bitter regret.

'Can I ask you something?'

Clayton opened his eyes. 'Depends what it is.'

'Don't look so alarmed. I was just wondering what it must be like to be such a hugely popular writer.'

'The first thing you have to understand is that writing is a compulsion. Maybe like acting is for you. The second thing is that as strong as that compulsion is, there's no security in it. You're living off your wits and if those wits pack up and leave home, you're a goner. The compulsion then is to disappear into a great big black hole of nothing.'

'Is that what happened to you?'

'Yes,' he said simply.

'Will you write again, do you think? Do you even want to?'

He thought of last night, how his brain had felt as if it had momentarily rewired itself. 'I've discovered a wood pile in one of the outhouses; why don't we make a fire, but in the room with the turret? I like that room.' Clayton's face was suddenly animated, his voice eager. 'Then you can tell me about the cherry liqueurs.'

Alice smiled. 'A bedtime story round the campfire?'

'It's what everyone wants, isn't it?'

Ten minutes later and Clayton was clearly in his element. Give a man the opportunity to play with a fire and he was transformed.

Sitting cross-legged on the floor, Alice watched Clayton, fascinated and amused. All his concentration was focused on building the perfectly constructed fire. How different he was from the dishevelled, bad-tempered, grumpy man she had met just a short time ago. He had mellowed beyond belief. Now that the beard was gone she could discern his features more clearly. To her surprise, she liked what she saw. He probably wouldn't ever be described as classically good-looking, but his eyes were a soft hazel colour, and his mouth had an appealing lopsided curve to it. He had a tall, rangy build with broad shoulders.

She watched him strike a match and hold it carefully against a screwed-up ball of newspaper, his face illuminated with a golden light. He seemed so contentedly untroubled now and she found herself hoping that he would be able to find a way to be happy again.

During supper, and although she was itching to know more, she had deliberately not pressed him on the exact details of his winding up here at Cuckoo House. He in turn hadn't asked her anything about her childhood, not until they'd finished eating and he'd raised the matter of the cherry liqueurs. Prior to that, he'd told her some anecdotes about working with the American studio that had made the US version of *Joking Aside*. He had also asked her about her work and she had enjoyed showing off her catalogue of voices—Marge Simpson, Victoria Beckham, Davina McCall, Anne Robinson and Hollywood greats such as Zsa Zsa Gabor and Bette Davis. He was a good audience.

'There,' he said, swinging round to her and wiping his hands on his trousers. 'Now we're all set for story time.'

Chapter Five

ALICE HAD KEPT HER PROMISE to Rufus not to tell anyone about them. But in truth, there wasn't an awful lot to tell. Very little had actually changed since that day he had kissed her and walked out of Cuckoo House.

Once he was back in London he wrote to her, but the letters were always a disappointment. Whereas she couldn't stop herself from opening her heart to him, he never spoke of his feelings for her. 'I'm no good with putting my emotions down on paper,' he'd written in one letter, 'but you know in your heart how I feel about you.' She hung onto that and veered from euphoric delight whenever she recalled their first kiss to desperate misery that she couldn't see him.

At Cuckoo House things were becoming increasingly difficult between Alice's father and Julia. The arguments escalated until they were no longer conducted behind closed doors. Julia was no match for Bruce's vociferous outbursts; she would break down in tears and accuse him of bullying her. Alice knew that tears were anathema to her father. He would walk away from Julia in disgust whenever she cried. Something that was happening more and more.

The worst of it was that this newfound hostility put a strain on Alice and Tasha's friendship. Predictably Tasha took her mother's side and described her stepfather as a heartless tyrant. When Tasha did that, Alice would rush to defend her father. One day she blurted out that Tasha should be grateful for having such a generous stepfather, that if it hadn't been for him, they wouldn't have anything. 'What do you mean by that?' Tasha had demanded.

'Nothing,' Alice had said, snapping her mouth shut. She had promised herself she would never let on to Tasha that she and her family were as poor as the proverbial church mouse for, as the days and weeks passed, and Bruce made himself yet more unpopular in Tasha's eyes, she had begun to mention her dead father more frequently. She would proudly show Alice the photographs she had of him. The stories Tasha told of her father—what a clever and successful man he'd been—

were untrue. Knowing how she felt about her own father, Alice couldn't bring herself to tell Tasha the truth

One day, during the summer holidays, she pleaded with her father to write to Rufus and say he was sorry and that he'd reconsidered. 'Nothing doing, Alice,' her father had said, 'and do you really want to know why I'm not going to reconsider?'

'You want to teach Rufus a lesson?' she said.

'There is that, but more crucially, the truth of the matter is that since your mother died, money has not been as plentiful as it once was. Look, Alice, I think it's time I told you something important. I was going to wait until your birthday, but now is as good a time as any. It was your great-aunt Eliza who had all the dosh. She left it in a trust to your mother when she died and when your mother died, a new trust was invoked which meant I would be paid a regular allowance to take care of you, but the bulk of the trust will pass to you when you turn eighteen. You see, your great-aunt Eliza never trusted me when it came to money; she was determined that you would inherit the bulk of everything she had, which is why this house isn't in my name. When your mother died, it became yours. Well, strictly speaking it does when you turn eighteen.'

Alice was astonished. 'Why didn't you tell me this before?'

He waved a tired hand. 'It all seemed such a bore to me. Plus I didn't want you growing up with the burden of it. And I'd strongly advise you not to tell anyone about this conversation. Especially not any young men you might become entangled with.'

Wondering if her father was thinking of a young man in particular, she said, 'Would I be right in saying that Julia has no money?'

He nodded. 'Of course, I've known all along that that was why she agreed to marry me. She thought I was the answer to all her problems.' He smiled. 'She had a nasty shock when she realised her mistake.'

'Why did you marry her, Dad?'

'Good question, Alice. Maybe I was lonely. Maybe I thought she'd make a good mother to you. Has Julia been a good mother to you?'

'I don't really know. She's not like Mum was.'

He smiled ruefully at this. 'Your mother was unique.'

'Do you miss her?'

'God, yes. It's not till you lose someone that you realise how important they were to you. Life was hell at times with Barbara, but it was never boring. A day doesn't go by when I don't miss her wit.'

'If Mum meant so much to you, why did you . . .' Alice faltered but then forced herself to ask the question she had always wanted to ask her father. 'Why did you mess about with all those au pairs?'

Without a flicker of hesitation or embarrassment, he said, 'Neither your mother nor I were saints, Alice, but no matter what we got up to, we always came back to each other. Some relationships are made that way. But let's not dwell on any of that. There's something else I want to discuss with you. In September, you'll be eighteen; I want you to have a party. A real do. A marquee on the lawn affair. A disco. The full works.'

She looked at him doubtfully. 'Can we afford it?'

He rolled his eyes. 'Now you see, that's exactly why I never told you any of this nonsense about money before.'

On the day of the party, Cuckoo House was crammed to the rafters with guests. Tasha and Alice were alone in Alice's bedroom getting dressed. For some weeks now there had been a truce in place between them; this was mostly down to Alice—forever the mediator—who had suggested that she and Tasha have a combined eighteenth birthday party.

Tasha was wearing a white dress that showed off her flawless olive skin. Alice's dress, made of red silk, was long and strapless like Tasha's. Tasha had done her make-up for her, making her eyes look dark and sultry.

'Here, have some of this,' Tasha said. She passed Alice a bottle of vodka.

Alice took a sip. Then another. And another. She wasn't planning on getting drunk, but she did want to drink enough to take away the pain that Rufus wouldn't be at the party. She had begged him in numerous letters to come. 'If you really care about me, you'll do this one small thing for me,' she had written. She knew she was taking a risk—emotionally blackmailing him—but she was desperate to see him. The risk had backfired; he hadn't replied to her letter. He hadn't even sent her a birthday card. She was devastated. She had lost him.

Alice was dancing with Jessica Lawton's brother, Magnus. He was studying politics up in Edinburgh and looked good in black tie.

'The question I've been asking myself all evening,' Magnus yelled in her ear, his hands creeping round her waist and towards her chest, 'is why a girl as beautiful as you doesn't have a boyfriend.' His thumbs had almost made contact with her breasts.

She shrugged. Flirting didn't come easily to her, but she'd had sufficient to drink and now thought what the hell? Rufus didn't love her;

why shouldn't she have some fun? It was her eighteenth birthday party. She leaned into Magnus and said, 'Maybe I was waiting for the right person to come along.'

He grinned and took her in his arms. 'Come on,' he said, 'let's go somewhere quiet so I can give you my full attention.'

She allowed him to lead her outside and round to one side of the marquee. 'Now then,' he said, 'here's your first lesson of the night.'

'And what lesson would that be?' said a voice directly behind Alice.

She spun round. 'Rufus!'

He smiled. 'Looks like I got here in the nick of time. Whoever you are,' he said to Magnus, the smile gone from his face, 'hands off. This one's mine. Go on, piss off before I get really angry with you.'

Magnus dissolved into the night.

'Rufus,' she said again. 'What are you doing here?'

'It's your birthday; did you really think I wouldn't come?'

'But . . . I wrote . . . and when you didn't reply, I thought that you didn't care about me any more.'

'Alice, how could you think that?' He encircled her waist with his hands, pulled her to him and kissed her fiercely.

When they finally pulled apart, he said, 'I'd say that was definitely worth coming back for.'

Suddenly light-headed, she could feel herself swaying, as if she was about to fall off a cliff. 'I think I'm going to faint,' she murmured.

He held her firmly. 'I've got you, Alice, and I'll never let you go.'

'Rufus? Is that you?'

They both turned to see Tasha standing a few feet away.

'Oh my God, it is you, Rufus!' But then the expression of delight at seeing her brother slipped and was replaced with an expression of confusion. 'Why are you holding Alice like that? What's going on, Alice?'

Alice didn't know what to say.

But Rufus did. Still keeping an arm round her, he said, 'I couldn't *not* come to my girlfriend's eighteenth birthday party.' As if to convince his sister, he bent his head and kissed Alice again.

'Since when?' Tasha looked horrified.

Embarrassed, Alice wriggled out of Rufus's arms. 'Since Easter,' she said shyly. 'We've kept it a secret, though.'

'Why?' Tasha demanded.

'Because of Alice's father,' Rufus said matter of factly. 'He's hardly likely to approve, is he? But I've decided he can stick his disapproval.'

'What about you, Tasha?' Alice said, nervously. 'Do you approve?'

Tasha looked uncertainly between Rufus and Alice. 'I don't know,' she said. 'It's weird. I mean, it's practically incest.'

Rufus suddenly laughed. 'Hey, if I didn't know better I'd say my little sister is jealous.'

'I'm not! Don't be ridiculous.'

'Only joking, Tasha.' He smirked as she stormed off.

Rufus was all for marching straight off to find Bruce and Julia. But not wanting anything to spoil the moment, Alice tugged at his sleeve and held him back. 'Let's go and see them later,' she whispered in his ear. 'For now I want some time on my own with you.'

Smiling, Rufus grabbed her hand. 'I know the perfect place.'

The perfect place turned out to be his bedroom. As soon as he had the door shut, he pressed her to the wall and kissed her hard. Their mouths locked tight, he somehow managed to fling off his jacket. When he started to unbutton his shirt, she suddenly realised what he was planning to do. She panicked. Oh God, what if she got pregnant? She broke the seal of their mouths. 'Rufus,' she murmured anxiously. 'I—'

'Oh, Alice,' he said gruffly, misunderstanding her. 'I want you, too.' One of his hands slipped round to the back of her dress. He found the zip and pulled on it. She felt the silk fall away from her body; he smiled, picked her up and carried her over to his bed. He stood over her and ripped off his trousers.

I want this, Alice told herself. Wasn't it what she'd fantasised about all this time? He lay on top of her, then as if by magic, her underwear was gone. His mouth and hands were exploring her body. She imagined herself on a beach, the hot sun blazing down on her, waves gently caressing her body. Her panic began to fade. She moved against him, enjoying the touch of his skin on hers. Maybe it would be all right.

Abruptly he leaned over her and yanked open a drawer on the bedside table. 'I'm sorry, Alice,' he said, 'but I can't hold on any longer.' Next she heard him tearing something open. Her nervousness returned in an instant. *Relax*, she told herself. He pushed gently at first, then as if losing patience he pushed harder still and forced his way in. She gritted her teeth, trying to ignore the burning sensation. He started to move, his hips working against hers. She lay there not knowing quite what to do. Nothing much, it seemed. With his eyes closed, Rufus seemed in a world of his own. She couldn't even tell if he was enjoying himself. How long would it go on for? she wondered. Oh God, why was she even thinking that? Why wasn't she enjoying herself? Why wasn't she making the kind of noises women in films did?

Above her, Rufus let out a long, shuddering moan then collapsed against her, his body hot and sweaty. Was that it? Was it over? A part of her was relieved. 'There,' he murmured. 'I've claimed you now, Alice. Happy birthday.' Just as she was about to shift position so she could stop her leg from cramping, the door flew open.

Now she did cry out.

Perfectly framed in the doorway was her father and there was nowhere to hide; both lying on top of the duvet, their nakedness was fully exposed. Rufus sat up and casually dealt with the condom. 'Hey, Bruce,' he said, 'a little privacy if you don't mind. How would you feel if I burst in on you and my mother?'

Alice trembled.

Her father made a low grumbling sound. He came into the room, scooped up her discarded dress and flung it at Alice. 'When you've got a moment, Alice,' he said, 'we're ready to cut your cake.' He turned and left, slamming the door after him.

Nothing was said the next day until their guests had all left.

At Rufus's insistence, Alice had spent the night in his room. 'You're a grown woman,' he'd said. 'You can sleep with whom you want.'

Actually she'd wanted to sleep alone. But she'd gone along with him. 'You'll enjoy it more this time,' he'd said. She must have been doing something wrong because she didn't enjoy it any more than the first time. She had been tense, horribly aware that her father, as well as all the guests, might hear what they were doing. Frankly, she couldn't see how they could miss it. Throughout it all Rufus had made loud grunting. The headboard had thumped against the wall and the bed itself had creaked. To make matters worse, Rufus had wanted a repeat performance in the morning. When they finally emerged downstairs for breakfast, everyone had stared at Alice. The girls sniggered together, with the exception of Tasha who looked at her as though she was smeared in something unspeakable, and the boys gave Rufus lewd winks and thumbs-up gestures.

She had wondered how her father had known where to find her last night. It turned out that Tasha had seen them sneaking off inside the house, had put two and two together and had helpfully pointed Alice's father in that direction.

She was glad when the last of the guests had left. Now all she had to cope with was her father. She found him sitting in his car.

'I forbid you to see him again, Alice,' he said.

'I don't think you can do that, Dad,' she said quietly.

'He's not good enough for you.'

'He said you'd say that.'

'He's . . . he's only doing this to get at me.'

'Oh, Dad, not everything's about you.'

'Is that something else he's filled your head with?'

She turned and looked at her father. Really looked at him. When was the last time she had done that? She let her eyes travel the familiar, yet at the same time unfamiliar track of his profile. His nose was a bit on the beaky side, but he wasn't bad-looking. His hair needed cutting but he hadn't gone grey yet. He was dressed in faded jeans and a blue denim shirt that matched the blue of his eyes. The collar of his shirt was askew: she could see he hadn't buttoned it correctly. She remembered how Mum used to say he couldn't be trusted to get himself dressed of a morning. She thought of him dressed as a pirate when she'd been little—the moustache he'd glued to his top lip, the peg leg he'd strapped on, the eye patch. He'd gone to so much trouble. And all for her. She felt her throat tighten. 'I love him, Dad,' she said.

'Is there nothing I can do to make you see sense?'

'What have you got against him?'

Her father gripped the steering wheel. 'I don't trust him. I never have. I once caught him snooping through my desk. Swear you'll never tell him about the house, that as of yesterday you now own it.' He whipped his head round. 'You haven't told him already, have you?'

'No, Dad, I haven't.'

They sat in silence again until her father said, 'If he ever hurts you, in any way, I'll make damned sure he pays for it.'

Not surprisingly, things were never the same again after that weekend.

Alice and Tasha returned to school for their final year, but not as friends. Tasha made that very clear. Bad enough that Alice and Rufus had been carrying on behind her back, but then, in Tasha's own words, to flaunt their relationship by shagging themselves senseless and for all to hear, was 'just plain disgusting'.

A fortnight after the party, Alice was working in one of the study cubicles in the school library when the door opened at the far end of the room. Knowing she was alone, she leaned out of the cubicle to see who had come in and spotted Tasha with Freya Maynard. 'Alice is nothing but a two-faced slut,' she heard Tasha say. Her cheeks burning, Alice rocketed forward in her seat to try and conceal herself.

Footsteps approached. 'Oh, it's *her*.'

Never had so much contempt been poured into so few words. Alice turned round as casually as she could. It was time for yet another performance of sparkling indifference. 'Oh, it's *you*,' she said in return. 'For your information, Tasha, I am not a slut.'

'Then why do you behave like one?'

'Careful what you say, Tasha. If you make me out to be such a slut, what does it make Rufus?'

Tasha recoiled. 'I don't know how you've done it, but you've blinded my brother. You want to be one of us, a Raphael. Well, it won't work. You're just a nobody. A weirdo Barrett. I'm embarrassed to be associated with you.' She linked an arm through Freya's. 'Come on, Freya, let's find somewhere more conducive to study.'

The door closed after them with a decisive thud.

Exhausted from the strain of her performance, Alice slumped forward and rested her head against her forearms on the desk. Not only was she a slut for loving Rufus, but she was a nobody. What was that all about? And what the hell was so special about being a Raphael? Anyone would think Tasha was a member of the royal family the way she carried on. Alice didn't know which of them was the more self-deluded—Tasha, or herself for believing that once Tasha had got things into perspective they would be best friends again.

Now, though, she was wondering if she wanted to be best friends with someone who could be such a vicious bitch.

Alice had always known that Tasha idolised her brother but now she understood that it was an exclusive right to idolise him. Well, tough luck, girl! Hadn't Rufus claimed her? Her heart lurched at the memory of him saying, *This one's mine*.

The day after the party and before he'd left Cuckoo House to return to London, Rufus had asked Alice to go for a walk with him. 'While you were talking to your father, I spoke to my mother,' he'd said. 'She seems to think that for the time being it would be better all round if we don't make too much of a big thing about our relationship. She doesn't want your father to be any more antagonised.'

'You don't regret telling them about us, do you?' she had asked him.

'Of course not. But last night I got carried away with the excitement of it all. Now I don't want you to worry over the coming weeks and months. I'm being assigned to a hospital as of next week, so I won't be easy to get hold of.'

'Can I write to you?'

'Of course. I'll do my best to write back, but I'm not much of a letter writer. But keep yours coming.'

Thinking now of Rufus's rock-sure certainty, Alice decided to write to him. She would tell him how awful Tasha was being; if Tasha was going to listen to anyone, it would be Rufus.

How wrong could she have been?

A month after Alice posted her letter—a long, worrying month during which she didn't hear from Rufus—she received a reply. She and Tasha were at home for half-term when his letter arrived.

Dear Alice,

I've always been honest with you and so I'll come straight to the point. I've met somebody else and being with her makes me realise that you and I were kidding ourselves when we thought we were in love with each other. Your father would never have accepted me, so this is best all round. I hope you can see the sense of what I'm saying and won't make any trouble. When all is said and done, you are my sister and we have to get along.

Regards, Rufus

P.S. At Mum's request, I'm planning on being at Cuckoo House for Christmas.

Somebody else? Alice couldn't believe it. How could he have tossed her aside so easily? In one sweep of his pen, he had broken her heart.

With each reading of the letter, she began to doubt everything he'd ever said to her. To end things so abruptly—had there ever been anything of a genuine feeling in his entire body for her? She thought of the many letters she had written to him, of how she had given herself to him the night of her birthday. Only now to be discarded so cruelly.

She lay on her bed and cried herself out. There seemed no end to her tears. A knock at the door had her lifting her head from the pillow. 'Go away!' she croaked.

The door opened. 'Alice?' Her father came over to the bed. He sat on the edge of it. 'What's wrong, love?'

She thrust Rufus's letter at him. 'See for yourself.'

She watched him read the letter, his eyes flickering along each line. 'I'm sorry,' her father said. 'I'm sorry I allowed him to hurt you. But I warned you. Didn't I say that I didn't trust him?'

'It's not him, Dad!' she wailed. 'It's you. You made him do this! He would have loved me if it hadn't been for you!' She didn't really believe what she was saying but she needed to blame someone.

'Oh, Alice, don't let him do this to you. He's not worth it. And don't think I've forgotten the promise I made to you. I said that if he ever hurt you, I'd make him pay.'

Things went even further downhill from then on. Alice and Tasha returned to school but a week later Alice was diagnosed as having glandular fever and because her father was away in Norway on an assignment, Julia had to come and fetch her home.

Alice had always considered Julia's vacuous presence at Cuckoo House as being little more than that of a shadow. Her input was minimal. Certainly this was the first time she had tackled the drive to school on her own. It was also the first time that Alice had spent more than ten minutes in her company alone.

'Do you feel very poorly?' she asked Alice.

'Yes,' Alice replied, her eyes closed. She couldn't recall ever feeling this ill before. The doctor had said it was unlikely she would return before school started again in January. Even then, he'd warned her she might not feel up to it.

'You'll probably want to go straight to bed when we get home.'

'Yes,' Alice replied again.

'Have you heard from Rufus?'

Alice said nothing.

'Love's a fickle thing, Alice.'

Shut up!

'Really, what you imagined you felt for Rufus was nothing more than a teenage crush. You'll soon get over it.'

'Could you not talk about it, please?' Alice said hoarsely.

'It's easy to get confused when our emotions are involved,' Julia said, as if Alice hadn't spoken. 'We all make mistakes.'

Yes, thought Alice. My father definitely did when he married you.

'Things have recently become very difficult between your father and me. He's not an easy man to live with. God knows I've tried, but I just don't seem to be able to make him . . .' Julia's voice faded away and she started to cry.

Oh, great, thought Alice. Just what she needed: a feeble, weepy Julia. 'If you're going to cry perhaps it would be safer if we pulled over,' she said wearily.

They pulled over into a lay-by. Cars and lorries thundered by, shaking the Range Rover Dad had bought Julia last year.

'I thought you would be able to help me,' Julia sniffled, her pale face spotted with ugly red blotches. 'Bruce never loses his temper with you.'

'That's because I don't annoy him.'

Julia cried even harder. 'I don't think I can take much more.'

'Then go. Just leave him.'

'It's not as easy as that.'

No, thought Alice, it isn't, is it? 'My father is nothing more than financial security to you, isn't he?' she said coldly. 'I *know* why you married him. So does my father. You're not a patch on my mother and that's probably what drives my father mad. He despises you. He despises the fact that you're so weak and can't stand up to him.'

More tears spilled down Julia's face. 'You hate me, don't you? You hate me nearly as much as your father hates me.'

'I don't, actually. You're nothing to me. Just as Rufus is nothing to me. Just as Tasha means nothing to me. Do you know what she's put me through at school? She's telling everyone I'm a slut for loving your precious son. I may be a fool, but I'm not what she says I am.'

'Tasha's very attached to Rufus. She . . . ever since her father died, she's worshipped the ground he walks on.'

'And you think that's healthy?'

'I don't really see anything wrong in it. But I'll tell you what *is* wrong, and that's how Bruce treats me. Have you ever wondered about the way your mother died?'

Alice stiffened. 'It was an accident.'

'Not suicide, then? You don't think that she woke up one morning and realised she couldn't go on living with a madman?'

Alice was consumed with loathing towards Julia, spewing toxic insults and spite at her for the slightest of reasons. Often for no reason at all. If she couldn't exact revenge on Rufus, she would settle for making his mother's life even more wretched than it already was.

After weeks of taking whatever Alice threw at her, Julia finally showed a hint of spirit and came close to fighting back.

It was three days before Christmas—Tasha hadn't yet come home from school as she had gone to stay with Freya—and Alice was in the kitchen rolling out pastry for mince pies while her father sat at the table reading aloud to her from P. G. Wodehouse's *The Code of the Woosters*. It was a comforting reminder of when she'd been little.

'That was Tasha on the phone,' Julia said, breezing into the kitchen and instantly destroying the cosy, tranquil atmosphere. 'She and Rufus will be arriving tomorrow afternoon.' She looked directly at Alice, an unexpectedly brave, challenging look of score-settling in her eye. 'Rufus is bringing his girlfriend with him. I trust you don't have a problem with that?'

'You don't think it would have been polite to have checked first?' her father asked without looking up.

'Polite, in the sense of tiptoeing round Alice's feelings? Is that what you mean?'

'You know damned well that's exactly what I mean.'

Julia laughed bitterly. 'Whoever considers *my* feelings?'

'Why should anyone else contribute to the stockpile of your self-absorption when you do such a fine job of it yourself?'

What little fight Julia had mustered was gone. 'Is that what this Christmas is going to be like?' she asked, her voice tight.

'We wouldn't be having this tedious discussion if you hadn't encouraged your son to flaunt his new girlfriend under Alice's nose. But thanks to you, I think it's safe to say that we're now set for a real old Rice Krispie Christmas. And by that, I mean there'll be plenty of snap, crackle and pop. Really, Julia, you have only yourself to blame.'

'Do not treat me this way,' Julia said slowly and a little breathlessly.

He said nothing. Alice resumed rolling out the pastry.

'"I am a shy man, Bertie,"' Bruce read aloud. '"Diffidence is the price I pay for having a hypersensitive nature."'

A stifled squawking sound came from Julia's direction and then the door crashed shut behind her.

'You OK?' Bruce asked.

Alice blinked. 'I can't believe Rufus could be so crass.'

'I could put my foot down and say he can't bring her with him, but that way he gets to play the hard-done-by stepson. By letting him bring his girlfriend with him, you and I are going to prove just how meaningless he is to you now.'

Her father was right. But he was also wrong. Horribly wrong. With her father so certain that Rufus now meant nothing to her, how could she tell him that she had secretly been hoping that when he returned to Cuckoo House for Christmas and spent some time alone with her, Rufus would see what a terrible mistake he had made?

From the moment Isabel Canning stepped over the threshold of Cuckoo House the following afternoon, she swept into their lives like a breath of fresh air. In Alice's mind this unknown quantity had been cast in the role of Public Enemy Number One. Meeting her made Alice realise that her cause to win back Rufus was lost. There wasn't a chance in hell of Alice competing with this incredible creature. Blonde, blue-eyed and beautiful beyond belief, she looked older than Alice had expected. She was charmingly jolly and she greeted Alice and her father like long-lost friends. Either Rufus hadn't explained the situation to her, or she was a better actress than Alice could ever hope to be.

Within an hour of being in Isabel's company, Alice could quite understand how Rufus had fallen under her spell. She had a knack for showing great interest in her surroundings or whatever somebody was telling her. She enthusiastically admired the curtains and sofa Julia had recently had made for the sitting room, she raved over the Christmas tree Alice had decorated, and she was particularly interested in Bruce's work, professing to dabble in photography herself—a remark that would normally elicit a snort of derision from him. She somehow managed to extract a promise from him to show her his darkroom before she left.

So much for Public Enemy Number One.

All the while, Rufus looked on with pride and adoration shining in his eyes. He was completely captivated.

However, Tasha was not so captivated. Maybe that was because she knew Isabel was a genuine threat. This was no teenage crush. It explained to Alice why Tasha had returned to Cuckoo House with a hand of friendship shyly extended towards her: she needed an ally. Who better than the girl whose heart had been broken by her brother? By anyone's standards, it was an audacious U-turn. Did she really think Alice would conveniently forget all that had passed between them?

Alice had assumed responsibility for cooking over the Christmas holiday. While stuck at home, and since she had been well enough, she had been teaching herself to cook to relieve the boredom. Tonight she was going to cook roast duck with an orange and cranberry sauce.

But Isabel wouldn't hear of it. 'We can't have you slaving away in the kitchen on your own,' she insisted. 'Tasha and I will help you.'

'What about me?' Rufus asked, 'I could help as well.'

Laughing, Isabel shook him off. 'This is girl time. I'm going to find out from your lovely sisters everything about you that you've tried to hide from me, and I don't want you butting in.'

Rufus exchanged his first direct glance with Alice and visibly paled. Oh my God, she thought, Isabel didn't know anything, did she?

Public Enemy Number One. Alice had to keep reminding herself. But how could she hate Isabel? How could she hate anyone who was such fun and who was showering such warmth, kindness and encouragement on her? They were standing together at the sink, peeling potatoes, and Isabel was promising that when the time came, she would put in a good word for Alice and Tasha with an old family friend who was a theatrical agent in London.

'I don't believe in nepotism,' Tasha said sulkily. She was sitting on the worktop, banging her heels against the cupboard below. 'I want to know I made it to the top through my own merit,' she added.

Isabel had to be aware of Tasha's brooding hostility towards her but nothing in her conduct betrayed how she felt about it. 'Gosh, Tasha, you're so right,' she said cheerfully. 'I applaud your conviction. I'm afraid I don't have half your talent, so am quite shameless in asking for a teensy leg-up when necessary.'

'What kind of work do you do?' asked Alice, curious.

'Officially I'm an events organiser, you know, organising parties, conferences, charity balls, that sort of thing. Hopelessly superficial.'

'And unofficially?'

Isabel laughed. 'Unofficially, I'm a free spirit looking for a sense of purpose to my life. I dabble here and there. One minute I want to be an artist, the next I want to be a photographer. That's why I'm so fascinated by your father. He really does take amazing pictures. But then you know that, don't you? You must have the most incredible photo albums of you growing up. I'd love to see them.'

Tasha's heels had taken up a faster and more vigorous beat against the cupboard door. 'That's the funny thing about Alice's father,' she said, 'I can't recall him taking a single photograph of us as a family.'

Alice smiled awkwardly. 'It's true. Dad's always preferred taking pictures of wildlife or landscapes.'

'Exactly how old are you, Isabel?' Tasha said suddenly. 'You seem so much older than Rufus. I reckon you're thirty.'

'Thirty,' Isabel repeated with a raise of her elegant eyebrows. 'Well, I've been told I look older than I am, but you're out by five years.'

'What's it like going out with a toy boy?' Tasha continued relentlessly.

'It can be a terrible pain sometimes,' Isabel said with a weary sigh. 'I can't tell you how often I've forgotten to blow his nose for him.'

Alice smirked, but knowing she'd been made fun of, Tasha looked furious. 'I'm bored,' she said. 'I'm going to go and talk to Rufus.'

When they were alone, Isabel said, 'Would I be right in thinking Tasha doesn't like me very much?'

'She's very protective of her brother.'

'What about you, Alice? Are you very protective of Rufus?'

'Are you asking me if I like you?'

Isabel smiled. 'That's exactly what I'm asking you.'

To her amazement, Alice replied, 'Yes, I do.'

'Thank you. Now tell me everything you think I should know about Rufus. No holding anything back. I want to know all his nasty habits. Apart from the fact he hates it when he can't get his own way.'

During dinner, Rufus was displaying this very trait. Tasha had laid the table and had put her mother and Bruce at each end of the table with Rufus between his mother and Alice and Isabel between Bruce and herself. Rufus was far from happy with the arrangement. Especially as Isabel was hanging on to Bruce's every word. Alice hadn't seen her father so animated in a long while. He was enjoying himself, she realised.

Unlike Rufus, who, stuck with his lacklustre mother and Alice for conversation, was clearly having a miserable time. They had moved on to dessert when he clinked his spoon against his glass. 'I have an announcement,' he said. 'I was going to wait until Christmas Day, but I've never been known for my patience, so here goes. Isabel and I are going to be married.'

There was a momentary silence. Not one of them had seen that coming. Not even Isabel, from the startled expression on her face.

'Well, isn't anyone going to congratulate us?' Rufus demanded.

At breakfast the next morning, Tasha said, 'I know a good joke. Would you like to hear it, Isabel? It's about Alice and Rufus.'

Alice froze. As did Rufus. 'Shut up, Tasha,' he said.

'That's no way to speak to me, Rufus. Not on Christmas Eve. Honestly, Isabel, you'll love my joke. Actually, Alice knows the joke better than me; she should tell it to you really. Alice?'

'I think I'll pass on breakfast,' Alice murmured. She pushed back her chair and stood up. She was halfway to the door when her father came in. 'Dad,' she said, 'why don't you show Isabel your darkroom?' She fixed him with a wildly frantic look, praying that he'd catch on.

'You must be telepathic, Alice,' he said brightly. 'I was just going to ask Isabel if she'd like to take a look.'

For once Rufus was in agreement and practically hustled Isabel out of her seat. When she was safely out of earshot, Rufus said, 'Alice, don't go. We need to talk.'

'Oh, well, if you two are going to have a cosy tête-à-tête,' Tasha said offhandedly, 'I'll leave you to it.'

Her brother turned on her. 'The fuck you will! Now sit down and tell me what the hell you thought you were playing at?'

Tasha's mouth dropped in shock. She quickly rallied, though. 'I just think your future wife should be aware that you screwed her future sister-in-law then dumped her. Don't you?'

'Why, Tasha?' Rufus replied. He turned to Alice. 'Is this your doing? Have you put her up to this as an act of revenge?'

'No! The last thing I want is for anyone else knowing how you humiliated me.'

His eyes narrowed. 'I didn't humiliate you, Alice. You and I had a bit of a thing for a while and then I came to my senses and finished it.'

'If that's all it amounted to, why don't you tell Isabel that?'

'Is this what you're going to do for the rest of my life? Hold me accountable for a moment of madness?'

'I'm not doing anything!' Alice had to stop herself from screaming the words in his face. 'If I could take a pill to make me forget what we did, then I'd take it right now. And in case you've forgotten, it was Tasha who wanted to reveal our dirty little secret, not me.'

He swung his gaze round to his sister. She stared back at him with a determined and defiant expression. 'I just think you should be honest with the woman you're going to marry, Rufus,' she said.

He went over to her. 'Tasha,' he said, his tone suddenly soft. 'I don't want to lose Isabel. She means the world to me and I don't want anything to spoil my happiness. Do you understand that?'

'But wasn't that how you felt about Alice?'

Alice moved quietly towards the door. She didn't want to hear Rufus's reply. But she was too slow.

'What I feel for Isabel couldn't be more different from what I felt for Alice,' he said. He glanced over to Alice. 'And that's the truth.'

'Fine,' she said. She fled, her eyes brimming with tears. She locked herself in her room and lay on the bed, exhausted. The doctor had warned her that it took a long time to recover fully from glandular fever. How about a broken heart? How long did that take?

She fell into a deep, dreamless sleep and two hours later she awoke to an eye-opening revelation. It was no longer her heart that needed mending: it was her pride. She didn't love Rufus any more. It was the shame of knowing she had allowed herself to be treated so shabbily that hurt. Well, it was time to hold her head up high again. Because if she didn't, the alternative was to turn into an emotional wreck like Julia.

Buoyed up with a new inner strength, she went over to the turret. Staring out of the window, she took in the grey half-light of the day. The end of the garden was hidden by thick freezing fog. Snow was predicted for tomorrow. A white Christmas. Would that cheer them all up?

She thought of Rufus's shock announcement last night at dinner. As a result of the announcement, they had learned a lot more about Isabel. Like Alice, she was an only child and her mother lived in America with her third husband—in a place called the Hamptons. Isabel described her mother's new home as being excessively overstated, but infinitely more civilised than the freezing mausoleum in Norfolk where she had grown up.

Alice's breath had formed a patch of condensation on the window. She wiped the pane of glass and below her in the garden she saw two figures emerge from the fog: her father and Isabel. In his hands was a camera and he was pointing it at Isabel, capturing her every pose, her every angle. Recalling how only last night Alice had said that her father rarely took photographs of people, she felt a shadow of unease settle on her. She pressed a finger to her top lip and tapped it. He wouldn't. Oh dear God, he absolutely wouldn't.

Would he?

For the past three years, much to Julia's horror, as well as Tasha and Rufus's disgust, Alice's father had invited George to join them for Christmas lunch. She always turned up late, tricked out in an actual dress and with a bottle of her famously noxious home brew. Today was no exception. She was introduced to Isabel, and Alice could see Rufus cringing, but Isabel took George in her elegant stride and was as charmingly interested in her as she had been in the rest of them.

It was after lunch, during present-giving time, that they took their places for the opening scene of the final act of the drama they were caught up in. Alice had always wondered just how much of what followed could have been avoided had it not been for those cherry liqueurs.

With his customary air of indifference, Alice's father handed Julia a present. He didn't wish her a Happy Christmas, nor did she utter a word of thanks. When Julia finally had the paper off, she looked over to where Bruce was sitting next to Alice. 'Why?' she asked. 'Why have you given me a box of cherry liqueurs when you know I hate them?'

'Do you?' he said with exaggerated astonishment. 'Since when?'

'Since for ever. Since before the very first time you gave me a box.' She flung the box across the room at him. It caught him on the chest then dropped to the floor at his feet. She ran from the room.

'Bruce Barrett, you are such a bastard,' Rufus said. He rose slowly. 'Is that all you think my mother's worth? A box of chocolates you know perfectly well she doesn't like?' He moved towards the offending box. He lifted a foot and they all knew what he was going to do next.

'I wouldn't do that if I were you,' Bruce said quietly.

Rufus brought his foot down with a vicious stamp and crushed the box. He then turned to Isabel. 'I want you to know here and now, Isabel, you will not be subjected to this vile man's company ever again.'

'Oh, don't talk such rubbish, young man.'

It was George who had spoken. Rufus glared at her with contempt. 'No one asked you for your opinion, you filthy, mad old hag.'

'Rufus!' This was from Isabel. She looked genuinely horrified. 'You can't speak to a guest like that.'

'She isn't a guest,' he responded hotly. 'She's a hanger-on. The local crazy woman.'

George smiled happily at the description but Alice was incensed. 'Rufus,' she said, 'apologise to George immediately.'

Rufus laughed. 'You have to be out of your mind.'

'Then I suggest you leave.'

'Isabel and I will leave when we're good and ready.'

Alice got to her feet. She squared up to Rufus. 'Isabel is welcome to stay as long as she wants, but you,' she pointed at him, 'are not.'

He laughed. 'Oh, do us all a favour and shut up, Alice.'

'Don't tell me what to do in my own house.'

Tasha joined in. 'It isn't your house, Alice, so stop telling Rufus what to do.'

Alice managed a wan smile. 'Actually, Tasha, this house does belong to me, so I'm perfectly entitled to say who is welcome and who is not. And right now, your brother isn't.'

Both Tasha and Rufus stared at her.

'Yes, you did hear me correctly. Cuckoo House became mine when I turned eighteen.' She turned to Isabel. 'I'm sorry you've had to witness this ugly scene, but you really ought to know what kind of a family you're marrying into. Oh, and by the way, Rufus and I slept together on my eighteenth birthday. Ask him about it. He'll tell you it was all very casual and meaningless. Well, it was on his part. I made the same mistake as you; I fell in love with him. Hard to fathom why now.'

Isabel's eyes grew wide and she stared at Rufus.

'You bitch!' He shouted at Alice. 'You total sodding bitch!'

'I'm warning you, Rufus, speak to my daughter like that again and you'll regret it.'

Rufus took a moment to compose himself. 'Tasha, Isabel,' he said, 'come on, let's leave them to it.'

Tasha was immediately at her brother's side, but as Rufus grabbed her hand and pulled her from the sofa, Isabel appeared less sure. At the door, she hesitated. Alice smiled at her, hoping to convey a look of understanding, that she knew Isabel was caught between a rock and a hard place.

'Are you coming, Isabel?' Rufus was glowering furiously.

'Yes,' she said.

'Bravo, Alice!' her father said when they were gone.

Alice sighed. 'Thanks, Dad. Sorry I had to pull rank on you.' She picked up the crushed box of chocolates. In Alice's hands, the flattened lid slipped off the box and, instead of smashed chocolates inside, there was a necklace, a delicate gold chain with a solitaire diamond. 'Oh, Dad, why didn't you tell Julia what you'd really given her?'

'What does it matter? What does any of it matter?' He went over to the tray of drinks. 'George, what do you fancy?'

It was three thirty in the morning and Alice couldn't sleep. Some Christmas it had turned out to be. Rufus hadn't left immediately as he'd threatened. The snow had started falling shortly after George's departure; only a fool would have set off in such treacherous conditions.

It was still snowing; Alice could see and hear it pattering softly against the window. It was years since they'd been snowed in, but if it kept up like this, in all likelihood no one would be going anywhere for the next twenty-four hours.

Rufus had apologised in a desultory fashion for losing his temper and Alice suspected that Isabel had had something to do with that. Alice had wanted her father to give Julia the necklace, but he had said that enough was enough. Alice wasn't sure what he had meant, but she hadn't pressed him. Having locked herself in her sanctuary after the cherry liqueurs fiasco, Julia had childishly refused to come out.

Alice decided to go downstairs to make herself a drink. She had reached the bottom step when she heard noises coming from the direction of the sitting room. The door was open a crack, letting a faint glowing light from inside spill out in the darkness of the hallway.

Alice went to investigate. The first thing she saw was the Christmas tree with the lights switched on. Then she saw the log fire burning in the grate and the two naked bodies directly in front of it. There was no mistaking what they were doing. Or that it was Isabel lying on her back with Alice's father moving languidly on top of her. They were gazing deeply into each other's eyes, wholly immersed in each other, their expressions intense.

Neither of them was aware of Alice or that she had crept away.

When Alice had finally managed to sleep she had fallen into a profoundly deep, dead-to-the-world kind of sleep. As she surfaced, heavy-headed and befuddled, she recalled a disturbing dream she'd had of her father and Isabel. But then her head cleared. It hadn't been a dream.

She threw on the first clothes to hand and hurried downstairs. If her father and Isabel had fallen asleep in the sitting room, there would be all hell to pay if anyone else discovered them. But the sitting room was empty. There was no sign that anything untoward had taken place there.

Alice took refuge in the kitchen and while she busied herself with making a pot of tea, she stared out of the window. Beneath an unwaveringly crystalline sky and a brightly shining sun, the snow was already melting. The sound of raised voices from upstairs and running feet broke the still quiet. What now?

Julia was on the landing. Her face was deathly pale and tears were streaming down her face. Next to her was Rufus; he was reading something. A letter? 'No!' he cried. '*No!*' He dropped the piece of paper to the floor, turned on his heel and shot off towards his room.

'What is it?' Alice forced herself to ask. 'What's happened?'

Julia crouched on the floor. 'How could he?' she wailed. 'How could he do this?'

Her heart racing, Alice picked up the discarded piece of paper. Her father's handwriting was instantly distinguishable. She had read no more than a few words when Rufus reappeared. 'Her clothes and case have gone,' he said.

Dreading the answer, Alice said, 'Do you know where my father is?'

Julia suddenly let out a manic scream. 'He's gone as well!'

'Go on, read the letter. It's all there,' Rufus seethed.

So it was. Bruce Barrett and Isabel Canning had run off together. There were no words of apology. No remorse. No regret. Just a few lines about living life to the full and seizing the day.

'Oh, Dad,' Alice murmured. 'What have you done?'

She was held personally responsible, as if it had been her job to control her father. The sad truth was, she *was* responsible. Her father had done this entirely for her benefit. He had exacted his revenge on Rufus in the cruellest way imaginable.

Julia had shut herself in her sanctuary and Tasha and Rufus had holed themselves up in the sitting room. Not really knowing why she was doing it, Alice put a tray of coffee and sandwiches together for them.

Standing by the fireplace, Rufus was jabbing a log into place. 'I thought she loved me,' he was saying. 'I really did. But she couldn't have felt anything for me, not when she could go off with a man old enough to be her father.'

Now you know what it feels like, Alice thought nastily.

'I suppose you're quietly cheering to yourself,' Tasha said as Alice put the tray down on the table in front of her. 'And you can take that away,' she added, pointing at the tray. 'We don't want anything from you.'

'Tasha, don't be such an idiot.' Alice kept her voice level.

'Don't call me an idiot. Not when your father has broken my brother's heart, not to mention what he's done to our mother. I bet you were in on it, weren't you?' Tasha continued. 'I wouldn't put it past you to have helped the pair of them slip away in the night.'

Rufus whipped round. 'Did you, Alice? Did you help them?'

'No! I'm as shocked as you are.' Well, that wasn't totally true, was it? She'd had a warning. She'd seen them in the garden. And then last night. Could she have stopped them if she had spoken to her father?

Something in Rufus's face made her think he didn't believe her. 'Our situation here is now untenable,' he said. 'Just as soon as our mother is feeling better, we'll leave. I certainly don't intend to be around when your father returns. Now, if you'd kindly leave us alone, Tasha and I have things to discuss.'

For months afterwards, Alice wondered if Rufus ever blamed himself for what happened next. Certainly she blamed herself. If Rufus had been more of a support to his mother or forced her to pull herself together, would the worst have been avoided? But instead he indulged her weeping and wailing and added to her hysteria by insisting they had to leave. The ill feeling escalated until, in the end, Alice did shout at him and his mother that she would be glad to see the back of them.

An excruciating twenty-four hours later, during which time there was no word from her father, Alice went out to the garage to sit in his car. She thought she might find some kind of solace there.

When she opened the garage, she found that his car had been trashed. The tyres had been slashed and the paintwork had been scratched. When she approached the driver's seat, she saw Julia slumped over the steering wheel. On the passenger seat beside her was an empty bottle of sloe gin, along with a selection of empty pill bottles.

Chapter Six

THE SILENCE WAS ABRUPT and long.

Clayton waited patiently for Alice to continue. After taking a steadying breath, Alice spoke again. 'I've never forgotten that moment,' she said, 'when it hit me that Julia had taken her own life. She had hinted that she might do as much, that day in the car when she came to fetch me home from school. She had even questioned whether my mother had killed herself for the same reason. But I didn't think she meant it. I should have done more for her.'

'You don't really think you were responsible for her death, do you?'

Alice shrugged. 'I was very cruel to her at times.'

Another moment of silence passed between them. 'Dare I ask what happened next?' he said quietly.

'I'll give you the shortened version. Julia's death was officially recorded as a suicide. There was talk of her having been under a lot of stress. Both Rufus and Tasha went as far as to say that my father was to blame, that he had as good as tipped those pills down her throat. Naturally that had everyone wondering for a while. Had Bruce Barrett murdered his wife? Then, of course, my mother's death was raked over again. The gossip machine was churning. The local newspaper and then a couple of the nationals picked up on it. My father's reputation as a photographer and his first wife having had a public persona was too tempting a story to pass up. Not to mention that he had scooted off with a woman so much younger than himself.'

'Where was your father when all this was going on?'

'He'd disappeared. No one could track him down. The police knew that at the time Julia had been sitting in his car swallowing handfuls of pills he and Isabel were on a flight to Chile, but from then on there was no trace of the pair of them. I remember him saying after my mother's death that he had been glad he was out of the country when she had died as then no one could point the finger in his direction. He must have been relieved it happened again in the same way.'

Clayton knew he was probing, but he couldn't stop himself. 'Did you ever seriously wonder about your mother's death?' he asked.

'No. My mother was not the suicidal type.'

'And when did your father finally surface?'

'A week after Julia's funeral. He telephoned to say sorry for having gone off without leaving a note for me. I told him about Julia. He went very quiet but when I asked him to come home, he said he couldn't do that. Not even when I threatened never to speak to him again if he wouldn't come back when I needed him most. He told me I'd be fine, that he was thinking only of me. "You don't deserve the shame of having me around," he said. "If people want to think I drove Julia to suicide, it's better for you if I'm not there." He went on to say that he was starting a new life with Isabel. She made him happier and more alive than he'd felt in years. I told him that as of that moment, since he obviously cared so little about me, he no longer had a daughter. My last words to him were to say that I would never speak to him again. Ever.' She sighed deeply and stared into the fire. She looked so very sad.

'Do you think your father really did plan to use Isabel to get back at Rufus?' Clayton said. 'Or do you think the attraction between them was real from the word go?'

She nodded. 'The attraction was genuine. Photographing her in the garden, there had been a powerful intimacy to what they were doing.'

Clayton could picture the scene all too well. 'And what of Rufus and Tasha?' he asked. 'What happened to them?'

'They left the day after the funeral. I never saw or spoke to them again. Rufus's last words to me were to say he hoped I was satisfied now, now that my father had destroyed his family.'

'He had a highly tuned sense of drama, that young man.' Clayton paused, then continued, 'Please don't take this the wrong way, but do you think he ever really cared about you?'

'I think Rufus had been playing a game. He hated my father and used me to get at him. He knew, or thought he knew, that I was the only thing my father cared about. In the end, he was proved wrong on that score. Bruce Barrett only ever cared about himself.'

'I'm sure that wasn't true,' Clayton said. 'Your father lost his head over a beautiful woman; he wouldn't be the first man to do that.'

'That may well be true and I know this is going to sound like I'm wallowing in self-pity, but he never came back. That hurt. He wrote to me, but I couldn't bring myself to read his letters. I threw them away. I didn't want to read about what a great time he was having, I just wanted him to come home. Then I made sure he couldn't. I completed my A-levels, sold Cuckoo House and took a gap year. I left no forwarding address. The only person who knew where I was, was the solicitor I used in Derby to handle the sale of the house, and he was under orders not to pass on my new address to anyone. I used the same solicitor to change my name by deed poll. A year later than planned, I took up my place at university—not my first choice, just in case I could be traced, and I pretended I was somebody completely different.'

'You were very thorough.'

'Anger and rejection can do that to a person. Also, I wanted a clean slate. I saw myself as the Queen of New Beginnings.'

'Do you have any idea if your father tried to find you?'

She shook her head.

'Do you ever regret that?'

Frowning, she said, 'The truth is, yes, I do regret what I did. Especially when I read of his death. It wasn't his obituary, just a reference to the fact that Bruce Barrett, the naturalist photographer, had died some five years earlier. In some ways, that was really what forced me to leave behind my life in London. The knowledge of his death seemed to compound the sense I had of having reached a dead end. The acting roles just weren't coming my way.'

After another prolonged silence, Clayton said, 'I know this is going to sound tactless, but when you learned of your father's death, did you find out anything about his life after he left here?'

She shook her head. 'All I know is that he died in Argentina about seven years ago.' She yawned hugely and looked at her watch. Clayton glanced at his: it was nearly midnight. 'I must go,' she said. 'It's late and the neighbours will start to talk.'

'George has this place watched, does she?'

'No, not George. I was thinking of my neighbours, Ronnetta and her son, Bob. Bob tends to keep rather a close eye on me.'

'In a good way? Or a bad way?'

'In a habitually tedious kind of way.' She was on her feet now.

'You'll come back, won't you?' he said.

'Of course. We had a deal; my story then yours.'

Clayton saw Alice to the door, then locked up, but instead of going to bed, he returned to the room where they had spent the evening. He threw another couple of logs on the fire and reflected on all that Alice had shared with him. He could only wonder at the effect that being back here must be having on her. With his back to the fire, Clayton closed his eyes and listened to the silence of the house. Only a matter of seconds passed before the silence was crowded with voices. The Armstrongs may have stripped the place of its superficial trappings, but nothing could erase Alice's childhood from the house. He could feel it as acutely as he could feel the warmth of the fire on him. He opened his eyes and took a deep breath. He went and settled himself at the desk, took another deep breath and switched on his laptop.

With the kind of assurance he so rarely experienced, he knew he was free of the crippling fear he'd lived with these past few years. He was zinging with creative energy. He hadn't felt like this since working on that first magical script for *Joking Aside*.

With no work booked for the next day, Alice treated herself to the luxury of a lie-in. She stayed in bed until nearly eleven o'clock and the only reason she dragged herself from the warmth of duvet heaven was because there was an insistent ring at the door.

She was wearing her warmest and thickest flannelette pyjamas so she didn't bother with a dressing gown, but at the sight of Bob leering at her when she opened the door, she felt as good as naked. 'Nice togs,' he said, looking her up and down.

'Is that for me?' she asked pointedly.

He looked at the parcel in his large, shovel-like hands. 'The postman left it with us when he couldn't get a response from you earlier.' He grinned. 'Looks like I succeeded where he failed.'

'It must be your superior technique.'

'I've certainly had no complaints over the years.' He gave her a wink, just in case she'd failed to catch the double entendre.

The parcel looked like the manuscript she had been expecting. 'I'll take that then, shall I?'

He hesitated. 'If I give it to you will you have a drink with me tonight?'

'If that's how you usually ask a girl out, Bob, you might want to work on it. In my experience blackmail isn't the best approach.'

'But I've used all my best chat-up lines on you and they haven't worked. What else is left for me?'

Oh, what the heck, she thought. Why not put him out of his misery and have a drink with him? What would it cost her? 'OK,' she said.

'You're serious?' He looked like he couldn't believe his luck.

'I'm only saying yes to a drink, Bob.'

'Eight o'clock suit you?'

'That'll be perfect.'

She closed the door and wondered if she had done the right thing. She blamed her rashness on last night. Too much rattling round in the past had addled her brain.

Eating a late breakfast and flicking through the manuscript, she thought of the incongruity of having shared so much of her life story with a stranger when she had never so much as breathed a word of her upbringing to anyone else. But then, really, whom would she have wanted to tell? Certainly not any previous boyfriends. Not when they'd all borne an uncanny resemblance to Rufus.

She had never consciously chosen to date men that were carbon copies of Rufus but that was the way it had gone. It was as if she had approached an old-fashioned sweetshop counter for boyfriends and asked for a quarter of dark, floppy-fringed hair, a quarter of olive skin, a quarter of penetrating blue eyes and a quarter of fatal charm. Even James Montgomery, who could in no way be described as a boyfriend, had fitted the profile. Nobody needed to tell her that it wasn't healthy to be drawn to Rufus clones. Yet how could she stop something she wasn't conscious of doing until it was too late? Perhaps her evening out tonight with Bob would help to broaden her horizons.

Breakfast dealt with, she decided it was time to tackle something that was long overdue.

When she arrived at Well House that afternoon, the light was already fading. As she had always done, Alice went round to the back door. She was pleased to see that the same tarnished brass bell was hanging in the same place in the untidy porch. She gave the bell rope a firm tug and waited. She suddenly felt nervous. George was the only living person who had known her since the day she was born and there was going to be some explaining to do.

'And about time, too,' George said when she opened the door.

The same George. A wave of regret swept over Alice. New beginnings were all very well, but here was a very poignant reminder of what Alice had so decisively put behind her. Of what she had lost.

Ushered into the kitchen, Alice felt as though she had truly stepped back in time. Nothing had changed. A large, brutish rooster eyed Alice from the hearth rug in front of the Rayburn. He scratched at the rug, puffed out his chest, stretched his neck and strutted towards her.

'Away with you, Percy!' George shouted.

As if understanding every word, the rooster deflated himself and went back to loitering with menacing intent on the hearth rug.

'He's full of hot air,' George said to Alice. 'Take no notice of him. So what'll it be? Tea, coffee or something stronger?'

'Since I'm driving I'll take the safe option: tea, please.'

The tea made, George eased herself stiffly into the armchair opposite Alice. 'Right then,' she said with an unnervingly direct stare, 'tell me all you know about my new neighbour at Cuckoo House.'

This was not the opening she had been expecting and Alice took a moment to recalibrate her thoughts. She also felt just a tiny bit slighted. Didn't George want to know what she had been doing all this time?

'And you can drop the charade about his name being Shannon,' George said. 'I saw a picture of him in a newspaper.'

A promise was a promise in Alice's book. 'I'm sorry,' she said with her best innocent face firmly in place, 'you've lost me entirely.'

George bristled. 'We both know exactly who he is, so how did our interesting visitor at Cuckoo House end up here?'

Alice could see she had no choice but to concede. 'Look, I made a promise to him. Please don't ask me anything else.'

The old woman slurped her tea noisily. 'Fair enough. I can respect that. He seems nice. I like him. Is he a friend of yours?'

'I've only just met him.' Alice explained briefly about Ronnetta and the cleaning agency, then she told George everything about her life after leaving Cuckoo House.

'Well, that's all that neatly clarified,' George said when she had finished. 'Apart from the one glaring omission of why you didn't come and see me when you moved back up here.'

'I think you were a connection too far. If I'm really honest, I was worried you'd tell me something I didn't want to hear.'

'Such as?'

'Such as my father might have been in contact with you at some point and . . .' Alice faltered. This was something she had steadfastly refused to let herself think about, that her father had tried looking for her, that he really had cared.

'And asked if I knew where you were?' George finished off for her.

Alice swallowed. 'Yes. Did he?'

Clayton had been up all night. Once he'd got started, the words had poured out of him with an unstoppable force. He'd written for most of the day as well. But now he could barely keep his eyes open. He decided to take a nap. He kicked off his shoes and lay on the sofa. He closed his eyes. Oh, that felt good.

He was in a hot-air balloon, looking down on Cuckoo House. He could see Alice staring at him from the garden. 'Don't go,' she called out. He floated away until finally he was hovering over the rooftops of London. The skyline looked like it did from that Mary Poppins film. He'd always loved the film as a boy; he'd secretly had a crush on Julie Andrews. He floated on, and then he was above Notting Hill, and oh, look, there was Stacey. And Barry. 'I've got something for you,' he shouted down to them. He leaned over the side of the basket to throw it to them. 'This is yours,' he called out. 'You left it behind.' 'No!' they shouted. '*No!*' But it was too late. The bundle was tumbling through the air; it was unravelling. First a tiny pink leg appeared and then a head and two hands. It was a baby. '*No!*' he screamed. 'That wasn't what I meant.'

He woke with a massive jolt; his heart was thumping hard. His mobile rang; light-headed, he snatched up the phone.

'Greetings!'

'This had better be good, Glen,' Clayton snarled.

'Love and kisses to you, sweetheart. How's it going?'

'You really want to know? I've started writing.'

Silence from the other end of the phone.

'Glen? You still there?'

'I'm in shock. You've started writing? What have you got?'

'A bit of a departure from anything I've written before.'

'I like the sound of it so far.'

'Are you saying you didn't like what I've written before?'

'Just when exactly did you get to be so needy?'

'Oh, go blow smoke up your gigantically oversized ego! Now shut up and listen. I think I've got something. It's about a family. A gold-carat, all-the-way-to-the-top, screwed-up family.'

'Mmm . . . remind me, has that ever been done before?'

'Of course it's been done before, but whoever got tired of watching other people mess up? Schadenfreude's never going out of fashion.'

'Good point. Talking of which, according to a site on the Internet, you're currently languishing on a beach in Mexico. There's even a photograph of you wearing nothing but a thong.'

Clayton groaned. 'Will it never end?'

'That is something we need to discuss. I've been wondering whether you should come back to London and deal with things.'

'I'm not going anywhere. I can write here. This place is working for me. I'm not leaving and that's flat.'

The point of Glen's call, other than to wind Clayton up, had been to let him know that Bazza and Stacey would be on *The Stevie McKean Show*. What the hell were they up to now? Could it be yet more 'charity' work? Whatever the cause, Clayton had no delusions that his name wouldn't be further besmirched during their television appearance—what chat show host could resist raising the subject? The last time he'd forced himself to watch them it hadn't ended well.

But it wouldn't happen now, would it? He could be trusted not to react and do something silly again? Couldn't he?

Don't watch the programme, Captain Sensible whispered in his ear.

Yeah right, like that was going to happen.

Well, if you must, Captain Sensible said priggishly, *but on your own head be it. However, I strongly advise against watching it alone.*

Just whom was he supposed to invite to watch it with him?

No sooner had he articulated the thought than it came to him whom he could, and *would* invite. OK, it was pretty weird, but it would provide a convenient segue to giving her his story. A deal was a deal, after all, and for one thing she had proved to be pleasantly agreeable to be around; interesting and fun. There was also the small matter of what he was writing to broach with her. It was only polite that he ask her permission to go ahead with it. Naturally, he'd abandon the project if she objected. No question.

Hmm . . . observed Captain Sensible with his arms folded.

Alice had intended to read through the manuscript of *Liar, Liar, Pants on Fire* one more time in preparation for going into the studio next week, but Clayton's phone call had made her change her good intentions. She hadn't needed much persuading; the chance for some company was a welcome diversion. Her visit to Well House had been a lot more distressing than she had expected. She had been so deeply upset she had called off her evening out with Bob, much to his disappointment.

What George had told her had left her feeling more alone and isolated than she had ever felt in her whole life. What hurt most was that she had to accept that she had made a terrible mistake and there was no way of righting it. How would she ever come to terms with that?

'You OK?' Clayton greeted her when she arrived at Cuckoo House.

Surprised that he should notice there was anything wrong with her, she shook off his concern. 'I'm fine,' she lied offhandedly.

With his back to her as he put the kettle on the hob, Clayton said, 'You mentioned on the phone earlier that you'd been to see George yesterday. Did she scold you very badly for not visiting her before?'

'She was remarkably lenient with her scolding,' Alice replied, 'but I ought to warn you, she knows who you are.' Alice explained about George seeing him in the newspapers. 'But don't worry about her telling anyone about you being here. She would never do that.'

'My agent seems to think that I should go home and face the music.'

Alice felt a pang of disappointment. 'When will you go?'

Clayton shook his head. 'Not yet, anyway. I also have another reason why I want to stay on. The thing is, I've started to—' He broke off. 'Is that your mobile?'

'Not guilty; it must be yours.'

He put down the teapot, looked about him, then eventually located his phone. While he took the call, Alice finished making the tea.

'No, Glen,' Clayton said wearily, 'I haven't forgotten. Yes, I'm well aware that it starts in ten minutes. Love you, too.' He ended the call.

'What starts in ten minutes?'

'*The Stevie McKean Show*. I thought you could watch it with me.'

'Why exactly are you putting yourself through the ordeal of watching Barry and Stacey being interviewed?'

Clayton passed Alice a biscuit. She was sitting on the floor just a few feet away from where he was fidgeting anxiously on the sofa. The first guest was banging on about a forthcoming comeback tour and album.

'I've decided it's time to see how I'll react. Or rather, I want to know whether I'm overreacting.'

'OK, but here's the deal. If you go psycho on me, I'm out of here.'

Finally, Stevie McKean was introducing his next two guests. Clayton slid off the sofa and joined Alice on the floor. His shoulder touched hers.

She turned and looked at him. Their eyes met and for the craziest of nanoseconds he contemplated kissing her. Anything to distract himself.

Erm . . . not a good idea, Captain Sensible cautioned.

'Well,' said Stevie as Lucky Bazza and Stacey took their positions on the sofa, 'you've had a busy time of it recently. I don't seem to be able to open a magazine or a newspaper without seeing the pair of you in it.'

'Yes, Stevie,' Stacey said gravely, 'we're hoping it's all going to calm down before too long.'

'Like hell you do!' Clayton muttered.

'Are you going to mutter like that throughout the entire interview?' Alice asked.

'Probably.'

'I hear congratulations are in order,' Stevie said with a twinkling, meaningful look. 'I hope there's an invitation in the post for me.'

Stacey reached for Lucky Bazza's hand and they gazed sickeningly into each other's eyes. After an eternity had passed, Stacey said, 'You're more than welcome to the wedding, Stevie, but I have to tell you, it won't be anything grand. It's going to be very low-key.'

'We don't want to do anything overly lavish,' Lucky Bazza said earnestly, speaking for the first time, 'not when there's so much human suffering in the world. It would seem obscene.'

'So no delicious photos in *Hello!* for us to enjoy?'

If it were possible, Lucky Bazza adopted an even more earnest tone. 'There will be pictures in *Hello!*' he said, 'but we won't be touching a penny of the fee; we're donating it to an orphanage in Malawi.'

There was a collective *Aaah* from the audience.

'After we lost our . . .' Stacey paused for unmistakable dramatic effect '. . . baby . . .' Another pause as she and Lucky Bazza exchanged doe-eyed glances, 'We just felt this was the right thing to do.'

'Oh, shit, here we go.'

'*Ssh!*'

'I know how painful the loss of your baby must have been for you, so perhaps it's better if we don't—'

'That's all right, Stevie,' Stacey said hurriedly, as if she were terrified she might be denied the chance to lay out her stall of well-publicised emotions. 'We don't mind talking about it. Especially if it will help other couples who have had to face the trauma of a miscarriage.'

'You're very brave.'

'I wouldn't say that,' she said. 'But if Clayton is watching this . . .' she snapped her head round to find the camera. 'I'd just like to tell him that we no longer bear him any malice.'

'Really?'

'Really, Stevie. In my opinion he needs help. You know, professional help. Barry feels the same way. Isn't that right, Barry?'

The camera zoomed in on Lucky Bazza's face: his forehead was shiny with perspiration. 'Clayton had more than his fair share of problems and bad luck,' he said, 'and I wish him nothing but the very best.'

The camera slowly panned to the show's host. 'Ladies and gentlemen, I think we should give this extraordinary couple a round of applause. And Clayton,' he added when the clapping was over, 'if you are listening out there, let me tell you, you look a right slapper in a thong!'

'It wasn't me in the thong!' Clayton shouted at the TV.

'That's all we've got time for today, folks,' beamed Stevie.

Clayton zapped the television with the remote control.

'That was pure Tate and Lyle,' Alice said. 'Any sweeter and our teeth would be falling out. As an antidote, do I get to hear your side of the story now?'

'I never meant for things to turn out the way they did,' Clayton started. 'It just got out of hand. I couldn't stand to see them constantly parading their smug happiness. Bazza had never been into all that celebrity crap. But with Stacey at his side he changed; he bought into what we'd always despised and he and Stacey became an obscene parody of a Showbiz Couple. Don't get me wrong, Bazza isn't stupid, he has talent, but Stacey's the literary equivalent of a footballer's WAG. She's in there for the main chance.'

'So what was the trigger that caused you to make the phone call?' Alice remembered some of the story from the newspaper James had shown her.

'If you know about the phone call, then you know they were on *This Morning*. Bazza was promoting a new film that was about to premiere in the States and saying how much he and Stacey were looking forward to flying out to LA the next day. They just looked so infuriatingly pleased with themselves. To cap it all, Stacey announced that she and Bazza were expecting a child. The first of many, she added.'

'But why did that matter so much to you?'

He shuffled awkwardly. 'I'd wanted children but she'd been dead against it. She'd said she couldn't think of anything worse than a screaming brat. And suddenly, there she was, flaunting herself as a nauseating celebrity mother-to-be.'

'So the red mist descended?'

'They were doing a phone-in, so I thought, right, I'll call in. I'll wipe the smirk off their self-satisfied faces.'

'Ooh,' Alice cringed, 'with or without the benefit of hindsight, that doesn't sound like a smart move.'

'I gave a false name to whoever it was operating the phone lines and when they put me through, I congratulated Bazza and Stacey on an outstandingly phoney performance. I told them, and the nation, exactly what I thought of them, how Stacey had been sneaking round my back seeing Bazza, how they'd both lied and cheated. And did they really think they'd make such good parents when Stacey had all the maternal instincts of a sea turtle and Bazza was nothing but a social-climbing twat.'

Alice smiled. 'You got all that out before you were cut off?'

'I can only imagine that somebody in the control room had a sadistic streak running through him or her.'

'What happened next?'

'I put the phone down before Bazza and Stacey could respond. Inevitably, an advert break followed and by the time the programme returned Bazza and Stacey had legged it. Phil Schofield said that owing to being terribly upset by my outburst, Bazza and Stacey were unable to continue. So I called in again and said that in future they should choose guests who had more guts and backbone, preferably with a bit of decency.'

'You were one angry man, weren't you?'

Clayton nodded. 'I need a drink. How about you?'

'A glass of wine will be fine. Thank you.'

Out in the kitchen, Clayton let out his breath. OK, so far, so good. He hadn't lost it. That was a good sign.

Behind him, on the table, his mobile rang.

'Yes, Glen,' he said.

'You watched the programme?'

'Every heart-tugging second.'

'But you're OK?'

'My God, Glen, is that a lump of concern I can hear in your voice?'

'No, it's a Custard Cream.'

'Well, bugger off and leave me alone.'

'Clay. I forgot to ask earlier, done any writing today?'

'Ah, I get it. Your new-found concern for me hangs on my writing again and the thought of yet more filthy lucre coming your way.'

'You're a hurtful swine.'

'As I've told you before, sweetkins, it's what keeps our relationship so fresh. Now if you don't mind, I'm busy. I have company.'

Clayton rang off, poured two glasses of Merlot and rejoined Alice. He found her standing at the window, looking out over the front garden.

She turned. Shocked, he saw an expression of intense sadness on her face. 'You all right?' he asked, and for the second time that evening he suddenly realised.

She did that jerky head-wobbling thing that people always did when they were far from all right.

He put down the glasses on the coffee table. 'What's wrong?'

'I'm fine,' she snapped. 'I'm absolutely . . .' Her voice cracked and she coughed. Then she burst into tears and turned away from him.

Oo-kay, tears. Right. And the best course of action would be? 'Tissues?'

She nodded.

He returned as fast as he could with a box of Kleenex from the kitchen. 'Man-size,' he said, holding the box out to her.

She wiped her eyes and started crying all over again.

Obviously something more than tissues was required. Reassurance of some kind. What if he hugged her? Would she think he was trying something on?

He cautiously touched her shoulder. She didn't flinch. He slowly turned her towards him, his arms encircling her. She sank into him, her head resting on his shoulder. With no ready words at his disposal, he started to rub her back, moving his hands in slow, self-conscious circles. He could feel the softness of her breasts pressed against his chest. That feels nice, he suddenly thought.

It also felt bad. Should he be enjoying himself this much when she was clearly so upset? His hands moved from her back to her shoulders. He noticed she had stopped crying now. Was that his cue to let go?

One of his hands had somehow found its way to the nape of her neck. He cradled her head gently. Now the whole of his body seemed to be working of its own accord; he was holding her closer still and his other hand was now heading towards the smooth, warm skin of her neck. He tilted her face up to his and placed his lips very lightly over hers.

How had that happened? His mouth still hovering over hers, he found himself staring into the dark, dark depths of her gaze.

'Are you going to kiss me?' she asked. 'Or just leave me dangling?'

'I must confess, a mad, crazy part of me was planning on kissing you. What do you think? Good or bad idea?'

'Let's see how it goes, shall we?'

He closed the tiny space between them and kissed her. And kept on kissing her.

There was a split second of awkwardness when they at last pulled apart, but after some lowering of eyes and some throat clearing, Clayton took matters into his own hands. 'You sit here and have an obscenely large glug of wine while I organise a fire,' he said.

She looked at him curiously, her head tilted. 'Did you have a shot of double-strength testosterone with your breakfast this morning?'

'Is that what's wrong with me? I thought there was something.'

She smiled and he felt a flicker of warmth spread through him.

When he had the fire lit and the curtains drawn, effectively shutting out the outside world, he went and joined her on the sofa.

'Do you want to tell me what it is?' he asked.

Again the smile. 'It was what George told me about my father,' she said. 'He came back to look for me. According to George he tried really hard. She told him the name of the estate agent who had sold the house; they passed him on to the firm of solicitors I'd used, but of course they were under strict instructions not to give out any information about my whereabouts. He gave them a letter to forward to me, but by this time I'd moved so many times in the space of two years there was no way anything could have reached me.' She wiped away two small tears. 'He was a crazy father, a wildly unpredictable and passionate man, but I loved him. I just wanted to hurt him in the way he'd hurt me. Why do we do that, hurt the ones we love?'

Clayton shifted uncomfortably. 'Did George know whether your father and Isabel stayed together?' he asked.

'No, she didn't know that. But it was highly unlikely that they would. She was so much younger than him. It had to have been nothing but a stupid fling.'

'If that's all it was, he paid a high price for it, losing his daughter.' It was the wrong thing to say. Alice's eyes filled. 'Sorry,' he said, 'big mouth syndrome. I'm told there is treatment for it. It's a tricky procedure, involves having my head removed.'

She blew her nose. 'You're really quite a nice man, aren't you?'

'That's not what the newspapers would have you believe.'

'I've read only the one piece about you. I didn't want to read any more; it didn't feel right. It seemed too much of an invasion of your privacy. I'd hate for anyone to do that to me.'

Having earlier planned to tell Alice *what* he'd been writing, Clayton knew that now wasn't the time to share this turn of events with her.

'Take my mind off things by telling me what really happened with Stacey and Barry,' she said, surprising him.

The morning after his telephone outburst on national television, and nursing a fearsome hangover, Clayton felt ashamed of his conduct. Glen phoned him. 'Had you been drinking beforehand?'

'I might have been,' he'd admitted.

'Perhaps you could find a way to make amends,' Glen had suggested. 'The public is capricious. They loved it when you outed that tosser and his highly entertaining proclivities, but one look at the papers this morning tells me they're siding with Bazza and Stacey in this instance. It's the baby thing. Perhaps you could make a gesture of deep regret, a touching display of contrition. As abject as you can manage.'

The next day Clayton came up with the perfect apology. He would surprise the Golden Couple with baby presents galore. He would buy up Baby Gap and have everything installed in the house ready for their return from LA. But why stop at Baby Gap? There was Mothercare, there was John Lewis. Moreover, there was the Internet. That was when it got out of hand, when his imagination took over and all coherent and rational thought fled from his head. All he needed to pull off his apology was access to Bazza's house.

Bazza had an astonishingly expensive property in Notting Hill. Clayton used to be a frequent visitor and had been entrusted with the code for the alarm system. Unfortunately he'd never been entrusted with a key, but a little thing like that wasn't going to stop him.

From reading the papers he knew that the Golden Couple would be returning late the following evening, and he had everything planned with military precision. He gained entry to the house in the dead of night by smashing a pane of glass in the French doors at the back. He stumbled in the dark to the hall where he knew the control panel was situated for the alarm system. He tapped in the alarm code and at once the red warning light on the panel stopped flashing. He was in!

He passed the night on the sofa and woke early to await the deliveries. The van for Baby Gap arrived first. Clayton instructed the delivery driver where to put everything. Then came John Lewis, and at the same time as Mothercare, a man came to fix the broken panel of glass.

Clayton was impressed with his selection. The ground floor of the house was full of everything that a couple could possibly want for their forthcoming offspring from birth through to about four years old.

He was beginning to get a bit twitchy by five o'clock that the last of the deliveries wasn't going to arrive, but then ten minutes later, the van showed up. Except it wasn't a van, it was a stonking great lorry. Oh, shit, Clayton thought, when the two enormous delivery men opened up the back of it. He could see now why the two men were so large. They'd have to be to lug these things about.

'I think there's been some kind of mistake,' he said.

'No mistake, mate,' the larger of the two hulks replied. 'Got it all down here on paper.' He thrust the paper at. 'Where do you want them?'

'You don't understand . . . I thought they'd be—'

'Come on, pal,' said Hulk Number Two. He had a skull and crossbones tattooed around his neck; it was a helpful clue to Clayton not to mess with him. 'We ain't got all day, you know.'

And with that, they began to unload and install the delivery. The final touch was for Hulk Number One to install the timer device Clayton had ordered. 'Unless you're a qualified electrician, mate,' he was informed, 'don't even think about messing with the electrics. We'll be back to collect the gear in four days' time.'

Ohshitohshitohshit! What in hell's name had he done?

Crammed into the garden, ablaze and each measuring approximately ten feet in diameter, was the grisliest sight he'd seen in the whole of his miserable life. Online they had looked like cartoon-cuddly-cute novelties to hire, but Holy Moses, how had he missed the measurements? These monsters were huge. They'd seemed scarily large in their unlit state, but now that the timer had switched on and they were illuminated, they seemed to have doubled in size and hideousness. There was a pale-blue elephant head, a russet squirrel head, a pink rabbit head, a yellow duck head and a purple pig head, all grotesque and demonically oversized. But it was too late to do anything about them. He just had to hope that Bazza and Stacey wouldn't be too freaked out, that they would see the funny side of what he'd done.

He left a note on the kitchen table—*I hope you like my present*—reset the burglar alarm, and slunk away into the night.

A little after five o'clock the next morning his telephone by the side of the bed rang. 'You psychopathic wanker!' Bazza yelled at him. 'What kind of a sick joke did you think you were playing on us?'

'OK,' Clayton apologised, 'the heads were a mistake. I accept that. But the rest of it, surely you like the rest of the stuff? The toys?'

'Stacey's lost the baby because of you,' Bazza shouted.

Stacey had gone outside to switch off the power and had received an electric shock that had thrown her off her feet. Two hours later she had started to miscarry and Bazza had driven her to the hospital.

Appalled at what had happened, Clayton had gone to Notting Hill to apologise, but his visit had only made things worse. Bazza had taken a swing at him and the next thing they were brawling in the street with Bazza shouting that he would personally see to it that he would become the most hated man in the country. Somebody called the police and at the sound of a siren, Clayton decided his best option was to leg it.

In the days that followed he kept expecting a heavily armed unit to crash through his door and arrest him. He'd been responsible for the death of a four-month-old foetus; could he go to prison for that? But prison wasn't what Bazza had in mind for him. His revenge was to hound Clayton through the press. With seemingly every journalist on his side, he painstakingly set about his task. Reporters and photographers set up camp outside Clayton's house, forcing him to stay inside. The newspapers vilified him as a psychotic monster who had caused an innocent woman to lose her baby, and every minuscule aspect of his character was dredged up and dissected. Lists were compiled of all the questionable things he had publicly said or done. Even his cleaner abandoned him to tell the *Sun* how some days he lounged about in his pyjamas with his hair uncombed while sitting at his desk not writing a single word. Clearly all signs of a mind seriously on the tilt.

In the end, Glen, the only one to stand by him, put out a statement to the press, stating very clearly just how sorry his client was and that Clayton had had no intention of causing anyone any harm. Then he spirited Clayton away and dispatched him to a place where no one would find him.

Chapter Seven

AS SHE SWITCHED OFF the light and slid beneath the duvet, Alice couldn't help but think it was just the sort of outlandish thing her father would have done. On the Richter scale of bad ideas it was certainly up there with the cherry liqueurs.

Unquestionably Clayton's heart had been in the right place when he'd planned his surprise for Barry and Stacey, and if the outcome hadn't been as it was, surely they would have seen the funny side of what he'd done. If it had been a scene from a film the audience would have laughed out loud. Clayton would have come across as a hapless yet wholly likeable and sympathetic character, not the evil monster the press had since portrayed him as being.

She rolled over and her thoughts turned to her father. How could she ever make up for what she had done, wiping her father out of her life? Only two days ago she could have justified her actions to herself, but now she couldn't. The Queen of New Beginnings had got it wrong. There was no such thing as a new beginning when you were devising it for the worst reason of all: revenge.

Acknowledging the sad truth of this had plunged her into a state of remorseful torment. Was that why she had turned to Clayton? Had he merely been a convenient shoulder to cry on?

She replayed inside her head the moment he had kissed her. She had experienced a jolt of pleasant surprise pass through her and had willingly kissed him back. She had liked the way he had held her, very close but unexpectedly gentle. Where had this new man come from? This kind, thoughtful, perceptive and curiously attractive man? Perhaps it was merely that he had decided to trust her, just as she had trusted him when she had decided to share her childhood with him.

At Cuckoo House, Clayton was flying. The words were coming so fast his fingers couldn't keep up with his brain. Clayton knew, absolutely *knew*, this was destined to be a Major Success. He had felt exactly the same when he and Bazza had started playing with ideas for the script that went on to become *Joking Aside*. His instinct had been right then and he was sure it was right now—if you'd suffered the debilitating horror of writer's block for as long as he had you knew when it was or wasn't happening. He reckoned writer's block wasn't unlike erectile dysfunction: the sort of thing a man just can't bring himself to discuss openly. Not that he'd actually experienced the latter. But then when was the last time he'd had the chance to put his equipment to the test anyway?

He immediately thought of Alice. He let his mind linger on the pleasurable memory of kissing her, then, with great effort, he shifted gear and dragged his thoughts away from her as an attractive woman and back to when she'd been a young girl shortly before her mother had died. Not once during her chats with him had Alice referred to how she'd felt about her mother's death. Was that deliberate? Or was she a natural storyteller, moving the narrative along to what she deemed the next important part of the story? Clayton wanted to write more about

Barbara Barrett. Could he use some artistic licence and flesh out her character himself? Or would that be insensitive of him?

Bit late for that, Captain Sensible butted in.

It occurred to him that maybe he could talk to George about Barbara Barrett. He'd have to tread warily, though. He couldn't let on to George what he was doing without having first OK-ed things with Alice. Telling her what he was writing would be his next priority. Well, he'd leave it a few more days. No point in rushing in when she might still be troubled by her father.

See, he could be sensitive when it was required.

'**Y**ou haven't brought any more of your diabolical brew, have you?'

'That, Mr Shannon, is not gracious.'

Clayton stood back and let George in. It was uncanny that she had come knocking on his door so soon after he had decided he wanted to talk to her. 'Alice told me that you know who I am,' he said, 'so I suggest we bury Mr Shannon. What can I do for you?' He knew exactly what she could do for him, but he needed to bide his time.

'No, it's more a case of what I can do for you, Mr Miller. Fetch your coat; you're coming out with me. Oh, and you'd better bring that ridiculously large-brimmed hat I saw you wearing when we first met; we don't want anyone cottoning on to who you are, do we?'

They were in the car, destination downtown Stonebridge. Above the noise of the engine and screaming gears, George shouted at him, 'You're looking a lot better than the last time I saw you. I think the sudden improvement in your well-being may have something to do with our sweet Alice. Am I right?'

'How in hell's name did you reach that conclusion?'

'No need to shout,' she said as his yelled and startled reply coincided with an unexpected lull in the noise of the car. 'But it stands to reason. You're all alone in that great big house with only Alice to keep you occasional company. What red-blooded man's thoughts wouldn't turn towards her. She's a very attractive young woman.'

'Nothing has passed between Alice and me.'

She shot him a sideways glance. 'Very well, if that's how you want to play it. I can respect that. But you're not a bad catch. Alice could do a lot worse than hook up with you.'

'George,' he said, 'while I'm inordinately grateful for you taking me shopping and showing such a sensitive interest in my personal life, do you think there's the remotest chance that you might shut up?'

'No chance at all. And anyway, I'm not just taking you shopping; you're treating me to afternoon tea at the Penny-Farthing.'

The café had been designed to appeal to those with a discerning eye for an overload of kitsch. A heavy hand had been given free rein to display all things Victoriana: black and white photos, copper kettles, doilies, a rocking horse, masses of crockery as well as a row of bed warmers. Clayton felt as if he was an extra in a costume drama; he kept expecting Dame Judi to drop a breathless curtsey at their table.

Instead of Dame Judi, a flame-haired, rosy-cheeked woman arrived to take their order. 'Afternoon, George,' she said. 'What's it to be today?'

'My usual for me, Theresa.'

'And you, sir?'

'I'll have the same,' Clayton said, from beneath the brim of his hat.

When they were alone, George said, 'You have no idea what my usual is; how do you know you'll like it?'

'It's crossed my mind that maybe this place offers the answer to your immortality. No way could you have cheated death for so long without consuming some kind of secret elixir of life. I thought I'd try it.'

She let rip with a deep-throated cackle. 'You're a ballsy mutt.'

With surprising speed and efficiency, their waitress reappeared with a large tray of dainty sandwiches and oversized scones, along with a china teapot, a milk jug and two sets of cups and saucers.

Clayton offered George the plate of sandwiches. 'Just out of interest, why do you keep going on about Alice and me? Has she said something to you?'

'It's what she hasn't said that interests me more. I've given the matter a lot of thought and I think you would be good for each other.'

'What on earth has given you reason to think that?'

'It's knowing Alice as well as I do.'

Seizing the opportunity George had given him, he said, 'Alice has told me the whole story about Rufus, Isabel and Julia, but I'm curious about her mother, Barbara Barrett. Alice doesn't talk about her in the same way she does about her father. Were they not very close?'

'Oh, I think they were close enough, but she idolised her father. He was a real larger-than-life character. Not an easy man to live with, but who wants a boring straightforward man? That's why I think Alice could well be attracted to you. You're complex. You're also a fair bit older than she is. In short, you remind her of her father.'

Clayton choked on his tea. Spluttering painfully, he croaked, 'I'm not sure I like the sound of that. My guess is that Alice is more likely to go for men who resemble Rufus.'

'That may well have been the case in the past. But have they made her happy? No, take it from me, the man she really falls in love with will be nothing like that dreadful so-and-so. You'll do very nicely.'

At the sound of tapping at the kitchen window, Alice looked up from the manuscript she was reading. 'The door isn't locked,' she said.

Ronnetta let herself in. 'It's freezing out there,' she said with an exaggerated shiver. She pulled out a chair and sat down. 'Alice, love, I was hoping you could help me out again.'

'Sorry, next week is pretty busy for me. I've got a book to do in the studio and then I'm down in London on Friday for a voiceover.'

'Something for the telly?'

In common with so many people, Ronnetta viewed television as the Holy Grail in Alice's line of work. 'It's for a budget airline,' Alice explained. 'The usual kind of thing: safety drills, flagging up the duty free. I'll put the kettle on, shall I? Tea or coffee?'

'Coffee, please. So how come you bailed out of your date with Bob the other night?'

Their drinks made, Alice carried the mugs over to the table. 'Bob's very nice, Ronnetta,' she said, choosing her words with care, 'but—'

'He's mad about you; you do know that, don't you?' Ronnetta said.

Alice's heart sank. 'I'm extremely fond of Bob,' she tried, 'but he's . . . he's simply not . . .' She faltered. How could she tell her friend and neighbour that her son just wasn't her type? 'Look, the thing is, I've met someone else,' she said with a flash of inspiration.

Ronnetta's face dropped. 'Oh, well, that's that then. So who is he? Some clever schmuck you've met through your work down in London?'

Alice had two choices. She could tell an all-out lie. Or she could tell a partial lie. She chose the latter option. 'It's the man staying at Cuckoo House,' she said.

Ronnetta sat up straighter. 'But I thought you said he was weird.'

'He is.'

'I don't understand. Why would you choose weird when you could have Bob?'

'When Cupid fires that arrow, it falls where it falls.' Alice winced. Did she really just say that?

Ronnetta pulled a face. 'Any more comments like that, you keep them firmly to yourself. You look glum though, what is it? Does the weird bloke not feel the same way about you as you do for him?'

Again Alice was faced with a choice: pretend she was all right, or go some way in being honest. 'It has nothing to do with him.' She then explained about growing up at Cuckoo House and how she had promised herself when she sold it never to set foot in it ever again. Too many bad memories, was as far as her sketchy explanation went—memories, she said, that had stirred things up for her.

'Well, I never,' said Ronnetta when Alice had finished. 'You think you know a person, and then out of the blue they completely throw you. You're a strange one and no mistake.'

'Bet you're now thinking Bob's had a lucky escape. Who in their right mind would want to be involved with me?'

'You mean, other than the weird bloke?'

It was the first week of December and Clayton didn't think he had ever experienced such bitter coldness. It bit deep, although Alice didn't seem to be aware of it. They were taking a walk across the moors. So far they hadn't encountered anyone else mad enough to be out.

'It's going to snow later,' she said matter-of-factly, tipping her head back to look at the sky; it was ominously grey and pendulous.

'A man could die up here all alone and no one would ever know,' he remarked. 'He would be forgotten entirely. All trace of him gone.'

She turned and smiled. 'But at least the coyotes and grizzly bears would remember him fondly.'

He smiled back at her and on an impulse reached for one of her gloved hands. 'Should we encounter any grizzly bears, you will protect me, won't you?'

'You have my word.'

They walked on, hand in hand. A week had passed since they had last seen each other. Clayton had thought about her a lot in those days. It was hard not to, given that he was secretly writing about her on a daily basis. He'd also thought about George's theory that he reminded Alice of her father. He didn't know what to make of that. He still thought charming bastards—men like Rufus—were Alice's type. Only one way to find out where he stood in her estimation.

'Alice, can I ask you something?' he said.

'Yes,' she said, turning to face him.

'Does James Montgomery bear any resemblance to Rufus?' he asked.

'Wow,' she said. 'What put that thought in your head?'

'Oh, you know, an inquisitive mind. Does that bother you?'

'I think that my answer bothers me more, because you're right, almost every man I've been attracted to bore some kind of resemblance to Rufus. You'd think I would have gone out of my way to avoid reminding myself of him, wouldn't you?'

'Would it be impertinent to suggest you try a different type of man?'

'Do you have a particular type of man in mind?'

'Well, there is this chap I know. He's a complete idiot and can be relied upon at all times to do or say the wrong thing.'

The corners of her mouth lifted. 'So much for his good points. What about his bad points?'

'Ah, much too numerous to go into.' He bent his head and kissed her very slowly, very lightly. Her lips were icy cold against his own cold mouth, but he soon felt a warmth spring between them. A powerful surge of desire made him want to get Alice back to Cuckoo House as fast as possible. 'Can we go home, please?' he whispered in her ear.

After a frantic search, Clayton found what he was looking for in the master bedroom. He shut the drawer and hurried back to where he'd left Alice in his bed. 'We're in luck!' he said, putting the box down.

She smiled and flipped back the duvet, inviting him to get in. He stripped off and slid in alongside her. He lay on his side and ran a hand the full stunning length of her naked body. She sighed at his touch and rolled on top of him. He held her face in his hands, took in the happiness of her expression and kissed her.

'Feeling any warmer now?' she murmured.

When they looked out of the window later, it was snowing. She was wearing his shirt—and nothing else—and Clayton could honestly say it had never looked better. 'You do know that I can't possibly let you leave here today. Not in this weather,' he said.

She turned and looked at him. 'You'd like me to stay?'

'You don't want to?' His heart plummeted.

She smiled and wrapped herself round him. 'I'd love to stay.'

It must have snowed persistently throughout the night.

Sculpted by the wind, bulging drifts of perfectly white snow had transformed the garden and the surrounding moorland into a landscape of exquisite beauty. Uncomfortably reminded of the very last time she had witnessed snow to this extent at Cuckoo House, Alice sat at the kitchen table watching Clayton get breakfast ready in his amusingly haphazard way. By rights they should both be exhausted after the night they'd had but Clayton looked as alert and bright-eyed as she'd ever seen him. 'How many eggs would you like?'

'Just the one, please.'

'Rashers of bacon?'

'Two.'

'Have you ever thought about the word "rasher"? Such a simple word, but the more you say it, the funnier it becomes. It's what we in the trade call a comedy word. The same goes for weasel. Rascal. Stout. Scuttle. Perky. Scoundrel.' He slid the pan under the grill and went over to the sink to wash his hands. 'Tomatoes or beans?'

'Are they comedy words?'

'No, they're options for breakfast.'

'In that case, tomatoes. You're much too full of beans as it is.'

He came over and kissed her. 'A man can't be happy?'

She put her arms round his neck. 'How shall we spend the day?'

He stroked her hair. 'Here's the plan. After we've eaten breakfast, I'll make a fire in the sitting room and we'll spend the day in there. And later, I might even do some more writing.'

She looked up at him. 'Writing? *More* writing? When did you start?'

His hands stopped moving. 'Um . . . just recently,' he said quietly.

'Why didn't you say anything?'

'I . . . I was—' He straightened up.

She took holds of his hands. 'It's OK,' she said, 'I understand. It was too soon, wasn't it? You didn't want to jinx things. But how brilliant.'

He sat in the chair next to her. His expression was unexpectedly serious. 'I couldn't have got going again if it wasn't for you. You'll never know how grateful I am. You've inspired me. The thing is, what I've started is—'

Her gaze flickered away from his. 'Sorry to interrupt you,' she said, 'but I think we have a grill-pan situation.'

'Oh, hell!' He leaped to his feet and went to deal with the smoke that was billowing from the grill. 'It's not as bad as it looks,' he said.

It*'s not as bad as it looks.*

The words were yet another damning indictment of his behaviour. He hadn't meant to open his great big gob; the admission that he had started writing had slipped out. And, of course, he should have had the courage to explain exactly what he was writing. The longer he kept quiet, the worse it would appear.

But the thing was, he couldn't tell her. He was terrified that if he did, two things could happen. One: the script would be jinxed. And two: she would freak out and ban him from writing another word. The net result would be that he would lose the best script he had ever written. He would also, despite it being early days between them, lose Alice, who was the best thing to have come into his life in a long while.

Whichever way he viewed matters, the situation had disaster written all over it if he opened his mouth. He'd come this far; he simply couldn't let this opportunity slip through his hands. If he could hold his nerve, he could finish the script, own up, and then somehow convince Alice that it really wasn't as bad as it looked.

'If you don't mind me saying, you're sounding remarkably chipper,' said Glen. Does that mean you're still writing?'

'Like a demon. What's more, I'm prepared to stake my life on you thinking this is easily the best thing I've ever written.'

'All right then, when do I get to read this stupendous work?'

'Give me another week. Then I'll email you some pages.'

'That'll take us to the middle of December. The week before Christmas.'

'Is that a problem for you? Don't tell me you're forcing yourself to endure yet another five-star holiday in some unbearably luxurious location for the festive season?'

'Of course I am. What else would I be doing for Christmas? Which brings me to the point of this call. I've got bad news. Craig and Anthea are coming home for Christmas. Some relic of a relation has died and, as we speak, they're on their way back for the funeral.'

'And what would that have to do with me precisely?'

'It has everything to do with you, you moron! You're staying in their house. You have to leave pronto.'

'But I can't!'

'Sorry, you have to. Craig and Anthea will be arriving in Derbyshire the day after tomorrow.'

'But I can't leave. I'm writing here. It's working for me.'

'I'm sure you'll continue to write when you come back to London.'

'LONDON! Are you mad? I can't possibly return there.'

'It'll be fine. You're no longer the focus of the nation's thoughts. But if you don't want to come back to London and the area up there is providing the necessary ambience for you, why don't you check into the nearest hotel? Meanwhile, start packing. I'll ring the cleaning agency and organise for someone to give the place the once-over before Craig and Anthea arrive. I'll give you a ring in the morning.'

The line went dead. Clayton stared at the mobile in his hand. He was all set to ring Glen back, to say heaven only knew what, when a flash of car headlights caught his attention at the end of the drive. He went to let Alice in. He hadn't seen her for ages. Absolutely ages. Well, not since breakfast that morning.

'I stopped off at the Indian takeaway,' Alice said, putting a large brown carrier bag on the table. 'I hope you like what I've chosen. Clayton? What's wrong? Did the writing not go well today?'

He helped her out of her coat. Then he kissed her, very slowly, very surely. 'I have to leave Cuckoo House tomorrow,' he said. 'The owners are coming back. Glen's suggesting I go home to London.'

'Oh,' she said. Her voice was flat. 'London. Right. Well, yes, I suppose you do have to leave, don't you?' He could see she was trying to hide how upset she was.

'I don't want to go back to London. I don't think I'll be able to work there.'

'Is that the only reason you don't want to go back?'

'No,' he said simply.

She swallowed. 'Then don't go back.'

'I'll have to find somewhere else to stay. Do you know of a good hotel?'

'What kind of hotel were you thinking of?' she asked quietly. 'Because there are only B&Bs round here.'

'That doesn't sound very promising.'

She took a step towards him. 'There is one place I know of that might suit you.' She looked up into his face and he felt his pulse quicken. 'The trouble is, the landlady is a stickler for rules,' she said.

'What, such as no guests after ten o'clock at night?'

'She also has a ban on muddy boots. And she's a total Nazi when it comes to toothpaste etiquette.'

He began to smile. 'And the bedroom arrangements?'

'Ah, now that's where things get interesting. It would be obligatory for you to keep her company at night.'

'You know, at a pinch I think I could manage that. But are you sure the arrangements would work? I would hate to intrude.'

She placed the tips of her fingers over his mouth; it made him want to take hold of her and carry her upstairs to bed. 'You wouldn't be intruding,' she said softly. 'Far from it.'

He kissed the tips of her fingers, then moved her hand aside and kissed her on the lips. 'So when do we tell George I'm moving in with her?' he said.

It was a long time since Alice had let anyone live with her. The two occasions she had tried it had been disastrous. So letting Clayton move in was a huge risk. But she had done it because the thought of him leaving had seemed infinitely worse.

In the split second when he had broken the news that he had to move out of Cuckoo House, she had felt as if the air had been knocked out of her. To her surprise, she had been close to tears. It was then that she realised how strongly she felt about him. In a knee-jerk reaction to this insight she had invited him to stay with her.

So far, a week into the new arrangement, things were going well. There was a sense of rightness about his presence in the cottage with her. It was something that scared her. With a track record for not holding onto a man for longer than a few months, she was in the daunting position of having found someone she didn't want to lose.

Initially she had been frightened to trust her feelings for Clayton, seeing the relationship as too good to be true. But the more time she spent with him, the more real it felt to her. She loved it when she discovered something new about him, such as the ease with which he could rattle off a cryptic crossword. Then there was his talent for juggling. OK, juggling wasn't exactly the most useful of talents, but given how cack-handed he often appeared to be, he really was rather good at it. She also discovered that he had never learned to drive and that he'd had a boyhood crush on Julie Andrews. Clayton had told her she was the first person he'd ever admitted this to.

Clayton's appearance at Dragonfly Cottage had not gone unnoticed by Ronnetta and less than two hours after his arrival, she was tapping on the kitchen window. Introductions were duly made—Clayton having reverted to his alias of Ralph Shannon—a full investigation carried out, and after she'd left, Clayton said, 'Is it my imagination, or would I be right in thinking your neighbour didn't approve of me?'

'She was measuring you against her precious son.'

Now as Alice weighed out dried fruit for the Christmas pudding, she could hear Clayton speaking on his mobile in the sitting room. He had been waiting for a call from his agent since yesterday morning when he had emailed some of his script to him. It gave her a thrill knowing that she had unwittingly been a part of curing his writer's block.

On the phone with Glen, Clayton was punching the air euphorically.

'I don't know how you've pulled this out of the bag,' Glen said, 'but I'm picturing you at the BAFTAs. Hell, this is Emmy stuff! Who do you think should play the character of Abigail? I've got Bill Nighy down as the father; he'd be perfect. How long before you've finished?'

'Not sure. Another month perhaps.'

'Well, what are you doing wasting time talking to me? Get back to your laptop and write! Meanwhile, I'm going to start talking to people at this end. I'm so excited about this I could kiss you!'

'Oh God, not one of your big wet kisses. But seriously, Glen, do you think we should hold back from putting my name on the script?'

'No. I think sufficient time has passed for us to cash in on your infamy. Now get on with the rest of it and I'll be in touch when I get back from Mauritius. Have a good Christmas.'

He ended the call and stared out of the window. The euphoric feeling had passed. Now that Glen was going to start pitching his script, he had to tell Alice what he'd done.

He knew he'd messed up. He should have gained Alice's approval and consent weeks ago. But he'd known all along that she would be horrified at what he'd done. She would see it as a betrayal of her trust. He was the first person with whom she had shared her story. And what did he go and do? Yeah, that's right, pinch it with the full intention of selling her innermost secrets to the highest bidder.

By God, he was a class act!

But he was consistent, if nothing else. He would keep quiet a little longer. He didn't want to ruin Alice's Christmas.

Alice had invited George and her neighbours for Christmas lunch. Ronnetta and Bob came bearing carrier bags clinking with bottles. Combined with what Alice already had and the bottle of deadly vintage brew George had brought with her, they had a dangerously well-stocked bar. Bob was applying himself with serious intent.

After a second glassful Bob was red in the face and as playful as a Labrador puppy. Jabbing Clayton on the shoulder, he was offering him advice on how to get in shape. 'No offence, Ralph, but I can see you've let your body go.' While Clayton smiled grimly back, Alice hoped the level of alcohol wouldn't turn the Labrador puppy into a spurned, snarling pit bull terrier. She also hoped that she could keep up the subterfuge of calling Clayton by his alias. She had warned George to remember that he was Ralph and not Clayton.

'Mistletoe moment!'

Alice looked up from where she was laying the table. Before she had a chance to react, Bob had clamped his mouth over hers. After she'd shaken him off and mentally disinfected her mouth, she saw Clayton looking on with a tight expression of disbelief on his face.

'Aren't you going to kiss me, young man?' asked George with a roguish twinkle in her eye. Bob couldn't have looked more terrified.

Just as she always used to, George had smartened herself up for the occasion. She was decked out in a tweedy dogtooth-check dress that emphasised her small, desiccated body. Alice felt a pang of sadness, acknowledging just how frail the old woman really was.

By the time they were midway through lunch everyone seemed less tense. The conversation round the table was relaxed and friendly. George was mostly responsible for that, regaling them with amusing tales about the inhabitants of Stonebridge.

'So what sort of work is it you do down in London, Ralph?' Ronnetta asked.

'Oh, this and that,' Clayton replied evenly.

'This and that?' repeated Bob. 'What's that supposed to mean?'

'It means I'm a lucky sod and can do as I please.'

'Loaded, are you? I might have guessed.' Bob stared at Alice accusingly, as if to say, so that's the reason you've hooked up with him.

'And what's your line of work, young man?' asked George.

'He's a telephone engineer for BT,' Ronnetta said proudly.

George narrowed her eyes. 'I hope you're not the engineer for whom I waited in all day and who never came.'

'Not my area,' Bob said. 'My patch is north of here.' He downed his glass of Merlot in one long gulp, then belched. 'Pardon me,' he said, 'better out than in.'

They were on the Christmas pudding course when the shaky balance that had so far been in place collapsed entirely.

Alice had just poured a dash of brandy over the pudding and reached for the matches, when Bob rose unsteadily from his seat and took the box out of her hands. He clumsily scraped a match along the side of the box, then tossed it vaguely in the direction of the pudding. When nothing happened, he reached for the bottle of brandy and poured it over the pudding. He struck three matches against the box at once and threw them at the pudding. There was a loud *whoomph* followed by a ball of fire shooting high into the air. It made instant contact with the lampshade that was hanging directly above the table.

With lightning speed, Clayton smothered the Christmas pudding with a plate then grabbed the oven gloves. He climbed onto his chair and wrapped his hands round the lampshade. Near-disaster was averted.

'Clayton Miller, you are my all-time hero!' George cheered. 'And you, young man,' she added, turning to Bob, 'are an idiot.'

'Don't you call my Bob an idiot!' Ronnetta responded indignantly.

Alice wasn't interested in the potential spat breaking out among the rest of her guests; she was more concerned with Clayton. He'd pulled off the scorched oven gloves and was blowing on his hands.

'Come with me,' she said.

Out in the kitchen, she ran the cold tap and made him put his hands under the gushing water. She could smell the unmistakable tang of singed hair. 'How bad does it feel?' she asked.

'I'll be fine. I'm just attention seeking.'

'Keep your hands under the water,' she said, when he tried to move them. 'How do they feel now?'

'I can't feel them; they're numb.'

The sound of raised voices, followed by a loud exclamation and footsteps had them both turning. Bob was standing in the doorway.

'So let me get this straight,' Bob said, swaying slightly but doing his best to focus on Clayton. 'Your name isn't Ralph Shannon, is it? George called you Clayton Miller. You're that bloke in the papers, aren't you? I thought there was something familiar about your untrustworthy mug the second I laid eyes on you.'

'Who'd have thought it,' muttered Clayton. 'The dumb-ass can read.'

'What did you call me?' Bob's expression darkened. 'Outside. You and me. Let's get this sorted.'

Alice put a hand on Bob's forearm. 'Come on, Bob, that's enough.' Seeing that Ronnetta was now standing in the doorway, Alice appealed to her with an anxious glance, hoping she would step in.

Luckily Ronnetta took the hint. She stepped towards her son. 'Bob, let it go, love. Just accept there's no accounting for taste.' She turned to Alice. 'I think we should probably leave, don't you?' To Alice's great relief, there was no animosity in her voice.

It was another Christmas to remember. Alice wished she had spent the day alone with Clayton. But no, she had to go and invite Ronnetta and Bob. As a consequence, poor Clayton had burned his hands—thankfully not badly—and heaven only knew how she was going to face Bob again. There was also the worry that Clayton's identity would soon be common knowledge in the village.

George had been mortified by her slip of the tongue in calling Clayton by his real name. Clayton had played down the potential consequences of people knowing who he was, even saying that it was going to come out sooner or later, so why not now? Alice had been taken aback by the effect this casual remark had had on her. Until he had uttered those words, she hadn't dared acknowledge the doubt she had been secretly harbouring, the worry that perhaps the reason Clayton had wanted to continue with the deception was because she didn't really matter that much to him, and that when it was time for him to return to London, he would do so without a backwards glance. But as a result of this exchange with George, the doubt had been quashed.

George had insisted then that it was time for her to go home. 'No, no,' she had said when Alice had tried to dissuade her, 'you two don't need me here playing gooseberry.' She had then whispered something to Clayton in a way that Alice could only describe as collusive.

Now, as she sprawled on the sofa with Clayton, while trying to decide what to watch on the television, she was intrigued to know what it was George had said to him. 'I feel it only fair to warn you,' she said, 'secrets are all very well when they're *my* secrets, but I draw the line at others withholding anything from me.'

Clayton looked up from the rumpled copy of the bumper Christmas edition of the *Radio Times* he was reading. 'Secrets?' he said. 'What makes you say that?'

She assumed a mock-serious expression. 'I'm just wondering what it is that you're keeping from me.'

'Why do you think I'm keeping anything from you?'

'You can't fool me, Clayton,' she said. 'I know there's something.'

He slowly put aside the *Radio Times*. He suddenly seemed tense. He wasn't looking at her. A small alarm bell started ringing inside her head. What had she unwittingly stumbled upon?

'What is it, Clayton?' she asked. 'Why do you look so serious?'

He swallowed. 'Because you're right. I do feel guilty. I've done something you're not going to like.' He still wasn't looking at her.

'You're leaving? Is that it? You've decided to go back to London?'

He shook his head. 'I've . . . I've been doing something behind your back,' he said. 'And you're going to be furious with me. I can't say I'll blame you. I think the best thing is for me to show you what it is. Then you can decide for yourself just how morally bankrupt I am.'

Clayton left Alice on her own with his laptop. He stood outside by the back door, as if punishing himself by being in the freezing cold. When he could no longer bear it, he went back inside to hear his fate.

She looked up. 'You were right,' she said, 'you are morally bankrupt. How could you do this to me? How could you have thought this was a good thing to do?'

'I don't choose what to write,' he said. 'It chooses me.'

'That's bullshit. You stole this. You stole my life story. How do you think that makes me feel?'

'Put yourself in my shoes. I haven't been able to write in over three years, then out of the blue I meet you and you banish the fear that had crippled me for so long.' He went and knelt on the floor in front of her. 'Alice, you have to believe me; if I could have stopped myself from grabbing hold of the lifeline you'd thrown me, I would have. But I couldn't. After the crap I'd gone through with Bazza and Stacey, life suddenly felt good again. Better than good. So much better. These past few weeks have been the best I've known in years. And that's all down to you.'

She pushed the laptop at him. 'With every word you've written, you've betrayed me. And I'll never forgive you for that. *Never*. Did George know about this? Was that why she whispered to you earlier?'

'George knows nothing about it. She . . .' he broke off. He could hardly tell Alice that George had been congratulating herself on knowing that he and Alice would be good together. 'She was saying goodbye,' he said.

'Well, I'm saying goodbye to you. I want you out of my house. If you'd ever really cared about me, you wouldn't have done this.'

'I do care about you. More than you'll ever know.'

'Then prove it to me. If you delete what's on your laptop, you can stay. But if you don't delete it, you have to leave. The choice is yours.'

He swallowed. 'That's not fair.'

'Fair? You want to talk fair? How about we discuss how you continually cross-examined me about my family just so that you could make sure you got the details right for your script? Does it sound fair to you that I kept my promise not to tell anyone who you were, while all the time you were preparing to tell the world the most intimate details of my life? My God, I've done some stupid things in my time, but thinking that we had something special going on between us was the dumbest thing I ever did.' She shook her head. 'I believed in you, Clayton. I think that's what hurts the most.'

Chapter Eight

'YOU KNOW WHO THAT IS, don't you?'

Clayton tipped his head to see to whom Glen was referring. It was the third time during their lunch that his attention had been drawn to the occupants of another table in the smart restaurant which, according to Glen, was now his favourite watering hole in Soho.

'Got me again, Glen,' he said.

'It's one of the Cheeky Girls.'

'Eyes on me, Glen. Come on, concentrate. Keep the focus.'

Two and a half months had passed since he had left Derbyshire—two and a half months since he had last seen Alice. After she had finished saying exactly how she felt about him, she had calmly explained that she was going to spend the night with George, leaving him at Dragonfly Cottage on his own. 'When I return tomorrow, I want you gone,' she had said.

At eight o'clock on Boxing Day morning, he had found a taxi firm willing to take him to the station and, after a two-hour wait on a freezing-cold platform, he had caught the only train to London that day.

Alice's parting look would stay with him for a long time yet. Her expression had cut him to the quick, knowing that he had wilfully hurt the one person he had come to think actually meant something to him. But the bottom line was, he clearly hadn't cared enough about her. Had his feelings been strong enough, he would have hit the delete button on his laptop, just as she had requested. But she had given him an impossible task, like asking a mother which of her two children she would save if they were both drowning. How could she have expected him to choose between her and resurrecting his writing career? Being able to write again had been akin to a blind man suddenly having his sight restored. Had she really expected him to be capable of throwing that away?

He had considered writing a letter of apology and justification to Alice, but had decided against it when he recalled the letters her father had sent her and which she had never read. Instead he had tried to convince himself that Alice had overreacted and needed time to cool down. That was pushing it, he knew.

He had even kidded himself that if Alice watched the series when it was shown on television—he still wasn't sure when that would be—it would help her realise that what he'd written wasn't exploitative. Those who had been involved in the production process were all saying that he had written with great sensitivity, not just when it came to Alice's character—or rather, Abigail's character—but in regard to all the other characters. Well, all of them except for Rufus, aka Lucius. Everybody also agreed that the two stars of the script were Abigail and her father. Clayton was pleased about that, because he had genuinely wanted Alice to be happy with what he'd written, and portraying her father, whom he'd renamed as Ralph, in an empathetic light had been crucial to gaining her approval.

Once he'd arrived back in London, he had got his head down and finished the script. Not only had Glen been right about Clayton no longer being of interest to anyone in Tabloid La-La Land, but he had found a production company eager to take on his script. Things had moved fast and, before he knew it, he was on set for most of the filming in North Yorkshire. Bill Nighy had agreed to take on the part of 'Ralph' Barrett—miraculously he'd been available at such short notice—and he had played the role brilliantly.

While Clayton liked to think the green light had been given to his script because it was a work of pure genius and therefore forgiveness had been a natural consequence, he had to accept that a far more important factor had been at work in his being welcomed back into the fold. Two factors to be precise: Bazza and Stacey.

As Glen had assured him, the public can be relied upon to be fickle, but the merry band of souls who make up the country's great unbiased press can be just as fickle. And so it came to pass that the sun began to go down on the Golden Couple. Their PR people wildly miscalculated the public's appetite for Saint Bazza and Mother Stacey when they let loose a press release announcing that Stacey had just signed a contract to write a book entitled *How to Forgive and Forget*. It had Major Stinker written all over it. The *Mirror* led the attack:

> When will it ever end, this obsession among publishers to print anything a D-rated celebrity has had ghosted for them? Who gives a stuff for what a nobody like Stacey Cook thinks? And who, by the way, is this woman? OK, she lost a baby, but millions of women have had a miscarriage. What makes her so special?

The next day a piece appeared in the *Mail* picking up on the theme:

> Am I alone in reaching for a sick bag whenever I hear the names Barry Osborne and Stacey Cook mentioned? If I have to stomach another good cause or publicity stunt that they've involved themselves with, I swear I will not be responsible for my actions.

From then on the tide turned and Glen suggested the time was right for Clayton to tell his side of the story. 'Bazza and Stacey's downfall ensures your reinstatement,' Glen promised him. 'And it'll give us a brilliant hook for your new show.'

Three days later, Glen set Clayton up with a journalist from *The Sunday Times* and the paper ran the interview the following Sunday. A few days after that, Glen received a call for Clayton to appear on Jonathan Ross's show. Clayton had given it his best shot in getting across his side of the story—how he'd tried to apologise to Stacey and Barry and how it had all gone hopelessly wrong. When he admitted how shocked he'd been at the size of the heads as they'd emerged from the truck, expecting them to be cute and adorable whereas they'd proved to be nearer a Tyrannosaurus in scale, the audience had laughed and he'd known then that the worst was over.

'**A**aah . . . Oooh . . . Yes . . . do that again . . .'

'Sorry, Alice, could we give that another go? Only you really didn't sound like you were enjoying it.'

That's because I'm not, Alice thought crossly. Sex to sell a toilet cleaner? Where would it all end? What she couldn't understand was why Johnny Phoenix had agreed to voice-over the product. He certainly didn't need the money—his career was going from strength to strength. Well, good luck to him. And good luck to her too; she was being paid more money today than she had received in a long while for a job. Now, if she could just get into character—that of a toilet—and pretend she was enjoying the experience of Johnny Phoenix tackling her stubborn build-up in one easy squirt, she would be home and dry.

Hazel had been overjoyed to nail this job for Alice. 'It'll become a series of ads, no doubt about it,' she had enthused. 'You and Johnny will be like the Nescafé couple back in the eighties. This could be the beginning of something big for you, Alice.'

Alice had heard it all before. What's more, she had believed it all before. Now she didn't. She didn't believe a word anyone said to her. Clayton had seen to that. He had robbed her of the belief that there would always be something better around the next corner. Once that was taken away from a person, what was left? Only the resounding conviction that life was pretty shitty.

She had read several articles in the newspapers about Clayton, including an interview in *The Sunday Times*. It was Bob who had brought the first of the articles to Alice's attention. Alice had told Ronnetta everything, about Clayton stealing her childhood to write a script, and, naturally, Ronnetta had kept Bob informed. Bob had been all for taking Clayton apart by telling the local newspaper what he had done to her, but Alice had made him promise he wouldn't. 'I couldn't take the shame of everyone here knowing what a fool I've been,' she had explained to him. To her relief, Bob had respected her wishes and backed off. He'd offered to take her out several times, 'just to take her mind off things' and now it had become a regular thing; every Friday evening he took her for a curry. 'I know you don't fancy me,' he said the last time they were dining at the Bombay Mix. 'Not now, but give it time and who knows, you might just change your mind. You've got to admit, I'm not a bad-looking bloke. And I'd always be straight with you. Not like some folk I could mention. What did you ever see in him, Alice?'

Good question. What had she seen in Clayton? It was hard now to remember. Had it been nothing more than getting caught up in the heat of what could only be described as a very strange moment?

George had been annoyingly bullish on the subject. If anything, she had taken Clayton's side. 'All I'm saying is that the man should have been given the opportunity to explain himself fully,' she had said.

'There was nothing he could say to explain or justify his actions,' Alice had retorted. 'He conned me. And he wrote about you as well.'

'I should hope so. And I hope he wrote about me warts and all. I'd hate to think he sanitised me into an insipid old dear.'

'He made you appear very eccentric. Positively off your trolley.'

'Excellent! I think Eileen Atkins would play me rather well.'

'It's not excellent what he did. It's awful,' Alice had said, exasperated. 'It's an infringement of our rights. He exploited us.'

'Really? I think he got drawn into a situation and found himself a changed man as a result. A happier man. You were mostly responsible for that. You enabled him to write again. Aren't you just a little bit flattered and proud that you were responsible for that and that he thought your childhood worth writing about?'

'He should have asked for my permission.'

'And you would have refused it. He couldn't take that risk. Any fool can see that.'

'You're saying I'm a fool?'

'Unquestionably so.'

Always nice to know where one stands, Alice thought now, as she stepped out onto the street, the recording session over.

Soho: it was a world away from her life in Stonebridge. But not so very far from Clayton, she supposed. How easy it would be to call him on her mobile and suggest they meet for a drink and a chat. Would he come? Would she manage to be civil? Not a chance.

Why, she wondered, when a relationship ended, could the happiness one had previously experienced not remain? After all, the past couldn't be changed. What she had experienced with Clayton had actually happened, so why could she no longer recall how happy she had been with him?

Because her happiness had been based on a falsehood. Clayton had deceived her into being happy. And that was unforgivable.

'Alice? Is that you?'

She spun round at the sound of the voice. '*James!*' she exclaimed.

'Well, of all the gin joints,' he said. 'What brings you here?'

'I've been in a studio all day recording an advert for the telly. With Johnny Phoenix,' she added.

'Wow!' he said. 'Good for you. Hey, you don't fancy a drink, do you?'

There were no tables free, so they grabbed the last two stools at the crowded bar. With two glasses of wine in front of them, Alice said, 'So what have you been up to since we last met? I miss Matilda.'

He pushed a hand through his dangling fringe. A gesture that reminded her all too uncomfortably of Rufus. 'I miss you reading Matilda,' he said, 'and if I'm honest, just between you and me, the new voice isn't half as good as you.'

'I'm delighted to hear it,' she said. 'Why didn't you tell me yourself that I was being dropped in favour of a big name?'

Another rueful push of his hand through his hair. 'God, Alice, I was all set to, but I lost my nerve. I'm sorry. But it sounds like you're going gangbusters. Working with Johnny Phoenix, no less. If I tell you something, do you promise not to tell anyone?'

'Of course.'

'I've just signed a contract for a TV adaptation to be made of the first book in the series. It'll go out next Christmas.'

'Congratulations.'

'Thank you. I still can't quite believe it. What's more, my agent found me a brilliant production company. Right now they're putting the finishing touches to Clayton Miller's new drama. Do you remember all that hoo-ha when he disappeared last year? Well, it transpires he was holed up somewhere in the frozen north working on a completely new project. The word is, this is his best work yet.'

'Is that so?' Alice said as calmly as she could.

'It's called *The Queen of New Beginnings*. Good title, don't you think?'

There was only one person Alice could talk to with regards to what she had just learned and that was George. She parked behind George's Morris Minor and went round to the back door. She didn't bother knocking or ringing the bell. Ever since she had arrived home from London last night, she had been in a foul temper.

There was no sign of George in the kitchen. Percy eyeballed Alice with ferocious hostility. He thrust out his chest and pulled himself up to his full height. 'Oh, put a sock in it, Percy,' she said, 'I'm not in the mood.' She called out to George. 'George, it's me, Alice.'

No reply.

Deciding George was either upstairs or in the garden, Alice climbed the stairs to rule out the first possibility. Percy followed a few steps behind her. He was acting his socks off, giving her the kind of manic stare Jack Nicholson had won awards for. 'You missed your calling, Percy,' she muttered. 'You should have gone to drama school.'

He cocked his head, giving her yet more attitude, then hopped up onto the next step, which had the effect of propelling her towards the landing. He continued after her. 'George,' she called out. 'It's me, Alice.'

Still no reply. Perhaps she was in the garden, Alice decided. Percy was now on the landing with her. Still eyeballing her with plenty of attitude, he came right up close and pecked at one of her shoes. She took a step back. He advanced and pecked again. Another step. Another peck. Their two-step continued until he had her jammed up against a door. 'Are you trying to tell me something, Percy?' she said.

He strutted past her into what was George's bedroom. The most obvious thing to do seemed to be to follow him.

The room was in semi-darkness, but Alice made out the shape of a body on the floor by the side of the bed. She rushed forward. 'George!' she cried out. Lying on her back, her head turned to one side, her mouth open at an unnatural angle, the old lady looked like a small, discarded doll dressed in oversized pyjamas. There was fear in her eyes. Relief too. And then tears.

The doctor explained things to Alice with brutal detachment. George had had a massive stroke. There was no question of her going home. 'It's possible that she might regain some movement,' he said, 'maybe even some speech, but right now, given her age and frailty, I think that's unlikely. The end will probably come sooner rather than later.'

Alice could have cheerfully pushed a knife between his ribs. How dare he pronounce George's life over?

'She can still see, hear and feel, can't she?' Alice said pointedly.

'To a degree, yes,' the doctor said.

'Well then, let's not write her off just yet, shall we? May I see her now?'

'Visiting hours are—'

Alice quelled him with a look that Percy would have been proud of.

'All right. But not for long.'

The ward smelled of institutional cleaning fluid and canteen food. Alice drew the curtain round them and sat by the side of the bed, on the right side so George could see her. She held her hand. 'I go down to London for a day,' she said softly so as not to disturb the other patients, 'and look what happens while my back is turned.'

George stared at Alice, pale and glassy-eyed.

Alice swallowed back the painful lump in her throat and dabbed at the old woman's distorted mouth, wiping away a small amount of dribble.

'We need to devise some form of communication,' she said. 'One blink is yes. Two blinks, no. Can you manage that?'

George blinked.

'Good. I'm going to help you get well, George,' she said. 'Together we'll soon have you up and about.'

George blinked twice.

'Wrong answer,' Alice said. Her chest tightened. 'You're just going to give up?'

George's eyes slowly fluttered as if alternating between yes and no and then stayed shut.

A swish of movement had Alice turning round. A nurse appeared in the gap in the curtain. 'I think she needs to sleep now. And don't worry, she'll be in safe hands here with us.' The girl had a gentle manner about her. Alice felt inclined to believe her.

'You'll call me if there's any change, won't you?' she said.

'Of course.'

Alice drove home tired and depressed. Poor George. How long had she been lying on the floor of her bedroom? If only Percy could use a phone. She almost smiled at the thought of Percy, who was clearly as smart a rooster that had ever lived. George would worry about Percy and his harem; Alice knew that she would have to take on their care herself. In the short term it wouldn't be a problem, but what if the doctor was right and George was never going to get better?

In her heart, Alice knew that this was the reality of the situation: unless a miracle happened, George would never return home. The severity of George's situation made what James had shared with her seem unimportant. Let Clayton Miller have his great comeback. So what if it was at the expense of anyone else. Yes, she could try to take out an injunction, but that might attract even more attention to herself. If she kept her mouth shut, maybe no one would ever know that it was her family he had written about.

But there were others who would know: Rufus and Natasha, and not forgetting Isabel. What if they saw the programme and tracked Alice down? What if they started screaming defamation of character? But there was nothing she could do about it. It was beyond her control. Besides, she had more pressing matters on her mind now: helping George. She hadn't hesitated to fill in the necessary forms describing herself as a niece and therefore next of kin. No one had questioned her. Just let them try.

As the days slipped slowly by George showed no sign of getting any better. Their method of communication had been extended; as well as yes and no, they now had established that a glance to the right meant that George agreed with Alice; a glance to the left meant she thought something was funny and a roll of her eyes meant what it always had—that she thought Alice was being an idiot.

There had been a good deal of eye rolling during this afternoon's visit. Alice had told George about her meeting with James Montgomery in London and the latest news on Clayton's script, soon to be put out as a two-hour drama called *The Queen of New Beginnings*.

'George, if you roll your eyes like that any more, they'll pop out,' Alice said. 'And I won't scrabble about on the floor looking for them.'

George glanced to her left.

'I'm glad you think I'm being funny. Because actually I'm being deadly serious.'

Two blinks.

'You don't think so, eh? Well, I'll tell you what I am serious about;

I have no intention of watching that lying cheat's programme when it goes out. Oh, for heaven's sake, you're rolling your eyes again.'

Two blinks.

'Stop saying no to everything.'

Two blinks again.

Alice wiped George's mouth. 'You're being very difficult today. I hope you're not trying to tell me that you want to watch his programme.'

One blink.

'I might have known. You're desperate to see how Clayton's portrayed you, aren't you? You're the vainest person I know.'

One blink. And a glance to the right.

Alice sat in silence for a moment. She stared off into the distance. When Alice returned her attention to George, she found herself confronted with a gaze so intense she sat back a little. It was as if George was trying to tell her something.

'Do you need something? Do you want me to fetch a nurse?'

George blinked twice and rolled her eyes.

'You think I'm being an idiot?'

One blink.

Alice took a stab in the dark. 'I'm being an idiot with regards to what we were just discussing? Clayton and *The Queen of New Beginnings*?'

One blink.

'You wouldn't be trying to blackmail me emotionally?'

One blink.

'Just because you're ill, don't for one minute think you can make me do something I don't want to do.'

George's eyes remained open and fixed on Alice.

'Oh, for heaven's sake, stop nagging me and I'll try to arrange it so that we watch the wretched programme together. OK?'

A month after being admitted to hospital, George defied the experts and regained a limited amount of movement and the ability to speak, although her speech wasn't at all easy to understand. More often than not, her words came out as fast as machine-gun fire and made little or no sense. It frustrated her immensely when Alice failed to grasp what she was saying. George had never been one to suffer fools gladly so it was no wonder she lost her temper when Alice had to apologise for the nth time that she had no idea what George was talking about. But it was a comfort to have more of the old George back. It was a comfort also when George would reach for Alice's hand and gently squeeze it.

Today, when Alice took her usual seat by the side of her bed, George was in a particularly agitated mood. 'Slow down,' Alice said after George had bombarded her with a breathtaking stream of incoherency.

George ignored her and let loose with a furious look and another torrent of incoherency. Her tone and frantic demeanour suggested that she had just explained the world was about to end.

'Start again,' Alice said patiently. 'I didn't hear you properly.'

'The teapot,' George said. *There!*' With great effort, she pointed vaguely towards her bedside locker. There was no teapot, only a plastic cup, a jug of water and a newspaper.

'You want a drink?' Alice asked.

George's eyes glinted.

'OK, you want me to read the newspaper to you, is that it?'

George's body visibly relaxed. But Alice's body did the opposite when she saw what it was that George had been so keen for her to read.

It was his big night and Clayton wasn't handling it well. With only minutes to go until *The Queen of New Beginnings* started, Glen was schmoozing a new client on the phone in the room next door, leaving Clayton to sweat out his apprehension alone.

He checked his watch. Six minutes to go.

Was he too old to watch his programme while hiding behind the sofa as he had as a child with *Doctor Who*?

Four minutes to go.

Would Glen ever get off the phone? It was worse than waiting to be taken to the gallows.

Not that he had ever waited to be taken to the gallows, but hyperbole had its place in situations like this.

In the old days he and Bazza had watched their work together. Presumably Stacey now kept Bazza company on the sofa when he had something new to watch. Lately Clayton had almost begun to feel sorry for the Golden Couple. Their collective halo had definitely lost its shine and their TV appearances had more or less dried up. The shots the paparazzi now snapped of them were less than kind. Only yesterday there had been a very unflattering series of pictures in a newspaper depicting a furious-looking Stacey emerging from a restaurant with Bazza; she appeared to be giving him hell.

Two minutes to go.

He wondered whether Alice was right now settled in front of her television. Perhaps she was there with a hotshot lawyer by her side, ready to take him to the cleaners. He had changed all the names though. And the location. He had done everything to cover his back. He had done everything except the one thing Alice had asked of him.

The voice of Captain Sensible kept muttering ad nauseam that as his agent, Glen should have been made aware that there was a potential glitch on the horizon. He had a right to know just how close to the wind Clayton was sailing. But Captain Sensible wasn't having it all his own way. He now had to contend with the voice of Signor Ego. Signor Ego stubbornly maintained that he needed this success to be back in the game. And at any cost. So what if he was accused of stealing somebody's life story? So what if he had trampled on the feelings of a person who had shown him nothing but friendship and kindness? *And trust*, Captain Sensible piped up. *Let's not forget that.*

Clayton squeezed his eyes shut. Just how much rope did a man need to hang himself by?

They had the television room to themselves. After the briefest of exchanges, both Alice and George kept their gaze on the screen. When the credits rolled at the end they looked at each other. But Alice couldn't speak. Her throat was tight and her eyes had filled with tears. From her wheelchair, George reached out to her and patted her arm. With great effort, she said, 'I was right. He did care about you.'

Alice felt bereft, as if she had lost her parents all over again. The actors hadn't looked anything like her parents, but the way they spoke was uncannily reminiscent, especially Bill Nighy. How had Clayton captured her father to such an incredible and insightful depth? Surely she hadn't described him to that extent? In contrast, her mother had come across as a far more unknown quantity. Was that how Alice had depicted her mother to him? Maybe so. After all, her mother had died when she was still quite young. And what of Rufus and his family? Alice gave a little shudder as she thought how cruelly devious and manipulative Rufus had been portrayed. How had her father stood by and let Rufus get away with what he had? But how could he have stopped him? He had warned Alice and she had chosen not to believe him.

There wasn't a hope in hell that Natasha and Rufus could be deceived into believing this wasn't a direct account of their time at Cuckoo House. Would they want revenge? Thank God she had changed her name and they wouldn't be able to track her down easily.

And what of her feelings for the man who had put her through this?

A part of her wanted to thank Clayton for writing what he had. As a permanent record of her father, it was as authentic as she could have wanted. Even when her father had run off with Isabel, Clayton had not shown him in a bad light. He had written the whole thing with extraordinary sensitivity. As loath as she was to admit it, it was just possible she had misjudged Clayton.

The way he had ended the drama, and the inclusion of one character in particular, had been the greatest surprise of all. Clayton had written himself into the script under the guise of a novelist suffering from writer's block. He meets a young woman with a story to tell . . . they fall in love . . . they part . . . they get back together . . .

It made her wonder. Why had Clayton written the ending like that? Was it because, as George had said, he had genuinely cared about her?

Something else that was making her wonder was the hard-to-ignore fact that she was really in no position to judge Clayton as harshly as she had. To condemn him was to condemn herself. For hadn't she wilfully misled people all her life? The word 'hypocrite' resounded in her ears.

Unable to sleep, Clayton lay in bed thinking about Alice. He was thinking about the ending he had written. Watching it play out had made him remember just how good his time with Alice had been. Would it have been the final straw and have had her throwing a very large, heavy object at the screen? Or was he flattering himself that she had even bothered to watch the programme?

He turned over and tried to force himself to sleep, but he couldn't stop thinking about Alice. The way she used to smile at him. And God help him, the way her body fitted perfectly against his when they were in bed together.

Three hours later he was still trying to sleep. He shouldn't be feeling like this. He should be feeling immensely pleased with himself. He'd got what he wanted: a slot on prime-time television and accolades aplenty. So why did it feel so pointless? Why did he feel like shit?

And why did he keep thinking that it wasn't until you lost something that you realised just how much you valued it?

He buried his face in the pillow. Maybe suffocation was the answer.

It was almost like the old days. *Joking Aside* had regularly attracted a sizeable mail bag and Clayton thought of those letters now as he flicked through the bundle of mail Glen had forwarded to him. He was a dozen letters into the pile and grateful that so far, in the nine days that had passed since *The Queen of New Beginnings* had aired, the letters were all complimentary, congratulating him on his comeback, saying they liked the change of direction he had taken and looked forward to more great drama from him.

More great drama, he mused. Well, that remained to be seen. Glen had already been on at him for his next Big Idea. The production company behind *The Queen of New Beginnings* had been muttering that he should write a sequel. Well, he didn't think he'd have the heart to do that. He didn't want to put Alice through any more pain or disappointment. On paper or in real life.

He stood up. Coffee. A shot of the hard stuff to stop him obsessing over whether Alice had watched his programme.

While he waited for the kettle to boil in the kitchen, he glanced through the rest of his mail that had arrived that morning. There, tucked in between a communication from BT and another from British Gas, was a handwritten envelope. The writing was instantly familiar.

This he hadn't expected. He made himself an extra-strong cup of coffee, grabbed a packet of Jaffa Cakes and went back to his office.

Dear Clayton,

I know this may come as a surprise to you, but I wanted to congratulate you on The Queen of New Beginnings. *You've really pulled it off with this one. Well done! At least now I know I did the right thing in splitting our partnership. I always knew I was holding you back. Remember I said you'd thank me one day? Hey, not that I'm expecting you to thank me!*

Once again, congratulations.

Cheers, Bazza

P.S. If you ever fancy meeting up for a drink, you know where I am.

What to make of it? Congratulations and the offer of a drink. Whatever next?

Next came far sooner than he could have imagined. Returning to the pile of fan mail, he opened another letter and began reading it.

Dear Mr Miller,

I watched with great interest The Queen of New Beginnings. *In fact I'd go so far as to say that I was spellbound by it.*

. . . Excellent. Obviously someone who appreciated quality . . .

The programme was of particular interest to me because I strongly suspect that it was not a work of fiction.

. . . He sat up straighter . . .

Moreover, I would very much like the opportunity to discuss this matter further with you. I'm intrigued to know how you came to write the piece. Of course, it could all be coincidence but I'm certain that this is not the case.

. . . His eyes flickered anxiously to the end of the letter . . .

Yours sincerely,
Isabel Blake

Isabel.

Rufus's girlfriend, who ran off with Bruce Barrett.

Clayton racked his brains trying to remember the surname that particular Isabel had gone by. It hadn't been Blake. But then it wouldn't be the same name if she had married. And she hadn't married Bruce by the looks of things. He read the letter again, this time taking in the contact addresses and number Isabel Blake had provided.

Canning! Yes, that was the surname Isabel had gone by.

He drank his coffee, then chewed on a Jaffa Cake, hoping it would quell the queasy feeling in his stomach.

Whether or not it was the injection of caffeine into his system, the writer in him suddenly saw something positive that could come of this letter. If this Isabel proved to be *the* Isabel Canning, then she might just turn out to be an answer to a prayer. A sequel . . . Captain Sensible cleared his throat. *Just one little thing: will you tell Alice about Isabel getting in touch? No? You don't think she has a right to know?*

Three days after receiving Isabel Blake's letter, Clayton had phoned the number she had supplied. They had arranged to meet and now, as the train pulled into Haslemere, he took a moment to steel himself. If she started making any unpleasant accusations, he would simply deny everything.

At the station, he gave the taxi driver the name of the restaurant she had suggested. It wasn't long before he was being dropped off.

When he spotted an attractive woman with shoulder-length blonde hair sitting at a table with a glass of white wine in front of her, there was no doubt in Clayton's mind that she was *the* Isabel. She was just as he had pictured. Just as Alice had described her: tall, slim and very elegant, simply dressed in a pair of white jeans and a cashmere top, with a string of pearls at her throat and earrings to match. She had class act stamped all over her. He clocked the absence of a wedding ring.

They shook hands. So far, so good. He cast a glance round the restaurant, checking for an army of lawyers to pounce on him. All he saw, he was pleased to note, were people eating their lunch.

'You made it,' she said. Her voice was light and friendly.

'Yes,' he responded. Oh, great, Mr Loquacious comes to town.

'Let me order you a drink. What would you like?' she said. She waved to a young waiter, who bounced over like an adoring puppy.

'The same as you,' he mumbled.

'Another glass of Chardonnay, Andrew,' she said to the puppy.

'So,' she said, when the puppy had left them two copies of the menu. 'Two words, Mr Miller. Cuckoo House.'

'Please, call me Clayton.' Make way for Mr Smooth.

She smiled, supremely composed. 'Two words, *Clayton*: Cuckoo House.'

'Do you know if the grilled sole is any good here?' he asked.

She laughed. It was a light, tinkling laugh, guaranteed to make the strongest of men weaken. 'I can recommend it,' she said.

They both ordered the Dover sole with green beans and crushed potatoes. 'So,' Clayton said, determined to take control, at the same time dispensing with his original plan. 'We both know exactly why I'm here.'

'Oh, yes,' she said happily. 'I knew there could be no coincidence in what you had written.'

Signor Ego tipped up the brim of his sombrero and peeped out. 'And what did you think of it?' Clayton asked.

'I thought it was very moving. I cried. For all sorts of reasons. Bruce loved Alice so very much, you know. I hope she never doubted that.'

'But he loved you more, didn't he?'

'There are different kinds of love. A father can't possibly love a daughter in the way he would a lover.'

'Well, one certainly hopes not.'

'Do I detect a dig at the age difference between Bruce and me?'

'Absolutely not. You were undoubtedly a woman to him.'

'Not to mention a woman who apparently belonged to Rufus?'

'You switched horses very easily, if you don't mind me saying.'

'Have you never done that?'

'Excuse the mix of metaphors, but I have at least let the sheets cool down before switching horses midrace.'

'Then I would suggest you've never lost your head. Or your heart.'

'Is that what you did with Bruce?'

She nodded 'And he with me. Nothing on this earth could have stopped us from doing what we did.' She lowered her eyes. It was as if the light had gone from her face. But then their waiter reappeared with their food and the smile and bewitching gaze were reinstated.

When they were alone again, she said, 'Now it's time for you to tell me how you came to write *The Queen of New Beginnings*.'

'I met Alice,' he said simply.

'Alice,' she repeated. 'How is she?'

'All grown up,' was all he could think to say.

'Married?'

He shook his head.

'Where is she living? In London? Is that where you met?'

'She lives about five miles away from Cuckoo House.'

'Her father was devastated when she didn't reply to any of his letters.'

'She was hurt by his selfishness. She was left to cope with so much, not least the aftermath of a suicide. She was only eighteen.'

Isabel put down her knife and fork. 'You sound protective of Alice,' she said. 'Are you involved with her?'

'I . . . I was.' It was the first time he had admitted this to anyone.

'Recently?'

'Why do you think that?'

She shrugged. 'If you'd met her a long time ago you would have written *The Queen of New Beginnings* then. What does Alice think of it?'

He hesitated. He could so easily lie. He could say that Alice had given it her full backing. But there was something about sitting here with Isabel—no longer a character he'd written about but very much the real deal—that compelled him to speak the truth.

'Before I answer your question,' he said, 'can I ask you what you thought about the way your character came across? Was it a faithful enactment of the events? These things are important to me.'

'I can speak only for the little that I took part in, but yes, I'd say you got it dead right. You could have done that only with Alice's help.'

'But you're not angry? You don't feel a libel suit coming on?'

'Relax. I didn't write to you with anything like that in mind. But tell me about Alice.'

He took a mental deep breath. 'I wrote it all without Alice's knowledge or permission after she had shared her story with me. She'd never told it to anyone else before. When she discovered what I was doing, she was furious.' He explained in more detail how once he'd started writing he just couldn't stop. Despite the inevitable consequences.

'Heavens,' Isabel said quietly. 'You're a bit of a bastard beneath that engagingly winsome exterior, aren't you?'

'No argument there.'

'Does she hate me very much?'

Clayton pushed his empty plate to one side and took a moment to consider Isabel's question. 'I'm not sure. But she never said as much.'

'I'd like to meet her. Do you think she would agree?'

'You're asking the wrong person. We haven't spoken since Christmas. I have no idea what's currently passing through her mind.'

'Good Lord, what is it with that family and Christmas?'

'People who come into their orbit and cock things up for them?'

'Is that what you think I did?'

'Well, you didn't exactly help, did you? Running off with Bruce was hardly the best way to bring about family accord. Not that my crime was any less serious: I flagrantly stole from Alice just as you stole from Julia.'

'Don't you think that love sometimes justifies our actions?'

'You can dress it up that way if you like, but I know what I did was out of self-interest. Was sleeping with Bruce an act of altruism? Or were you driven by your own needs?'

'You can play dirty, can't you?'

'There really doesn't seem any point in shirking the truth. I did that for long enough with the woman with whom I was previously involved.'

'That would be Stacey Cook, wouldn't it? If the tabloids are to be believed, that could not have been a happy relationship. What made you stay together for as long as you did?'

'Habit. That and a reluctance to change the status quo.' It was another thing he'd admitted aloud for the first time.

'And what if you had met Alice while you were still with Stacey? Would habit have stopped you from falling in love with her?'

'Who said anything about me falling in love with Alice?'

'Are you saying she meant nothing to you? That she was nothing but a handy shag while you sneakily robbed her of her life story?'

'No!' His voice rang out so loudly a couple at a nearby table turned and stared. 'Certainly not,' he denied more quietly.

Isabel's face broke into a slow smile. 'I didn't think so. You cared about her, didn't you? Otherwise, you couldn't possibly have written what you did, not with so much sensitivity.'

'And your point?'

'I'm just trying to say that nothing we do is as simple as it first appears. My running off with a man so many years older than me wasn't a mindless fling. As unbelievable as it sounds, it was love at first sight. And mutual love at that. Bruce and I were crazy about each other.'

'How long did you stay together?'

'We were together right up until he died.'

'How did he die?'

'Pancreatic failure. There'd been no warning signs.'

'Did you marry?'

She shook her head. 'We never felt the need.'

'Yet you later married someone else?'

She looked him dead in the eye. 'And divorced him fifteen months after we married. It was a ghastly mistake. A bit like the mistake Bruce made with Julia.' Her gaze softened. 'Bruce was irreplaceable. He really was the love of my life. I still miss him.'

'So does Alice,' Clayton said. 'She cried when she found out that he'd persisted in trying to find her.' Clayton went on to explain about George telling Alice all that she'd known.

Their waiter reappeared to take away their plates and to offer them the dessert menu. They both declined. 'Just coffee, please,' Isabel said.

'The same for me,' Clayton added. 'And the bill.'

While they were waiting for their coffee to arrive, Clayton asked Isabel if she had ever heard from Rufus in the intervening years.

'No, we never spoke again. But then I never expected to.'

'What did you see in him?'

'A handsome, clever and charming man. Plus he was head over heels in love with me. I knew it would never last, though. That was why I was so surprised when he suddenly announced our engagement. I thought I'd made it clear to him that I believed we were far too young to consider getting married.'

'By leaving him for Bruce you couldn't have squashed his enormous ego more effectively.'

'That wasn't ever my intention. I did feel guilty about what we'd done, but when Bruce told me just what kind of a man Rufus was, I felt I'd had a lucky escape. As did Alice.'

'What about Julia? She wasn't so lucky, was she?'

'Bruce told me that Julia had tried to kill herself before, when the children were away at school. He came home late one night and found she had taken an overdose of sleeping pills, not enough to kill her, but enough to make a point. Another time she locked herself in the bathroom and taunted Bruce by saying she was going to kill herself in exactly the same way as his first wife had. Even though he knew it was impossible because he'd had the electrics changed after Barbara's death, he broke the door down to ensure she couldn't harm herself in some other way. It was a nightmare for the poor man.'

'Being so unstable couldn't have been much of a picnic for Julia.'

'Exactly right.'

Their coffee arrived, and after offering each other milk, Isabel said, 'Was there ever any communication between Alice and Rufus? Or his sister?'

'Nothing. Not a word from either of them. Although there's every chance that could change now if either of them saw the programme and they choose to write to me as you did.'

'I meant what I said earlier,' Isabel said. 'I really would like to get in touch with Alice. Why don't you pass on my number to her?' She let loose one of her dazzling, white-toothed smiles. 'At least then you'll have the perfect excuse to get in touch with her yourself.'

'How do you know I want to?'

'Because it's written all over your face, you silly man.'

Chapter Nine

RONNETTA HANDED ALICE a tumbler of green liquid. 'This,' she said, 'will cheer you up better than anything else I know. I call it the Last Resort.'

Alice took it doubtfully. 'And the key ingredient would be?'

'Crème de menthe. With a dash of pernod, ouzo, rum, amaretto, limoncello and a hotly guarded secret ingredient.'

Alice took a cautious sip and willed her liver to forgive her.

'What do you think?' Ronnetta asked.

'It's very sweet,' Alice murmured.

'Another few sips and you'll get beyond that. Now then, what's the latest on George?'

Alice had just arrived home after her day spent at the hospital when Ronnetta had knocked on her door. She had taken one look at her and ordered her to come round for a drink and a bite to eat.

Alice risked another sip of her drink and brought Ronnetta up to date on the news that George had had another stroke in the night. What little strength and mobility she had gained had gone again. The only upside was that she hadn't lost her limited speech. 'Oh, Ronnetta, if you'd seen her today . . . I'm worried there isn't any fight left in her, that she'll simply give up.' At the memory of how defeated and wretched poor George had looked, Alice took a large mouthful of her drink. Then another. She held the glass up to the light. 'How extraordinary,' she said. 'You were right about this stuff: it does get better.'

'As if I'd lie to you. And talking of lying, have you heard anything from that dreadful man?'

'Clayton?'

'Well, of course, Clayton. Who else would I mean? Or perhaps you were thinking of that atrocious stepbrother of yours.'

It had come as no surprise to Alice that, three weeks ago, when she had been watching *The Queen of New Beginnings* with George at the hospital, Ronnetta and Bob had been at home watching it as well. After Alice had admitted that Clayton had done an excellent job of being faithful to what she had told him, Ronnetta had thrown her arms round Alice and hugged her tightly. 'You poor thing!' she had cried. 'What a dreadful life you've had!' From then on, it was as if Ronnetta had assumed the role of surrogate mother to Alice.

Now, up on her feet and clattering round in her drinks cabinet again, she seemed intent on pitching Alice headlong into oblivion with a refill. But Alice was beyond caring. 'You know, I've always thought of myself as having been lucky,' she said.

'Lucky?' repeated Ronnetta with a dubious expression. 'Your mother died when you were a kiddie, your stepbrother played you like a cheap violin, your stepmother topped herself, and your dad . . . oh, and let's not forget what that rogue Clayton Miller did to you. You call that lucky? Bob's got a list of scalps he wants on your behalf.'

Alice laughed. 'Where is Bob, by the way?'

'He's helping a mate over in Matlock with some DIY work. You see, that's the kind of man he is—always willing to give up his free time to help people. Honest too. Unlike some people I could mention.'

Smiling, Alice said, 'You're never going to forgive me for making the mistake of choosing Clayton over Bob, are you?'

Ronnetta waved a hand round in the air. 'He was attractive enough, I'll grant you, but he was a bit dull. No real pizzazz to him.'

Alice thought about Clayton. He'd had something. Maybe not pizzazz, but a sort of understated, enigmatic quality she had liked. She had liked his sense of humour, too, and that he'd never taken himself too seriously. Time spent with him had never been boring. She thought of how she had fooled him with Katya. That had been fun. She sighed, suddenly overcome with a very real sense of regret.

'You've got a strange faraway look in your eyes,' Ronnetta said.

'It's this cocktail of yours,' Alice replied. 'It would give anyone a strange faraway look.' She downed another mouthful, thinking that she was in danger of acquiring a taste for it. Not only that, but in her happily mellowed state she was in danger of losing her animosity towards Clayton. She missed him. Many a time when she had been at the hospital with George she had experienced the urge to talk to him, to find out how he was, to share with him her concerns for George.

Before last night, George had been annoyingly vocal in her opinion that Alice should congratulate Clayton on his programme. George also wanted him to know how delighted she was with the way she had been portrayed. 'Just don't start boasting to all and sundry about your moment of fame,' Alice had begged her.

Alice's fear that suddenly everyone would know that the programme was about her had not proved to be the case. Either no one in the area had watched it or they simply hadn't made the connection.

Hours later, Alice stumbled home. Acutely aware that she needed to take preventative measures to ward off a stinker of a hangover, she filled the kettle for some coffee. While she waited for it to boil, she drank a glass of water. And another. That was when she noticed that the red light on her answer phone was winking.

'Hello, Alice. I'm not sure which one of us will feel more awkward about this, although right now I reckon I might be out in front, but I'm pretty sure you'll still be furious with me. And I don't blame you for being angry. Anyway . . . um . . . look, something's come up and if you could bear to return my call, I've got something to tell you—'

The answer phone cut him off at this point. Alice could see there was another message waiting for her attention. She pressed play again.

'Sorry,' Clayton's voice said, 'I'm rambling on. Nerves. Well, fear actually. Maybe even terror. Not that I'm saying you're scary, Alice. Well, you were when you were Katya. Oh, hell, I'm off again. Look, here's my number, just in case you threw it away.'

The kettle clicked off. Alice made a cup of coffee and then made a decision. It was time to bring back an old friend.

The ringing of his mobile roused Clayton from a deep sleep. 'Hello,' he said groggily.

'Hello, mister.'

He switched on the bedside lamp and checked to see what time it was: five minutes past midnight. 'Who is this?' he demanded.

'Don't tell me your memory is as bad as your manners.'

OK, a wrong number. And from someone who wasn't English. 'Whoever you are,' he said, 'try concentrating on what you're doing and dial correctly next time.'

'Hey, mister, you the big idiot! Not me. I dial very carefully. I always do things carefully. Not like you. You the most careless man I know.'

He sat up. His brain suddenly made itself half-useful. *Katya?* 'Hey,' he said, 'you can't just ring up and hurl abuse at me like you used to.'

'No? Well, we see about that. I no lose my touch.'

'That much is clear. How have you been?'

'I've . . . I've been better.'

If he didn't say it, he knew he'd regret it. 'I've missed you,' he said.

The line went quiet.

'Alice? Are you there?' he said, concern making him dispense with playing along with Katya. He could hear something faint and muffled in his ear. 'Alice?' he repeated. 'Are you all right?'

'No.'

'What's wrong?'

'I'm crying, you horrible, insensitive man!'

'Oh, Alice. I'm sorry. I'm sorry for what I did, that it upset you.'

'Who said it was anything to do with you?'

'I'm sorry.'

'And stop saying you're sorry.'

'Sorry. Oh, hell.' From the other end of the line came the sound of Alice blowing her nose. 'I've missed you,' he said again.

'I've missed you, too,' she said so softly he very nearly didn't hear her. 'Especially recently since—since George had a stroke.'

Shocked, it was now his turn to fall quiet.

'It happened several months ago,' Alice went on. 'She's been in hospital ever since. Then last night she had a second stroke. I . . . I don't think she's going to recover from this one.'

'Alice, I'm genuinely sorry. It doesn't seem possible. Not George.'

'She wanted you to know that she thought you'd done a great job with *The Queen of New Beginnings*. She was pleased with her screen-self.'

'She was a gift. It took no effort at all to shape her character.'

'You did a wonderful job with my father.'

'You watched it, then?'

'George insisted. We watched it together in the hospital.'

Clayton suddenly knew there was something hugely important he should do. 'Would you mind if I came up there to visit George?' he asked. 'I'd like to see her. To thank her.'

'I'm sure she'd love to see you. She must be sick of seeing me.'

'What about you? Would . . . would you like to see me?'

'I can think of worse things to do.'

'In that case, I'll come up tomorrow. Which hospital is she in?'

Alice woke early the next morning. Relieved that Ronnetta's Last Resort hadn't inflicted too much damage, she ate a hurried breakfast and got down to work at the kitchen table. She had the last hundred pages of a manuscript to read before going to the hospital to see George. She had read solidly for an hour when her mind began to wander from the text to Clayton.

She was both anxious and excited about seeing him later that day. It hadn't been her intention last night to admit that she had missed him, and certainly not to cry, but the moment he had said he had missed her, something had cracked inside her.

In bed afterwards she had realised that ringing Clayton while pretending to be Katya had been nothing but a means to speak to him without having to talk to him honestly. Except Clayton had snatched the cloak off her, leaving her emotions vulnerably exposed.

She looked at her watch and wondered if Clayton was already on the train and on his way. It was good of him to go to so much effort.

What wasn't so good was that he hadn't told her what it was he had called her about in the first place. Why the mystery?

She made herself a cup of tea and got back to work.

Clayton blamed Signor Ego. If only he hadn't been so damned greedy for yet more back-patting affirmation, Clayton wouldn't have stuffed the letters Glen had forwarded to him in his pocket to read on the train.

Captain Sensible rolled his eyes and muttered something about there being only one person who should shoulder the blame. It was Clayton who had set this particular ball rolling and it would be Clayton who would have to explain matters to Alice. How she would take this latest turn of events, he didn't know. Isabel surfacing from the past was one thing, but Natasha and her brother?

Alone in the first-class carriage he read the letter again. How tempting it was to throw the piece of paper out onto the track. Yet the decision wasn't his to take. He plugged himself into his iPod and tried to sleep. But he was too agitated to nod off.

He simply had to protect Alice. And there was only one way to do that. He neatly folded the letter, ripped it into four evenly sized pieces, then opened the window. He watched the bits of paper get whipped away.

There. Problem solved. The letter had never existed.

Captain Sensible groaned. *How do you live with yourself?*

I'm protecting Alice, Clayton silently replied.

Yourself, more like it, Captain Sensible fired back with disgust.

Clayton followed the directions Alice had given him to George's ward. At the entrance, he saw Alice. She was sitting by the side of a bed, a book on her lap. He could see her lips moving, as if she was reading aloud. The withered husk of a woman in the bed bore little resemblance to the spirited woman Clayton had last seen on Christmas Day. He hoped he would be able to mask his shock.

He approached the bed slowly. As Alice turned a page and raised her head slightly, she caught sight of him. She beckoned him nearer. When he was standing beside her, she smiled fleetingly then leaned closer to George. 'Look who's come to see you, George,' she said.

The old woman's eyelids flickered open. Her eyes settled on Clayton. Her expression didn't change; the mischievous face was now devoid of all animation. But then he saw something; the dullness lifted from her eyes and was replaced by a sparkle of vibrant emotion. He bent to kiss her cheek. 'George,' he said, 'it's got to be said, I've seen you looking better.' He showed her the flowers he'd brought. 'The best that money could buy. I had them specially flown in this morning.'

'Li . . . ar.' Her voice was faint and strained.

'I'll see if I can find a vase,' Alice said.

Clayton handed her the bouquet and when she'd gone he sat down. George stared at him. Clayton stared back at her. 'If you could keep quiet for just a few moments,' he said, 'and let me get a word in edgeways, there's something I want to say, something important.'

Her eyes sparkled. 'Sur . . . sur . . . surprise,' she said. 'Nice.'

'Hey,' he said with a smile, 'what did I say about keeping quiet? I want to thank you for giving me a lift to the shops that day when we first met. If you hadn't done that, I would never have had the pleasure of getting to know you and that would have resulted in a massive gap in my script where you should have been. You really added something to it.'

'Youwer . . . youwer a beaky bastard fwhat you did.'

'You're right, George, but you understand why I did it, don't you?'

'Dint intrupt me. You have to makebings right floliss.'

'Floliss?'

'For . . . Alice.'

'Do you think there's any chance she'll ever forgive me?'

'Time. Give . . . her . . . time.'

'I hope you two aren't talking about me.'

Clayton started. 'Of course not,' he said much too quickly.

'Hezlibing,' George said.

Clayton looked to Alice for help.

Alice smiled sweetly. 'She said you were lying.'

'Traitor,' Clayton hissed good-humouredly at George.

'You . . . need . . . to . . . talk.'

Again Clayton looked at Alice. 'She's right, we do. Or maybe the three of us could talk.' He suddenly saw a way to deliver his news to Alice with a safety net in place. He positioned himself on the other side of the bed from Alice. *Nice going*, muttered Captain Sensible. *Using a dying old lady as a human shield; it gets better and better. I'm so proud of you.*

'So, Clayton,' Alice said, 'what was it you wanted to tell me?'

He swallowed. 'I've received a letter from a woman called Isabel Blake.' He paused, seeing the look of two and two making four in Alice's face. 'And yes, she did indeed turn out to be Isabel Canning. I've met her and she says she would really like to meet you. But she quite understands that you might not be so keen to meet her.'

'What about Rufus and Natasha?' she asked quietly. 'Have you heard anything from them?'

'No,' Clayton lied without hesitation. And with that easy lie came the certain knowledge that he had just blown things for ever with Alice. He wasn't to be trusted. Even if what he had done had been to protect her. She deserved somebody decent. Somebody who wouldn't look her right in the eye and lie so effortlessly. He cared too much for her to put her through the misery of being involved with him.

They were seated at a table in the hospital cafeteria. The place was a tip, but if their surroundings were grim, it was nothing compared to the gloomy expression on Clayton's face. Alice sensed he wanted to tell her something. Something that he believed would upset her more than his earlier revelation about Isabel. Which actually didn't seem that bad to Alice. A meeting with Isabel would be all right. What she wasn't so sure about, if it ever happened, was a meeting with Rufus and Natasha.

'Alice?'

Realising that Clayton had been talking, she said, 'Sorry, I was thinking. How long do you think it will be before we can rule out Rufus and Natasha getting in touch via your agent?'

'Um . . . it won't work quite like that,' he said. 'There are repeats and DVD sales.'

'You mean I'll never be able to stop worrying that they'll suddenly reappear in my life?' Her old anger resurfaced. And in that instant, gone was her intention to say that it had been hypocritical of her to condemn him for something she was also guilty of doing. 'Just what gave you the right to go sneaking round behind my back the way you did! How the hell did I ever trust you?'

'You're right,' Clayton said quietly. 'I'm not to be trusted.'

'And admitting that doesn't bother you?'

'Would it make you feel better if it did?'

The heat of her anger cooled. She sighed. 'I no longer know what would make me feel better any more. Other than George making a miraculous recovery or dying sooner rather than later so that her last days are still worth something to her.'

Clayton said, 'I'm glad I came up to see George.'

His words further calmed the atmosphere. 'I'm glad, too,' Alice said.

'She seemed to think I made a reasonable fist of *The Queen of New Beginnings*,' he said, 'if that doesn't sound like I'm blowing my own trumpet.'

'You have every reason to be proud of it; it was good.'

'Is that the nearest I'll get to an honest appraisal from you?'

'You want more? You want me to shower you with flattery? Is that it?'

He shook his head. 'I just want your honest opinion. Whatever else, that's important to me.'

Whatever else . . . That sounded ominous. 'OK,' she said, 'since it seems to matter to you, I thought you did a great job. For that reason alone I thought I could forgive you for what you did. You gave George a fantastic amount of pleasure, too. So that adds to your stock.'

After a lengthy silence, he said, 'I never set out to hurt you. But I had to write your story. It was a lifeline to me; I'm just sorry it was at your expense. I'm also sorry for everything else that may happen as a consequence of what I did.'

Again his words had an ominous ring to them. 'Such as?' she asked.

'Such as Isabel wanting to meet you.'

'Right now, I think it'll be OK. How did she seem? Has she changed?'

'I never met her before so I don't know.'

'Of course. It's easy to forget that you weren't there with us all. You captured the mood and feel of everyone involved so well.'

'I was only able to do that because you told me your story so well.'

'At last, I get some credit.' Her voice was heavy with scorn.

'I would have loved nothing more than to give you all the credit, Alice, but I didn't because I thought it would make everything worse for you.' He glanced at his watch.

'In a hurry?' she asked.

'I don't want to miss my train. There isn't another for several hours.'

'Oh,' she said flatly. 'You're not stopping the night then?'

'No,' he said. 'Why? Did you think I would?'

'I thought maybe . . .' She stopped herself. How had she leaped to the ridiculous conclusion that Clayton might want to spend the evening with her? Stupidly, oh, so stupidly, she had imagined that because he had said he'd missed her he might want to make things right with her. As shaming fury with herself grew, she was forced to acknowledge how much she had hoped the outcome of today would be that Clayton would be back in her life. She knew exactly where that hope had sprung from. It had been because he'd given *The Queen of New Beginnings* a happy ending with her living happily ever after. Yeah right!

She looked at him across the table. He was now fiddling with a napkin, meticulously folding it in half and in half again. She had never seen him like this before. So distracted. So on edge.

'I really enjoyed our time together, Alice,' he said. 'It meant a great deal to me. It still does. Not only that, you inspired me to write again. And with that came the confidence and belief I could do it. You'll never know just how grateful I'll always be to you for that.'

She sensed the but of all buts just seconds away.

'But *because* of what you mean to me, I have to be completely straight with you. I can never be the man you'd want me to be.'

'How do you know what kind of a man I'd want you to be?' she said indignantly. 'Or indeed if I want you to be anything at all?'

'OK, I may have got that wrong, but . . . Oh, well, you have to know that I can't give you what you deserve. Remember, I'm the one we both agreed is morally bankrupt. I wish I weren't the man I am because then things could be different between us. But I can't change. I am who I am. If I've shafted you once, who's to say I wouldn't do it again?'

'Put like that, how could I possibly argue with you? I'd have to be mad to want to have anything to do with you. I appreciate your honesty.'

But really. No, *really*. How could Clayton have tried that old it's-not-you-it's-me crock of shit on her? She would have expected better of him, something considerably more creative. Anything but some pathetic I'm-not-the-man-you-need number. Who was he to say what kind of man she needed? Who was he to say she even needed a man?

Another anxious glance at her watch. Alice had been doing this for the past twenty minutes. Isabel was due to arrive any time now.

After Clayton had left the hospital yesterday evening, Alice had returned to George. They agreed Alice should meet Isabel as soon as possible.

When Alice got home, she had emailed Isabel. Within half an hour of sending the email, she received a reply. Ten minutes later and it was all arranged: Isabel would drive up to meet Alice the next day.

Today.

The sound of a car engine had Alice hurrying to the window. In the process of being parked on the road behind Alice's car was a large four-by-four. She took a deep breath and opened the door.

The first thing Alice noticed was the enormous bunch of flowers Isabel was carrying. The second thing she noticed was just how beautiful Isabel was. And when she smiled, Alice felt inexplicably tempted to hug her guest. It was an echo of all those years ago when Isabel had arrived at Cuckoo House as the enemy and yet Alice had still fallen helplessly under her spell. 'Come in,' she said.

'What a lovely cottage,' Isabel exclaimed after Alice had led her through to the kitchen and had offered to make some coffee. The smell of freshly made bread greeted them. Seeing the plaited loaf on the table surrounded by plates of cheese, quiche, olives and slices of chorizo, Isabel let out another exclamation. 'Oh, Alice, you've gone to so much trouble. Please don't tell me you made that bread. Although I just know you're going to say you did.'

Alice gave a little shrug. 'When I have the time I like to cook.'

'I remember what a good cook you were. I'm so glad you agreed to meet me. When I asked Clayton to try and arrange it, I didn't hold out much hope. He's an interesting man, don't you think?'

'That's one way to describe him,' Alice said noncommittally.

'He mentioned that you had been involved for a while and that—'

'I don't know what he told you,' Alice interrupted, 'but if you don't mind, I'd rather not talk about him. Milk? Sugar?'

'Just milk, please. I'm sorry for appearing to pry.'

Really! Just what had that wretched Clayton been saying! 'I think it's warm enough to sit outside,' Alice said, her tone clipped.

When they were settled in the small courtyard garden, after Alice had felt her scrutinising gaze sweeping over her once more, Isabel said, 'You have a lovely home, Alice. How long have you lived here?'

Alice provided her with a potted history.

'You seem settled,' Isabel commented when she'd finished. 'I envy you that. I've never been able to fill the gap your father left in my life after he died.'

At last, thought Alice, the elephant in the room had been referred to.

'I want you to know that I really did love your father. It wasn't a mere passing fancy taking off with him the way I did. Since then, with one exception, I've never felt so sure about something as I did that Christmas. Your father was genuinely the love of my life.'

'Did he feel the same about you?'

'Yes.'

'You made each other happy?'

'Yes. Very happy.'

'Then it was all worth it, wasn't it?'

'And that, if you'll forgive me, was said with great feeling. But then you've had a long time to wait before having the opportunity to say it.'

Alice took a sip of her coffee. 'I hope you're not going to be so annoyingly reasonable throughout this entire conversation.'

They stared at each other. Very slowly, they each began to smile, and then they laughed. Easily and companionably.

'You know, Alice, that's exactly the kind of thing your father might have said. Do you suppose he's looking down from on high and willing us to straighten this mess out on his behalf?'

'And wouldn't it be just like him to leave it to us to sort it out?'

'Well then, let's show him how it's done. I might be overstepping the mark, but can I do what I wanted to do when I first arrived?'

'What's that?'

'I'd like to give you a hug.'

They were just letting go of each other when Alice saw Bob's head appear over the garden wall. He whistled loudly. 'I hadn't got you pegged as being into girl-on-girl action, Alice, but now I see where I've been going wrong all this time.'

His head disappeared from view but his voice could still be heard. 'Say nice things about me, Alice. I can still hear you.'

'Come on,' Alice said to Isabel, 'we'll have lunch indoors, away from Big Ears.'

'I heard that!'

'You have some very interesting men in your life,' Isabel remarked when they were back inside. 'I take it Bob has a soft spot for you?'

'For some strange reason he refuses to give up on the idea that eventually I'll fall madly in love with him. He's actually been very kind to me recently. He—' She stopped herself abruptly. She didn't want to go into all that business with Clayton. 'Glass of wine?'

'Thank you. But only a small one. Finish what you were saying. Was it to do with Clayton?'

'Now why would you say that?'

'Because I know he was upset about what happened between you.'

'I don't believe he could have been that upset, not after his visit yesterday. He gave me a very nicely prepared little speech about him not being good enough for me. Have you ever heard a more lame or more clichéd excuse for bailing out?'

'You don't think he was being sincere? Maybe he truly believes he isn't worthy of you after what he did.'

'Do you always try to think well of everyone?' Alice asked.

Isabel laughed. 'Certainly not. But Clayton struck me as being quite a complex character. But a good man at heart. Which I know you won't agree with, given the way he went about writing *The Queen of New Beginnings*, but I can imagine how that happened. There he was, presented with a fantastic opportunity to cure himself of his writer's block—how could he not follow it through in the hope that, eventually, he would be able to convince you he wasn't betraying you or your father?'

'Yes, yes, yes!' Alice snapped impatiently. 'But you can't deceive or trample on other people's feelings without there being consequences.'

'You don't need to tell me that. If I hadn't given in to my feelings for Bruce, Julia might still be alive and you would never have been separated from your father. You don't think I've had to consider those consequences all these years? But you know, the truth is, if you were to rewind time and put me back at Cuckoo House that Christmas, I'd do exactly the same thing again. I wouldn't be able to stop myself. I think Clayton found himself in a similar situation with the golden opportunity your story gave him. He simply couldn't stop himself.'

Irritated that Clayton had found himself such a staunch defender,

Alice said, 'Look, can we leave Clayton out of the conversation, please? Tell me what you did when you left Cuckoo House on Boxing Day.'

Isabel smiled. 'First let me say something I've always wanted to. I'm sorry your father and I left in the way we did. It was wrong, and I've always regretted that we never explained or said goodbye to you. Your father felt the same way, too. It was why he wrote all those letters to you. You did receive them, didn't you?'

'I received lots of letters, none of which I read.'

Isabel suddenly looked profoundly sad. 'Oh, Alice, your father feared as much, but you must believe he never gave up.'

'I know. George told me about him going to see her.'

'Have you forgiven him? Tell me that you have, Alice. If not for my benefit, for the sake of your half-sister.'

'For Natasha's sake? Why on earth would I do that?'

Isabel's expression changed again and a smile radiated back at Alice. 'Your father and I had a child. Her name is Grace and she's eleven.'

'A child? You have a daughter?'

Isabel's face shone with happy pride. 'Yes, and what's more, she looks very like you, Alice. She has your father's blonde hair, mine too, but her eyes are dark just like yours and she has the very same smile. That's why I keep staring at you. Would you like to meet her?'

Alice's eyes widened. 'Has she been sitting in your car all this time?'

Isabel laughed. 'Of course not! She's at school right now. She's staying the night with her best friend so I don't have to rush back.'

'Eleven years old,' murmured Alice. 'I can't take it in. Does she know about me?'

'Most definitely. She wanted to come here with me today. You do want to meet her, don't you?'

Alice nodded mutely. A sister. She had a sister. 'Do you have a photograph?' she asked.

Isabel gave Alice a cream leather wallet.

'She's lovely,' was all Alice could say after she had studied the two photographs.

'And why wouldn't she be when she looks so like you?'

'I'm not lovely. I deliberately pushed my father away. I . . . I hated him for leaving me. I wanted to punish him. And he must have hated me for what I did to him.' She put a hand over her mouth but it did nothing to stop her from breaking down and crying.

Isabel put her arms round Alice. 'Oh, Alice,' she said softly, 'he never hated you, not for a single moment. He loved you unconditionally.'

Clayton was wondering how things were going up in Derbyshire. Late last night, Isabel had telephoned to explain that Alice had been in touch with her and that a meeting had been arranged. She had promised to ring him to let him know how it had gone. He hoped that the meeting would have a positive outcome.

During the train journey home yesterday he had wanted repeatedly to call Alice but that would have only muddied the waters. He had to stand firm and believe that cutting the tie with her was the one decent thing he was going to get right in his life.

Oh, very sporting of you, murmured Captain Sensible. *Very altruistic. A pity you didn't listen to me in the first place!*

Go to hell! Clayton fired back. He screwed up the piece of paper he'd been doodling on and chucked it at the wastepaper bin. As with all the other pieces of screwed-up paper he'd thus far thrown, it fell wide of its target. He was trying to write—and he was failing miserably. It was just like it used to be. No matter what he did, the words just wouldn't come.

He sighed and wondered what to do by way of displacement activity. He could sit here for only so long pretending he was working. He thought of the letters he had yet to reply to regarding *The Queen of New Beginnings*. One letter in particular stuck in his mind. He rummaged through the overflowing in-tray. Eventually he found it: the one from Bazza. He pondered his old friend's postscript. Had he meant it? Or had it been one of those superficial, showbizzy, throwaway remarks made by the kind of people Bazza now hung out with? He forced his brain to remember Bazza from the old days; the Bazza who would no more have gone all luvvie on him than he would have . . . would have slept with a mate's long-term girlfriend.

He rubbed his unshaven chin. Moments passed.

Why not? Why not have a reconciliatory drink with Bazza? What harm could it do?

Bazza had suggested a bar in Covent Garden and Clayton strongly suspected that an alcoholic beverage or two may have already passed Bazza's lips before Clayton arrived. Bazza rose unsteadily from his chair and stuck out his hand. 'S'brilliant that you made it,' he slurred.

Clayton shook hands with him. It felt a very odd thing to do. How could two people who had once been so close be reduced to acting so formally? More to the point, why was Bazza three sheets to the wind?

'You look well, Clay,' Bazza said. 'What do you fancy to drink? I've made a start.' He indicated the near-empty bottle of Sancerre.

'I'll order us another,' Clayton said.

'S'how have you been?' Bazza asked when he'd drained his glass.

'So, so,' Clayton replied. 'How about you?'

'Oh, me, I'm fine. Life is tippety-top. Got it all goin' on. That waiter is taking his time with the wine, isn't he?'

This, thought Clayton, is going to be an interesting evening.

Their waiter materialised, opened bottle and glass in hand.

'To old friends,' Bazza said, his glass already against his mouth.

'To old friends,' Clayton echoed quietly. 'Thank you for your letter.'

Bazza swatted the air with his hand. 'Meant every word. You wrote a bloody good script. Better than anything I've ever written.'

'Oh, I wouldn't go that far. You've done some great work.'

'Crap! All crap. All meaningless crap. Yours had substance.'

Bazza's talk was making Clayton queasy. 'What's wrong, Bazza?'

Bazza shook his head. 'Don't know what you mean.'

'Come on, Bazza, I know you better than anyone. Something's up with you. You don't get drunk. What's going on?'

'You really want to know? You care? After what I did to you?'

'As strange as this may seem, I do care.'

Bazza put down his glass. 'You promise you'll keep this to yourself?'

Clayton nodded. 'I promise.'

'My life is shit. I've got writer's block and a bitch of a girlfriend who seems to think she can resolve the world's financial crisis by patronising every sodding shop in town with my money. *My* money.'

Clayton blinked. He didn't know how to react. Only a short while ago he would have been punching the air that Bazza had got his come-uppance. But he'd never felt less like cheering. He felt nothing but pity for his old friend. He topped up their glasses. 'Bazza,' he said, 'welcome to my world.'

The wine flowed. As did Bazza's confessions.

Clayton listened to his old friend describing how his life with Stacey had become a waking nightmare.

'All she cares about,' Bazza said, 'is fame. She's hired her very own PR firm. I don't think I can take much more of it.'

'Then don't,' Clayton said. 'End it. If I recall, you're rather good at ending partnerships.'

Bazza looked at him blearily. 'Ouch, man. That hurts.'

'The truth always does.'

'You're still cross with me?'

'Wouldn't you still be cross if you were me?'

'I'm sorry, Clay. I got it wrong. Horribly wrong.'

'So why not just tell her it's over?'

'Because I'm terrified of how she'll make it play in the press if I back out of the wedding now. I'll be accused of God knows what. Wife beater. Paedophile. Tory voter. My career will be over.'

'Just like mine was.'

Again Bazza stared at him. 'But you bounced back.'

'Yeah, I bounced back. Just like that. It was a piece of cake.'

'I'm sorry.'

'What are you actually sorry for, Bazza? For breaking up our partnership? Or for sleeping with Stacey behind my back?'

'For more than you'll ever know. C'mon, let's have another bottle.'

Clayton was a bottle of wine behind Bazza and was marginally the more capable of the two when they staggered outside. Clayton propped Bazza against a lamppost while he waited for a taxi to show. Just as one drew up and lowered its window, Bazza groaned and vomited messily just inches away from the vehicle. The driver cursed and drove off.

'And for your next party trick?' Clayton said with a sigh.

'Sorry,' Bazza murmured, 'I never could hold my drink.' He staggered and Clayton caught hold of him before he fell into the gutter. 'Clay, you're not leavin' me, are you? Please come back home with me.'

'Not one of your finest ideas, Bazza. Not with Stacey around.'

'She's away. C'mon, come back with me. We could pick up a curry on the way. It'll be like old times.'

Clayton winced at the thought of the putrid mess he'd have to clean up if Bazza was sick after a curry. 'OK,' he said, 'but let's skip the curry.'

Bazza put his arm round him. 'You're a good friend. The best. That's why I regret what we did.'

'All water under the bridge.'

'But it's not. Not for me, anyway. Not until I tell—'

'Hey, we're in luck,' Clayton interrupted him, 'here's a taxi. Try not to look so drunk. And whatever you do, no throwing up.'

They made it to Notting Hill without mishap. When they were inside Bazza stumbled in the direction of the kitchen. Clayton caught up with him and watched him select a bottle of wine from the rack. Clayton took it from him. 'Maybe we should pass on that,' he said. 'How about some coffee?'

'No. It'll sober me up and I want to stay drunk for ever.'

'A genius plan if ever I heard one.'

Bazza suddenly slumped heavily against the nearest wall. 'Don't mock me, Clayton. I'm on the edge here. One push and it'll all be over.'

Concerned, Clayton said, 'Bazza, how about I get you upstairs to bed. You strike me as a man who's had a long day.'

'I told you, I'm a man on the edge.' He tried to focus on Clayton's face. His eyes were wobbling all over the place. 'I have to confess something to you,' he said. 'If I don't, I might just lose what little reason I still have.'

'Fine. You do that. But first, let's get you upstairs.'

'OK, but you have to promise not to judge me harshly afterwards.'

'Yeah, yeah, I promise.'

Bazza allowed Clayton to help him up the stairs to his bedroom, where he threw himself straight onto the bed. Clayton eased off his shoes. He spied a wastepaper bin and placed it on the floor beside the bed. He drew Bazza's attention to it. 'Keep your aim true,' he said. 'We don't want Stacey ticking you off for puking on the carpet.'

Bazza groaned. 'Don't remind me of her!' Then he did something Clayton would never have dreamed possible; Bazza started to cry. 'Clay!' he howled. 'Come closer.'

Clayton reluctantly got down onto his knees.

'Clay,' Bazza said, 'I've got to tell you something. It's important. You weren't responsible for Stacey's miscarriage.'

'What?'

'Losing the baby had nothing to do with you.'

'But you phoned me. You were furious. You told the press. You—'

'It wasn't Stacey who got the electric shock. It was me. And it wasn't that bad. Whatever caused Stacey to miscarry, it wasn't anything to do with you. Maybe it was the flight coming back from LA. Maybe her losing the baby was nothing but a coincidence.'

Clayton was struggling to make sense of what he was hearing. 'So why did you blame me?'

'It was Stacey's idea. I went along with it because I was as mad as hell with you for getting into our house. When Stacey realised she was losing the baby, I was so upset I wasn't thinking straight. I really wanted that child and I needed someone to blame. When it was official that Stacey had miscarried, the first thing she said was that she blamed you. I just took it from there. Of course, once the story started to roll there was no going back. Stacey made me swear that I would stick to the story.'

'You publicly humiliated me.' Clayton's voice was low. 'You as good as destroyed me. You could have stopped it. But you didn't. Every opportunity you got, you drove home another nail in my coffin.'

Bazza nodded. 'It's all true. I'm sorry.'

'Sorry? Is that it?'

'What else can I do or say?'

Clayton got to his feet. He looked down at his old friend with disgust. 'If you don't know the answer to that, then I give up on you. And there was me thinking I was as low as it gets. Why, I'm a rank amateur compared to you.'

Chapter Ten

AFTER A WEEK of flitting about the country from one recording studio to another, it was Saturday morning and Alice was driving south to Sussex, on her way to meet her half-sister, Grace.

She had never once considered that her father may have had another child. Just as she had never considered that he and Isabel would have stayed together. Even George had been surprised. But she'd also been happy for Alice. 'It means you're not alone now,' she had said. 'You have a family again.' It was a bittersweet observation. If only she hadn't been so pig-headed she would have known this young girl from birth.

Squirrel's Patch was isolated, approached through a dense wood of beech trees. Built of stone with a low sloping roof, the house was neatly placed in a clearing. There were two small chimneys and a porch draped by a rambling rose. There was a small front garden in full flower and with the sun shining, the scene was a tableau of idyllic enchantment. Alice felt instantly at home.

The door opened and Isabel stepped out. Behind her a slightly built girl with shoulder-length blonde hair appeared. Alice recognised her at once. While her mother came over and hugged Alice, she remained shyly where she was. Rendered shy herself, Alice offered the girl a small, tentative smile. She badly wanted Grace to like her.

Isabel said, 'Come and meet Grace; she's been dying to meet you.

She was up at six o'clock this morning, she was so excited.'

'I've been dying to meet you, too,' Alice admitted.

Grace smiled and Alice saw that Isabel hadn't been exaggerating when she'd said that her daughter had the same smile as Alice. 'I've made you some flapjacks,' Grace said. 'Do you like flapjacks?'

'I love them.'

Isabel put her arm round Grace's shoulders. 'Let's go in.'

Inside, the decor was pure country house and Alice felt embraced by the warmth of its welcome. They were now in the kitchen, a large L-shaped room with French doors leading onto a gorgeous cottage-style garden. 'Who has the amazing green fingers?' asked Alice.

'Believe it or not, it's Mum,' said Grace. 'Would you like me to show you round the garden?'

'Thank you, I'd like that.'

All trace of her earlier shyness now gone, Grace escorted Alice round the raised beds devoted to herbs and salad vegetables, then the beds that seemed to be overflowing with colour. Beyond a weathered summerhouse there was a hammock strung between two apple trees.

'This is my bit of the garden,' Grace said proudly as she led Alice away from the hammock. 'Do you like it?'

'Very much,' Alice said as she took in a mostly bare patch of soil containing a crown of rhubarb and two orderly rows of lupins.

'I'm going to sow some spring cabbage tomorrow.'

'Well, good for you. I've only got a tiny garden compared to yours. Perhaps you'd like to see it one day?'

'That would be great. I've never been to Derbyshire. Will I be able to see the house where Mum met my dad?'

Taken aback, Alice said, 'We'd certainly be able to see it from the outside, but not inside. Other people are living in it now.'

'That's a pity. Never mind. It'll still be cool to see Cuckoo House. I've heard a lot about it. And about you. You're just as I pictured you. Mum said you were pretty and you are.'

'Now you're making me blush.'

'Why? I'm only telling the truth. I think it's going to be the coolest thing in all the world having you as my big sister.' She suddenly spun round on the spot and laughed gaily. She was as uncomplicated as a summer's day and just as lovely. 'My friends at school are all really jealous,' she said.

'Why?'

'Because you're famous. After Mum went to see you and found out what an amazing job you have, we bought one of your CDs. *Matilda and the Grumpy Dragon*.'

Flattered, Alice said, 'Did you enjoy it?'

'I thought you did the voices really well.'

Isabel called to them from the terrace. 'Tea and flapjacks.'

Grace took hold of Alice's hand. 'Come on,' she said. 'Let's go.'

It was such a small gesture, but Alice felt her heart soar.

Late that evening Isabel sat on the sofa next to Alice and placed a large photograph album on her lap. 'I wondered if you'd like to look at this,' she said.

Alice opened the album and turned to the first page. Her father stared back at Alice, his gaze as penetrating as if he were in the room with her. He looked as if he was trying to decide whether to turn his head from the lens in annoyance or to laugh out loud. It was a look Alice remembered all too well. 'He hated having his picture taken,' she murmured. 'Who took this picture?'

'I did.'

'Really? You've captured him perfectly.'

'Thank you. He did his best to teach me his craft. That's what I do these days. Portrait photography.'

'You work as a photographer?'

Isabel laughed. 'I have a small studio but honestly, Alice, I dabble. I'm one of life's great dabblers. It's probably because I inherited a stonking amount of money when I was young. I've been lucky.'

'I've been lucky as well,' Alice said thoughtfully. 'When I sold Cuckoo House, I hardly touched a penny of the money. And, of course, there was the money my great-aunt Eliza left for me.'

'Bruce always hoped you'd be financially secure.'

Alice turned the page and looked at another picture of her father. In this one he was sitting in an armchair, engrossed in a book.

'I caught him unawares when I took that photograph,' Isabel said.

Again, Alice had to admit that Isabel had captured her father perfectly. 'I think you're being modest about your ability. This is more than mere dabbling. You must be very successful at what you do.'

'People seem to like what I do for them.'

Alice continued turning the pages of the album. She stopped at a photograph of her father with Grace.

'That was taken in Buenos Aires,' Isabel said.

'Was that where you lived?'

'For a time. It was where Bruce did some of his best work. He did very little freelance work for magazines then and more gallery and exhibition work. He was in great demand.'

'He looks so happy,' Alice said wistfully.

'He was. But please don't think that Grace replaced you in any way. There wasn't a day when he didn't wish things could have been different. But he respected your right to punish him and left you alone.'

Alice looked up from the album. 'I feel awful that I behaved so badly. That I felt the need to punish him. It was cruel and needless.'

'Whatever guilt *you* may feel, think how bad I felt knowing that if I hadn't walked through the door of Cuckoo House, your father would never have left you. But neither of us can change the past so perhaps it's time to put that behind us. Grace deserves the best of both of us, not two miseries hung up on guilt. Why not award ourselves a new beginning?'

Alice smiled. 'I think that's a great idea.'

With promises made that they would get together soon, Alice left Squirrel's Patch after lunch the next day. It had been one of the most enjoyable weekends she had experienced in a long while and, best of all, she felt as though she had finally made peace with her father.

She was stuck in a long tailback of traffic on the M1 when her mobile rang.

When she heard what the person on the other end of the line had to say, her happiness evaporated in an instant.

Stacey had once said that Clayton was a natural for attending funerals. Something about him being a miserable sod. Fair enough. As far as he was concerned, funerals were meant to be sombre occasions. When he had got the call from Alice, he had immediately taken his black suit to the dry-cleaners and bought himself a new white shirt. He was wearing both now, complete with a black tie. George was to be buried in the cemetery of Stonebridge's Methodist Chapel and he would treat her with due deference.

He had spoken to Alice almost every day on the telephone since she had called to tell him about George. She had seemed so lost and vulnerable. So alone. It made him want to be with her, so he could offer more than a long-distance sympathetic shoulder.

He had contemplated telling her about Bazza and Stacey, by way of a distraction for her, but he had deemed it inappropriate, given that she had more important things on her mind right now.

When he'd told Glen about his night out with Bazza, Glen had been all for leaking Bazza's confession to the press, but Clayton had put a stop to that. Despite the depth of Bazza's duplicity, Clayton couldn't help but feel a degree of pity for his old friend.

He had no idea how to go about it, but what Clayton wanted was for Stacey to be forced into making a full confession, and the more public the better. He wanted her to feel just a fraction of the humiliation and guilt she had put him through.

The morning after that revealing night out with Bazza, Bazza had called Clayton. 'Um . . . I've woken up with the . . . with the vague recollection that something important took place last night,' he had said.

'What exactly do you remember?' Clayton had asked him. He hadn't reached the magnanimous stage at this point.

'I remember telling you something,' Bazza had replied.

'Can you remember what?'

'Oh, come on, Clay, don't do this to me. Help me out. Tell me what I said.'

'Nice one, Bazza. You screw me over, then ask me for my help.'

'Just tell me,' he said, 'what did I say?'

'Well, let me clue you in.' And Clayton had. Every incriminating word of Bazza's confession.

'What are you going to do?' Bazza had asked.

'I haven't decided yet. I'm waiting until the urge to kill you has passed.'

His train arrived on time and as he stepped down onto the platform, Clayton looked for a familiar face. Isabel had offered to drive him to Stonebridge for the service. Isabel had met George only once, and a long time ago at that, but as she had explained to Clayton, apart from wanting to support Alice, she felt it was something Bruce would have wanted her to do.

He spotted Isabel before she saw him. As Clayton made his way across the platform towards her, he did a double take. Alice had told him about Grace, but seeing the young girl in the flesh, he was struck by her likeness to Alice. It was all in the eyes and the mouth. Amazing.

'Clayton!' Isabel greeted him as if he were a long-lost friend. She turned to her daughter. 'Grace, this is Clayton.'

'Hello,' she said politely to Clayton.

'Hello to you, too.'

They drove straight to Stonebridge. The area round the Methodist chapel was jam-packed with cars. They managed to find themselves a space to park and walked the short distance back to the chapel. Inside, the place was full to overflowing. Isabel led the way to the front, where Alice had seats reserved for them.

George's coffin arrived, borne aloft on the shoulders of six burly, ruddy-faced men. Behind it and looking pale but composed, was Alice. Clayton thought she'd never looked lovelier. Was it weird of him to think that, given the circumstances? She slipped into the pew next to Isabel and leaned forward to give him the faintest of smiles. It felt good to be on the receiving end of a smile from her, even as fleeting and strained as this one was.

The service had been conducted in a simple but traditional manner, and afterwards everyone had enjoyed drinks and sandwiches at The Hanging Gate, a pub just a short walk from the chapel. When the guests had finally drifted away, each taking the time and trouble to thank Alice, they had all said the same: 'It was just as George would have wanted.'

Now, as Alice kicked off her shoes and sank gratefully into the softness of the cushions of her favourite armchair, she listened to what was going on in the kitchen. Isabel, Grace and Clayton were putting some supper together.

She had been banned from helping. 'You've done quite enough,' Isabel had said firmly. 'Now do as you're told and sit down.' Alice hadn't put up any argument; she was exhausted. It had been ten days since she had got the call from the hospital to say that George had died, but it felt longer. She had been devastated that the old lady had died alone and it still bothered her now. She should have been with her. With no official next of kin on hand, the task of organising George's funeral had fallen to Alice. She had done it willingly.

She closed her eyes and listened to the clatter of crockery and the soothing murmur of voices. Isabel and Grace were staying with her for a couple of days. Clayton was staying the night at The Hanging Gate and returning to London in the morning. No matter what had passed between them previously, she had known that she had to let Clayton know that George had died.

She didn't know how it had happened, but since that phone call, she and Clayton had slipped into a routine of him ringing her every evening. Knowing that he cared sufficiently to do that had meant a lot to her. It was proving impossible to stay angry with him. He was, she had to admit, a good man at heart.

'Are you asleep, Alice?'

She opened her eyes and found herself being stared at by Grace. 'No, I was just thinking. How's it going in the kitchen?'

'That's why I'm here. Mum wanted to know what you wanted to drink with your supper. Red wine or white wine?'

'I'll come and help now.' She said. No sooner had she stood up than Isabel's voice rang out loudly from the kitchen. '*No!* I don't believe it! How could they have done that to you?'

Alice looked at Grace. 'Any idea what they're talking about?'

'Clayton was telling Mum something I don't think I was supposed to hear. Do you know someone called Bazza?'

'I know *of* him.'

'Well, Bazza drank too much wine and he got drunk and then—'

Isabel burst in. 'Alice! You'll never guess what Clayton's just told me!'

Following Isabel was Clayton. 'I'd rather we discussed this later,' he said. He cast a meaningful glance in Grace's direction.

'We need a plan,' Isabel said. 'We need to teach Stacey a lesson.'

'What's with the "we"?' Clayton asked. 'Who said I needed any help?'

'Don't be silly, Clayton,' Isabel replied, 'of course you need help!'

They were in the sitting room; Grace had gone to bed and finally Alice had been let in on the big secret. She was shocked that anyone could have been so duplicitous, that Bazza and Stacey had not only blamed Clayton for something he hadn't done but made it their business to take advantage of his downfall. 'If Clayton doesn't want us interfering, then I really think we should respect his wishes,' she said.

'Oh, don't be boring. Come on, everybody, think!'

Alice looked over to the sofa where Clayton was sitting. She thought of the first time he had kissed her. It was after they'd been watching that awful chat show on television with Bazza and Stacey. How Stacey had had the nerve to put on such a breathtakingly sanctimonious act she didn't know. All faked to gain public sympathy.

If there was one thing Alice couldn't abide it was injustice. But how to right the awful injustice Clayton had suffered? A thought skittered through her head. She looked away from Clayton, thinking. Moments passed. She slowly returned her gaze to Clayton and was surprised to see him looking at her with an intensity in his expression that she was sure hadn't been there before.

'It may sound a bit far-fetched,' she said, 'but I think I've come up with something, a way to exact revenge on Stacey.'

The make-up girl dabbed Clayton's face one more time then declared him ready. He thanked her profusely. Oh, yes, Mr Congenial was in town. It was all preparation for his impending television appearance. Normally before he appeared in front of a camera he would be snapping and snarling with nerves but today was different. Today he was sweetness personified, ready to give the performance of his life.

Glen had been delighted when Clayton had suggested he try to get him on a chat show for some extra publicity. 'What's our hook?' he'd asked. 'What are we selling? Have you started on that sequel?'

'We're selling my innate charm and affability,' Clayton had told him.

'That won't get us ten seconds on hospital radio,' Glen had huffed.

Initially they didn't get any takers, just as Glen had warned, but then two days ago a call had come in from *The Stevie McKean Show* saying they'd been let down by a guest and could Clayton fill in?

From that moment, the first part of Alice's plan was up and running.

Next it was down to Bazza to play his part.

When Clayton had returned to London after George's funeral, Clayton had called Bazza and asked to meet him for a drink. 'You're not going to hit me or anything, are you?' Bazza had asked warily.

'No. But I am going to hit you with a brilliant idea.'

They had met for lunch. After Clayton had outlined what was going to happen, Bazza very nearly turned all weepy on him again. 'But why?' he'd asked. 'Why would you do this for me?'

'Because I'm a soft-in-the-head bugger and old friendships mean something to me. I also want retribution.'

Across London, in Clayton's sitting room, Alice checked her watch. 'Time to give Isabel a call, then we'd better put the television on.'

Bazza nodded and also checked his watch.

Isabel eventually answered her mobile. 'Everything OK your end?' Alice asked.

'I said I didn't want to be disturbed,' Isabel replied haughtily. 'You know I don't like to be interrupted when I'm with a client. Especially one as important as this one.'

'Well done.'

'Whatever it was you wanted to discuss, I'm sure it can wait until tomorrow when I'm back in the studio. Goodbye.'

Alice ended the call on the pay-as-you-go phone and turned to Bazza. 'Everything's going according to plan at your place.'

'I still can't believe we're going to get away with this,' Bazza said. He pointed the remote at the TV; *The Stevie McKean Show* had just started.

'I do hope you're not questioning my ability,' Alice said.

'Oh, no,' Bazza said quickly. 'Clayton's told me you're awesome.'

'You're sure you've got the recording stuff organised?'

'Yes. It's all set up. Don't worry.'

They sat on the sofa, both of them waiting for Clayton to make his appearance. He looked almost jaunty as he ambled down the steps to the interview area. Dressed in a pair of faded jeans, sporting a trim new haircut, he took his seat on the sofa, leaning back and crossing one leg over the other. 'He looks so casual,' Alice remarked. 'So at ease.'

'It's an act,' Bazza said. 'He hates chat shows. He'd rather gnaw one of his hands off than do this.'

'I know; that's what makes it all the more incredible.' Alice thought he had never looked better or more attractive. Since George's funeral they had grown closer again, but only as friends. She wished it was otherwise, that Clayton would view her as he once had, but he clearly didn't.

Meanwhile, on the television screen Clayton was going through the motions of the interview, talking about *The Queen of New Beginnings* and how it had set him off in a new direction with his writing. Which was exactly what they'd planned for him to say. Then, inevitably, Stevie turned his questions in the direction of ancient, well-trodden ground.

'So, tell me, Clayton, how are things between you and your old writing partner, Barry Osborne? Any chance of a reconciliation?'

Clayton shuffled a bit. He smiled ruefully. He looked exactly like a man who had been put on the spot. Again, it was what they had planned. 'Are you working up to asking me how things are with Stacey?'

Stevie laughed lightly and exchanged a look with the audience. 'Well, since you've raised the matter, how are things?'

There was a bit more shuffling from Clayton. Another rueful look. 'Not good, if you want the honest answer,' he said. 'I still feel so guilty about Stacey losing the baby. I don't think I'll ever get over the guilt.' He suddenly snapped forward in his seat. 'You know, Stevie, I'd give anything to hear Stacey say she forgives me. I know that she's said it in interviews, but, the thing is, she's never said it directly to me.'

After lingering on Clayton's pained expression, the camera turned to Stevie. Stevie took his cue. 'Well, Clayton,' he said, 'who knows, maybe Stacey is watching us right now.' And in one of the cheesiest moments in television history, he said, 'Stacey, if you are watching us, why not get in touch with Clayton? Why not put the man out of his misery?' Then he announced they'd be right back after the break.

Bazza turned to Alice. 'Ready?'

'Yes.'

The make-up girl was dabbing at his face again when he heard Stevie replying to someone who was talking to him in his earpiece. 'You're kidding me? It's for real? Are you mad? Of course, we'll go with it. This could be television gold!'

They were counted back in and once again Clayton assumed an air of nonchalance. Which was the last thing he was feeling.

Face to camera, Stevie was telling the audience about his next guest. 'But first, girls and boys, we've got a surprise guest on the phone. Some of you might be thinking we've set this up, but hand on heart, this is one of those spontaneous television moments we all live for.' He turned to Clayton. 'We've got Stacey on the phone for you!'

'No!'

'Oh, yes! She was watching the programme and felt compelled to call in.' Stevie swivelled his head and stared into the appropriate camera. 'Hi, Stacey,' he fawned. 'It's good to speak to you again. How are you?'

There was a silence and then what sounded very like the chink of glass against glass and liquid being poured.

'Err . . . Stacey, are you there?'

'Oh, hi, Stevie, I'm sorry, I didn't think you were ready for me yet.'

'We're more than ready for you, my darling. How are you?'

'Is Clayton still there with you?'

'He is. Is there anything you want to say to him?'

There was another silence, another chink of glass and the sound of more liquid being poured. A lot of liquid. Practically a bucketful.

'Stacey?'

'Sorry . . . I'm just in the most awful state here. There's something I have to say to Clayton. I can't go on unless I do.'

Stevie turned his caring face to Clayton. 'Clayton, would you like to say something to Stacey?'

'What is it, Stacey?' asked Clayton. 'You don't sound well.'

'I'm sorry,' she mumbled. 'I'm really sorry for . . . for everything! I've treated you atrociously.' She started to cry.

Clayton exchanged a look with Stevie, as if getting his permission to go on. 'Is this about you sleeping with Barry behind my back?'

'*No!* Well, I am sorry about that, but not as sorry as I am about . . . Oh, God, I've spilled my drink now!'

'Stacey, what *exactly* are you drinking?'

'Um . . . just a little something to get me through the day. It's all there is in my life these days,' Stacey said with a loud and messy sniff. 'I should never have left you for Barry. He's not half the man you are. He's too weak. I need a man who can stand up to me.'

'Stacey, darling,' Stevie cut in with his ultra-caring voice, 'what about forgiving Clayton, can you do that? That's what we all want to know.'

'But it's Clayton who has to forgive me. I lied about him causing my miscarriage. I made Barry lie, too. He didn't want to, but I forced him. I wanted someone to blame for losing the baby and Clayton was perfect. Oh, this feels so liberating, finally to tell someone the truth.'

Clayton turned to Stevie, his expression all wide-eyed shock. 'I don't believe I'm hearing this. I was . . . I was cast as a child killer.'

For once, Stevie seemed lost for words. 'I'm as shocked as you,' he finally managed. 'What we all want to know now, Clayton,' he said, 'is can you forgive Stacey for what she did?'

Milking the moment for as long as he could get away with, Clayton hummed and aahhed and eventually he said, 'You know, I think I can. After all, harbouring a grudge never did anyone any good, did it?'

From down the line came a tearful howl. 'Thank you, Clayton. Thank you, thank you, *thank you*. You're a wonderful man.'

Bazza's kitchen table was littered with newspapers. Alice, Bazza, Isabel and Clayton were studying the results of their handiwork.

All the papers had covered Stacey's drunken confession on live television. Condemnation was sweeping and total. Not a single journalist had a good word for Stacey. No one had rushed to defend her. Bazza had also come in for criticism but he'd been portrayed as merely weak rather than a hard-nosed malevolent schemer.

'I think we can safely say,' Clayton said, looking up from the copy of the *Express* he was reading, 'your fall from grace will be short-lived, Bazza. The press are effectively siding with you.'

Bazza looked doubtful. 'I still don't think I deserve to come out of this so well. I should have stopped Stacey.'

'I agree,' Alice said flatly.

While Clayton had forgiven his old friend for what he'd done, he knew that Alice wasn't so easily inclined. It was understandable; she didn't know Bazza. He was touched, however. Her censure meant that she cared about him. But then he'd known that already, as why else would she have gone to such lengths to help him? That night in her cottage, on the day of George's funeral, when she'd been trying to think of a way to expose Stacey's deception, he had very nearly given in to his ever-increasing desire for her. Had Isabel not been sitting in the room with them, he would have leaped from his chair and, well . . .

Her voice light, Isabel broke into his thoughts. 'Alice,' she said, 'don't be so hard on Bazza. I spent only a few hours with the woman, but I swear I've never known a more vain, pretentious or demanding client. I think Bazza and Clayton deserve medals for putting up with her for as long as they both did.'

Finished with the *Express*, Clayton closed it and pushed it aside. 'Speaking for myself, I hardly think I deserve a medal for having a woefully ineffectual nature when it comes to that woman.'

'Never mind a medal, an Oscar more like it, after your performance with Stevie McKean. Don't you agree, Alice?'

Alice smiled. 'Isabel's right: you were utterly convincing, Clayton.'

He returned her smile. 'And your impersonation of Stacey was scarily spot-on. I was shaking inside at that voice. You were fantastic.'

'Barry?' said Isabel. 'Tell us again how Stacey reacted when you arrived home.'

Was it Clayton's imagination or was there a mutual admiration society taking shape between Bazza and Isabel? Clayton glanced at Alice and saw by her smile that she was thinking the same thing. Well, well.

Bazza's response to Isabel's request was to grin like an idiot and say, 'Really? You really want me to go through it all again?'

Amused, Clayton said, 'Tell you what, Bazza, why don't you oblige the lady while I make us some more coffee.'

'I'll help you,' Alice said.

When they were at the other end of the kitchen, Alice whispered to Clayton, 'You thinking what I'm thinking?'

'And some,' he whispered back.

'Do you think it could work?'

'You're asking the wrong person. I'm a total dud when it comes to understanding how relationships work.'

Alice frowned and looked away. Clayton immediately regretted his words. He plugged in the kettle and tuned into what Bazza was saying to Isabel. Bazza had always been a master storyteller. Right now he was describing how when he'd returned to Notting Hill, timing his arrival so that he missed Isabel's departure, he had suggested to Stacey that there was something on YouTube she might be interested to see. Downloading the recording he'd made onto the Internet had been one of the tasks Alice had assigned to him, along with hiding Stacey's mobile and disconnecting the land line so that no one could ring her before he got back. According to Bazza, Stacey had watched the recording with her eyes and mouth wide open.

'But it's not me!' she had cried. 'That isn't me speaking on the phone. I've been here all afternoon. I swear it!'

'Well, it sure as hell sounds like you.'

'But I can prove it isn't me!' she had screeched. 'The photographer will verify I never went near the phone.'

'What photographer?' Bazza had asked.

'The one you arranged to come here, of course.'

'I did no such thing.'

'You did! The photographer said you'd been in touch with her.'

A few more denials from Bazza and apparently the penny had dropped. 'What's going on?' she had demanded.

'I've had it with you, Stacey. You may thrive on all the arguments we have, and you may also be able to live with the guilt of what we did to Clayton, but I can't. I want you out of my house and my life.'

She had then turned on him, just as Bazza had known she would. She had threatened to go to the press and tell the world that not only had it all been his idea to blame Clayton for the loss of their baby, but he did unspeakable things to her in bed.

That was when Bazza had slipped a CD into his laptop and said, 'I knew that's how you would react, so listen to this.'

The CD had been made earlier in the week with Alice's help. It contained yet more confessions made by Stacey. She spoke of her drink problem. How it had been fuelled by the shallowness of her existence. She spoke of the strain of living a life of lies, especially the one she had devised about Clayton.

'One wrong word to anyone from you and I'll leak this to the press. And a lot more besides,' Bazza had said.

'You hate me so much?'

'I hate what you've turned me into.'

Hearing Bazza repeat those words to Isabel now as he came to the end of his story, Clayton thought they made a pretty good punchline.

The kettle clicked off and while Clayton spooned coffee into the row of mugs, he said, 'Alice, I'm so grateful for how fantastic you were. God only knows how you had the patience to listen to those hideous chat-show recordings Bazza got hold of.'

She shrugged. 'It's what I do; it's how I learn a new voice.'

'Well, you did it brilliantly. I want you to know how much I really appreciate everything you've done. You were the brains behind it all.'

She gave him one of her flickering, tentative smiles. 'Be quiet and make the coffee,' she said, 'you're embarrassing me.'

He had just finished pouring water into the mugs when his phone rang. It was Glen. Again. There had been dozens of calls that morning, all from Glen, all following up on *The Stevie McKean Show*. Journalists were in a frenzy of eagerness to interview Clayton.

'Your life is turning into a soap opera, my friend,' Glen said now. 'I think you'd better get yourself over here. As in pronto.'

'Any reason why?'

'I currently have two people in my office claiming they're going to whip your ass with a libel suit.'

Clayton turned his back on Alice and lowered his voice. 'Are they brother and sister by any chance?'

'As a matter of fact they are. And if you don't mind me saying, your reaction sounds worryingly like you were expecting this.'

'You know me; I always expect bad news. For the sake of clarification, tell me the names of the two people in your office.'

'Natasha and Rufus Raphael.'

Now that was what Clayton called a punchline.

'Who was that?' asked Alice. 'Whoever it was, they've turned your face a whiter shade of pale. To coin a phrase. What's happened?'

Isabel and Bazza had heard Alice's tone of voice and looked anxiously at him.

Clayton's pulse quickened. Time to come clean. No more hiding anything. He did his best to look Alice square in the eye. 'It's Rufus and Natasha,' he said. 'They're with Glen. In his office. And they're none too happy.'

It had to happen. Alice had known that eventually Rufus and Natasha would reappear.

Once she had recovered from the initial shock, she had felt surprisingly calm. She still did. She didn't even feel angry with Clayton. Yes, he was responsible for creating the situation, but it was time to face up to Rufus and Natasha. And what did she have to feel bad about? It wasn't as if the way they had been portrayed had been an exaggeration of their behaviour. If anyone needed to feel bad, it should be Rufus and Natasha.

She was now in the back of a cab with Clayton, on their way to his agent's office. They were both silent. Clayton hadn't wanted her to come, but she had refused to listen.

The traffic was horrendous. 'We might as well walk,' Clayton said. 'It'll be quicker. Do you mind?'

'Whatever gets us there fastest. I'm keen to get this over with.'

They completed the rest of the journey in continued silence. It was a sultry, blurry-skied early summer's day and the streets were crowded. They had reached Soho now, and Clayton halted in front of a small door. 'Is there anything I can say to make you change your mind about me doing this alone,' he said.

'Clayton, this is my battle. Let me sort it out my way.'

He shook his head slowly. 'I can't do that. I've made many mistakes in my life, but this is one I have to rectify personally.'

'Why? Why does it matter to you so much?'

'Because . . . because I care about you. I care about you a lot.'

She frowned. 'Caring is such a vague term. What do you actually mean by it?'

'I'm trying to tell you I made a mistake,' he said at length. 'About us. I should never have kidded myself I didn't want to be with you.'

'But you did. That day at the hospital, you couldn't have made your feelings for me clearer.'

'Another mistake. I thought I was doing the right thing, only to discover it was entirely the wrong thing. You're the most amazing person I know, Alice. You're the first thing I think of when I wake up in the morning and the last thing when I go to bed at night. Tell me, is there anything I can do to make you think well of me again?'

'You choose *now* to tell me all this? Why? What's changed?'

'Maybe it's got something to do with the thought of Rufus hurting you all over again. The very idea of it makes me want to tear him apart.' He ran a hand over his face. 'Perhaps only love can make a person feel that way. What do you think?'

Stunned, Alice paused. *Love*. He'd used the word 'love'. But did he mean it?

His answered her question by taking her in his arms and kissing her.

'We're making a terrible spectacle of ourselves,' she said, when a crowd of drinkers outside a nearby bar started whistling and cheering.

'I've made a terrible spectacle of myself all my life,' he said, still holding her close. 'I'm beyond caring.' He tipped his head to kiss her again.

She gently pushed him away. 'Not so fast, mister. We have serious business to attend to.'

Glen's office was on the ground floor. Clayton led the way to a reception area. There was no sign of anyone behind the sleek, curving desk. He took Alice's hand. 'Please,' he said, 'will you let me try and smooth the waters on my own? A few simple but adamant denials on my part and we'll soon have this wrapped up.'

'Sorry, Clayton, I'm afraid that's not good enough for me. But I will meet you halfway. I won't come in with you, so long as you don't deny anything. You're to tell them the truth about how you came by the story. And if they want to meet me at a later date, tell them they can.'

'You're sure?'

She kissed him on the cheek. 'I'm convinced Rufus and Natasha won't pursue a libel suit. The shame would kill them. Let's see what they've got to say for themselves, shall we? I believe that it's me they want. And to get at me they have to go through you. They probably want my silence on any further revelations they're worried I might come out with.'

Clayton gave in. 'OK, but I want you out of sight for now.'

'Don't you worry about me. I'll make myself invisible.'

Clayton didn't bother knocking on Glen's door. He strolled in casually. 'Glen,' he said volubly, 'I hope you appreciate that you've probably ruined the best day's writing of my life.' He turned his head to get his first sighting of Rufus Raphael. *Come on, you bastard, let's be having you!* He almost jumped back in surprise. Holy shit! This was not what he had been expecting.

With her ear pressed against the door, Alice was straining to hear what was going on. So far only some indistinct mutterings, and then came Clayton's voice. 'So what exactly is it you're accusing me of?' he asked.

Alice held her breath, waiting to hear who would answer.

'Let's get straight to the point, shall we?'

It was Rufus. No question. Still the same patronising and superior arrogance in his voice. Still the same dismissive drawling lilt to his words. She could picture him looking down his nose at Clayton. He probably hadn't changed at all. She shuddered.

'And what point is it that you want to get straight to?' asked Clayton.

'That your grubby script was not a work of fiction, as your abysmal agent here has been claiming, but was based on a pack of lies told to you by a conniving bitch my sister and I once knew.'

Conniving bitch! Alice was ready to crash through the door and have her say, but hearing Clayton speak, she held back. 'Now listen, you ingrate,' he said in a commanding voice she had never heard him use before. 'First, my agent is not abysmal and secondly, the misfortune was entirely that young woman's.'

'You admit it then! Your script was based on what that wretched girl told you.'

Natasha had now joined in. There was no mistaking her voice.

'And what if it was? What are you going to do? Sue me? Yeah, why don't you? Tell the world that it's you in the script. But the consequences will be far more damaging to you than they ever would be to me. I have first-hand experience of how the press will treat you. You'll be social pariahs. Meanwhile, I'll be riding high on a wave of free publicity that you'll have provided for the sequel I'm currently writing.'

Alice froze. *Sequel*. She didn't like the sound of that.

There was silence then. Clayton had out-manoeuvred them.

Rufus eventually spoke. 'We want to speak to Alice.' He uttered her name as if it was poison on his tongue. 'We want to know why she did this to us. After all this time, what did she hope to gain?'

'Not everyone does something in the hope of gain. Very likely that's a concept you don't understand. Given your behaviour towards Alice, I think unrepentant self-interest is a way of life for you both.'

'And you're basing this on lies and exaggerations by a fool of a girl who threw herself at me? She was a fantasist, imagining that I was in love with her. What's more, she was as unbalanced as her father. A man who pushed two women to their death. The man was a dangerous lunatic.'

Alice had heard enough. She could countenance being branded a liar and not right in the head, but she would not stand and hear the memory of her father being disparaged. She pushed open the door. Despite what she had said to Clayton, it was time for her big entrance.

It was difficult to know just who was the most shocked when Alice entered the room. Everyone stared at her. But it was Alice who stared the most. She openly gaped, robbed in a flash of her murderous anger.

'Well, well, *well*,' Rufus drawled. 'Here she is at last. The person everybody's talking about. What a stir you've caused.'

'What happened to you?' she asked.

'This?' he said, tapping the arm of the wheelchair he was sitting in. 'How very rude of you to come right out with such a question. But of course, we couldn't really expect polite discretion from you, could we? Hardly your style, is it? Blabbing is more your forte.'

'Alice didn't blab,' Clayton said sharply. 'She merely recounted her childhood to me.'

'That's all right, Clayton,' Alice said, 'I can handle this.'

'Handle what exactly, Alice?' asked Natasha. 'The fact that you've tried to destroy our reputations?'

'That was never her intention.'

'Clayton, please,' Alice said gently. She looked at Natasha, no longer a teenager but a young woman the same age as Alice. She seemed older, though. And very tired. She looked as if life had worn her down a long time ago.

Beside her, in his wheelchair, Rufus sat defiantly implacable. He was wearing a pair of jeans and Alice could see by the way the fabric lay that beneath it his legs were withered and useless. Her anger was now replaced with pity. How he would hate to know that. 'Perhaps the three of us should talk about this in private,' she said.

'Why? Are you worried that we'll expose you for a lying bitch?'

Clayton lurched forward. 'Listen, you little shit! Just because you're in a wheelchair don't think for one moment it wouldn't give me the greatest of pleasure to kick your sorry arse.'

'Oh, oh! Fighting talk. Alice, would I be right in thinking you and this man are bedfellows? I'm hearing the sound of someone keen to protect your honour. Which means, of course, that he's blind to your faults, namely that you're a born liar and given to fantasising.' He tutted. 'Really, Alice, hiding behind a man just as you once hid behind your father.'

'Why can't you face up to the truth of what happened to us?' Alice asked quietly. 'Are you now going to deny that your mother killed herself? And that it wasn't the first time she'd tried it?'

'What are you talking about?'

'It's true,' Alice replied calmly. 'I recently found out that your mother tried or threatened to take her life on several occasions.'

'How did you come by this information?'

'From Isabel.'

At the mention of Isabel's name, Rufus visibly stiffened.

'After what Isabel did to Rufus I hardly think we're inclined to believe a word she has to say on the matter,' Natasha said. 'And anyway, if our mother was unhappy, there was a good reason for it. She was married to a monster. That man put her through hell.'

'You think it was easy for my father, knowing that Julia's only reason for marrying him was financial security?' The earlier rush of adrenaline that had coursed through Alice was fading fast and she began to feel drained by the effort of sparring with Rufus. 'If you're not going to accept the truth,' she said wearily, 'what is the point in any of this?'

'The point, Alice, is that you have trashed our family name and I won't stand for it.'

'Yeah, we can see that!' Clayton snapped.

Alice winced and behind his desk, where he was looking like a man who had gate-crashed the wrong party, Glen drew in his breath. Rufus glared at Clayton. 'A cheap shot if ever I heard one.'

'Trust me, Bambi, there's plenty more where that came from. Tell me, what did you do, fall off your high horse? Or trip over your bloody great ego?'

'How dare you talk to my brother like that?'

'That's OK, Tash, let him have his sport. If you must know, Mr Miller, the summer after my mother died, in a moment of maudlin inebriation, I dived into a pool of water that was shallower than I was expecting and surfaced with a broken back. And in case you were wondering, Alice, as a consequence of that accident I didn't finish medical school.'

'I'm sorry, Rufus,' Alice said. 'That must have been awful for you.'

'Please don't insult me with your phoney sympathy; I've managed perfectly well up to now without it.'

The sour acrimony of his words spoke of a life not lived to the full. Of grudges harboured. Of blame and hatred carefully nurtured.

After glancing over at Clayton, and keeping her voice as level and reasonable as she could, Alice said, 'Natasha and Rufus, as far as I can see, you've had a wasted trip. You don't have any kind of a case against Clayton. If you can't accept that *The Queen of New Beginnings* was a fair representation of our lives at Cuckoo House then you have to take a good look at yourselves.' She opened her bag and pulled out a card. She handed it to Rufus. 'If you have anything further to say on the subject, you can contact me via *my* agent.'

He looked at it and his mouth curved into a sneer. 'Alice Shoemaker, voiceover artist. That's quite a comedown from your lofty ambition of being an actress, isn't it? Here's what I have to say about getting in touch with you, Alice.' He ripped the card in half, then in half again. He threw the pieces at her. It was a nasty, petty little gesture, intended to make Alice feel as worthless as her business card. 'Come on, Tash,' he said, 'let's get out of here. I've had enough.'

As they watched Natasha carefully steer her brother out of Glen's office, Alice wondered if Natasha was solely responsible for taking care of Rufus. If so, it meant that she had got her wish; she had the brother she adored all to herself.

When they were left alone, Glen said, 'Would either of you two care to fill me in on what I've just witnessed?'

'Later,' said Clayton. 'I need to talk to Alice on her own.'

Chapter Eleven

PLEASE FORWARD TO ALICE SHOEMAKER

3 Abbey Court House,
Brayton,
Hertfordshire

Dear Alice,

I do hope your agent forwards this letter to you. It is not an easy letter for me to write. The sad and embarrassing truth is that we have found ourselves in financial difficulties. The recession has hit Rufus's IT consultancy work badly and, to make things worse, I have just been made redundant from the hospital where I worked part-time as a dietician. Of course, my main job is to take care of Rufus, which is why I can work only part-time. We bought this house when he finally left Stoke Mandeville Hospital and have lived here together ever since.

Rufus has no idea that I am writing to you, but, Alice, I am asking whether you could help us. We could call it a loan, if you like; a loan to tide us over until this wretched recession has passed. I hesitate to bring up the matter, but I'm sure you must have benefited financially from The Queen of New Beginnings *and since the story included the Raphael family, I don't think it's unreasonable for us to benefit in some way as well. I am sure you know in your heart that it would be the right thing to do.*

With kind regards, Natasha

P.S. I've read about the many awards Clayton Miller has received, including a BAFTA and an Emmy. I've also read how he says he owes the success of The Queen of New Beginnings *to one person in particular; he didn't name you, but clearly he was referring to you. Has he started work on the sequel he mentioned during our meeting last year?*

Dragonfly Cottage,
Stonebridge,
Derbyshire

Dear Natasha,

I'm sorry to hear of your troubles. It must be a very distressing time for you and Rufus. This may surprise you but I did not benefit financially in any way from The Queen of New Beginnings. *I have, though, had a run of luck with a series of television adverts I've voiced in the past year and I am enclosing a cheque for you. I hope you will take it in the spirit it is given in, not as a loan, but as a gift.*

I wish you and Rufus well.

Best wishes, Alice

P.S. Clayton has been working on a new project that has nothing to do with the events of Cuckoo House. I managed to talk him out of that!

3 Abbey Court House,
Brayton,
Hertfordshire

Dear Alice,

Please find enclosed your unwanted crumbs of charity. I want nothing to do with it. If you thought you could buy us off to assuage your guilt for what you did, you are very much mistaken.

Rufus

It had been a small wedding, no unnecessary frills. When exiting the church, never had a couple looked more thoroughly relieved to get things over and done with. And never, in Alice's opinion, had a groom looked more terrified throughout the proceedings. He was a lot more relaxed now, now that he had a plate of food in his hands and had a few drinks inside him. With the aid of a chicken drumstick he was adding extra emphasis to his words by jabbing at the air in front of Alice's face.

'I've got to tell you, Alice, I hardly knew you when you walked into the church. You've scrubbed up a treat. Nice dress.'

'Thank you, Bob.'

He winked. 'And to think you went to so much trouble specially for me.'

'How is your poor new wife ever going to put up with you?'

'Kim will manage well enough. She's a sensible woman and knows when she's on to a good thing. Where is that man of yours, then?'

Alice turned and pointed across the lawn to where Clayton was hunkered down beside Kim's five-year-old son, Jake.

Eleven months ago Bob had met Kim through work. He had been sent to fix a fault on her phone line and had ended up being fixed himself. Well, that was the way he told the story.

'So when are you and Clayton going to get spliced?'

'Why change things when we're both happy? Anyway, we're too busy right now to think about anything like getting married.'

'Busy with the house?'

They redirected their gaze; this time they both stared up at the house behind them. 'We're hoping to start work on the kitchen and bathrooms next month,' Alice said.

'It was good of you to let us have our wedding shindig here.'

Alice shrugged. 'My wedding present to you. No point in having a lovely garden like this and not sharing it with friends.'

Shortly after George's funeral, Alice had received a solicitor's letter saying that his client, a Miss Georgina Harrington-Smythe, had left Alice Well House. 'But she couldn't have,' Alice had said when she went to meet with the solicitor who had written to her.

'I was summoned to visit my client when she was in hospital. She was very clear on her wishes, namely that she wanted you to have Well House. There is also a not inconsiderable amount of money. There is just one condition, though. You inherit only if you promise to take care of Percy for the rest of his life, and his girlfriends. Do you know who Percy is? Does this make sense to you?'

Alice had roared with laughter in the car on her way home. Then she had cried. Dear old George; what a wonderful woman she had been.

Looking about her now, Alice took in the garden that she remembered so fondly from her childhood and thought of all the plans she had for it. She even fancied the idea of keeping some bees. Clayton teased her that she was going to end up as eccentric as George.

Two days later Alice and Clayton were woken by the sound of a clanging bell: it was the postman. Alice went downstairs. The package was addressed to them both. Taking it upstairs with her, Alice got back into bed with Clayton. She opened the package knowing what was inside—photographs that Isabel had taken last weekend when she and Grace, along with Bazza, had come to stay at Well House. They had been celebrating the success of Clayton and Bazza's *Reasons to be Cheerful*, which had hit people's TV screens to enormous popular and critical acclaim. The boys were back.

Having previously made the mistake of turning himself into a very public figure, Bazza wasn't making that mistake again and had spent the past year keeping his relationship with Isabel under wraps. The press knew that there was someone new in his life, as they did with Clayton, but fortunately no one was hounding them over it.

The first photograph was a group shot. 'I'm going to frame this one,' Alice said decisively. 'It shows everything wonderful in my life. This is my new family: you, Isabel and Grace and Bazza.'

Clayton put his arm round her. 'I'm glad you've forgiven Bazza.'

'How could I not when I know he's going to marry Isabel?'

'You really think they'll marry? Even though Bazza's completely different from Bruce?'

'Perhaps that's why they're perfect together. Bazza isn't a replacement for my father.'

'George once said to me that she thought I was right for you because I reminded you of your father. Would I be foolish to ask if that's true?'

'Only in that from time to time you make the same sort of wacky decisions he used to make. And you can be wildly unpredictable, like the day we went to Glen's office to meet Rufus and Natasha. I had absolutely no idea how you felt about me until then. And then afterwards you surprised me again when you bundled me into a taxi and whisked me off to the Ritz for cocktails.'

'Where better to convince you that I really did love you?'

'Lucky for you the concierge was able to supply you with a tie or you would have been declaring your feelings out on the street again.'

'I like to do things spontaneously. I can't prepare for all contingencies.'

'And that's one of the many things I love about you. So don't ever think of changing.'

'You must be the only woman in the world who doesn't want the man in her life to change. Can I ask you something else?' he said.

'Of course.'

'What would you say if I asked you to marry me?'

Alice looked at him. 'Is that a trick question?'

'It wasn't meant to be, but I take your point; my question was too ambiguous.' He suddenly slipped out of the bed and came round to her side of it. 'OK, same question but with a hundred per cent clarity.' He got down on one knee. 'Alice Shoemaker, will you marry me?'

She stared at him in shock. Her heart hammered. 'I don't know what to say.'

He looked disappointed. 'That wasn't quite the answer that I was hoping for.'

'I'm sorry,' she said, flustered. 'I just wasn't expecting this. I thought you weren't the marrying kind.'

'When did I ever say that? I love you, Alice, and I want to spend the rest of my life with you.'

'You really want to get married? To *me*?'

'No, Alice, I'm down here wrecking my knee on a whim, in the hope that a passing stranger will want to marry me.'

'You've thought about this? I mean, you've really thought—'

'Geez, Alice! Stop dickering about and say yes before—'

'Before what?' she interrupted him. 'Before you change your mind?'

'No, before my knee gives out completely.'

Laughing, she pulled him back into bed. 'Clayton Miller, I absolutely love you! And I love it when you're so romantic.' She kissed him but no sooner had her lips touched his than he pushed her away.

'Oh no you don't, no distractions. I want my answer.'

'The answer is an unequivocal yes,' she said. And a rousing cheer sounded inside her head. *Hurrah for the Queen of New Beginnings!* This was one beginning that wasn't going to end badly. She had finally cracked it.

Erica James

Where did the idea for *The Queen of New Beginnings* start?

With Clayton Miller. He was a character who had been rattling around in my mind for some time. A self-absorbed man, drifting through life with the world against him—a modern-day Reginald Perrin. I enjoy looking at life from a male perspective and exploring male vulnerability in my novels.

Alice does voiceovers and is a mimic. Is this a skill you have?

No, definitely not, though I would imagine it would be a great one to have. Alice began with her name: Alice Shoemaker. I then wanted to give her an interesting occupation, and since many of my novels have been made into audio books I thought I would put her in that world. But it wasn't until I was writing the scene in which she knocks on the door of Cuckoo House and it's opened by Clayton, that in my head I heard her speaking with a Latvian accent. It surprised me as much as Clayton! I love to let my characters roll—to let them cook, so to speak.

You have homes in Cheshire and on Lake Como. Where do you write best?

I think and write anywhere and everywhere. When I am in the planning stage I am like a magpie, storing away anything that might come in handy. I jot ideas down and make lots of lists. When I'm writing I am totally immersed in my story and when I'm at the lake in Italy, I feel as though I am on holiday and have a true sense of well-being. Being by the water has a calming effect and I have a wonderful network of friends. Then there's the food! In contrast, my writing is more structured when I am in Cheshire, where I usually write from 8.30 to 7.30, Monday to Friday. These hours stem from the time my sons, Samuel and Edward, were young and I was fitting writing around being a mother, and the habit has stuck.

How would you describe yourself in just a few words?

Independent, creative, happy.

How would your sons describe you?

Oh, barking mad!

Have you any dreams or ambitions that you still want to fulfil?

To own a Bentley Convertible before the fuel runs out! To have continued writing success and to keep pleasing my readers. I would also love to spend more time in Italy.

What book are you currently reading?

I've returned to the classics and am reading Tolstoy's *Anna Karenina*.

What was the worst/best film you have seen recently?

Worst was *Bright Star*. It was a shocker. Best was *The Reader*. So moving.

On a Saturday night would you be curled up on the sofa watching *X-Factor* or *Strictly Come Dancing*?

X-Factor. No competition. I also watch Italian *X-Factor*, which is not as good as ours. When I am watching the television I have to be doing something else as well, though—needlepoint, tapestry or learning Italian grammar.

Do you prefer crosswords or sudokus? Or do you hate them both?

Hate them both. Don't have the time. Could have written another chapter in the time it would take me to complete one. Am very stingy with my time.

If your house was burning down what would you save?

Well, assuming that no one needed rescuing, it would be the manuscript of the current book I was working on. The thought of all that hard work going up in smoke would be too awful.

What do you do when you are not writing?

I relax by reading, going to the gym (in an effort to stave off the dreaded writer's bum!), gardening and travelling. But I'm not an adventurous traveller who enjoys roughing it. I spent Christmas in Phuket and enjoy a little bit of luxury.

You have just turned fifty—what are your thoughts on this big birthday?

It's scary, but I had a big party and invited lots of friends I hadn't seen in a very long time. It was a very special evening and was the perfect distraction from worrying about being fifty. But, seriously, I think I feel happier, more content with myself now than ever before. I am more fulfilled, more in control of my life. I am The Queen of New Beginnings at Fifty!

The Girl Who Chased the Moon

SARAH ADDISON ALLEN

In North Carolina, barbecue means pork—pork and sauce and coleslaw and hush puppies. Our idea of barbecue is just a part of the odd loveliness of my home state, part of its distinctive flavour. So, of course, I decided to make Mullaby, the fictional town in 'The Girl Who Chased the Moon', a barbecue town, where the air is always tomato-sweet and hickory-smoked. I hope you enjoy this taste of it.

Sarah

Chapter 1

It took a moment for Emily to realise the car had come to a stop. She looked up from her charm bracelet, which she'd been worrying in slow circles round her wrist, and stared out of the window. The two giant oaks in the front yard looked like flustered ladies caught mid-curtsy, their starched green leaf-dresses swaying in the wind.

'This is it?' she asked the taxi driver.

'Six Shelby Road. Mullaby. This is it.'

Emily hesitated, then paid him and got out. The air outside was tomato-sweet and hickory-smoked, all at once delicious and strange. It was dusk, but the streetlights weren't on yet. She was taken aback by how quiet everything was. No street sounds. No kids playing. No music or television. There was this sensation of otherworldliness, as if she'd travelled some impossible distance.

She looked round the neighbourhood while the taxi driver took her two overstuffed duffle bags out of the trunk. The street consisted of large old homes, most of which were showpieces in true Southern fashion with elaborate trim work and painted porches.

The driver set her bags on the sidewalk, nodded and drove off.

Emily watched him disappear. She tucked back some hair that had fallen out of her short ponytail, then grabbed the handles of the duffle bags. She dragged them behind her as she followed the path from the sidewalk, through the yard and under the canopy of fat trees. When she emerged from under the canopy on the other side, she stopped short at the sight before her.

The house looked nothing like the rest of the houses in the neighbourhood. It had probably been white at one time, but now it was grey, and its Gothic Revival pointed-arch windows were dusty and opaque. It was flaunting its age, spitting paint chips and old roofing shingles into the yard. There was a large wraparound porch on the ground floor, the roof of which served as a balcony for the first floor, and years of crumbling oak leaves were covering both.

This was where her mother grew up?

She could feel her arms trembling, which she told herself was from the weight of the bags. She walked up the steps to the porch, set the bags down and knocked. No answer.

She tried again. Nothing.

She opened the rusty screen door and called into the house, 'Hello?' No answer.

She entered cautiously. No lights were on, but the last sunlight of the day was filtering through the dining-room windows, directly to her left. The dining-room furniture was dark and ornate, but it seemed incredibly large to her, as if made for a giant. To her right was obviously another room, but there was an accordion door closing off the archway. Straight in front of her was a hallway leading to the kitchen and a wide staircase leading to the first floor. She went to the base of the stairs and called up, 'Hello?'

At that moment, the accordion door flew open and Emily jumped back. An elderly man with coin-silver hair walked out, ducking under the archway to avoid hitting his head. He was fantastically tall and walked with a rigid gait, his legs like stilts. He seemed badly constructed, like a skyscraper made of soft wood instead of concrete. He looked as if he could splinter at any moment.

'You're finally here. I was getting worried.' His fluid Southern voice was what she remembered from their first and only phone conversation a week ago, but he was nothing like she expected.

She craned her neck back to look up at him. 'Vance Shelby?'

He nodded. He seemed afraid of her. She found herself monitoring her movements, not wanting to startle him.

She slowly held out her hand. 'Hi, I'm Emily.'

He smiled. Then his smile turned into a laugh, which was an ashy roar, like a large fire. Her hand completely disappeared in his when he shook it. 'I know who you are, child. You look just like your mother.' His smile faded as quickly as it had appeared. He looked around awkwardly. 'Where are your suitcases?'

'I left them on the porch.'

There was a short silence. Neither of them had known the other existed until recently. How could they have run out of things to say already? 'Well,' he finally said, 'you can do what you want upstairs—it's all yours. I can't get up there any more. Arthritis. This is my room.' He pointed to the accordion door. 'You can choose any room you want, but your mother's old room was the last one on the right. Tell me what the wallpaper looks like. I'd like to know.'

'Thank you. I will,' she said as he turned and walked towards the kitchen, his steps loud in his wondrously large shoes.

Emily watched him go, confused. That was it?

She went to the porch and dragged her bags in. Upstairs, she found a long hallway that smelled woolly. There were six doors. She walked down the hall, the scraping of her duffle bags magnified in the hardwood silence.

Once she reached the last door on the right, she dropped her bags and reached inside for the light switch. The first thing she noticed when the light popped on was that the wallpaper had rows of tiny lilacs on it, and the room actually smelled like lilacs. There was a four-poster bed against the wall, the gauzy remnants of what had once been a canopy now hanging off the posts like maypoles.

There was a white trunk at the foot of the bed. The name *Dulcie,* Emily's mother's name, was carved in it in swirly letters. As she walked by it, she ran her hand over the top of the trunk and her fingertips came away with puffs of dust. Underneath the age there was a distinct impression of privilege to this room.

It made no sense. This room did not feel like her mother's room.

She opened the set of French doors and stepped out onto the balcony, crunching into ankle-deep dried oak leaves. Everything had felt so precarious since her mother's death. When she'd left Boston, it had been with a sense of hope. She'd actually been comforted by the thought of falling back into a cradle of her mother's youth, of bonding with the grandfather she hadn't known she had. Instead, the lonely strangeness of this place mocked her. This didn't feel like home.

She reached to touch her charm bracelet for comfort, but felt only bare skin. She lifted her wrist, startled. The bracelet was gone.

She frantically kicked the leaves on the balcony, trying to find it. Then she rushed back into the room and dragged her bags in, thinking maybe the bracelet had caught on one of them. But it wasn't anywhere. She ran downstairs and out of the door. After ten minutes of searching, she realised that either she had dropped it on the sidewalk and someone had taken it, or it had fallen off her wrist in the cab.

The bracelet had belonged to her mother. Dulcie had loved it—the crescent-moon charm in particular. That charm had been worn thin by the many times Dulcie had rubbed it while in one of her faraway moods.

Emily walked slowly back into the house. She couldn't believe she'd lost it. She heard what sounded like a clothes-dryer door slam, then her grandfather came out of the kitchen. 'Lilacs,' she said when he met her in the hall.

He gave her a cautious look. 'Lilacs?'

'You asked what the wallpaper was in Mom's room. It's lilacs.'

'Ah. It was always flowers when she was a little girl. It changed a lot as she got older. Once it was lightning bolts on a tar-black background. Another time it was this scaly-blue colour, like a dragon's belly. She hated that one, but couldn't seem to change it.'

That made Emily smile. 'It doesn't sound like her at all. I remember once . . .' She stopped when Vance looked away. He didn't want to know. The last time he saw his daughter was twenty years ago. Wasn't he even curious? Stung, Emily turned from him. 'I guess I'll go to bed now.'

'Are you hungry?' he asked as he followed her. 'I went to the grocery store this morning. I bought some food.'

She reached the staircase. 'Thank you. But I really am tired.'

He nodded. 'All right. Tomorrow, maybe.'

She went back to the bedroom and fell onto the bed. Mustiness exploded from the mattress. She stared at the ceiling, trying not to cry. She could survive a year here, surely.

She heard the wind skittering dried leaves around the balcony, and turned her head to look out of the open balcony doors. The light from the bedroom illuminated the trees in the back yard. She sat up and crawled off the bed. Once outside, she looked around.

Something suddenly caught her eye in the woodline beyond the gazebo in the overgrown back yard. There! It was a bright white light—a quick, zippy flash—darting between the trees. Gradually, the light faded into the darkness until it disappeared completely.

Welcome to Mullaby, North Carolina, she thought. Home of ghost lights, giants and jewellery thieves.

She turned to go back in and froze.

There, on the old metal patio table, sitting on top of a layer of dried leaves, was her mother's charm bracelet.

Where it hadn't been just minutes ago.

Too much wine. That's what Julia would blame it on. When she saw Stella in the morning, she would say, 'Oh, and that thing I said about Sawyer last night, forget it. It was just the wine talking.'

As Julia made her way up to her apartment that evening, she felt vaguely panicked and not at all mellow—as wine on the back porch with Stella usually made her. She only had six months before she was free of this town again, the downhill slope of her two-year plan. But with one slip of the tongue, she'd made things infinitely harder. If what she said got back to Sawyer, he wouldn't let it rest.

She opened the door at the top of the staircase and stepped into the hallway. Nothing had been done to the upper storey of Stella's house to make it look like an apartment. There were four doors off the hallway. One led to the bathroom, one to Julia's bedroom, one to a second bedroom that had been converted into a kitchen, and another to a tiny third bedroom that Julia used as a living room.

Years ago, after Stella's ex-husband had spent his way through Stella's trust fund, he'd decided they should bring in lodgers, so he'd put a curtain at the top of the staircase and said, '*Voilà!* Instant apartment.' Then he'd been surprised when there were no takers. Men of thoughtless actions are always surprised by consequences, Stella said. The last year of their marriage, when Stella had found out about the other women, she had kicked him out. Afterwards she got her brother to put a door at the top of the staircase, and a sink and an oven hookup in one of the bedrooms. Julia was her first tenant.

Initially, Julia had been uneasy about renting a place from one of her old high-school enemies. But Stella's apartment had been the only place Julia could afford when she'd moved back to Mullaby. She'd been surprised to find that, despite their pasts, she and Stella actually got along. Stella had been one of the most popular girls at Mullaby High, a member of Sassafras—what the elite group of pretty, sparkly girls had called themselves. Julia had been the girl everyone avoided. She'd been sullen, rude and undeniably strange. She'd dyed her hair bright pink, worn a studded leather choker every day, and used eyeliner so black that she'd looked bruised.

And her father had tried so hard not to notice.

Julia walked to her bedroom. But before she turned on the light, she noticed a light coming from Vance Shelby's house next door. She went to her open window in the darkness and looked out. All the time she'd lived in Stella's house, she'd never once seen a light in the upstairs bedrooms next door. There was a teenager on the balcony, staring into the woods behind Vance's house. She was willow-branch thin and had a cap of yellow hair. A sad vulnerability wafted from her. That's when Julia remembered. Vance's granddaughter was coming to live with him. This past week at Julia's restaurant, it was all anyone could talk about. Some people were curious, some were fearful, and some were mean. Not everyone had forgiven this girl's mother for what she'd done.

Julia didn't like the thought of what the girl was in for. Living down your own past was hard enough. You shouldn't have to live down someone else's. Tomorrow morning, Julia decided, she'd make an extra cake at the restaurant to take to her.

Julia undressed and got into bed. Eventually the light went off next door. She sighed and waited to cross another day off her calendar.

After her father's death almost two years ago, Julia had taken a few days off work to come back to Mullaby to get his affairs in order. Her plan had been to quickly sell his house and restaurant, then take the money and go back to Maryland and finally make her dream of opening her own bakery come true.

But things hadn't gone exactly the way they were supposed to.

She'd quickly discovered that her father had been deeply in debt, his house and restaurant mortgaged to the hilt. Selling his house had paid off his home mortgage and a small part of his restaurant mortgage. But even with that, she would have barely broken even if she'd sold the restaurant then. So she came up with her two-year plan. By living very frugally and bringing in more business to J's Barbecue while she was there, in two years she would have the mortgage paid off and could sell the restaurant for a tidy profit. She'd been perfectly up-front about it with everyone in town. She would be staying in Mullaby for two years, but that *did not mean she lived here any more.* She was just visiting. That was all.

When she took over the restaurant, J's Barbecue had a modest but loyal following, thanks to her father. He had a way of making people feel happy. But Mullaby had more barbecue restaurants per capita than any other place in the state, so competition was fierce. Julia knew the restaurant needed something to set it apart. So she started baking and selling cakes—her speciality—and it was an instant boon. Soon, J's Barbecue was known not just for fine barbecue, but also for the best cakes and pastries around.

Julia always got to the restaurant well before dawn, and the only person there before her was the pit cook. They rarely talked. She left the day-to-day running of the place to the people her father had taught and trusted. Even though the barbecue business was in her bones, she tried to stay as uninvolved as possible. She loved her father, but it had been a long time since she'd wanted to be like him. When Julia was a child, before she'd turned into a moody, pink-haired teenager, she used to follow him to work every day before school and gladly help with everything from waitressing to tossing wood into the smokehouse pit. Some of her best memories were of spending time with her father at J's Barbecue. But too much had happened since then for her to be comfortable here again. So she came in early, baked that day's cakes, and left as the first customers arrived for breakfast. On good days, she didn't even see Sawyer.

This, as it turned out, wasn't a good day.

'You'll never guess what Stella told me last night,' Sawyer Alexander said, strolling into the kitchen just as Julia was finishing the apple stack cake she was going to take to Vance Shelby's granddaughter.

Julia closed her eyes for a moment. Stella must have called him the moment Julia left her last night and went upstairs.

Sawyer stopped next to her at the stainless-steel table and stood close. He was like crisp, fresh air. Charm sparkled round him like sunlight. Blue-eyed and blond-haired, he was handsome, smart, rich and fun. And he was disgustingly kind, too, filled with Southern gentility. Sawyer drove his grandfather to Julia's restaurant every morning just so he could have breakfast with his old cronies.

'You're not supposed to be back here,' she said.

'Report me to the owner.' He pushed some of her hair behind her left ear, his fingers lingering on the pink streak she still dyed in her hair there. 'Don't you want to know what Stella told me last night?' he asked.

She jerked away from his hand. 'Stella was drunk last night.'

'She said you told her that you bake cakes because of me.'

Julia knew it was coming, but she stilled anyway, the icing spatula stopping mid-stroke. 'She thinks you have low self-esteem. She's trying to build up your ego.'

He lifted one eyebrow in that insolent way of his. 'I've been accused of many things, but low self-esteem is not one of them.'

'It must be hard to be so beautiful.'

'It's hell. Did you really say that to her?'

She clanged the spatula into an empty bowl. 'I don't remember. I was drunk, too.'

'You never get drunk,' he said.

'You don't know me well enough to make blanket statements like,

"You never get drunk."' It felt good to say that. Eighteen years she'd been away. *Look how much I've improved*, she wanted to say.

'Fair enough. But I do know Stella. Even when she drinks, I've never known her to lie. Why would she tell me that you bake cakes because of me if it wasn't true?'

'I bake cakes. You have an infamous sweet tooth. Maybe she got the two tangled up.' She walked into the storage room for a cake box, taking longer than necessary, hoping he'd go away.

'You're taking a cake with you?' he asked when she came back out. He hadn't moved.

'I'm giving it to Vance Shelby's granddaughter. She got in last night.'

That made him laugh. '*You're* actually giving someone a welcome cake?'

She didn't realise the irony until he pointed it out to her. 'I don't know what came over me.'

He watched her as she put the cake in the box. 'I like this colour on you,' he said, touching her white long-sleeved shirt.

She pulled her arm away. A year and a half of avoiding this man since she'd been back, then she had to go and say to Stella the one thing that would draw him to her like a magnet. He wanted to get closer to her. She knew that. And it made her angry. How could he even *think* of picking up where they left off after what happened?

She closed the window above her table. It was the last thing she did every morning, and sometimes it made her sad. She picked up the cake box and took it with her out into the restaurant without another word to Sawyer.

J's Barbecue was plain, as most barbecue restaurants in the South were—linoleum floors, plastic tablecloths, wooden booths.

She set the box down and picked up the chalkboard on the diner counter. She wrote the names of the day's cakes on the board: traditional Southern red velvet cake, peach pound cake, green tea and honey macaroons and cranberry doughnuts.

Sawyer walked out as she set the chalkboard back on the counter. 'I told Stella I'd come over with pizza tonight. You'll be there?'

'I'm always there. Why don't the two of you sleep together and get it over with?' Sawyer's Thursday pizza courtship of Stella had been going on since Julia had moved back to Mullaby. Stella swore nothing was going on, but Julia thought Stella was being naive.

Sawyer leaned in close. 'Stella and I did sleep together,' he said. 'Three years ago, after her divorce. Before you think that sounds indiscriminate, I try to keep my actions regret-free these days.'

She gave him a sharp look as he walked away. His casual, almost flippant, mention of it took her by surprise.

She couldn't blame him for being a scared teenager when he'd found out she'd got pregnant from their one night together all those years ago. She'd been a scared teenager, too. And they'd made the only decisions they were capable of making at the time.

But she resented how easily he'd got on with his life. It had been just one night to him. One regretful night with the freaky, unpopular girl at school. A girl who'd been madly in love with him.

Oh God. She wasn't going to fall into this role again.

Six months and counting and she would leave this crazy place and never think of Sawyer again.

Chapter 2

WHEN EMILY WOKE, her hairline was wet with sweat and she felt bone tired. She also had no idea where she was. She sat up quickly and pulled the earbuds of her MP3 player out of her ears. She looked round—the lilac wallpaper, the tattered furniture. That's when she remembered. She was in her mother's old bedroom.

Even though she knew her grandfather was downstairs, having the upstairs to herself made her uneasy. All night, there had been periods of quiet punctuated by loud wooden pops of the house settling. And leaves kept rattling outside her balcony doors. She'd finally turned on her MP3 player and tried to imagine herself someplace else. Someplace not so humid. Scared or not, tonight she was going to have to sleep with the balcony doors open, or else perish into a puddle of perspiration. Her mother might have been the most politically correct person on the planet—an activist, an environmentalist, a crusader for the underdog—but even she ran the air conditioner when it got too hot.

She made her way to the antiquated bathroom and took a bath because there was no shower. Afterwards she dressed in shorts and a tank top, then went downstairs. She noticed the note taped to the inside of the screen door right away.

Emily: This is Grandpa Vance. I forgot to tell you that I go out for breakfast every morning. Didn't want to wake you. I'll bring you something back, but there's also teenager food in the kitchen.

She took a deep breath, still trying to rearrange her expectations. Her first day here, and he didn't want to spend it with her.

Standing at the screen door, Emily heard a swish of leaves and, startled, looked up to see a woman in her thirties walking up the front porch steps. She had light brown hair that was cut into a beautiful swinging bob just below her ears.

The woman didn't see Emily until she reached the top step. She instantly smiled. 'Hello! You must be Vance's granddaughter,' she said as she came to a stop. She had pretty, dark brown eyes.

'Yes, I'm Emily Benedict.'

'I'm Julia Winterson. I live over there.' She turned her head slightly, indicating the yellow and white house next door. That's when Emily noticed the pink streak in Julia's hair. It wasn't something she expected from someone so fresh-faced, in flour-stained jeans and a white peasant blouse. 'I brought you an apple stack cake.' She opened the white box she was holding and showed Emily what looked like a stack of very large brown pancakes with some sort of filling in between each one. 'It means welcome. I know Mullaby has its faults, as I'm sure your mother told you, but it's also a town of great food. You're going to eat very well while you're here. At least there's that.'

Emily couldn't remember the last time she'd had an appetite for anything, much less food, but she didn't tell Julia that. 'My mother didn't tell me anything about Mullaby,' Emily said.

'Nothing?'

'No.'

Julia seemed shocked into silence.

'What?' Emily looked up from the cake.

'It's nothing,' Julia said, shaking her head. She closed the lid on the box. 'Do you want me to put this in the kitchen?'

'Sure. Come in,' Emily said, opening the screen door for her.

As Julia walked in, she noticed the note from Grandpa Vance still on the screen. 'Vance asked me to take him grocery shopping yesterday so he could get some things for you,' she said, nodding towards the note. 'His idea of teenager food was Kool-Aid, fruit chews and gum. I convinced him to buy crisps, bagels and cereal, too.'

'That was nice of you,' Emily said. 'To take him shopping.'

'I was a big fan of the Giant of Mullaby when I was a kid.' When

Emily looked at her, not understanding, Julia explained, 'That's what people round here call your grandfather.'

'How tall *is* he?' Emily asked.

Julia laughed. It was a great laugh, and hearing it was like stepping into a spot of sunshine. That she came bearing cake seemed oddly fitting. It was like she was *made* of cake, light and pretty and decorated on the outside—with her sweet laugh and pink streak to her hair—but it was anyone's guess what was on the inside. 'Tall enough to see into tomorrow. That's what he tells everyone. He's over eight feet tall. I know that much.'

Julia knew the way to the kitchen, so Emily followed. The kitchen was large and kitschy, like something out of the 1950s. It was overwhelmingly red—red countertops, red-and-white tiled floor and a large red refrigerator. Julia put the cake box on the counter, then turned to stare at Emily. 'You look a lot like your mother,' she said.

'You knew her?' Emily asked, perking up.

'We were in the same class in school. But we weren't close.' Julia stuffed her hands into her jeans pockets. 'She didn't tell you *anything*?'

'I knew she was born in North Carolina, but I didn't know where. I didn't even know I had a grandfather. She never talked about him and I always assumed he had passed away. Mom didn't like to talk about her past. She always said there was no use dwelling on the unfixable past when there was so much you could do to fix the future. She devoted all her time to her causes.'

'Her causes?'

'Amnesty International. Oxfam. Greenpeace. She travelled a lot when she was younger. After I was born, she settled down in Boston. She was very involved locally there.'

'Well. That's . . . not what I expected.'

'Was she like that here? Was she involved in a lot of causes?'

Julia took her hands out of her pockets. 'I should be going.'

'Oh,' Emily said, confused. 'Well, thank you for the cake.'

'No problem. My restaurant is called J's Barbecue, on Main Street. Come by anytime. That's where your grandfather is right now, by the way. He walks there every morning for breakfast.'

Emily followed Julia to the front door. 'Where is Main Street?'

As they stepped onto the porch, Julia pointed. 'At the end of Shelby Road here, turn left onto Dogwood. About a half-mile later, turn right. You can't miss it.' Julia started towards the steps, but Emily stopped her.

'Wait, Julia. I saw some sort of light in the back yard last night. Did you see it?'

Julia turned. 'You've seen the Mullaby lights already?'

'What are the Mullaby lights?'

Julia scratched her head as if deciding what to say. 'They're white lights that sometimes dart through the woods and fields round here. Some say it's a ghost that haunts the town. Don't pay any attention to it and it will go away.'

Emily nodded.

Julia said, 'Listen, I'll be next door if you ever need me. This place takes some getting used to. Believe me, I know.'

Emily smiled and she felt her shoulders lose some tension. 'Thanks.'

It didn't take Emily long to decide to walk to Main Street and greet her grandfather. She thought it would be nice to walk home with him, establish some sort of routine. Maybe his hesitancy around her came from simply not knowing how to act. Don't wait for the world to change, her mother used to say. Change it yourself!

Emily wondered if her mother had been disappointed in her. She didn't have her mother's passion, her courage, her drive. Emily had always been in awe of her mother, but it had been hard to get close to her. Dulcie had wanted to help, but never wanted to be helped.

Emily found Main Street easily. It was a long, beautiful street, with brick mansions in grand Federal style, sitting close to the sidewalk. Across the street from the mansions was a park with a bandstand that had a lovely silver crescent-moon weather vane on top. Past the houses and the park, the street turned commercial, with touristy shops and restaurants. Emily counted seven barbecue restaurants, and she was only halfway down the street. They were obviously the source of the smell that settled over the town like a veil.

There were a lot of tourists around, mesmerised by Mullaby's old-fashioned beauty. The sidewalks were crowded. She kept looking, but she couldn't see J's Barbecue and, out of nowhere, panic set in. What if Julia had been wrong? What if Grandpa Vance wasn't here? What if she couldn't find her way back?

She started to feel light-headed. It was like being underwater, this pressure against her eyes, always followed by sparkling confetti swimming along her periphery. She'd been having anxiety attacks ever since her mother died. The business end of Main Street was lined with benches, so she sat on the nearest one. She'd broken out into a cold sweat. She wouldn't faint. She wouldn't. She leaned forward, her head down.

A pair of expensive men's loafers suddenly appeared on the sidewalk in front of her.

She slowly looked up. It was a young man about her age, wearing a white summer linen suit. He had on a red bow tie and his dark hair was curling round his starched collar. He was handsome in a well-bred kind of way, like something out of a Tennessee Williams play. She felt self-conscious in her shorts and tank top.

He didn't say anything to her at first, just stared at her. Then he finally, almost reluctantly, asked, 'Are you all right?'

She didn't understand. He was treating her as if associating with her was going to hurt. 'Fine, thanks,' she said.

'Are you sick?'

'Just light-headed.' She looked down at her feet, in ankle socks and cross-trainers, and seemed strangely detached from herself. Socks that only cover the ankle are not acceptable. Socks must be mid calf length or knee socks only. So said the Roxley School for Girls handbook. She'd been at Roxley all her school career. Her mother had helped found it, a school to empower girls.

Silence. She looked up again and the young man was gone, like smoke. Had she been hallucinating?

She felt someone take a seat beside her on the bench and she caught a nice, clean scent of cologne. The loud aluminium crack of a soda can being opened startled her, and she sat up with a jerk.

The young man in the white linen suit had returned. He was sitting beside her now, extending a can of Coke.

'Go on,' he said. 'Take it.'

Still bent over, she reached for the can, her hand shaking. She took a long drink and it was cold, sweet, and so sharp it made her tongue burn. She couldn't remember the last time something had tasted this good. In no time she had emptied the can. When was the last time she'd had something to drink? When she thought back, it was long before she'd got on the bus in Boston yesterday.

She heard a crackling of paper. The young man said, 'Don't be alarmed,' and she felt something cold on the back of her neck. Her hand went instantly to her neck, covering his hand with hers.

'What is that?' she demanded.

'It's a Creamsicle,' he said. 'It was the first thing I grabbed from the freezer in the general store.'

For the first time, she noticed that they were sitting in front of a deliberately old-fashioned place called Zim's General Store. The door was propped open and Emily could see large barrels of candy near the cash register.

'It's mostly for the tourists, so it's been a long time since I've been in there,' he said. 'How are you feeling?'

She turned back to him and realised just how close he was, close enough to see that his ivy-green irises were rimmed in black. Strangely, she thought she could actually feel him, feel a sort of energy emanating from him, like heat from a fire. He was so odd and lovely. Then she realised her hand was still on his on her neck. She moved her hand and shifted away. 'I'm fine now. Thank you.'

He took the paper-covered Creamsicle off her neck and held it out to her, but she shook her head. He unwrapped it and took a bite.

'I'm Emily Benedict,' she said, extending her hand.

He didn't turn to her, nor did he take her hand. 'I know who you are.' He took another bite of the Creamsicle.

Emily's hand fell to her lap. 'You do?'

'I'm Win Coffey. My uncle was Logan Coffey.'

She looked at him blankly. This was obviously something he thought she should know. 'I just moved here.'

'Your mother didn't tell you?'

What did her mother have to do with this? 'Tell me what?'

He finally turned to her. 'Good God. You really don't know.'

'Know what?' This was beginning to concern her.

He stared at her. 'Nothing,' he said, then stood. 'If you're not feeling well, I can call our driver to take you home.'

'I'll be fine. Thank you for the Coke.'

He hesitated. 'Sorry I refused to shake your hand. Forgive me.' He held out his hand. Confused, she took it. She was shocked by the warmth of him, stretching out to her like wandering vines. He made her feel *tangled* in him, somehow. It wasn't bad, just strange.

He released her hand and she watched him walk down the sidewalk. His skin almost glowed in the morning summer sun. He looked so alive. For a moment, she couldn't look away.

'Emily?'

She turned and saw her giant grandfather walking towards her carrying a paper bag. People were watching him in awe. She could tell he was trying not to notice, but his enormous shoulders were hunched, as if attempting to make himself smaller.

She stood and Vance came to a stop in front of her. 'What are you doing here?' he asked.

'I thought I'd meet you so we could walk home together.'

The look on his face was almost indecipherable, but if she had to guess, she'd just made him sad. She was horrified.

'I'm sorry,' she immediately said. 'I didn't mean to—'

'Was that Win Coffey you were talking to?'

'Do you know him?'

'Yes, I know him,' Vance said. 'Let's go home.'

'I'm sorry, Grandpa Vance.'

'Don't apologise, child. You did nothing wrong. Here, I brought you an egg sandwich from the restaurant.' He handed her the bag.

'Thank you.'

He nodded and put one impossibly long arm round her, then walked her home in silence.

'You'll never guess who I met today,' Win Coffey said as he stood in front of the large sitting-room window and watched a whale of grey sky swallow the pink evening light.

There was a sound of tapping heels on the white marble floor of the hall, and Win could see the reflection of his mother as she entered, followed by Win's younger sister. His mother sat beside his father on the couch, and his sister crossed the room to the settee.

Win's father, Morgan, set aside his newspaper. He took off his reading glasses and focused on Win. 'Who did you meet?'

Right on schedule, the blinds began to automatically lower in the sitting room. Win waited until the window was completely covered before turning round. The room was filled with antique furniture—Federal-style highboys and couches tastefully upholstered in blue and grey florals. 'Emily Benedict.'

Her name was instantly recognised. His father's anger was sudden and tangible. Win returned his father's stare, not backing down. It was something Morgan himself had taught him. And they had been butting heads enough lately that this was a familiar dance.

'Win, you know my brother would be alive today if it weren't for her mother,' Morgan said. 'And our secret would still be safe.'

'No one in town has ever said a word about that night,' Win said calmly.

'But they know. That puts us at their mercy.' Morgan used his reading glasses to point at Win. 'And no one should be more angry than you, the first generation to grow up with everyone knowing, with everyone looking at you differently.'

Win sighed. It was something his father could never understand. Win *wasn't* angry. If anything, he was frustrated. If everyone knew, why did no one talk about it? Why did his family still stay in at night? If people looked at Win differently, it was because of that, not because of the story of some strange affliction the Coffeys had, seen only once, over twenty years ago. Who was to say things couldn't be different now? No one had even tried.

'I don't think Emily knows,' Win said. 'I don't think her mother told her.'

'Stop,' his father warned. 'Whatever you're thinking. Stop. Emily Benedict is off limits. End of discussion.'

Win walked over to where his sister, Kylie, was sitting in the far corner of the room. She was texting someone. This was traditionally reading time in the Coffey household, at dusk, just before dinner. It was a family tradition, dating back hundreds of years, structuring their time at night when they were forced to stay inside because of their secret, even on beautiful summer nights like this one. Win didn't see the point of it now. He didn't want to sneak around like there was something wrong with him any more.

He sat beside his sister. Win was almost two years older than Kylie. She was about to turn sixteen. 'You shouldn't test him,' Kylie said. 'If I were you, I'd stay far, far away from that girl.'

'Maybe I'm just getting to know my enemy.' It was unsettling, his unexpected fascination with Emily, with her unruly blonde hair and the sharp edges of her face and body. He'd been thinking about her all day. 'I'm going out again tonight,' he said. 'Don't tell Dad. And don't follow me.'

Kylie rolled her eyes. 'Why do you keep trying? I can tell you from experience, it's not all that great.'

'What?'

'Being ordinary.'

'Julia! Will you get the door?' Stella called from downstairs that same evening, just as Julia was taking her second attempt at madeleines out of the oven. She frowned at the pan. Still no good.

Stella bellowed again, 'Julia! It's Sawyer, and I'm in the bathtub!'

Julia sighed. She'd already seen Sawyer once today. That was enough. She wiped her hands on her jeans and went downstairs. Through the sheer curtains on the front-door window, she could see a figure haloed by the porch light.

She took a deep breath and opened the door. But she smiled in relief when she saw who it was.

Emily shifted from one foot to the other. She was wearing the same clothes she'd been wearing that morning, black shorts and a black tank top, and her quirky blonde hair shone like meringue in the light by the door. 'Hi, Julia,' she said. 'Am I interrupting something?'

'No, of course not.' She waved Emily in. When Julia had told her that she'd be here if Emily ever needed her, she didn't think she'd take her up on her offer so soon. Still, Julia's heart went out to her. It was never easy being the outsider.

'You have a nice house,' Emily said. Stella's part of the house was warm and lovely, thanks to her decorator mother—golden wood floors, lively flower arrangements, and a striped silk couch.

'It belongs to my friend, Stella. I have the apartment upstairs.'

As if on cue, Stella yelled, 'Hello, Sawyer! I'm wearing nothing but steam, want to see?'

'It's not Sawyer,' Julia called to her. 'I can't believe you're waiting for him in the bathtub. Get out before you turn into a prune.' Emily's brows rose and Julia said, 'That's Stella. Don't ask. Come on, I'll show you my part of the house.' She started up the stairs and motioned Emily to follow.

At the top of the staircase, Julia had to step back in the narrow hallway to let Emily enter, then she reached round her to close the door.

'Just let me turn off the stove,' she said as she walked to the tiny kitchen. There was a mood of magic to the room. Swirls of sugar and flour still lingered in the air like kite tails. And then there was the smell—the smell of hope, the kind of smell that brought people home. Tonight it was browning butter and lemon zest.

The window in the room was wide open, because that was the way Julia always baked. Bottling up the smell made no sense. The message needed some way out.

'What are you making?' Emily asked.

'I experiment with recipes here before I make them for the restaurant. My madeleines aren't up to snuff yet.' Julia picked one up from her first batch. 'See? Madeleines should have a hump. This is too flat.' She placed the small cake in Emily's palm. 'Try it.'

Emily took a bite and smiled. She covered her lips with her hand and said, her mouth full, 'You're a really good cook.'

'I've had a lot of practice. I've been baking since I was sixteen.'

'It must be nice to have such a gift.'

Julia shrugged. 'I can't take credit for it. Someone else gave it to me.' Sometimes she resented the fact that she never would have found this skill on her own, that she had only discovered what she was truly good at because of someone else. Emily looked as if she was going to ask what Julia meant, so Julia quickly said, 'How was your first full day here?'

One more bite and Emily had finished the madeleine. She took a moment to chew and swallow, then said, 'I guess I'm confused.'

Julia leaned a hip against the ancient refrigerator. 'About what?'

'About why my mom left. About why she didn't stay in touch with people here. Did she have friends?'

Julia paused with surprise. Emily had a lot to learn about the havoc her mother had wreaked. But Julia certainly wasn't going to be the one who told her. 'Like I said, I didn't know her well,' Julia said carefully. 'We weren't in the same social group in school. Have you talked to your grandfather? He's the one you should ask.'

'No.' Emily tucked back some of her short, flyaway hair. Her whole demeanour was so achingly sincere. 'He's been hiding in his room all day. Did he and my mom not get along? Do you think that's why she never came back?'

'No, I don't think that's it. Everyone gets along with Vance. Come and sit down.' Julia led Emily out of the kitchen and into the living room. This room contained the only nice thing in her apartment—a royal-blue love seat. There was also a television and a bookcase full of pots and pans—overflow from the kitchen. When they sat down, Julia said, 'Your mother was the most beautiful, popular girl in school. Perfect clothes. Perfect hair. Confident. She was in a group that called themselves Sassafras, made up of girls in school whose families had money. I wasn't one of them.'

Emily looked astonished. 'My mom was popular? Grandpa Vance had money?'

There was a knock at her door. 'Excuse me,' Julia said as she got up. Her whole body gave a start when she opened the door, felt a gust of air that smelled like freshly cut grass, and saw Sawyer.

'I brought pizza,' he said with a smile. 'Come down.'

Something was definitely afoot. A year and a half of Thursday-night get-togethers, and Sawyer had never asked her to have pizza with him and Stella before. 'Thanks, but I can't.'

He tilted his head at her. 'If I didn't know better, I'd think you were embarrassed.'

That got her. 'Embarrassed? By what?'

'By the fact that I now know you've been baking cakes for me.'

She snorted. 'I never said I baked them for you. I said I baked them because of you.'

'So you did say it,' he said.

Yes, she'd said it. The one night they'd had together, they'd lain side by side on the high-school football field, staring up at a starry night, and he'd told her a story of how his mother used to bake cakes on summer afternoons and, no matter where he'd been, it had sent him to her, a beacon of powdered sugar flowing like pollen in the wind. He'd sensed it, he'd said. He'd seen it.

Cakes had the power to call. She'd learned that from him.

'Actually, what I think I said was I baked cakes because of people like you,' she finally said. 'You're my target customer.'

He looked as if he didn't believe her. 'That's a nice save.'

'Thank you.'

His eyes went over her shoulder. He'd never been in her apartment before, and she wasn't going to ask him in now. Sawyer had grown up with money, and she hadn't. She didn't want him to see this. 'It smells good up here,' he said. 'I want to live in your kitchen.'

'There's not enough room. And I only bake here on Thursdays.'

'I know. Why do you think I always come by on Thursdays?'

She'd never even suspected. He was that good. 'I can't come down because I have company. You and Stella have fun.' She closed the door and leaned against it, letting out a deep breath.

She went back to the living room. 'Sorry about that.'

'I can come back later if you're busy,' Emily said.

'Don't be silly.'

'So, everyone must have liked my mom, if she was so popular.'

Julia hesitated. But before she could speak, there was another knock at the door. 'Excuse me again.'

'Who do you have up here?' Stella demanded when Julia opened the door. Stella had a wide, exotic face, with almond-shaped eyes. She was wearing a kimono-style robe and her dark hair was pulled up into a bun. 'Sawyer said you had company. Are you seeing someone? Why didn't you tell me? Who is it?'

'It's none of your business,' Julia said, because she knew it would drive Stella crazy. She still hadn't forgiven her for telling Sawyer about the cakes.

She closed the door, but as soon as she walked back into the living room, the knocking started again. Incessantly.

'She's not going to stop until she meets you,' Julia said to Emily. 'Do you mind?'

Emily seemed game, and followed her into the hallway.

As soon as Julia opened the door again, Stella said, 'I'm not leaving until . . .' She stopped when Julia opened the door further, revealing Emily standing beside her.

'This is Vance Shelby's granddaughter,' Julia said. 'Emily, this is Stella Ferris.'

Stella seemed incapable of speech.

'Emily came by wanting to know what her mother was like when she lived here.'

Stella recovered quickly. 'Well, it's so lovely to meet you, Emily! Sawyer and I were friends with your mother. Come downstairs and have pizza with us. I'll pull out my yearbooks.'

When Stella stepped to the side, Emily didn't hesitate and bounded down the stairs.

Before Stella could follow, Julia grabbed the sleeve of her robe. 'Don't talk about what her mother did.'

Stella looked insulted. 'I'm not an ogre.'

Emily waited eagerly for them to come down. Once they did, Stella led the way to her kitchen. Sawyer had his back to them and was staring out of the kitchen window. He turned when he heard them enter. His brows shot up when he saw Emily.

'Hello, who is this very lovely young lady?' There was something inherent in Stella's and Sawyer's manners around strangers, something that always gave away their breeding.

'This is who Julia was entertaining, Sawyer, so you can stop pouting. This is Emily, Dulcie Shelby's daughter,' Stella said.

Sawyer didn't miss a beat. 'A pleasure.' Sawyer held out his hand and Emily shook it. She actually giggled, and Emily didn't strike Julia as a giggler. 'Let's eat the pizza while it's hot. Julia?' Sawyer pulled out a chair for her, not giving her much of a choice.

Stella set out drinks and napkins, then they unceremoniously ate the vegetarian pizza out of the box. Julia tried to eat a slice quickly so she could leave. Sawyer was relaxed, smiling at her as if he knew what she was doing. Stella was as comfortable wearing a robe at the dinner table as she would have been in a Dior suit. And Emily was watching the three of them as if they were unopened presents.

'So, you two knew my mom?' Emily finally asked.

'Dulcie and I were in a close-knit group of friends,' Stella said.

'Sassafras?' Emily said.

'Right. Sawyer dated a girl named Holly who was in the group, so he was one of our honorary boys.'

'You weren't friends with Julia?'

'I wasn't friends with anyone back then,' Julia said.

Emily turned to her, curious. 'Why not?'

'Being a teenager is tough. We all know that. Sassafras made it look easy. I looked like the truth.'

'What did Sassafras do?' Emily asked. 'Community service? Fundraising?'

Stella laughed. 'We weren't that kind of group. Let me get the yearbooks.' She left the kitchen, and swished back in minutes. 'Here we are.' She set a green and silver book on the table in front of Emily, then opened it. 'That's Sassafras, with your mother in the middle. We held court on the front steps of the school every morning before classes. There's your mother at homecoming. There she is as our prom queen. There's Sawyer on the soccer team.' Stella turned the next page. 'And there's Julia.'

It was a photo of her eating lunch by herself on the top row of the bleachers on the football field. That was Julia's domain. Before school, at lunch, sometimes even at night, that was her safe place.

'Look how long your hair was! And it was all pink!' Emily said, then looked closer. 'Are you wearing black lipstick?'

'Yes.'

'No one knew what to think of Julia back then,' Stella said.

Julia smiled and shook her head. 'I was harmless.'

'To other people, maybe,' Sawyer murmured, and Julia automatically pulled her long sleeves further down her arms.

'Julia's father sent her to boarding school after our sophomore year,' Stella told Emily. 'She didn't come back for a long time. And when she did, no one recognised her.'

'I did,' Sawyer said.

Stella rolled her eyes. 'Of course you did.'

Emily was poring over the yearbook now, stopping every time she came across a photo of her mother. 'Look!' she said. 'Mom is wearing her charm bracelet! This one!' Emily held up her wrist.

Julia found herself staring at Emily's profile, a familiar yearning in her heart. Without thinking, she reached over and pushed some of Emily's hair out of her eyes. Emily didn't seem to notice.

'Who is this with my mom?' Emily asked, pointing to an elegant dark-haired boy in a suit and bow tie.

'That's Logan Coffey,' Julia said.

'That's who he was talking about.' Emily smiled. 'I met a boy named Win Coffey today. He mentioned that his uncle was Logan Coffey. He seemed surprised that I didn't know who he was.'

Oh, hell, Julia thought. *That can't be good.*

'Was Logan Coffey her boyfriend?' Emily asked.

'We all wondered. He and Dulcie denied it,' Julia said cautiously. 'Basically, he was just a shy boy your mother tried to coax out of his shell.'

'Does he still live here?'

There was a conspicuous silence. No one wanted to tell her. Julia finally said, 'Logan Coffey died a long time ago, sweetheart.'

'Oh.' As if sensing the change in atmosphere, Emily reluctantly closed the yearbook. 'I guess I should get back home. Thank you for letting me look through the book.'

Stella waved her hand. 'Take it with you. That was twenty pounds ago. I don't need to be reminded.'

'Really? Thank you!' When Emily stood, so did Julia. Julia walked her to the door and said good night, watching until Emily evaporated into the darkness under the canopy of trees next door.

When Julia walked back in, Stella was standing there. 'OK, what's going on? Why are you acting that way around her?'

'I'm not acting any way around her.' Julia frowned. 'Why are you looking at me like that?'

'I'm just surprised, that's all. You're the least maternal person on the planet.' Stella laughed, but stopped when she saw the look on Julia's face. Julia had got used to people saying that to her, but it didn't make it any easier to hear. It was the price you paid when you were thirty-six and had no apparent interest in sharing your life with anyone. 'Oh, I didn't mean it in a bad way.' And Julia knew Stella didn't. Neither did Julia's friends in Baltimore when they said, *You love your independence too much.* Or, *You couldn't be a mom because you'd be cooler than your teenager.* 'Let's go out on the back porch and have wine.'

'No, thanks.'

'Julia . . .'

'I know you have something sweet in here,' Sawyer called from the kitchen, followed by the banging of cabinet doors.

Stella rolled her eyes. 'That man can find my stash of Hershey's Miniatures no matter where I hide them.'

'Let him have them before he tries to raid my kitchen,' Julia said as she headed for the staircase. 'I have work to do.'

Emily sat on her balcony when she got home, the yearbook on her lap. Earlier that day, she'd gone through the closet and all the drawers in her bedroom, in search of . . . something. Some clue to her mother's time here. But there were no photos, no old letters. That's why Emily had gone over to Julia's. She'd felt awkward about it at first, but now she was glad she'd done it. The yearbook was a treasure, if a little confusing. How could her mother have been prom queen?

Emily remembered that her mother never let her go to the mall. She always said that fashion should never be a factor in determining someone's self-worth. So of course Roxley School had uniforms. Yet, here in the yearbook, her mother was in the trendiest clothes of the time. Maybe she'd been embarrassed by who she'd been as a youth. Maybe she thought her grassroots reputation might have been hurt by her tiara-laden past.

Still, that seemed like such a peculiar reason never to return.

Sitting at the old patio table she'd cleared of leaves, she leaned back. The stars looked like Christmas lights. She took a breath of the sweet evening heat, and began to get sleepy. She only meant to close her eyes for a moment. But she dozed off almost immediately.

When she woke up, it was still dark. She blinked a few times, trying to figure out what time it was. The yearbook had fallen from her lap to the leaves on the balcony floor. Her body stiff, she leaned down to retrieve it. When she sat up again, her skin prickled.

The light was back! The light Julia said people thought was a ghost. Frozen, she watched it in the woodline beyond the old gazebo in Grandpa Vance's back yard. It didn't disappear like it had last night. It lingered instead, darting from tree to tree.

Was it . . . was it watching her?

She made herself stand and slowly walk into her room. She didn't know what came over her, but suddenly she took off in a run, her bare feet slapping against the floors. She slowed as she went down the stairs and past Grandpa Vance's room, but then she took off again. After fumbling with the locked kitchen door, she finally opened it and ran out.

The light was still there! She ran after it, into the wooded area behind the gazebo. The light quickly retreated and she heard footsteps in the leaves. Footsteps?

Ghosts don't have footsteps.

After about five minutes of chasing it through the gloomy, moonlit woods, it occurred to her that she had no idea where she was going.

When the light suddenly disappeared, she felt the first twinge of real worry. What was she doing? But a few more steps and she unexpectedly broke through the trees. She stood there for a moment, out of breath and painfully aware that she was barefoot. She lifted her foot and saw she'd cut her heel.

Out of the quiet came the distinct sound of a door being closed.

She looked round and realised she was on the residential end of Main Street, standing in the middle of the park facing the old brick mansions. The woods behind Grandpa Vance's house must zigzag through other neighbourhoods in a crazy labyrinth, ending here, by the bandstand with the crescent-moon weather vane. She looked up and down the street, then into the woods. Surely she saw the light end here?

She limped back home the long way, taking the sidewalks. Her mind was whirling. She couldn't believe she'd just run through the woods in the middle of the night, chasing a so-called ghost.

When she reached Grandpa Vance's house, she saw that the back porch light was now on. Obviously, Grandpa Vance had heard her run out and was waiting for her. How was she going to explain this? She hobbled up to the kitchen porch and almost tripped over something as she approached the door. She bent and picked up a box of Band-Aids.

A crunching of leaves invaded the quiet, and she turned with a gasp to see the white light disappearing back into the woods.

And she would also soon discover that Grandpa Vance had slept through everything.

Chapter 3

FROM HIS BEDROOM WINDOW the next morning, Win watched Vance Shelby walk down the sidewalk towards the business end of Main Street. He looked like a praying mantis, as if biologically suited to grab things, to hide things, to shield. He wouldn't like Win's interest in Emily. It was unfortunate, but it couldn't be avoided.

'Win!' his father called from downstairs. 'It's light. Let's go.'

Win left his room and walked down the marble staircase to where his father was waiting in the hall. He didn't mind these outings with his father. Morgan Coffey liked to get out bright and early to greet shop owners and tourists. From the time Win was about five, Morgan took him on these PR treks, to groom him, Win guessed. They went to a different restaurant every morning, where Morgan chatted up everyone. Win liked to get out of the house at first light.

'Ready?' Morgan asked when Win met him by the front door.

'If I said no?' Win said as his father opened the door.

Morgan inspected Win, from his red bow tie to his loafers. 'You look ready.'

'Then I suppose I am.'

Morgan reined in his anger. 'Don't get smart with me,' he said.

And Win had to concede that it really was too early in the morning for such antagonism.

They walked down the sidewalk. Vance had disappeared—no easy feat for a giant. This morning, Morgan had decided to go to Welchel's Diner. When they entered, he led Win to a table by the door. Morgan liked to greet people as they came in. He liked to zero in on the tourists first. For someone so seemingly content with his cloistered life, Morgan Coffey was genuinely thrilled to meet new people. It gave Win hope that, in the end, his father would understand why Win was going to go through with his plans.

Win didn't know how long they'd been there when he saw her.

Emily walked past the diner, staring straight ahead, the sunlight at her back. Her arms and legs were long. She didn't favour her grandfather in any way but this one. But where Vance looked as if he'd grown too long, Emily looked . . . perfect.

Win turned to see if his father had noticed. He hadn't. In fact, Morgan had left the table without Win even being aware. He was across the room now, shaking hands with someone. Win pushed his chair back and quietly slipped out of the diner.

He followed Emily at a distance, noticing she had on flip-flops that morning, and a Band-Aid on her heel. He stopped when she reached the bench outside J's Barbecue. She didn't go in. She was waiting. Waiting for her grandfather to come out. The gesture was both charming and uncomfortably lonely.

He was only two or three storefronts away from her, close enough for Emily to look up when Inez and Harriet Jones approached him from behind and said in unison, 'Hello, Win!'

He returned Emily's stare before reluctantly turning to Inez and

Harriet. They were spinster sisters who lived next door to the Coffey mansion on Main Street. The sisters went everywhere together.

'Hello, Miss Jones.' Win nodded to Inez. 'Miss Jones.' He nodded to Harriet.

'We saw you staring at that pretty thing there,' Inez said, though Win wished she hadn't. Emily could hear every word.

Harriet clutched her sister's arm. 'Do you know who that is?'

'Could it be?' Inez said, clutching her back.

'Yes, it is!' Harriet answered.

'What brings you two out so early this morning?' Win asked, trying to change the subject.

Inez tsked. 'Oh, she does look like her mother, doesn't she?'

'She does.' Harriet shook her head. 'She's never going to fit in.'

'And how is her grandfather going to take care of her? He can barely take care of himself.'

'I don't know, sister,' Harriet said. 'I don't know.'

'Can I escort you home?' Win interrupted. 'I'm headed that way.' He held out his arm, trying to herd them away.

Inez wagged her finger at him. 'Don't turn into your uncle, Win. Don't get fooled by a pretty face like he did. What a tragedy.'

The sisters turned and left, walking towards home, one arm each looped into the handles of a single handbag.

Win turned towards Emily. She looked unsettled and he didn't blame her. He walked up to her, trying to seem casual. 'Hello again.'

She didn't answer. Her eyes went to the Jones sisters.

Win hated that they had been so indelicate. 'Where is your grandfather? I saw him earlier,' he said.

'Inside,' she said. 'I'm waiting for him.'

'Instead of eating with him?'

'I don't know if he actually wants . . . I just thought I'd wait.' She gave him a once-over that tried to be subtle, but wasn't. 'Are you always up and dressed like that this early?'

'It's sort of a tradition.' He indicated the bench. 'May I?'

She nodded. 'Where do you come from?' she asked as he sat.

He crossed his legs, trying not to seem too eager, too suspicious. Getting into someone's good graces was second nature to him, but he was nervous. 'Here. I'm from here.'

She hesitated, as if he'd answered an entirely different question. 'No, I meant yesterday and today. Where did you just come from?'

He laughed. 'Oh. Breakfast with my father. Every morning.'

'Does everyone here come to Main Street for breakfast?'

'Not everyone. How is your foot?' he asked. He stared into her true blue eyes. She wasn't what he'd expected. Not at all.

'My foot?'

'It looks like you scratched your heel.'

She turned her right foot slightly to see the bandaged cut. 'Oh. I cut it running barefoot through the woods.'

'You should put on shoes next time.' She looked back up to see that he was smiling.

She narrowed her eyes. 'Thank you. I plan to. Who were those ladies you were talking to?' she asked.

'Inez and Harriet Jones. They're my next-door neighbours.'

'They knew who I was,' she said. 'They knew my mother. It sounded like they didn't like her.'

He picked at imaginary dust on his sleeve. His heart was knocking against his chest. 'If you want me to tell you the story, I will.' *God, what was he going to say?* 'I'm not sure I should be the one, though. Your mother should have told you. At the very least, your grandfather should have said something by now.'

'About what? They mentioned your uncle. Is this about him?'

'Yes. We have history, you and I.'

She tilted her head curiously. 'That's a strange thing to say.'

'Just wait. It gets stranger.' A flashy older woman in heels and shorts clicked by them and walked to the door of J's Barbecue. That's when Win saw that Vance Shelby was inside, watching them. It was disconcerting to have someone that large give him such a forceful look. Emily hadn't noticed, so she seemed surprised when he suddenly stood and said, 'I think I should go.'

'What? No, wait, tell me about my mother and your uncle.'

'Next time I see you, I will. Goodbye, Emily,' he said as he walked away. No going back now.

Julia had the day's cakes baked and was writing on the chalkboard before there were even four customers in the restaurant. Vance Shelby had arrived and was sitting by himself, waiting for the rest of the old men in his breakfast group. He was drinking his coffee from his saucer instead of his cup, because the lip of the saucer was larger and his giant hand could more easily manage it. Julia was tempted to go and talk to him about Emily. But then she thought better of it. It wasn't any of her business.

Vance was watching something outside, a frown on his face.

Julia had just finished writing the names of the day's specials on the board—Milky Way cake, butter pecan cake, cigar-rolled lemon cookies and vanilla chai macaroons—when the bell over the door rang. Beverly Dale, Julia's former stepmother, walked in.

At least it wasn't Sawyer. But it was almost as bad.

'Julia!' Beverly said as she teetered up to the counter in her white kitten heels. 'I haven't seen you in a month of Sundays. I always try to get here early enough, but I'm not a morning person. Last night I said to myself, "Beverly, you're going to get to the restaurant early enough to see Julia." And here I am!'

'Congratulations,' Julia said, glad that the counter was between them and Beverly couldn't hug her. Beverly could choke an elephant with the scent of her Jean Naté perfume.

'I see you're still wearing those long sleeves,' Beverly said, shaking her head. 'Bless your heart. I can't imagine you're comfortable, especially in this summertime heat.'

'It's cotton. It's not so bad,' she said.

'I understand. Scars aren't pretty on a woman.' Beverly leaned in and whispered, 'I have a tiny scar here on my forehead. That's why I have my hairstylist, Yvonne, fix this curl just so.'

Julia smiled and nodded, waiting for Beverly to get to what she was really there to talk about.

Julia had been twelve the first time her father had brought Beverly home. He'd told Julia that he thought she needed another female around to talk to about girl things—as if he'd brought Beverly into their lives for her sake. Beverly had been attentive to Julia at first. Julia had been a baby when her mother died, so she'd begun to think having Beverly around would be nice. But then Beverly and Julia's father had got married, and Julia felt the power shift. Julia's father's attention had been drawn to the person who'd demanded it the most. And that person had been Beverly. No amount of temper tantrums, and, later, pink hair or cutting, could ever have competed with Beverly, sexy Beverly with her puff of blonde hair, the low V of her shirts, and the high heels she wore even with shorts.

Beverly and her father had stayed together until four years ago. When her father told her about the divorce during Julia's annual Christmas call to him, he'd said in his kind, simple way, 'Beverly is a vibrant woman. She needed more than I could give her.'

What she needed, Julia later found out, was a man with cash. Julia's father never had a lot of money, but he'd done very well for a man with only an eighth-grade education. He'd owned his own home and business by the time he was thirty. And he'd been an excellent money manager, which was why Julia had been so shocked when she'd discovered the extent of his debt after his death. She could only assume Beverly had spent her way through what he had, and when there was nothing left, she'd left him for Bud Dale, who had just opened his second muffler shop in town.

Julia remembered seeing Beverly for the first time in years at her father's funeral. 'I'm sorry about your daddy,' she'd said. 'Let me know if there's any money left. Some of it should go to me, don't you think? We had twenty beautiful years together.'

When Julia sold her father's house and took what little was left after paying off the mortgage and applied it to his restaurant mortgage, Beverly had been livid. Some of that money could have gone to her, she'd insisted. But once she realised what Julia was doing, working to get the restaurant mortgage paid off in order to sell it for a profit, she periodically accosted Julia to remind her that some of the money should go to her.

'Is it always this slow at this hour?' Beverly asked.

'The place will fill up soon,' Julia assured her. 'I was just on my way out, Beverly. What can I do for you?'

'Oh, stop with that. You don't have anywhere to go. You never do anything but work and go home. You're like your daddy.'

Julia tried to hold her smile. At one point in her life, she would have welcomed the comparison. Now, she wanted to scream, No! I've done so much more!

'I know it's only a few more months until you're going to sell this place. Rumour has it that Charlotte is interested in buying it. I just wanted to tell you that I don't think that's a good idea.'

'Oh?' Charlotte was the day manager of the restaurant, and the perfect person to sell it to. She not only knew the business, she cared about it. And that meant something to Julia.

'I think you might give the restaurant to her for less than you should, just because she's worked here a long time. But the whole point is to get as much money as possible for it.'

'Thank you for your input, Beverly.'

'I'll see you soon,' Beverly said. 'We can go over arrangements. Make it all nice and official, OK?'

Julia didn't say a word, but she had absolutely no intention of giving

Beverly any money from the sale of the restaurant. She watched Beverly leave. Then she headed for the door.

Only to have it open, and there was Sawyer.

Julia rubbed her forehead. How could a day be this bad so early?

Sawyer was bright and attentive, even at this hour. He smiled. 'Julia, you look lovely. Doesn't she, Granddad?' Sawyer asked the elderly gentleman he was helping through the door.

The old man looked up and smiled. He had deep blue eyes like Sawyer. Alexander men were a sight to behold. 'You do look lovely, Julia. That pink streak in your hair adds pizzazz.'

Julia smiled. 'Thank you, Mr Alexander. Enjoy your breakfast.'

'Wait for me, Julia,' Sawyer said. 'I want to talk to you.'

'Sorry,' she said, and slipped out of the door. 'Gotta go.'

She walked down the sidewalk towards home. Julia knew she could have driven to work, but gas was a luxury. Sometimes her walks home reminded her of walking to high school because her father couldn't afford to buy her a car. With envy, she used to watch members of Sassafras in their BMWs and Corvettes.

It was all going to be worth it, this sacrifice. When she got back to Baltimore, she would pick up where she'd left off. She'd find the perfect spot for her bakery. She would bake with all the windows open and make nothing but purple cookies if she wanted to. *Blue-Eyed Girl Bakery.* That was going to be the name. That Julia's eyes were brown didn't matter. It wasn't about her, anyway.

'Julia!' Sawyer called. He jogged up and fell into step with her.

She cut her eyes at him. 'Did you actually run after me?'

He looked indignant. 'I wouldn't have had to if you had waited.'

'What do you want?'

'I told you. I want to talk to you.'

'So talk,' she said.

'Not like this.' His hand wrapped round her arm and made her stop. 'I've kept my distance since you've been back, because I thought that's what you wanted. When I heard you were moving back to Mullaby, I had . . . hope. But the moment I saw you, and you gave me a look that could kill, I knew it was still too soon.'

'I haven't moved back,' she said, wriggling her arm free.

'But I've been doing us both a disservice,' he continued, as if she hadn't spoken. 'This has gone on too long. I want to talk about it, Julia. I have some things to tell you.'

'Talk about what?' she asked.

He was silent.

She tried to laugh it off. 'Does this have something to do with thinking I've been baking cakes because of you?'

'I don't know. You tell me.'

They stared at each other before she said, 'I have nothing to say to you. And I doubt you have anything to say that I want to hear.'

Undeterred, he said, 'Have dinner with me tomorrow.'

'I have plans on Saturday,' she said.

'Oh?' He rocked back on his heels with surprise. This was a man who wasn't used to being turned down. 'With whom?'

'I was thinking of taking Emily to the lake,' she said, off the top of her head.

'You're showing a remarkable amount of interest in this girl.'

'Does it surprise you that much, Sawyer?' she shot at him.

She could tell that hurt him. He hesitated before asking quietly, 'Are you ever going to forgive me?'

'I forgave you a long time ago,' she said as she turned and walked away. 'That doesn't mean I've forgotten.'

His voice carried after her. 'Neither have I, Julia.'

The weight of Julia's unhappiness took her breath sometimes when she was sixteen. It had been building for years: adolescence, her father remarrying, her unrequited love for the cutest boy in school. Still, until high school, she'd always had friends. She'd always been a good student. But then a gradual depression settled over her. By the time her sophomore year rolled round, she'd given up on trying to compete with her stepmother, Beverly. Her pink hair and black make-up were attempts to fight the overwhelming sense that she was disappearing. Her friends started avoiding her as her appearance changed and she became more sullen, but she didn't care. She would gladly lose them if it meant her father would look at her.

It didn't work.

Sometimes she would hear Beverly tell her father not to pay her any attention, that it was just a phase, that she would grow out of it. And, of course, he did exactly as Beverly suggested.

Then the cutting started.

Her unhappiness and self-loathing got the better of her one day when she was in history class. Mr Horne was writing on the board and Julia was sitting at the back of the room, Dulcie Shelby a few seats in front of her. Julia looked up to see Dulcie whisper to one of her friends, then take something out of her bag. Seconds later, a canister of flea powder rolled down the aisle and stopped at Julia's feet.

Dulcie and her friends laughed and Mr Horne turned round.

He demanded to know what was so funny, but no one said a word. Julia kept her eyes down, staring at the canister.

Mr Horne finally turned back round, and as soon as he did, Julia took the sharpened pencil she was holding and dragged it heavily across her forearm. She watched the pebbles of blood form on her skin with a weird sense of satisfaction, of release.

At first it was random, using whatever she had to hand, but it soon became more deliberate and she started using razor blades. Every time she cut herself, it was intense and dramatic, like being jerked from the gaping maw of nothingness and back into life. It not only made her feel, it made her feel good. It wasn't long before her forearms were covered in scabbed-over cuts, and she wore long-sleeved shirts even on the warmest days.

She'd been cutting her arms for months before Julia's father and stepmother found out. It was Beverly who first saw the marks. Julia had just stepped out of the shower one morning and had wrapped a towel round herself, when her stepmother tapped on the door and waltzed in, saying, 'Don't mind me. I'm just getting my tweezers—'

She stopped short when she saw Julia's bare arms.

When Julia's father got home from work that evening, he came into her bedroom. His face was pinched and worried and he approached her cautiously. He wanted to know what was wrong, and Julia resented the question. How could he not know?

Her sophomore year ended not long after, and her father and Beverly never let her out of their sight that summer. Instead of feeling as if she'd got what she wanted, she hated that they were trying to stop her from doing the one thing that made her feel better.

She actually started looking forward to the school year so she could get away from them. And of course, the new school year meant she would get to see Sawyer. Beautiful Sawyer. But a few days before the start of school at Mullaby High, Julia's father told her that he was sending her to boarding school. It was a special school, he said. For troubled teens. They were supposed to drive to Baltimore to the school the next day. He'd given her only one day's notice. He'd been planning this behind her back all summer!

That night, she had crawled out of the laundry-room window and run away. If her father didn't want her around, fine. But she wasn't going to some stupid school. The problem was, she had no idea where to go. She ended up on her favourite perch on the school bleachers.

She'd been there a few hours when Sawyer showed up. It was after midnight, but suddenly there he was, walking round the track. The moon was out and he was wearing white shorts and a white polo shirt, so she could see him clearly from her seat.

She didn't move, so she didn't know what made him look up. But he did, and her breath caught, as it did every time he looked at her in school. They stared at each other for a long moment. Then he crossed the track and walked up the bleachers towards her.

Sawyer had never approached her before, but he had always watched her at school. A lot of people watched her, so that in itself wasn't unusual. But he was always so deliberate about it. She'd often wondered if that was why she had these strange feelings for him, because she thought he really saw her.

He came to a stop in front of her. 'Do you mind if I sit?'

She shrugged.

He sat, but didn't say anything more for a while. 'Do you come out here at night a lot?' he finally asked.

'No.'

'I didn't think so. I've walked round this track at night all summer, and I've never seen you, like I do during the school year.' She wondered why he walked the track at night. She was too nervous to ask. 'Are you ready for school to start?'

She suddenly stood. Being this close to him made her heart feel lighter. He made her whole world seem lighter. But it was all a horrible illusion. 'I've got to go.'

'Where are you going?' he asked as she clomped down the bleachers in her heavy black boots.

'I don't know.'

'I'll walk you,' he said as he stood and followed her.

'No.'

'I'm not going to let you walk alone at this time of night.'

She stepped off the last bleacher and walked onto the football field. She looked over her shoulder. 'Stop following me.'

'I'm not letting you walk alone.'

That made her stop and turn to him. 'What is the matter with you? Stop being so . . . so . . .'

'What?'

'*Nice to me.*' She lowered herself to the ground and sat cross-legged.

'I'm sitting here until you go away.' This didn't exactly have the effect she wanted. 'Don't sit beside me. Don't . . .' She sighed when Sawyer sat beside her, right on the fifty-yard line.

'What is the matter with you?' he asked.

'My dad is sending me away to boarding school tomorrow.'

'You're leaving?' he asked incredulously.

She nodded.

Finally he said, 'Can I tell you something?'

'Not unless it's goodbye.'

'Stop being such a smart-ass.' That made her swing her head round. It was surprising to hear someone willing to call her on her attitude. 'This past year, sometimes I would get up in the mornings and actually look forward to going to school because I knew I would see you. I would wonder what you were going to wear. I loved lunch because I could sit in the cafeteria and look out of the window and see you up there on the bleachers. I've been looking for you all summer. Where have you been?'

Her mouth gaped. He had a girlfriend named Holly who, despite being in Dulcie Shelby's group, Sassafras, was mostly nice. And they'd been going together forever. 'What is wrong with you?' Julia said. 'You and Holly belong together. You match.'

'I'm just saying I'm sorry I never talked to you. I've always wanted to. I've always wanted . . .' His eyes went to her lips, and she was suddenly very aware of how close they were.

She turned away. 'Go away, Sawyer. Go back to your perfect life.' She felt tears come to her eyes, and she wiped them with her hands. They came away streaked with her black eyeliner. The tears kept coming and she kept wiping her face, knowing she was making it worse. Why didn't Sawyer just leave her to her misery?

Sawyer very calmly took off his white polo shirt and handed it to her. 'Go on. Use it.'

She reluctantly took it and scrubbed her face with the shirt. When she finally stopped crying, she looked at the shirt in her hands. She balled it up, embarrassed. She'd ruined it. 'I'm sorry.'

'I don't care about the shirt. Are you going to be OK?'

'I don't know.' Her eyes started watering again. 'I don't want to go away. But my dad doesn't want me any more. He has Beverly.'

'I'm sure that's not true,' Sawyer said. He reached over to her and hesitantly pushed some of her crisp pink hair behind her ear. 'I forgot what you looked like without make-up.'

'I disappear.'

'No. You're beautiful.'

She didn't believe him. 'Go to hell, Sawyer.'

'You can believe whatever you want. But I don't lie.'

'Of course you don't. You're perfect.' She paused, then turned to him. 'You think I'm beautiful?'

'I've always thought that.'

'What about these?' she said, drawing up the sleeves of the button-down she was wearing. She showed him the lines on her arms. 'Do you think these are beautiful?'

Sawyer actually recoiled. 'Did you do that to yourself?'

She pulled the sleeves down. 'Yes.'

She expected him to leave her then, but he didn't. They sat in silence for a long time. Finally she got tired and leaned back so that she was stretched out on the ground. He lowered himself beside her.

The sky was incredible that night, the moon nearly full and the stars littering the sky like tossed stones. She'd never been away from Mullaby before. Would the sky look like this in Baltimore?

When Sawyer's stomach growled, he laughed. 'I haven't had anything to eat since the cake I had for lunch,' he said sheepishly.

'You had cake for lunch?'

'I'd have cake all the time if I could. You know how some people have a sweet tooth? Well, I have a sweet sense. When I was a little boy, I could be playing across town and know exactly when my mother took a cake out of the oven. I could literally see the scent, how it floated through the air. All I had to do was follow it home.'

It was such a surprising thing to admit. She turned and saw that he was staring at her again. 'You're charmed,' she said. 'But you probably know that already.' She stared at him for a moment, gorgeous in the moonlight. 'Yes, you know what power you have.'

'Do I have a power over you?'

Did he honestly think she was immune? 'Of course you do.'

He lifted up on one elbow and looked at her. 'Can I kiss you?'

She didn't hesitate. 'Yes.'

She was confused when he carefully pushed her long-sleeved shirt off her shoulders. Even though she was wearing a tank top underneath, her arms were exposed. She tried to cover them again, but then he did the most extraordinary thing. He kissed her arms.

And she was done for.

He not only saw her, he accepted her. He wanted her.

They made love that night, and stayed on the field until dawn. He walked her home and they made promises to stay in touch, promises, it turned out, only one of them meant to keep. She left for Collier Reformatory in Maryland thinking she might be able to get through this, because she now had Sawyer to come home to.

Looking back, she found that she could forgive him because it had been her fault for putting her happiness in the hands of someone else. It had been so easy to do, though. He'd made her feel true happiness that night. How could she not have succumbed to it?

But sometimes she wondered if she'd lost true happiness that night, as well. And she'd been looking for it ever since.

Chapter 4

THAT AFTERNOON, with nothing better to do, Emily started cleaning. She tackled her room first, then went to the other rooms, opening blinds and shedding light into corners that looked as if they hadn't seen the sun in years. It was an adventure at first—learning the story of the house. But she soon realised the story was a sad one. There was a room that had obviously once been a little boy's room. There were blue sailboats on the wallpaper and safety rails still on the bed. Then there was a room with a bed that was twice as long as a normal one. There was a vanity table in the room, too, a feminine touch. Grandpa Vance had shared this room with his wife. Where was his wife? Where were all the people who had once lived here?

Her mother had told her nothing. Nothing. Why?

She went to the balcony outside her room for some fresh air. She kicked at the leaves, and decided to sweep them away. She swept until she had a large pile pushed against the balustrade. She gathered some leaves in her arms, then tossed them over the side. It wasn't until they hit the head of the person standing on the front porch steps that she had any idea someone was there.

'Julia!' she called. 'Hi!'

Julia smiled up at her, leaves in her hair. 'Bored, are we?'

'I'm so glad you're here! I have something to tell you.'

She ran downstairs and out of the front door. Julia was standing on the porch with two large brown paper bags in her arms.

'I saw the light again last night!' Emily said excitedly. 'It's not a ghost, Julia. I chased it, and it had footsteps.'

Julia looked dismayed. 'You chased it?'

'Yes.'

'Emily, please don't do that,' she said gently. 'The Mullaby lights are harmless.'

Before Emily could ask why Julia didn't think this was a huge discovery, the screen door squeaked behind her and Emily turned round to see Grandpa Vance duck under the doorway.

He'd changed clothes since she'd last seen him that morning, when she'd followed him to breakfast. She'd intended to wait for him outside the restaurant and walk home with him again. But then Win had distracted her. She'd followed Win to a diner, where she'd watched him go in and vanish in the crowd. She'd gone home after that and waited for Grandpa Vance there, but when he'd got home, he'd disappeared into his room.

'Julia,' he said. 'I thought I heard your voice.'

'I brought you a gift.' Julia handed the bags to Vance, who looked as if he'd been given the Holy Grail of foodstuffs. 'With this heat, I thought cooking dinner would be the last thing either of you wanted to do today. Maybe the two of you could eat together,' she said with a significance that wasn't lost on Emily.

Grandpa Vance nosed around in the bags and surprised her with his zeal. 'You're in for a treat, Emily! Julia's barbecue is the best in town. My mouth is watering already. Will you join us, Julia?'

'No, thanks. I have to be going.'

'You're right neighbourly. Thank you.' Vance disappeared inside, leaving Emily on the porch with Julia.

'That's the first time he's been out of his room since this morning,' Emily said, amazed.

'Barbecue gets him every time.'

'I'll remember that.'

'Listen,' Julia said, 'how would you like to go to Piney Woods Lake with me on Saturday? It's the place for kids your age to go in the summer. Maybe you can meet some people.'

It felt nice to be included. 'OK. Sure.'

'Great. See you tomorrow. Now go and talk with your grandfather.'

Julia gave her a backward wave and jogged down the front porch steps.

Emily went back into the house. When she reached the kitchen, she heard the dryer door close and Vance came out of the attached laundry room. He'd been looking in the clothes dryer again. He was inordinately preoccupied with it, which was strange because just that afternoon, someone from the dry-cleaner's had come by to take a bag of laundry he'd left on the porch.

Vance stopped when he saw her. 'Emily.' He cleared his throat. 'So, um, has the wallpaper in your bedroom changed yet?'

'Changed?' she asked.

'It does that sometimes. Changes on its own.'

It sounded like something you would say to a child. The moon is made of cheese. Wish on a star. There's magic wallpaper in your room. He probably thought of her as a little girl, she realised, and he was trying to make her smile. 'No, it's still lilacs. But I'll be on the lookout,' she said to humour him.

He nodded seriously. 'All right, then.'

Emily looked around and found where he had set the bags on the table in the breakfast nook. 'Are you going to eat now?' she asked.

'I thought I might,' he said. 'Would you like to join me?'

'You wouldn't mind?'

'Not at all. Have a seat.' He took plates and utensils out of the cabinets and put them on the table. They sat opposite each other, and together they unloaded the contents of the bags, mostly Styrofoam containers of various sizes, plus a few hamburger buns and two slices of cake.

'What is this?' Emily asked, looking in the largest Styrofoam container. There was a lot of dry-looking chopped meat inside.

'Barbecue.'

'Barbecue is hot dogs and hamburgers on a grill,' Emily said.

Vance laughed, which made Emily smile. 'Ha! Blasphemy! In North Carolina, barbecue means pork, child. Hot dogs and hamburgers on a grill—that's called "cooking out" around here,' he explained with sudden enthusiasm. 'And there are two types of North Carolina barbecue sauce—Lexington and Eastern North Carolina. Here, look.' He excitedly found a container of sauce and showed her. 'Lexington-style is the sweet sugar-and-tomato-based sauce that you put on chopped or pulled pork shoulder. Julia's restaurant is Lexington-style. Eastern North Carolina-style restaurants use a thin, tart, vinegar-and-pepper-based sauce. But no matter the style, there're always crispy, hot hush puppies and coleslaw. And, if I'm not mistaken, those are slices of Milky Way cake.'

'Like the candy bar?'

'Yep. The candy bars are melted and poured into the batter.'

Emily watched as Vance forked some chopped pork onto a hamburger bun. He poured some sauce on it, then topped it with coleslaw. He capped it all with the top bun and handed it on a plate to Emily. 'A barbecue sandwich, North Carolina-style.'

'Thank you,' Emily said, smiling. He really was a nice man. She liked being around him. 'This was nice of Julia to do.'

'Julia is a wonderful person.'

'I was just talking to her about the Mullaby lights,' Emily said, hoping he'd be more interested in what she'd discovered than Julia had been. 'I've been seeing them at night.'

Vance paused. 'You have? Where?'

'In the woods behind the house,' she said.

'I'll only ask you to do one thing while you're here, Emily,' he said seriously. 'Just one. Stay away from them.'

'But I don't think it's a ghost,' she said. 'I think someone is doing it on purpose.'

'No one is doing it on purpose. Trust me.'

Emily had to bite her tongue to keep from pointing out that leaving her a box of Band-Aids last night seemed pretty intentional.

'Your mother would get that same look on her face when she was a little girl,' he said. 'She was stubborn, my Dulcie.' He hastily looked away. Suddenly that old awkward tension was back.

Emily toyed with the food on her plate. 'Why don't you want to talk about her?'

He said, 'I get all confused about it. I don't know what to say.'

Emily nodded, though she didn't really understand. Vance's relationship with his daughter must have been a complicated one. But then, her mother's relationship with everyone had been complicated. She'd been a hard woman to know.

Emily wouldn't push him. And she would try not to be hurt by his avoidance. He'd taken her in when she had no other place to go, after all, and she was grateful. So she would talk to other people in town about her mother, find out more from them. Maybe she'd even see Win Coffey again and ask him about the relationship his uncle had had with her mother.

She liked that thought. Seeing Win again.

They ate in silence. Afterwards, Grandpa Vance again checked the clothes dryer, as if something might have appeared during dinner. But again he found nothing, so he went to his room. Emily went upstairs and finished sweeping, then sat on the balcony and waited for the lights. And so ended her second full day in Mullaby.

Later that evening, when Vance ducked out of his room to check the dryer one last time before bed, he paused to look up the staircase. He didn't hear any more shuffling. No more scraping of a broom. Emily had settled in for the night.

It was a peculiar thing, he thought, having someone in the house again. He was surprised by how he felt with Emily near, and he didn't know how to handle it. Being needed was like being tall—it was never an issue until other people were around.

Vance had towered over all the other kids in kindergarten. That was his first memory of truly understanding how tall he was. Up until then, while he was big for his age, he was still the shortest member of his own normal-sized family. Some kids teased him at first, but there came a point when they realised that maybe it wasn't the best idea to pick a fight with someone who could knock them over with only the wind he caused by walking past them.

His family was gone now. Vance was the only one left of the Shelbys, and he had inherited the existing fortune. It wasn't supposed to all come down to him—the Shelby legacy. There were supposed to be normal brothers and sisters who would do great things. For a while there were. But his older sister drowned in Piney Woods Lake when she was eleven. And his younger brother died from a fall out of the tree house in the front yard when he was six. His parents tried for more children after that, but to no avail.

His parents died when he was in his twenties. He thought he saw disappointment in their faces when they passed away. Their legacy was all going to the giant. What was Vance going to do with it? they probably thought. He'd never get married. Who'd want him?

He was thirty-two and living alone, rarely venturing outside, when he met Lily. She was related to the Sullivans down the street and, while attending State, came to visit them one weekend. She was happy and intelligent and afraid of nothing. The Sullivan boys had taken to throwing balls into Vance's yard and daring each other to fetch them and risk getting eaten by the Giant of Mullaby. Lily was appalled. She took them by their ears and forced them into the yard and up the front porch steps, determined to get them to apologise. When Vance came to the door, Lily was so stunned that she let go of the boys. They instantly ran away.

A few hours later, when Lily hadn't returned home, they cried to their mother that the Giant of Mullaby had eaten her. When their mother went to investigate, she found Lily and Vance sitting on the front porch steps, drinking iced tea and laughing. She'd paused, then backed away. Something wonderful was happening and she could see it.

Vance and Lily married after Lily graduated, and Lily taught second grade until she became pregnant with Dulcie. Those were halcyon days. Lily didn't let him stay in the house. She insisted they go grocery shopping together, go to the movies. Once he left the house, he came to realise that Mullaby easily accepted him. He was, in a town full of strange things, just another oddity.

He almost died himself when Lily passed away. Dulcie was twelve when it happened. It was like snow had settled over their world, turning everything cold and silent. It was only Vance's memory of Lily's faith in him that made him survive. How Dulcie got through it, he had no idea. That was one of his biggest shames.

Vance thought a person could only bear going through that once in a lifetime. Then he learned that his daughter had died.

When Dulcie's friend, Merry, called and told him that Dulcie had been in a car accident, Vance couldn't even speak. He had hung up the phone and crawled upstairs to Dulcie's old room. He stayed there a week, the wallpaper in her bedroom turning grey and wet, like storm clouds. He wanted to die. What reason was there to go on?

When Julia next door finally got to him, he hadn't eaten in so long he couldn't walk. He spent a week in the hospital. After he got home, there were phone messages left by Merry. Dulcie had a daughter, she said. And she needed a place to live. Merry couldn't keep her because she was moving to Canada. She'd hired a private detective to try to find any close relatives. And Vance was it.

He'd always taken a passive stance in life. His parents had left him a fortune. His wife had found him. Lily had always taken care of everything. And Dulcie had basically been on her own since she was twelve. Now he had to step up and take care of something.

He hadn't done a very good job of taking care of Emily so far. Dulcie hadn't told Emily anything about Mullaby, about what had happened, so Vance was terrified of saying something Dulcie wouldn't want her daughter to know. When Dulcie left, she'd sworn him to secrecy. *Don't speak of it*, she'd said. *And maybe it will go away. Maybe one day everyone will forget.* He'd let his daughter down in countless ways, so he'd been determined to keep his word about this. And he had, for twenty years.

Now he didn't know what to do. Emily had attracted the attention of the Mullaby lights already. She was going to want answers.

He walked to the kitchen in the darkness. But instead of going into the laundry room to check the dryer, he went directly to the back door and opened it. Sure enough, like Emily said, there was a light in the woods in the back yard, not moving, as if watching the house.

Vance stepped onto the porch, making himself seen. The light immediately disappeared. He heard a gasp, then footsteps on the balcony above. He stepped off the low kitchen porch and looked up.

Emily was standing there, staring out into the woods.

She didn't see him, so he quietly moved away.

He'd made this mistake once. He wasn't going to again.

Piney Woods Lake was exactly that—a lake in the middle of a thick nest of pine trees. Julia parked her old black Ford truck, which had belonged to her father, in one of the last spaces in the crowded parking lot above the boardwalk. It had been a long time since she'd been here. She'd forgotten how beautiful it was. When she and Emily got out, they were assaulted by summertime scents and sounds. Coconut oil, boat motors, kids laughing, music playing.

'It's so loud!' Emily said. 'I like it already.'

'Your mother liked it out here, too. I remember hearing about a place in the cove where Sassafras would meet and rule over the beach all summer,' she said as she led Emily across the parking lot.

They walked down to the boardwalk, and then on down to the beach. Emily smiled the entire way.

They finally stopped at a place halfway between the boardwalk and the cove. There were houses above the beach on this end of the lake, large houses with glass walls overlooking the glittery blue water. As Julia took two towels out of her bag and spread them on the sand, Emily looked round. 'Were you meeting Sawyer here?'

'No. Why?' Julia asked as she shimmied out of her white shorts, revealing the bottom half of her red bikini. She left her gauzy long-sleeved shirt on over her red bikini top, though.

'Because he's coming this way.'

Julia turned to see him walking towards them. Sawyer stood out too much to blend in anywhere, but the closest he came was here, with the sun and the sand. He was golden. A sun king.

'He's nice,' Emily said wistfully. 'The moment I saw him, I knew he'd have an accent like that. I don't know why.'

'Some men you know are Southern before they ever say a word,' Julia said as she and Emily watched Sawyer's progress. 'Southern men will hold doors open for you, they'll hold you after you yell at them. Be careful what they tell you, though. They have a way of making you believe anything, because they say it that way.'

'What way?' Emily asked as she turned to her, intrigued.

'I hope you never find out,' she said softly, just as Sawyer stopped at their towels.

'Hello, ladies.'

'Hi, Sawyer,' Emily said as she sat down.

Julia sat on the towel next to her. 'What are you doing here?'

'Oh, I don't know, Julia,' he said. 'Bear hunting?'

She squinted up at him. 'Is that a euphemism for something?'

He ignored that and sat on her towel at her feet. She could see her reflection in his sunglasses as he stared at her. What was he doing? The eighteen years of silence while she was gone, along with the year and a half of cold shoulder she'd given him since she'd been back, should have been more than enough to discourage him from sitting on her towel on the beach, inches away from her bare legs.

Yet here he was. And all because she'd told Stella that she made cakes because of him. Stupid, stupid, stupid.

'My sister is in town,' he said. 'She and her daughter are staying at the family's lake house. I came to see them.'

'So this has nothing to do with my telling you I was taking Emily out here today?' she asked sceptically.

'Now, that would be too easy, wouldn't it?'

'Everything is easy for you, Sawyer.'

'Not everything.' He nudged his chin in the direction behind her. 'There's my niece. Ingrid!' he called.

Julia and Emily turned to see a pretty redheaded teenager walk over to them. Julia seemed to remember Sawyer's older sister having red hair.

'This is Julia Winterson,' he said to his niece.

Ingrid smiled. 'I recognise the pink streak in your hair. I see you sometimes in town when my mom and I visit,' she said. 'I love it, by the way.'

'Thanks,' Julia said. 'This is Emily. She just moved here.'

'Some kids over in the cove are having a cookout party and they asked me if I wanted to come. I'm going to ask my mom. Do you want to come, Emily?' Ingrid asked.

Emily looked at her blankly. 'What is it for?'

'What do you mean?'

'Is it a club?'

'It's a party,' Ingrid said, giving Emily a questioning look as she turned to leave. 'I'll be right back.'

Emily still looked confused.

'You're making this out to be harder than it really is,' Julia said, laughing as she patted Emily's hand. 'All you have to say is "I'd love to come!"'

'Like this,' Sawyer said. 'Julia, would you like to go out with me Monday night?'

'I'd love to!' she play-acted. 'See? Easy. It's just a party. Didn't you go to parties at your old school?'

'I helped organise parties with my mom. Usually fundraisers. And some community-service clubs at school used to have parties.'

'What kind of school did you go to?'

'Roxley School for Girls. My mom helped found it. It's a school based on social activism and global awareness. Volunteering is part of the curriculum.'

There again was that hint that Dulcie might have done some good with her life. As unbelievable as it seemed, Dulcie must have changed when she left here. 'Well, there's no reason for this party. It's just for fun.'

Emily gave her a dubious look.

Julia laughed again. 'You'll be fine. I'll be right here.'

Ingrid came back shortly and said, 'Are you ready, Emily?'

Emily stood, put on a smile, and walked away with Ingrid.

'Who would have thought Dulcie would have raised such a decent girl?' Sawyer said.

'She is a nice kid, isn't she?'

'You're good with her. And no, I'm not surprised.'

Julia shrugged uneasily, realising she was alone with him now. 'I figure she needs someone she can turn to until she gets settled.'

Sawyer was quiet for a moment as he studied her. She wished he would take off his sunglasses. It was natural, she supposed, to be tense around him. Around Sawyer, she was the old Julia—the messed-up daughter of a man who cooked barbecue for a living. Sawyer never did anything to make her feel that way, but it inevitably happened. She could blame a lot of things on him, but not that.

'Why don't you take off your shirt?' he finally asked.

'I bet you say that to all the girls.' When he didn't respond, she said, 'You know why.' She reached over to her beach bag for a bottle of water, but Sawyer caught her arm.

He held her arm and slowly pushed the sleeve up. It took great effort not to snatch her arm away. She had to remind herself that he'd seen them before. He trailed his thumb over the scars. It was a surprisingly tender thing to do and it made her heart ache a little.

'Who did you turn to when you were her age, Julia?'

You. 'No one. That's how I know.' She slid her arm out of his grasp. 'I don't like to get sun on them. A tan makes them look worse.'

'Did you ever turn to your dad or your stepmother?'

'Dad didn't know what to do with me. And Beverly considered her job taking care of Dad, not being a mother to me. But she was the one who convinced him to send me away to school. I'll always be grateful for that. Leaving this place probably saved my life.'

'And you can't wait to leave again,' he said.

'Six months and counting.'

He sprawled out on his side in front of her, his head propped on his hand. 'So, what time should I pick you up?'

'Pick me up for what?' she said.

'For our date. You accepted my invitation. I have a witness.'

She snorted. 'Don't be ridiculous.'

'I'm serious.'

'No, you're not. Go coax the shirt off someone else. Your charm doesn't work on me. I have a force field deflecting it.'

'You'd have no idea what to do if I turned it on full blast.'

'You're not scaring me.'

'Yes, I am. And that's why I'm stopping. I want to talk about it, Julia,' he said. 'But not now.' He rolled onto his back, the golden hairs on his legs and arms sparkling like spun sugar.

'You don't get to decide that,' she told him. He didn't respond. She waited for him to go away, but he didn't. He might have even fallen asleep. She took a book out of her bag and moved as far away from him as she could, wondering what pitiful part of her heart actually enjoyed this, his nearness.

The part that would always be sixteen years old, she supposed, frozen for ever before everything changed.

The closer they got to the party, the more nervous Emily became. She wouldn't have thought twice about it if it hadn't been for those old ladies. Now she was worried about what everyone would think of her. She kept telling herself there was no reason she shouldn't fit in.

The group was assembled away from the beach, in a small grotto formed by the trees at the back of the cove. Music was playing. A couple of guys were playing touch football. There were a few adults there, one of whom was manning the grill and seemed to be master of ceremonies. He was a large, gregarious man with black hair and a booming voice.

Once they got into the thick of things, Ingrid left her alone. Emily walked to the periphery of the party, towards the back of the grotto by the trees. She took a few deep breaths. No reason to panic.

Julia said this was where Sassafras had gathered in the summer. Emily could tell that it had been a popular spot for kids, because the tree trunks were covered with carvings of names and initials. One carving in particular caught her eye. It was a large heart with the initials D.S. + L.C. inside. She wondered if the D.S. stood for Dulcie Shelby. It was nice to imagine a boy who had once loved her mother so much that he'd carved their initials into a tree. Her mother hadn't dated much in her adult life. As far as Emily could tell, the only serious relationship her mother ever had was with Emily's father. They'd met during a high-seas stand-off with fishermen over the killing of dolphins. They'd spent ten days on a boat together, and Emily had been the result. Her father had died in a boating accident two years later. Her mother and father had never married and Emily had no memory of him.

As she was standing there staring at the tree, she suddenly felt something odd, like ribbons of warmth wrapping round her from behind. It was alarming, but she realised that it didn't feel bad. Not at all. She closed her eyes and felt almost . . . comforted.

She opened her eyes again, and something made her turn round.

There was Win Coffey. He had on long swimming trunks. His hair was wet and dripping, and he smelled like warm lake water.

She cleared her throat. 'I almost didn't recognise you without your suit,' she said.

A corner of his mouth lifted, amused. 'It's a different kind of suit.'

'But no bow tie.'

'Hard to swim in. I've tried.'

Her eyes went from his lips to his chin, then to the rivulets of water running down his bare chest. Embarrassed, she quickly met his eyes again. It looked as if he'd come right out of the water and made a beeline for her. But how could he have known she was there? Over his shoulder, she could see that some kids were watching them and whispering. Win didn't seem to care. He clearly fitted in. 'Do all these kids go to the same school?' she asked.

'Some are summer lake residents who leave in the fall,' he said. 'Some are permanent residents who, yes, go to school here.'

'Mullaby High?'

'Yes.'

'I'll be a senior there in the fall.'

'I know. I will, too.' He ran his hands through his dark wet hair, slicking it back. It almost made her breath catch. 'Not that it isn't nice to see you again, but I have to ask: What are you doing here?'

'Here?' she asked. 'You mean at this party?'

'Yes.'

'Trying to blend in.'

'It's not working. Prepare yourself.'

'For what?' And no sooner did she ask than a dark-haired girl in an orange bathing suit came to a stop beside Win.

'You're Emily Benedict, aren't you?' she asked, with the same combination of aversion and curiosity Win had had the day she'd met him, but with a little more bite.

'Yes,' Win said before Emily could. 'Emily, this is my sister, Kylie.'

'You weren't invited,' Kylie said bluntly. 'You're going to ruin my party.'

'I . . . I came with Ingrid,' Emily said, feeling embarrassment.

'You should leave.'

Win gave a look of censure to his sister. 'Kylie, stop being rude.'

'I'm not being rude. I'm serious. She should leave.' Kylie pointed over her shoulder. Win turned to see that the big man, the master of ceremonies, was slowly making his way towards them.

Win cursed. 'Let's go.' He took Emily by the arm and together they skirted the party, following the tree line. When they reached the regular part of the beach, Win stopped once they were out of sight of the grotto.

She rubbed her arm. The place where he'd touched her felt warm. 'I'm sorry,' she said. 'I didn't know it was a private party.'

They faced each other on the crowded beach. 'It's not.'

It took a moment to sink in. 'Oh.'

'Has your grandfather told you yet?' Win asked out of the blue.

'Told me what?'

'About your mother and my uncle. That's what that was all about.' He nudged his chin back towards the grotto.

Confused as to why being kicked out of the party had anything to do with her mother and his uncle, Emily said, 'Actually, I was hoping to run into you again so I could ask. You said next time I saw you you'd tell me.'

'I did say that, didn't I?' Win hesitated before he said, 'My uncle committed suicide when he was a teenager.'

She didn't know how to respond. The best she could come up with was, 'I'm sorry.'

'He did it because of your mother.'

She felt a jolt of alarm. She suddenly thought of the initials on the tree. D.S. + L.C. Dulcie Shelby and Logan Coffey.

'They were in love,' Win said. 'Or, he was in love with her. His family didn't want him to be with her, but he went against their wishes, against years of tradition. Then your mother turned round and broke his heart, like what he sacrificed didn't matter.'

Emily was desperately trying to make sense of this. 'Hold on. Are you saying you blame my mother for his death?'

'Everyone blames her, Emily.'

'What do you mean, everyone?' She could hear her voice rising.

Win noticed, too. 'I'm sorry. I should have thought how to say that in a nicer way. This is harder than I thought it would be.'

'Than you thought what would be?' she demanded. 'Convincing me that my mother was responsible for your uncle's suicide? I have news for you, my mother was a wonderful person. She would never do anything to hurt another person. Never.'

Win suddenly looked over his shoulder, as if sensing something about to happen. 'My dad is still looking for me. Come this way.' He took her hand and led her towards the pine trees.

Her bare feet kicked up sand as she jogged to keep up with him. 'Where are we going?'

'Out of sight,' he said, the moment she stepped onto the cool, pine-needle floor. The smell of resin was strong. It reminded her of Christmas wreaths and red glass ornaments.

'I don't have shoes on,' she said, pulling him to a stop.

He turned to her. 'You seem to find yourself without shoes in the woods a lot.'

She wasn't amused. 'Why are you doing this?'

'Believe it or not, I'm trying to help you.'

'Help me do what?' She threw her hands in the air, frustrated.

'Adjust.'

She scoffed at him. If adjusting to this place meant believing what he said about her mother, she was never going to adjust.

Before she could turn to go back to the beach, he said, 'OK, here are the basics. Your mother was known to be spoilt and cruel. My uncle was gullible and shy. She used his feelings for her to trick him into revealing a long-held Coffey family secret to the entire town, just because she could. Then she turned her back on him. Devastated, he killed himself. She left town without so much as an apology. I know it's hard to hear. But this might go a long way in explaining why people here act a certain way around you.'

'Act what way?'

His dark, arched brows rose. 'You haven't noticed yet?'

Emily hesitated.

'You have noticed.'

She shook her head. She was angry at him for saying these things. 'You didn't know my mother. I knew my mother. She would never turn her back on anyone.'

Win's eyes went soft. It was clear he was sorry she was hurt by his words, but he didn't look sorry that he'd said them in the first place. This was what he meant by the two of them having history?

'Why should I trust you, anyway?' she challenged him.

He shrugged. 'You probably shouldn't. You probably shouldn't have anything to do with me. I'm surprised your grandfather hasn't told you to stay away from me already. He will soon, though.'

The wind picked up for a moment, brushing the treetops. A cascade of pine needles fell down around them. Emily watched Win through the swarming needles, a peculiar enchantment coming over her. Who was this strange boy? What did he want from her?

'What secret did your uncle reveal?' she found herself asking.

He took a long time to answer. His lips finally lifted into a cynical smile. 'You wouldn't believe me if I told you.'

He gladly shared some secrets, yet he wouldn't reveal his own. And that made her furious.

She turned stiffly and walked back to the lake. She made her way across the beach to where Julia was sitting on her towel, reading. Sawyer was stretched out at her feet like a large marmalade cat.

Julia looked up when Emily's shadow fell over her. 'Emily? What's wrong?' she asked, setting her book aside.

'Nothing. I'd like to go home, if that's OK.' She suddenly wanted to talk to her grandfather. He was her one true connection to her mother. He would tell her that what Win said was a lie.

Sawyer sat up. He took off his sunglasses. 'You look upset.'

'I'm fine.' She tacked on a smile for good measure.

'My sister was rude to her. I apologise.' Win's voice behind her made her turn. She wasn't aware that he'd been following her.

Sawyer stood. For someone so beautiful, he could certainly be imposing when he got angry. He was as tall as Win, but much bigger. 'What did she say that upset Emily?'

Before Win could answer, Julia said, 'That was your party?'

'My sister's birthday party.'

She grabbed her bag and quickly stuffed it with their towels. 'I didn't know. Come on, sweetheart. Let's go home.'

'I can take her,' Win said. 'It's on my way, and I need to be home before sunset anyway.' He held out his hand and, without thinking, Emily took it. She immediately came to her senses and tried to take it back, but he held firm. His hand was warm and dry.

'I'm taking her home,' Julia said.

'It would be no trouble.'

Sawyer stepped forward. 'I don't think that's a good idea, Win.'

Win stared at Emily for a moment before saying, 'That does seem to be the consensus.' He finally let go of her hand. She missed the contact. It was crazy.

Julia put her arm round her and led her away. 'Come on.'

'Do you need me to go with you?' Sawyer called after them.

'No.' Julia looked back at him, then added, 'But thanks.'

Julia and Emily walked to the parking lot in silence. When they climbed into the truck, Julia immediately put the key in the ignition. As much as Emily didn't want to believe it, Julia's reaction was giving some credence to what Win had told her.

'Win said his uncle committed suicide because of my mother,' Emily blurted out.

Julia started the engine. She obviously didn't want to comment.

'That's not true, is it?'

'Whether it's true or not, he shouldn't have told you,' Julia said.

Emily almost came undone. 'He said she was cruel,' she said.

That made Julia wince. 'This is something your grandfather has to tell you. Not me. And certainly not Win.' Julia stared at her a moment, her sympathy clear in her every pore. 'It took me a long time to realise this: We get to choose what defines us. It doesn't make a lot of sense right now, but it will. OK?'

Emily reluctantly nodded.

'All right, then.' Julia put the truck in reverse. 'I'll take you home to talk to your grandfather.'

Chapter 5

'GOOD, YOU'RE HOME,' Grandpa Vance said as Emily came in at the front door. 'I was thinking, you need a car so you can go out to the lake whenever you want to. I happen to have one, you know.'

'Grandpa Vance—'

'I don't actually drive it. I've never been able to drive. Not with these legs. But your grandmother had a car. Come, I'll show you.'

What was this all about? Just last night they were eating barbecue in silence. She followed him out and round the side of the house. There was an old garage there that looked as if it hadn't been used in ages. The driveway no longer existed, so the garage stood in the grassy side yard like an island that had lost its mainland bridge.

When Vance pulled the garage door up, dust motes sparkled in the sunlight. He reached round and felt for the light switch. The fluorescent light popped on reluctantly.

'It's a 1978 Oldsmobile Cutlass,' he said. 'If you wouldn't mind driving something this old, I'll have someone look it over.'

Emily stared at it. 'Did my mom drive this?'

'No. She wanted a convertible, so I bought her one.' He paused. 'If you want something different, I can arrange that.'

'No,' she said. 'I think I like this one. It looks like a muscle car.'

'A muscle car, huh? Lily would have liked that.'

She turned to him. 'Who is Lily?'

Vance looked shocked. 'Lily was my wife, child,' he said. 'Did your mother never talk about her?'

'She didn't tell me anything.' Emily tucked her hair behind her ears. *Talk to him.* 'Grandpa Vance, today at the lake, there was this party. It turned out to be a party thrown by the Coffeys, and I was asked to leave.'

If indignation were something you could see, it would look exactly like an eight-foot man pulling himself to his full height. '*You were asked to leave?*'

'Well, not in so many words,' she said, still embarrassed by it. 'But it was clear enough that the Coffeys don't like me.'

'That was the one thing I asked you to do, Emily!' he said. 'To stay away from them.'

Win had said Grandpa Vance would soon tell her that. 'You asked me to stay away from the Mullaby lights, not the Coffeys. I didn't know I was doing anything wrong.'

Vance took a deep breath. 'You're right. None of this is your fault.' He looked at the car before turning off the light. 'I had hoped, with all the time that had passed, these old wounds had healed.'

'Is this because of my mom?' she asked hesitantly. 'Win told me some pretty unbelievable things. He said she was cruel. But that can't be true. Mom was a wonderful person. Wasn't she? I know you don't want to talk about her. But please, just tell me that.'

'Dulcie was a handful when she was a young girl,' Vance said as he pulled the garage door down. 'She could actually sting people with her energy. But she was also bright and happy and curious. She got that from Lily. Dulcie was twelve when Lily died.' He rubbed his eyes. 'I didn't know how to handle her on my own. The only thing I could think to do was give her everything she asked for. So she got the best of everything. As she got older, she began to take pleasure in teasing people who didn't have as much as she did. She could be cruel sometimes. Julia was a target.'

'My mom was cruel to Julia?'

He nodded slowly. 'And others,' he added reluctantly.

This couldn't be her mother he was talking about. Her mother had been a good person, selfless. She'd wanted to save the world.

'She was the queen bee of her social circle, and her word was law. Who she accepted, they accepted. Who she shunned, they shunned,' he said. 'When she took this troubled boy named Logan Coffey under her wing and told everyone to accept him, they did.'

'Win said he committed suicide.'

'Yes.'

Emily paused. 'Did my mom have something to do with it?'

She waited, holding her breath, until he finally answered. 'Yes.'

'What did she do?' she whispered.

Vance struggled with what to say. 'What did Win tell you?'

'He said Logan loved my mom, but his family didn't approve of her. He said Logan broke tradition to be with her, but all my mom wanted was to trick him into revealing a Coffey family secret.'

Vance sighed. 'The Coffeys are much more social these days, but back then they were very exclusive. Status was important to Dulcie. It started with me, giving her everything she wanted. It all got wrapped up in her grief over losing her mother. If only she had more, then she'd be happy. When the Coffeys wouldn't let her into their social circle, when they frowned on her relationship with Logan, it made her angry. Not just angry. Livid. She had a hard time with her temper after Lily died.' Vance paused, then continued. 'The Coffeys had, and still have, one particular quirk: they never come out at night. But Logan came out that night for Dulcie. She assembled most of the town in front of the bandstand in the park, saying she was going to perform for them. She had a lovely singing voice. Instead, she led Logan onstage.'

She waited for more. There had to be more. 'That doesn't make any sense,' she said. 'He committed suicide because she made him come out at night? That's the big secret? That's ridiculous.'

'Tradition has always been important to the Coffeys,' Vance said. 'And Logan was a sensitive, troubled young man. His suicide almost drove the Coffeys away. If they'd left and taken their money with them, Mullaby would have been ruined. That was the last straw. No one wanted anything to do with Dulcie after that. She had finally done something I couldn't buy her way out of.'

Emily realised she was backing away from him.

'I haven't spoken of it in twenty years,' Vance said. 'And I was going to keep it from you, because you were better off not knowing. The Coffeys obviously thought differently. I'm sorry.'

Emily continued to back away. Vance simply watched her go, as if leaving him was what he expected, what he was used to. Without another word, Emily turned and walked back into the house.

When she reached her room, she just stood there. Coming here had been a mistake. She should have known her mother had a good reason for keeping this place from Emily. This place wasn't right. There was something distinctly off about it. And this person everyone remembered as Dulcie Shelby wasn't her mother at all.

As she stood there, she began to hear a fluttering sound, as if something was in the room with her. She looked up and couldn't believe what she saw. She turned in a circle, staggering slightly.

The wallpaper didn't have lilacs on it any more. It had changed to tiny butterflies of every imaginable colour. There wasn't a pattern, they were simply everywhere. There was a static frenzy to them, like they desperately wanted out. Out of this room. Out of this town. Setting aside her incredulity for a moment, she knew exactly what they felt like.

She slowly backed out of the room, then she ran down the stairs. Vance was making his way into the kitchen from the yard.

'The wallpaper in my room,' she said. 'When did you change it?'

He smiled. 'The first time is always hard. You'll get used to it.'

'The wallpaper looks old. How did you get it to look like that? How did you get it up so fast? How do you get it to . . . move?'

'I didn't do it. It just happens.' He waved his arms like a magician. 'It started with my sister. No one knows why.'

She shook her head. This was too much craziness for one day. 'I'm not a child. Wallpaper doesn't change on its own.'

Instead of arguing, he asked, 'What did it change to?'

As if he didn't know. 'Butterflies. Crazy butterflies!'

'Just think of that room as a universal truth,' he said. 'How we see the world changes all the time. It all depends on our mood.'

She took a deep breath and tried to be tactful. 'I'm sure it took a lot of effort, but I don't care for that pattern. Can I paint over it?'

'Won't work,' he told her, shrugging. 'Your mother tried. Paint doesn't stick to that wallpaper. Won't tear off, either.'

Emily blew out a puff of air in frustration. No one in this town would give an inch. Not with her mother. Not with this . . . wallpaper situation. Grandpa Vance watched her silently. 'I'm waiting for someone to tell me this is all just a trick being played on me,' she finally said.

'I know that feeling well,' he said quietly.

She met his eyes. 'Does it get better?'

'Eventually.'

Not the answer she wanted. But she was going to have to live with it. She had nowhere else to go.

Over seventy years ago, during the full moon in February, the house beside the Coffey mansion on Main Street caught fire.

Flames were jetting out of the windows of the house by the time the fire engine arrived. The town gathered in the park across the street to watch, huddled together under blankets. Vance was only four years old at the time, and his height was not yet a concern.

Everyone watching the fire was riveted by the undulating yellow-golds and blue-oranges. First one person saw it, and then another, and soon the entire crowd was watching, not the fire, but the house next door—the Coffey mansion. All the servants were leaning out of the windows on the side of the house facing the fire, and they were throwing whatever liquid substance they had to hand at the flames next door, trying to keep the fire away from the Coffey mansion. They threw water from flower vases, jars of peaches swimming in juice, a leftover cup of tea from breakfast.

The town slowly began to realise that the Coffeys weren't coming out and their loyal house staff was trying to save them.

The fire was eventually extinguished and the Coffey mansion wasn't affected. The next morning, the story began to circulate that the Coffeys had huddled in their basement while the fire had raged next door, claiming they would rather die than come out at night.

People had always known about the Coffeys' aversion to the dark hours, but no one had ever realised just how serious they were about it. It was the first time the citizens of Mullaby began to wonder, What if it wasn't that they didn't come out at night . . .

What if it was because they couldn't.

Dulcie had loved that story when she was a little girl. Dulcie had always been close to her mother, but she'd never wanted much to do with Vance. Maybe because he'd been so cautious around her when she was a baby. She'd been so unbelievably small compared to him. So when he'd found something, like stories of the Coffeys, that brought Dulcie closer to him, he'd been thrilled. He hadn't known that he'd been building the framework for disaster. By the time she was a teenager, she'd been obsessed with the Coffeys.

He didn't want that for Emily.

After Emily had gone to bed that night, Vance moved a chair to the back porch and waited, flashlight in hand. The full July Buck Moon was out—a time for the young and randy.

The Mullaby lights had been around a long time, and there were dozens of stories about them. But after the fire, the rumour started that the Mullaby lights were really the ghosts of Coffey family members who had passed on. That rumour stuck, and to this day, it was still what the people of Mullaby told all outsiders who asked.

When the light appeared in the woods that night, he stood and turned on his flashlight.

'Go back to where you came from,' he called softly, knowing it could hear him. 'I know what my daughter did to you. But you can't have Emily.'

Late on Monday afternoon, Julia was walking home from the post office, reeling from the postcard she'd just received.

The postcard was from Nancy, one of her best friends in Baltimore. Because Julia couldn't afford a phone, once a month or so Nancy would write with what was going on with Julia's friends—a rowdy group of young professionals. This postcard had thrown Julia into confusion. On it, Nancy—whom Julia didn't even know was seeing anyone—had written that she had suddenly got married. She'd also written that their friend Devon had moved to Maine and Thomas was taking a job in Chicago. Nancy promised to give Julia details as soon as she got home from her honeymoon in Greece.

Julia hadn't expected everything to remain static while she was away, she just didn't think things would change so much. Now, when she left Mullaby and moved back to Baltimore, there would be hardly any friends to reconnect with.

She tried to rally. She still had her Blue-Eyed Girl Bakery dream. The bakery, after all, was the reason she had confined herself to this hell for two years. Growing apart from her friends had always been a risk. She knew that. She'd dealt with losing much worse.

She heard a splashing sound, and looked down the sidewalk to see Emily in front of Vance's house. There was a sudsy bucket by her feet, a sponge in her hand, and a large old car at the kerb.

Julia walked over to Emily. She hadn't seen her since Saturday and wondered if Vance had finally told her everything. 'Nice car.'

Emily looked up. Her fine blonde hair, as usual, seemed suspended in midair, half-up in a ponytail, half-down around her face. 'Grandpa Vance is letting me drive it. His mechanic is picking it up tomorrow, but I pushed it out of the garage so I could wash it first.'

'I didn't know Vance still had this.' Julia walked over to the car and looked in at a dusty window. 'It belonged to his wife, didn't it?'

'Yes.'

Julia watched Emily scrub the hood for a few moments. 'Have you talked to your grandfather?'

'Yes.' That word conveyed all Julia needed to know. 'I didn't know it was going to be like this. But my mom knew. I'm sure that's why she never came back, and why she never told me about this place. I'm beginning to think she wouldn't want me here.'

Julia looked from Emily, to the car, and back again. If Julia had had a car at Emily's age, she knew exactly what she would have done. 'Planning to leave?'

Emily looked surprised that Julia had caught on so quickly. She shrugged. 'I don't have anywhere to go.'

'Well, if you'll hold off for a little, the Mullaby Barbecue Festival is this weekend. It's a big deal round here. Do you want to go with me?'

Emily didn't look at her. 'You don't have to do this, Julia.'

'Do what?'

'Try so hard to be nice to me. My mom was cruel to you.'

Oh, hell. 'So Vance told you that, too?'

'He said my mom used to tease you. What did she do?' Emily finally met her eyes. If she were any more sincere, she would dissolve into fresh air and blow away.

'You shouldn't worry about it. It has nothing to do with you.'

'Please tell me.'

'It's not exactly my shining moment, Em,' Julia said. 'But, if you must know, aside from the pink hair, black clothes and black lipstick, I used to wear a studded leather choker that looked like a dog collar to school every day. Your mother would bring dog treats to school and throw them at me in the hallways. Once, she even gave me flea powder.' She paused at the memory. She hadn't thought about that in a long time. 'To be fair, I gave her a lot to make fun of. I probably brought it on myself.'

'Don't. Don't justify it. No one should ever compromise the dignity of another human being.' She shook her head. 'My mom taught me that. Can you believe it?'

'Yes, actually,' Julia said. 'I can.'

'You told me she was popular.'

'She was popular.'

'But no one liked her?'

Julia thought about it for a moment. 'Logan Coffey did.'

Emily dropped the sponge she was holding into the bucket at her feet. 'I'm sorry for what she did to you.'

'I would never blame you for something your mother did, sweetheart. No one worth your time would. You're not who your mother was. In fact, I'm beginning to think you are who your mother became. It might be worth staying, if just to prove that to everyone.'

Emily seemed to be thinking it over when they both heard a car door slam. They turned to see Sawyer standing beside a white Lexus hybrid parked behind Julia's truck next door.

He walked towards them.

'Is he here for your date?' Emily asked.

Julia turned to her. 'What date?'

'He asked you out for Monday night. When we were at the lake.'

Julia threw her head back and groaned. 'Oh, damn.'

Emily laughed. 'You forgot?'

'Sort of.' Julia looked at her and smiled, glad that at least Emily was finding some humour in this.

'Hello, ladies,' Sawyer said from behind her.

'Hi, Sawyer. Julia didn't forget you were going out,' Emily said.

'She's . . . just running late. It's my fault. She was going to change when I stopped her to show her my car. Right, Julia?'

Julia looked at her strangely before realising that Emily thought she was helping. 'Right,' Julia said. 'Let me know about going to the festival.'

'I will.'

Julia led Sawyer next door. 'She thinks you're here to take me on a date,' she whispered. 'She just went to a lot of trouble to help me save face because she thought I forgot. Go along with it, OK?'

'All right,' he said as they walked up the steps to Stella's house. 'But I am here to take you out. And obviously you did forget.'

They entered the house and Julia set her mail on the table in the hall. 'I'm not going on a date with you,' she said.

'You accepted in front of Emily. And she just covered for you. What kind of example are you setting?'

'That's a low blow. Just wait here until she goes inside.'

He went to the living-room window and pushed the curtain aside. 'That might take a while. That car is filthy.'

Julia smiled. 'She seems thrilled with it.'

'How was she when you took her home on Saturday? She seems OK now.'

'She's coping. Her grandfather finally told her some things about her mother's time here. I think she'll be better prepared for snubs from the Coffeys now.'

'She really is nothing like Dulcie.' He let the curtain fall, then walked over and sat on Stella's striped couch. Julia found herself staring at him. He was so perfect. 'You do realise that the longer I stay in here, the more likely she is to think we're doing something scandalous,' he said.

'You're being manipulative.'

He shrugged. 'If that's what it takes, I have no problem with it.'

'Careful, Sawyer, you're acting a lot like you did when you were sixteen. And here I was thinking you'd improved so much.'

'And there it is,' he said with satisfaction. 'Exactly what I want to talk about.'

'No,' she said. 'Stella will be home any minute.'

'She won't be home for an hour or more.' He locked eyes with her. 'You said you've forgiven me. Is that true?'

'I'm not having this conversation.' She shook her head.

'Why?'

'Because it's mine, Sawyer!' she said. 'It's my memory and my regret. I'm not sharing it with you. You didn't want it then. You can't have it now.' The words were strung in the air like garland. She could almost see them.

Sawyer stood and walked to the fireplace mantel. He stared into the empty fireplace. 'Holly and I couldn't have kids.'

Julia paused at this sudden change in subject. Sawyer and Holly had got married right out of college. Her father had told Julia about it in passing one year. It had hurt a little, but hadn't surprised her much. Sawyer and Holly had dated since middle school. What had surprised her was discovering that their marriage had lasted less than five years. Everyone thought they'd be together for ever.

'The ironic thing is, I was the problem,' Sawyer continued. 'I contracted chickenpox in college and had an unusual reaction to it. Not a week goes by that I don't think of what happened between us, and how I responded. My fear and my stupidity not only made what was already a horrible time in your life worse, it destroyed what turned out to be my only chance to father a child. That's what I wanted to tell you. I knew the moment I saw you again that you were holding on to what had happened, that I was still, in your eyes, that stupid boy. Maybe this will make you feel a little better.'

'Feel better?' she asked incredulously.

He shrugged. 'To know that I got what I had coming.'

For the first time, Julia realised Sawyer might be just as messed up as she was about what had happened. He was simply better at hiding it. 'What is the matter with you?' she demanded. 'How could you possibly think that would make me feel better?'

'It doesn't?'

'Of course not.'

Still staring into the fireplace, he said, 'I've read that an abortion rarely affects a woman's ability to bear more children. Is that true?'

She hesitated. 'I assume so.'

'I'm glad,' he said softly.

She didn't think he cared, or even deserved, to know what she'd been keeping so close to her heart, this hope she'd been carrying around for so long. 'You bastard. I was happy being mad at you. Why couldn't you have just left it at that?'

He smiled slightly. 'Because I get such a kick out of telling beautiful women that I'm sterile.'

At that moment, the front door opened and there was Stella. She always smelled like carnations from her florist shop when she came in from work. The scent ran ahead of her into the room.

'I told you she'd be home any minute,' Julia said.

'Am I interrupting something?' Stella asked hopefully. 'I can come back later. As a matter of fact, I can be gone all night.'

'You're not interrupting anything. Good night.' Julia turned and jogged up the stairs to her apartment.

'Night?' Stella said. 'It's barely five o'clock.'

Julia locked the door behind her and went straight to her bedroom. She sat on the edge of the bed. She suddenly had a very big decision to make, one she thought she'd never have to make.

Coming back here had messed up everything.

Her first six weeks at Collier Reformatory in Maryland were hard. Julia spent a lot of time crying, and using all her allotted phone time trying to call Sawyer. His maid always said he wasn't home. Julia refused to talk to her father when he called. Her therapist didn't pressure her. Her therapy sessions were odd at first, but then she started looking forward to them. In fact, her therapist was the second person she told when she realised she was pregnant.

Julia was thrilled when she found out. In her mind, it meant she could go home and be with Sawyer. They would get married and move in together and raise their child. He could make her happy.

She called his house incessantly until she wore the maid down. When Sawyer got on the phone, she was taken aback by his tone.

'Julia, you have to stop calling here,' he said brusquely.

'I . . . I've missed you. Where have you been?'

Silence.

'This place is horrible,' she continued. 'They want to put me on medication.'

Sawyer cleared his throat. 'Maybe that's a good idea, Julia.'

'No, it's not.' She smiled. 'It might hurt the baby.'

Silence again. Then, 'What baby?'

'I'm pregnant, Sawyer. I'm going to tell my therapist, and then my dad. I should be home soon.'

'Wait, wait, wait,' he said quickly. 'What?'

'I know it's a surprise. But, don't you see? It's the best thing that could have happened. I'll come home and we can be together.'

'Is it mine?' he asked.

She felt the first string tighten round her heart, thin and sharp. 'Of course it's yours. That was my first time. You were my first.'

He waited so long to say something that she thought he'd hung up.

'Julia, I don't want a baby,' he finally said.

'What do you mean?'

'I'm sixteen!' He suddenly exploded. 'I can't be a parent! And I'm with Holly. I have plans.'

Her insides tightened. 'You're with Holly?' She knew he'd been dating Holly, but she'd assumed, after what had happened on the football field . . . How could he still be with Holly?

'I've always been with her. You know that. We're going to get married after college.'

'But that night—'

He interrupted her, saying, 'You were upset.'

'It's not just the baby?' she whispered. 'You don't want me?'

'I'm sorry. I really am. I thought you knew.'

You thought I knew? Her eyes started filling with tears.

'I'll take care of it,' she said, turning to hang up the payphone. Sawyer might not want the baby, but she did.

Sawyer misunderstood. 'That's good. It's the right thing, Julia. I know it'll be hard, but it will be over before you know it. Just get an abortion and everything will be fine. Let me send you some money.' His voice was so nice now, so relieved.

She felt a wave of hatred so strong that it popped off her skin. He wanted her to get an abortion? How could she ever have thought she was in love with such a person? 'No. I can do it by myself. You've done enough,' she said, and hung up.

Telling her father was horrible. When her therapist made her call him, he wanted her to come home right away, thinking she'd got pregnant at Collier. But she admitted that it had happened before she left Mullaby. Though he demanded to know who the father was, she never told him. In the end, everyone agreed that she should stay at Collier. She wasn't the only pregnant girl there, after all.

She started craving cakes around her third month. Her therapist told her it was just a normal pregnancy craving, but Julia knew better. This child growing inside her obviously had Sawyer's magical sweet sense. Julia started sneaking out of her dorm to go to the cafeteria. That's where she baked her first cake. She became pretty good at it because it was the only thing that settled the baby. It had an unusual effect on the rest of the school, too. The smell of cake would waft through the hallways while she baked at night, and even the girls whose dreams were always dark would suddenly dream of their kindhearted grandmothers and long-ago birthday parties.

Julia's therapist started talking to her about adoption. She refused to consider it. But every session her therapist would ask, *How do you plan to care for this child on your own?* And Julia began to get scared. Her only choice was her father, but when she brought it up, he said no. Beverly didn't want a baby in the house.

In the spring, in a flood of pain and fear, Julia went into labour. It came on so quickly that she gave birth in the ambulance on the way to the hospital. She could feel the baby's impatience. Her daughter had a mind all her own. After it was over, the baby fussed about how hard her journey had been. It made Julia laugh, holding the squawking infant in her arms. She was perfect, with Sawyer's blond hair and blue eyes.

Julia's father came to Maryland to see her in the hospital the next day, and she asked him one last time to take her and the baby home. Standing at the foot of the hospital bed, his ball cap in his hands, looking shy and out of place, he again said no. She gave up on ever having a real relationship with her father after that.

It was the hardest decision Julia had ever made, giving up her little girl. She knew she couldn't take care of her baby alone. She could barely take care of herself. She hated Beverly for not wanting a baby in the house, and she hated her father for being so weak. But most of all, she hated Sawyer. If only he had loved her, she could have kept the baby.

She was told that a couple from Washington, DC, adopted the baby. Julia was given two photos. One was the official hospital photo, the other was of Julia in the hospital bed holding her—warm and soft and pink. Julia put the photos away immediately, because it hurt too much to look at them, only to find them years later in an old textbook when she was packing to move after college.

It took a long time to feel fine. She started cutting herself again after she was released from the hospital. Her school therapist worked tirelessly to get her admitted into a summer programme sponsored by Collier because Julia wasn't ready to go home. Julia still felt too vulnerable to go back to Mullaby, so her father agreed that she should stay at Collier for her senior high-school year.

She applied to and was accepted to college the next year. Though she hadn't baked since she was pregnant, those months of practice made her proficient enough to get a job at a grocery store bakery to help pay for tuition. By this time, Julia was able to think of Sawyer without the world turning a furious ember red around her, and she remembered what he'd told her about following the scent of his mother's cakes home. It became a symbol to her. Maybe one day, baking cakes would bring her daughter back to Julia. At the very least, it would carry Julia's love to her. Wherever she was.

Nearly twenty years later, Julia was still calling out to her. Knowing she was out there somewhere was what got Julia through every single day. She couldn't imagine a life without knowing that.

Sawyer was living that unimaginable life.

It was then that she knew she had to tell him.

Julia heard a tapping at her door. She opened her eyes and was surprised to see that the sky was blackberry blue and the first star of the night was out. She got up and went to her bedroom doorway.

'Julia?' Stella called. 'Are you all right? You've been awfully quiet. Sawyer's gone, if that's what you're waiting for.' There was a pause. 'I'll be downstairs if you need me. If you want to talk.'

She heard Stella walk back down the stairs.

Julia rested her head against the doorjamb for a moment, then she walked into the kitchen. A hummingbird cake, she decided as she turned on the kitchen light. It was made with bananas and pineapples and pecans and had a cream cheese frosting. She would make it light enough to float away. She reached over to open the window.

To float to her daughter.

Chapter 6

THE CAR HAD AN EIGHT-TRACK PLAYER. The steering wheel was huge. The interior smelled like cough drops. *And she loved it.*

When Vance's mechanic dropped the car off that next day, Emily eagerly sat behind the wheel. But then she realised that she couldn't think of anywhere she wanted to go. The more she thought about it, the more she didn't really want to leave Mullaby. Although she would never say it, a part of her found an odd comfort in her mother's fallibility. Dulcie had set an impossible standard in Boston, and Emily had thought she could never do enough, care enough, work hard enough. And sometimes she'd resented it.

Emily sat in the car until it became too hot, then she got out. She couldn't go next door to visit, because Julia had left earlier. And she didn't want to go back inside her own house, because Grandpa Vance was taking a nap, and the new butterfly wallpaper in her room made her nervous. She walked aimlessly to the back of the house. The yard was so overgrown that, at eye level, it was hard to even see the gazebo at the back of the property.

With nothing better to do, she began to pick up twigs and fallen branches from the yard. She checked the garage for some shears, and went to the gazebo and began to trim back the wild boxwood bushes, flustering a large frog who was hiding in the shade there.

As she worked her way round the gazebo, shortening the bushes so the latticework could be seen, the fat frog followed her. At one point, she lobbed off a bit of boxwood and a twig fell onto the frog. She laughed and bent to lift it off him, and that's when she saw it. A large heart with the initials D.S. + L.C. carved inside.

It was carved onto a back post of the gazebo, near the bottom.

Her fingers reached out to trace the lines of the heart. Logan Coffey had been in this back yard. She didn't know why her eyes went to the woods, just a hunch, but there, on one of the trees that formed the border into the woods, was another carving. D.S. + L.C.

She set the shears down and went to it. She saw another heart further in the woods. Then another. They formed a trail, too irresistible not to follow. She spent fifteen minutes slowly making her way through the woods, until she finally broke into a clearing. This was the same place the light had led her the night she'd chased it. The park on Main Street.

She looked over to the bandstand, and carved into the base of the structure, next to the side steps, was the heart with the initials.

She walked to the bandstand and knelt, touching the carving.

Why did they lead here? Did they have something to do with her mother leading Logan Coffey onto the bandstand stage that night?

She looked around the park. It was full of people. Some were having lunch. Some were sunbathing. And there was Win Coffey.

He was standing with a few adults in the middle of the park. One was the big man from the party at the lake. She didn't realise it before, but he was clearly related to Win—if the dark hair, the suit and the bow tie were any indication. The adults were gesturing towards the street, to the festival banner, but Win was looking at her.

Without thinking, she ducked behind the bandstand, then regretted it. What was the matter with her? She straightened her shoulders and walked back around the bandstand. It was a public park. She had as much of a right to be here as he did.

As soon as she came round from the back, she gave an exclamation of surprise. There he was, facing her, his hands in his pockets.

'Are you hiding from me?' he asked.

'No,' she said quickly. 'I mean, I didn't know you'd be here. I didn't even know I'd be here. I was just following a trail of these from the back of my grandfather's house.' She pointed to the carving.

'They're all over town. After my uncle died, my grandfather tried to scratch over them, until he realised there were too many.'

'Dulcie Shelby and Logan Coffey. That's what they mean?'

He nodded.

'Despite what everyone thinks, she wasn't this person,' she found herself saying, indicating the carving. 'Not when she left.'

'I know,' he said. 'I Googled her name the day after we met. I found out a lot about her. I read about the school she helped found in Boston. And I saw your photo on the school's website.'

That made her cheeks feel like she'd bitten into a green apple. She hoped it wasn't the photo of her at the Christmas food drive, but it was always the one they used in the school literature. When Emily had protested, her mother had said, *Don't be vain. What you look like doesn't matter. It's the deed that matters.* Emily used to think her mother had no idea what it was like to be a teenager. 'You know a lot more about me than I know about you,' Emily finally said. 'I don't think that's fair.'

Win leaned in towards her, making her heart do a strange kick. His eyes went to her lips, and she suddenly wondered if he was going to kiss her. The crazy thing was, a tiny part of her wanted him to. 'Does this mean you're curious?' he asked.

'Yes,' she said. 'Especially about why coming out at night caused your uncle to commit suicide. My mother might not have been very nice, but what kind of secret is that to kill yourself over?'

He suddenly pulled back and gave her an assessing look. 'You've learned a few things since we last talked.'

'My grandfather said he didn't tell me because he thought I was better off not knowing. He's not thrilled that you took it upon yourself to be my tour guide into my mother's past.'

'And how do you feel?'

'I still love my mom.'

He hesitated. 'I wasn't trying to make you feel otherwise. I'm sorry. I was just trying to help.'

Something made her wonder if he meant help her, or help himself. 'Why was it such a big deal to be seen at night?' she suddenly asked. 'I mean, you come out at night now, don't you?'

'No.'

'No?' she asked, surprised. 'Why?'

'You wouldn't believe me if I told you.'

'You've said that before. How do you know?'

He gave her a look that made every nerve in her body feel alive. 'Be careful what you wish for,' he said.

'Win, what are you doing back here?' The man dressed like Win suddenly appeared from round the front of the bandstand. He was bulky but not fat, as if his own importance made him take up so much room. He looked at Win, who tightened with clear animosity. The man's eyes then fell on Emily. 'Ah,' he said, as if something suddenly made sense. 'You must be Emily Benedict.'

'Yes.'

He gave her a politician's smile, lots of teeth, but it didn't quite make it to his eyes. 'I'm Morgan Coffey, mayor of Mullaby. And Win's father. I believe I saw you at my daughter's party last Saturday? I don't recall you being invited.'

'I didn't know I needed an invitation. I apologise.'

'Well then.' He held out his hand and she shook it. His grip was bone-crushing. 'Welcome to town.'

'Thank you,' she said, trying to draw her hand back.

But he held on, his eyes on the silver charm bracelet she was wearing. 'Where did you get this?' he demanded.

With another tug, she slid her hand out of his and hid the bracelet with her other hand. 'It was my mother's.'

Morgan Coffey looked completely poleaxed. 'My father gave that to my mother when they got married.'

Emily shook her head. Surely he was mistaken. 'Maybe they just look the same.'

'The moon charm has an inscription: *Yours from dark to light.*'

Emily didn't have to look. The words had almost been rubbed off, but they were still there. She could feel tears come to her eyes. 'I'm sorry,' she said, fumbling as she took it off. She held the bracelet out to him, her heart breaking. 'She must have stolen it.' After what she'd learned, she wouldn't put it past her mother.

A muscle twitched at his jawline. 'She didn't steal it. Win, let's go.' Morgan Coffey turned and left without another word.

Without taking the bracelet.

Win watched him go, then said to Emily, 'That went better than I thought it would, actually.'

She looked away, blinking back the tears. 'I don't think I want to know how you thought it would go.'

He smiled and stepped over to her. He took the bracelet, which she was still holding out in her palm, and put it back on her wrist.

His touch was warm, and she could feel it beyond the places he actually touched. And there again was that comforting feeling. How did he do that, make her feel so wary, and yet so fond of him?

He looked up from fastening the bracelet and met her eyes. He was still touching her wrist, and she was trembling with the effort to remain still. 'Will I see you at the festival this weekend?'

Julia had asked her, but Emily hadn't given her an answer yet. But she had the answer now. 'Yes.'

'Friends?' he asked, and it sounded as if he was asking her to do something perilous. He made her feel brave for standing there, and she didn't know why. She'd never felt brave before.

She nodded. 'Friends.'

When Sawyer pulled into his driveway after work that day, he saw Julia sitting on the front steps of his town house, a white cake box on her lap. It never occurred to him that she knew where he lived. It made him feel important to her, somehow. Though that was probably his delusion speaking. It spoke to him often about Julia. But this explained the black pickup truck he saw parked at the kerb a couple of blocks away. As he'd passed it, he'd thought it looked like Julia's, though he had no idea why she chose to park so far away. He wondered if she didn't want to be seen associating with him.

He stopped in front of his garage and stepped out of his Lexus. He'd been looking at potential rental properties. His family's property management business was expanding into neighbouring counties. His father had been against it at first. Now business was so good they were considering opening a satellite office.

As he approached her, Julia stood. She was wearing blue jeans and a dark blue peasant blouse. She looked so beautiful, with her big brown eyes and her light brown hair shining. He couldn't see the pink streak, and he had an incredible urge to find it. He'd always been fascinated by her. But he'd done a spectacular job of ruining any chance he'd ever had of being with her.

The night he and Julia had had was amazing, and something he'd dreamed about for years. He'd been the popular preppy kid; she'd been the school's punk hard-ass. He'd never thought he'd have a chance with her, so he'd watched her from afar. That night was everything he'd dreamed it would be. He'd meant everything he'd said at the time, but then he'd got scared. He and Holly had the approval of everyone. Especially after what had happened with Dulcie and Logan that same summer, he'd wanted to hold on to what he had, and he didn't have Julia. He'd reacted badly when she'd told him she was pregnant. When he thought back to that conversation, it was like watching a movie. That wasn't him. That was some horrible boy who'd forced a girl to have an abortion because he hadn't wanted to face the consequences of his actions.

But he ended up facing the consequences anyway. He thought he'd moved on, first with Holly, then by throwing himself into the family business. But then Julia came back to town and he realised for the first time that he hadn't moved on at all.

He'd just been waiting for her to come back and forgive him.

'I didn't know you knew where I lived,' he said as he walked up the steps towards her.

'Apparently, I didn't. Someone told me once that you owned that big house on Gatliff Street. I assumed you lived there. But Stella told me you'd moved here after the divorce.'

'Holly and I still own that house jointly, actually. When she moved to Raleigh, we agreed to rent it out and split the income.'

'Why didn't you just keep living there?'

'It was too big. My family gave it to us as a wedding gift. Five bedrooms. It was a big hint for grandchildren.'

'Oh,' Julia said awkwardly.

'Don't be embarrassed. I'm not. I've come to terms with it.'

She gave him a look that said she didn't believe him. Then she thrust the cake box at him. 'I made you a hummingbird cake.'

He took the box from her, stunned. 'You baked me a cake?'

'Don't get all emotional on me. I have to tell you something. A couple of things, actually. I'll save the big thing for later.'

Later. That was encouraging. 'And the cake is to soften me up?'

'The cake is because I know you like it.'

He gestured towards the door. 'Come in,' he said.

She shook her head. 'I can't. I ran out of gas coming over here. I was waiting for you to come home to give you this and tell you something, then I have to walk to the gas station.'

'I can take you.'

'I'll be fine,' she said dismissively. She didn't want anything from him. Yet he wanted so much from her. 'I do bake cakes because of you. Well, I started baking cakes because of you. That's what I wanted to tell you.'

He wasn't expecting that. He rocked back slightly on his heels.

'It was what you told me about how you always sensed when your mother baked cakes. I loved that story. I started baking when I was away at school. That's a whole story unto itself. The point is, at a time in my life when there were a lot of bad things happening, you gave me something good. I'm opening my own bakery when I move back to Baltimore. And it all started with you.'

He felt incredibly humbled. 'I didn't give you anything but a hard time. How can you possibly appreciate that?'

'I've learned to hold on to the good parts.'

He didn't know what to say. He struggled for a few moments before saying, 'And that's not even the big thing?'

She smiled. 'No.'

On the one hand, he wanted to know. On the other, he wanted to make this last. As curious as he was, he would live with the anticipation for ever if it meant being able to be with her like this.

He shifted the cake box and opened it. He loved hummingbird cake. It was all he could do not to dig his hand through it like a shovel right now. His mother had tried to hide cakes from him when he was small, but he always found them. He couldn't help it. He'd inherited his sweet sense from his grandfather. His grandfather had taught him how to turn it off, after too many stomachaches. He'd also told Sawyer that not everyone could see what he saw, so be careful who he told. Sawyer normally left it off now, unless he was distracted or tired, then he would unwittingly see the silver glitter undulating out of house windows, or the sparkle trailing out of a child's lunch box. The only time he consciously switched it on was when Julia baked on Thursday nights. She was hidden from him, but he could see her do this. She was so good at it, the smell so beautiful. And he'd inspired it. He was overwhelmed.

'You're the only person I've ever told about my sweet sense,' he said. He'd never even told his ex-wife.

'I hate to break this to you, but your secret is out.'

He closed the lid to the box before temptation got the better of him. He shook his head. 'Uh-uh. That's not going to work any more. You can be as hard and sarcastic as you want, but we both know you really have a soft spot for me. You just admitted it.'

'If you tell anyone, I'll deny it.'

'Come on,' he said, feeling as light as high cotton. 'I'll take you to your truck. I think I have some gas in a canister in my garage.'

'No, I . . .'

But he was already walking down the steps. By the time he had the cake in the back seat of the car and the gas canister in the trunk, she was in the driveway, looking uncomfortable and lovely.

He opened the passenger door for her, and she sighed and got in.

When Sawyer started the car, she busied herself by playing with his navigation system. He just smiled when she programmed his GPS to take them to Frank's Toilet World on the highway.

Instead of Toilet World, in a matter of minutes, he was at her truck. They both got out and he put the gas from the canister into her tank. She thanked him, but before she could get in, he said impulsively, 'Have dinner with me tonight.'

She shook her head. 'That's not a good idea.'

'Come on. You have six months left here. Live a little.'

She snorted. 'Are you asking me to have a fling with you?'

'Absolutely not,' he said, feigning shock. 'I said dinner. It was your lascivious mind that went to the bedroom.'

She smiled, and he was glad. This was much better than the bristle she'd given him since coming back. Without thinking, he lifted his hand to her hair, petting it, then threading his fingers through it so that he could see the pink streak. He'd often wondered why she kept it. Was it her way of remembering?

When he met her eyes, he was stunned to see that they were huge. They darted to his lips. She thought he was going to kiss her.

And she wasn't running away.

Suddenly his blood was pumping thickly until it was roaring in his ears. And he leaned down and put his lips to hers.

Touching her, kissing her, was everything he remembered. There was such chemistry between them. He remembered from the football field, how it had felt like this. And he remembered thinking at the time, This girl must be in love with me.

He lifted his lips from hers, startled.

'I have to go,' she said quickly, not meeting his eyes, obviously embarrassed. 'Thank you for the gas.' She wrenched open the door to her truck and jumped in.

He was still standing on the sidewalk long after she drove away.

What just happened here? he thought.

Chapter 7

STELLA HAD BEEN GONE for hours before Julia finally left the house. Stella considered the Mullaby Barbecue Festival her day of debauchery. She started early and wouldn't be home until the next day. Sometimes Julia worried about her. She couldn't help it. She'd never seen anyone *try so hard* to be happy with what she had.

The Stella that Julia knew now was very different from the Stella she'd known in high school. Back then, Stella had been conspicuously showy, just like Dulcie Shelby. She'd driven a shiny black BMW bought specifically to match her shiny black hair. When Julia came back, she'd been surprised to find Stella still living here. Julia had always imagined those rich girls from school going on to live exotic lives.

Stella's problem, it turned out, was falling for the wrong guy. A tale as old as time. Her ex-husband had done a number on her by cheating and spending his way through her trust fund. The experience had turned Stella into a funny, self-deprecating woman who worked in a flower shop, lived in a house she could barely afford, and drank wine out of a box. Sometimes Julia wondered if Stella would trade all she'd learned to be that envied girl again.

Julia had never asked. Their pasts were touchy subjects, which was why Julia hadn't told her about Sawyer and the kiss, even though she really wanted to. And the fact that she couldn't bring herself to tell something that personal to Stella meant that they weren't as close as Stella thought they were. It made her sad.

It was noon when Julia finally walked over to Vance's house to take Emily to the festival. She knocked on the door and heard Emily race down the staircase with uncharacteristic enthusiasm. Julia was instantly suspicious.

Emily stepped outside, and Vance followed shortly.

'Are you sure you won't come?' Emily asked her grandfather.

'I'm sure,' Vance said. 'You two have fun.'

Emily ran down the front porch steps. 'I'll have her back before dark,' Julia told Vance. 'And we'll bring you some festival treats.'

'That's right nice of you, Julia. She seems awfully excited, doesn't she?' Vance said as Emily disappeared under the trees.

'Yes,' Julia said thoughtfully. 'She does.'

'Getting excited about barbecue. She's a lot like me.' He paused. 'I mean, there's not a lot about me I'd want her to favour, but . . .'

Julia put her hand on his arm. 'She is a lot like you, Vance. And that's a good thing.'

When Julia met her on the sidewalk, Emily asked, 'Why won't he come? He loves barbecue.'

'Vance tries to stay away from crowds,' Julia said. 'So, how are the two of you getting along?'

Emily shrugged, distracted. 'OK, I guess. Better.'

'That's good.'

Once they reached Main Street, Julia could tell that Emily was a little taken aback. People assumed that because Mullaby was small, the festival would be small. But the Mullaby Barbecue Festival was actually the largest barbecue festival in the Southeast. The street was closed to cars, and white tents stretched as far as the eye could see. In the distance, a Ferris wheel could be seen. The smell was delicious.

As they wove their way through the crowded street, they passed numerous barbecue tents in which the barbecue sandwiches were made in an assembly line. Sauce, no sauce? Coleslaw? There were also tents selling chicken on a stick and bratwursts, fried pickles, fried candy bars and funnel cakes. Craft tents dotted the area, too.

'I didn't know it would be this big,' Emily said, trying to take it all in. 'How do you find anyone in all of this?'

'Looking for someone in particular?' Julia asked.

Emily hesitated. 'No. Not really.'

But to test her theory, Julia purposely led Emily to the main stage. There were several stages staggered around the festival where bands were playing—folk and bluegrass mostly—but the main stage was right in the middle of Main Street.

There was a group of people, most of them Coffeys, clustered at the bottom of the stage steps, the men in hats and the women in crisp belted dresses. Win was wearing a straw boater. Sure enough, Emily's eyes went right to him. And he seemed to know exactly when it happened, because he looked up and saw her.

'Why is Win . . . why are the Coffeys so dressed up?' Emily asked. 'I mean, more than usual.'

'Because this festival belongs to them. Their family created it about sixty years ago. In a while, they'll do all their grandstanding on that stage, then they'll judge some barbecue and pie contests.'

Win's father looked over to his son, then followed his stare. He immediately called Win over to him, at the same time Julia ushered Emily away.

She and Emily had a good time for the next few hours. They ate way too much and bought commemorative T-shirts that read I WENT HOG WILD AT THE MULLABY BARBECUE FESTIVAL. Julia hadn't been to the festival in years. Her restaurant had a tent here, somewhere. She didn't have anything to do with it, though, her managers had set it up. She remembered how her father had loved the festival, and there had been a time when Julia had loved to come with him. She thought the event had lost its appeal for her, but she liked seeing it through Emily's eyes. She realised she missed something about this place.

Tired and sweaty and happy, they finally reached the amusement park rides at the other end of the street. It was getting late, so their plan was to go on a few rides, get treats for Vance, then go home.

But that's when Sawyer appeared, in khakis and a polo, winding his way towards them. Julia would have steered Emily away and lost him if Emily hadn't seen him first and said, 'There's Sawyer!' as if he were a rare and colourful bird they had to stand still to watch.

No one could deny that he was a sight to behold. But the muscles in her shoulders tightened as he approached. She'd been purposely avoiding him since last Tuesday. She didn't know what to do without her animosity towards him. It had been her companion for years, and now that he'd broken through that, she felt vulnerable.

As he walked towards them, he gave Julia a look so hot she was almost embarrassed. Contrary to this look, however, the first words out of his mouth were, 'I hope you're happy. My navigation system has been trying to take me to Frank's Toilet World all week.'

Emily laughed, and Julia said, 'Sorry.'

'I get the feeling you like pointing me in the wrong direction.' Before she could respond, he turned to Emily. 'Are you having a good time?'

'We've had a great day,' Emily said.

'We won't be staying much longer,' Julia added. 'We were about to take in a few rides, then go home.'

He chose to interpret that as an invitation. 'Great, I'll join you.'

'We don't want to keep you,' Julia said. 'Surely you're here with someone.'

'I came alone. I met up with Stella earlier, but her entourage got too big. Stella is like a comet collecting space debris as she passes.'

That made Emily laugh again, but Julia, curious ever since Sawyer had told her he'd once slept with Stella, asked seriously, 'You didn't want to be a part of Stella's comet tail?'

'I was distracted by another heavenly body.' He met her eyes.

Emily cleared her throat. 'I'm sure you two want to be alone. Why don't you go on a ride? I'd like to walk around by myself for a while anyway.'

'I don't think that's a good idea, Em,' Julia said.

'Why not?' Emily asked.

'Because I told your grandfather I'd keep an eye on you.'

'I'll be fine,' Emily said reasonably. 'I'm seventeen, not four.'

Julia knew she wasn't going to win this one. 'Meet me by the bandstand in one hour. One hour.'

Emily kissed Julia's cheek. 'Thanks.'

'One hour,' Julia called after her as she watched the crowd swallow Emily. She turned back to Sawyer, who had his brows raised. 'She's been looking for an excuse to get away from me. Win Coffey has been eyeing her all afternoon.'

'It was inevitable,' Sawyer said. 'Those two were going to have magnets attached to each other. The lure of the forbidden.'

'I don't want her to get hurt. She's been through so much.'

'Win is a pretty good kid. But if he does hurt her, he'll have me to contend with. Now,' he said, leaning in slightly, putting his face close to hers, 'let's talk about last Tuesday.'

'I have a better idea,' she said. 'Let's go in the fun house.'

Sawyer looked confused. 'That's a better idea?'

'It's the fun house. Who doesn't love the fun house?' she said as she walked over to the small structure. It sounded ridiculous, even to her. But talking about last Tuesday was too far ahead of her plans. He wanted her. But there was the little matter of telling him about their daughter first. That was going to change everything.

Sawyer bought their tickets. When they entered, the undulating floor threw her off-balance and she fell back against him. He took her hand and pulled her across the room. Many kids chose to stay in that room and ride the wooden waves, so when Julia and Sawyer tripped into the hall of mirrors, they were the only ones there.

She had to hold out her hands to make her way forward. Which was the walkway and which was just reflection? Which was the real Julia? She turned when Sawyer disappeared from behind her.

'Where did you go?' she called.

'I'm not sure,' he called back.

She tried to follow his voice. She almost walked into a mirror, then followed the corner of that mirror to the corridor she thought he'd taken. The strobe lights didn't help.

'If you want me to say I'm sorry for kissing you, I will,' Sawyer said. She caught sight of him, then he disappeared again. 'But I won't mean it. I'm sorry for a lot of things, but not that.'

There! There he was again! No, he moved. 'Stand still so I can find you,' she said. 'I don't want you to say you're sorry. It's just . . . I'm leaving soon. If you can accept that, then . . .'

'Then . . . what?' Sawyer asked. 'I can kiss you again?'

'That's not what I meant. There's a lot you don't know.' She turned a corner, only to find herself in a dead end. She backed out.

'It's starting to make sense,' Sawyer said. 'I even put the idea in your head, didn't I? "Live a little, since you only have six months left here." Or was this your plan all along, wait until a few months before you left, and then have one last hurrah?'

She stopped in her tracks, stung. 'You think I'm capable of that?'

'You're capable of leaving for eighteen years without so much as a look back. Do you regret that at all?' His voice was moving away.

She charged forward, determined to catch up to him. 'I wasn't the one who barrelled ahead without looking back. And how do you know I didn't look back? Were you looking? No, you weren't. And you have no idea what my regrets are, Sawyer, so don't go there.'

'You're right. I don't. You never shared them. You wanted them all to yourself. But you're saying the only way you can do this is if it's temporary. The only way you can let me in is knowing you get to leave me. No strings. No dealing with our complicated past.'

'*Where are you?*' she yelled in frustration.

'I have news for you. You can't have temporary. As a matter of fact, you're nowhere near where I want you to be.'

'What does that mean?'

'Stay in Mullaby, Julia, and find out.' She heard a door close.

'Sawyer? Sawyer!' It took a few minutes for her to make her way out. She went through the door and found herself in the rolling barrel. She ran through it, then through the air jets, but when she was finally outside again he was nowhere to be found.

What she'd been trying to say was she didn't think it was a good idea to pursue a relationship in light of what she had to tell him. He might hate her after she told him.

She walked down the street towards the bandstand, huffing with indignation. This was good. The animosity was back. She didn't owe him anything. She could just walk away now.

Oh God. If only she meant that. If only he hadn't kissed her . . .

Julia had barely made it out of the amusement ride area when she heard, 'Julia! Jooooooooolia!'

She turned and saw Beverly walking up to her with tiny clips of her high-heeled sandals. Her husband, Bud Dale, was walking beside her, looking like a pack mule as he carried all her bags.

'Beverly,' Julia said flatly. Then she turned to Beverly's husband. 'I haven't seen you in a while, Bud. How are you?'

'I'm doing real well, Julia. You're nice for askin'.' Something about the way he said it gave Julia pause. It was something her father would say, in that same good-ol'-boy kind of way. Beverly had left Julia's father, but then married a man just like him.

'I have a big surprise for you,' Beverly said. 'I don't have it with me now,' she said. 'But I'll come by to see you tomorrow around lunchtime, OK? I'm so excited about it.'

'Sure.' Julia started to turn. 'See you later.'

'Why do you have to act this way, Julia?' Beverly asked, putting her hands on her hips. 'Why are you always so unhappy? It's not an attractive quality. Why don't you spruce yourself up a little? Take that awful streak out of your hair. Smile at men, show a little skin.' Beverly adjusted herself, pulling at the low V of her shirt.

'Thanks for your input. Goodbye, Bud.'

'Good seein' you, Julia,' he said as she walked away.

'I always tried to be a mother to her,' she heard Beverly say. 'But I think there's something wrong with her that can't be fixed.'

Julia fought with herself, trying not to turn round and confront Beverly. Beverly had been no kind of mother to her. Julia kept walking, telling herself she wouldn't have to put up with this, or Sawyer, for long.

Emily walked around slowly, surrounded by the hot mist from food vendors and the tinny music from the kiddy rides. She was trying not to look as if she was looking for Win. She'd seen him several times, just glimpses before Julia pulled her away, or his father distracted him. Emily was so relieved that Sawyer had come up to them when he did. It had given her the perfect excuse to go off on her own.

Barely five minutes later she felt a familiar warm hand on her arm. She turned round and smiled.

Win had taken off his jacket and tie and his sleeves were rolled up. He'd lost the boater, too. His eyes were intense and green as he looked down at her.

'Hi,' was her brilliant opening line.

'Hello,' he said.

'Have you noticed there's a conspiracy to keep us at least twenty feet away from each other at all times? Who would have thought being friends would be this hard?'

He indicated they should walk. 'I think that's the difference between us,' he said. 'I knew how hard it would be going in.'

'So you get the badge of courage?'

'I'm sorry,' he said. 'I didn't mean it like that. I'm glad to finally spend some time with you.'

Slightly mollified, she said, 'I wish I could figure you out, Win.'

That made a side of his mouth lift into a smile. 'If you only knew how refreshing it is to hear that.'

'Oh, come on. You mean everyone has figured you out but me?'

He shrugged. 'Everyone in Mullaby, at least.'

'Gee, as if I didn't feel like such an oddball already.'

'See, that's exactly what I mean. You live in such a strange town, and yet you feel odd.'

As they walked, their arms touched as they were jostled by the crowd. She liked the unintentional nature of it. Everything else about Win was so deliberate. 'Well, I'm glad I could shake things up for you,' she said, which made him laugh.

They'd only been walking for a few minutes before he stopped and led her to a short queue. 'Let's go on this ride,' he said.

'Why this one?' she asked, following him.

'Because it's closest,' he said. 'And my dad is nearby.'

Emily looked back, trying to find Morgan Coffey, but she couldn't see him. Win paid for their tickets and they crossed the deck to the Ferris wheel. They took the next available seat.

Win put his arm over the back of the seat behind her and focused on the sky as the wheel slowly lifted them up. Emily, however, looked down at the crowd. She finally found his father. He was watching them with an expression made of ghosts and anger.

'He'll leave soon,' Win said. 'He won't want anyone knowing that it bothers him that we're together.'

'You and your dad don't get along, do you?'

'We're alike in many ways. But we don't see eye to eye. For example, he's very attached to doing things the way they've always been done. I don't agree.'

The Ferris wheel came to a stop two seats down from the top. 'I've been thinking about you a lot this past week,' she said, and it came out a lot more moony than she intended.

He met her eyes. His smile was mischievous. 'Oh?'

'Not like that,' she said, laughing. She stopped laughing when their seat swayed back and forth in the wind. She grabbed the safety bar in front of them. 'I just can't get my mind around something.'

'What is it?'

'You wouldn't happen to be a werewolf, would you?'

'Excuse me?' he said.

She slowly loosened her hold on the bar and sat back. 'There are only two reasons I can think of for why you don't come out at night: night blindness or werewolf.'

'And you decided to go with werewolf?'

'It was a toss up.'

Win didn't answer for a few moments. He finally said, 'It's tradition. It's gone on for centuries.'

'Why?'

'A good question. I guess because that's what traditions do.'

'Is this something you and your father don't see eye to eye on?'

The wheel started moving again. 'Yes. But going against this tradition is a big deal.' He turned to her. 'Of all the things I'm going to tell you, you need to understand that the most.'

She felt excited. 'What things are you going to tell me?'

'Strange and wondrous things,' he said in a dramatic voice.

'And why? Why are you doing this?'

'I told you before, we have history.'

'Technically, we don't,' she pointed out. 'Your uncle and my mother had history.'

'History is a loop. We're exactly where they stood twenty years ago. What's theirs is ours; what's ours will become theirs.'

'You've thought about this a lot.'

'Yes, I have.'

The wheel made one more rotation before stopping again. This time they were at the very top of the ride. Their seat creaked as it swung precariously back and forth. Emily grabbed the bar again.

Win smiled at her. 'You're not afraid, are you?'

'Of course not. Are you?'

He looked out over the horizon. 'I like seeing things from this perspective. I know what everything looks like from down there. I like seeing the possibilities of what's beyond that.'

She didn't realise she was staring at him until he turned to stare back. The air around them suddenly changed. His eyes went to her lips. Something warm and desperate filled her body. She'd never felt anything like it. But the moment passed and he moved his arm from the back of the seat.

After another rotation, the wheel stopped and the attendant unhooked the safety bar. They both got off the ride without a word.

'I'm sorry, but I've got to go,' he said.

She was still feeling strange, sort of buzzed and prickly. 'OK.'

But he didn't leave. 'My dad is round the corner, waiting,' he explained. 'I want to spare you whatever it is he might say.'

'OK.'

And still he didn't go. 'And it's going to get dark soon.'

'And you don't want to grow fur and fangs in front of me,' she said. 'I get it.'

His dark hair was curling in the humidity. He ran his hands through it. 'No, I don't think you do.'

'Then explain it to me. Tell me these strange, wondrous things.'

That made him smile. 'I will. Next time.' He turned to leave.

'Wait,' she called. 'I need to ask you something.'

'What is it?'

She decided to come right out and say it. 'Do you blame me for what my mother did?'

'Of course not,' he said immediately.

'But your father does.'

He hesitated. 'I can't speak for him.'

'My grandfather told me that my mom got angry because the Coffeys wouldn't let her into their social circle and that's why she did what she did.'

'That's how the story goes,' he said. His eyes bored into her with a sudden and intense curiosity.

She pushed her hair behind her ears, and his eyes followed the movement. 'I just want you to know that . . . I'm not mad that your family doesn't like me. I understand why. And I'm not mad.'

'Oh, Emily,' he said. 'You're making this very hard.'

'What? Leaving?'

'That too. Next time?'

She nodded. She liked that, the continuance, the anticipation. What would he do? What would he say? She was too enamoured of him, too fascinated. But she couldn't seem to help it.

'Next time,' she said as he walked away.

Emily met Julia by the bandstand as promised, and she could tell that both their moods had changed since they'd last been together. They bought Grandpa Vance a barbecue sandwich and a fried pickle, then headed home. Neither of them was particularly chatty.

Julia said a distracted goodbye when they reached Grandpa Vance's house. Something was definitely on her mind.

When Emily walked into the house, she knocked on the door to Vance's bedroom. 'Grandpa Vance, I'm home.'

When he opened the door, she caught her first glimpse of his bedroom, which had obviously once been the living room. The curtains were drawn to keep the heat out, but the light through the rust-coloured material cast a glow of permanent sunset over the room. There was a faint scent of sweet perfume lingering in the air.

There were rows of photographs on the shelves on the far wall, older photos of the same woman, a pretty woman with blonde hair and Emily's mother's smile. That must be her grandmother Lily.

Emily held up the foil-wrapped food. 'I brought you some stuff from the festival.'

'Wonderful! I think I'll eat in the kitchen. Will you join me?' He led the way. As soon as they reached the kitchen, Vance went directly to the laundry room. Emily heard the dryer door open, then close. Then Vance walked back out. 'So, how did you like our little barbecue shindig?'

Emily smiled. 'It wasn't little at all.'

'What did you do?' He went to the breakfast nook and sat.

'Wandered around. Ate too much. Julia bought me this T-shirt.' Emily placed the food on the table, then sat opposite him. She brought the T-shirt out of the small bag she'd been carrying.

'Ha! That's a good one,' Vance said as he read what was on the shirt. 'Did you see any kids your age?'

Emily hesitated before she said, 'Just Win Coffey.'

'Well, it is their festival,' he said as he unwrapped his food and began to eat. 'You need to meet some other people your age. School doesn't start until next month.' He suddenly looked worried. 'That friend of your mother's, Merry, said she would take care of getting you registered and your class credits transferred. Do you think I should check with the school, just in case?'

Emily had been so focused on what was going on here, she hadn't given Merry much thought lately. That startled her. 'Merry probably handled everything. She's very detail-orientated, just like Mom.' Emily looked down to the T-shirt in her lap. 'Mom helped found the school I went to. Did you know that?'

He nodded. 'Merry and I had a long talk. Your mother had a remarkable life. Merry told me a lot about you, too. She said you were involved in a lot of activities.'

Emily shrugged. 'They were school requirements.'

'I bet there are a lot of activities you can get involved in here.'

She knew what he was doing, being about as subtle as an eight-foot-tall man. He didn't want her associating with Win. She understood why. At the same time, she wondered if she could change this. Like her mother said, *Don't wait for the world to change.* She'd been thinking a lot lately about clues her mother might have given her over the years, either on purpose or unconsciously, about her time here. Who she'd become, Emily was beginning understand, was her penance. She'd hurt people when she was young. She'd saved them when she got older. But for all the good she'd done, she'd never thought it was enough.

After Grandpa Vance ate, he got up and threw the food wrappers away. Then he went back to the laundry room to check the dryer.

She couldn't stand it any longer. When he came back out, she asked, 'Why do you do that? Check the dryer so often?'

He laughed and gave her a sly look. 'I was wondering when you'd ask,' he said. 'I was a little uptight when Lily and I first married. I'd lived alone for quite a while. I would follow her round when she would do housework, to make sure it was done the way I'd always done it. The thing that bothered Lily the most was my checking the dryer after her to see if she'd left any clothes behind.' He shook his head at the memory. 'Because I'm so tall, I can't see that low into the dryer, so I just feel. One day, I went in and stuck my hand in the dryer . . . and felt something cold and slimy. She'd set a frog in the dryer for me to find! I jerked my hand out so fast that I fell down. Then out jumps the frog. Lily was standing in the doorway, laughing. Over the years, she'd tell me to go check the dryer as a joke, and I'd always find a small gift from her. After she died, I just kept checking. It makes me think of her. And when I get worried, I go check, just in case she wants to tell me something.'

'I think that's sweet,' Emily said. 'I wish I'd known her.'

'I do, too. She would have liked you.'

They said good night at the staircase, and Vance went into his room. Emily made it halfway up the staircase before she stopped. She hesitated, then walked down and went to the laundry room.

She studied the dryer for a moment. Before she knew what she was doing, her hand went to the handle and she quickly opened the door, jumping back as if something inside might fly out at her.

She cautiously peered in. Nothing was there.

She almost laughed at herself as she walked out. What had possessed her to do that? What sign was she looking for?

Hours later Emily slowly opened her eyes, not sure what had awakened her. She stared at the ceiling and it gradually came to her. Something was wrong. The room was normally brighter than this.

When she'd gone to sleep, light from the moon was shining in through the open balcony doors. She turned her head on the pillow to see that the balcony doors she'd left open were now closed, and the curtains had been drawn over them.

Her heart suddenly gave a single hard thud of surprise. Someone had been in her room. She reached under her pillow and turned off her MP3 player, then she slowly sat up. She knew it was him. She could feel the lingering warmth of him still in the air.

She pulled the earbuds out of her ears, got up and and went to the light switch. When she flicked it on, the chandelier bathed the room in cobwebby light. But no one was there. From across the room, she saw a piece of paper peeking out from the curtains. The twin doors had been shut with a note tucked between them. She hurried over and pulled the note out. *I'm sorry I had to leave the festival. I didn't want to. Will you spend the day with me? Meet me on the boardwalk at Piney Woods Lake this morning. Win.*

Emily immediately swung open the doors and stepped out onto the balcony, looking round.

'Win?'

Nothing. The only sound was the rustling of leaves in the wind.

Her heart was still thumping, but not so much from fear now as an incredible sense of anticipation. It had been months since she'd looked forward to anything. He made her remember how it felt.

The edge of her nightgown was fluttering against her legs, and the air around her was charged with energy. She didn't want to move. She didn't want to let go of this feeling.

A few minutes later, she heard an engine turn over. The lights of Julia's truck, parked in front of her house, suddenly sprang to life. Emily watched the truck pull away and drive down the street. She guessed she wasn't the only one who wasn't going to sleep that night.

Chapter 8

WHEN SAWYER OPENED the door, he was irritated, as anyone would be if they were forced out of bed by the incessant ringing of a doorbell. The door flew open and hit the wall as he flicked on the porch light.

Julia took her hand away from the doorbell, and the grating shriek inside his house stopped.

He blinked a few times. 'Julia?' he asked, just to be sure.

'I need to talk to you.'

'Now?' He wasn't at his best.

She rolled her eyes. 'Yes, now.'

He took a good long look at her. She hadn't changed clothes. She was wearing the same faded jeans and white peasant blouse she'd been wearing at the festival. He should have stayed there with her, but he'd been angry. She thought he only wanted a fling. While he'd had his share of flings, he wanted to be nobler than that with Julia. *And she wouldn't let him.* 'Are you drunk?' he asked.

'No, I am not drunk. I'm mad.'

'Oh, good, because for a moment there I thought it was going to be something unusual.' He stepped back. 'Come in.'

She walked past him into his darkened living room. The only light came from his kitchen, where he kept the hood light over his oven on at night. She looked round, nodding slightly, as if his space was exactly what she expected it to be.

'Is this about the big thing you wanted to tell me?' he asked.

She turned to face him, her brows lowered. 'What?'

'Last Tuesday, you gave me a cake, told me you started baking because of me, then said there was some big thing you were going to tell me later. Is this later?'

'No, this has nothing to do with that. Why would I be mad about that?'

He sighed. 'I don't know, Julia. When it comes to you, it's all guesswork.'

She began to pace. 'I was fine here until you went all humble on me. And you almost had me, too. I almost trusted you.' She made a scoffing sound. 'And you accuse me of being conniving.'

'What are you talking about?'

'I'm talking about what you said today.'

He rubbed the side of his face. 'Refresh my memory.'

'You said that I'm only letting you in because I'm planning to leave. *And then you walked away from me.*'

'Ah.' He let his hand drop. 'That.'

'I wasn't saying that at all, which I would have told you if you'd stuck around. But it doesn't matter that it wasn't what I meant. Because, so what?'

He was beginning to think it wasn't his sleepy mind after all. She really was making no sense. 'Excuse me?'

'So what if I was only letting you in because I'm planning to leave? Why would that matter to you? You've been trying to get into my pants ever since I came back, and you were going to let something like my leaving get in your way? It didn't get in your way last time.'

His head suddenly felt hot. She'd struck a nerve. 'You know as well as I do that I could get into your pants at any time.' He took a step towards her. 'Because I know exactly how to do that.'

'So do it now,' she said, but her voice faltered a little.

'I want in here, too.' He put his finger to her temple.

'You are there.'

'What about here?' He put his hand on her chest, over her heart. Her heart was racing. Was it anger? Fear? Lust?

She stepped back. 'You're not going to do that to me again.'

'What?'

'Weasel your way into my heart. Charm me and make me think that it's for ever. It took years to get over it last time. You're not going to promise me anything, and I'm not promising you. So that "Stay, because you're nowhere near where I want you to be" crap isn't going to work. Do you know how much easier it would have been if you had just promised me one night? That night? Do you realise how much I hated you for making me think you loved me?'

'Julia . . .'

'No. Promise me one night,' she said. 'Don't promise to love me. Don't ask me to stay.'

To hell with nobility. He reached for her and kissed her. It was all at once passionate, as if there was too much in him to contain.

'You want one night, I'll give it to you,' he said as he picked her up and carried her to the couch. 'But it's going to be one hell of a night.'

It had never been like this with anyone else. They held on to each other as if the force of their bodies coming together could make everything that had ever separated them disappear. And it did, for a short period of time.

Afterwards, clinging to each other, Sawyer managed to say, 'Contrary to my lamentable lack of restraint just now, I have actually learned a few things since I was sixteen.'

She gave a sudden laugh.

'And as soon as I have the strength to get up, I'm taking you to my bedroom and showing you.'

It was morning, but still dark in his bedroom when she woke up. Sawyer watched as she blinked a few times and turned her head on the pillow to find him staring at her. Her hair was rumpled, the pink streak curling round her ear. She took a deep, defeated breath. 'I thought I had everything figured out.'

'Do you think promising you another night might clear things up?'

She smiled, but didn't answer.

He brushed one finger lightly against her forearm. He saw the moment she realised he was following the lines of her scars. She immediately pulled her arm away. He pulled it back.

'Why did you do this to yourself?' he asked.

She watched him as he watched his finger trace the lines. 'It was my way of dealing with the depression I felt. All my anger was turned inwards, so this is what I did. Don't think I'm naturally this enlightened. That's years of therapy speaking.'

He met her eyes. 'Do you ever think of doing it again?'

'No. In case you hadn't noticed, I'm very good at expressing my anger these days.' She shifted slightly.

'Why didn't you come back to Mullaby, Julia?'

'I didn't think there was anything left for me.' She rolled her head back on the pillow and stared at the ceiling.

'Didn't you ever get homesick?'

'I'm homesick all the time,' she said, still not looking at him. 'I just don't know where home is. There's this promise of happiness out there. I know it. I even feel it sometimes. But it's like chasing the moon—just when I think I have it, it disappears into the horizon. I grieve and try to move on, but then the damn thing comes back the next night, giving me hope of catching it all over again.'

'Is that the big thing you were going to tell me?'

'No.'

He groaned. 'You're killing me. Is it something good?'

'Yes.'

He put his hand on her thigh. 'Better than last night?'

'No comparison.' She put her hand on his. 'What time is it?'

He lifted himself on his elbow and looked over to the clock on the nightstand. 'A little after nine.'

She gasped and jumped out of bed. She went to the heavy curtains and threw them open. Morning light cut into the dark room.

'I can't believe it's morning! Why didn't you tell me? What kind of curtains are these?' She grabbed the offending material and looked at it.

'They're insulated light-blockers. I'd be blinded every morning if I didn't have them.' He sat up against his pillows.

'I've got to go,' she said. 'I have to make the day's cakes at the restaurant. I'm usually there and gone by now. Where are my clothes?' She looked around. 'Oh, downstairs.' She darted from his room.

He smiled and got up. He took his robe from the back of his door and put it on as he walked down the stairs after her.

She was quick. She already had on her jeans and shoes, and was pulling her shirt over her head. By the time her head poked through the collar, he was there, backing her against the wall by the door.

'We're back where we started. I think this is a sign that we need to do it again.'

Suddenly there was a knock at the door, directly to the right, which startled Julia so much she let out a small scream.

Sawyer winced and rubbed his ear.

'Who is that?' she whispered.

'I don't know.'

'Don't answer it. Maybe they'll go away.'

'What's the problem? You don't want people to know we've been together?' He turned and went to the door before she could answer, because he was afraid of what that answer might be. When he saw who was standing there, he thought, *Oh, damn.* This wasn't going to help things at all.

'Hi, Sawyer,' Holly said as she walked in. 'Was that you screaming like a girl?'

Holly stopped when she saw Julia. There was an awkward moment when the three of them didn't say anything, just stared at one another.

'Holly,' Sawyer finally said, 'you remember Julia Winterson?'

'Of course,' Holly said, giving Sawyer a pointed look before turning to Julia and smiling. 'It's nice to see you, Julia.'

'You too. I'm sorry to run, but I'm late.' In seconds, she was gone.

Sawyer turned to his ex-wife. 'I forgot you were coming by.'

Holly kissed him on the cheek, walked to his kitchen and began to make coffee. He followed her, remembering the feeling he had when he first asked Holly to be his girlfriend in sixth grade. She was his best friend all through school, but he didn't know if he was ever in love with her. That night with Julia on the football field should have told him that, but he'd been too afraid to give up on the future he'd planned.

He was the one who had ended the marriage. Holly would have stayed once they'd found out he couldn't have kids. In fact, she'd become determined to stick it out. She'd brought home information on adoption and tried to be enthusiastic. Kids were an integral part of their plan, but he realised she wanted them so much because what they had together wasn't enough. It never had been.

'You finally did it,' Holly said. She was scooping coffee grounds out of the can. 'I can't believe it.'

Sawyer pulled out a stool and sat at the counter. 'What are you talking about?'

'Don't play dumb with me.' She looked over her shoulder with a grin. She looked good. Happy. Her hair was in a ponytail, revealing that her face was fuller. She'd put on weight. 'I know you too well. You've had a thing for her since we were kids. And you finally got her.'

Sawyer sighed. 'I'm not so sure about that.'

Holly's smile disappeared. 'Oh, hell. I didn't . . .'

'No, it's not your fault. You look fantastic, by the way.'

'Are you really OK with this? With me getting married again? With this?' She put her hand to her stomach.

'I'm happy for you, Holly. I truly am.'

She snorted and turned back to the coffee. 'I think you're only saying that because you got some last night.'

Sawyer slid off the stool. 'I'll get the papers for you to sign.'

Liquid morning light was rippling through the open balcony doors when Emily woke up. She had no idea what time it was.

The note. She turned quickly to the bedside table. The note was still there, where she'd left it. She picked it up and stared at it.

Was she going to do it? Was she going to meet him?

Win said he didn't blame her for what her mother had done, but how could she know for sure? What were his motives?

Her mother was the bravest person she had ever known, yet even she hadn't been able to face down her past. So Emily would.

She would do something her mother couldn't do. In order to find her place here, she had to set herself apart from who her mother had been, but she also had to try to make it right.

She thought about the history loop Win had talked about. Here she was in the same place her mother had been, at about the same age, and involved with the Coffeys in a way no one approved of, just like last time. There had to be a reason for it.

She got up and walked to her wardrobe for shorts and a tank top. She was getting used to averting her eyes to avoid looking at the frenzied butterfly wallpaper. Getting used to it meant she was fitting in, according to Julia. Either that, or she was going crazy.

When she reached the wardrobe, though, she suddenly realised the butterfly wallpaper was gone. It had been replaced by a moody, breathless wallpaper of silver, sprinkled with tiny white dots that looked like stars. It made her feel an odd sense of anticipation.

Did it really change on its own?

It was beautiful. It made the room look like living in a cloud. She put her hand against the wall by her wardrobe. It was soft, like velvet. How could her mother not have told her a room like this existed?

She dressed quickly and went downstairs. Thankfully, Grandpa Vance had already left for breakfast, so she wrote him a note telling him she'd be at the lake. She didn't mention who she was meeting.

She was about to get in her car when she heard her name being called. Already jittery, she jumped in surprise. She turned to see Stella walking towards her from next door. She looked strangely overdressed for that time of morning, in a strapless red dress and heels. Her wide face had blotches of make-up on it, and her exotic eyes were tired. She looked as if she'd had a bad night. Or maybe a very good one. Emily couldn't decide which.

'Have you seen Julia?' Stella asked. 'I just went by J's Barbecue and she wasn't there.'

'I haven't seen her since yesterday. But I did hear her leave in her truck around one o'clock this morning.'

Stella looked confused. 'I wonder where she went. Julia never goes out that late. Do you think she's been acting weird lately?'

'Only around Sawyer.'

'Hmm. Something's on her mind.'

Emily looked over her shoulder anxiously, half expecting to see Grandpa Vance coming home. 'She hasn't said anything to me.'

'Well, if you see her, tell her I'm looking for her.' Stella nodded to the Oldsmobile. 'Where are you going at this time of the morning?'

'To the lake. What about you?'

'Oh, I'm just getting in,' Stella said, then paused. 'Crap. I can't believe I said that to you. Erase that. Just . . . do as I say, not as I do.'

That made Emily laugh as she got in her car. Stella walked back to her house, taking off her heels and shaking her head to herself.

There was so little traffic at that time of the morning that Emily arrived at Piney Woods Lake in record time. She knew she was too early, but she'd wanted to leave before Grandpa Vance got home.

She parked the car, then walked to the boardwalk in the murky morning air and sat on one of the benches overlooking the lake. She propped her feet on the railing while watching the fog roll off the water. Some of the lake houses had their lights on, but not many.

She heard footsteps approach behind her, then Win appeared by the bench. He sat beside her and put his feet on the railing beside hers. He had a strong, angular profile. Proud, full of secrets. She wanted to know those secrets. Was this how her mother felt?

'Come to my family's lake house and have breakfast with me,' he finally said.

'How long have you been waiting?'

'A while. I didn't want to miss you.' He took a deep breath, then stood. 'I'm glad you came.' He held out his hand to her.

They walked down the empty beach, then Win led Emily up the steps to the large deck of his family's lake house. He gestured for her to sit in one of the Adirondack chairs. She did, pulling her legs up and wrapping her arms round them.

She relaxed this stance only when Penny, the housekeeper, came out and served them frittatas. Penny was sixty-three years old, widowed, and set in her ways. But she had a soft spot for Win, and Win adored her.

He and Emily ate breakfast in silence. He made her nervous and she made him feel off-balance. He'd spent his life accepting what his father had told him he could never change, and forcing himself not to covet the freedom other people had. Things had to change. If Dulcie Shelby's daughter, of all people, could accept him for who he was, then his family would have to take notice. Emily was the first step to a new way of life.

After breakfast, they sat side by side, quietly watching the sun burn the morning fog away. The beach was now slowly filling with people.

'Are you out here a lot in the summer?' Emily finally asked.

He'd been waiting for her to say something, not wanting to rush her. 'My family uses this house all year round. It's a home away from home. It drives Penny crazy, though. She likes to keep to a schedule and we throw her off it by showing up unexpectedly, like I did this morning.'

'I get the feeling she doesn't mind. I think she adores you.' She looked over to him with a smile that made his chest feel full. All he could think was how different she was than he thought she would be. She was striking and sweet . . . and had endearingly quirky hair.

In the silence that followed, her smile faded and her hands went to her hair. 'Do I have something on my head?'

'No, sorry. I was just thinking about your hair. I was wondering if you ever wore it down.'

She shook her head. 'It's in that growing-out stage right now. My mom wore her hair short, so I wore mine short, too. But I started growing it out a little over a year ago.'

'What made you stop wanting to be like her?'

'I've never stopped wanting to be like her. She was a wonderful person,' she said vehemently. 'It was just a lot to live up to.'

This wasn't working. They had to shake some of this awkwardness off. 'Let's go for a walk,' he said as he stood.

They left their shoes by their chairs and went down the deck steps. They walked close to the water and got their feet wet. They didn't talk much, but that was OK.

When they reached the cove, Emily looked towards the grotto where Win's sister's birthday party had been held. He knew what she was going to do before she took the first step. Without a word, Emily walked away from the water, towards the trees. She went to the tree where her mother's and his uncle's initials had been carved.

The past few months of her life had been marked by a chaos Win could only imagine. Looking at her, he could see her grief.

'Will the kids at Mullaby High know about my mom? About who she was here?' Emily finally asked, staring at the tree.

'If their parents tell them. You probably got the worst of it from my dad. I wouldn't worry about Mullaby High.' He hated seeing her like this. He wanted to distract her. 'Tell me about your old school. The website made it seem . . . intense.' That was putting it mildly. Roxley was full of righteous, politically correct indignation.

She shrugged. 'After my mom died, I wanted to find some sort of comfort in the school, but I couldn't. There was just this *legacy.* People there wanted me to fill my mom's shoes, and I couldn't.'

'What about your friends there?'

'I started having panic attacks after my mother died, so I started spending a lot of time by myself.'

He suddenly thought of her sitting on the bench downtown with her head down. He'd seen the way she'd stopped short on the sidewalk, the colour draining from her face. It had been alarming. 'Were you having a panic attack the first day we met?'

She nodded.

'What brings them on?'

'They come when there's too much going on in my head.' She suddenly seemed wary. 'Why do you want to know?'

'I'm just curious.' She continued to look at him, her brows low over her bright blue eyes. 'Why are you looking at me like that?'

'I've never told anyone about my panic attacks,' she said, as if he'd somehow forced it out of her. 'You now know my weakness.'

'We all have weaknesses.'

'Do you?'

'Oh, yes.' She had no idea.

'And you're not going to tell me?'

He took a deep breath. 'It's complicated.'

'I get it,' she said, and turned to walk back to the shoreline. 'You don't want to tell me.'

He jogged after her. 'No. It's more like . . . I have to show you.'

She stopped. He almost ran into her. 'So show me.'

'I can't. Not now. You'll have to trust me on that.'

'I don't have much of a choice, do I?' she said.

They headed round the lake, quiet again, and eventually circled back to the house. It was a long walk, and when they got back, Penny brought lunch out to them unasked. After she set out the plates of sandwiches and fruit, she passed behind Emily's chair, still in Win's view. She smiled as she pointed to Emily and gave him a thumbs up before she went inside to answer the ringing phone.

He smiled back at her.

After they'd finished, Emily stood and walked to the railing. 'I wish I had my bathing suit,' she said. 'I'd go cool off in the water.'

'Come inside where it's cool. I'll show you around,' he said. He walked into the cavernous living room off the deck and Emily followed.

She was silent when she stepped inside. This place actually looked as if his family spent a lot of time here, which they did. The furniture was comfortable. One wall was dominated by a flat screen, and the floor under it was littered with a Wii and tons of DVDs. Overnight travel was inconvenient for them, so their vacations usually consisted of coming to the lake and staying here.

'This is a lot more homy than I expected,' she finally said.

'They can't all be ivory towers.'

He led her to the first floor with a cursory wave to the four bedrooms there, then up to the second-floor loft, through a door in the linen closet. The space was occupied by a low couch, a stack of books, a television and some storage boxes. No one came up here but him.

'I spend a lot of time in this loft when I'm here,' he said as she looked round. The only light was from the windows on the far wall, stacked in the shape of a triangle.

'I can see why. It has a secret feel to it. It suits you.' She walked to the bank of windows. 'Great view.'

He watched her from across the room. He was moving before he was aware of what he was doing. He stopped behind her, inches away. Awareness immediately radiated from her like electricity.

A full minute passed before he said, 'You're suddenly quiet.'

She swallowed. 'I don't understand how you do this to me.'

He leaned in slightly. Her hair smelled like lilacs. 'Do what?'

'Your touch.'

'I'm not touching you, Emily.'

She turned round. 'That's just it. It feels like you are. How do you do that? It's like you have something surrounding you.'

That startled him. She felt it. No one had ever felt it before.

She waited for him to say something, to explain or deny it, neither of which he could do. He took a step past her, closer to the window. 'Your family once owned all of this,' he said.

She decided to accept the change of subject. 'All of what?'

'All of Piney Woods Lake. Years ago, that's how the Shelbys made their money, by selling it off, parcel by parcel.' He pointed to the trees in the distance. 'All that wooded acreage on the other side of the lake still belongs to your grandfather. That's millions of dollars of potential development. It drives my father crazy. He wants your grandfather to sell him some of it.'

'Why?'

'Coffeys like to have a say in the growth of Mullaby.'

'Why?' she asked again.

'Because this is our home. For years and years, we thought this was the only place we could live.'

'Is it?'

He turned to face her. 'Do you really want to know? My weakness?'

'Yes. Yes, of course I do.'

This was it. There was no going back after he told her. He had to show her then. 'The men in my family have an . . . affliction.'

She looked confused. 'What sort of affliction?'

He paced across the room. 'It's genetic,' he said. 'A simple mutation. My grandfather had it. My uncle had it. My father has it. I have it.' He paused. 'We call it The Glowing.'

Emily stared at him, still not understanding.

'Our skin gives off light at night,' he explained. It was liberating, actually saying that to someone outside his family. 'That's what you feel,' he said eagerly, walking back to her and putting his hands on either side of her face, almost, but not quite, touching her.

She met his eyes. 'You want me to believe that you glow in the dark,' she said in a monotone.

Win dropped his hands. 'You'll believe I'm a werewolf, but not this?'

'I never believed you were a werewolf.'

He stepped back, trying not to feel defeated. He had to go on. 'It goes back generations. My ancestors left the old country to avoid persecution, because people assumed their affliction was the work of evil. They settled here when it was nothing but farmland, but slowly the town grew around them. No one knew their secret. That changed the night your mother tricked my uncle into coming out at night. He stood on the bandstand that summer night, in front of the entire town, and for the first time, everyone saw what we could do.'

'That's a very elaborate story,' she said.

'Emily, you've even seen me. In your back yard at night.'

That gave her a start. 'You're the light in my back yard? You're the Mullaby lights?'

'Yes.'

He could tell her mind was working, trying to sort it all out.

'Then why have you stopped coming round?'

'I come every night. But your grandfather sits on the kitchen porch and tells me to go away before you can see that I'm there.'

'My grandfather knows?' Her voice was pitching higher.

'Yes.'

'Prove it.' She looked round and saw the closet door. She walked over to it and opened it. 'Here, come here.'

He walked over and she herded him into the closet, closing the door behind them. She waited a few moments in the pitch black before she said, 'Ha! I don't see you glowing.'

'That's because it takes moonlight,' he said patiently.

She snorted. 'Well, that's convenient.'

'Actually, no, it's not.'

'This is ridiculous,' she said, fumbling to find the doorknob.

'Wait,' he said, and reached out to stop her. His hand landed on her hip and she suddenly stilled. 'Meet me tonight at the bandstand. At midnight. I'll show you.'

'Why are you doing this?' she asked in a whisper. 'Is this some elaborate plan? For getting back at my mother for what she did?'

'No,' he said. 'I told you, I don't blame you for what she did.'

'But you're re-creating that night with my mother and your uncle.'

'It has nice symmetry, doesn't it?'

'OK,' she said unhappily. 'I'll be there.'

He almost laughed. 'You don't have to sound so enthusiastic.'

'This would be easier if I didn't like you so much.'

'You like me?' He felt both elated and ashamed. She didn't answer. 'How much?' he asked quietly, the air filling with tension.

'Enough to meet you tonight, even though I'm pretty sure you have something else planned other than glowing in the dark.'

'That isn't enough?' He could sense her holding her breath when she realised how close his face was to hers. 'I'm knotted up with you,' he said. 'Don't you feel it? I was meant to show you.'

'I need to go.' She opened the door, and was gone in seconds.

He caught up with her on the deck as she was putting on her shoes. 'Don't go through the woods tonight. Come into the park from the street.'

She stood and stared at him for a long time. He started to reach out his hand to touch her, but she gave him a brief nod before turning and quickly making her way down the steps to the beach.

He watched her walk away, then walked slowly back into the house. He stopped when he entered the living room. His father was sitting in the big black leather chair by the couch, his legs crossed.

Win was astonished. He could usually feel when his father was looking for him. Finally he said, 'When did you get here?'

'Just now. I called earlier to ask you not to block your mother's car when you come home, because she's leaving early tomorrow with Kylie to go to Raleigh to shop for school clothes. Penny said you were on the beach with a girl. I asked her to describe the girl, and it sounded like Emily Benedict. But I thought, no, Win knows better than that.'

That must have been the phone call Penny had answered earlier.

'So you came out to see for yourself,' Win concluded. He took a deep breath and said, 'I like her.'

'I liked a girl once, when I was your age,' Morgan said. 'Her name was Veronica. She was new to Mullaby, too. I asked her to a matinée, and your grandfather found out. He slapped me, then locked me in my room. When I didn't show up at the movie theatre, Veronica came to the house to ask if I was all right. Your grandfather was horrible to her. He told her that my asking her out was just a joke. She hated me after that. But he made his point.'

'What point?'

'That we weren't made for normal lives.'

'Did your father treat your brother the same way?' Win asked as he took a seat on the couch.

'The rules weren't any different for Logan.'

Win had never known that his grandfather hit his father. Win remembered the old man vaguely. He was very quiet when Win knew him. It made sense now that Logan and Dulcie Shelby had to sneak around. Win's grandfather obviously would have slapped Logan and locked him in his room if he'd found out. It all seemed so ridiculous now. The furtive prowling. The secret was out and it couldn't be taken back.

'It's different now,' Win said.

'You say that as if different is better,' Morgan said. 'If we wait long enough, people will forget what they saw, and things can go back to the way they were.'

'I don't want to go back to the way things were.'

'You don't have a choice. You're grounded. And you're not allowed to associate with Emily any more.'

That wasn't unexpected. 'That girl you liked. Didn't you ever want to tell her?'

Morgan stared at his hands. 'No,' he finally said. 'I liked the illusion. When I was with her, I was . . .'

'Normal,' Win finished for him.

Morgan nodded. 'It was like that with your mother for a while. Then Logan was tricked into showing everyone. Your mother and I had only been married for two years. She's never forgiven me for not telling her, for making her find out with the rest of the town.'

Every Coffey man had a different way of telling the woman he married, but it was always after the ceremony.

'Mom loves you,' Win said, certain that it had been true at least once.

Morgan got up and headed for the front door. 'She loves me in the daytime. Trust me, Win. I'm trying to save you some misery.'

Chapter 9

JULIA PARKED HER TRUCK behind the restaurant and thought, *What in the hell have I just done?* Sawyer had got her so mad that she'd slept with him. Or was that really the reason? Maybe it had just been the excuse she'd needed. And now she had to go into her restaurant wearing the same clothes she'd been wearing yesterday.

She groaned and put her head on the steering wheel. She could go home, she supposed. But then people might come by and ask if something was wrong. It wasn't worth all the additional explaining.

She tried to smooth her hair back a little, but it didn't help much. She sighed and got out. Coming in through the back meant walking a few steps into the seating area itself, just past the rest rooms. She tried to sneak in, but found herself stopping when she saw just how full the place was. She knew how well the business was doing from a financial standpoint, but it was a different experience to see it for herself. Her father would have loved this. He would have been out there talking to people, making them feel welcome. She suddenly wondered, when she left this place, would his memory live on?

'Hey, Julia!' someone called from a table, and several people turned and waved. Normally, she was here so early that she never saw these people. Julia smiled at them and stepped into the kitchen.

Hours later, in the thick of the lunch rush, Julia finally finished her cakes. They were being served even as she stood behind the counter, writing their names on the chalkboard.

She didn't know it, but while she was in the kitchen, her stepmother, Beverly, had come in, but not to eat. She was waiting for Julia at a table near the door.

'Julia!' Beverly said as she approached, waving a large brown envelope. 'I stopped by Stella's house looking for you. What are you doing here at lunchtime?'

Julia was too tired to deal with Beverly today. She set the chalkboard down. 'Let's talk some other time, Beverly. I'm exhausted and I want to go home.' And where was that, exactly? she thought. Her apartment at Stella's? Her dad's old house? Baltimore?

'No, no, no. I'm put out enough with you already, missy. If I had known you'd be here, I would have come here first instead of stopping at Stella's house and waiting for you. That woman is such an odd duck. What are you doing here at lunchtime?' she asked again.

'I own this place, Beverly. I can come and go anytime I please.'

'Speaking of which . . . Excuse me, hon,' she said to a man sitting at the counter as she hipped her way between him and the man beside him. It was a tight fit, but she didn't seem to mind. Neither did the men. 'Here's the surprise I was talking about!' She slapped the envelope on the counter. 'I had my lawyer draw up partnership papers for this place. All you have to do is sign over half of J's Barbecue to me. That way, when we sell it, we can split the profit.'

The men on either side of Beverly looked at Julia curiously, waiting for her to say something. People at a nearby table heard, too.

Julia stared at the envelope. This shouldn't have mattered, but it did. Just like last night shouldn't have mattered, but it did.

At least a full minute passed before Beverly began to look uncomfortable. 'Now, Julia, you know I deserve this.' She leaned in and said in a softer voice, 'I thought we had an understanding.'

'My understanding,' Julia said, 'is that my father loved you, but you left him.' That had the restaurant quiet in seconds.

Beverly scooped up the envelope. 'Obviously, you're cranky. From the look of you, you haven't had much sleep. And don't think I haven't noticed that those are the same clothes you were wearing yesterday. Clean up a little, and I'll meet you outside.'

'No, Beverly. This ends here,' Julia said, and it all came flooding out. 'You were everything to him, to the detriment of his relationship with me. I ceased to exist when you came into his life. He worked hard at this business, but it was never good enough for you, was it? When it stopped making money, as paltry as it had been, you left him. Do you honestly think I'm going to give you half of it? That you *deserve* it?'

Beverly pursed her thin lips, which were lined in pearly peach. 'You could learn a thing or two about casting stones. You left him first. And you were the reason he was so deeply in debt. It was all your fault, missy, so don't get all high and mighty on me.'

Julia couldn't believe her gall. 'How could I be the reason he was in debt?'

Beverly laughed resentfully. 'How do you think he paid for that reformatory you went to? He mortgaged everything he had for you, you ungrateful girl. And I still didn't leave him then. I only left when Bud started showing an interest in me and your father didn't say a word. He stopped appreciating me a long time ago. All he talked about was you. How you were the first in his family to go to college, how you were making your dream come true. He conveniently forgot that you tried to shred yourself to pieces, that you got knocked up at sixteen, that you took his money and never came to see him.' Julia could see the surprise on the faces of some people in the restaurant. No one knew she'd been pregnant when she left.

As blindsided as she was by this news, something clicked, and it made perfect sense. He'd never been good at expressing himself. She'd spent a long time in therapy, trying to adjust her expectations, especially from the men in her life. She'd thought she'd wanted grand gestures and expressive declarations, because her father never gave her that. But how could she have missed this? Everything her father did was quiet. Even loving her. The tragedy was that everyone in her father's life had left him because they hadn't been quiet enough to hear him. Not until it was too late. But no, she thought. It wasn't too late.

Tears came to Julia's eyes. She wiped them away. She couldn't believe she was doing this in front of everyone. 'He was a good, uncomplicated man,' she said. 'And he deserved better than us both. You're not going to get this restaurant, Beverly. No one is. This was the one thing that never let him down. Too many people have taken too many things from him as it is.' She pointed to the door. 'You're not welcome here ever again.'

'Oh, I'll be back,' Beverly said, sashaying to the door. 'When you leave, I'll be back and there won't be a thing you can do.'

'I'll be sure she knows she's not welcome,' Charlotte, the day manager, said from behind Julia.

'So will I,' one of the men at the counter said.

'Me too,' said someone across the room. The restaurant then became a chorus of agreement.

Beverly looked aghast. She glared at Julia. 'See, this is what you do! You go and leave all sorts of trouble behind.'

'I've got news for you,' Julia said. 'I'm not leaving.'

The restaurant erupted into applause as Beverly left.

Julia stood there, breathing heavily, and thought again, *What in the hell have I just done?*

'There you are!' Stella said, meeting her at the door when Julia finally got home. She was wearing what she called her day gown, a silk robe with buttons. 'I've been so worried! Where were you last night? Even your evil stepmother came by looking for you.'

'Why did you sleep with Sawyer?' Julia blurted out. She hadn't meant to say it. She was as surprised as Stella looked.

'What?' Stella said.

'Sawyer said you slept together three years ago.'

'Oh, that,' Stella said. 'I was a mess. My divorce had just been finalised and all my money was gone. Sawyer came by that evening to give me a bottle of champagne to celebrate my freedom. I got drunk and I climbed all over him. I'm not proud of it. Believe me, I never wanted to be the woman men had sex with out of pity. It was just once, and I tried to avoid him after that, but he wouldn't let me. Sawyer's a good guy. A good friend. Why do you ask?' Stella clutched at her heart dramatically. 'Oh my God! That's where you were last night! You totally did it with Sawyer!'

Julia must have given something away with her look.

Stella drew her into her arms for a hug. 'I'm so happy. That man has always had a thing for you. I have no idea why he waited so long.' She led Julia to the living room, where she'd been fortifying herself with a pitcher of Bloody Marys. 'So, tell me everything that's happening!'

Julia shook her head as she sat down and accepted the drink Stella gave her. 'Uh-uh. No way.'

'You have to. You're my best friend,' Stella said, which startled Julia. 'It's the code. I tell you everything in my life.'

'You didn't tell me about Sawyer,' she said.

'Sawyer happened a long time ago.'

Julia set the glass on the tray. 'Am I really your best friend?'

'Of course you are.'

'But you used to laugh at me in high school.'

Surprised, Stella sat down heavily on the chair opposite Julia. 'High school was a long time ago. Are you saying you can't be my best friend now because of what happened back then?'

'No,' Julia said, being honest with herself. Her friendships in Baltimore had never felt like this. Her friends there had accepted her for who they thought she was. Stella accepted her for who she really was. This place defined her. It always had. Stella knew that. 'I think you're the best friend I've ever had.'

'That's more like it,' Stella said. 'Now, tell me *everything*.'

The first thing Sawyer said when Julia opened the door a few hours later was, 'Let's get this out of the way. There's nothing going on between me and Holly.'

Julia leaned against the doorjamb. It was so nice to see him, but there was so much that needed to be said. 'The two of you look good together. Have you ever considered getting back together?'

'I don't want to. Holly is selling me her part of the house we own together here. She's getting remarried in a couple of weeks. She's pregnant. I forgot she was coming to town this weekend.'

'That was my fault. Sorry.'

'Don't be sorry. Do it again.'

She opened the door wider. He stepped inside with a deep breath and a satisfied smile. 'I've wanted to come up here ever since you've been back. And it's not what you're thinking. On Thursdays when I have pizza with Stella, that incredible smell from whatever you happen to be baking . . . it never fails to make me heady.'

'Could you see it?' Julia asked.

'I can always see it. It's on you now, sparkling in your hair.' He pointed to her hand. 'You have some in the cuff of your sleeve, too.'

Julia turned the cuff inside out and, sure enough, flour and sugar from that morning sprinkled out. 'That's amazing.'

'Are you going to give me a tour?' Sawyer asked.

'We can do it from here.' She pointed to each door. 'Bedroom, bathroom, kitchen, living room.' She led him to the tiny living room and invited him to take a seat. She remained standing, too nervous to sit. 'Stella's mother gave me that love seat. I have a nice couch of my own in storage up in Baltimore.'

'Do you think you'll bring it down?'

'I don't know.'

He sat back, obviously making a concerted effort not to push the subject. 'Did you actually get into a fight with Beverly at your restaurant this morning?'

Julia laughed. 'Did Stella tell you, or did word travel that fast?'

'Both. I heard that you said you weren't selling the restaurant,' he said.

'What can I say? I'm as surprised as you are.'

He hesitated. 'Does this mean you're staying?'

She didn't answer right away. 'You know that big thing I wanted to tell you? I'm going to tell you now. Then I'm going to leave you alone to let you think about it, OK?'

A guarded look came to his face. 'OK. Lay it on me.'

'Stay right there.' She went to her bedroom and found the old algebra textbook she had hidden under her bed. She opened the book and looked at the two photos she had of her baby. Sawyer's baby. She took the photos to the living room.

He looked up at her as she entered. Before she could talk herself out of it, she held the photos out to him and he took them.

She watched as he looked at them, confused at first, then alert. He met her eyes with a short, quick jerk of his head.

'She was born on May the 5th,' she said. 'Six pounds, six ounces. She looked nothing like me and everything like you. Blonde hair and blue eyes. A couple from Washington, DC, adopted her.'

'I have a daughter?'

She nodded, then left before he could ask any more questions.

Heat radiated from the metal bleachers. Julia's spot when she was a teenager was where the top bleacher butted against the enclosed media box, forming a pocket of concrete shade. She hadn't been here since she was sixteen. From where she was sitting, she could see down on to the fifty-yard line where it had all happened, where her life had changed.

She'd been there for at least an hour, wondering how much time he needed with this, when something suddenly caught her eye and, on the left side of the field, she saw Sawyer walking towards her.

He stopped at the base of the bleachers and looked up at her. The photos were in his hand. It was hard to tell his expression. Was he mad? Would this change everything all over again?

He started up the bleachers towards her. The first step he took, he was sixteen, blond and cherubic. With every step he took, he got older, the cherubic cheeks giving way to sharper cheekbones, his skin growing golden, his hair a darker blond. By the time he reached her, he was the Sawyer of today, of this morning . . . of last night.

Without a word, he sat beside her.

'How did you know I would be here?' she asked.

'Just a hunch.'

'Go ahead,' she said. 'Ask.'

'I don't have to ask the big question. I know why you didn't tell me.'

She nodded. 'OK.'

'Do you know where she is now? What she's doing?' He looked at the photos. 'Her name?'

'No.' She tugged on the cuffs of her sleeves. 'The papers are sealed. I can't find her unless she wants to find me. You said you followed the scent home when your mother baked, so I have it in my head that if I just keep baking, she'll find me.' Julia looked down, then across the field. 'I think she has your sweet sense. I couldn't eat enough cake to satisfy her when I was pregnant.'

'That's what my mother said when she was pregnant with me.'

'I wanted to keep her so badly,' she said. 'For a long time, I was angry at everyone for not helping me make that happen. It took a while to realise that it was just misplaced guilt, because I wasn't well enough to care for her on my own.'

He was the one to look away this time. 'Saying I'm sorry doesn't feel like enough. I feel like I owe you so much more. I owe you for her.' He shook his head. 'I can't believe I have a daughter.'

'You don't owe me anything,' she said. 'She was a gift.'

'Your hair is still pink in this photo.' He lifted the one of her holding the baby in the hospital. 'When did you stop dyeing it?'

'When I went to school. I cut it off after that photo was taken.'

'When did you start with the pink streak?'

Julia nervously tucked it behind her ear. 'In college. My friends in Baltimore think I do it to be edgy. But I do it because it reminds me of what I can get through. It reminds me not to give up.'

There was a long silence. A maintenance man on a sit-on lawn mower drove onto the football field and started taking wide loops round it. 'Are you going to stay?' Sawyer finally asked.

How did she answer that? 'I spent so much time telling myself that this wasn't home that I started to believe it,' she said carefully. 'Belonging has always been tough for me.'

'I can be your home,' he said quietly. 'Belong to me.'

She stared at him, stunned by his whispered grand gesture, until he turned to her. When he saw the tears in her eyes, he reached for her. She held on to him and cried, cried until the football field was all mown and the air smelled of cut grass.

To think, after all this time, after all the searching and all the waiting, after all the regret and the time she'd spent away, she came back to find that happiness was right where she'd left it.

On a football field in Mullaby, North Carolina.

Chapter 10

EMILY STUFFED HER HANDS in her shorts pockets as she walked down the sidewalk that night. There were no cars out, but she kept listening for them, stepping into the darkness in between each streetlight and pausing, waiting for some indication that Win had invited the whole town to this, like her mother had done.

Since coming to Mullaby, Emily had discovered that her disbelief could be suspended further than she ever thought it could. If giants exist, if wallpaper can change on its own . . . why couldn't Win do what he said he could do? If it was real, that meant this wasn't about revenge. This wasn't about what her mother had done. The closer she got the more she wanted it to be true.

When she reached Main Street, she stopped on the sidewalk by the park. No one was there. Grey-green moonlight lit the area. She walked to the bandstand and stood a few feet away from the main staircase.

'You came. I didn't think you would.'

His voice startled her, coming out of nowhere. 'Where are you?'

'Behind you.' She spun back to the bandstand. Looking closely, she could make out a figure at the back of the stage. Her heart sank.

'You're not glowing.' she said, and it was an accusation. It hurt, and she felt stupid for letting it. There wasn't anything supernatural to this. It was simple, and simple was good. Easier to understand. That was why she'd shown up tonight, after all. To let him play his trick on her. To try to right some wrongs.

He walked to the steps and slowly descended. He stopped on the grass a few feet away from her, his white suit standing out against the shadows. She met his eyes defiantly.

It took a moment for her to realise that Win looked nervous. That's when it happened. Like blowing on embers, a light began to grow around him. It was as if radiant heat was emanating from his skin, surrounding him in white light. It was utterly, terrifyingly beautiful.

He stood there and let her stare at him. His shoulders seemed to relax when he realised she wasn't going to run away. But it wasn't because she didn't want to. She couldn't. Her muscles felt frozen.

He took one step towards her, then another. She could see the light as it began to stretch towards her. Then she felt it, those ribbons of warmth. It was usually comforting, that feeling, but it was a decidedly different experience to actually see what was happening.

'Stop,' she said, her voice thin and breathless. She turned her back on him and put her hands on her knees. 'Make it stop!'

'I can't. But I can get out of the moonlight. Come over to the steps.'

'Don't,' she said, looking over her shoulder and seeing that he was making another move towards her. 'Just make it go away.'

He took the steps two at a time and retreated into the shadows of the stage. She sat gratefully on the steps and put her head down.

She eventually lifted her head as the spots faded from her eyes. She felt chilled from her cold sweat.

'I didn't mean to make you panic,' Win said from behind her. 'I'm sorry.'

It helped not having to turn round to look at him yet. 'Are there people here watching? Is that what this is all about?'

'This isn't a trick,' he said, an ocean of heartache in those words. 'It's who I am.'

She took a deep breath. If this was real . . . she understood why the town was shocked when her mother brought Win's uncle out at night.

'How do you feel?' he asked. 'Can I get you something?'

'No, just stay there.' She finally stood and faced the bandstand again. 'Everyone here knows?'

'Everyone who was there that night,' he said from the darkness. 'My family made sure no one has seen it since.'

'But they know that you're the light in the woods?'

'Yes. I've been doing it since I was a kid, but plenty of my ancestors did it before me.'

'Why did you want me to see it?'

He hesitated, as if he wasn't sure now. She suddenly felt horrible, like she'd let him down. Her mother had raised her to accept and respect, to help and to never be afraid to get involved. All her life had been leading up to this, and she'd failed. She'd failed Win. She'd failed her mother.

She was still in the history loop. She was scared now, scared for herself, scared for Win, knowing how this had turned out last time.

'I've never known how to say to people, "This is me. Accept me for who I am,"' Win finally said. 'I knew from the moment I met you, I was meant to show you. I thought you were meant to help.'

'How?' she asked. 'How can I help you? I don't understand.'

'You can tell me that, now that you've seen this, your feelings are no different than they are in the daytime. That's all.'

She squared her shoulders and backed further into the open park. 'Come down here, Win.'

He walked back down and his skin started burning again. When he finally made it to her, she took his hand. She was surprised that it was simply warm, not hot. 'Does it hurt?' she asked.

'No.'

She swallowed. She was trembling. Could he feel it? 'I think it's beautiful. I think it's the most beautiful thing I've ever seen.'

He stood there, glowing like the sun, and stared at her as if she was the unbelievable one. He angled closer to her, and the closer he came, the more the glowing seemed to stretch out to her. It felt like walking into sunshine from the shade. She saw him tilt his head.

He's going to kiss me. She knew it in a way she couldn't explain. She'd thought about this a lot, but it was nothing like she'd expected. And yet . . . it was perfect.

But before it could happen, they jerked away from each other, startled, when they heard quick footsteps. Win's sister was running across the park towards them.

'Win! What are you doing?' Kylie said breathlessly, skidding to a stop on the dewy grass. 'Dad wants you to come back inside.'

Emily and Win exchanged glances. She wasn't used to seeing him this unsure. 'What happens now?' Emily asked.

'Now we deal with the consequences. Just like last time, only—'

'Better,' she finished for him.

He touched her cheek, then ran across the park towards his house. Emily and Kylie watched him go. What a ravishing sight he was.

'It's beautiful, isn't it?' Kylie said.

Emily turned to her warily, surprised she was being so nice to her now. 'Yes,' she said softly.

'I would love to do what he does. He has no idea.' Kylie paused. 'All my life, I've heard stories of that night with my uncle and your mother. I thought you'd be like her. I'm glad you're not.' She smiled, as if she'd just given a compliment. Emily took it in the spirit it was intended, but would never get used to how the town thought of her mother. 'I'd better go and see what's going on in there. I'll see you around. With Win, no doubt.'

With no light to her skin, Kylie soon faded into the night. Emily stood there for a while before finally walking home.

Emily woke to the sound of someone pounding on the front door. She sat up quickly. She'd been too exhausted to turn on her MP3 player before she'd gone to bed. When she looked around, the new phases-of-the-moon wallpaper took her aback for a moment. That's when it all came rushing back to her. He glowed.

Then, out of nowhere, the thought: *He almost kissed me.*

The pounding continued and Emily climbed out of bed. She'd slept in her clothes, so she jogged to her door and down the stairs.

To her surprise, the front door was closed. Vance usually left it open when he went to breakfast. She'd just reached the bottom stair when the accordion door to Vance's room swung open. Grandpa Vance walked out. He hadn't left for breakfast yet.

Vance didn't notice her on the staircase as he walked to the front door and unlocked it.

'We need to talk,' Morgan Coffey said from the porch. His white linen suit was rumpled. His dark hair, normally gelled, was falling across his forehead. It made him look younger, more like Win.

'Morgan?' Vance said, obviously surprised. 'What are you doing here at this hour?'

'I would have been here earlier, but I had to wait until light.'

'Come in.' Vance stepped back and Morgan entered the hall. 'What's wrong?'

Morgan noticed Emily and stiffened. His hatred rushed at her in one great wave. 'I take it your granddaughter hasn't told you yet,' he said, nudging his chin at her. His stare was so hard that Vance put himself between them. 'Why did you let her come here in the first place, Vance? Hasn't your family done enough to hurt mine?'

'What happened?' Vance demanded.

'It happened,' Morgan said. 'Your granddaughter lured my son into the park last night. Just like last time.'

'Emily had nothing to do with it,' Win said from the porch. He opened the screen door and stepped inside. 'I asked her to meet me. It was nothing like last time. We were the only two in the park.'

'I told you to stay at home,' Morgan said.

'This has to do with me. I am going to be here for it.'

Grandpa Vance looked confused. He turned to her. 'Emily?'

'I thought I would show up and he would do something to humiliate me, to get back at my mom for what she did. I didn't believe him when he said he glowed. I didn't believe him when he said to meet him and he'd show me.'

'Child, why did you go if you thought he was going to humiliate you?' Vance asked incredulously.

'I thought it would help make up for—'

Vance held up one skillet-sized hand. 'Stop. You don't have to make up for anything your mother did. Morgan, this ends now.'

'You're letting her off the hook, just like you did your daughter.'

Grandpa Vance was angry. And an angry giant was a sight to behold. 'I never made excuses for Dulcie, and I have always accepted blame for what happened, for not being able to control her. But my granddaughter is not Dulcie. I will not have her treated this way.'

Morgan coughed. 'I'd feel more comfortable if you sat down, Vance.'

Vance didn't give an inch. 'No one is ever comfortable around me. You, of all people, should know how that feels.'

'I want her to stay away from my son.'

'I've been watching your son in the woods behind my house. Emily staying away from him isn't the problem,' Vance said.

Morgan shot an angry look at Win.

'You can't make me stay away from her,' Win said.

'Did you learn nothing from your uncle?' Morgan asked him.

'Yes, I did. I learned from him that it takes courage to love someone your family doesn't approve of.'

'You don't seriously love this girl,' Morgan said with disbelief.

Emily couldn't take her eyes off him. He loved her? But Win simply stared at his father, a power struggle going on.

'My brother committed suicide because of her family,' Morgan told Win. 'Doesn't that mean anything to you?'

'It was his decision,' Win said, and she was amazed by how composed he was. 'But I think ignoring what he sacrificed is stupid. He gave us an opportunity to live normal lives here.'

'My life has not been normal since it happened! Your mother has never forgiven me for not telling her.'

'And you want the same for me? I wanted to show her. I didn't want it to be a secret. And the world didn't end. She didn't reject me, Dad. This isn't you and Mom. This isn't Dulcie and Logan. This is me and Emily. It's an entirely different story.'

Vance said, 'Let them live their lives without our baggage, Morgan.'

But Morgan wasn't going to let it go. 'Your daughter lured my brother into that park that night! She tricked him!'

'I'll say this only once more. My granddaughter is not Dulcie, and I will not tolerate you blaming her for her mother's sins.'

'And what are you going to do about it?'

Vance took a single step towards him. 'I'm going to tell the truth. You've made Logan and your family out to be the victims, and I let it happen because Dulcie wanted it that way. She left knowing she would be vilified. She left to make things easier on you, which was the first selfless thing she'd ever done.'

Emily, who had been staring at Win all this time, suddenly turned her head sharply. 'What are you talking about, Grandpa Vance?'

'Let's go, Win,' Morgan said quickly.

'No, I want to hear this.'

'Logan was troubled long before Dulcie came into his life,' Vance said. 'He'd tried to commit suicide several times, something no one but his family knew. But Logan told Dulcie. He and your mother were in love. At least, your mother was in love with him. I'd never seen her like that before. All over town, she carved their initials onto every wooden surface she could find.'

'Wait, Mom carved those initials?' Emily asked. 'Not Logan?'

He nodded. 'She was smitten. She was usually such a forceful girl, always getting her way, but she was very deferential to Logan. He could control her like no one else. Knowing how angry it would make her, he told Dulcie that they couldn't be together because his family didn't approve. He said his family had secrets and wouldn't let him marry just anyone. But there was a solution, he told her. So Dulcie went along with inviting everyone in town to a so-called performance by her, aware that it was a ruse, an opportunity for Logan to come out at night in front of the whole town. But she thought it was simply going to be his symbolic declaration of love for her. Dulcie had no idea that the reason the Coffeys didn't come out at night was because they glowed. She thought, as we all did, it was just one more thing they did to keep themselves elite.'

'She didn't trick him?' Emily asked.

'If anything, he tricked her. Dulcie was as stunned as the rest of us. Logan reached out to her after it happened, but she didn't want to talk to him. I don't know if it was his plan all along to commit suicide after he exposed his family's secret, or if he was just overcome with remorse afterwards, possibly fuelled by Dulcie's rejection. Only his family knows that. I do know he wanted to reveal himself. He wanted people to know.'

Morgan's face had raspberry-red splotches on it now. 'No one is going to believe you. I will always maintain that Dulcie could have stopped him from stepping out onto that bandstand. She could have stopped him from killing himself. He did love her. He gave her that family heirloom.'

He pointed to Emily's wrist, to the charm bracelet. 'Our mother gave it to him to give to the woman he married, like it had been given to her on her wedding night. That he gave it to Dulcie had to mean something. But if he had fallen for someone less selfish, he might be alive today. Our secret might still be a secret. The way it was always meant to be.'

'Emily knows the truth now,' Grandpa Vance said calmly. 'That's all that matters. I have no intention of telling anyone else.'

She didn't know why it was so important for Morgan to have people believe his brother was tricked. Maybe it helped his family, knowing the town didn't think Logan was troubled. It could only help, she thought, that there wasn't a stigma like that attached to their glowing. It probably made it easier for the town to accept what they'd seen, to sympathise. Emily realised that her mother had known this. That's why she'd taken the blame. 'I won't tell anyone, either,' she said.

Morgan turned to Win. 'I'll think about it,' Win said.

'You'll think about it at home. You're grounded.'

Morgan walked to the front door. He held the screen door open for Win. But Win walked over to Vance. 'I'd like to take your granddaughter on a date when my punishment is over, if I have your permission.' Win held out his hand.

'Win!' Morgan said.

Vance seemed as surprised as Morgan, but he shook Win's hand.

Win looked up at Emily and said, 'I'll see you soon?'

She nodded. He gave her a reassuring smile, then turned and left.

Emily and Vance stared at the door. Emily finally turned to her grandfather. 'Why didn't you tell me the truth from the beginning?'

'She made me swear not to tell anyone.' He looked tired. He sat on the stairs, sinking like an anchor. She was still standing, but he was taller than she was, even when he sat. 'Lily had a cousin who lived in San Diego. I arranged for Dulcie to live with her. I gave her a large chunk of cash, and she left the day before Logan's funeral. She tried to make it work, but a few months later she ran away. I got postcards for a couple of years. Then nothing.'

'Why didn't you look for her?' Emily said.

He shrugged. 'Because I knew she didn't want to be found. A good, decent life for her was only possible if she left everything behind. The Coffeys, Mullaby . . . me.'

'She could have come back and told the truth!' Emily said. 'She could have been redeemed.'

'I think she found redemption in other ways,' Grandpa Vance said. 'When she left, she told me that when she had children, she would never raise them the way I raised her. She said she would teach them responsibility. I like to think that at some point in her life she forgave me. But I deserve it if she didn't.' He took a deep breath. 'One thing is for sure, she did raise a remarkable daughter.'

Emily sat beside him. 'So did you, Grandpa Vance,' she said.

And for the first time, she thought it was OK that they were the only two people who knew that. The point was, they knew.

When Vance came in from breakfast a few hours later, he was exhausted. He was more than ready to lie down and take a nap. But instead of going to his room, he went to check the dryer. He hadn't meant to get so angry at Morgan. He didn't often get angry at other people. There was no sense in it. Now, getting angry with yourself had some merit. It showed you had sense enough to chastise the one person who had any hope of benefiting from it. And he was plenty angry with himself.

For many things. For living in the past. For not being a better parent to Dulcie. For missing so much of Emily's life already.

He walked to the laundry room and opened the dryer. He reached in and expected to feel the smooth curve of the dryer drum. Instead, his fingers brushed something slimy. He jerked his hand away.

Out jumped a large frog. He stared at it, frozen.

He watched it hop to the laundry-room door, and for a moment he expected to see Lily. But no one was there.

He quickly stepped out of the room, and when he crossed through the doorway, he felt as if he'd walked through a fragrant breeze. His hair even moved. The sleeves of his shirt billowed.

He closed his eyes and took a deep breath. Lily.

The air was sprinkled with her spirit. He stood still for a long time, his heart aching as, with each breath, the scent faded.

When he opened his eyes, he saw the frog sitting at the kitchen door. It wriggled through a tear in the screen. Vance followed.

He opened the door to see the frog hop across the back yard. He walked after it, all the way to the gazebo. The frog stared at him.

Vance hesitated, then looked around. Emily had obviously been back here, trimming the boxwoods. He suddenly remembered that Dulcie had done that, too, after Lily had died. She'd tried so hard to keep things going on her own, and she'd only been twelve. He should have been there for her. But he'd fallen apart.

Lily wouldn't have wanted things like this. Maybe that's what she was trying to tell him. The last time she'd put a frog in the dryer was to tell him to stop being afraid of change, of what came next.

He had to stop squandering what time he had left. He had a granddaughter to take care of. He nodded to the frog. OK. He would call his old gardener. He'd get this place fixed up. He turned to look at the house. He'd hire a roofer. A housepainter. And he'd give Emily an allowance. He'd have a talk with her about college. Maybe she would want to come home on breaks . . . and live here after she graduated.

He would build her a house on the lake, as a wedding gift, maybe.

What if she married Win Coffey? Lily's wedding dress was in the attic. Maybe she'd want to wear it.

Julia, of course, would make the cake.

He gave a short laugh at how far ahead of himself he was getting.

He might be tall enough to see into tomorrow, but he hadn't looked there in a long, long time. He'd forgotten how bright it was.

Seven days later, Emily felt as if she was living in a bubble, waiting for Win's punishment to end. Not that there wasn't plenty to distract her. Vance was suddenly on a home improvement kick. Every morning Emily woke up to hammering on the roof, or the roar of a lawn mower.

A heatwave had hit Mullaby that week. But every time she would come downstairs, irritable from the heat, Grandpa Vance would tell her not to worry, rain was coming to cool things off. When she asked how he knew, he told her his joints told him so.

Every day, when Vance took his afternoon nap, she would go next door just as an excuse to spend some time in an air-conditioned house. Despite the heat, every day Julia made a cake with her kitchen window wide open. When Emily asked her why, she said she was calling to someone. Emily didn't question this. While Julia baked, Emily told her about Win and Julia seemed glad that Emily now knew. Emily knew that Julia had forgiven her mother for what she'd done. Julia seemed to be doing a lot of forgiving lately.

At five o'clock every day, Julia would leave with the cake she'd made, just as Stella came home from work. On the seventh day of this happening, Emily finally asked Stella where Julia was taking the cakes. At first she'd assumed she was taking the cakes to her restaurant, but she became curious when she realised Julia never returned in the evenings.

'She takes them to Sawyer,' Stella said. 'Don't worry. He burns it all off.' Stella looked shocked at herself. 'Erase that. You didn't hear that.

Crap. I need a glass of wine. Remember, do as I say, not as I do.'

As she headed back home that evening, Emily realised that the heat made things in Mullaby move even more slowly. It was as if everyone was waiting for something to happen.

Finally, that night, it did. A terrific thunderstorm erupted and Emily and Vance had to race round the house closing the windows. Then they stood on the front porch and watched the sheets of rain. Later, they played cards and looked through photo albums that Vance magically produced, full of photos of her mother.

Finally, Grandpa Vance said he was tired and she reluctantly said good night to him. She went upstairs and walked into her room, and realised that she'd forgotten to close her balcony doors. Rain was flying in and the floor was soaked. She spent nearly an hour wiping down the floor, the walls, and all the nearby furniture.

She put on a cotton nightgown and fell into bed. The temperature had dropped sharply. The clatter of drops against the windows on the balcony doors sounded like raining coins.

A few hours later, she woke up. The storm had passed and it was uncomfortably hot in her room now. Moonlight was filtering in through the gaps in the curtains on the closed balcony doors. She slowly got out of bed and went to the doors to open them.

The light from the moon spread inside far enough for her to suddenly notice that the phases-of-the-moon wallpaper had gone. It was now a dark colour she couldn't quite make out, punctuated by long strips of yellow. It looked almost like dark doors and windows opening, letting in light. The wallpaper was usually some reflection of her mood, but what did this mean? Some new door was opening? Something was being set free?

When she finally realised what it meant, she spun round, her eyes darting round the room until she found him.

Win was sitting on the couch opposite her bed. He was leaning forward, his elbows on his knees, his hands clasped.

'My punishment ended as of midnight,' he said.

Her heart began to race. It was so good to see him. Yet, she felt awkward. 'So . . . you were just going to sit there until I woke up?'

'Yes.' He walked to the balcony doors. She was standing in a square of moonlight and he stopped just short of it.

'I'd almost forgotten what you looked like,' she said. A bad joke. Why was she so nervous? *Because he had almost kissed her.*

'I spent all my time remembering what you looked like,' he said.

'I had people hammering and sawing and mowing all round me. It was hard to concentrate.'

He gave her a funny look. 'That's your excuse?'

'And there's no air conditioning in this house. Do you know how hard it is to concentrate when you don't have air conditioning?' She needed to stop, but couldn't seem to.

'Your grandfather had the limb of the oak that stretched to your balcony cut down. I had a hell of a time getting up here this time.'

That finally drew her up short. She stared at him in the shadow. 'How many times have you come up here?'

'A few.'

She suddenly thought back to the day she'd arrived in Mullaby. 'The day I arrived, my bracelet on the table . . .'

'I knew you were coming in that day,' he said. 'I was curious about you. I found the bracelet on the front walk.'

'You don't have to sneak in here any more,' she said. 'Everything's out in the open now, right?'

His answer was to step into the light in front of her. The glow round him started to blaze. He was watching her closely.

'I lied,' she whispered.

He looked concerned and started to step back. 'About what?'

She reached out and stopped him. 'About forgetting what you looked like. I could never forget this,' she said. 'Not in all my life.'

He smiled and took her face in his hands.

Then he finally kissed her.

Chapter 11

MADDIE DAVIS ADJUSTED the backpack on her shoulder as she walked down the sidewalk. She'd arrived in Mullaby yesterday and was staying at the Inn on Main Street. Her parents had arranged it. She'd wanted to do this alone, but she understood that her parents were worried, and if paying for her stay at a swanky inn made them feel better, then she would suffer through it.

She hadn't slept well the night before. The full moon had poured through the window in her room. At breakfast, the innkeeper had told her that the full moon in August was called the Sturgeon Moon. It made people restless, he'd said, like there was too much to do, too many fish to catch.

After breakfast, Maddie had talked to her mom and had tried to keep it light. 'Maybe my sarcasm will finally be explained,' Maddie had joked. 'Maybe it's simply hardwired. That means it's not your fault.' Her mother hadn't laughed. Maddie should have known. Her parents were the kindest people she knew, but they didn't share Maddie's sense of humour.

It was a perfect, sunny Monday morning. As Maddie walked, she took a deep breath of the tangy-sweet air. She liked this town.

She saw the sign hanging over the door ahead. J's Barbecue.

For some reason, she stopped. She'd thought about doing this for years, and it was time. She'd sandwiched it between the end of her summer internship at her father's law firm and her first day back at Georgetown for her sophomore year. But now she wasn't sure she wanted to go through with it. She had a great relationship with her adoptive parents. And she already knew enough about her birth mother to piece together why she'd given Maddie up for adoption. Julia Winterson had been sixteen and a student at Collier Reformatory. She now lived in a small barbecue town in North Carolina and owned a restaurant. She'd never married. Never had more kids. The private investigator her parents had hired on Maddie's behalf had even supplied a photo of Julia. She was pretty and fresh, but Maddie, with her blonde hair and blue eyes, didn't look much like her. She figured she must take after her birth father, whoever he was. His name wasn't on her birth certificate.

She started walking again, but her heart was racing. She was almost at the front window of the restaurant when she stopped again. Don't be a wuss, she told herself.

She was standing opposite two teenagers sitting on a bench outside the restaurant. The girl had quirky flyaway hair and was dressed in shorts and a tank top. The young man was in a white linen suit and red bow tie. The guy had the girl's hand in his. They were in their own world. They made Maddie smile.

They both looked up when the door to the restaurant opened. Maddie's eyes widened. The elderly man walking out had to duck under the doorway to get out. She'd never seen someone so tall.

The teenagers stood when they saw him. The giant walked over to them with an awkward gait. The young man held out his hand and the giant shook it. They said a few words, laughed, then the guy in the white suit turned and walked down the sidewalk.

When he passed Maddie, he smiled slightly and gave her a polite nod. She watched him walk away, then turned back to the giant and the girl. The giant handed the girl a paper bag. She took it and together they walked down the sidewalk. Maddie craned her head to look up at him as he passed.

She felt as though she was in some strange fairy tale.

The door to the restaurant opened again and two men walked out. Silver sparkles from inside caught in the air and rolled in the wind past her. Sugar and vanilla and butter. That relentless scent had been following her round all her life. Sometimes she could see it, like this, but most of the time she just felt it. When she was a kid, the smell would appear out of nowhere and make her inexplicably restless. Even now, sometimes she would wake up at night and swear someone was baking a cake in the house. Her room mates thought she was crazy.

It was the familiarity of the smell that gave her the courage to look inside the restaurant. It was a nondescript place, but packed.

Maddie's eyes went to a woman behind the counter. There she was. Julia Winterson. The woman who'd given birth to her.

She was smiling, talking to a handsome man with blond hair sitting on the other side of the counter. Maddie had spent countless hours staring at the photograph from the private investigator. In real life Julia looked happier, more settled.

Maddie kept her eyes on her through the window as she slowly walked to the door. When she reached the door, she saw that there was a flyer taped to it that read:

Blue-Eyed Girl Cakes:
Speciality cakes for any occasion. Enquire within.

Someone else walked out and, seeing her, held the door for her.

'Are you ready?' the man asked.

The ending of one story. The beginning of another.

Sarah Addison Allen

Did you always want to be a writer?
When I was a kid, I wanted to be a trash man. But I gave up my dream of waste management and decided to pursue writing as a career when I graduated from college. Writer was a close second.
Was it difficult getting your first novel, *Garden Spells*, published?
I wrote for twelve years before writing *Garden Spells*. But I was lucky enough to find the right people to champion that quirky and otherwise hard-to-market novel. It turned out to be the right book at the right time.
Is quirky the word you would use to describe your writing style?
I call my books 'Southern-fried magical realism'. But, at their heart, they are love stories.
Which authors, writing in your genre, do you admire?
My favourites continue to be the first I ever read in college. I think the newness, the way this literary device opened a whole new world for me when I discovered it, made these titles unforgettable, like first loves: *The Passion* by Jeanette Winterson, *I Am One of You Forever* by Fred Chappell, *Like Water for Chocolate* by Laura Esquirel, *A History of the World in Ten and a Half Chapters* by Julian Barnes. I also think Stephanie Meyer's *Twilight* series of

books are great. They've shown a generation of young readers what it's like to fall in love with a book. The films have been fantastic, too.

What's the best advice you've ever been given as a writer that you would pass on to others?

A bestselling author once told me that the secret of successful writers is to wear comfortable shoes. Wise words that I pass on to you now.

Do you have a writing regime? Do you work 9 to 5 or are you a middle-of-the-night-ideas kind of person?

My typical writing day consists of large chunks of time lost to procrastination and daydreaming. But the closer I get to a deadline, the more hours I spend in front of the computer. Up to fourteen hours a day!

Where did the idea for *The Girl Who Chased the Moon* start?

The idea started with barbecue. I wanted this book to be set in a North Carolina barbecue town. It was the only constant throughout many drafts, and it actually ended up influencing the story and the characters.

Who was your favourite character in the novel?

Grandpa Vance, the elderly giant. But I like to call this book my ode to the Southern man. My previous books had heroes who weren't from the South. All the men in this book are purely Southern. Starched cotton, sexy drawls and all.

Julia's story evolves slowly. Did you enjoy teasing the reader with her tale?

Julia's storyline was a surprise to me while I was writing it. I never know where these characters will take me.

Do you bake cakes as well as Julia?

I don't bake. I'm a horrible cook. But I make up for this shameful inability to prepare food with an unbounded joy in consuming it. I love food. I love the comforting, sensual nature of it. And it always finds its way into what I write. I did a lot of delicious research on North Carolina barbecue. It's a tough job but someone's got to do it . . .

If you were having a dinner party, who would be your ideal guests, dead or alive, real or fictional? And what would your signature dish be?

Being a notoriously bad cook, I will spare everyone—real and fictional—the horror of attending a dinner party thrown by me.

What do you do to relax?

I unplug everything in the house and take to my bed, a good book in hand.

As we have just begun a new decade, do you have any particular ambitions that you have yet to fulfil?

I haven't thought that far ahead. I'm still trying to remember what year it is.

If you were given three wishes, what would they be?

A perfect glass of wine, a perfect piece of chocolate, and at least one hundred more wishes.

The Saffron Gate

Linda Holeman

Unlike my other novels, which found their beginnings in characters so persistent that I had to write about them, this book began with a city. From the moment I stepped off the train in Marrakesh, unprepared for anything more than another adventure, and looking forward to learning about a new culture, I felt the city's heat and rhythm and mystery wrap themselves around me. Within a day, I knew that I would write a book set in this astounding place.

With that realisation I opened myself to Marrakesh—and it was waiting. It whispered to me, it called to me, it sang to me. It murmured secrets I couldn't quite hear.

And so I wrote a story about Marrakesh for Sidonie, my heroine, so that I could uncover the secrets of the city with her. I hope you enjoy it.

Linda

Chapter One

Strait of Gibraltar, April 1930

We were caught in the levanter.

I heard this word as a small knot of Spaniards huddled on the deck, pointing and shaking their heads. *Viento de levante*, one of them said loudly, then spat and said a word with such vehemence I knew it could only be a curse. He kissed the crucifix hanging about his neck.

The Spaniards moved to the wall of the ferry, crouching on the balls of their feet, their backs against the building as they cupped their hands around small rolled cigarettes in an attempt to light them. The air had a sudden texture, one of moist, thickening fog. This, as well as seeing the Spaniard kiss his crucifix, seemed a troubling portent.

'Excuse me,' I said to the middle-aged man standing beside me at the railing. I had heard him speaking English to one of the porters as we boarded, and knew that he was, like me, an American. 'What are they saying? What is *levante*?'

'Levanter,' he said, buttoning his topcoat. '*Levante*, Spanish for east. *Levanter* is to rise. It's a terrible wind blowing in from the east. We may have to turn back if we can't outrun it.'

'Outrun it? Will it not just blow over us?'

'Can't tell. Reaches its maximum intensities here, on the western side of the strait.' His hat suddenly lifted as if by unseen hands, and, although he grabbed for it, it swirled briefly in front of us before disappearing into the air. 'Damn!' he shouted. 'You must forgive me, Mrs . . .?'

'O'Shea. Miss O'Shea,' I said. My cape billowed up and then swirled around me as though I were a whirling dervish; I clutched it against my chest with one hand while I held on to my own hat with the other.

I couldn't catch my breath; it was partly the wind and partly fear.

'Could . . . could the boat . . . overturn?' I couldn't bear to say *sink*.

'Overturn?' He looked over my shoulder, towards the stern. 'Doesn't happen too often any more, ships going down in the strait. Not with the sturdy engines these ferries are equipped with now.'

I nodded, although his words didn't calm me as I'd hoped. I had recently sailed from the port of New York to Marseilles, and then from Marseilles to the southern tip of Spain, and hadn't encountered anything worse than a day or two of rough waves on the Atlantic. I hadn't considered that this brief stretch of sea could be the worst.

'Levanters usually last for three days,' the man went on. 'If the captain makes the decision not to go ahead, we shall have to return to one of the terrible little port towns in Spain and wait until at least Saturday.'

Saturday? It was Wednesday. I had already been forced to wait far too long in Marseilles. Every day that passed added a layer to the slow, yet ever-growing panic that had been building since the last time I'd seen him, seen Etienne.

As the wind blew a salty spray into my face, I rubbed at my eyes with my gloved fingers, partly to clear my vision and partly to attempt to wipe away the image of my fiancé. Wherever he was now.

The man added, 'You'd better get inside. This spindrift . . . you'll soon be soaked by both the sea and the very air itself. You don't want to be falling ill as you arrive in Tangier. North Africa is not a place where one wants to be ill.' He studied me further. 'North Africa is a place where one must keep one's wits about one at all times.'

At his words I thought of lying in the narrow bed in Marseilles, less than ten days ago, feverish and weak. Utterly alone.

'Have you travelling companions, Miss O'Shea?'

'No,' I shouted. 'No, I'm on my own. Do you know Tangier?'

'Yes,' the man yelled back at me, 'yes, I've been a number of times. Come now, come.' He touched the small of my back, directing me towards the door of the ferry. As we stepped inside the narrow passageway leading to the main salon, the door slammed behind us, and I realised what a relief it was to be out of the wind. I pushed back the hair stuck to my cheeks, and adjusted my cape.

'Could you recommend lodgings in Tangier? Just for a night or two; I need to get to Marrakesh. I'm not sure . . . I've read varying reports of the route one takes from Tangier to Marrakesh, but whatever information I could find was a little confusing.'

'The Hotel Continental in Tangier would be the appropriate choice,

Miss O'Shea. It's the most fashionable; there are always a number of Americans and Brits there. It's within the old city walls, but a safe haven.'

'Safe haven?' I repeated.

'You'll most certainly feel a little wary in Tangier. All the narrow, twisting streets and lanes. Quite disorientating. And the people . . .' He stopped, then continued. 'But the Continental should suit your needs.'

I nodded.

'But you said you're going on to Marrakesh?' he asked.

Again I nodded.

His eyebrows rose. 'Surely not on your own. Are you meeting friends in Tangier?'

'I hope to take a train,' I said, not answering his question, but as his expression changed, I added, 'There *is* a train to Marrakesh, isn't there?'

'You don't know North Africa, I take it, Miss O'Shea.'

I didn't know North Africa.

It was also abundantly clear now that I hadn't really known Etienne.

When I remained silent, the man continued. 'Not a journey for the faint-hearted. And especially not a journey I'd recommend for a woman on her own. Foreign women in North Africa . . .' He stopped. 'I don't recommend it at all.'

Suddenly I was hot and light-headed. I couldn't faint. Not here.

'You're not well,' the man said. 'Come and sit down.'

I felt his hand under my elbow, pressuring me forward, and my feet moved involuntarily. With my leg as it was, walking on board a ship presented its own difficulties for me even when the sea was calm. I kept a hand on the wall for support, and at one point I leaned against the man's solid upper arm to avoid stumbling. And then there was a firm push on my shoulders, and a hard seat beneath me. I leaned forward, my arms crossed against my stomach and my eyes closed as I breathed deeply, feeling the blood thud back into my head. When I finally sat up and opened my eyes I saw we were in the narrow, smoky salon, lined with metal chairs bolted to the floor. It was filled with a mix of those identifiable as Spanish or African by their features and dress, as well as many more that I found impossible to name by physical description alone. The man was sitting beside me. 'Thank you. I'm feeling better.'

'You're not alone feeling ill in these conditions,' he said. I grew aware of the moans around me, and realised that many of the passengers were experiencing the effects of the violently rocking ship.

'Now. You were asking about the train,' he said. 'You're correct: there is a train that goes into Marrakesh—but it's unreliable at the best of times. Besides, it doesn't run from Tangier. You'll have to get to either Fez or Rabat first. I don't recommend going to Fez. It's far inland and quite out of the way; Rabat is a safer bet. Even so, you'll have to hire a car and driver to get you there. Why don't you stay in Rabat, if you want to leave Tangier and see Morocco?'

'No. It must be Marrakesh. I must go to Marrakesh.'

'To be honest, I really wouldn't count on the train from Rabat to Marrakesh, Miss O'Shea. Unreliable, as I've said: the rails are always shifting, or are blocked by camels or those infernal nomads. Best to hire a car and drive all the way there, really. Then again, you'll surely run into problems even on the roads, and be forced to take the old routes, simply tracks in the sand made for camels and donkeys and not much else.'

'Thank you for the information,' I told him. He was trying to help, but he couldn't possibly understand my urgency in reaching Marrakesh.

'Think nothing of it. I take it you have family in Marrakesh. Or at least friends. Nobody goes to Marrakesh unless they've someone there. And they're all French, you know. You do have someone there?'

'Yes,' I said, hoping I sounded confident, when I didn't know whether I spoke the truth or not. The answer would be revealed only when I arrived in Marrakesh. Suddenly I didn't want to hear anything more, or answer any more questions. Instead of making me sure that I could and would do this thing—travel across the expanse of North Africa on my own—the conversation was filling me with even more uncertainty and dread. 'Please, don't feel you have to sit with me any longer. I'm fine, really. And thank you again,' I said, attempting a smile.

'All right then,' he said, standing. Did I see relief in his face? How must I appear to him—so alone, so uninformed, so . . . desperate?

The levanter grew worse, and because of the roughness of the sea I couldn't tell whether we had turned back, as the American had suggested we might, or were still going ahead. The ferry forced its way through the waves blown up by the wind, and we rose and fell with a rolling regularity that made me feel even more ill than I had previously. Others did as well; some hurried out to the deck, where I assumed they hung over the railing to be sick. I ran my sleeve across my face, grateful now that I had eaten nothing all day. If only I had thought to bring a flask of water, like most of the other travellers. Everyone was now still, bodies rising and falling with the ship, and, in contrast to the earlier cacophony of voices when we left Spain, silent.

And then, so slowly that I wasn't at first aware of it, the heaving of the ship grew less severe. I sat straighter, no longer able to see the sea rising and falling through the windows. The floor beneath my feet was once more solid and familiar, and my stomach settled.

As relief came over me, one of the Spaniards from the deck opened the door and shouted, 'Tangier. *Ya llegamos!*' and a low rumble of relief went up. I assumed he meant that he had spotted the city, or that we were approaching it. So we had managed to outrun the levanter. I closed my eyes in thankfulness, and when I opened them again, everyone was stretching and moving about, chattering as they gathered children and packages. I stood as well, but immediately felt light-headed and nauseous again, whether a lingering result of the rocking of the vessel, or my thirst and lack of food that day, or from my recent illness.

I sat down.

'Miss O'Shea? Pity you didn't get out to the deck to watch our arrival. Quite magnificent, with the sun . . . Oh. But you're still feeling under the weather, I see,' the American said, frowning, and I knew my face must be damp and pallid. 'Can I help you find—'

I shook my head. 'No, no,' I said, interrupting him. Although his offer to help me was tempting, I was embarrassed by my weakness. 'I'll just rest another moment, and then I'll be all right. Thank you so much; you've been very kind. But please, go on your way. I insist.'

'Very well,' he said. 'But watch out for the touts. Lots of them hanging around the docks. Take *un petit taxi*, or a cart. And pay half of what they demand. Half. They'll give you a story about their hungry children, their ailing mother, but stay strong. Pay no more than half,' he repeated.

I nodded.

'Goodbye, then, Miss O'Shea. I wish you luck. You'll need it, if you do truly go on to Marrakesh on your own.' His footsteps were slow and heavy as he walked away.

After a few more moments, I shakily stood in the empty salon. Then I went out to the deck, into warm sunshine. As soon as I stepped through the door my head cleared; the air was fresh, smelling of the sea and also something else, something tangy, perhaps citrus. I breathed deeply, feeling stronger with each intake of breath, and looked at what I could see of Tangier.

It was indeed magnificent, as the American had said. There was the sense of an amphitheatre, white houses rising up from the dock amid a sea of palms. Minarets stood high above, the sun gleaming on their towers. There was a foreign beauty, unlike the teeming and industrial docks of New York or Marseilles. Drawing my eyes from the city,

I looked at the people moving about the docks. There were only men—where were the women?—and I thought, for one odd moment, that there were monks everywhere . . . yet how could this be? Was not Tangier a city of Muslims? In the next instant I realised my mistake: it was simply the hooded robes the men wore.

I made my way down the gangplank. There were no guards, no border inspection. Tangier was a free port, an open zone called an international protectorate, and there were no restrictions on who might enter or leave.

As I reached the bottom of the gangplank I spied my luggage, my two heavy cases wet from sitting on the ship's deck. I was the last passenger to leave the ferry. As I went to them, wondering how I would find the strength to lift them, a small dark man with a filthy white turban came towards me, leading a shaggy grey donkey attached to a cart. He spoke to me, but I shook my head at the unknown language. Then he spoke in French, asking me where I wished to go.

'Hotel Continental, *s'il vous plaît*,' I told him, because I knew no other name, and he nodded once, putting out his hand, palm up, as he quoted me a price in French sous.

I thought of the American's warning: *North Africa is a place where one must keep one's wits about one at all times*. What if this man had no intention of taking me to the hotel? What if he were to take me to some hidden spot and leave me, taking my money and my bags? Or worse.

The enormity of what I had done—travelling here, with no one to call upon should I need assistance—came over me again.

What choice did I have?

I licked my lips and named half the price the small man had asked for. He slapped his chest, frowning, shaking his head, speaking again in the unknown language, and then named another price in French, halfway between his first offer and mine. I was almost woozy with the heat, and knew I couldn't carry my own luggage more than a few steps. I reached into my bag and pulled out the coins. As I placed them on the man's palm I saw, with a small start of surprise, that there was a fine line of dirt under my fingernails.

It appeared that this dark continent had become a part of me from my very first footsteps on its soil.

The man lifted my two bags into the open back of the cart with amazing ease. He gestured to the seat beside him, and I climbed up. As he lightly slapped the reins against the donkey's back and the cart rolled forward with a jerk, I took another deep breath.

'Hotel Continental,' the man said, confirming where we were going.

'*Oui. Merci*,' I answered, and stared straight ahead.

I was in Tangier, and the architecture, the faces of the people and their language and clothing, the foliage, the smells, the very air itself, were all foreign. There was nothing to remind me of home—my quiet home in Albany in upstate New York.

And as I looked back towards the ferry, I knew also that there was nothing left for me in America—nothing and no one at all.

Chapter Two

I HAD BEEN BORN on the first day of the new century, 1 January 1900, and my mother named me Sidonie, after her grandmother in Quebec. Apart from their shared religion, they were an unlikely match, my lanky Irish father and tiny French-Canadian mother. I was born late in their lives; they had been married eighteen years when I arrived; my mother was thirty-eight and my father forty. They had never expected to be so blessed. I heard my mother give thanks for me every day in her prayers, calling me her miracle. When she and I were alone we spoke French; when my father entered the room we switched to English.

As a child I truly thought myself to be a miracle. My parents had little to give me in terms of material possessions, but I felt loved.

And very special.

All through the uncharacteristically warm spring of 1916—shortly after my sixteenth birthday—I imagined myself in love with Luke McCallister, the boy who worked in the feed store on Larkspur Street. All the girls in my class at Holy Jesus and Mary had talked about him since he'd arrived in our neighbourhood a few months earlier.

We argued among us over who would be the first he would talk to, go for a walk with, or share an ice cream with.

'It will be me,' I told Margaret and Alice Ann, my best friends.

'Just because you always have the most dance partners doesn't mean you can have all the attention whenever you want, Sidonie,' Margaret said, her chin lifted.

I smiled at her. 'Maybe not. But remember Rodney? You didn't believe me when I said I'd get him to take me on the Ferris wheel at the fair last year. But I did, didn't I?'

Alice Ann shrugged. 'That's just because your mother is friends with his mother. I'll bet Luke talks to Margaret. Especially if she wears her pink dress. You're beautiful in pink, Margaret,' she added.

'No, it will be you, Alice Ann,' Margaret said, obviously pleased by Alice Ann's comment.

'Think what you will,' I said, laughing now. 'But he'll be mine.'

They laughed with me. 'Oh, Sidonie,' Alice Ann said. 'You always say the silliest things.' We linked arms as we walked along the narrow street, our hips and shoulders touching as we matched our steps.

One steamy Sunday at the beginning of June, at Our Lady of Mercy church, I prayed so hard to the Virgin Mother for Luke to fall in love with me that I was suddenly overcome with a strange sense of leaving my body. My neck had been stiff that morning when I awoke, my head aching to such a degree that my stomach churned. I begged my mother to let me stay home, but she refused.

It wasn't uncommon for me to try to find a way to avoid church.

My body, usually light and quick, was heavy and cumbersome as I knelt alongside my mother, the smell of the incense was overpowering to the point of making me more nauseous, and the incantations of Father Cecil were as garbled as though he spoke in other tongues. It hurt the back of my neck to lower my chin to pray, and so instead I looked at the Holy Mother and saw tears, like glass, on her cheeks. The Virgin's lips parted, and I leaned forward, my chin on my arms on the back of the pew in front of me, my knees numb on the stone floor.

Yes, Mother, yes, I begged, *tell me how to make Luke love me. What can I do to make him want me? I beseech you, Holy Mother. Tell me.*

I had to close my eyes against the sudden brilliant light in the church, but on the insides of my eyelids I saw the Virgin Mary reach her arms to me. And then, effortlessly, I was flying towards her. I soared over the nave and the confessional, the rows of pews, the altar boys, Father Cecil. I knew the Holy Mother had heard my prayer, and had deemed that yes, I deserved this wish. She would answer my prayers.

She let me see Luke's face, and then I was no longer flying but falling, falling towards Luke, who put out his arms to catch me, a gentle smile on his beautiful mouth.

I smiled back at him, my lips parting to touch his, and the colour and heat and light all became one, and I was overcome with a rapture I had never known.

When I awoke, I was in my own small bedroom. The light was still too bright; it hurt my eyes when I blinked, trying to focus.

My mother sat by my bed, humming my favourite lullaby. I hadn't heard it since I was a child. *Dodo, l'enfant, do*. Sleep, child, sleep.

'*Ah. Ma petite Sido*,' she said, and her voice was thick in her throat.

I tried to open my lips, but they were stuck together. My mother gently swabbed them with a damp cloth, and then held a straw to my mouth. 'Come, drink,' she said, and I drank, the liquid so cold and somehow fragrant that it seemed to me I had never before tasted water.

But the effort of simply swallowing was so great that I had to close my eyes. I must have fallen asleep again, for when I next blinked, the light in the room had changed, and was softer, shadowed, and I could see more clearly. My mother still—or again—stood over me, but now, strangely, my father was at the open window, looking in.

'Dad?' I whispered. 'Why are you outside?'

His face folded in on itself, his chin quivering in the oddest way. I suddenly realised he was crying.

'What's wrong?' I asked, carefully moving my eyes from him to my mother, and finally back to my father.

'It's the infant paralysis, my girl,' he said.

I tried to make sense of it. I wasn't an infant. Paralysis I understood, and, although the word sent a shiver of horror through me, I was too weak to do more than close my eyes again.

That summer, the polio epidemic of 1916 raged through the state of New York. Most of those who contracted it were children under ten; some, like me, were older.

So many died. And I was told, by my parents, that I was one of the lucky ones. *It's another miracle*, my mother had whispered into my ear, the first day I understood fully what had happened to me.

It was well known that polio was contagious; I was in quarantine. My mother stayed with me. But my father didn't enter our house again for a number of weeks; he needed his job, chauffeur to one of the wealthy families who lived throughout our county.

For those first weeks my mother followed the recommendations given out by the health-service nurse, agreed upon by the doctor who had come to see me. She bathed my legs daily in almond meal. She made endless poultices of camomile, slippery elm, mustard and other nasty-smelling oils, putting the hot plasters on my legs. She massaged my thighs and my calves. When I found the strength to sit up for a few moments, she pulled my oddly heavy legs to the edge of the bed, and put her arm around my waist, trying to help me stand, but my legs wouldn't support me, and I wept with anger and frustration.

For the first few months I wept often—tears of impatience, tears of disappointment, tears of self-pity. My parents were sympathetic and did what they could to make me feel better. It was a long time before I could understand what an effort this was for them: to put on a positive face and attitude when they must have been as shattered and grieving as I was.

After some time I grew weary of my own burning eyes and the headaches brought on by the crying, and one day I simply stopped, and didn't cry again.

When the quarantine had passed and I felt well enough, my friends came to see me. It was the beginning of the new school year, and during those initial visits, when my life felt like a strange, disturbing twilight from which I couldn't quite awaken, I listened to their stories, nodding and imagining myself back in school with them.

Every Friday my mother picked up my schoolwork from Holy Jesus and Mary, and returned it the following Friday.

One Friday, along with my new assignments, my mother handed me a sealed envelope from one of the sisters who had formerly taught me. When I opened it, a letter and a small prayer card, edged in gold, fell from its folds onto the blanket.

My dear Sidonie, I read. *You must not despair. This is God's will. You have been predestined for this test. God found you wanting, and so chose you. Others have died, but you have not. This is proof that God has protected you for a reason, and has also given you this burden, which you will carry for the rest of your life. In this way, He has shown you that you are special to Him.*

As a cripple, now God will carry you, and you will know Him with a strength that those with whole bodies do not.

You must pray, and God will answer. I will also pray for you, Sidonie.

Sister Marie-Gregory

My hands were shaking as I folded the letter and put it and the prayer card back into the envelope.

'What is it, Sidonie? You've gone pale,' my mother said.

I shook my head, carefully placing the envelope between the pages of a textbook. *As a cripple*, the sister had written. *For the rest of your life.*

Even though Sister Marie-Gregory had also said that I was special to God, I knew, with sickening reality, that it didn't mean, as my mother told me, that He would let me walk again. But I also knew that the polio wasn't a test sent by God, as the sister had said. I alone knew why I had contracted the disease. It was punishment for my sinful thoughts about Luke McCallister. I had committed one of the seven cardinal sins—lust—and for this I was punished.

A week after the sister's letter, I was again visited by the doctor from the public health services. Openly weary and speaking with a sighing resignation, he agreed, after moving my legs about and testing my reflexes and having me try a few simple exercises, with Sister Marie-Gregory's written prediction. He told me that I would never again walk, that I should be grateful the disease had affected only my lower limbs, and that I was better off than many of the children totally paralysed by the epidemic.

After the doctor's visit I resumed my prayers. But this time they had nothing to do with Luke McCallister.

Heavenly Father, Gracious Mother, I repeated, over and over, week after week, month after month. *If you allow me to walk I shall have only pure thoughts. I will never again give in to the desires of my body*.

During that first long year I was forced to remain in bed, propped up by cushions; it hurt my back to sit upright for longer than a few minutes. Margaret and Alice Ann still came to see me, but it was not as before. I began to see that they had, in a few short months, grown taller and brighter, while I had shrunk and lost colour. I listened to them, but now, instead of cheering me, their stories made me see only that I was missing out on life. It soon became apparent that they sensed this as well, for they began speaking more haltingly, sometimes stopping in the middle of an anecdote about what someone at school had said or done, as if they too suddenly realised that they were only reminding me of a life that was no longer mine. Would never be mine.

The visits eventually grew less frequent. Although I knew my mother was saddened by my lack of visitors, I was relieved when, after a month of no one knocking on our front door, I knew I wouldn't have to worry about another strained afternoon.

The second year passed, and slowly, changes came about. I was finally able to sit up without assistance, and I moved from the bed into a wheeled chair. This gave me a certain freedom; after many attempts and many falls I learned to pull and swing myself from my bed into the chair without help. I no longer had to wait for my mother to come and assist me in bringing the pan or washing myself; I could wheel myself to the bathroom and into the kitchen. I could eat at the table with my parents. If my father or mother pushed the chair over the high doorway sill, I could sit on the porch in pleasant weather.

With this my spirits rose. On the porch one warm evening, I played with Cinnabar, the copper-coloured kitten my parents had bought me. The little creature turned out to be deaf, but it didn't matter to me; perhaps it made me love her more. I laughed now to see her leap straight into the air, frightened by a cricket that hopped over her paws. My parents came to the doorway, and I told them about Cinnabar and the cricket.

My father opened the door and walked to me, standing behind me and putting his hand on my shoulder, squeezing it. 'It's the first we've heard you laugh since . . .' he said, and then stopped, turning away abruptly and going into the house.

In that instant I understood how much my parents had wanted—and waited—for that most simple and human response: my laughter. I understood how they waited for me to smile, to talk about ordinary things, to paint with passion, something I'd shown promise in as a child, although I hadn't had the patience then to sit still for long. They wanted me to be happy.

I knew how much they had done for me. Even if I would never accept what fate had handed me, I could pretend, for their sakes, that I still found pleasure in life. I owed them this, at the very least.

By the end of that second year, I proved the doctor—and Sister Marie-Gregory—wrong.

I was fitted with heavy metal braces from ankle to thigh. They bit into my skin, but they kept my legs from buckling. And with the aid of crutches, I was able to pull myself out of my chair. At first I did little more than drag my legs behind me, but eventually I was able to swing my legs from the hips, putting pressure on the bottom of my feet. My right leg was now shorter than the left, and so sturdy boots with one built-up sole were made for me. It was only a parody of walking, but I was once again upright, and able to move about, although very slowly.

I stood, I walked. My prayers had been answered. In body I was like the old Sidonie. But inwardly she was gone.

And life was altered in another way. I didn't want to leave the yard. I never resumed my old friendships for, by now—over two years later, and approaching my nineteenth birthday—all the girls I had gone to school with had left Holy Jesus and Mary. Although neither Margaret or Alice Ann had gone to New York as we'd once planned, Margaret was training to be a teacher, and Alice Ann had a job selling hats in a fancy shop.

Even though I now found great pleasure in my painting, I hadn't finished my final year of school, despite the fact that the teachers offered to bring the exams and supervise while I wrote them. I simply lost interest in doing the school assignments. Besides, I told myself, what difference would it make? I would never go out into the world—or even into the main streets of Albany.

My father had been aghast when I told him I didn't care about achieving a high-school diploma.

'I didn't come to this country—nearly dying on the journey in the hold of that stinking, cholera-infected ship—to have my own child refuse the education handed to her. What I would have given to have your opportunity . . . don't you want to *be* something, Sidonie? You could learn to use a typewriter, and work in an office. Or become a telephone operator. There are many jobs where you don't have to walk or stand for long periods. You would make your mother proud, learning a trade. Wouldn't she, Mother?'

I glanced at my mother. She gave a small, encouraging smile. 'She could be anything,' she said.

I held my lips together tightly. Of course I couldn't be *anything*. I wasn't a child, and I was a cripple. I opened my mouth to argue with her, but my father spoke again.

'Just until you marry, of course,' he said.

Marry? Who would marry me, with my heavy black boots, one built an inch higher than the other, and my noisy, dragging limp?

'No. I don't want to be a secretary or telephone operator.'

'What is it you might like, then? Don't you have some dream? *Leprechauns, castles, good luck and laughter; lullabies, dreams and love ever after*,' he quoted. He had so many clichés about life, so many useless Irish sayings.

It was the beginning of the many arguments I would have with my father over the next few years. After a time I had been able to walk without dragging my legs. I eventually exchanged the hated crutches for canes. And then, after wearing the full leg braces for two more years, my legs growing stronger all the time, I exchanged them for small metal ankle braces, which could be almost hidden by high leather boots. My left leg was now quite sturdy, but I was unable to walk without dragging my right leg in a limping gait.

I knew that earlier I had felt sorry for myself, embarrassed at my affliction and, as my father had said, regretful to the point of bitterness. But those feelings passed, and now I accepted my small, quiet life. It suited me; everyone in our neighbourhood knew me, and there was no need to explain anything. I was Sidonie O'Shea: I had survived polio and I helped my mother care for the house on Juniper Road, which we rented from our next-door neighbours, Mr and Mrs Barlow.

My mother suffered from arthritis and, when it grew worse, I took over the running of the house. I cooked and baked, I did laundry and ironed and kept the house clean. Through the winter I studied gardening books, painting my visions of new designs for the garden, which now filled most of both the front and back yard. As soon as the last of the snow melted in the spring, I walked among the pebbled paths I had had my father lay, exulting over the first crocuses and snowdrops, and then the hyacinths and tulips and daffodils, willing the first tiny pink shoots of the peonies to stretch into the warming air.

In the summer I persuaded my father to borrow Mr Barlow's truck to drive me out to the marshes of nearby Pine Bush, where I sketched the flora and wildlife, so that I could create watercolour paintings from my charcoal renditions.

And through every season I kept my vow. I had promised, in my endless prayers, that in return for being able to walk I would have no unclean thoughts. I knew I would never meet anyone, living the way I did. It certainly wasn't as though a man ever came to the door of our house on Juniper Road, looking for Sidonie O'Shea.

Shortly after my twenty-third birthday my mother became ill. First it was bronchitis, and then a virulent strain of pneumonia that would clear up but kept recurring. After one terrible bout, the doctor told us that it was now only a matter of time; her lungs couldn't take any more.

My father and I sat up with her that night, after the doctor left. My father spoke to her, and although she was incapable of answering, it was clear from her eyes that she understood. And I—what did I do? I walked about their bedroom. It was difficult to swallow around the burning pain in my throat. My mouth hurt. My eyes hurt.

And then I understood. I needed to cry. I hadn't cried in eight years, since I'd wept as a sixteen year old in the aftershock of polio.

I went to the bed and sat down beside my mother, picking up her misshapen hand. I opened my mouth, trying to let the pain in my throat out. But nothing came, and the pain increased.

My father touched my arm. I looked at him, seeing tears running down his cheeks, and I whispered, in a choking voice, 'Dad,' wanting him to help me. My mother was dying, and yet it was me asking for help.

He shifted his chair closer and put his arm around my shoulders. 'Cry, Sidonie. *A rain of tears is necessary to the harvest of understanding*,' he said. Another of his Irish quotes, but I needed it at that moment.

I cried. I cried and whispered to her until she died, just after midnight. And after that I couldn't stop crying.

My father was a gentle man, with a beautiful lilting Irish voice, but he spoke less and less after my mother's death and seemed to grow smaller and more hesitant in his movements. And then—whether it was his reflexes or something about his eyesight, even with his eyeglasses—it was soon evident that his vision wasn't strong enough to continue his chauffeuring. His first minor accident was simply brushing against a lamppost when he attempted to park his employer's expensive car, but that was quickly followed by him nudging the front of the car into the garage door.

After this his employer told him he couldn't keep him on any longer. But the employer was a kind man, and had given my father an unexpectedly large dismissal package. We lived frugally, but managed.

The years passed. The seasons came and went, and both my father and I grew older. Little changed until a late March day in 1929, when an icy rain blew in from the east, and all that I knew disappeared for ever.

Chapter Three

AS I WAITED at the front desk of Tangier's Hotel Continental for the key to my room, I saw that the American on the boat had described it accurately: the other guests were fashionable, and the hotel itself was quite beautiful—a combination of European and Arabic influences.

I was shown to my room by a young boy wearing a maroon fez; the fabric was discoloured where it sat on his head, and the tassel was a bit ragged. He nodded and smiled broadly as he set down my bags. 'Omar,' he said, patting his chest. 'Omar.' I put a few centimes in his hand.

'Thank you, Omar. Is there somewhere I might get something to eat at this time of day?' I asked him, and he studied my lips carefully, in the way one does when trying to understand a language one is not comfortable with. '*Manger*,' I repeated, touching my mouth.

'Ah, *oui*. Downstairs, madame, downstairs,' he said, backing out, nodding and smiling. Suddenly the smile left his face. 'But please, madame, not to go on roof,' he told me, in tortured French. 'Roof bad.'

'*Oui*, Omar,' I said. 'I will not go to the roof.'

When he'd left, I went to the narrow windows. They overlooked the port and the strait beyond, fed by both the Atlantic and the Mediterranean. The strait was perhaps only eight miles across, but it divided two continents and an ocean and a sea. And it was as if Tangier itself was caught somewhere in the middle, belonging to neither European Spain nor African Morocco.

Suddenly I shivered, overcome with melancholy. It was unexpected, this odd sense of isolation. I didn't like crowds, and avoided situations where I would have to make conversation, yet now I didn't want to sit alone in my room. And, most importantly, I had to speak to someone about renting a car and driver to take me to Marrakesh.

I went back down the winding staircase to the lobby, remembering the lounge I had passed. There were people at different tables, some with heads together in corners, others laughing loudly as they sat at the bar. I took a deep breath and stepped in.

I had never before gone into a drinking lounge. I sat at one of the small round tables. Almost immediately a man in a short white jacket bowed before me, setting a tray with a glass of reddish liquid and a small carafe of water onto my table.

'*Non, non*, monsieur,' I said, shaking my head at the man. I had planned to order a mineral water.

'Campari, madame,' he said, firmly. He pointed to a line on the paper he handed me, and, rather than argue, I signed my name.

Nobody noticed me, and in an attempt to appear that I was used to these situations, I breathed deeply, sitting back and taking a tiny sip of the Campari. It was bitter and had a medicinal quality.

A shadow fell over the carafe as a woman passed my table. She walked in long, easy strides, and wore a rather mannish shirt tucked into a simple skirt. She glanced at me, then looked away. I watched her go to a table and join four others—another woman and three men. They all greeted her with a burst of enthusiasm. She looked like the type of woman who would know about hiring a car.

I rose from my chair and went to the group, aware, as I grew close, that they had turned to watch me. I stumbled, slightly, on the heavy carpet. A silence fell as I stood to one side of the raw-boned woman.

'Excuse me,' I said.

'Yes?' There was something slightly unfriendly in her manner. She openly studied my hair and my face, her eyes lingering on the scar on my cheek. I fought not to raise my palm to cover it.

'I . . . I'm newly arrived in Tangier. Just a few hours ago, in fact. And I'm in need of hiring a car. I thought perhaps you could help.'

As I spoke, her demeanour changed. 'Well, hello,' she said, extending her hand as if we were men. I responded, putting my hand in hers. She gave my hand one abrupt shake and then let it go. 'Elizabeth Pandy,' she said, adding, 'from Newport, Maine. And you?'

'I'm Sidonie O'Shea.'

'O'Shea. Hmmmm. Of the Boston O'Sheas?'

'No. No,' I repeated, shaking my head. 'I'm from Albany.'

Now she smiled. 'Well. New York. I wouldn't have—' She stopped herself. 'Look, when I first saw you I thought you were French. You—' She stopped for the second time.

I knew why she had made this distinction. But her tone made me realise it might be better not to tell her about my mother's background.

'Join us, why don't you, and have a drink.'

'Oh, I already have one, thank you. A . . .' I looked back at my table. 'A Campari. Although I didn't order it.'

She nodded in a knowing way. 'I don't know why these bloody boys think that every foreigner in Tangier drinks Campari. Come now, and have a proper drink with us.'

She raised her chin at one of the men, who immediately stood and pulled a chair from the next table in beside hers.

'I . . .' How could I leave without appearing impolite? But these confident men and women made me so aware that my life was nothing like theirs. That I didn't fit in. 'I really . . . I'm hoping to hire a car, as quickly as possible. And a driver, of course. I was wondering if you knew how I could go about this. I need to get to Marrakesh. I was told . . .' I thought of the American, 'that it would be best to get to Rabat first.'

Elizabeth Pandy dismissed my question with a wave of her hand. 'Marrakesh? Don't be silly. There's nothing to see there. Come, now,' she demanded, 'do have a drink. Marcus, order Miss O'Shea a whiskey sour. Isn't it lovely being away from the tedium of Prohibition back home? All that silly clandestine behaviour. So tiresome.'

There seemed no alternative without appearing horribly rude to Miss—or was it Mrs?—Pandy. As I manoeuvred myself into the chair, she glanced down. 'Have you turned your ankle on the terrible streets here? I noticed you limping heavily.'

'No,' I said. 'No, I haven't. It's . . .' I stopped, unsure how to continue.

'Well, never mind, sit down and take a load off.'

She introduced me to the men and one woman, although the only name I remembered was Marcus. All of them, including Elizabeth, were in various stages of intoxication.

One of the men asked me which room I'd been given, and the other woman interrupted him, asking in a demanding voice how long I was planning on staying, but I had no time to answer before the conversation swung. A glass was set in front of me; upon trying it I decided it was more pleasurable than the Campari, and occasionally took a very small sip.

'Well?' Elizabeth finally demanded. 'What has brought you to Tangier? Nobody comes to Tangier without a story.'

'Story?' I repeated, sudden panic coming over me as all their eyes turned in my direction.

'Yes, yes,' Marcus encouraged. 'What brings you to Tangier?'

'I'm going to Marrakesh.'

'I've told you, my dear, it's nonsense. No point going way down there. Marrakesh is such an outpost. Nothing of interest, I'm sure,' Elizabeth said. 'Although who was it—Matisse, I believe—who worked there some years back? Tangier has much more to offer in terms of entertainment.'

The others joined in, a rumbling chorus of agreement.

'No. I must. I'm . . .' I stopped. 'I'm looking for someone. In Marrakesh,' I said, unnecessarily.

'Ah. I see,' Elizabeth said, her eyebrows arching. 'Gone off and left you, has he? Perhaps he's a spy. Is he a spy, Miss O'Shea? The country is awash with them, you know.'

I stood so suddenly, pushing back my chair in one swift movement, that it caught the passing waiter in the hip. He uttered a small, surprised yelp, but kept going.

'No. No. He's not a spy. Thank you. For the drink,' I added, and then left the lounge, feeling that all eyes were on my limp, surely more pronounced by the unfamiliar alcohol swirling in my empty stomach.

I lay on my bed in the shadowed coolness, my head still pounding from the whiskey, annoyed by the idiotic way I must have come across to Elizabeth Pandy and her friends. I didn't know how to share the easy camaraderie they possessed, nor how to make small talk so openly.

I rose and drank a glass of the bottled water on the dressing table, and then, despite the boy's earlier warning, went out into the hallway, looking for the stairs to the roof. They were steep, with no handrail. Such steps usually presented difficulty for me, but still I set off up them, thankful the passageway was so narrow that I could help pull myself along by planting my hands firmly on each side of me. There was a strong smell of sewage wafting from somewhere, but when I reached the top and stepped up into blinding light, the darkness and odour were washed away, and I could smell the sea.

The climb had left me panting, and I had to lean over, my hands on my knees. But when I straightened, what I saw threatened again to take away my breath. On one side of me the sea tilted away, glinting in the sun, and on the other I saw mountains. The glorious Rif mountains, the setting sun staining them a blood red.

Standing alone in the sweet breeze, Tangier encircled me, the buildings blinding-white in the late afternoon sun. Unfamiliar feathery and broad-leafed trees, as well as palms, stood in variegated shades of green. There was a clarity to the scene in the play of light that made me think of the most brilliant of paintings—the colours were not blue and red and yellow and green, but cerulean, indigo, they were vermilion and crimson, amber and saffron, celadon and olive and lime.

I closed my eyes and opened them, each time letting the thrill run through me. I knew my box of paints, stored away on the bedroom shelf of my small house across the ocean, could never create such colours.

I walked, slowly, to the far end of the roof and peered down into a shadowy labyrinth of streets, surely the medina, the oldest part of the city. There the crowds milled in a kind of frenzy; there were calls and shouts and the braying of donkeys and barking of dogs and the occasional roar of a camel.

And then came a sound I hadn't before heard, a high and yet carrying voice, coming from somewhere behind me. I turned to see the spire of a minaret, and knew it was a muezzin, calling the Muslim believers to prayer. Suddenly another voice joined in, and then another, as voices from the various minarets throughout Tangier called out. I stood on that roof, surrounded by the sonorous, rhythmic phrase that to me sounded like *Allah Akbar*, watching the scarlet-stained mountains.

Was Etienne hearing these same sounds? Was he looking at the sky, at mountains, at the sea? Was he thinking of me, at this lonely hour, as I was of him?

I had to close my eyes.

When the echo of voices ended there was a sudden quiet, and I opened my eyes and drank in the sense that the foreign prayers had somehow reached inside me. Without thinking I crossed myself in the old, reflexive habit.

And then I made my way down the stairs. I was impossibly hungry. I went back to the lobby, passing the doorway of the lounge. From the laughter and boisterous voices it was obvious that Elizabeth Pandy and her friends were still there.

Out on the spacious terrace—empty but for me—with its gently swaying potted palms and wooden furniture and views of the harbour, I ordered a pot of mint tea and a *pastilla*, which the server explained was a kind of bird—I couldn't understand if he was saying partridge or pigeon—mixed with rice and chopped egg in layers of thin pastry.

While I waited, I laid my head against the tall back of the chair, listening to the muted babble of unknown languages, to the rustle of the palm fronds in the warm early-evening breeze. I was weary, and overcome with a listlessness that was not unpleasant. But I would not—could not—stop and rest in Tangier. I sat up, shaking off the languor that had set in. Tomorrow I would set out to find a driver to take me to Rabat, as the American on the ferry had instructed.

When the tray was set before me, the server lifted the small brass teapot. He poured the tea in a thick amber stream, holding the pot high over the small painted glass in a silver holder. I expected the tea to splash out of the glass from that height, but he filled it with the foaming liquid without spilling a drop. He set down the teapot, picking up the glass with both hands and extending it to me with a slight bow.

'*Très chaud*, madame,' he said. 'Wait, please, for it to cool.'

I nodded, holding the glass by the silver holder, and lifted it to my nose. The odour of mint was almost overwhelming. I took a sip; it was intensely sweet, like no tea I had ever tasted, but it was delicious.

I thought of home, of my garden and the silence of this time of evening. It all seemed so far away. It *was* far away, geographically, of course. But it wasn't just the distance. It was what had happened to me since those days, those endless, quiet days when my life consisted of small, certain pieces of a larger, but basically simple, puzzle.

When I was sure that I always knew where each piece fitted.

Chapter Four

IT WAS TWO YEARS earlier—1928—when my father received a letter from a lawyer.

'Read it for me, darlin', he'd said, anxiety on his face. 'I can't think what I've done wrong.'

'It doesn't mean anything's wrong, Dad,' I told him, opening the letter and scanning it.

'Go on, then. What does it say?'

I looked at him. 'Dad. Mr Harding has passed away.'

'Well,' my father said, sitting at the kitchen table. 'Poor auld soul. I knew he'd been ill some time.'

Mr Harding had been my father's last employer, the one who had been so kind when he'd had to terminate my father after fourteen years.

'And why would a lawyer be writing to me about it?' he asked.

I licked my lips, trying not to rush. I was sorry, of course, that Mr Harding had died, but he'd been ninety-two.

'You remember his car,' I stated.

'Which one, now? For he had quite a fleet of them,' my father said.

'The one you loved to drive the most. You always talked about it.'

He was smiling now. 'Ah, that would be the Silver Ghost. Such a thing of beauty. Driving it was like floating on a cloud.' He picked up his pipe and tapped it on the ashtray; a clump of dottle fell from the bowl. 'I did love to drive that grand thing,' he said.

'Dad?' I stood, unable to keep my own smile from my face any longer. 'Mr Harding has left it to you. It's in his will, Dad. The car is yours.' My voice had risen with excitement.

But my father grew very still as I spoke. I waited for something—an exclamation, a burst of laughter, something—but he didn't move.

'Aren't you happy about it, Dad? You just said—'

'I know what I said. But it's too late, Sidonie. The time for me to own a car like that is gone. You know I can't trust my own eyes.'

I sat down, running my fingers over the embossed letterhead. 'But it's yours,' I said.

'What would I do with it?'

I sat straighter. 'I could drive it, Dad. You could teach me, and I could drive it for you. Wherever you want to go.' I was speaking quickly, thrilling myself at the idea.

'No, Sidonie,' he said, filling his pipe. 'It takes coordination, hands and feet. Feet, Sidonie. You have to be able to use the pedals—the gas and brake and clutch. You'd have to be able to bend your knees freely. I don't think . . .' He glanced at my built-up shoe.

My mouth twisted. 'I can learn,' I said, loudly. 'I want that car.'

My father looked surprised. 'Well. It's a rare day I hear that tone from you.'

I knew my voice was loud. But it excited me—the thought of driving. I couldn't remember the last time I had learned something new.

I lowered my chin and tried to modulate my voice. 'It's just that . . . it's been given to you, Dad. If you don't want it, I'll have it.'

He shook his head. 'As I said, you couldn't—'

'Can't you let me do this for you? You spent most of your life driving other people. You've spent all your life doing things for me. Please. Let me do something for *you*.'

He didn't answer, but his expression changed, softened, and I knew then that the Silver Ghost would be mine.

Once the car was delivered to our yard, my father did teach me to drive it, and I took pride in the fact that he was obviously surprised at how quickly I mastered it. It was true, as he'd said, that I had a certain difficulty because I didn't have a lot of strength in my right leg, and the knee didn't bend freely. But even though he saw that I could manage, my father still worried, knowing my foot's reflex was poor.

Immediately I discovered that I loved driving the Silver Ghost; from the first time I took it out on my own I felt a sense of power I had never before experienced. Behind the steering wheel I forgot my heavy limp; with the top down and my hair loose, I achieved the almost-forgotten pleasure of moving quickly. Perhaps it reminded me a bit of running.

It was the very tail end of winter when my father told me he was going to the next county to watch a car auction. He said he would go with Mike Barlow.

'No, I'll drive you,' I said. 'The snow has melted enough to get the Ghost out. Last week I took the tarp off and started the engine and let her run a bit. She's all ready to go, Dad.'

'There's no need, Sidonie. Mike has said he'll take me in his truck, and the roads are icy after yesterday's wet rain and then the freezing. With your leg—'

'Stop fussing about my leg. And I want to go as well. We haven't been to an auction in months.' I put on my coat, glancing at myself in the mirror over the sideboard and smoothing back my hair. 'I'm taking you, and that's all. It'll be fun, Dad,' I added.

Something was different now; I had a new confidence.

My father shook his head, his lips tight, but he put on his coat and his galoshes.

I didn't want us to leave with bad feelings, and put my arms around him, hugging him. 'Wear a scarf, Dad,' I said.

'*No man ever wore a scarf as warm as his daughter's arms around his neck*,' he quoted, and I smiled.

While it was indeed wonderful to drive the Silver Ghost again, I hadn't ever driven on anything more challenging than surfaces wet from summer or fall rain. As my father had predicted, the roads were slippery, and if I accelerated too quickly the car's thin tyres slid to one side, just enough to surprise me and make me turn the wheel sharply to line up the car again. My father said nothing, but I could hear his teeth working the stem of his unlit pipe.

I shifted gears slowly, and occasionally one would grind. Each time this happened I saw, from the corner of my eye, my father's head turning sharply towards me, but I ignored him. Even though it was just past noon, as we drove out of the city the sky was growing grainy.

'Turn on the lights, Sidonie,' my father said.

I shook my head, the concentration I needed making me tense. 'It's not dark, Dad,' I said, annoyance in my voice. Later I would remember that my last words to him had been in this slightly strident tone. 'It's just your eyes.'

'But it's growing foggy.'

'There are no other cars on the road,' I said, looking at him, and suddenly his expression changed. I thought it was anger I saw, and shook my head at him. 'I'm quite capable of—'

'Sidonie!' he yelled, and I looked back at the road. A truck loomed on the other side of us, and its unexpected presence startled me so that I gasped, wrenching the wheel sharply away from the truck. When I relived this split second and my reaction, over and over and over, in the ensuing days and weeks and months, I saw, in my head, that there had been no need; the truck was on its side of the road, and we were on ours. It was only that I hadn't seen it coming as I looked over at my father, and my reaction was an instinct born of surprise.

The land blurred, and there was a sickening spin of the car as I fought to get it under control.

'Don't brake,' my father yelled. 'Downshift. Downshift!'

I tried, but my foot, in its heavy shoe, slipped off the clutch. The wheel whirled beneath my palms. There was the unbelievable sensation of flight, and then darkness.

I don't know how long it was before I opened my eyes. The view through the windshield was odd. I kept blinking, trying to understand what I was seeing. Finally I realised the car was on its side, my cheek against the side window.

'Dad?' I whispered, moving my head. There was an odd crunching under my face, and a dull bite in my cheek; I raised my hand and touched something unfamiliar, something embedded in my cheek. I pulled it out, feeling no more than a slight sting, and dully looked at a long shard of glass covered in blood.

'Dad,' I said again, dropping the glass and looking for him. He wasn't in the passenger seat. For a brief moment I thought perhaps he'd gone to get help, but as clarity came back I saw, with horror, that his side of the windshield was completely smashed. I struggled to pull myself up. The side of my head hurt, but it was just a dull throb. In order to get out of the car I had to climb over the gear stick and drag my lower body across the passenger seat, fighting to open the door straight up into the sky. When I was finally able to swing it open, I pulled myself out, the uncooperative weight of my lower body similar to my earlier days of polio. I clambered out, falling the short distance from the open door to the ground. The car was half on the road and half in a shallow depression leading to a field of frosted stubble.

'Dad!' I called, my voice low and hoarse. I wandered into the middle of the road. 'Dad,' I cried, turning in a slow circle, 'where are you?'

And then I saw a mound in the ploughed field a number of yards from the car, and knew with certainty it was my father. When I reached him I kneeled beside him, saying *Dad, Dad, Dad*, and stroking his bloodied face. He lay on his back, one arm thrown over his head, but other than the wide gash on his forehead and so much blood he looked as still and calm as if he was sleeping. I lay my cheek against his chest. It was warm, and I felt it rise and fall, slowly.

It was only then, knowing he was alive, that I cried.

'You'll be all right, Dad. You'll be all right,' I said, over and over, weeping as the cold, damp air swirled around us.

Something woke me, and I lifted my head in a hopeful rush. But my father still lay unmoving in the hospital bed, and in the next instant I knew that what had woken me was a painful throbbing in my cheek. I reached up to touch it, and felt gauze and tape. I explored it for a few seconds, only mildly curious, and then again took my father's hand, as I had when they first allowed me to come into his room.

His breathing caught for a moment, and I squeezed his hand, looking at his face. A spasm passed over his features, but in the next instant both his face and his breathing settled, and I sat back again.

'Dad,' I said, quietly. 'Dad. Please.'

Please what? Wake up? Don't die? Forgive me?

'You should rest while he sleeps,' a voice said, and, dully, I looked over my shoulder. It was a man, a doctor, I assumed, from the stethoscope around his neck. I put down my father's hand and stood.

'Can you tell me anything?' I asked. 'What . . . will he be all right?'

The doctor looked at my father, then back at me. 'There were many injuries. Internal. And because of the age . . . it's . . . Miss O'Shea, yes? You must prepare yourself.'

I sat down. 'Prepare myself?'

'You would not wish to go home for a while? The man and woman who brought you and your father here—did you know them? Could you call them to take you home?'

I shook my head once. I had only a vague recollection of a car stopping on the road, of a man lifting my father into the back seat, a woman pressing a handkerchief against my cheek. 'I'll stay with him.'

The doctor was silent for a moment.

'Has someone called your mother?' he asked. 'Or perhaps a brother, sister—'

'There's only me,' I interrupted, my voice hoarse.

'The medication,' he said then. 'It has helped?'

I looked at my father. 'I don't know.'

'No,' he said. 'Your face. It pains a great deal?'

I reached up to touch the dressing as I had a few moments earlier. 'No. I . . . I don't remember. . .'

'It's the deep cut, Miss O'Shea. There were many small pieces of glass; I took them out and stitch it for you.'

His English was similar to my mother's. I had a recollection: the stinging smell of disinfectant, this man's face close to mine, a tugging at my flesh, which was cold, and unfeeling. 'No,' I said. 'It doesn't hurt.'

Why was he talking about my insignificant injury? It was my father he should be attending to. 'Can't you do something? Is there some surgery you can perform, something . . . something to help him?'

The doctor shook his head. 'I'm sorry,' he said, and it was clear that he meant it. 'Now it is only the time we wait.' He glanced at a round watch he pulled from his waistcoat pocket. 'I must go now, but I return in a few hours.'

'It's my fault,' I said, not sure why I felt the need to confess to this doctor. His forehead was high and intelligent, his cheeks ruddy. He couldn't have been a doctor too many years; he was surely only a little older than I. 'He told me not to drive.'

He didn't reply, but kept looking at me, his hands in the pockets of his jacket, as if waiting for me to continue.

Again I lifted my father's hand, pressing it against my forehead.

'I am Dr Duverger,' the man said. 'If you wish to speak to me about your father, or your face, you ask the nurse for me. Dr Duverger,' he repeated, looking at me intently.

But I was suddenly so weary, so overcome, that I simply nodded, and turned back to my father.

My father died just before sunrise, without regaining consciousness, without forgiving me. I was there, in the room with him, but at the moment of his death I was asleep.

It was a nurse who came in and discovered he was no longer breathing. She roused me with a hand on my shoulder.

'I'm sorry, Miss O'Shea,' she said. 'He's gone, dear. Come now. Come and we'll get you a cup of tea.'

I remember sitting in a small room with a cup of tea in my hands, and the young doctor—what had he said his name was?—speaking to me. But I couldn't understand him. I walked from the room, but the doctor followed me, putting something—a small container—into my hand. Then he draped my coat over my shoulders. I smelled my father, the scent of his tobacco, and swayed for a moment. The doctor put his hand on my wrist to steady me.

'You must put the ointment on your cheek,' he said. 'The ointment—there, in your hand. Put it on every day. And a clean bandage. Come to see me in one week. How will you go home?' he asked.

'Home? I . . . I don't know. The car . . . my car . . . is it . . . where is it?' I asked, as if he would know.

'I don't know about your automobile, but I think it is better if you do not drive. We will find someone . . . It's very early . . . Where do you live, Miss O'Shea?' he asked then.

'Juniper Road,' I said.

'I will find someone to drive you,' he said. 'You may have to wait.'

I stood there, trying to process his words. 'No,' I said, my senses returning. 'My neighbour, Mr Barlow. Mike Barlow. He'll come and get me. He'll take me home.'

'He has a telephone?'

I nodded. All I wanted to do was leave this place, with my father's lifeless body. 'Yes,' I said. Suddenly I was very cold. Shivering. 'But . . . I can't remember the number. I can't remember it,' I said.

The doctor nodded, moving his hand from my wrist to my shoulder. 'It's the shock, Miss O'Shea. Please. Sit here. Mike Barlow on Juniper? I will find this number,' he said.

I sat where he indicated, my teeth chattering, and watched his back as he left me, going to a nearby desk and speaking to a woman there. She looked at me, nodding, and then he looked back at me as well.

'Put on your coat, Miss O'Shea,' he said, his voice carrying across the small space. 'Keep yourself warm.'

We drove through the thin early-morning light. The sky had cleared and the rising sun shone tentatively, as if unsure of itself. Mr Barlow rolled down the window, and there was the sweet smell of the promise of spring. Suddenly my cheek throbbed so terribly that I drew in my breath and closed my eyes. 'You all right, Sidonie?' Mr Barlow asked.

I opened my eyes and looked at his stubbled face. 'You all right?' he asked again, and I nodded, looking away to stare through the windshield.

And then I saw it. The beautiful Silver Ghost, overturned. There was an overwhelming sense of sadness about it. It lay as though it were a great hulking white beast, beaten and defeated, in the muddy gravel.

'Your dad was a good man, Sidonie,' Mr Barlow said.

And I killed him. I killed him, I thought.

It was Mr Barlow who drove me back to the hospital three weeks later. He came to the door, turning his cap in his hands.

'Nora says you got a phone call. You're supposed to go back to the hospital. They say you missed your appointment.'

'My appointment? For what?' I asked.

Mr Barlow cleared his throat. 'Most likely about your face, Sidonie,' he said, touching his own cheek.

Mr and Mrs Barlow had been good to me for the past few weeks. They had helped with the funeral arrangements and Mrs Barlow had brought me something to eat every day. Sometimes I ate it, sometimes I didn't, and sometimes I didn't remember if I'd eaten or not.

Mr Barlow had taken me to the lawyer's office in Albany, and sat with me while the lawyer explained that my father had left a simple will. He had managed to put away a small amount of money, left to me. I looked at Mr Barlow as we left. 'Is it enough for the rent?' I asked.

'Don't worry about that, Sidonie,' he said. 'It will keep you for a little while. But . . .' He stopped. 'Don't worry about paying any rent,' he said, and I nodded. 'You'll have to open your own account, at the bank,' he added, and again I nodded. Nothing made sense, those first weeks.

Now Mr Barlow was still standing at my door, his cap in his hands. 'Sidonie?' he said, and I jumped, lost in thought.

'Oh. Yes, sorry. When am I supposed to go to the hospital?'

He shrugged. 'Nora didn't say. Just that you missed your appointment and you should go. I can take you today.'

I set down Cinnabar—she was thirteen years old and heavy now—and pulled my coat from its hook behind the door. As we walked out into the spring sunshine, I put my hands in my pockets, and felt something in the left one. It was a small vial and a folded paper. I had worn my coat since the accident—to the funeral, to church, to the lawyer's office, when I sat on the porch, and when I walked to the store—but hadn't discovered these things before. Had I fingered them without even the curiosity to pull them out and look at them, or had I not put my hands into my pockets?

The vial was the ointment the doctor had given me the day my father died, and the paper gave instructions to use it three times a day. It could be renewed if more was needed. There was also a date for me to return to see the doctor. It was for two weeks earlier. On the top of the paper was a small letterhead: *Dr E. Duverger, MD*.

We drove in silence, and when I got out, Mr Barlow touched my arm and said, 'I'll wait for you.'

I nodded, and went up the steps of the hospital. But at the door I stopped, thinking of the night my father died.

I took a deep breath and went through the door. I gave my name at the front desk and was shown into a small room, and after a short wait the doctor came in. Dr Duverger. I remembered his ruddy cheeks. His hair was very dark, as were his eyes. Like mine.

'Good day, Miss O'Shea,' he said, smiling, a very slight smile, and studying me. In the next instant the smile fled, and a line appeared between his brows. 'I phone to your friend—the number for your ride home—because I look at my active patient records, and see that you have not return to have the stitches remove,' he said.

He was standing over me, and I was looking up at him. 'You should have come back when it was the time. Miss O'Shea—did you not see what was happen?'

'Happen?' I echoed, rather faintly. 'What do you mean?'

'The flesh grow over the stitches, and the wound, it turns . . .' He said something in French just under his breath, too low for me to hear the words. Then he said, in English, 'Keloid. It become keloidal.'

I lifted my shoulders a fraction. 'What's that?'

'The tissue—it grows too fast. Look,' he said, pulling a round mirror from his desk. He held it so I could see my own face, and his fingers running up and down the red scar. 'This mound is the formation of fibrous scar tissue. We could have stop it. Did you not feel the itch, the pull?'

I shook my head. 'It doesn't matter.'

He stared at me, and something in his expression suddenly shamed me. I put my hand over my cheek. It was hot. 'My father . . . the funeral and . . . and everything. I . . . I forgot. Or . . . I don't know,' I finally said.

The doctor's face softened, and he sat down in a chair across from me. 'I understand. It is the difficult time. I have lose my own parents,' he said, and with those words, from this man I didn't know, my eyes burned. I hadn't been able to cry at the funeral. I had stayed strong, telling myself I had no right to cry for my own pig-headedness, for my own fatal error in judgment.

So what power did this man have, to make me feel, so unexpectedly, that I wanted to lean my head against his chest and weep? That I wanted him to put his arms around me? I swallowed and blinked, and was relieved that my eyes remained dry.

'Let me look again, Miss O'Shea,' he said. I lifted my chin, and again he leaned closer to me, his fingers gently exploring my cheek.

'You're French,' I said, and then immediately felt foolish. I had no idea why I had made that obvious proclamation.

But he just sat back in the chair, putting on a pair of spectacles and looking at my file. '*Oui*,' he said, reading.

'My mother was French. Not from France. From Canada.'

'*Je sais*,' he murmured, still reading.

'You know?' I asked, surprised.

He put the folder on the desk and took off his spectacles. This time he smiled again, that small, slightly unsure smile. 'Not about your mother. But I hear you pray in the French of this country. And singing. I hear the French song.'

'Singing?' I asked, surprised a second time.

'*Dodo, l'enfant, do*. The night . . . when your father died. When I pass the door I hear you sing . . . what do you call the night song for children?'

'Lullaby,' I said.

'Yes. My mother also sing this lullaby to me. Very traditional,' he said, his smile unself-conscious, warm and sincere. In the next instant it faded. 'Miss O'Shea. You wish your face to be better?' He picked up the small hand mirror and extended it to me for the second time.

I took it, and looked at myself. The scar was angry and red, raised and lumpy, and ran vertically from my cheekbone all the way to my jaw. I was startled at its ugliness. How had I not seen it like this before?

'If I do the very small surgery, I can correct it. There will be new stitching, but it will leave a less noticeable scar. Finer, and more flat. Do you wish to have this done?'

When I didn't immediately speak, Dr Duverger said, 'Miss O'Shea?' and I looked from my own reflection to him.

'No.'

It was obvious that my reaction puzzled him. He couldn't see the great guilt I carried. It was so heavy. And ugly, like the scar.

I didn't want to be here. The antiseptic smell of the hospital, the sounds of the nurses' rubber shoes on the floors, the occasional quiet cry from behind a door . . . it was too real. I just wanted to go home, and stay within the security of my own walls.

'I just don't know if it's worth it,' I said. 'It doesn't matter to me, and it surely doesn't matter to anyone else.'

His eyebrows rose. 'You don't feel you are worth it, Miss O'Shea?' He waited for an answer, but I was silent until he eventually shrugged. 'If this is the case, of course it's your right.' He stood. 'I'm only sorry you care so little for yourself. To carry this mark for ever is not necessary.'

He left then, and I stayed where I was. There was no way to explain to the doctor that the scar would be my reminder of the kind of person I was, and what my stubbornness had wrought. It *was* necessary to carry it.

Chapter Five

I SPENT A WEEK in Tangier. It was quite clear that word travelled quickly throughout the twisting alleys and bustling souks, for apart from Elizabeth Pandy, I had mentioned only to Omar—the boy who had carried my bags to my room my first day in Tangier—that I was looking for someone with a car to take me to Rabat. But almost immediately a seemingly endless array of men came to the front door of the Hotel Continental. They were stopped by the doorman, and not allowed inside the grand lobby. They waited until I was called and came to meet them.

Most of them immediately proved unsuitable, for they didn't possess a car. They assumed I would provide it, but, I explained, I needed a driver *and* a car.

During those first days I learned a great deal about the North African attribute of persuasion. Some said they had a cousin with a car; others said they would find me a car. One arrived who said he didn't yet know how to drive, but surely, once he was actually in a car, he would figure it out. I thanked them but told them it would not work out.

The days were warm and fragrant, the scent of orange blossom everywhere. But I was overcome with frustration and anxiousness. Each day I didn't leave for Marrakesh was another day wasted.

Although I regularly saw Elizabeth Pandy and Marcus and other Americans, I tried to avoid them. I found their constant drinking and loud voices and laughter exhausting. One afternoon I sat in the empty lounge, partly hidden by a high banquette, sipping a mineral water as I attempted to understand a rough map of Morocco I had purchased in Le Grand Socco—the Large Square. I finished my water and folded the map, but before I had a chance to stand I heard Elizabeth and her crowd enter. They had come from Rue de la Plage, where Elizabeth had braved the wild Atlantic waves and plunged into the frigid water.

'Marvellously refreshing,' Elizabeth said, her voice carrying. I was desperate to escape and to go back to my room. I rose in a half-crouch, But at that instant Elizabeth walked around the banquette, and stopped when she saw me.

'Well, hello, Sidonie,' she said, and my cheeks flushed. 'What are you doing sitting here by yourself? I'm off to the Ladies'. Go over and join the others. I'll be back in a moment.'

'Thank you, but I'm . . . I must go to my room.'

She shrugged. 'As you wish,' she said, and then added, 'Oh, have you managed to find a car and driver yet?'

I shook my head.

'I was speaking to a British fellow at the Red Palm Café today. He told me he had just been driven up from Casablanca, and the fellow was on his way back down south tomorrow.' She opened her bag and dug around in it, finally pulling out a crumpled paper and handing it to me. 'Here's his name. Ask one of the boys to locate him; he's staying somewhere in the medina. But if you do find him, hire him for all the way to Marrakesh. From what I've heard, you could end up waiting days for a train in Rabat.'

Now I didn't know how to react. In spite of her brashness and lack of sensitivity, Elizabeth Pandy had just provided what I had been waiting for. I took the paper and unfolded it. *Mustapha. Tall. Red waistcoat. Yellow Citroën*, was scrawled on it.

'Thank you, Elizabeth,' I said, tentatively.

'We all must stick together, mustn't we?' she said, lifting her hand in a kind of salute.

I nodded and smiled, and then left the lounge, stopping to talk to Omar on my way through the lobby. Finally something was happening.

Mustapha presented himself to me on the veranda the following morning. I was relieved that he could speak a smattering of French. He was, as the note had described, tall, and wearing a decidedly filthy red waistcoat over an equally dirty, once-white robe. A very short man, his jellaba hood down and a small round white hat on the crown on his head, stood beside him.

Mustapha clapped his hand on the shorter man's shoulder. A puff of dust rose from his jellaba.

'*Mon cousin*, madame,' he explained. 'Aziz. He go always with me.'

I nodded at both men. There was no point in correcting Mustapha's use of the title madame. All Arab men referred to non-African women in that way.

I didn't want to get my hopes up; I had seen too many men like Mustapha and Aziz. Still, they did come with a form of reference, from the British man Elizabeth had spoken of. 'May I see the car, Mustapha?'

'Oh yes, madame, very fine auto. Very fine.' His chest seemed to expand under the red waistcoat as he spoke. 'I very fine driver. Very fine. You ask. Everybody say Mustapha very fine. Auto very fine.'

'I'm sure it's . . . fine,' I said, as obviously this was a word beloved by Mustapha. 'But please. I must see it first.'

'What price madame pay?'

'I need to go all the way to Marrakesh. But first I must look at the auto, Mustapha.' I spoke softly, smiling at him, knowing, from this one week in North Africa, that he would have difficulty dealing with a woman giving him instructions. 'May I look at your auto?'

He waved his arm down the street, pointing at a lemon-yellow Citroën. It was covered in dust, its wheels caked with mud. It was rusted and dented, its ragtop torn in spots, but compared to the others I'd been offered, it was more promising. I followed Mustapha to it and peered inside. It was filthy, littered with scraps of rotting food. It was a three-seater; the third seat was in the rear in the middle, forcing the passenger to put his feet between the two front seats. On the floor was a stacked pile of goatskins.

It would do. This car would do. I didn't want to appear overanxious, or too excited.

Aziz came up beside me. 'What you are thinking, madame? It suits you?' he asked, speaking for the first time. His voice was surprisingly deep for such a small man; his French was better than Mustapha's.

'I have two large cases. Will there be enough room?'

'We make room, madame,' Aziz said.

'Is very fine car, *oui*, madame?' Mustapha repeated.

'Yes, Mustapha. Yes. I would like you to drive me to Marrakesh.'

'*Inshallah*,' Mustapha said, the phrase—God willing—already familiar to me. I noticed the North Africans said it about every single thing, from the weather to the food to their own health. God willing, I thought to myself, nodding at Mustapha. And then the necessary game of haggling over the price began.

We set out the next morning, Aziz crammed in the back, one of my cases on either side of him. I don't know why Mustapha wouldn't put them in the trunk; he had simply shaken his head when I'd suggested it. Although the car was far from clean, he had removed all the rotting food, and had strapped the skins to the roof with long strips of rag.

Before we drove away, Mustapha and Aziz had walked around the car, reverently touching it and murmuring.

'This auto already has *baraka*,' Aziz said. 'It has made many journeys. No trouble. It has much *baraka*.'

'*Baraka?* What is that?' I asked.

'Blessing. It is fine auto, very fine,' Mustapha said. I was beginning to think this was the extent of his French vocabulary. 'And I fine driver.'

'Oh yes, madame,' Aziz said. 'The very best. It is difficult, very difficult, to drive an auto, madame. Very difficult for the man, impossible for the lady.' He stood straighter, but was still shorter than me.

I looked at the steering wheel, knowing what it would feel like beneath my hands. And then I clenched my fingers into fists, burying them in the sides of my skirt. I had vowed never to put my hands on the steering wheel of a car again.

As I left Tangier with Mustapha and Aziz, the rising sun turning the white buildings various shades of pink and red, I let out a long, shaky breath. I was on my way to Marrakesh. I had come this far.

I let a sensation of relief wash over me, but in almost the next instant I asked myself if I really knew what I was doing, setting out in a car in a foreign land with two men about whom I knew nothing more than that they had an automobile and could drive it. I was trusting my life to unknown men based on a note handed to Elizabeth Pandy by a stranger.

And yet . . . and yet . . . somehow I had a perhaps misguided belief that it would be all right. That *I* would be all right, and would uncover what I needed to find. Or maybe it was more a new, unexpected faith in myself. Hadn't I crossed the Atlantic, coped with Marseilles, survived the Strait of Gibraltar in a levanter, and managed to hire these men to transport me to my final destination? I, who had never left Albany, who had never even played with the possibility of a life anywhere but safe.

As we left the city on the bumpy macadam road built by the French, the striking peaks of the Rif mountains were on our left, while the blue Atlantic sparkled along the right. There were few other automobiles on the road, although occasionally one passed, so close on the narrow road that I tensed, waiting for the sides of the cars to scrape together. More often there were caravans of dromedaries, small, one-humped camels, led by draped figures.

The road turned and weaved, and we would lose sight of the ocean for a number of miles, and then, suddenly, over the top of a dune or at an estuary, it would spread out before us again. This region of Morocco appeared to be a paradise of sea, with long stretches of sandy beach punctuated by sudden groves of olive trees or flat agrarian land. We passed many tiny villages, each one walled, each with the spire of a minaret rising above its parapets.

When we finally stopped, a few hours outside of Tangier, and stepped out of the car, I stretched, and the men went to a grove of palmetto palms off the road. Curious, I watched them, but as they turned their backs to the car, I quickly looked away, realising what they were doing. This had also been a concern for me for the past hour, although it was too embarrassing to speak of with these strange men. But when Mustapha and Aziz sauntered back to the car, Aziz pointed at the palms and said '*Allez*, madame, *allez*,' and I did as he said, going behind a thick cluster, hoping there was enough privacy to ensure my dignity.

I felt acutely uncomfortable returning to the car, wondering how I would face them, but Mustapha and Aziz were leaning against the car with arms crossed, talking and occasionally gesturing down the road. It was my own American sense of modesty that was distressing me in this wild land; the men were completely unconcerned.

When we again stopped, this time on the outskirts of a village Aziz identified as Larache, I opened my door.

But Aziz shook his head. 'No lady go,' he said. 'Bad for lady.' He gestured in a circle in front of his own face, and I knew he meant that it wouldn't be proper for me to go into the town with my face exposed. 'Stay in car,' he said. 'And look children do not take skins.' He pointed to the roof of the car. 'Mustapha and I go for food. Come back soon.'

I had to content myself with looking at what I could see through the open gates of the walls surrounding the town. The buildings were all painted a brilliant blue, with red-tiled arced roofs, giving the small town the rather charming look of a Spanish mountain village. Donkeys were tethered outside the walls, standing in the shade with their heads down. As I sat there, little boys, the oldest no more than eight or nine, slowly gathered at the open gates, and then, as if daring each other, left the safety of the walls and came closer and closer. They were dressed in ragged robes, their heads shaved and feet bare. Eventually they clustered around the car, silently staring in at me, frankly studying my face. Did I look so strange? There was a sudden shout, and the boys scattered, throwing up dust.

It was Mustapha and Aziz, coming back to the car. 'The boys are bad?' Aziz asked, looking at the small crowd as they raced back through the gates, and I shook my head.

'No, they're not bad. Just . . . boys,' I said. 'Just boys,' I repeated, realising how true it was. And wishing I could see their sisters and their mothers. Their fathers. I wanted to see them within their walls.

I took the thick round of aromatic bread and a waxy paper of soft white cheese, the sticky figs in a paper cone and the cashews Aziz handed me. I wasn't hungry, but I ate it all, licking the last bits of cheese and figs from my fingers, keeping the cashews in my lap and nibbling on them as we drove on.

I needed to stay strong, and to keep my wits about me. I needed to be ready for Marrakesh, and for finding Etienne.

We continued along the road, moving a little farther inland at times, so that I could no longer see or smell the sea. My back ached from sitting so long and continually bumping along the rough road. I tried not to think about the evening: where would we stop? Where would I sleep? I was covered in dust; would I be able to bathe? If I hadn't been allowed to go into Larache because of my uncovered face, how would I be accepted in other places?

It had been different in Tangier; it was a city welcoming those from abroad, but I had left Tangier, and it was rapidly appearing that in the middle of Morocco I would not just be another woman from the Western world. Here I was an anomaly, an outsider, one who might easily offend or repel.

How would I be treated in Marrakesh? My hurried planning for this voyage had been, I realised as we drove along the dusty road, one of singular notion and narrow vision—of finding Etienne.

I wanted him now. I wanted to feel I belonged with someone, that I wasn't alone. I wanted once again to feel the way I had with Etienne.

'We come city Salé, and river—Bou Regreg,' Aziz said. He leaned forward to see more clearly, resting his arms on the backs of the seats. 'And on different side of river, Rabat,' he added. 'Salé and Rabat like . . .' he touched Mustapha's shoulder, 'cousins. Or the brothers.'

Salé, also a white city like Tangier, was walled, terraced and spiky with minarets. In the distance, south, was another city, this one with the same walled appearance and silhouette against the early-evening sky, although its buildings were all a tawny colour: Rabat.

'We take you to house, you eat and sleep,' Aziz said.

House? Did he mean a hotel?

'And how much farther is Marrakesh from Salé?' I asked him.

'Tomorrow we come take you, drive past Casablanca, stay one night at Settat. Next day, Marrakesh. *Inshallah*,' he finished.

'You come take me? What do you mean? You aren't staying in the house?' I felt even more alone now, frightened at the idea of the only two people I knew leaving me in an unknown place.

He shook his head. 'Oh no, madame.'

We drove through the massive arched gates into the city, past a market shaded by trees, where I saw rough white wool hanging from ancient scales on tripods. In the next souk were stalls rich with melons and figs and olives, with bright red and green peppers and purple onions and the sizzle and smells of cooking meat. In front of the stalls, covered women argued with the vendors, shrieking, I could only reason, about the thievery of their prices. Surely it was part of the game of the Moroccan culture, for the women did indeed buy the goods, and the sellers, although shaking their heads in a parody of anger and disappointment, handed over the purchases.

I was leaning out the window, and as I stared at one of the sellers, he looked back at me with an expression of animosity, frowning, and then his lips pursed and he spat towards the car. I immediately pulled my head in, sitting as far back as I could so that the line of the car hid my profile. I was again filled with unease. Even though Salé was a good-sized city, I didn't see any foreigners—men or women.

As I was worrying about this, Mustapha stopped in front of a splintered, locked gate, and Aziz got out, gesturing for me to come as well. He carried my bags to the gate, putting one of them down to pound on the wood with the palm of his hand. If it was a hotel, it was unlike any I had ever seen.

Through a small grilled opening came a feminine murmur, and Aziz spoke into the metal lattice. There was another answering murmur, and the gate was opened by a woman in black, her face covered but for her eyes. 'You go inside,' Aziz said, and I did as he said. He followed me into the tiled courtyard, bringing my bags. Unlike the shabby, unpainted door, the courtyard was lovely, filled with beds of roses and orange trees.

'Woman is Lalla Huma,' Aziz said, setting my bags on the tiled floor. 'She give you food, you sleep, give her only one franc,' and then he turned to leave.

'What time will you be back for me?'

'Starting time, madame,' he said, and uttered one sentence to the woman. She picked up my cases—she was smaller than I but lifted them with apparent ease—and climbed a set of stairs that ran up one of the outside walls of the building.

As the gate shut with a clang I stood alone in the courtyard. Then

I hurried to follow the woman up the stairs, to a tiny room on the second floor of the house, the one window with an elaborately decorated wooden grille overlooking the street. There was nothing in the room but a hard pallet on the floor, with a thick woven blanket folded neatly in the middle. At the foot of the bed was a bowl covered with a wooden lid. There was a candle in a little decorated jar on the windowsill; beside it a box of wooden matches.

I had barely time to wonder what I would do—how I would communicate with Lalla Huma—when she left for a few moments and then returned with a large ceramic bowl of steaming water and a long strip of clean cloth. As soon as she left again, I took off my shoes and stockings and began unbuttoning my dress to wash, but stopped, going to the door to lock it. There was no lock.

I washed hurriedly, dressing again, as I had no idea what was expected. In a short time Lalla Huma again opened the door and entered, this time carrying a tray with a plate of unidentifiable shredded meat and long fingers of cooked carrot and a pot of mint tea.

She took the bowl of water and the damp cloth and left.

I ate and drank, my eyes heavy, and then put on my nightdress and lay on the narrow pallet, pulling the heavy blanket over me. The street outside was quiet, although as darkness fell I heard the call from the minarets: *Allah Akbar*—God is Great. I had, since I'd arrived in North Africa, become accustomed to the calls, which came five times a day.

The sound, so familiar now, only increased my loneliness. 'Etienne,' I whispered into the darkness.

I was awakened at dawn by the first call to prayer, and rose, glancing through the wooden grille. Parked below, in the still street, was the dusty Citroën, and outside it, their foreheads pressed to the ground, were Mustapha and Aziz. I dressed and Lalla Huma silently appeared with breakfast. I quickly ate and hurried out to the car. There was an assortment of sacks and bags on the floor, perhaps food for the rest of the journey. The skins were gone from the roof. Mustapha retrieved my bags and again put them in on either side of Aziz.

As we drove away, Aziz asked, 'Your night is good?'

'Yes,' I said, smiling. 'Yes, thank you, Aziz.'

I had been able to wash off the dust and grime from the road, I'd eaten well, and had had a deep sleep. I'd been lonely, and sad, but I had felt that every night since the last one I'd shared with Etienne.

'Where does your family live, Aziz?' I asked him.

'Settat,' he said. 'Same Mustapha.'

I didn't know how big Settat was, and wondered if there would be another house like Lalla Huma's for me to stay at, or whether I would stay with Aziz or Mustapha's family.

'Today I see wifes, children. I don't see one month. I am driving many places with Mustapha.'

Had he said *wifes*? Did he mean wife, or wives? I knew from Etienne that Muslims could have up to four wives. 'How many children do you have?' I asked him then.

He smiled proudly. 'Six. Four from wife one. Two from second wife. But she is young, second wife. More will come, *Inshallah*.'

'And Mustapha?' I asked, looking from Aziz to the driver.

'Mustapha has bad luck. No money for second wife. But maybe soon fate gives him another wife.' Aziz said something to Mustapha in Arabic, and Mustapha gave a wry smile.

'Your husband,' Aziz said to me then, 'why he lets wife go alone to Marrakesh?'

'I don't have a husband,' I told him.

He frowned, shaking his head. '*Quoi?*' he said, drawing out the word, sounding incredulous. 'What?' he repeated. 'Why no husband?'

I took a deep breath. 'Maybe . . . maybe bad luck, like Mustapha,' I said. It was a question I'd never been asked outright before.

Aziz nodded sadly. 'This is not good. I pray for you, madame.'

'Thank you, Aziz,' I said, and turned to look out the side window. Aziz understood the gesture, and sat back, not saying anything more.

We drove downwards from Salé, the road sloping to the mouth of the river, where I could see what looked like a steam ferry moored.

'We must cross Bou Regreg,' Aziz said, and, as we inched towards the landing stage for the ferry, I stared around at the crowds who had also gathered to cross the river to Rabat. There were the usual camels and donkeys and goats, as well as crowds of women in their voluminous robes, babies peeping from the front or the back, small children clutching their mothers' skirts.

When the steam ferry was packed so tightly there wasn't room for another man or even goat, we were transported across the brown river. We were the only car on the ferry, and I was viewed, much like at Larache, with open stares. One woman stooped to look in the window and hissed something through her covering, her dark eyes narrowed.

I drew back, leaning to one side, so that I was away from the open window and closer to Mustapha. 'What did she say?' I asked Aziz.

'Womens think you bad, show face to all men,' he said, and after that I kept my eyes fixed straight ahead, looking neither right nor left, and was relieved when we docked on the other side of the river.

The Rif mountains had died away before we reached Salé, but now I saw the outline of others far to the east.

'Atlas mountains,' Aziz told me. 'But not big Atlas. Smaller. Big is later, near Marrakesh. High Atlas,' he said.

We passed Casablanca on the edge of the sea, white, huge and glorious, all spires and towers and ramparts. We left the magnificent white city, turning away from it and the Atlantic, ready to move inland towards my destination, Marrakesh.

'In three hours, maybe four, we come Settat,' Aziz said, smiling, and I knew how anxious he was to see his family.

But a few miles later the macadam road came to an abrupt end, blocked off by stacks of uprooted, rotting cacti and rusting barrels. Beyond the blockade the road had caved in, and there were jumbled chunks of macadam as far as I could see.

'Aaaaahhhh,' Aziz breathed. 'Not good. Road is broken,' he said, then spoke to Mustapha in Arabic.

Mustapha turned the wheel sharply, onto simple hardened tracks that ran away from the macadam. The tracks were sandy soil woven with some sort of tough vegetation. Mustapha pointed to the narrow ruts that led into what appeared to be a blank canvas of earth and sky.

'We drive the *piste*,' Aziz said. 'The tracks of caravans. Roads no good, drive *piste* through the *bled*. Maybe road come back, maybe not.'

'*Bled?*' I repeated.

'*Bled*,' he said. '*Bled*, madame. No city. Country. Big.'

We rattled along the rough *piste*. Here the land was occasionally dotted with circles of mud huts with roofs made of woven rush. There was always a well and corrals of a sort—defined by low hedges of cacti or wattled thorn—containing hundreds of piteously bleating goats. Under their shade a group of swathed figures sat. These villages, Aziz said, were called *nourwal*. When, some miles farther along the road, we passed dozens of tents made of dark hair—goat or camel—perched on a rocky slope, Aziz said *douar*. After the different forms of habitat had sprung up a few more times and Aziz had again named them, I understood that the mud hut villages were permanent, with the wells and the ancient trees, while the skin tents, with children guarding small groups of camels and goats, were nomadic villages.

When we had first started on the *piste* it had appeared that the countryside was flat. But I was mistaken. We suddenly plunged downwards, and then almost immediately upwards again. This went on for what felt like an interminable time. I clutched the dashboard, aware that my hairline and collar were damp with perspiration and gritty with sand. My stomach rolled with the landscape. It was almost like being at sea again, sailing up and down on the waves.

'Mustapha,' I said, 'will we be able to get back on the road soon? So that we can reach Settat before nightfall?'

Mustapha didn't answer.

'Too far from road now,' Aziz said. 'Better we stay on *piste*. And tonight, sleep in *bled*.'

'Here?' I asked, looking around at the empty expanse.

'Sleep in *bled*,' he simply repeated. I thought of how disappointed Aziz and Mustapha would be, so close and yet unable to get home after a month away from their families. But I was also thinking about a long Moroccan night in a small car with two men, in the middle of nowhere.

Before darkness fell, Mustapha stopped the car under a stand of palmettos just off the *piste*.

As the men opened the trunk of the car I got out, trying to ease the kinks from my hips and back. They pulled out some old rugs, taking them to the smaller palms, and somehow fashioned a draped shelter, one rug on the ground and two more creating the roof.

'You sleep,' Aziz said, and I smiled my thanks at him, grateful that I didn't have to sleep in the car. I sat on the rug and watched as they took a lantern and a tin box from the trunk. Aziz emptied the box onto the sandy earth; it was coals. Next Mustapha pulled out a can with a spout and poured some of its contents into a battered teapot.

Now I understood why they hadn't put my cases into the trunk of the car; it was filled with their travelling necessities. In the sudden darkness, as the sun dropped behind the mountains, they lit the kerosene lamp and made mint tea. In the circle of light we chewed strips of salty dry meat and ate bread and more figs and olives and drank our tea.

The men stayed around the glowing coals, but I went back to my shelter. I sat in the opening, hearing their quiet murmurs. The sky was like nothing I had ever seen, not at home and not at sea and not in Marseilles or Tangier. I lay on my back, looking up at the starry dome over me.

In a shell we think we hear the ocean; in this desert I felt I heard the sky. I counted three shooting stars. And then there was a soft, rhythmic pattern, a kind of plopping noise. I listened, trying to understand what it was. 'What is that sound?' I finally called into the darkness.

'Only wild camel, madame,' came Aziz's voice. 'Walking, walking, looking us and smelling us.'

I smiled at the thought of that lone creature, circling our car and the shelter in interest and perhaps wonder, its clumsy-looking feet so sure on the sandy soil. Then I pulled one edge of the rug over me and watched the stars until my eyes closed.

The next day, after morning tea and bread, we set off.

'This day finish we are Marrakesh, madame,' Aziz said.

Tonight we would be in Marrakesh. I had come all this way to find Etienne. Shouldn't I be excited, and relieved? But instead, a strange unease came over me. I didn't understand it.

It was a long one, this final day, with only a quick village stop for some *harira*—a thick lentil soup—and then the seemingly endless *piste*.

As the sun lost its intensity in the late afternoon, I saw something far ahead on the tracks, shimmering in the waves of heat as if a mirage. At first I could determine only that it was a solitary human figure, but as we drew nearer, I made out blue robes. They fluttered out from the figure like a semaphore, signalling something important, although unknown. Closer still, I could tell it was a man. But as we drove straight towards him, he didn't step to the side of the *piste* for us to pass. He continued towards us, forcing Mustapha to stop the car.

The man stood tall and unmoving in front of us. He was covered from his neck to his ankles by his long pale-blue robe, and had a dark-blue turban around his head, one end covering his nose and mouth.

Mustapha went out and faced him; they spoke, then Mustapha came back to the car and said something to Aziz. Aziz dug in the bags at his feet and handed Mustapha a round of bread. Mustapha gave it to the man, and the man put something into Mustapha's hand.

When Mustapha returned, the man in blue passed on my side of the car, staring in at me. I could see only his eyes and the aquiline bridge of his nose, but a small shiver went through me as he walked on, down the road behind us, straight and dignified, almost haughty.

Mustapha tossed something onto the floor near my feet, a beautifully ornate tile, painted with an abstract geometric design in greens and blues.

'That's lovely,' I said, picking up the tile.

'You take this *zellij*,' Aziz said, leaning forward. 'Is only trade for bread. Always l'Homme Bleu give something for trade.'

'A Blue Man? You call him this because of his robe?' I asked, studying the tile. A *zellij*, Aziz had called it.

'Tribe is Blue Man. All life they wear robe and turban made blue from indigo plant. After many years indigo is in their skin. *Et voilà!* Blue.'

'They're Arabs?'

'*Non*. Berbers. But different Berbers: Tuaregs. Nomads, from Sahara. Speak like us, but also separate language. They have the camel caravans, bring goods forward and back. Salt, gold, slaves. Walking always in desert. They walk all Morocco, more Africa. Far. To Timbuktu.'

'And they're Muslims as well?'

Aziz shrugged. 'Some, but more not care Muslim. The woman show face, the man cover face. They are like . . .' he searched for a word, 'like backward side Muslim. The Blue Man and their womans do what they want. They are the desert people.'

I would like to paint a man like that, I thought, holding the tile between my palms and trying to visualise his features. A Blue Man.

I was still thinking about him when Mustapha took one hand from the wheel, pointing ahead of us. 'Madame. Marrakesh,' he said, and I peered through the dirt-encrusted windshield.

In front of us a wall of red rose up. Suddenly my breath came too quickly in my throat, and my heart beat in hard, rapid thuds.

I had arrived. I was in Marrakesh, the city where I hoped to find the answers I was seeking. Where I hoped to find Etienne.

Chapter Six

TWO MONTHS AFTER DR DUVERGER had talked to me about the scar, and I'd told him I wasn't interested in having it operated on, I looked at my reflection in the bathroom mirror and found it disturbing. The scar was dreadful, and a far greater disfigurement than my limp. As I had told Dr Duverger, I had little vanity, yet did I wish to go through life like this? Yes, the scar was a horrible memento of what I had done to my father, but now I questioned whether I needed it to be so obvious.

I thought of Dr Duverger's fingers, lightly exploring the deadened scar tissue. I thought about the concern in his eyes, and the way he had tried to make me feel that he understood when he saw my distress in his office, telling me he'd also lost his parents. I thought about the ruddiness of his cheeks, and the smoothness of his forehead.

The next day I used the Barlows' telephone, making an appointment to consult with Dr Duverger about the surgery.

When I met with him a week later I wore my best dress—a soft green silk with a wide fabric belt—and took special attention with my hair. I told myself I was being ridiculous. It was only my scar he was interested in, but no matter what I told myself, my fingers were damp with nervousness when he shook my hand. I hoped he didn't notice.

'So. You have change the mind?' he said, gesturing for me to sit.

'Yes,' I said. 'I needed time, I suppose. To think about it.'

He didn't respond.

'Unless . . . it's not too late, is it? Have I waited too long?'

He shook his head. 'No. But it requires more work now, I'm afraid, because you leave it longer,' he said. 'And you must understand, Miss O'Shea, you will always have a scar. But as I first tell you, it can be much finer.' He started to talk about the procedure, but I stopped him.

'I don't care to hear about it,' I said, with a small, apologetic smile. 'Just do what you can to minimise it.'

He scheduled me for the operation in three weeks' time, and on a muggy, late June day, it was done.

When I awoke I had a thick bandage on my cheek, and Dr Duverger told me that I must return within ten days to have the stitches removed.

'This time I will definitely be back,' I said, my tongue thick from the ether. He smiled, and I attempted to smile back, but the numbness from the medication was wearing off, and the new stitching throbbed.

Ten days later I was at the hospital, again wearing my best dress, again asking myself why I was acting like a silly schoolgirl.

While I waited for Dr Duverger, I took out the pencil and small sketchpad I always carried in my bag, and worked on my rendition of the Karner Blue butterfly. They lived in Pine Bush, and were an endangered species, difficult to spot. And yet I had finally caught a glimpse of one last summer; it was a stunningly beautiful little butterfly with a wingspan of only an inch. When Dr Duverger entered I put the pad and pencil on the chair beside me.

'Now, Miss O'Shea,' he said, 'we will see the result.'

I nodded, licking my lips.

'Don't be worry. I think you will be happy.'

He gently pulled off the gauze covering, and leaned close to remove the stitches. I didn't know where to look with his face so close to mine. He had put on his glasses, and I could see myself reflected in them. I smelled the faint clean scent of his crisp shirt and stiff collar.

Suddenly I realised he might be married.

As Dr Duverger removed the stitches there were tiny clipping noises and a slightly painful jerk with each one, making me wince occasionally. Each time I did, he murmured *pardon* in an unconscious way. And then, with the last stitch removed, he studied my face, moving my chin from side to side with his fingers. They were dry and warm.

'*Oui. C'est bien*,' he said, nodding.

'It's good?' I repeated.

'Yes,' he said, and again nodded, looking into my eyes this time. 'It was success, Miss O'Shea. Good success. And it will continue to heal with time, and within one year it will be less; it will fade. Look. You see.'

He handed me the round mirror.

'Thank you very much,' I said, looking at myself for a moment, then giving the mirror back. 'For the surgery. You were right.'

'I'm happy you agree to it,' he said, standing. I also rose, and we faced each other. He stared at me then, not just at my cheek, but somehow more deeply. It was only a moment, but it was somehow awkward.

'Well,' I said, needing to fill the silence that was both uncomfortable and exciting, and Dr Duverger said *très bien* at exactly the same time, echoing my word.

We both smiled, and then Dr Duverger said, 'So. Good day, mademoiselle. Please call if you have a question . . . or any pain . . . *oui*?'

'*Oui*,' I agreed.

I left the hospital and walked home in the warm late-morning sunshine, thinking about the effect the doctor had had on me. I tried to understand the sensations I had felt, standing close to him in the noisy hospital. I hadn't had a similar feeling since . . . I stopped. Had I ever felt this way?

I thought back to my adolescence, and the fantasies I had entertained about Luke McCallister. But I had been a young and silly girl then, not a woman who lived a practical and quiet life, with no room for whimsical daydreams.

It was all in my head. Dr Duverger hadn't looked at me a moment too long, and he hadn't felt the same strange confusion as I.

It was all in my head.

The next evening I opened the front door to let Cinnabar out, and saw a car slowly pull up. It stopped, and Dr Duverger stepped out.

It was so unexpected that I didn't have time to think about how I felt. As he walked towards the house, I saw that he carried my sketchpad.

'You leave this,' he said, coming up the steps. 'I look at your address on the file, and see that I have to drive nearby to visit a patient, so think I will return it.' He held it out to me.

'Thank you so much,' I said, taking it. 'Yes, yes, I looked for it this morning. I couldn't remember where I might have left it . . . there's a particular image I've been working on, but I can't quite get it right, and . . .' I was babbling. 'Well. Thank you,' I said again.

'I look to your work,' he said. 'It is good. The work.'

'Thank you. But they're just line drawings,' I said, embarrassed and yet pleased at the thought of him going through the pages.

'But you like this. To . . .' He stopped. 'My English,' he said, then licked his lips. 'To draw. The . . . the . . . talent to draw is obvious.'

'Thank you,' I said, feeling ridiculous repeating *thank you* over and over, my mind darting about for something else to say.

'Would you care to come in and have a cup of coffee?' I asked. As soon as the words were out of my mouth I wanted to take them back. What was I doing? Now it would be more uncomfortable when he found a reason to decline politely. Or . . . if he didn't decline.

'Yes. I would like to take *le café. Merci*,' he said, and I had little recourse but to step inside.

After he drove away I sat on the porch, staring at the street. I was twenty-nine, and this was the first time in my life I had been alone in my own home with a man who wasn't my father or a neighbour. As Dr Duverger had followed me through the living room into the kitchen, my heart was racing and my throat woolly. But once he sat at the kitchen table and I busied myself preparing the coffee, I realised there was something different about Dr Duverger today. As a doctor, with his files and stethoscope, he was in control. But away from the hospital I recognised in him an insecurity, as though he was as unsure of himself as I was when I left the safety of Juniper Road. And seeing this filled me with something I hadn't felt before, some very small confidence.

He's a doctor, but he's also just a man, I told myself.

He asked more questions about the sketches in my notepad, struggling with some of the words, and I told him to please speak French if he wished. 'It's very different from the French my mother and I spoke,' I told him, 'and I haven't used it since she died six years ago, so I'll answer in English, but I like to hear it.'

He nodded, smiling as he sipped his coffee. 'Thank you,' he said in French. 'Even though I speak English daily, and am usually comfortable with it, sometimes . . . in some circumstances . . . it fails me,' he said, and even that small confession gave me more confidence. Did I make him nervous, as he made me, and if so, why?

I asked where he was from in France, and he told me that he'd studied medicine in Paris. He had been living in America for over five years now.

After half an hour and two cups of black coffee, he rose. 'Thank you for the coffee,' he said.

I followed him to the front door. He opened it and stood there for a moment, looking at me. Suddenly it was hard to breathe.

'I'm glad you made the decision about the operation,' he said, finally. 'Now you will again be beautiful.'

Before I could respond, he went out into the deepening dusk. When he opened his car door he looked back at me.

'Perhaps we will take coffee again,' he called, and I didn't know whether it was a question or a statement, and just nodded in a dumb way.

I watched his taillights until they disappeared from Juniper Road, and then sat on the top step while darkness fell around me.

Beautiful, he had said. *Now you will again be beautiful.* Surely it had simply been the doctor—not the man—speaking, pleased with his work on a patient. Surely, for I had never been beautiful.

I went back into the house and turned on the light over the bathroom mirror, looking at myself, tracing the pink but smoother and narrower line of the new scar.

Had he said *Perhaps we will take coffee again* in a nonchalant way, knowing we never would? Or had he meant it?

I had no idea how to interpret a man's words or actions.

For the next four days I was in a state of anxiety. I didn't want to walk to the store to buy groceries in case Dr Duverger came when I wasn't home. Every day I wore one of my two good dresses—either my green silk or a deep plum that emphasised my waist—and periodically checked that my hair was held back securely. I made a spice cake. I constantly went to the front window, thinking I heard a car door slam.

By the fifth day I was so annoyed with myself for my stupidity—of course Dr Duverger hadn't really meant it when he talked about having coffee again—that I cut up the drying cake and threw it out for the birds.

And then I put on my overalls with the muddied knees over an old shirt of my father's, rolling up the sleeves. I braided my hair into one loose plait, and went out into the back garden and started on the weeds. I hacked and cleared, attacking the coarse thistles and twining bindweed. I was angry with Dr Duverger for acting as though he might really be interested enough to come again, but also angry with myself for four days wasted on daydreams.

'I knocked, but there was no answer.'

I jumped, turning to see Dr Duverger standing at the edge of the garden. He had spoken in French.

'I'm sorry to have startled you, Mademoiselle O'Shea. As I said, I knocked . . . then I heard the whistling.'

'Whistling?' I wanted to answer him in French, but didn't.

'I think it was Grieg. Solveig's Song, wasn't it?'

I hadn't realised I was whistling. I didn't think I'd whistled since my dad's death.

'Mademoiselle O'Shea? I can see I've disturbed you.'

'No, no, Dr Duverger. I just . . .' I rolled down my sleeves, seeing smears of dirt on one forearm and palm. 'I wasn't expecting you.' Only a short time earlier I had been angry with him, but now that he was here, I was glad. Excited.

'I know it was rude just to stop by. I had extra shifts this week, but today I unexpectedly had some time off. So I took a chance. . .'

'Of course it's all right. But I must wash and change,' I said.

He gestured at two old Adirondack chairs in the shade under the basswood tree. 'There's no need. We can sit out here. Please, stay as you are. You are looking very . . .' he put his head on one side, 'relaxed. Very relaxed and, if you will allow me to say, it's a charming effect.'

I half smiled, still aware of the tightness of my cheek. I tried to act as if men regularly came into my garden and called me charming, as if smiling was natural for me again. 'As I said, you just caught me off guard. I didn't expect . . .' I stopped, knowing I was repeating myself.

'Come then,' he said, making a sweeping motion towards the chairs. 'I'll stay only a few moments. But it's so glorious, this weather. And I'm glad to be out of the hospital, even for an hour.'

I sat on the edge of the seat of one of the Adirondacks, and he sat across from me.

'Do you mind if I remove my jacket?' he asked.

'No. And it *is* a glorious afternoon,' I said, sitting farther back.

The world became a different place. I became a different person. Over the next month I fell in love with Etienne Duverger.

He came to see me twice a week. The day and time depended on his shifts at the hospital, but, unless there was an emergency, he would arrive when he said he would.

He always left my house by ten o'clock; it was only after we'd seen each other four times that he picked up my hand as he was leaving and pressed his lips to it. At the end of that first month he put his arms around me as we stood on my front step, and kissed me.

I knew, by the look on his face, and the way he moved closer to me as we said our goodbyes, what would happen, and was trembling with both excitement and anxiety. It was the first time I had been kissed, and I was embarrassed by this fact and didn't want him to know, but I was so overwhelmed by the feel of his lips on mine, of my body against his, that my trembling increased.

'It's all right, Sidonie,' he said, and I leaned against his chest.

After he'd left, the night he kissed me, I sat on my bed in the dark, reliving the moment. I wanted to hold on to this feeling of wonder, but I was also troubled in a vague way.

Dr Duverger was handsome. He was clever and witty; he laughed easily. He had an exciting career, and had lived a life out in the world.

I didn't understand why he wanted to spend time with me. Me, with my wild hair and dark eyes and skin. Me, with a built-up shoe and limp, with a permanent, although now less noticeable, seam down my face. Me, with my small and narrow life, lacking experience in so many areas.

I tried to hide how little I knew about the world by making sure Etienne always talked about himself.

He had an exotic background. Although he'd been born in Paris, and had received his medical training there, he now explained that he'd spent much of his youth with his family in Morocco, in the city of Marrakesh.

'But how is that?' I'd asked, when he'd first told me. 'Why were your parents living in Morocco?'

'The French Protectorate. They took over the government of Morocco early in the century, and a good number of people from France moved there. My father was a doctor and went out to set up clinics there.'

'Tell me about Marrakesh.'

'It's a city so full of colour and sound and movement that it all bleeds together. It's almost like a thrumming, a vibration, under the feet. And the sun . . .' He looked towards the window; we were sitting in the living room. He was drinking bourbon—he had brought a bottle—and I lemonade. 'The sun has an intensity unlike here.'

'When were you there last?'

His face changed, and he didn't answer my question, reverting to our former conversation. 'Once the Protectorate was in place, my father was assigned a permanent position in Marrakesh, and of course we moved there as a family. I was a young boy. My father treated only the French; the Moroccans stuck to their own cures. Especially the women in the harems.'

'Are they really full of hundreds of beautiful women? The harems?'

Etienne raised his eyebrows, smiling. 'Harems in Morocco are simply the women's quarters within a house. The word *harem* derives from the Arabic word *haram*,' he said, 'which means shameful or even sinful. But in everyday language all it means is forbidden. No man is allowed in the women's quarters in the home, apart from husbands and sons, brothers and fathers.'

'They see no men but those they're related to, by blood or marriage?'

He nodded. 'It's a difficult life for them; depending on a man's success, he can have up to four wives. It's a Muslim convention.'

My face must have showed my surprise.

'Complex for us to fathom, I know. My father said the women were sometimes driven to what we might call witchcraft by their own need for some attempt at dominance. Some way to regulate the behaviour of their men, and their own status with the other wives.'

'What do you mean by *witchcraft*? What do they do?'

He looked into his glass. 'They make potions they believe will create a certain circumstance, either positive or negative—a birth, an illness, love, even death—or to protect themselves from the harmful spirits they believe lurk around them. There's a great deal of ignorance and superstition that rules their lives.' His voice had grown hard.

After a moment of silence, during which Etienne drained his glass, I said, 'Of course,' as if I knew what he spoke about, even though all I knew about Morocco by then was that I'd located it in my atlas, at the tip of North Africa, and had found, in a history book, a bit of information about the French conquest of the country in 1912. Although so often his descriptions of his life were joyful and candid, there were also times when I heard a hesitancy, as though he was sifting through his memories and choosing only those he wanted to share. As if there was something he was deliberately avoiding.

'Do you plan to return again soon? Is your family still there?'

'There's nothing left for me there now. It's a place of sadness; my parents and my brother Guillaume are buried there. They all died within three years,' he said, and then sat quietly for a moment. I knew he wasn't yet finished, and sat, waiting.

'There is nothing—and no one—for me in Marrakesh any longer. Nothing but sad memories. Nothing could make me return.'

When Etienne asked me about the botanical and bird paintings on the walls of my home—it was the next time he came to see me after he'd first kissed me—I had admitted, nervously, that yes, they were mine.

'After seeing your sketches in the notepad, of course I wondered if you'd painted these. They're very well done.'

'It's just a hobby,' I said.

'Can you show me more of your work?'

I rose from my chair and he followed me into my studio—my parents' former bedroom. I was very conscious of their double bed, against the far wall.

Half-finished paintings lay on the table; I had finally started the Karner Blue butterfly the day before, and it was clipped onto the easel near the window. He went to it and leaned closer, studying it.

'You don't paint anything else, apart from nature?'

'I paint what I see around me. In the woods, and the ponds and marshes,' I said.

'Of course they are very pretty,' he said, and then lightly stroked my forehead with his index and middle finger. 'I think there is so much more in here,' he said, putting a bit more pressure against my forehead. 'You understand what I mean, don't you? You see other things. In here.'

I closed my eyes, hoping he would leave his fingers on my forehead. 'Yes. But . . . this—botany, and the birds—is what I've always painted.' I reached up and took his hand in mine, and then brought it, slowly, down my scarred cheek. I was surprised at my own boldness.

We stayed like that for a few moments, my hand over his on my cheek, and then he put his other arm around me and pressed me against him.

'It's enough?' he whispered. 'For a woman like you, a woman with a wild heart, to live in seclusion, and paint only what is in front of her?'

Was this how he saw me? A woman with a wild heart?

That may have been the moment I fell in love with him.

I lifted my face so that he understood how much I wanted him to kiss me. He did. This time I didn't tremble, but my body was suddenly so heavy and yet light, liquid, that my legs were weak.

Still kissing me, he gently guided me backwards until the back of my knees touched the edge of my parents' bed, and I lowered myself, without taking my lips from his. He sat beside me, but as he started to push me down gently, I pulled away, sitting up and straightening my hair. We were on my parents' bed, the bed they'd shared for as long as I could remember, the bed where I'd seen my mother die.

I stood.

'I apologise,' Etienne said, also standing. 'I've acted inappropriately, Sidonie, I'm sorry. I should go.'

I shook my head. 'No, don't go. You haven't upset me. That's not it. I took his hand, pulling him towards my bedroom.

Of course he knew it was the first time for me; even so, I told him so, and also told him that I didn't know what to do, and that I wanted him to show me.

'You're sure . . .' and I nodded. He loved me. He would never do anything to hurt me.

Etienne and I fell into an easy pattern; over the next months, through the autumn and into December, we spent his free evenings—sometimes once a week, sometimes twice—at my house, or in Albany, eating out or attending concerts and plays. He stayed with me for the night, although sometimes he had to leave early, while it was still dark, to go back to his rooms to change for work. He lived in a rooming house—a rather bleak place near the hospital, he told me, but fine for the small amount of time he spent there.

We were sitting side by side on the sofa one December evening at dusk. Cinnabar leaped onto my lap, and I stroked her, absently running my hand down her back.

'She was born deaf?' he asked, and I nodded.

'I assume so. I've had her since she was a kitten, and she's always been deaf.'

'Hopefully you didn't allow her to mate.'

I looked at him. 'She hasn't. But what do you mean, hopefully?'

'Her deafness. It would be wrong to allow her to breed and possibly pass on that trait.' He took another mouthful of his bourbon. 'She's an aberration, after all. And the problem with an aberration is that if allowed to procreate, it can weaken the species.'

Etienne was particularly fascinated by human genetics, and when he spoke on the topic he grew animated. He could somehow make the study of genes sound intriguing. 'Remember when I told you of Mendel's Unit of Inheritance? That every living organism is made up of half of the paternal genes and half of the maternal?'

'Yes,' I said.

'So it's quite simple. Only the strong, the perfect, should be allowed to create offspring. Think, Sidonie. Think of the possibilities of a world without the weak. Without the sickly, the damaged in mind or body.'

I caught my breath. Did he not realise I was particularly sensitive to this? That I was one of the damaged he spoke of? 'But don't you think there can be something attractive in that which has a flaw?'

He knew me too well. 'Sidonie,' he said, smiling, slightly. 'You had an illness. It's not genetic. And you have been made stronger by it, not weakened. You know you're beautiful to me, in every way.'

He never failed to make me feel precious, and wanted. I leaned my head on his shoulder.

'But your cat,' he went on, his breath, just above my ear, moving my hair, 'is a different situation. It's a good thing that when Cinnabar dies she will not have passed on her unfortunate disability.' He gently brushed my hair from my cheek and kissed my scar.

Although I wanted to argue further, I didn't want him to stop kissing my cheek. I turned to him and pushed Cinnabar from my lap.

It was in early February, eleven months after my father died, that I realised what had happened.

I waited an extra week to make certain before I shared the news with Etienne. I didn't know how he'd react; he had made a point of assuring me that I wasn't to worry about any consequences of our lovemaking. I understood. He was a doctor; he knew how to prevent it. But somehow, in spite of his reassurances, his precautions had failed.

I was excited and nervous, wanting to find the right moment to tell him this unexpected news. We lay facing each other in my bed, our bodies still heated, although our breathing had resumed the normal rhythm. It was the perfect time. I smiled, running my hand up and down Etienne's bare chest, and said, 'I have something to tell you.'

He leaned up on one elbow to study my face. 'What do you have to tell me, with this expression? You look pleased, and yet shy.'

I nodded, taking his hand. 'It's unexpected, I know, Etienne, but . . .' I could barely say it, such was my joy and wonder. 'It's a baby, Etienne. I'm expecting a baby.'

I held my breath, waiting for his reaction. But it was not as I expected. He lost all expression. His skin took on the texture and colour of a bleached fossil. He pulled his hand from mine and sat straight up, looking down at me with his mouth slightly open.

'Etienne?' I said, sitting up to face him.

'You're certain?' he asked.

I nodded.

'But I use the . . . what . . . *la capote*, the rubber, prophylactic,' he said. 'Always I use it.' He was still frightfully pale, and, for a completely unknown reason, had switched to English.

I was stunned. 'Etienne? Aren't you . . . don't you . . .' I stopped, not knowing how to continue.

Now he stared over my head at the window and the darkness beyond, as if he couldn't bear to look into my face. 'You see a doctor?' Without waiting for an answer he turned in the other direction, reaching for the pill bottle on the bedside table; he said he suffered headaches.

'No. But I know my body, and the signs are unmistakable.'

Finally he looked at me, and there was a heavy, dull thud in my stomach. 'No. *C'est impossible*. Perhaps there is other reason for the symptoms. On Thursday—one day behind the next day—I have the late . . . what is it . . . the shift. I take you, in the morning, to the clinic I know, in the next . . . next place, county . . . and you will be examine,' he said, his tongue tripping on every word. 'Not at my hospital.'

His strange way of speaking, combined with his almost-blank stare, made me feel that I might be sick. This wasn't what I had envisioned, the hundreds of times over the past few weeks I'd imagined myself telling him this remarkable news.

I hadn't doubted, for even a moment, that he would immediately propose, and we would marry without delay. But now . . . I swallowed, and knew that even though it was close to midnight, I would be sick, as I was most mornings now. I rushed from the room, retching over and over in the bathroom.

When I had finished, I shakily washed my face and rinsed my mouth, and then returned to the bedroom. Etienne was dressed, sitting on the bed tying his shoes. He looked up at me with such an unreadable expression that something like fear came over me.

He stood. 'I'm sorry, Sidonie,' he said in French. 'It's . . . it's just the shock. I need to think. Don't be hurt.'

Don't be hurt? How could I not be hurt by his reaction?

'I'll come on Thursday morning then, at nine, and take you to the clinic. For a professional opinion,' he said.

'Etienne,' I said, putting my hands on his arms.

He did pull me to him then, pressing my head against his chest. I heard his heartbeat, too fast, as though he'd been running. And after too brief a time he stroked my hair once, and then was gone.

The almost silent ride to the clinic—where my pregnancy was confirmed—had been bad enough, but as we approached the outskirts of Albany I could bear it no longer.

'I know it's a surprise. But perhaps we should view it as fate.'

Staring straight ahead, his hands gripping the steering wheel so intensely that his knuckles were white, he said, 'I'm sorry, Sidonie. I know I'm not behaving in the way you hoped.'

I wanted to ask him, *Don't you want a child, Etienne? A child with me? Don't you want to marry me and be a husband and father?* So many emotions: shock, and sadness and disappointment, and also, yes, also anger, all combined in a swirling fusion of dark colours.

I looked at him again. 'So what will we do, Etienne?' I spoke slowly, clearly, my voice low and controlled. 'I know it's not what we planned. But . . . but I want this baby. I want it more than anything.'

Finally he spoke. 'Of course we will marry,' he said, his voice hoarse, as if his throat was too tight, and then his face softened, and he cupped my chin. 'Of course, *ma chère* Sido,' and at that a sob caught in my throat. Tears came to my eyes, tears of relief, and he pulled me to him.

I cried against his lapel.

He did love me. He would marry me. It was not the proposal I had hoped for, but it would be all right.

When he walked me to my door he said he would come by in three days—his next day off—so that we could discuss our plans.

He put his hand against my abdomen. 'You will sing to it. *Dodo, l'enfant, do*. I can see you as a mother. I can hear you sing a lullaby to our child.'

I put my arms around him and again pressed my head against his chest, my eyes filling with tears for the second time. *Our child*, he had said.

Our child.

Etienne didn't come three days later. I told myself he'd had an emergency at the hospital. Of course, for what else could keep him from coming? I waited through the evening, every hour carrying a heavier dread. Finally I undressed and went to bed, but couldn't sleep. What if he'd had an accident? I remembered the steering wheel wrenching in my hands, the sensation of rising into the air. I saw my father lying in the cold field, and then the image of his body turned into Etienne's.

Would anyone from the hospital come to tell me if he'd been hurt?

I tossed and turned. Cinnabar refused to stay on the bed, and finally I rose as well, and walked around and around the house.

By eight o'clock I was next door.

'Do you mind if I use the telephone?' I asked Mrs Barlow.

'Of course not,' she said. The kitchen was warm and fragrant. There was a bowl covered with a tea towel sitting on the back of the stove, and another round of dough on a floury board on the table. 'I'm making raisin bread,' she said, kneading the dough.

'Thank you,' I said, taking the receiver from its hook and pulling the hospital phone number from my dress pocket. When I was put through to the hospital operator I asked for Dr Duverger. There was a moment's silence, and then the woman said, 'Dr Duverger is no longer at the hospital. Can I give you another doctor?'

'No longer . . . What do you mean?' I turned so that my back was to Mrs Barlow. There was a dull thump as she slapped the dough on the board. My ears were humming, and I cleared my throat.

'We're referring his patients to Dr Hilroy or Dr Lane, ma'am. Would you care to make an appointment with one of them?'

I hung up the receiver, but didn't turn around. I was vaguely aware of Mrs Barlow's endless thumping.

'Is everything all right, Sidonie?' Mrs Barlow asked.

'Yes,' I said, and then shook my head. 'Not really. Etienne—Dr Duverger—was supposed to be here yesterday. I'm worried that something has happened to him.'

'There's no reason to worry yourself, dear. Give it another day or so.'

I didn't want to tell her what I'd just heard on the telephone.

I was too ashamed to ask Mr Barlow to drive me to the hospital, so I walked there.

At the front counter I asked for Dr Duverger. Somehow I hoped that my physical presence in the hospital would actually produce him. When I was given the same answer, that he was no longer in the hospital's employ, I asked to speak to one of his colleagues.

'Dr Hilroy or Dr Lane?' the woman asked.

'Either. Could I speak to one of them? I simply have a question. It's not anything medical.'

'Have a seat then, please. Dr Hilroy is almost done with his shift. When he's finished I'll have him speak to you.'

I waited for what felt like a long time, and finally a tall, white-haired man came from behind swinging double doors.

'I'm Dr Hilroy,' he said, after speaking to the woman at the desk. 'May I help you?'

I stood, explaining that I had expected to hear from Dr Duverger. 'I'm a friend of Dr Duverger's. A good friend,' I stressed. 'I'm concerned for his well-being. As I said, I expected to hear from him, and now I'm afraid something must have happened to him.'

The doctor frowned. 'Well, he did leave a month early, but it was quite straightforward.'

I blinked. 'He was leaving next month? For where?'

'I really don't know of his plans once his term contract was up. But frankly, none of us got to know Dr Duverger very well. He never spoke of his family before this, although I assume they're in France.'

Etienne's family? But . . . they were all dead.

'He's gone to France?'

Now Dr Hilroy looked vaguely displeased, shifting and glancing at his watch. 'He simply said it was impossible for him to stay on, due to family circumstances, and that he had to return home.'

Return home. Family circumstances.

'Did he leave an address? Some way to contact him?' I asked.

'I'm afraid not,' Dr Hilroy said. 'I'm sorry.'

'Is there anything, anything more at all, you can tell me?' I heard the beseeching tone of my voice. 'What about . . . can you tell me the address where he lived? A rooming house nearby. I know that much.'

I know that much. The words only emphasised how little I did know.

'I don't believe I should be giving out that information.'

'I don't see how it could hurt to give me the address now. If Dr Duverger has truly left Albany, it won't matter, will it?'

He studied me for a moment longer.

'Please,' I said, in little more than a whisper, and he shook his head, as if to himself, and then walked away from me, speaking to the woman at the front counter in a low tone, glancing towards me. Then he motioned me towards the desk, leaving before I stepped up to the high counter, and the woman handed me a slip of paper.

The rooms Etienne had rented were ten long blocks from the hospital. I told myself he was actually still there; that he hadn't left Albany. He wouldn't leave me like this, especially not now. He had said we would marry. He had said *Our child*.

The house was tall and narrow, the red brick well maintained. In one of the front windows there was a hand-printed sign: *Furnished Rooms for Rent*. I told myself the sign didn't have to refer to Etienne's rooms.

I knocked on the door, and it was opened by an elderly lady in a neatly pressed brown housedress with a white lace collar.

'I'm sorry,' she said, immediately. 'The rooms haven't been properly cleaned yet. If you would come back in a few days, I can show—'

'No,' I said, interrupting her and taking a deep breath. 'Actually, I'm a friend of Dr Duverger's.'

'He doesn't live here any more,' she said.

'I know,' I said, panic filling me even more than it had at the hospital. 'I know,' I repeated, 'but he asked that I see if he left a black leather case behind.'

'A leather case?'

'Yes. Black. With a brass clasp.' As I spoke, I stepped into the hall.

'Well, it wouldn't surprise me if the doctor forgot something. He certainly left in a hurry.'

'I'll only take a moment, if you'll point out his rooms.'

'I suppose it won't hurt.' She turned and pulled out the drawer of a cabinet in the hall, handing me a key. 'Upstairs, first door on the left. There are two connecting rooms.'

'Thank you,' I said, and went up the stairs. 'Oh,' I said, turning to look back at the woman. 'Did Dr Duverger remember to leave you his forwarding address, so that any mail might be sent on?' I struggled to keep my voice casual, but I heard the beat of my heart in my ears.

'No. Although he got only one or two letters the whole time he was here. Foreign, they were.'

I nodded, but just as I put my foot on the next step she added, 'He got one just days before he left, too.'

Without answering I climbed to the top of the stairs and unlocked the door. The room was simply furnished with a tufted couch and small table with two straight-backed chairs, as well as a sturdy desk with a swivelling wooden chair. There were a few papers in a pile on the desk. Through the open door into the next room I saw a neatly made bed with a candlewick bedspread.

I sat in the chair in front of the desk; my fingers were shaking as

I scrabbled through the papers. But they were only printed pages of a study on throat ailments. I opened the drawer on the right of the desk. It was empty but for a pair of spectacles. I picked them up and ran my fingers over the thin frame.

'Etienne,' I whispered into the empty room. 'Where are you?'

I set the spectacles on the desk and slowly pulled out the other drawers. They were empty.

I looked under the desk; there was a trash container. It held a small pill bottle for a drug with the long and unpronounceable name of oxazolidinedione, and was prescribed for Etienne. I knew the bottles that held the pills for his headaches and the ones to help him sleep. There was another he sometimes took before he left my house in the morning. *To help keep me alert through the long day ahead*, he had said, in an offhand way. But this was one I hadn't seen before.

I put the spectacles and empty pill bottle into my handbag. I needed something—anything—of Etienne to hold on to.

I wanted to go home, but first I knew I had to go into the next room. The room contained only the bed, a dresser and a wardrobe. Again I pulled out each of the dresser drawers. There was nothing. Like the drawers, the wardrobe was empty, but as I turned to leave, I noticed a book on its floor. It was one on famous American watercolourists I had given to Etienne for Christmas.

For some reason, seeing this book left behind—abandoned—filled me with overwhelming grief, and I sank to my knees, staring at it. I picked it up, running my hand over its cover. A small edge of paper, emerged from the top, only a few pages in. I opened the book at the folded piece of paper, so thin that I could see writing through it.

Still on my knees, I pushed the book from my lap onto the floor and unfolded the paper. The spidery writing, from a fine nib, was in French, and the delicacy of the script indicated a woman's hand.

My eyes darted to the signature—the single name—at the bottom.

I held the paper in both hands and read.

3 November 1929
Marrakesh

My dearest Etienne,

I write to you yet again. Although you haven't replied to my former letters, I once more, with even more desperation, beseech you not to abandon us. I have never given up the hope that after all this time—it is now more than seven years since you have been home—you would find it in your kind and loving heart to forgive me.

I shall not give up, my dear brother. Please, Etienne. Come home, to me, and to Marrakesh.

Manon

The onionskin paper in my hand trembled violently.

Manon.

Come home, she had said, *to Marrakesh*.

I looked down at the letter again. *My dear brother*, she had written. *It is now more than seven years*. Manon was his sister . . . but when I'd asked about his family, he had said there was only Guillaume, hadn't he? *There is nothing and no one*, he'd said, *in Marrakesh*. Had he left me without a word—abandoned me, like the book—because of his sister?

'Did you find the case?' a voice asked, and I turned my head to see a pair of sturdy laced shoes. I looked up.

The woman was staring down at me.

Clutching the letter, I managed to get to my feet. 'No,' I said, and pushed past her.

As I limped heavily down the stairs, holding the railing to steady myself, she called after me, 'Who did you say you were?'

I didn't answer, leaving the front door open behind me.

I fled as if hounds were at my heels. I wanted to be within the safety of my own walls, where I would take out the letter and read it, over and over, trying to make some sense of it all.

The letter was the only link I had to Etienne.

Back home, I took out everything I'd brought home from Etienne's rooms: his eyeglasses, the pill bottle and the letter. I spread them out in front of me on the kitchen table and sat down, staring at them. I read the letter three more times; there was no reason to read it again, as by then I knew the words by heart.

Now I looked at the pill bottle, then rose and went to the bookcase in the living room, pulling out a thick medical journal. I took it back to the kitchen and turned to the index. There it was, this oxazolidinedione.

It was a medication for neurological pathologies, I read, prescribed to help deter both epileptic conditions and palsy.

But surely Etienne was not epileptic. He had never experienced a seizure in the times I'd been with him. And he didn't have any signs of palsy. He was occasionally slightly clumsy, stumbling against a piece of furniture or tripping on the edge of a rug. I remembered watching him carving a chicken I had cooked for dinner, and how suddenly the knife appeared to jerk to one side. I hadn't thought anything of it at the time, but now I also remembered how these seemingly inconsequential acts upset him, and how he'd tersely brushed off my enquiries or concerns.

I didn't know what to make of the prescription. If Etienne had an illness, I would have known. Wouldn't I? I picked up the letter again.

This woman, his sister Manon, was related to the secret I was sure Etienne felt he was unable to tell me. This was why he had left. But he didn't realise that I could accept anything he told me. He had to know that. He had to know that I loved him enough to not care what his past held. That it was our future that would cleanse him of what plagued him.

But to find him . . . the only clues I had were the Christian name of his sister—a woman he had never mentioned—and the city where she lived. Where Etienne had grown up. I would go there. I would find him, in Marrakesh, and tell him this.

'I'm going abroad, Mrs Barlow,' I told her, standing in her kitchen.

'Abroad?' Mrs Barlow said. 'How will you do that?'

I swallowed. It had been over a week since I had made my decision, and in that time I had been planning and acting. I had already done what was necessary to obtain a passport. I had taken the stack of money from the sale of the repaired Silver Ghost to the bank, changing most of it into francs. I had also withdrawn almost everything but a few dollars from my bank account, and had gone into the travel offices on Drake Street and purchased a ticket for a ship leaving from New York to Marseilles in two weeks. 'It's all organised,' I said now.

'And when will you return?'

'I don't know yet,' I told her. 'But could you and Mr Barlow watch the house while I'm gone? And could you keep Cinnabar for me?'

Mrs Barlow's mouth closed in on itself. 'Correct me if I'm wrong, but I get the sense this is to do with that missing doctor of yours.'

'Mrs Barlow, please. I just have to go. I love him. And he loves me too. I know he does.'

At that Mrs Barlow put her arms around me. 'You know so little about the world, my girl,' she said. 'And about men,' she added. 'I saw this trouble coming from the first. I saw it, Sidonie, but you were still sorrowing over your dad, and I thought, now, Nora, let the girl have a little pleasure.'

She pulled away from me. 'But there's no pleasure without pain, Sidonie. No pleasure without pain,' she repeated. 'And you can count on that, as surely as you can count on the first frost each year.'

I had to stop overnight at Marseilles; the ship for Tangier sailed late the next afternoon. I looked at the port with little interest as my cases were loaded into a taxi, and we drove through the streets to the hotel recommended on board.

The room was small but clean, with the luxury of an attached *salle de bains*. As soon as my bags were deposited on the floor near the wardrobe, I took out my nightdress. It was only seven in the evening, but I had an unfamiliar, persistent pain in my back. I fell into the single, hard bed with a sigh of relief, and in spite of the discomfort in my back, fell asleep almost immediately.

My body woke me in the night. The pain had moved into my abdomen, more painful now. I thought a warm bath might help. I slowly put back the covers, and, as I stood, there was a rush of fluid down my legs. Horrified, I looked at the wet darkness on my ankles. My hands over my belly, I made my way to the bathroom and switched on the light. The brilliance of the blood made me weak—not because of the sight of it, but because I knew what it signified.

'No!' I cried out into the empty bathroom, my voice echoing. 'Etienne,' I said, aloud. 'Etienne,' I repeated, quietly now, but of course there was only my own voice bouncing off the walls and ceiling.

And there appeared nothing for me to do, no way to stop the life rushing from me.

I believe I was in a state of shock; I was unable to think of anything more than the death of that little being. I know that at some point I clasped my hands and prayed for its soul.

I don't know how much time passed. I had had a bath and got into bed and slept, when I heard the clanging of a pail in the hall, then there was knocking at my door. I called out.

'Please,' I said, as loudly as I could. 'Ask the concierge to come to my room. Tell her to come in. I'm ill.'

When she arrived, unlocking the door and standing in the doorway, looking at me across the room, I told her, flatly, that I had been sick during the night, and wished to have a doctor visit me. I had pulled myself into a sitting position in the narrow bed, the blankets piled haphazardly over my legs.

She nodded, her face unreadable, but when her eyes flickered to the open bathroom door I saw her chest rise. She went to the bathroom and glanced in, then closed the door with a firm thud, bordering on a slam. She stared at me, her head giving an almost imperceptible shake, and left.

I think I slept, for within what felt like a very short time she returned, this time with a middle-aged man with a thick moustache. He carried a black bag, and his fingers were chapped.

'Mademoiselle O'Shea,' she said, adding, 'American, just arrived,' as if she smelled something unpleasant. The doctor nodded at me. She stayed in the room, by the door, her hands clasped in front of her.

The doctor asked her—I wondered why he didn't speak to me—the nature of the visit.

'There is every indication it was a miscarriage, Doctor.'

Glancing back at me, the doctor spoke quickly. 'She's alone?' he said, turning to the woman, and by his tone it was clear he knew the answer.

Then he asked the concierge what I was doing in Marseilles, and she told him I was going on to Tangier.

He looked back at me and shook his head. '*C'est impossible*. Oh, but it's not possible, mademoiselle,' he said in English. 'You must not make the travel,' he said, and then I knew why he had been ignoring me and speaking only to the concierge about my situation. Because she had emphasised that I was an American, he didn't realise I spoke French, and she hadn't told him. He switched back to French as he again faced the concierge. 'She'll never make it there alone, having just gone through a miscarriage. It will take her some time to recover. Tell her to return to America as soon as she's able.'

'*Monsieur le Docteur*,' I said, in French, 'I understand. Please speak to me directly. I must get to Tangier, as quickly as possible. There's no reason I shouldn't recover quickly, is there?'

'Mademoiselle. As I've said, you must rest and let your body grow stronger. How many months were you?'

'Three,' I said.

'Has the bleeding stopped?'

'Almost.'

'And the miscarriage was complete?'

I swallowed. 'I think so.'

'All right. Stay in bed for the next few days, and don't exert yourself in any way. I'm leaving you something'—he took a green bottle from his bag—'that helps in these situations. Take two spoonfuls morning, midday and evening for the next two days. You will experience some cramping. If the miscarriage wasn't complete, this will help to dispel everything from the womb.'

At those last words, the enormity of what had occurred came over me again with a pain so deep that my body trembled. I knew I had to ask the question. I didn't know how I would deal with the answer.

'Could it have been my fault?' I asked. 'Was it the travel, on the ship from America? Or . . . I've had a great deal of worry lately. Is it my fault I lost my baby?'

'Mademoiselle,' the doctor said, more kindly now. 'Sometimes this is just the way of nature. You mustn't blame yourself. Try to rest. Madame Buisson, have another blanket brought up for her, and some soup. You have to regain your strength. And please, if you have more pain, or other difficulties, you must go to the hospital. Do you promise you will do this, mademoiselle?'

His unexpected gentleness with me was more than I could take. I covered my face with both hands, weeping, rocking back and forth, while the doctor and the concierge silently left the room.

Perhaps I should return to Juniper Road—return home, where I would be safe. But alone. I knew that if I decided to go on to Marrakesh, there was no guarantee I'd find Etienne, or even his sister.

And yet I could not turn back now. As the room darkened, I knew I could not return to my former life until I completed what I had started, no matter the final outcome.

Chapter Seven

'MADAME? HERE IS MARRAKESH, as you wish,' Aziz said, his voice puzzled. 'You are not happy to come Marrakesh?'

I couldn't speak or look at him. Instead, I stared ahead as we approached the outskirts of the city. Grand rows of date palms lined the road, and groves of them stretched out on either side. Mustapha drove with studied concentration and decision, although, like most of the other drivers, he constantly blew the horn.

'Where are we going?' I asked Aziz. 'Where are you taking me?'

'We go French Quarter, madame, La Ville Nouvelle. There are the hotels for foreigners in the new city.'

The long red parapets of the city's walls were made richer by the lowering sun. I had no visual image of Marrakesh in my head, other than knowing that many of its buildings were built of the deep red-brown soil of the countryside, and that there was the newer city, built by the French—where Etienne had lived—as well as the centuries-old one within the walls. French was the official language spoken in La Ville Nouvelle, while Arabic was, of course, the language of the old city.

There was a profusion of trees: olive, lime, pomegranate, almond and orange. In spite of my trepidation, I couldn't help but see that they gave a beautiful and verdant sense to La Ville Nouvelle, with its wide boulevards and small taxis weaving between donkeys and their carts. Brilliant fuchsia blooms tumbled over garden walls.

I stared at the trees and flowers, afraid that if I looked at the faces of the people, I might suddenly see Etienne. I knew it was rather ridiculous, imagining I would see him within moments of arriving, but still, my heart wouldn't stop racing.

Mustapha stopped the car in front of an impressive, elegant hotel surrounded by tall, swaying palms. *Hôtel de la Palmeraie*. A dark-skinned man in a pressed red jacket with gold braid and a red fez with a golden tassel stood at attention outside the doors.

Mustapha jumped out of the car and opened my door, bowing low and sweeping his arm towards the building as if suddenly he had acquired new-found manners. 'Hôtel de la Palmeraie, madame,' he said, and, as I stepped out of the car, Aziz hauled out my cases and set them down. The man in red and gold hurried over and took them, bowing too.

'*Bienvenue*, madame,' he said. 'Welcome to Hôtel de la Palmeraie,' and carried my cases up the steps and inside the hotel.

I opened my bag and took out the decided-upon payment, as well as a number of extra francs. I put them into Mustapha's hand, and then took out additional francs and gave them to Aziz, who was standing beside the open passenger door. 'Thank you, Aziz. I appreciate your help,' I told him, and he bowed his head.

'*De rien*, madame, you're welcome, it's nothing. Goodbye, madame.'

I stepped back from the car. 'Goodbye, Aziz, goodbye, Mustapha,' I said. 'Thank you. Have a safe journey home.'

'*Inshallah*,' both men murmured.

The concierge—a short man, his smile a sly glint due to a gold front tooth—watched me as I approached the front desk. His eyes travelled from my hair down my dress to my shoes.

'Welcome, madame,' he said, although his voice wasn't particularly welcoming. 'You wish to stay with us?'

'Yes. Please.'

He turned the registration book, pushing it across the counter. 'Certainly, madame. If you would sign here,' he said, handing me a pen. As he watched me write my name, he corrected himself, his eyebrows rising. 'Ah. Mademoiselle. It is . . . Osh . . . I'm sorry. What is the name?'

'O'Shea,' I said. 'Mademoiselle O'Shea.'

'You have taken the train?'

'No. I was driven from Tangier.'

'A difficult journey, I am sure,' he said, his eyes going to my hair. I was suddenly aware of how filthy I was. I had worn the same clothing for the past two days, sleeping in it overnight in the *bled.*

'Yes.'

'And how long will you stay with us, mademoiselle?'

I looked down at the cost of the hotel per night. It was far beyond my means. And yet I had no idea where else to stay. 'I . . . I don't know.'

His face gave away nothing. 'As you wish, mademoiselle. You are welcome at Hôtel de la Palmeraie for any duration. I am Monsieur Henri. Please call upon me for whatever you may need. May I reserve you a table for dinner? It is served until nine o'clock.'

Did I want to eat dinner? Did I propose to rush out into the streets and blindly begin my search? I opened my mouth to say *I don't know* again, and then realised I needed to eat, to sleep. To keep up my strength. 'Thank you, yes,' I said. 'I will have dinner.'

'Seven o'clock? Eight? What is your preferred time?'

'I . . . seven o'clock,' I said.

He wrote, nodding. 'And now, I'm sure you would like to go to your room, to relax and refresh yourself after your arduous voyage.'

'Yes,' I said again.

He lifted his hand, snapping his fingers, and immediately a wiry boy in the same uniform as the man who had opened the front doors for me ran over and picked up my cases.

My room was sumptuous, with walls of burled wood panels and oil paintings of mountains and Moroccan vistas in thick gilt frames. The bed's white coverlet was scattered with a pattern of rose petals. I had never imagined such a thing.

I went into the attached bathroom. There were fluffy white towels folded into shapes of flowers and birds, and a pair of slippers of soft white leather, and a white silk robe.

I would quickly have to find a less expensive place. But I would stay here the night, and hopefully tomorrow be more clear-headed. I drew a bath, pouring in sweet-smelling oil from one of the containers on a glass shelf over the sink.

I lowered myself in and leaned back. My hands and wrists were so much darker than the rest of my body; I turned my head and looked at myself in the mirrored wall beside me. My reflection showed that my face and neck were the same deep colour; my three days of travel in the sun and wind had given my complexion a hue I hardly recognised.

I lay back again, looking at the length of my body. My hipbones jutted out and my knees were knobby.

My abdomen lay flat under the warm, scented water.

After I'd washed my hair I pinned it up, still damp. Then I put on my best dress, attempting to shake out the myriad of wrinkles. Then I took my second pair of shoes from my case: although still ugly, black, with the right sole built up, at least they weren't ingrained with red dust.

I went down to the dimly lit lobby; in the middle was a huge, gently splashing fountain.

'Madame?' A boy, tall and thin, with the first hint of a moustache, appeared at my side. He wore the hotel's red and gold uniform, as well as white cotton gloves. 'You wish the dining room?'

'Yes, please,' I said.

At the door of the dining room he stopped, speaking in a low tone to the maître d', dressed in a tuxedo with long tails, a burgundy cummerbund and white gloves.

'Your name, madame?' he asked. When I told him he nodded once to the boy.

As soon as I looked into the grand room I knew I was terribly underdressed. The men wore dark suits or tuxedos, while most of the women were in long evening gowns of satin and net, their hair either short and curled, or in elaborate upsweeps.

I stood in the doorway in my creased green silk, my damp hair springing out of its pins, knowing that everything about my appearance was wrong. But the young man gave me a beautiful smile under his new moustache, saying, 'Come, please, madame,' and his smile gave me the confidence to walk through the room with him. Thankfully the boy didn't place me in the middle of the other diners, but led me to a small table set for one beside a window overlooking the gardens. He pulled out my chair for me, and I settled into its wide burgundy velvet seat.

The room was filled with quiet laughter and chatter, the clink of silver against porcelain, and the soft strains of a harp from one corner. But in spite of this formal atmosphere, from somewhere beyond the garden outside the window I was very aware of a distant, muted roar and the rhythmic pounding of drums.

I sipped the mineral water instantly poured for me, and chose a simple ratatouille from the extensive menu held in front of me by more gloved hands, and then looked through the window.

In the dusk I could see rows and rows of trees and tall, flowering bushes with paths weaving throughout. At the far end of the garden was a high wall covered with bougainvillea. And beyond the wall were snow-capped mountains: the High Atlas.

It was a backdrop of such unbelievable beauty that for that moment I forgot, or perhaps was just distracted from, my purpose in Marrakesh.

I came back to my senses when a server murmured, 'To start, madame. *Bon appétit*,' and set a plate of tiny millefeuille pastries in front of me. I put one of them in my mouth, and tasted something that reminded me of the *pastilla* I had had in Tangier. The noise from outside grew in frequency. I looked around the dimly lit, fragrant room, but nobody else seemed aware of it.

'Excuse me,' I finally said to the couple at the next table. 'What is that sound?'

The man put down his knife and fork. 'The main square in the medina—the old city of Marrakesh,' he replied, in a British accent. 'D'jemma el Fna. Quite a place,' he said. 'I take it you've just arrived?'

'Yes.'

'Well, you certainly must experience the medina during your visit. It's purported to be the greatest souk in Morocco, centuries old. But I wouldn't recommend going there—or even venturing into the old city—without an escort. Allow me to introduce myself, and my wife.' He stood, giving a small, dignified bow from his waist. 'Mr Clive Russell,' he said. 'And Mrs Russell.' He extended his hand towards the tall, slender woman with alabaster skin sitting across from him.

I introduced myself, and Mrs Russell nodded. 'Mr Russell is right. The medina is frightening. Snakes and their charmers, aggressive monkeys, fire- and glass-eaters. Ghastly beggars pulling at you. And the way the men stare . . . it positively gave me shivers,' she said.

'Its name—D'jemma el Fna—means Assembly of the Dead, or Congregation of the Departed—some such grisly thing,' Mr Russell went on, sitting down again but turning in his chair to continue speaking to me. 'They used to display decapitated heads throughout the square, warnings of some sort. The French put an end to that.'

'Thankfully,' Mrs Russell added.

'Have you been here long—in Marrakesh?' I asked.

'A few weeks,' Mr Russell answered. 'But it's far too hot now. We're leaving next week. Off to Essaouria, where we can enjoy the sea breezes.'

'Charming seaside town. Charming,' Mrs Russell added.

'You haven't, in your time here, run into a Dr Duverger, have you?' I asked. The hotel was obviously full of wealthy foreigners; perhaps Etienne had stayed here. Or was here now. My heart gave one low, heavy thud, and I quickly surveyed the room again.

Mr Russell shook his head. 'I'm sorry. We don't know a Dr Duverger. But you should ask at the desk if you think he may be here.'

'Thank you,' I said. 'I will.' It hadn't occurred to me to ask the pompous Monsieur Henri if Dr Duverger had stayed here recently. How could I not have thought of such a simple question?

'I'd suggest you try the Napoleon for dessert. The hotel has a very talented French pastry chef,' Mr Russell said, then, turning in his chair ever so slightly, so that I knew the conversation was over, 'We do enjoy it, don't we, darling?' he said to Mrs Russell.

After I'd finished my dinner, I wandered out through huge glass doors into the garden. Many of the guests were now dancing in one of the ballrooms I had passed, and the empty paths of the garden were lit by flaming torches. There were orange and lemon trees and thousands of rosebushes amassed with bright red roses. Nightingales and turtledoves nested in the palm trees that lined the pathways. There was an abundance of sweet-smelling mimosa, and plants that were surprisingly like many I knew from my own garden at home: geraniums, stock, snapdragons, impatiens, salvia, pansies and hollyhocks.

Suddenly my memories of home—and my former life there—were so distant. It was as though the woman who had lived that simple life, so out of touch with the world beyond Juniper Road, couldn't possibly have been me.

Under new skies, I was no longer that Sidonie O'Shea. Since I'd left Albany, the things I'd seen, that I'd heard and smelled, touched and tasted, had been unexpected, unpredictable. Some had been beautiful, others frightening. It was as if all the new scenes were photographs in a book, photographs I'd captured within my mind. I could look at them as if slowly turning pages.

And the enormity of my final challenge—the one I had journeyed this distance to confront—still lay ahead. The thought of how I might face it, perhaps as soon as tomorrow, filled me with such anxiety that I hurried back through the paths towards the hotel, wanting to return to the safety of my room.

I slept restlessly in spite of the soft bed smelling of rose petals, and in the morning went immediately to the front desk.

I asked Monsieur Henri if Dr Etienne Duverger was—or had been—a guest at Hôtel de la Palmeraie. When Monsieur Henri shook his head, I asked, 'You're certain?'

'I assure you, mademoiselle, I have been here since the opening of the hotel over five years ago, and have an excellent memory.'

'Thank you,' I said quietly, turning to leave, then looked back at Monsieur Henri.

'What of a Manon Duverger?' I asked. 'I believe she lives in Marrakesh, surely here, in La Ville Nouvelle. Do you know her?'

Again he shook his head. 'I know of no Duvergers. But. . .'

'Yes?' I said, perhaps a bit too eagerly, approaching the desk again.

'Try the Bureau of Statistics on Rue Arles. They have a list of home-owners in Marrakesh.' He pulled a small folded pamphlet from under the high desk. 'Here is a map of the French Quarter; it will help you find your way about.'

'Thank you, Monsieur Henri,' I said. 'I appreciate your assistance.'

On the way out, I noticed a series of watercolours on one wall of the lobby. I was anxious to start my search, but glanced at them as I passed. They were by various French artists, none of whom I recognised. But some had managed to capture a particular essence of light in the renditions of what appeared to be the daily nuances of life in Morocco.

I easily found Rue Arles and waited while a clerk looked up the Duverger name. 'Yes,' he said, and I leaned closer. 'The Duvergers owned a home on Rue des Chevaux. But . . . it was sold some years ago. Now it is owned by a family named Mauchamp.' He looked up at me. 'That's all I have here. Now there is no indication of any Duvergers owning a home in the French Quarter.'

I thanked him and went out into the street. Now what were my options? I couldn't have reached a dead end so quickly. Somebody must know of Etienne Duverger. He had lived here; his parents had died and were buried here, as was his younger brother Guillaume. And somebody must know of Manon Duverger.

I searched La Ville Nouvelle for three full days, but every time I said the name Duverger I was met with blank stares. I had wandered through all of its wide boulevards, looked into all the cafés, asked about Etienne at the Polyclinique du Sud, the small French medical clinic, and had sat in the main square, studying each European man who passed.

I saw a few men who, from the back, resembled Etienne: wide, straight shoulders, dark hair curling over the collar, confidence in the step. Each time I felt faint for a moment, and then hurried after the man, realising, when I was a few feet from him, that it was not Etienne.

It was the same when I enquired about Manon Duverger, but I reasoned that she might have married and now have a different surname.

Staying at the luxurious Hôtel de la Palmeraie, my money was depleting at an alarming rate, and I knew I must find less expensive lodgings. And yet, at the end of each of those first three days, when I returned to the hotel hot and exhausted, I no longer had the energy to begin the process of searching out a different hotel and moving.

The fourth day of my search was like the first, and the second and third. At noon, weary and despondent, I returned to the hotel and sat, rather numbly, in the lobby.

Mr Russell stopped in front of me.

'We haven't seen you about, Miss O'Shea,' he said. 'Not even in the dining room.'

I smiled wanly. 'Yes. I've been . . . busy. And taking my meals either in my room, or . . .' I realised then that I'd been eating little.

'Mrs Russell and I are leaving for Essaouria tomorrow, but we thought that this afternoon we'd visit the Majorelle Garden,' he told me. 'It's a bit farther northwest in the city. Do you know of it?'

I shook my head.

'Have you looked at these paintings?' he asked, gesturing at the watercolours on the wall. 'They're for sale; a lot of people who stay here like to take home images of Morocco. They go for a pretty price. Some of them are by Jacques Majorelle,' he said.

I didn't comment, not interested in having a discussion on painting with Mr Russell.

But he liked to talk. 'Majorelle had this idea, supposedly a few years back, to build a magnificent public garden. He bought a few acres of land in the date palm groves on what was then the outskirts of the city. He's planted an impressive array of cacti, succulents, bamboos, bananas, tree ferns and so on. Parts of it are still being worked on; he's trying to bring in every tree and plant imaginable that will survive this climate.'

In the sudden silence I felt I couldn't be rude as Mr Russell stood over me as though waiting for something. 'Does Monsieur Majorelle no longer paint, then?'

Mr Russell waved one hand airily. 'I'm led to believe he's an artist of little importance. Nobody outside of Marrakesh seems to know much about him. But please, Miss O'Shea, do feel free to come along with us. It will be quite relaxing.'

'Oh, no. I shouldn't . . .' I began, and then stopped. The thought of spending time in a beautiful garden away from the busy streets in the oppressive heat was appealing, and I knew I didn't have the energy to search any further this day. Perhaps it would be a relief to think of something other than Etienne for a few hours. 'Well, yes. Thank you. I'd like to join you.'

Most striking about Le Jardin Majorelle was the sensation of shade and filtered sunlight, and the colour of many of the arches and huge terracotta vessels containing plants. They were painted green and yellow and blue. The colours of the garden matched Marrakesh's brilliant hues.

Almost immediately Mr Russell introduced me to a man in a white Panama hat—it was Monsieur Majorelle—and he welcomed us graciously. 'I'm happy to show my vision to visitors,' he said in French. Mr Russell could speak a little French, and he translated for Mrs Russell. Monsieur Majorelle led us down a shady path of beaten red earth. Other paths crossed it. Sunlight dappling through the tall, swaying foliage created a rhythmic pattern on our faces. There were a number of young Moroccan men, dressed in white, digging and planting.

It was clear that the design of the garden had a certain composition and placement of colour in both its structures and its plant life that immediately brought to mind a painting. I looked at the shallow tiled pool nearest; carp and goldfish wove through the clear water, turned aquamarine by the tiles. I recognised water lilies and lotus, but there were other aquatic plants unfamiliar to me. 'What is that, Monsieur Majorelle?' I asked, pointing to tall stalks topped with a large, tassel-like head.

'Papyrus,' he said. 'I wish to bring in forms representing the continents that sustain life. Please. Enjoy yourselves. Stroll about.'

We said goodbye. Mr Russell wanted to shoot photographs with the Brownie camera he wore around his neck.

'I'll go off on my own,' I told him and Mrs Russell. 'I'd love to explore some of the plantings.'

We parted, agreeing to meet back at the entrance in an hour.

I wandered down the pleasant paths, touching the profusion of vermilion bougainvillea twining over trellises.

Although the garden was beautiful, it hadn't lifted my despondency. There were few other people, apart from the Arab workers, but I noticed a frail, very elderly woman sitting on a bench under a banana tree. She held a tiny dog with feathery gold fur. The old woman stroked the dog with gnarled fingers, each one decorated with a ring bearing a different gem. I thought of Cinnabar, and the soothing feel of her fur.

The shaded bench was inviting. '*Bonjour*, madame,' I said.

'*Bonjour*,' she answered in delicate French, her voice tremulous with age as she peered up at me. 'Do I know you? I don't see well any longer.'

'No, madame. You don't know me. I'm Mademoiselle O'Shea,' I said, sitting beside her.

'I am Madame Odette. This is Loulou,' she added.

'Are you enjoying the gardens?' I asked.

She smiled. 'Oh yes, my dear. I come every day. My son brings me after our noon meal, and picks me up at five. Is it nearly five?'

'I believe so, madame. Do you live nearby?'

'Yes. I have lived in Marrakesh for a number of years. Now I stay with my son and daughter-in-law. My husband was in the Foreign Legion, you know. He died many years ago.'

She stopped, looking into the distance.

Madame Odette refocused on me. 'But she is unpleasant, my daughter-in-law. Every day some difficulty. So I come here, and enjoy the garden.' She looked towards a stand of bamboo.

I nodded, leaning down to pick up a fallen bougainvillea blossom and looking into its deep red centre.

'And you, mademoiselle? You live in Marrakesh as well?' Madame Odette asked.

I looked up, shaking my head. 'No.'

'You're visiting family?'

'I'm here to find someone, but . . .' I reached towards Loulou, stroking one ear. 'It's proving very difficult, I'm afraid.'

'I have lived in Marrakesh many years,' she repeated. 'The heat of Africa is good for my bones, although my daughter-in-law's chill is not good for my heart. But I have known many French families. My husband was in the Foreign Legion. Very handsome in his uniform. What day is it?' she asked, suddenly looking at me.

'It's Tuesday,' I said.

'What time is it?'

'Almost five,' I told her again.

'He comes at five. Who is it you seek, mademoiselle?' Madame Odette asked.

'The Duvergers, madame,' I said, without expecting her to answer.

'Marcel and Adelaide?'

'Yes, yes, Madame Odette. The family of Marcel Duverger. You knew them?' I said, still refusing to grow hopeful.

'Marcel and Adelaide, oh yes. And the son . . . I remember some tragedy. I remember the past, mademoiselle, but often not this day. They had a son. It was a tragedy,' she repeated. 'I have a son.'

'Guillaume was their son. He died.'

She studied me, her head on one side, her eyes suddenly more alive. 'And there was an older one.'

'Etienne. You know Etienne?' My voice was quick, loud now.

'Clever young man. He went off to Paris.'

'Yes, yes, that's him, Madame Odette. Have . . . have you seen him? Recently?'

She stroked the dog's chest. 'They died some years ago. First Adelaide, and then poor Marcel. There are no longer any Duvergers in La Ville Nouvelle. He was a doctor.'

'Yes. Yes, Etienne is a doctor,' I said, nodding, encouraging her. 'I'm trying to find him.'

'And he is willing to be found?'

I let her words sink in for a moment. 'Willing?'

The old woman smiled, a strange smile. 'Sometimes . . . well, if one can't be found, it is because one is hiding.'

I knew I had refused to think of this: that Etienne was indeed in Marrakesh, and had seen me, but had not approached me because he was, as Madame Odette had just said, unwilling to be found.

'Madame Odette,' I said then, not wanting to think about Etienne hiding from me. 'What of the daughter? She's gone as well?'

Now Madame Odette frowned. 'Daughter?'

'Manon Duverger,' I said, but the old woman shook her head.

'I don't recall a daughter.'

'She may have a married name now.'

'I forget many things,' Madame Odette said. 'I don't remember this Manon. You believe she lives here, in Marrakesh?'

'She did a few months ago,' I said, thinking of the folded letter I carried in my bag at all times.

'And it's with certainty that she lives in La Ville Nouvelle?'

'I . . . I assume so. She's French, after all.'

'Perhaps she's gone Arab. She may have moved into the medina to live with the Moors.'

'You think it's possible that she lives in the medina? I don't . . .' I stopped. I knew nothing about Manon.

'You should try there, among the Moroccans. Outside the walls live the emigrés. The native people of Marrakesh do not live in La Ville Nouvelle. Poor, rich, they all live in the old city; even the sultans and nobles have their fine homes and their harems, their *riads* with their glorious gardens, all within the medina walls.'

'The medina is large, Madame Odette. How could I even begin to look there?'

'Yes. It's large, the medina, and you must venture through the souks to the little *rues*, which run in every direction. Very confusing streets—more like alleys, narrow and dark. The homes are windowless on the outside walls. The people believe that conspicuous exteriors are a very poor show. Like their women, the men keep their riches hidden.' She drew a deep breath. 'Always look for the minaret of La Koutoubia.'

She stopped speaking and stroking Loulou, closing her eyes as though her explanation had exhausted her. I knew she was talking about the imposing red mosque I had seen. 'What day is it?'

'It is Tuesday, Madame Odette.'

'I myself have not gone into the medina for many years. I am old,' she said, yet again.

'Thank you, Madame Odette, for your help,' I said, standing.

'You know I have a son, mademoiselle,' Madame Odette said. 'He comes for me at five. Do you have a son?' she called after me, and those last five words travelled into me like five sharp jabs.

The following morning I stood and looked through the tall gates at the sun filtering through the medina. I clutched my handbag tightly and walked under the high portals, hoping I looked purposeful, with a destination in mind, and not like a woman only pretending to be unafraid.

Everywhere were African men and boys, some leading donkeys and small horses pulling carts piled with all manner of produce. The men's faces fascinated me because of their diversity. There were those so fair-skinned as to look European, with long, narrow faces and light brown or reddish beards, their heads covered by their turbans. There were the Berbers of the desert, often high-cheekboned, their faces chiselled and dark from the sun. And there were those with skin so black it shone ebony, their heads covered with tight curls. Slaves, or the descendants of slaves.

Also Moroccan women, although, as elsewhere throughout the country, nothing was visible but their eyes above their veils. Their bodies were also made completely indistinguishable by a white cloth—I knew it was called a *haik*—draped over their heads and completely covering them to the ground. Under the *haik* they would wear their daily dress, a flowing gown called a kaftan.

With every woman was a man or older boy, walking closely in front or behind. No woman was without a male accompanying her.

I was immediately aware of the stares of the men, and how the women gave me a wide berth. I looked straight ahead. I didn't know where I was going, but I had told myself that once I was inside the medina I would figure out my next move.

On this first street, every square inch under the faded straw or cloth awnings was crammed with tables or simple threadbare strips of carpets on the ground holding everything imaginable—as well as some things which were, to me, quite unimagined.

There were women's kaftans and endless jellabas of every colour and every fabric. Other stalls held hundreds of *babouches*—the backless leather slippers dyed bright shades of yellow and orange and red—dangling overhead from hooks. There were camel-bone teapots and red felt fezzes and arrays of perfumes: jasmine and musk and sandalwood.

I passed trays of sweetmeats and juicy dates and figs and live chickens and pigeons in crates. Thick swarms of flies buzzed and settled, lifted and settled over everything.

And then suddenly I came into a huge open square with stalls and kiosks lining its edges. It had to be at least three city blocks square. I didn't dare walk through the open centre; already I felt too conspicuous and uneasy. Instead, I edged along the perimeter of the square. Even here I was pushed and jostled, usually simply caught up in the bustle, but on occasion I suspected I was knocked into intentionally. I refused to listen to the voice in my head telling me that I was not wanted here, and should leave.

And yet I had no choice. I had run out of options in the French Quarter. I would stay in the medina, and try, somehow, to find out if Manon lived here. I had no plan other than asking about the Duvergers.

I heard a running string of Arabic in a loud, authoritative voice, and saw a man on a box, waving his arms, his eyes wild and his face stubbled. He wore a magnificent robe of brown and blue velvet, so different from the other men in the square in their drab jellabas. Around him some men squatted in a circle, or stood; all were mesmerised and silent. The man on the box went on and on, and I began to realise, by his pauses and the fire of his words, that he was telling a story. In front of him lay a square of dark cotton, and on it glinted coins. A professional storyteller.

Farther on I came across a man sitting on the ground with a cloth filled with pulled teeth in front of him. They were of all sizes, some rotted and some whole. I hurried away.

I walked down one of the alleys that led from the square like spokes of a wheel. I was now in the souks, and looked ahead and behind, trying to find clues to remind myself of the way back to the square. Here were endless stalls and tiny shops, with a man standing in front of each. It took me only a few moments to see that the souks were organised by trade, with the cloth-sellers in one alley, and the silversmiths in another. There were rug merchants and perfume dealers. I saw conical piles of spices of every shade of red and yellow and orange and green and brown, their smells mingling. The men visited back and forth, calling to each other, and sometimes to me, with murmurs of 'Madame, *venez*, madame.' Come, madame.

I stopped, looking backwards and then ahead; had I turned left or right at the last corner? I looked up, hoping to see the tower of La Koutoubia, but all that was visible was the slash of azure sky.

Would I be able to retrace my steps? I turned in all directions. Suddenly every man's eyes were on me; every woman pushed past me, banging my shoulders or hips as though in warning.

I edged closer to the stalls, away from the middle of the crowded, narrow streets. Occasionally the owner would spring to life, chattering in Arabic or French, trying to sell me a scarf or a decorated hand mirror or a bag of dried rosebuds or a sack of mint for tea. Each time I asked about the Duvergers. Some of the men shrugged, either because they didn't know the Duvergers, or perhaps because they didn't speak French, or simply didn't care to answer me if I wasn't purchasing something from them. Some shook their heads.

I was too hot, hot and thirsty; it was making me light-headed. It had been a mistake to come here, blindly looking for an unknown woman.

Suddenly my skirt was yanked, almost violently, and I gasped. Three small children—no older than four or five—stood around me, pointing dirty fingers into their mouths, screeching, '*Manger! Manger,* madame!'

I dropped a few sous onto the ground, because the children made it impossible to put them into their hands, clinging to my skirt and jumping up and down. As they stooped to gather the coins, I pulled free and hurried away, but suddenly there were more children running after me, again grabbing at my skirt.

'*Non, non*,' I said, trying to free myself from their hands, and suddenly, as I reached the end of the alley, I was back in D'jemma el Fna. But the children persisted, and as I pushed their little hands from my skirt, there was a flurry near my ear, and a weight on my shoulder. Shocked, I turned my head and stared into a tiny scowling face next to mine. I shrieked involuntarily, and the little thing also screeched in response. It was a monkey, I told myself, only a monkey.

A voice shouted in Arabic, and the children scattered. I stood, trembling, the monkey perched on my shoulder.

'Madame, oh madame, this is truly good luck,' said the man who had run off the children. He held a long chain, and the chain led to a leather band around the monkey's neck. 'I am Mohammed, and my monkey, Hasi, has chosen you,' he told me. 'If you give a sou, only one sou, madame, your luck will be threefold. Oh, it is a blessed day that Hasi has chosen you. He goes only to the good.'

I knew the monkey would jump on anyone Mohammed directed him to. Hasi now slid down my arm, looking up at me. He bared his pointed teeth in a smiling grimace, putting his tiny hand out, palm up.

'Madame,' Mohammed entreated. 'You must wish for this good luck. Only a fool would turn down such an opportunity.'

I reached into my bag and put a sou into that minute, almost human hand, and was rewarded with an ear-splitting screech. In a practised routine, he tucked the coin into the pocket of the waistcoat Mohammed wore over his robe. Then he pressed his teeth against Mohammed's ear. Mohammed nodded seriously.

'Madame, Hasi has informed me that a change will now take place in your life. An important change. You have come to Marrakesh to find something. You have lost something, something of importance. Hasi tells me that you are sad, but this will soon change. Very soon. Under the Southern Cross you will understand that what you look for may take a different shape. You may not recognise it.'

'The Southern Cross?'

Mohammed squinted at the sky. 'The constellation, madame. Here, in Africa. The Southern Cross. You look for it in the night sky. And under it you will find what you search for. But remember, madame, remember, here are the Others, the jinns. They masquerade in human form. Be careful. Be very careful you do not choose unwisely.'

I walked on, ignoring the cries of the begging children and the clanging bells of the water carriers, with their high domed hats and their brass cups and goatskins of water. I moved from stall to stall, saying *Duverger, Duverger, do you know the Duvergers?* Finally one man unfolded his arms and picked up a pair of bright orange *babouches*, studying me. 'These shoes will fit you, madame,' he said in French. 'Good shoes; I sell only the best shoes in Marrakesh. Where are you from? England?'

'America,' I said, and he nodded.

'Ah, America. I once had a beautiful American bride. She was my third wife. But she returned to her home.'

I nodded, although I didn't know if I believed his story. 'Good, good,' I said. 'But the Duvergers . . . do you know of them?'

'I knew Monsieur le Docteur,' he said.

'You knew him? Dr Etienne Duverger?' I said it calmly. Instinctively, I didn't want this man to know the importance of his words.

'What about the *babouches*, madame? You will buy them?'

I took the orange slippers from his hands. 'Yes, yes, I'll buy them. But please, what do you know of Dr Duverger?'

He shrugged. 'First we must discuss what price you will offer. We will have tea, and discuss,' he said, waving his hand in the air. I shook my head, but a boy of about ten appeared beside me. The man spoke in Arabic, and the boy ran off. 'He will bring tea. Sit, sit, madame, and we will drink tea and discuss the price.'

All I wanted was for him to answer my questions, but I realised I must play the game first. I sat down. 'Please, monsieur. About Dr Duverger.'

'I knew Monsieur le Docteur Duverger,' he repeated. 'He came to the souks to buy *kif*, what you call cannabis, and leather goods. He came to my stall because I speak French. Of course, that was before. Afterwards . . .' he threw up his hands, 'nobody saw him.'

'What do you mean, afterwards?'

'His illness. He did not leave his house.'

'What illness?'

'Madame, that is all I know. You asked if I knew the Duvergers. I told you yes, I knew the old man Duverger, who had the sickness.'

'The old man?' I said. 'Not the son? Not Etienne?'

'I found for him the *kif* he wanted, when he could still walk in the souks. We drank tea. Now you and I will drink tea. Soon my nephew will return with it. Maybe you will buy two pairs of *babouches*.

I make you a good price. Best *babouches* in Marrakesh, best prices.'

The slippers were soft in my hands. 'Perhaps . . . the daughter?' I said.

'You ask about the daughter of Marcel Duverger? That Manon?'

'Yes, yes.' I nodded, my voice again rising in hope, but the shop owner suddenly looked secretive, or disgruntled.

'That's what I've said, monsieur. Manon Duverger.'

'You are mistaken, madame. The Manon you ask about is not Duverger. She is Manon Maliki.'

'That's her married name?'

Now the man made a face of disgust. 'Hah!' he said.

I ignored his critical tone, fighting to keep my voice even, my face expressionless. 'But you are certain she's Monsieur Duverger's daughter?'

'I am certain.'

'Can you tell me where she lives?' I licked my lips. I was so close.

He was still staring at me. 'Sharia Zitoun.'

'How do I find it? Is it nearby? Please, monsieur.'

'It is past the dyers' alley. *C'est tout*,' he said, slapping his palms together as if to rid them of dust. 'There's nothing more I can tell you. You have taken me from my duties for too long.' He had abruptly lost his earlier friendliness. From the moment I made it clear I looked for Manon Duverger, his attitude had changed.

'I'm sorry to have troubled you, monsieur,' I said. 'I . . . what price do you wish for these?' I held up the orange *babouches*.

But he rather brusquely took them from my hands. 'You do not need to purchase anything from me. It will not be a good sale; now there is no *baraka*. Instead, I will give you something. I give it freely. It is this: do not seek out Manon Maliki. No good will come of it. Good day, madame.' He turned then, putting the *babouches* on another shelf. It was clear he would speak no more to me.

'*Merci*, monsieur,' I said to his back, and left the stall. I passed the man's nephew hurrying up the alley, a tin tray with two glasses of steaming tea on it. He stopped, staring at me, but I ignored him.

Now I asked anyone who looked at me for directions to the dyers' alley, or to Sharia Zitoun. Occasionally a man would point behind me or in front of me. And then, with a turn, there were no more stalls, and I was out of the souks. I was in an alley lined with the windowless house fronts Madame Odette had described. Straight walls and gates, and behind the locked gates lived the people of Marrakesh.

As I wandered deeper, it grew quieter; the noises of the souks had long died away. The peacefulness of this alley was a relief after the continuous noise and array of colour and wares and milling humanity. I stopped, leaning against a wall, wiping my forehead and upper lip with my sleeve. The cobbled alley stretched ahead, shaded and dim, with only the gates and the continuous walls. I couldn't tell where one house began and one ended except by the different gates.

I lost track of time. Occasionally I met a figure, and would speak the words *Sharia Zitoun*. Some turned their faces from me, unwilling to speak to an uncovered foreigner; others stared but didn't respond. I wandered deeper and deeper through the tunnelled streets; it felt as though I had walked for hours in the hot alleyways. My leg ached, and occasionally I leaned against a wall to rest it. I heard the slight splashing of fountains in the courtyards behind the high walls, or the slow clopping of hoofs on stones, echoing from another alley. It was cooler here, with the high stone walls and the sun unable to reach its long fingers into such narrow passages, and I understood why the streets were built in this fashion.

I turned down another street, and suddenly heard, from nearby, continual mechanical humming. I went towards the sound and walked into an alley lined with tiny niches. In every one an old man hunched over an antiquated sewing machine, working the needle with the hand wheel. The tailors' alley, then.

In the next alley were men working wood in their own alcoves. These men weren't as old as the tailors, and used an assortment of tools, some with their bare feet. The smell was aromatic and clean.

When I next turned I found myself in a small square. Over the entire square, from crossed ropes strung between the roofs, hung huge skeins of wool: a ceiling of colour. The dyers' alley. The skeins were scarlet and tangerine and sunflower-yellow, greens deep as the ocean and pale as the newest leaves, purples and blues both brilliant and muted. I stood in awe for a moment, looking up.

Sharia Zitoun was just past the dyers' alley, the *babouche* dealer in the souk had told me. I stopped at the end of the alley; I could go only left or right. There was a tiny sign on one wall, but it was in Arabic. Choosing left, I started down the alley, and almost immediately a gate opened and a heavyset woman stuck her head out of the doorway, holding a calico kerchief in front of her face. '*Pardon*, madame,' I said to her.

She looked over the kerchief at me with an unfriendly stare.

'*Je cherche* Sharia Zitoun,' I said.

The woman pointed at the ground. I looked down, not understanding until she said, 'Sharia Zitoun.'

'Ah. *Ici?* Here is Sharia Zitoun?'

The woman nodded again.

'Please, madame,' I said, 'I am trying to find Madame Maliki.'

At that the woman took a step back.

'Manon Maliki,' I said, again, nodding encouragingly.

Then the woman did an odd thing. She reached down inside her kaftan and pulled out a small leather pouch, clutching it. I knew it to be an amulet to ward off the jinns; Aziz had worn one. What I didn't know was whether she held it to protect herself from me, or because I had said Manon's name.

But then she raised her other hand and flung it in the air, pointing over my left shoulder. I turned and looked at the gate she indicated.

'*C'est là?*' I asked. 'That's where she lives?'

Now the woman simply tucked her amulet into her kaftan and stepped back inside, slamming the gate.

I went to the gate she'd indicated. It was a brilliant yellow-gold, in the way of many of the gates: the colour of saffron. There was a heavy, tarnished brass knocker in the shape of a hand: the *hamsa*, to afford protection from the supernatural.

I stood in front of the gate, breathing heavily. Had I actually found Manon?

I lifted my hand to grasp the knocker, then dropped it to my side. What if I knocked and it was Etienne who opened the door? Wasn't that what I had hoped would happen? Hadn't I made this terribly difficult journey, all the way to Marrakesh, for this very reason, this very moment?

Here was the moment.

And I was terrified.

What if he simply looked at me, frowning, shaking his head, telling me to go, that I had no right to come here? What if—when I tried to tell him that I could forgive him, that whatever he was hiding from me couldn't be so terrible—he simply closed the door in my face?

No. Etienne wouldn't do that to me. He wouldn't.

And what if it was Manon who opened the door? What if what she had to tell me about her brother was unbearable?

Instinctively I put my ear against it, but could hear nothing.

Then I lifted the heavy *hamsa*, raised it, and brought it down, once, twice, three times, with firm, heavy thuds.

There was no sound from the other side of the door. I knocked again, harder this time. Finally I heard footsteps, and the door creaked open.

A woman, holding her *haik* to cover her face in the way I was now accustomed to, peered through the narrow opening. I assumed her to be a servant.

'*Bonjour*, madame,' I said, hoping she spoke French. 'I'm looking for Madame Maliki.'

When she didn't answer, I assumed she didn't understand. I used the Arabic greeting—*assalaam alykum*, peace be upon you—and then slowly repeated Manon's name.

She studied my face. 'Why do you seek her?' she asked, in perfect French, her voice slightly muffled by the *haik*.

'I . . . I have come to speak with her,' I said, not wanting to divulge the complicated reason as I stood in this dim alley. 'I have gone to great lengths to find her. If she is at home, I should very much like to speak to her. Would you fetch her, please?'

'Come,' she said, pulling the gate open farther, and I caught my breath as I stepped into the courtyard. My eyes darted over every surface. What did I expect? To see Etienne sitting there? Or perhaps a sign of him: a familiar jacket, a book with a pair of spectacles on it?

But there was no such indication. Some sort of house-cleaning was under way, as there was furniture sitting about the tiled courtyard—stuffed ottomans and stools and long, narrow mattresses covered in multicoloured fabric, which I knew were used for both sitting during the day and sleeping at night. There was a fountain in the centre of the courtyard, but instead of water it contained only dead, dry leaves and the small, stiff body of a yellow bird. There was a set of steep, narrow tiled steps leading to an upper floor with shuttered windows.

The woman latched the gate and walked across the courtyard. I was uncertain whether to follow her. A child, perhaps four or five, ran into the courtyard from the house. 'Maman,' it said, but the woman ignored it, sitting on one of the mattresses. And then a girl appeared in the doorway. She was ten or eleven, her skin the colour of milky coffee. She was painfully thin in her simple muslin shift. Her right arm was covered in bruises, and one of her eyes was bloodshot, the eyelid puffy.

I couldn't tell if the younger child was a boy or girl; the thick black hair was cut in a straight line across the nape of the neck as well as the forehead, almost hiding large eyes that were as black as its hair. The child's skin was pale. It wore a long draped garment, and cotton trousers, torn off at the knees. Its feet were bare. 'Who is the lady, Maman?' the child cried. 'Who is she?'

Like its mother, the child's French was impeccable. It came to stand in front of me, its little neck tilted back to look at my face.

'Please, madame,' I called to the woman. 'Please. Would you ask Madame Maliki to come to the courtyard?' My heart was thumping. I realised, as I spoke, that if Etienne was inside the house he might have heard my voice. I looked up at the upper-floor windows, but the shutters remained closed.

'What's your name, madame?' the child asked me, with no hint of shyness.

'Mademoiselle O'Shea,' I said, in a distracted way, still watching the woman. Why did she not do as I asked?

'I am Badou.' It was a French name used for a boy or a girl.

The woman spoke in Arabic, and Badou and the girl pushed a cork stool until it was across from the woman.

'Sit,' the woman said to me, languidly pointing to the cork stool. Badou climbed into her lap, leaning against her, but she paid no attention. The girl had gone back to the doorway.

'Madame, please. Is Madame Maliki at home?' I asked, sitting stiffly on the stool. 'Or . . . or is anyone else here? Is . . .' I stopped.

At that the woman dropped the hand holding her *haik*, and it fell open. She had a straight nose and well-formed mouth. Her eyes were as dark as mine, but her skin tone was paler. She was definitely older than I. Hers was a sad and delicate face. It was obvious that she had, at some point, been quite beautiful. Although now she looked drawn, she still had a certain sensuousness to her. I realised that while I had seen a few uncovered Berber women in the square, I hadn't seen behind the face coverings of any other Arabic woman since I'd arrived in this country.

'I am she,' the woman said, calmly.

'*You* are Manon Maliki?'

She nodded, and at that I stood. 'No.' I said. 'The woman I'm trying to find is . . .' I stopped, careful of my wording. 'I have been given the wrong information. I'm sorry to have disturbed you.'

'Why do you seek this woman?'

'She's the sister of . . . of a friend.'

'The sister of whom?'

'The Manon I'm looking for is the daughter of Marcel Duverger,' I said. 'Someone in the souk told me that Manon Maliki was this woman.'

She sat without moving. The child played with a bit of string, its large dark eyes on me. The girl's mouth was open as she now crouched, motionless, in the doorway, watching.

'It is correct. I am the daughter of Marcel Duverger.'

'But . . . if you are Manon . . . I'm sorry, madame,' I said. 'It's just that I . . . I . . .' Was this not a Moroccan woman sitting in front of me? 'The Manon I seek is Dr Duverger's sister,' I finally said.

The woman didn't speak for a moment, then she said, 'How do you know Etienne?'

The way she said *Etienne*, with such familiarity, made me catch my breath. I hadn't said his name. 'You are his sister?' I repeated.

She nodded.

The courtyard was far too hot, even though I was in the shade. I tried to open my mouth to speak further, but my lips stuck together. I finally managed to say. 'Is Etienne here?'

The woman lifted her hands and pulled the *haik* completely off her head, so that I saw her hair, long and heavy, falling about her face and to her shoulders. Dark and wavy, as was mine, but with a few threads of white. She wore a dark-purple kaftan under the *haik*.

'You are from England? Or America? I cannot tell from your accent.'

I again struggled to lick my lips. 'America,' I said.

'Bring our guest water, *mon cher garçon*,' Manon said to the child—so it was a boy—and he slid off her lap and ran lightly through the doorway of the house. 'Falida. Go and help him,' Manon said, and the girl leaped to her feet and disappeared.

I studied my hands, clenched in my lap, hearing clinking and splashing. Within a moment the boy returned, crossing the courtyard slowly and very carefully, holding a tin cup in front of him with both hands. He didn't spill a drop, and proudly offered it to me. I drank; it was cool and refreshing, with a hint of lemon.

Badou waited in front of me; I handed him the empty cup and he took it and went back into the house.

'Madame. Is Etienne here, in Marrakesh? Please. I must know,' I said, my voice louder, an edge of sharpness creeping into it. There was something about this woman that troubled me. I didn't like her, I realised, even though I'd known her only a few moments. 'I have come from America to find him. I have been travelling and searching for over a month now.'

Manon sat very still. Falida and Badou came back from the house, and again Badou climbed into his mother's lap. He leaned against her chest and, as before, his mother didn't touch him. In spite of her stillness, I felt that beneath her calm exterior was a great deal of fire.

'You look hot, and perhaps a bit ill. Are you not well, Mademoiselle . . . what did you say your name was?' Her eyes suddenly left my face, running down my body.

I took a deep breath. 'O'Shea. Sidonie O'Shea,' I said, something painful in my chest, for at that moment I realised she didn't know who I was. That meant that either Etienne truly wasn't here, or, if he was, he hadn't mentioned me. 'You don't know who I am,' I said, stating what was now obvious.

'How could I? You are a stranger, from America, arriving at my door, unexpected and unannounced, speaking of my brother.'

I swallowed. 'I am Etienne's . . .' What to call myself? 'I am his fiancée,' I said then. 'We were to be married,' I added, unnecessarily.

At that, Manon's expression changed. She no longer looked curious. Something dark came over her face, and her hands clenched once, and then loosened. She spoke to Falida in Arabic. Badou rose without question, and Falida took his hand. They went through the gate, shutting it behind them with a clang.

'So you are Etienne's lover?' Manon asked, her voice toneless.

'I . . . I said I was his fiancée.'

'And why have you come to me, Sidonie O'Shea?'

I pulled the single page, now tearing slightly along the delicate creases, from my handbag. 'Your letter to Etienne.'

She glanced at the paper in my hands, then back to my face. 'A man leaves you, and you find an old letter, and you travel so far to find him?'

I hadn't said, specifically, that he'd left me, although it was an evident observation. I looked down at the thin sheet of paper. 'There is . . . there was more to it.'

'Mademoiselle. There is always more to it for the woman.'

We sat in silence. The heat was intense; it was almost as though I could hear it fluttering, like a flock of tiny birds, or perhaps butterflies, around my ears. Finally I looked back at Manon. 'He isn't here?'

She shook her head.

'Do you know where he is?'

At that, she studied me for so long—the silence stretching and stretching—that I felt one bead of sweat run down my temple and along my jaw. Finally she nodded.

I took a deep, shaky breath. 'Is he here, in Marrakesh?'

Again the wait, and then she shrugged. 'Perhaps.'

What was wrong with her? Why was she playing this silly game with me? I stood and walked the few steps to where she sat. I looked down at her. 'Madame Maliki,' I said, my voice hard. 'Do you not understand how important it is that I find Etienne?'

Now she rose as well. 'It's impossible for me to say, right now, where he is. Impossible,' she said. 'The fates are not correct. I can't speak to you any further right now. You will have to leave.'

'But . . . no. I can't leave until you tell me about Etienne. I have come so far to . . .'

At that she moved right in front of me. Her face was close enough for me to see her pupils, dilating. 'You will leave. This is my home, and you will leave when I tell you to leave. You have no right to be here.'

'Madame Maliki,' I said, quietly now. It was clear she wished to antagonise me, to challenge or frighten me. It was also clear she would tell me nothing at this moment. 'Perhaps tomorrow will be a better day to speak of this. Tell me when you wish me to come.'

I had been right. Her expression changed, and I knew it was because I had become submissive, acquiescing, and this pleased her. For an unknown reason she needed to wield some power over me, and I had no alternative but to bow to her wishes.

Finally she met my eyes. 'All right. You may come at two o'clock. Not before. Do you understand? Not before two.'

I moved my head in one slow nod, then went through the gate and down the alley. When I got to the end of it a small voice said, 'Mademoiselle.' I peered into a dark recess in the long wall and saw Badou and Falida, sitting on the ground in a niche. Each of them held a kitten. I would have passed by them if Badou hadn't spoken.

He held up the kitten.

'How old are you?'

'*Six ans*,' he said.

I had thought him to be five at the oldest. 'And your sister?' I asked, looking at her. 'How old are you, Falida?'

She didn't answer, but Badou did. 'Falida's not my sister. She's our maid.'

I looked at the girl's bruised arm and bloodshot, swollen eye.

'There are always kittens here,' Badou said. 'The mother cats live in there.' He pointed to a low hole in the wall. He stroked the kitten gently.

He was Etienne's nephew. Did I see something of Etienne in him? Maybe the long neck, the serious expression. I thought of my child, and wondered if he or she would have looked like this little boy.

'Do you like kittens?' he asked, and I nodded again. Then I drew in a deep breath, and walked away from Sharia Zitoun.

Chapter Eight

MANON HAD TOLD ME I shouldn't come to the house on Sharia Zitoun until two o'clock, but it was ten minutes to one when I knocked.

The heavy door was pulled back by Falida. I nodded at her, and she lowered her head in a submissive reflex. Today the courtyard wasn't jumbled with furniture, but held a long day bed with a thick, bright cover, an assortment of cork stools, and a low round table, all arranged in an orderly manner. Badou was walking around the edge of the empty fountain, balancing with outstretched arms. He jumped down and came to me as Falida shut the heavy gate.

'*Bonjour*, Badou,' I said.

'*Bonjour*, mademoiselle,' he said, holding out his little hand. '*Venez*. Come. Maman is inside.'

I looked down at his hand, surprised by the unexpected gesture. I took it, and together we crossed the courtyard.

We stood in the doorway, and the first thing I was aware of was a strong, sweet, smoky odour. I blinked, trying to focus in the dimness after the brilliance of the sunshine in the courtyard.

'Mademoiselle O'Shea.' Manon's voice was sharp. 'I specified you were not to come until two o'clock. You are too early.'

I couldn't see her in the darkened room.

'Madame Maliki. Please. I won't stay long; all I wish is for you—'

'Badou. Open the shutters,' she interrupted, and Badou took his hand from mine and ran to open one of the tall wooden shutters that faced the courtyard. Louvred lines of light illuminated a long, narrow room furnished with day beds, several camel-hide ottomans and a low table of intricately carved wood. There was a thick, rich-looking rug of red and blue and black, and tall mirrors leaning against two walls.

And then I saw them: the paintings on one wall. There were at least ten, unframed oils of various sizes. All were in violent colours, with disregard to smaller details, as though the images had come straight from the palette to the canvas with no structure or careful reflection. And yet there was a raw beauty that could be created only by one with a natural talent.

'I did not expect such inconsideration,' Manon said, her words followed by a deep inhalation. She was underneath the paintings on a green velvet day bed, a long curling tube in one hand. It was attached to a container like the *sheeshas*, the huge bubbling contraptions I had seen in Tangier. She exhaled, and a long line of smoke came from her mouth.

Badou left the windows and sat beside her.

'I apologise, Madame Maliki,' I said. 'But certainly you can understand my need to find out about Etienne. It was difficult to wait, as you asked, but now I'm here, please tell me where I can find him. Or anything that you know of his whereabouts.'

She wore a kaftan of green and orange silk, and another type of Moroccan overdress—a *dfina*. It was soft green, and had slits in the sides that allowed the skirt of the kaftan to be exhibited.

'Please make your way out, Mademoiselle O'Shea,' Manon said now. 'And fetch my bag, Badou.'

I stayed where I was while the child ran to a chest against the wall and returned with a decorated cloth bag. He gave it to his mother and then sat cross-legged on the floor at her feet.

Manon stared at me, but I didn't move. She raised one shoulder in a nonchalant shrug, and I knew I had won this very small battle. She drew a comb, a mirror and some vials from the bag. In silence, she slowly combed through her long, shining hair, but left it hanging loose. She applied rouge to her cheeks and lips. Then she dug once more into the bag, taking out what I knew, from seeing them in the shops in the French Quarter, to be a wood *merroud* containing kohl.

I wanted to shout at Manon, to shake her, to force her somehow to tell me about Etienne. But I knew it would do no good.

She would tell me what she wanted, when she wanted.

'My kohl is special,' Manon said, the *merroud* in one hand and the mirror in the other. As she outlined her eyes, she started to sing, her voice low and rich, '*I will make my eyes the moons in a dark sky. I will madden men with desire; one man or many. All will desire me*.' She looked away from her reflection, and straight into my eyes.

'Has any man ever been mad with desire for you, Mademoiselle O'Shea?' she asked then. Her voice held a sarcastic tone.

I didn't reply. I had told her I was Etienne's fiancée. Was it so impossible for her to believe he desired me? 'And your husband, Madame Maliki? He's at work?' I asked, partly because she angered me, and also because somehow I knew that she wouldn't like me questioning her.

I was correct. Her face changed again, her eyes narrowing.

'I will not ask—demand—again that you leave,' she told me. 'You may return in an hour. And consider yourself lucky that I will see you at all, in spite of how you have angered me.'

'Madame Maliki,' I said, exasperated. 'What difference does one hour make? Can't you simply—'

'Manon?'

We all turned to the doorway. A man stood there; he was so tall that his turban brushed the lintel. He wore a dark-blue cotton jellaba with yellow embroidery at the neck. The deep purple-blue turban was wrapped around his head and neck, one end of it tucked over his nose and mouth. Because of the light behind him I couldn't see his eyes. He carried a basket under one arm.

I immediately remembered the man on the *piste*. L'Homme Bleu.

Badou ran to him, first kissing the man's hand in the Arabic gesture of respect for an elder, and then winding his arms around the man's leg. 'Oncle Aszulay,' he said.

Uncle, I thought. But Etienne was his uncle. Why did he call this man uncle as well? He must be Manon's husband's brother.

I glanced at Manon; she was smiling at the man in a coquettish way. Suddenly I knew that Manon didn't want me here because she was waiting for this man. Her lover.

'*Assalaam alykum*, Badou,' the man said, greeting Badou in Arabic, smiling warmly at him and smoothing his hair. He set down the basket and looked at us.

Manon, no longer smiling, said, offhandedly, 'This is Mademoiselle O'Shea. But she is leaving now.'

The tall man studied me for a moment, then solemnly bowed his head. 'Good afternoon, Mademoiselle O'Shea,' he said, his French quite clear, but with a strong accent of his mother tongue—Arabic, I assumed.

'Good afternoon, Monsieur . . .' I hesitated.

'I am Aszulay, mademoiselle,' he said simply. He stepped out of his *babouches* before entering the room, and once across the threshold pulled down the end of his turban, uncovering his face. Then he unwrapped it from his head, pushing it down so that it encircled his neck. His head wasn't shaved in the way of the Arab men I'd seen throughout the souks, but was thick and wavy, very black. His eyes were a surprising blue.

'Falida,' Aszulay said, 'take the food into the kitchen and set it out for the meal in the courtyard where it is cooler.'

The girl took the heavy basket and lugged it across the room.

'You join us to eat, mademoiselle?' Aszulay asked.

'No,' Manon said, 'she will not stay. She is going now.'

'We are hospitable, Manon,' Aszulay said, in a firm voice. 'When a guest arrives we offer tea and food.' He said this patiently, as he might to Badou. Then to me, he said, 'You must stay, Miss O'Shea. Hospitality is the Moroccan way, ' as if he were indeed the master of the house.

I nodded and as we moved to the courtyard, I saw how completely at ease he was with Manon, putting a cushion behind her to make her comfortable, tousling Badou's hair.

Aszulay had an attractiveness that was due not only to his features, but from within. He didn't treat me with anything like the curious or disapproving attitude of the other men of Morocco. He treated me and, I saw, Manon, with a distinctly European air. And his French was formal, the grammar close to perfect.

Manon was watching Aszulay with what I could interpret only as a sultry look. Although he didn't respond, I knew this man was Manon's lover. Certainly. There was no doubt.

L'Homme Bleu. Again I thought of the man in blue robes on the *piste*, appearing out of nowhere and trading the tile for bread. How he had intrigued me, with his height and his direct stare, his slow walk of dignity and grace, disappearing down the dusty track as mysteriously as he had appeared.

Falida returned carrying a tagine—the large round earthenware plate with its high, cone-shaped cover to trap the steam. She then brought a circular brass tray that held a heaping platter of flat round bread, a teapot, three painted glasses in tin holders and four small porcelain bowls of water with a slice of lemon floating in each.

She set everything on the round table, then filled the three glasses with tea, before backing away from the table to run into the house.

'Please. Drink,' Aszulay said.

I nodded, taking a cautious mouthful—the familiar mint and so much sugar, as always—and set it down.

Aszulay didn't speak, but appeared relaxed as he sipped his tea. For me, the silence was too large. 'What is it you do in Marrakesh?' I asked.

He swallowed his mouthful of tea and said, 'I dig, and plant trees, and flowers in La Ville Nouvelle.'

'I'm staying at Hôtel de la Palmeraie. In La Ville Nouvelle.'

'*Bien entendu*,' Aszulay said. 'Naturally. It is very . . . it is luxurious.'

I nodded.

'I'm working in the garden of Monsieur Majorelle,' he said. 'But many days I bring the midday meal for Manon and Badou.'

'I went to Le Jardin Majorelle.'

He was a Blue Man of the Sahara, working as a gardener, and yet he spoke and carried himself with a sophisticated air.

I shook my head slightly, annoyed that I was having these thoughts. I was also annoyed at having to sit here, actually attempting to eat and drink and act as a polite guest. To wait for Manon to bestow me with information when and if she felt the time was right.

Aszulay took the lid off the tagine and gestured at it, looking at me now. It was a pyramid of couscous with long slices of carrots and a green vegetable—courgette?—arranged up its sides. Bubbling pieces of chicken poked from within the couscous.

'Please,' Aszulay said to me. 'As the honoured guest. Begin.'

There was no cutlery, no plates to put the food upon.

'May I eat, Oncle Aszulay?' Badou said. 'I am very hungry.'

Aszulay looked at me; surely my face portrayed my confusion. 'No, Badou. You know we must wait for our guest.'

'Please, Badou,' I said, 'please eat.'

Badou glanced at Aszulay, and he nodded. The little boy scooped up some of the couscous with the fingers of his right hand, kneading it until it was a small ball, and then put it in his mouth. Aszulay tore a thin round of bread in half and, folding it, used it to spoon the couscous into his mouth.

I suspected he had seen that I didn't know how to eat in the Moroccan way, and so was showing me. I was thankful to him for not embarrassing me further, and took a piece of bread and used it as he did. The couscous was delicious, and I realised I had eaten nothing today, and little the day before. Suddenly I was very hungry, and scooped up more of the couscous. When Aszulay picked up a chicken leg with his fingers, I reached into the hot couscous and extracted a thigh.

'For the Moroccan, the fork is unnecessary,' Aszulay said, and I looked at him, still thankful for his understanding, and saw that Manon was staring at me with open antagonism. She didn't like him paying any attention to me. She was jealous.

'Manon,' Aszulay said, turning to her. 'Eat. You love *les courgettes*.'

Manon looked at the long slices of courgette, but shook her head weakly. 'I cannot,' she whispered. 'I'm not well today. It's not a good day for me.' She sighed, an overdone sigh.

'Do you promise to eat later?'

'Yes, Aszulay,' she said, demurely.

When we were done, we rinsed our fingers in the cool lemon water, and then Badou went back to the fountain and once more walked carefully around its narrow edge, his arms out for balance.

'So,' Manon said, at last. 'What do you think of my Tuareg?'

I ran my finger around the rim of my tea glass. Aszulay said nothing.

'You know of the Tuaregs? The Abandoned of God, the Arabs call them, because no one can impose a will on them. They obey no laws in the desert. Aszulay obeys no laws anywhere, do you?' she asked him.

Again, he didn't answer, nor did his face show any expression.

'His name is a Berber Amazigh name. It means *man with blue eyes*. Quite unusual, aren't they?' she went on, still staring at me.

How was I to respond?

'How do you know Manon, mademoiselle?' Aszulay asked.

I licked my lips, glancing at her, and set my empty glass on the table. 'I've come in search of Manon's brother,' I said.

Aszulay's face became very still. 'You're looking for Etienne?'

I stood so quickly the edge of my skirt knocked my glass to the tiles of the courtyard. It shattered. 'You know him?' I asked, moving around the table. He stood; I had to look up to study his face. 'You know Etienne? Is he here? Where is he? Please, where is Etienne?'

'Mademoiselle O'Shea,' he said. 'Are you—'

Now Manon stood as well. 'Leave us, Aszulay,' she said, her voice loud and firm, suddenly changed from the weak woman she had appeared throughout the meal. 'I will speak to her about it.'

About it, she said. Not *him*.

'Mademoiselle O'Shea,' Aszulay said again. 'Etienne—'

Again Manon stopped him. 'Aszulay!' she said, her voice harsh. 'This is my home. You will do as I say.'

So. She spoke to him the same way she had spoken to me.

He opened his mouth as if to argue, then closed it. He grabbed up the long expanse of indigo cloth from the end of the day bed—his turban—and strode across the courtyard, his blue robe flashing behind him as he went through the gate. It closed behind him with a bang.

'Falida, Badou. Take the dishes and wash them,' Manon ordered.

I stayed where I was. When the children had carried away the dishes and glasses, Manon patted the day bed. 'Come. Sit beside me,' she said, 'so I can tell you where you will find Etienne.'

Swallowing, I did as she asked, and as soon as I was beside her she picked up my hand. 'So small,' she said, stroking it. 'Your hands tell me you have worked, but not so hard, eh, Sidonie?' I noticed her use of my Christian name. 'The way I have worked just to survive.'

I thought of what Etienne had told me of his upbringing. 'But . . . Etienne said his life was one of privilege.'

When she didn't respond, I said, 'And you have this house. To live like this . . . surely your life can't have been so difficult—'

She made a sound with her tongue against the roof of her mouth, shushing me, and I fell silent. 'I have not always had the luxury of this kind of home,' she said, confusing me. She ran her own fingers over the raised bump on my middle finger, and the callus on my palm where my paintbrush had rubbed for so many years.

'What is this from?' she asked.

'A paintbrush,' I said.

She smiled that awful smile. 'It grows ever more interesting.'

'What? What do you mean?'

After another endless moment she said, 'But you saw my paintings.'

It took a moment for her meaning to register. 'In the house? Those . . . you painted those?' My voice rose a half-tone.

Another mystery. Etienne had grown up with a sister who painted, and yet had never mentioned this fact to me.

'How did you learn to paint like this? Was it in France?'

'In France, Sidonie?' Manon gave a croak that was perhaps meant to be a laugh. 'In France?' she repeated, as though amused.

'But Etienne—his schooling in medicine. And Guillaume . . . Yes, I assumed you had, as well . . .' Again my voice faded as I saw the expression on Manon's face. She was no longer amused now, but angry.

'Of course I didn't study in France.' Her tone implied I was an idiot. And then she suddenly smiled again. I shivered. 'Now tell me about your paintings.'

'Please. Can we not—'

'But I insist. We are having a nice friendly chat. You tell me what I want to know, and then I'll tell you what you want to know.'

'I don't paint like you. I use watercolours. I paint plants. Birds.'

'So Etienne liked his little American *souris* to make pretty pictures?' There was a mocking tone in her voice.

I wanted to shout at her, *I am not a mouse! How dare you?* Instead I said, as calmly as possible, 'Yes. Etienne liked my paintings.'

'He *liked* your paintings? You think he liked such tame subjects? What do you think he thought of my work?'

I shook my head. 'I don't know. And I don't know why you're so angry with me. I made your brother happy, madame. Don't you want him to be happy?'

Manon sat back, her grip on my hand lessening but not releasing. 'Etienne is no more, Sidonie. He does not live. He is buried in the cemetery behind Eglise des Saints Martyrs.'

'You can't mean this, Manon.' I used her first name without thinking. My head moved swiftly from side to side, as if by its motion I could erase her words. I violently yanked my hand from hers. 'It's not true. It's not true,' I repeated, shaking her. 'Tell me Etienne isn't dead!'

She nodded, no longer smiling, but staring at me, her eyes, ringed with kohl, huge. I couldn't look away from them. I couldn't catch my breath; it came in great rolling heaves, and Manon's form thinned and wavered. I stared at her, choking now, while she simply sat, nodding, holding me with her eyes.

I don't remember how I found my way back to Hôtel de la Palmeraie. I lay on my bed, a handkerchief pressed against my face. *He's dead*, I thought, over and over. *Etienne is dead. He's dead.*

My eyes and throat and head ached as I thought of my lost baby, and of never again seeing Etienne. Flat on my back, rocking with my arms around myself, a low keening came, unbidden, from my mouth. How had Etienne died? Had he called out for me as he lay dying, or had he died so quickly that there was no time for even a word to pass his lips?

Now I would never know why he had left me. I relived the hours I had wrestled with my choices in Marseilles: to travel on to Marrakesh or return home. But I had made the decision to find some answers.

And now I had. I had an answer. It wasn't why he had left me. But it was an answer, a terrible, and totally unexpected answer.

I didn't think I would sleep, but the morning sun on my face woke me. I lay still for mere seconds, before the memory of what had happened the day before came back with a hard rush.

'Etienne is dead,' I said, aloud. 'Etienne is dead.' *Dead.*

I lay on the bed all day, watching the sun move across the room. I stayed there, not bathing, not drinking or eating. Once someone tapped on my door and I called out for them to go away. I watched the shadows lengthen and turn to darkness.

When the sun again shone through the windows, I was suddenly immensely thirsty. I wanted fresh orange juice. I rose and tugged the bell cord to call one of the staff.

Within a few moments there was a quiet knock on the door.

I opened the door to instruct the boy to bring me a pitcher of orange juice. But it was Monsieur Henri.

'Mademoiselle,' he said, looking, for the first time since I'd seen him, flustered. 'There appears to be a very uncomfortable situation. In the lobby. There is a man,' he said. 'A man who says he knows you.'

My legs suddenly felt as though they might give way. 'Monsieur Duverger?' I cried out. 'Is it Etienne Duverger?'

'I assure you, Mademoiselle O'Shea, that it is not this Monsieur Duverger you speak of. It is . . . an Arab. An Arab with his child.'

I blinked. 'An Arab?'

'Yes. I assured him that we, at Hôtel de la Palmeraie, are not in the habit of allowing non-European men into the hotel, let alone upstairs to the rooms. He insisted I come to speak to you. He was . . .' He stopped. 'He was rather menacing in his insistence. He has brought you something. Food.' He drew back. 'It's quite unacceptable. I told him that if you were hungry you would order from our extensive menu. But he stood there—and is standing there, I'm sure, as we speak—with a tagine and the child. And although fortunately, at this time of day, not many of our guests are about, I—'

'You may send them up, Monsieur Henri,' I said, and his eyes widened, but I didn't care.

'Are you certain, mademoiselle? The safety of our guests is—'

Again I interrupted. 'I can assure you that there is absolutely no reason for your concern. Please allow them up to my room. And also have a pitcher of orange juice sent up.' It wasn't my voice speaking. It was someone else's, someone who wouldn't be trifled with.

'As you wish, mademoiselle,' he said, and then, without the courtesy of a goodbye, turned and walked down the hallway, his back stiff.

I picked up my dress from the floor, where it lay in a crumpled heap, and put it on. I jammed my bare feet into my shoes, leaving them undone, but had no energy to attempt to comb through my hair.

Within moments there was another knock on the door. I opened it to Aszulay and Badou. Aszulay carried a tagine.

'Aszulay. And Badou,' I said, as if they didn't know their own names. 'What . . . why have you come?'

Aszulay studied me. I was aware of how I looked, my eyes red and swollen, my hair a disgusting tangle.

'What's wrong with your eyes, Sidonie,' Badou said. 'They—' Aszulay put his free hand on the boy's head, and the child was immediately quiet.

'I thought perhaps . . .' Aszulay said, and then stopped, as if unsure how to continue. 'Yesterday Badou told me . . . he said that the day before you had cried out, and fallen to the ground. He came to you, but you only stared at him, without speaking. Then you got up and . . . left the courtyard. I knew then that Manon had deeply upset you. I'm sorry for what she had to tell you. About Etienne.'

There was silence. I had cried out, fallen? Finally I looked at the tagine and said, 'Thank you. But . . . I think it's better if I'm alone at this time. But thank you, Aszulay,' I repeated. 'And thank you, Badou.'

Aszulay nodded. He still had his hand on Badou's head. He took it off and set the tagine on the floor just inside the door. A lovely smell rose from it—lamb and apricots. Rosemary. 'Come, Badou.'

I knew Badou had expected to share the meal with me. Even in the short time I had been in Morocco, I understood its hospitality, and how utterly rude—no matter what my mood—I appeared.

'Wait,' I said, and they both turned. 'No, no. Of course, you must come in and eat with me.' At that moment a boy appeared behind them with a carafe of orange juice and a glass on a silver tray.

'You may put the juice on the table, and fetch two more glasses, for my guests,' I told him.

He nodded, putting down the tray and leaving.

'Come in,' I said to Aszulay and Badou, 'come in, and sit.' I picked up the tagine and set it on the table beside the juice. Aszulay and I sat on the two chairs, Badou on Aszulay's lap.

I took the lid from the tagine. Steam and the fragrant aroma rose into the air. 'Please, eat. I . . . I don't know if I can,' I said, and Aszulay and Badou put their fingers into the dish and ate.

Once again, to me the silence, as Aszulay and Badou ate, was uncomfortable, but they didn't seem aware of it.

The boy returned and set down two more glasses.

'I have only a few hours—simple work—at the gardens today. I will take Badou with me,' Aszulay said, when they had finished.

I nodded, distractedly.

'Perhaps you would like to join us.'

'No,' I answered immediately. Did Aszulay not realise what I was going through? 'I don't . . . I . . .' Tears came to my eyes, and I turned my head so that he wouldn't see them.

'It's a difficult time. I understand,' he said, standing. 'I'm sorry you have come all this way only to be disappointed. Come, Badou.' He held out his hand to the child.

'His death is far more than a disappointment,' I said, quietly.

At this Aszulay turned his head sharply. 'His death?' he repeated.

I looked at him, and something in his expression made me catch my breath. 'Yes,' I said, still staring at him.

'But . . . Mademoiselle O'Shea,' he said. 'Etienne . . . he's not dead.'

I couldn't breathe. 'But . . .' I covered my mouth with my hand, then took it away and looked back at Aszulay. 'Manon . . . she said . . .' I stopped. 'She said Etienne was dead. Buried, in the cemetery.'

In the silence, Aszulay and I stared at each other.

'It's not true?' I finally whispered, and Aszulay shook his head.

'Tell me the truth, Aszulay. Just tell me what's happened to Etienne. If he's not dead, where is he?'

Aszulay didn't speak for a long moment. 'It's not my business,' he finally said. 'It's between you and Etienne, you and Manon. Between Manon and Etienne. It's not my business,' he repeated. 'But for Manon to . . .' He didn't finish the sentence.

I reached across the table and put my hand on his forearm. It was hard and warm under his blue sleeve. 'But why? Why would Manon do this to me, lie like this? Why does she not want me to be with Etienne? Why would she go to this length—to announce him dead?'

Aszulay looked at Badou then, and I looked as well. He had seen and heard far too much, I knew. Not just today, but all his short life.

'She has deep unhappiness within her,' Aszulay said. 'The reasons are hers alone. I don't know why she told you this.'

'And what is the truth, then? Where is Etienne?'

'Etienne was here, in Marrakesh. He stayed with Manon for perhaps two weeks. Then he left. Left Manon, and left Marrakesh.'

'Did he go back to America?' Could I have passed him, missed him as he journeyed one way and I the other?

'No. He said he would remain in Morocco, now that . . .' He stopped, looking at Badou again. 'Perhaps we can speak of this another time.' He took Badou's hand and left.

The rest of the day passed in a strange twilight. I alternately lay on the bed or sat at the table, looking out the window. I wanted to rush back to Manon's house, to confront her, to demand that she tell me the truth. And yet I was filled with an odd exhaustion. Only a few days ago, upon meeting Manon, I had been filled with hope at finding Etienne. Then Manon had told me he was dead, and I despaired. And now . . . according to what Aszulay had told me—and I believed him over Manon—Etienne wasn't dead, but alive, somewhere in Morocco.

I was no closer to finding him, no closer to understanding why he had abandoned me, without telling me why. But something had shifted. Something very small. I had grieved for Etienne, convinced he was dead. Something in me had gone cold. Was missing. And finding out he was still alive hadn't brought it back.

Next morning, I went again to Sharia Zitoun. Badou was in the courtyard, playing with a yellow pup with white paws and one ragged ear.

'*Bonjour*, Badou,' I said, after Falida let me in and went back to listlessly sweeping the courtyard. 'Where is your mother?' I asked him.

'She's sleeping,' he said, cradling the little dog against his chest. 'Look at my dog.'

I sat down on the wide edge of the fountain. 'Is he yours, really?' I asked, and Badou shook his head.

'*Non*,' he admitted, sadly. 'He belongs to Ali, across the lane. Sometimes Ali lets me play with him. But I would like him to be mine.'

I thought of Cinnabar, and the comfort she had brought me, even though I had been ten years older than Badou when she came into my life. 'I know,' I said. 'Maybe one day your *maman* will get you a dog.'

But Badou shook his head again. He put down the dog and came to stand in front of me. 'Maman said no. She said I can never have one, and not to ask any more.'

'But it's good that you can play with this little dog,' I said.

I studied his features as he played with the dog. I saw Etienne again: this look, right now, of intensity.

'Sidonie, I do not like your *dar*,' he suddenly said.

'You don't like my house?' I said. Basic Arabic words were becoming familiar to me now.

'Yes. I do not like it,' he repeated. 'It's too big, with too many people. And they do not love you,' he added, gravely.

'Oh, Badou, that's not my house. It's a hotel,' I said, realising, as I spoke, that he didn't understand the word. 'Not my house. I'm staying there for only a short while. And the people aren't my family.'

'Who are they?'

I shrugged. 'I don't know them. Strangers.'

'You live with strangers?' His eyes grew even wider. 'But where is your mother, and your father? Where are your children?' Badou already understood the Moroccan importance of family. In spite of the coldness of his mother, he spoke of love.

Perhaps he read something, some small and subtle thing, in my expression. He then added, so casually and yet with such weight, in the way of a child who knows too much of the world, too early, 'Dead?'

There was only one way to respond to a child like Badou. I nodded, slowly. 'Yes. They are all dead.'

Badou came to me then, climbing onto my lap as I had seen him do with his mother and with Aszulay. He laid his cheek against mine.

I couldn't speak, but simply put my arms around his small back. I moved my fingers to feel his ribs, and then the faint bumps of his vertebrae. At my touch he relaxed into my lap, so easily. The yellow pup settled at my feet, lying on its side on the smooth, warm stones. Falida continued her languid sweeping, the sound of the soft broom a rhythmic lull. We sat in the dappled light of the courtyard, Badou's head under my chin, and waited for Manon to awaken.

Eventually footsteps came down the courtyard steps; I braced myself, ready to face her.

But it wasn't Manon. A man, his dark-blond hair roughly smoothed across his forehead and his face shadowed by the night's whiskers, looked as surprised to see me as I was to see him. He was quite handsome, and wore a well-cut, although rumpled suit of cream linen, and carried his wide-brimmed hat.

'Oh. Madame,' he said, stopping halfway down the stairs. 'Good day.'

'Good day,' I responded.

'Manon is waiting for her morning tea. I don't think she's aware she has a visitor,' he said. 'Shall I tell—'

'No,' I interrupted. Too many things were swirling through my head. This man had obviously spent the night here. Was he her husband, then? No. He couldn't be. As the man had come down the stairs, Badou had jumped off my lap and was now pointedly petting the dog, his back to the man. And what of Aszulay? 'I'll wait here for her,' I said.

'As you wish,' he said, bowing slightly at the waist, and then left the courtyard. He had completely ignored Badou.

As the gate closed behind him, Badou ran upstairs. I heard his high, clear little voice telling his mother I was in the courtyard.

'What does she want?' Manon responded, her voice cranky.

'I don't know, Maman,' he said. 'Maman, her papa and mama, her children, they're all dead.'

There was rustling. 'She doesn't deserve a family,' Manon said, shocking me, not only because of her open resentment towards me, but because it was a terrible thing to say to a child.

'Manon!' I called, rising from the edge of the fountain before she could say anything more to him. 'I must speak to you.'

'You will wait until I'm ready,' she said. I had no choice but to sit down again, and wait until she appeared at the top of the stairs.

Finally she descended slowly, as if she had all the time in the world. She wore only a loose, almost diaphanous kaftan; I could clearly see the slender and yet curvaceous outline of her body through it as the light touched her. Her hair was uncombed, and her kohl was smeared around her eyes. Her lips were puffy, as though slightly bruised.

As I watched her come down the stairs with such studied nonchalance, I wanted to pull her hair, to slap her. I wanted to shout at her that she was a liar, and a deceitful person not worthy of her beautiful little son, her gracious home. Not worthy of Aszulay, who treated her and Badou with such consideration. Did he know she deceived him?

But I didn't do or say anything. I stayed on the edge of the fountain, my hands gripping each other, my mouth a tight line.

She seated herself on the day bed, and called, sharply, to Falida, and the girl hurried out, carrying a tray with a teapot and one glass, rounds of bread and a bowl of something that looked like dark jam. She set it on the low table. Badou, moving almost stealthily, had come down the steps and now sat beside his mother.

'Did you see my man, Sidonie? The charming Olivier?'

I didn't respond, staring at her.

'You look poorly, Sidonie,' Manon said now, as if it pleased her. 'Pale, and shaken. Not well at all.' There was the hint of a smile on her lips. She first took a sip of tea, then spread a spoonful of the fruity substance on the bread and bit into it.

'How do you expect me to appear, after what you told me?' I didn't attempt to keep the anger from my voice. 'Manon. Did you think I wouldn't find out about your lie? That I would simply believe you, and quietly leave Marrakesh?' Of course that was what I would have done, had Aszulay not told me the truth. 'What kind of cruel game were you playing with me? And why?'

Manon's mouth worked at the bread and jam. She swallowed. 'I have had many things to survive in my life. Many things,' she repeated. 'My level of unhappiness far surpasses anything you might ever feel.' She lifted her chin as if daring me to argue, then glanced at Badou. 'Go away,' she told him.

Badou crossed the courtyard and went out the gate, making kissing sounds to call the pup.

'Etienne would not have married you,' she said. 'So I thought it easier that you believed him dead. Then you would go home and put your silly dreams out of your head.'

She didn't fool me. She would never have thought of making it easier for me, of doing what she did out of perverted kindness.

'How do you know he wouldn't marry me?' I knew he hadn't discussed me with her, or she would have known who I was when I first came to her door.

'Etienne would not marry because he would not wish to father a child,' she said, with a distinctly goading look.

I swallowed. 'Why do you say that?'

Now she sat back and smiled. There was a tiny blob of the red jam in the corner of her mouth; she licked it off. '*Majoun*,' she said, taking another spoonful from the bowl. 'Do you like *majoun*, Sidonie?' she asked, the spoon in midair.

'I don't know what it is, and I don't care,' I said.

'Cannabis cooked with fruit and sugar and spices,' she said, eating the spoonful without even bothering to put it on bread. 'I give it to Badou, to make him sleep. When I need him to sleep,' she added, and I thought of her entertaining the man the night before.

I was so sickened by her that I stood. 'I came here today hoping you would give me the truth about how to find Etienne. And that perhaps I would also uncover the reason for your behaviour towards me,' I said. 'I should have known there's no explanation. You're simply spiteful.'

She rose, facing me. 'I lied to you because I can. Because it gave me pleasure to see you cry out, to see you so weak. You and Etienne made a good pair. He's weak, like you. He didn't even tell you, did he, about his illness.' It was a statement, not a question.

'His illness?' *But it had been his father who had been so ill.*

Manon sat again, pouring herself another glass of tea and then leaning back and languidly crossing one leg over the other. 'He had only the earliest signs, but can you really tell yourself you didn't see it?'

I envisioned Etienne at the hospital, and then at my home. Small, unimportant images flashed through my mind: the way he sometimes dropped his fork or knife with an unexpected clatter on to the table, his occasional trips over the edges of carpets. I thought of the empty pill bottle I'd found in his room, the medication that could be taken for palsy.

'Etienne inherited everything from our father,' she said. 'I was left nothing. But now I'm glad, for along with his wealth, Marcel Duverger left his son something else.'

I felt behind me for the stool, and lowered myself to it.

'Our father also left Etienne the jinns he carried in his body. The disease that killed him will now kill Etienne. But not for a long time. First he will suffer, as our father suffered.' She smiled, a calm, slow smile. Her voice was bitter. 'This house,' she waved one arm in front of her, 'was bought for me by Etienne, before he left for America. But it wasn't enough. There will never be enough to even the score. I was glad when my father died, and now I'm glad Etienne will suffer in the same way. He's welcome to the inheritance, and now he will live with it until it kills him. The jinns travel from parent to child. Father to son. There is only one way to prevent the disease. Only one. Etienne was very despondent, Sidonie, when he came here.'

'Of course,' I stated. 'He realised his future.'

'Yes. But also something else. He told me he had failed.'

'Failed?'

'He told me about you. I know everything, Sidonie.'

I blinked. So she had known who I was from the first time I came to her door. But why had she pretended she knew nothing about me?

'He told me about the child.'

I instinctively put my hands to my abdomen, and her eyes followed.

'I saw with the first glance there was no child. Foolish woman. You wanted Etienne to marry you, and so you lied to trap him. But the trap caught you. Because of your lie, you lost him. He came here because I wanted him to. Unlike you, I could get Etienne to do my bidding. But you had driven him away anyway. The only sure way for the jinns to die, he told me when he came, was for those possessing them never to procreate. Within a generation it would have disappeared. *Just one generation, Manon*, he told me. That's all it would take.'

Light fell in soft shafts through the leaves, shimmering across Manon's face, making it look as though waves passed over it. Her pupils were huge, perhaps an effect of the *majoun*.

'So, Sidonie, in essence you pushed Etienne away when he thought you would produce a child who might carry the jinns. Because he realised he was a hypocrite.'

I thought about Etienne's face when he learned I was pregnant. About his expression, which I had presumed to be shock, but now, with Manon's words, thought, suddenly, could have been panic.

I thought of the child we had created, half-me and half-him. Etienne knew there was a chance that he had passed on the gene, as his father had to him. He had seen the child we had created possibly as one of nature's aberrations, a mistake.

'You were just a diversion, a plaything for a short time,' Manon said now. 'He had no intentions of anything serious. He told me this himself.'

'There *was* a baby, Manon. And I lost it—before arriving in Tangier.' I didn't care if she believed me or not. 'If he had felt so strongly about this, about not procreating, he wouldn't have been with me. Nobody forced him.' I hated the way my voice faltered on the last sentence.

She waved one hand dismissively in the air. 'He was a man, Sidonie. He grew lonely for a woman, and acted on impulse. He had planned to have the procedure he said was the answer—the sterilisation—when he finished his year at the hospital in America. But he grew impatient. And he knew you were a safe bet, naive and inexperienced.'

But Etienne was not the kind of man she described. He had loved me. I knew I couldn't count on Manon for any truths. Etienne was protecting me. I needed to tell him I was strong enough; I could live with his disease. I would marry him, and stay at his side. He could put his fears to rest.

I was done with Manon. She would continue only to lie and confuse me. She wouldn't tell me anything about Etienne's return. There was only one other person in Marrakesh who could help me now.

I took a *calèche* to Le Jardin Majorelle. I saw three men in white clothing, digging in one of the flowerbeds close to the entrance. The middle one was Aszulay.

'Aszulay,' I said. 'Please. May I talk to you? It's about Etienne. I . . . I need . . .' I stopped, closing my mouth. What did I need?

The other two men watched as Aszulay stepped over the piles of red earth and came towards me. 'Please, Mademoiselle O'Shea,' he said, 'go and sit there, in the shade. I'll finish here soon. Wait for me.'

After some time, he left his shovel standing in a pile of earth, and came to me.

I stood. 'I need to ask you—'

But he interrupted by raising one hand. 'Please. We won't talk here. Come. We'll go to my house.'

I nodded numbly, following him through the garden and into the street. I didn't question going to his home.

He hailed a *calèche* and we climbed in. I stared at my shoes as we rocked and swayed, only looking up when I felt the *calèche* stop. Aszulay climbed down and took my hand to help me step out.

We walked into the medina, but didn't pass through D'jemma el

Fna; obviously there were other entrances to the old city. I didn't know where we went, or how far through the narrow alleys. Finally Aszulay pulled a large key from within his robe and opened a blue gate. I followed him into a courtyard. He stepped out of his *babouches* and gestured at an open doorway. I hesitated, knowing it was ill-mannered to leave one's shoes on when inside someone's home. And yet . . . I glanced down at my shoes, thinking of the time it would take to undo them, of hobbling across the room without my built-up sole.

'Please,' he said, and by the way he put out his hand, indicating I was to enter, I knew he didn't expect me to remove my shoes. Once inside, he gestured at a day bed, and I sat on its edge. He disappeared, and I closed my eyes and put my face into my hands.

After a few moments I heard the whisper of fabric, and looked up to see an elderly woman carrying a tray with a teapot and two glasses. She set down the tray and poured one glass, handing it to me.

I took it, saying *shukran*, then set it on the table. The woman poured another glass and put it on the table beside mine, and left.

And then Aszulay appeared; he still wore his work clothes, but he had washed his hands and face and taken off his turban. His hair was damp and curling along his collar.

'Aszulay, I need you to tell me what you know about Etienne. When you came to the hotel, when I thought . . . when Manon lied to me . . . you said we would talk about him again. I must have some answers now.'

Aszulay looked into my face, his fingers wrapped around the glass.

'I was his . . . we were to be married.' It was suddenly difficult to say this with Aszulay's intense blue eyes looking into mine. 'He left America so unexpectedly.' I didn't say *he left me*, and yet I imagined Aszulay would hear the unspoken words. 'His abrupt departure . . . we didn't have a chance to speak of . . . of important things. I came here to find him, to try and understand . . .'

My voice kept faltering. Why, in front of this man, was I feeling humiliated? 'I have just spoken to Manon again,' I went on. 'I know more. I know about his illness. Now I believe I know why he left. But I must find him, and tell him . . . I know you can tell me more than Manon will. It's clear she's keeping things from me.'

Aszulay hadn't taken a drink, but he still held his glass, small in his large hand. 'Manon's secrets are hers,' he said. 'I have little more to tell you, apart from regarding Etienne's behaviour when he was here.'

I nodded, leaning forward. 'Yes, yes. Tell me about that, then.'

'He mentioned that he couldn't sleep, that he hadn't slept in many nights. He suffered from anxiety; I saw him take tablets from a bottle.'

'He always took them,' I said, encouraging Aszulay.

'The last evening I saw him,' Aszulay said, 'he drank a bottle of absinthe, all of it, one glass after another. He smoked *kif*, more *kif* than is good. He took even more tablets. Yet he couldn't find peace.'

'So he simply left? He must have said something about where he was going. Or when he'd return.'

We sat in silence. Finally Aszulay said, 'He mentioned both Casablanca and Rabat. But he will return to Marrakesh.'

I sat straighter. 'When, Aszulay? When will he come back?'

'Perhaps he will return next month. Because of Badou. To see Badou.'

'Next month,' I repeated.

'He asked that I care for him—for Badou—in any way I could, while he wasn't here. But then . . . I have always cared for Badou.'

'Because Manon can't be trusted to look after him properly,' I stated, waiting for him to defend her.

The late afternoon call for prayer came, but Aszulay didn't kneel and press his forehead to the floor. He simply rose, saying, 'Now I must go back to the garden, to my work. I have been gone too long.'

'Of course. I'm sorry. Thank you, Aszulay, for . . . for speaking to me about Etienne. Now that I know with certainty he'll return to Marrakesh, I'll wait.'

Chapter Nine

THE NEXT MORNING I told Monsieur Henri I would no longer be staying at Hôtel de la Palmeraie. If I was to bide my time in Marrakesh I could not afford to stay at such a sumptuous place. Monsieur Henri had the good grace not to look relieved, although since I'd allowed Aszulay and Badou into my room, he'd treated me with even more coolness. 'You're leaving Marrakesh, Mademoiselle O'Shea?'

'No,' I said.

I went into the street and booked a room at a small, inexpensive hotel far off the main street of La Ville Nouvelle. The place was shabby and less than clean. I would have to share a bathroom with other guests, but there was also a small communal kitchen, so I could cook for myself. It would do while I waited for Etienne to return.

Two days after I had settled into the small hotel, I went back to Le Jardin Majorelle. I was embarrassed to seek out Aszulay again, and yet I had to tell him that I was no longer at Hôtel de la Palmeraie. Then, when Etienne returned, Aszulay would tell him where I could be found; I knew that Manon would not pass on my information to her brother.

This time Aszulay, obviously finished for the day, was walking towards the entrance as I was coming in.

'Mademoiselle O'Shea,' he said, looking . . . what? What was his expression? I couldn't decipher what I saw, but somehow it warmed me.

I moved into the shade of thick overhanging branches, and he stepped under the tree as well. 'I have moved hotels, and came to tell you. I know you will tell Etienne where he can find me when he returns. I'm at Hôtel Nord-Africain, on rue—'

'I know of it,' Aszulay interrupted.

'Oh. Well. You'll tell him, then, when he comes?' I asked.

'Yes.'

'And . . . what of Badou? Is he well?' I asked. I had been surprised by how many times I'd thought of the little boy since I'd seen him last.

'Badou is fine,' he stated. 'I passed by Sharia Zitoun yesterday.'

I wondered how Manon kept her lovers from running into each other. For all I knew, she had more men than Aszulay and Olivier.

'And Badou's father, Monsieur Maliki,' I suddenly said. 'Does he ever see his son, or help with his needs?'

Aszulay's expression changed. 'There is no Monsieur Maliki.'

'But . . . Manon is Madame Maliki,' I argued.

'She is Mademoiselle Maliki.'

'Mademoiselle?' I realised no one else had ever called her Madame. Only I, because I had assumed it was her married name. 'How is this? If she isn't married . . . why isn't she Mademoiselle Duverger?'

Aszulay ran his sleeve across his face. I saw the dirt of the garden on his hands and wrists, a fine red dusting on his dark skin.

'I'm not asking you to disclose secrets. I'm trying to understand Manon so I can understand Etienne. Manon is Etienne's sister, but . . . it's puzzling. Her hatred for her father; even her anger towards Etienne. Is it only over the fact that she wasn't left what she thought her fair share when their father died? Is it this that's made her so bitter and full of rage?'

'How do you not see it, Mademoiselle O'Shea?' Aszulay said then, frowning down at me. He seemed, somehow, upset with me.

I frowned back at him. 'What do you—'

He shook his head. 'Manon's mother—Rachida Maliki—was a servant in the house of Marcel Duverger. Monsieur Duverger and she . . .' He stopped. 'Manon told me that Monsieur Duverger came to Marrakesh and went back to France for some years before the French began to rule, and she was born during that time. But after the French took over Morocco, Monsieur Duverger brought Madame and Etienne and Guillaume from Paris, and they made their lives in Marrakesh. Still Rachida Maliki worked in the Duverger house.'

He stopped. It was the most I had heard Aszulay say at one time. I realised I was staring at him, watching his lips. He had a sensitive mouth, I suddenly thought. His mastery of French, with the Arabic influence, had an undercurrent of rhythm that was almost a melody.

'When Manon was small, her grandmother took care of her, but when she was older, her mother often took her to the Duverger house, to help with the work. Manon knew who her father was. In Marrakesh, in the medina, all the families know the father of the child. It's not a secret in the medina. In the French Quarter, yes, but in the medina, no.

'When Manon was helping her mother, she sometimes played with Etienne and Guillaume. But she knew she couldn't speak of the secret—that Etienne and Guillaume's father was also her father—because then it would go badly for her mother. She would lose her job and the extra luxuries Monsieur Duverger gave her.'

'So Etienne . . . he didn't know, then?'

Aszulay's face changed slightly. 'He didn't know for many years. Manon was simply a servant's daughter. But Manon has great strength, great determination. She educated herself. She learned to speak French as if born to it. She was—is, as you can see—very beautiful. Very . . .' He shook his head in frustration, saying an Arabic word. 'I can't think of the right word. But she could always make men come to her, and want her.'

I knew the word he was searching for. *Sensuous. Desirable.*

'Manon would never be a subservient Moroccan wife, confined to the house and courtyard and roof,' Aszulay continued. 'She wanted a French husband, a man who would treat her as she saw the French women treated. And she had French men, many of them.' Again I thought of Olivier, leaving her bedroom. 'But none would marry her.'

I watched his face; had he begged Manon to marry him? Had she spurned him because he was a Tuareg, and yet he loved her still?

'But . . . when did Etienne find out Manon was his sister?' I asked.

At that, Aszulay stepped out of the shade and looked at the sun. 'I must go,' he said.

I stayed where I was, not wanting him to leave. The story, and his voice, had mesmerised me.

He looked back at me. 'I have your information to pass on to Etienne, Mademoiselle O'Shea,' he said.

'My name is Sidonie,' I said, not sure why.

He nodded once. I wanted him to say it. I wanted to hear how he would say my name. But he turned and strode away.

One morning, as I bided my time at the Hotel Nord-Africain, listening to the morning call to prayer, I reached to my bedside table and picked up the tile from the Blue Man on the *piste*. I traced the bold blue and green design. How had the tile-maker created this depth of colour?

I thought of the wildness of Manon's oils, then compared them to the painful attention I had always taken with my pretty flowers, pretty birds and butterflies, true replicas, but what did they make me feel? What part of myself had I put into those re-creations?

I again saw myself in my old room in Albany, holding a brush, trying to capture a small, quiet image. But I knew that those paintings were not part of my world any more—not this world, this new world.

I thought again of the journey with Mustapha and Aziz, of the bright moored boats along the Atlantic, the sky yellow at the end of the day. I thought of the palms lining the main street of La Ville Nouvelle, and the richness of the flowers growing in tangled profusion in gardens. I closed my eyes, seeing, on my lids, the vibrancy of Moroccan colours everywhere: the fabrics, the clothing, the tiles, the walls and shutters and doors and gates.

I sat up.

Suddenly I wanted to paint it all. I had no idea if I could produce any of the images with even the slightest sense of authenticity. But I had to try.

I went to an art shop I had often passed and purchased watercolours and paper and an easel and brushes of various sizes. The purchases took more of my hoarded bills and coins, and yet I felt the need to paint so strongly that I knew I must.

I came back to the hotel and set up the easel near the window, and spent the rest of the day experimenting. The brushes felt so right in my hand. My strokes were sure and strong.

When I realised the light was failing, and my neck and shoulders were stiff, I stopped, studying what I had done. I thought of the watercolours in the lobby of the grand Hotel de la Palmeraie, comparing mine to them.

A thought came to me. Preposterous, perhaps.

A few days later, as I tried to capture the look of a Moroccan woman on paper, I tied one of my white linen handkerchiefs around the bottom of my face. With a *haik* draped over me and only my eyes and eyebrows visible, I would be indistinguishable from the other women in the souks.

Although D'jemma el Fna and some of the markets were, by now, more familiar, I was still uncomfortable going into the medina. The few times I ventured in I cringed at being stared at, at being set upon by small bands of demanding children, at being shouted at by all the vendors to buy their wares, at being surreptitiously touched.

I went out, stopping to look at the expensive silk kaftans in the windows in the French Quarter, and then went into the medina and found a souk selling them for a fraction of the price. I fingered the simplest of the kaftans, and finally bought one, after a great deal of bargaining. It was calico, small red flowers on a yellow background. I bought a long, wide piece of coarse white fabric—the *haik*—and a veil. I took it all back to my room at the hotel and put it on.

I stared at myself for a long time, then took it off and finished my painting. The next day, dressed as a Moroccan woman, I left the hotel and went to D'jemma el Fna, walking slowly through the square, looking around me. I had become invisible. And with the invisibility came a freedom. I could move about as I chose. I could watch and listen. It was so much easier to learn things, to understand, when one didn't have to be aware of oneself.

I stopped to watch the snake charmers, seeing that when the sun was at its brightest, the snakes reacted in the liveliest fashion. I saw children swarming a European couple trying to escape as I once had. One of the smaller boys in the little group reminded me of Badou, and I was overcome with a rush of wanting to see him again. I hoped that when Etienne returned I would have the chance; when Manon saw that Etienne welcomed me, she would have no choice but to accept me. She might not like it, but she would have to accept it.

At the end of my first week in the small hotel, I took two of my watercolours and, putting on my green silk, went back to Hôtel de la Palmeraie. When Monsieur Henri saw me approach the desk, his features tightened.

'*Bonjour*, monsieur,' I said. 'How are you?'

'Fine. Fine, mademoiselle. How can I help you?' He glanced to see if I had my suitcases.

'I wish to discuss something.'

'You don't wish to stay with us?'

'No, I will not be staying here again.' I took out the watercolours. 'But I have completed these, and wondered if you would be interested in placing them with the others, to be sold on commission.'

He studied them, then looked up at me. 'You say you have done these, mademoiselle?'

I nodded. 'Do you not agree they would fit with the others you have displayed?' I repeated, willing myself to appear businesslike, and not show too much hope. If I was to stay on in Marrakesh, waiting for Etienne to return, I needed money. This was my only option.

'I'll see what I can do,' he said. 'We've sold a number recently, and perhaps a new artist would be of interest.'

My relief was so great that it took me a moment to answer. 'Fine,' I said. 'Yes, fine. I'll leave them with you, and come back in a few days to find out if they have sold. I have more, as well,' I said. I had completed two more, with another started only that morning.

'Thank you, mademoiselle,' Monsieur Henri said, bowing slightly, and I raised my chin and smiled at him, an open, thankful smile.

As I walked out of the hotel, I thought of his words, *a new artist*, and walked more briskly, swinging my arms. When an elderly man looked at me, lifting his hat as I passed, I realised I was still smiling.

On the morning that marked a month since Aszulay had said Etienne might return, I counted my money again. I could stay perhaps two more weeks. That was all. Neither of my paintings had sold; I checked every few days. I had painted three more, but had run out of paper and some colours of paint, and couldn't afford to buy any more.

But Etienne was expected any day. Then everything would be all right.

I now wore kaftans and a *haik* and a veil at all times, quietly going about my daily shopping with my woven bag. As usual, I went down to the splintered hotel counter and asked if there were any messages for me. The man shook his head. 'Not today,' he said, and I nodded.

'Thank you,' I said, but before I could leave he said, 'Mademoiselle,' and his cheeks reddened. 'I know you are American. But the other guests . . .' He stopped. 'Some have mentioned to me that they stay here because it is a hotel for visitors to Marrakesh. Visitors from France, from Germany, from Spain and Britain. Also from America, like you.'

I waited.

Perspiration gleamed on the man's forehead. 'I'm sorry, mademoiselle. It's not suitable that you dress as a Muslim woman while staying here. It is unsettling for the others. There have been complaints. If you insist on dressing in this way, I will have to ask you to leave the hotel.'

'I understand,' I said, blinking, then turned and went out into the hot sunshine.

Aszulay was there, standing on the street in front of the hotel, in his blue robes, the bottom of his face covered by the end of his turban. He was looking down the street, so I saw his partly obscured profile, and I caught my breath.

As I approached him, my breathlessness was, surely, because seeing him meant he had news of Etienne.

At the sound of my footsteps, he glanced at me, then turned away.

I said his name, and he looked at me again, then said something in Arabic, his tone questioning.

I pulled my veil from my nose and mouth, and he drew back, just the slightest. 'Mademoiselle O'Shea,' he said, his voice muffled. Then he said, 'But why are you—'

'Have you news? News of Etienne? Has he arrived?'

'Manon has had a letter,' he said, pushing down the bottom of his turban, uncovering his lower face as I had. I'd forgotten how white his teeth were. His skin had grown darker from working in the intense summer sun, making his eyes appear even bluer.

I stepped closer. 'A letter from Etienne?'

He nodded. 'It arrived yesterday.'

I waited, but by his expression I knew, before he said it, what he would tell me. 'I'm sorry. He wrote to say he couldn't come this week. Perhaps in a few weeks, another month, the letter said.'

I swallowed. Another few weeks, a month. I couldn't stay that long; I didn't have enough money. 'Did he say where he was?' I asked. 'Did the envelope—'

'She didn't show it to me, Sidonie,' he said. 'She told me only that he wasn't coming yet, not for a few more weeks or a month.'

'But I'll go to her and ask her. Or no, you go, she'll tell you if you ask. She won't tell me, Aszulay, but she'll tell you.'

He shook his head. 'She's not here right now,' he said, and suddenly the air was too hot, the sun a white, burning disc on my face.

'She's not here?' I repeated. 'What do you mean?'

'She's gone on a holiday. For a week, maybe two, with . . .' he stopped, then continued, 'a friend.'

I knew that Manon had gone off with the Frenchman. Olivier. Surely Aszulay knew as well.

'Did she take Badou?'

'No. She left him with Falida.'

'She's only a girl,' I said. 'They're just children.'

'She's eleven. She could marry in two or three years,' he said. 'I'll go to Sharia Zitoun every few days, to bring them food and make sure they're all right,' he added.

I looked at him now. I knew he was a man of dignity, of honesty. How could he allow Manon to use him like this? How could he continue to be with her when she showed him so little respect? He didn't deserve to be treated in this way.

'So you will continue to wait?' Aszulay said, something odd in his voice. 'You'll stay in Marrakesh and wait for him—for Etienne—no matter how long it takes?'

I licked my lips. 'I . . .' I stopped, embarrassed to say I didn't know how I would manage it. 'Yes.'

'Sidonie, I think . . . maybe you shouldn't wait any longer. Maybe you should return to your life.'

'My life?' He still didn't understand. But how could he? How could he understand there was nothing for me in Albany? Suddenly I was angry at him, at Aszulay, for telling me I shouldn't wait. I was angry with Manon, for thwarting my efforts to find Etienne. And perhaps I was the most angry with Etienne.

I was so hot, and I was hungry; I hadn't eaten anything since the day before. 'As you'll wait?' I said to him, my voice louder, stronger. I stared into his eyes.

He shook his head the slightest. 'Wait for what?'

'For her. For Manon.' I couldn't keep the venom out of my voice as I spoke her name. 'You'll wait for her, doing her bidding, while she's off with another man?'

He shrugged. 'It's for the child,' he said, as if surprised, but this didn't satisfy me.

'I can tell you think I'm a fool to wait for Etienne to come back to me,' I said. 'Go ahead. Tell me you think I'm a fool. And then I'll tell you that I think you're a fool to wait for Manon. She's only using you to look after her son. How can you allow her to do that to you?' I didn't want to say these things; Aszulay had been nothing but kind to me.

What was wrong with me? Why did I care how Manon treated him? Why was I annoyed that he cared so much for her?

His nostrils tightened. 'Perhaps the same way you allow Etienne to do what he does to you.'

We stared at each other. His words stung me. *What Etienne was doing to me*. And then suddenly I couldn't look at him any longer, and put my head down. Instead of shaming him, as I'd tried to do, he'd shamed me. Suddenly I realised how he must see me, waiting endlessly for a man who . . . I was dizzy. The sun was too bright; it was making everything too clear, too transparent.

Still looking down, I said, 'I'm sorry, Aszulay. I don't have a right to tell you what to do. I'm sorry,' I repeated. 'All this waiting. And now. . .'

'I understand,' he said, and I looked at him again. Did he? His voice was a little stiff, as was his expression.

'There's something else,' I said then, because I knew I would have to make another change in order to stay in Marrakesh.

'Yes?'

'I need to find a place to stay. I . . . I will no longer stay at the hotel. I wonder . . . could you help me?'

'But the hotels in La Ville Nouvelle are for foreigners. For people like you. Why don't you continue to stay there?'

'The truth, Aszulay, is that I can no longer afford to stay in any of the hotels in the French Quarter. Perhaps there's someplace, someplace you know, that's very inexpensive. In the medina.'

He looked startled. 'There are no hotels in the medina. When Moroccans from other cities come, they stay with relatives, or friends.'

'All I need is a room. One room, Aszulay.'

'It's impossible,' he said, again shaking his head. 'A woman, a Nasarini, alone, in a Muslim house. It's not proper.'

Nasarini. A Nazarene, a Christian, the name foreigners were called by the Moroccans. I had heard it before, in the souks, as I understood more and more Arabic.

'But otherwise I can't stay in Morocco any longer. All of this will be for nothing. I'm so close, Aszulay,' I said. 'Please understand how important this is to me. Haven't you . . .' I stopped. I wanted to say *haven't you ever loved someone so much you would do anything for her*, but it was too intimate a question. What did I know of this man, his feelings?

'I'll see what I can do, Sidonie,' he said, but he looked troubled now.

'Thank you,' I said, and, relieved, and on impulse, I touched the back of his hand to show my gratitude.

He looked down, and I looked as well; my fingers were small on his hand. I pulled my fingers back, and he looked at me then.

I was sorry I'd been so forward. Obviously I'd made him uncomfortable. It was only later that I remembered he'd called me Sidonie.

The man with the withered arm, his jellaba sleeve rolled up over it, didn't appear pleased when Aszulay brought me to the house on Sharia Soura two days later. Aszulay said it wasn't yet a sure thing, but this man—his friend—might allow me to stay there for a short while.

It was early evening, and as we stood in the courtyard—my face covered but for my eyes—the man stared at me. I immediately looked at the ground, knowing I couldn't appear bold.

Aszulay spoke to him. They argued back and forth, quietly, in Arabic. I realised it was simply the usual haggling over price as at the market. Except this time it was over me.

Aszulay's tone remained the same, calm and firm, and finally the man threw up his hand in resignation. Aszulay quoted me the price of the room as well as my meals for a week; it was a tiny fraction of what I had paid for one night at the cheaper hotel. I nodded, and Aszulay took my cases and went inside the house. I was carrying my painting supplies in my woven basket, and my easel in the other hand.

I climbed the stairs after Aszulay, fixing my eyes on his heels in his yellow *babouches*. The stairs were narrow and steep, and my right leg ached with the effort of lifting it so high on each tiled step.

Aszulay opened a door and set my cases in the middle of the room. He turned to look at me.

'It's all right?' he asked, and I nodded, not even having time to take in my surroundings, but knowing I had no choice. There was a pleasant smell in the room, something woody and fresh.

'Yes. Yes, it's very good, Aszulay. Thank you.'

'There are two wives. They will give you tea and bread in the mornings, and a meal midday and evening. Downstairs, off the kitchen, is the lavatory.'

I nodded.

'But you must understand that you can't leave the house without a male escort. Although my friend understands you are not Muslim, if you wish to stay here you must act in the way of a Muslim woman, or he will be shamed. He has two sons, and one will accompany you when you want to go out. And if they will allow it, you can help the wives with the work of the house, although I believe they'll resent you.'

'Why? I'm not—'

'They'll see you as a rival, perhaps to be a new wife. If the husband enters when you're with the wives, turn your face to the wall so he can't look at you. He's doing this because he owes me a favour, but he isn't happy. So you must do all you can not to create any upset.'

'Thank you,' I said. 'For getting me this room. And for . . .' I wanted to say more. 'Thank you,' I repeated.

He looked into my face, opened his mouth as if to speak further, then nodded, tucking the end of his turban over his nose and mouth. He left, shutting the door firmly behind him.

I had been living in the house on Sharia Soura for three days. I was never confronted by the husband, although in the morning and evening I heard his voice, and saw him in the courtyard when I looked down from my window. He was often with twin boys of perhaps fourteen or fifteen; they must be the sons Aszulay had mentioned.

The older wife and servant ignored me, but it was clear the younger wife was interested in me. There was little we could do to communicate, but I appreciated her smiles. She told me her name was Mena, and laughed as she tried to pronounce Sidonie.

When I pointed to objects, Mena said their names in Arabic. In a short time I had learned many words and simple phrases. She chattered constantly, showing me how to make couscous—rolling and shaping the moistened semolina wheat, coating it with finely ground wheat flour before steaming it. I watched as she made *harira*, the lentil, chickpea and lamb soup. She ignored the disapproving glances of the servant, but when the older wife—Nawar—entered the kitchen, Mena would fall silent.

By the fourth day I grew restless and expressed to Mena that I wished to go out. She consulted Nawar, who looked a bit sour, but called out a name—Najeeb—and one of the boys materialised from a back room. She spoke a few lines to him, raising her chin at me, and Najeeb went to the gate and stood, waiting. I covered myself and followed him through the twisting lanes. I recognised some of the streets, and realised that we passed Sharia Zitoun on the way to the souks. I saw the niche in the wall—with the kittens—where Badou and Falida went when they were sent out by Manon.

Once Najeeb had led me to the souks, where I was sure he expected me to shop, I walked ahead of him, and he followed.

I went through D'jemma el Fna into the French Quarter, and all the way to Hôtel de la Palmeraie. I gestured for Najeeb to wait while I went into the hotel, pulling off my *haik* and veil as I did so. He immediately turned from me.

In the lobby, Monsieur Henri saw me coming, frowning at my kaftan, but then nodded. 'Ah, mademoiselle. Yes. Splendid news. Both your paintings have sold, and the buyers are interested in more. They are a young couple decorating their home in Antibes, and wish at least four additional paintings in the same vein.'

A strange heat filled me. I had no idea it would feel this way to be told such news: that my paintings were sought after.

'Mademoiselle? You said you have more paintings. The couple leave next week, and would like to look at them before then.'

I nodded. 'Yes. Yes,' I repeated. 'I'll bring them. Tomorrow.'

'Fine. Now, let me see,' he said, turning to open a drawer in the cupboard behind the desk. 'Yes. Here you are. The hotel has taken the fifty per cent commission, as usual. The details of the sale are written out.'

I took the envelope from him, still nodding. 'Thank you, Monsieur Henri,' I said. 'Thank you,' I repeated.

'I shall see you tomorrow, then,' he said, and turned, making it clear our business was over.

I went out to Najeeb, covering myself before embarrassing him again. I couldn't wait, and ripped open the envelope. Along with the typed receipt, there was a cheque, with an amount I hadn't expected. The sum I'd received for my two paintings filled me with euphoria. It was the first time in my life I had received payment. For anything.

The next day I again expressed that I must go out, and Nawar looked just as annoyed, but again called Najeeb.

First I went to Hôtel de la Palmeraie, leaving Monsieur Henri the other four paintings I had completed. Then I went to a bank and opened an account, paying in the cheque and withdrawing the money I needed, and after that I went to the art store. I purchased more paper and paint. On a whim, I bought a wooden box containing tubes of oil paint and a few canvases and different brushes. I thought of how much more depth I could achieve by painting with oils. It would be a completely new technique, and yet I was eager to try.

I was excited to try the oils immediately; I had painted in my room, but at this time of day there wasn't enough light. I brought my easel down to the courtyard, set up the canvas and squeezed paint onto my palette.

Mena came out, pulling up a stool and watching, her eyes bright, as she watched the courtyard slowly emerge from my brushes.

I turned to her, pointing at her face and then putting my brush back to the canvas. But she cried out, putting her hand on mine and shaking her head, saying, '*la, la.*' No.

'What's wrong?' I asked her, and she went to great lengths with words and gestures, and I understood enough to know she was telling me I couldn't paint her. I would capture her soul on the canvas.

I nodded, asking in my simple Arabic if I could paint a man.

She nodded. A man's spirit was strong enough not to be taken. But I couldn't paint a woman or a child.

We were sitting in companionable silence, Mena watching as I worked, when Nawar came into the courtyard. She shook her head, her lips tight, and spoke in a torrent of words to Mena, leaving with a great flurry of her kaftan.

I looked at Nawar disappearing into the house, and then at Mena. Mena shook her head slowly, and with a few sentences I knew I was not allowed to paint in the courtyard. Nawar felt it would draw in evil spirits.

The next day I was upstairs with Mena and Nawar when the old servant shouted something from the courtyard. Mena leaned out the window and called back, then looked at me.

'Aszulay is here,' she said, in Arabic. I jumped up, perhaps a little too quickly, and went down the stairs.

Aszulay stood in the courtyard, holding Badou's hand.

'Hello,' I said, a little breathless from hurrying, looking from Aszulay to Badou. 'Is Etienne in Marrakesh?' I asked.

Aszulay lifted one shoulder; the small movement gave me the impression he was annoyed with my question. 'No.'

'Is it that I'm no longer allowed to stay here?' I asked, swallowing.

'No. I have spoken to my friend. You may stay on.'

I nodded, relieved that I would be here a bit longer, and yet disturbed that time was stretching out with no more word from Etienne.

I let out a long breath. 'Thank you. How are you, Badou?' I asked, looking at the child.

He smiled, and it pleased me to see that his hair was trimmed, and shone, and that his little jellaba and cotton trousers were clean. 'We're going to see the turtles,' he said.

'At the garden,' Aszulay explained. 'I finished early today, so I'm taking Badou there. We were passing near to here, and I thought perhaps you would care to join us.'

He said it in a casual tone, but also with a slight hesitation.

'You will come, Sidonie?' Badou asked.

'Yes,' I said. 'I'll get my veil and *haik*.'

We rode to Le Jardin Majorelle in the back of a cart pulled by a donkey.

'We'll go to one of the bigger ponds,' Aszulay said, when we were in the garden. 'The turtles there are the largest.'

We went to a reflecting pool, and while Badou ran to its edge, I set my *haik* on a stone bench and untied the veil from my face.

Badou crouched beside the motionless water, which mirrored the sky, his little shoulders tense, staring into the smooth surface dotted with lily pads. Aszulay spoke to him in Arabic, and Badou put his fingers into the water and wiggled them, breaking the glasslike surface. Almost immediately a turtle popped its head up, only inches from Badou's fingers, and then quickly plopped back under the water.

Badou laughed, delighted. He was a different little boy like this, the usual serious expression gone.

'This is the first time I have heard your laughter,' Aszulay said.

I covered my mouth with my hand, unaware that I had laughed along with Badou.

He studied me. 'Why do you look as though you regret laughing?'

I blinked. 'I'm not sure.' I thought about the baby, about Etienne, about all that had happened in the past number of months. I realised I hadn't laughed since Etienne had left me. Did I feel I had no right to laugh? No right to happiness?

I looked down at Badou, flicking his fingers in the water. He had made me, for this brief moment in the sun, forget about the heaviness of my recent life. I glanced back at Aszulay. He wasn't looking at me, but I had the distinct impression he pitied me.

I didn't want this man to feel sorry for me. I left the bench to kneel beside Badou. 'Let's make the turtle come out again,' I said, and lightly splashed the surface of the water with my fingers.

As we left the gardens, Aszulay spoke to Badou in Arabic. Badou's mouth opened and his eyes shone. 'Yes, Oncle Aszulay, yes, when will we go?'

'In one week. Seven days,' he said, lifting Badou into the cart, which had waited for us. Badou looked at his fingers, his lips moving as he counted. 'Every few months I visit my family,' Aszulay added, turning to me. 'Badou likes to come with me. He likes to play with the children there.'

His family.

'Oh. You have children?' I asked, somehow startled. Somehow . . . disturbed. Why? I realised I presumed he had no wife, no children, mainly because when I'd gone to his home I'd seen no one but the older woman who served me tea. Was it also because of his association with Manon?

'No,' he said, then pointedly turned to Badou and spoke to him about the turtles.

Once we had left the cart, Aszulay and Badou walked me back to Sharia Soura. Badou asked, 'Sidonie, are you coming with us to the *bled*?'

'No, Badou,' I answered, stopping at my gate. 'But I hope you have a good time.' I turned, knocking on the gate.

We waited, and then Aszulay said, 'Do you wish to come?'

I thought he was just being polite. But that was my assumption: an American assumption. It was not Aszulay's way.

He added, 'We will be gone two days.'

The gate was opened by Najeeb.

Two days meant we would stay overnight. As if reading my mind, Aszulay said, 'There are women's quarters.'

I thought about my night in the *bled* with Mustapha and Aziz: the stars, the silence, the wild camel.

'I have *une camionnette*,' he said. 'We will go in it.'

'A truck? You own a truck?'

He nodded. Somehow I was surprised. I had only imagined him walking down the dusty *piste*, like the first Blue Man I had seen.

'And so? Do you wish to come?'

'Yes,' I said. 'I'll come. Unless . . .' Unless Etienne had arrived by then.

'Unless . . . ?' he asked.

'Nothing,' I said.

'I will come for you in seven days, after breakfast,' he said.

'Will you bring us food tomorrow, Oncle Aszulay?' Badou asked.

Aszulay put his hand on the boy's head. 'Tomorrow I must work too many hours. But I have left food. Falida will cook it for you,' he said.

'Will Maman come home soon?' Badou then asked.

Aszulay nodded. 'Soon.'

I looked from Badou to Aszulay. 'I could go to Sharia Zitoun and check on Badou and Falida,' I said.

'Yes. Come to my house, Sidonie,' Badou said.

'As you wish,' Aszulay said.

'I'll see you tomorrow, then, Badou,' I told him, and he nodded.

Aszulay took Badou's hand, and I went inside my gate.

When I went to Sharia Zitoun midmorning the next day, I had Najeeb bring my new oils and easel and a canvas. I stopped first in one of the souks and bought a simple French children's book for Badou.

Falida had made a goat stew. I realised how capable she was, and how different she seemed without Manon's menacing presence.

As she and Badou looked through the book, she laughed aloud at one of the pictures, and poked Badou with her elbow. He poked her back, and laughed with her.

I read the book to them with Badou on my lap and Falida sitting beside me. Then I set up my easel and canvas under the shade of the jacaranda in the courtyard. I asked Badou to open my box of paints. He set the box on the ground and, with a look of concentration, snapped it open, reverently laying back the lid as if opening a sacred container. He watched as I took out tubes and squeezed them onto my palette. After a while he sat at my feet, again turning the pages of the book.

The paint was brilliant on the canvas. There was a freedom with oils. Watercolours required much more delicacy, each fine line precise. But with the oils I could attempt bolder, freer strokes.

And then there was a knock on the locked gate, and I jumped.

Badou rose and ran to open the gate. When Aszulay came in, carrying a sack, he looked at me standing at my easel.

'I knew you were here when I saw Najeeb,' he said. 'I came on my midday break and brought more food.' He handed the sack to Falida.

'Falida made a goat stew, and we've eaten. Are you hungry?'

He nodded, and I looked at Falida. She went into the house. Aszulay came and stood beside me.

'You paint,' he stated.

'Yes. I brought my supplies here because the first wife at Sharia Soura doesn't want me to paint in the courtyard, and the light in my room is only right for a few hours. But I'm not used to painting in this heat.' I was babbling. 'Or using oils. I usually paint with watercolours; I always painted with watercolours in Albany,' I said, glancing sideways at him. 'My home. But the colours here—they're so brilliant and vibrant, and the subjects require more depth, more strength. I can't capture them the way I want to with watercolours.' I put down the brush, wiping my hands on my kaftan. 'My hands are damp, and the paintbrush slips.'

'Is it ever hot like this in your part of America?' he asked. 'Albany. Where is this?'

'It's near New York City. In the state of New York. The summers there can be very hot, and humid. But nothing like this. And the winters are long and bitter. There's snow. All white, and somehow untouchable.'

'Do you miss it? Your home in New York?' Aszulay asked, not looking at me, but at the canvas.

I didn't answer. Did I miss it?

'I have always been amazed that . . .' Aszulay stopped speaking. I waited. He looked intense, staring at the canvas as if mesmerised.

And then I heard it, and realised why he had so abruptly gone quiet. Birdsong, a soft trilling from the thick branches of the tree that spread its shade over us. Aszulay didn't look above, searching for the small creature responsible for the beautiful melody, but kept his gaze fixed on the canvas, almost, I think, unconsciously, for it appeared he was using all his concentration on the song.

The sound ceased. Aszulay blinked, and then continued, as if that tiny lapse in his speech had not occurred. 'That there are animals in America who make their home in the snow.'

And I believe it was at that moment—watching this tall Blue Man, his face glistening in the sun, his forearms corded from recent digging, stopping his conversation to listen, somehow respectfully, to birdsong—that something inside me tore. Not a painful tearing, but a slow, careful breaking apart.

The next day I went to check on Badou and Falida, taking Najeeb—or perhaps it was the twin brother, as I couldn't tell them apart. I knocked and called out, smiling, waiting for Falida or Badou.

But it was Manon who pulled open the gate.

I drew in my breath; although I knew she could come back at any time, somehow I hadn't expected to see her.

'What do you want?' she asked.

I lifted the basket I carried. 'I brought some food. For Badou,' I said, knowing it was wiser not to mention Falida.

'You don't need to feed my child. I'm quite capable of that,' she said.

'I know. It's only because you were away, and Aszulay . . .' I stopped. I knew I should say as little as possible to Manon about Aszulay.

'You and Aszulay are becoming friendly. Is that it?' she asked, staring.

I was still standing in the doorway. 'As long as you're home, I won't worry about Badou, then.'

'You have no reason—no right—to worry about my child,' she said. 'Come in. I don't like the neighbours watching everything.'

I stepped inside. She closed the gate behind me, and slid the bolt. 'Where's Badou?' I asked. The courtyard and house were quiet.

'I have sent him and Falida to the souks. What have you brought?'

She took the basket from my hands and lifted the cloth, then took the lid from the pot of couscous with vegetable stew. 'You cook Moroccan food now?' she asked.

'I'll go then, and, as you say, you don't need the food.' I reached for the basket's handle, but she didn't let go.

'Badou has told me you're going to the country with him and Aszulay,' she said, no expression in her voice now.

I didn't answer.

'You know he has a wife,' she said, with a wily smile, putting her thumb on top of my fingers, pinning them against the basket handle.

I felt a jolt at her words. Manon was lying, as she had lied about Etienne dying.

'Really?' I said. 'I was in his house. I saw no wife.'

Now her smile disappeared as quickly as it came, and the pressure of her thumb on my fingers grew more intense. 'You went to his house.'

I looked at her but didn't attempt to move my fingers. 'I didn't see a wife,' I repeated.

'What were you doing there?'

'That's my business.' Suddenly I stood straighter. I saw that I had caused a reaction in *her*. I could match this woman. She couldn't harm me with her words.

'Of course you didn't see her there. She doesn't live in the city.'

What had Aszulay said, exactly? I tried to remember our conversation, when he had invited me to come with him and Badou. *Every few months I visit my family*. I pulled my fingers from under hers. 'And so? What of it if he has a wife?'

'She's a real country girl. So beneath him,' she said, with contempt. 'She stays where she belongs, surrounded by her goats.'

'Oh?' I said, with feigned lack of interest.

'You still want to go to the *bled*? You want to go and watch Aszulay with his wife?'

'Why should it bother me?' I asked, troubled at this game we were playing. She was trying to make me jealous but it was she who was jealous—of the wife. And of me, because Aszulay had shown me attention. But she had Olivier. And she had Aszulay, in spite of his wife. Wasn't that enough? How much of Aszulay did Manon want, and need?

I tugged, slightly, on the handle of the basket, and she finally relinquished it. 'I'm going now,' I said, and turned to the gate.

'Oh, please, Sidonie, please wait,' Manon said, in a polite voice I hadn't heard before. 'I meant to give you something. I'll be right back.'

It was too suspicious; Manon had never treated me with any courtesy. But I was curious. She hurried up the stairs, and within a moment came back down, holding something in her hand.

'It's a pen and inkwell,' she said. 'An antique, used by scribes in the past.' She held it towards me. It was an egg-shaped silver container, the sides etched with designs. 'Look. Here's the pen,' she said, pulling on one end of the container, and a long metal implement slid out. Something dark—ink?—gleamed on its tip. She made as if to lay it in my right palm, but somehow its point jammed into my flesh, making a small nick in my skin. Instinctively I jerked away, and a bead of blood rose up on my palm.

'Oh, I'm so sorry,' she said, licking her fingers and putting them to the blood. With her fingers on the cut she murmured a line, very quietly.

I felt a chill. 'What did you say?' I asked, pulling my hand away and rubbing my palm against my *haik*.

Her look was intense. 'I just said how clumsy I was,' she answered, but I knew she lied. There was something in her look, something that I could almost call pleased.

I looked at the pen and inkwell she still held. 'I don't want it.' I turned and slid back the bolt of the gate and left without closing it.

I grew ill during dinner. The husband and sons had been served, and now I sat on cushions at the low table in the sitting room with Mena. Nawar was still in the kitchen, and we were waiting for her. But as I stared at the food on the table it blurred. My hand was aching, and I looked at it. My palm was swollen, the small wound puffy and dark red around the edges.

I wanted to lie down. I tried to get to my feet, pushing with my left hand on the table.

'Sick,' I said in Arabic, and Mena rose and came to me.

My face was wet with perspiration, and I wiped my forehead with the back of my right hand.

Mena put her hand on my wrist, looking at my palm. She held it for an instant too long. I understood her Arabic question: *what is this?*

How could I explain, with so little Arabic? *Woman. Hurt me.*

'*Sikeen?*' she asked, and I shook my head, not understanding. She picked up a knife from the table with her other hand. '*Sikeen*,' she repeated, and gestured at my palm.

I shook my head, making a writing motion with my other hand. What was the Arabic word for pen, and why was Mena making a fuss over something so insignificant when I felt so sick?

'*Qalam?*' she said quickly, and this time I nodded.

'Yes. *Qalam*. Pen. She just poked me with a pen,' I murmured, knowing she couldn't understand my French. Again I tried to pull my hand away, but Mena held it firmly, calling out for Nawar and the servant. They both came from the kitchen, and Mena spoke rapidly, gesturing at my hand.

The old servant let out a wail, throwing her apron over her face. Nawar's eyes widened, and she let out a stream of Arabic, as if praying.

Mena spoke to me again, saying a word over and over, then turned to Nawar, and I heard Aszulay's name.

The room was too hot, too bright. Mena's voice and Nawar's prayers mixed with the old woman's wailing, turned into gibberish, demonic shrieks. The room tilted, and the floor rose up to meet my cheek.

The smell was strong, burning my nostrils, and I turned my head from it. But my forehead ached at the movement, and when I opened my eyes my sight was blurry. It took me a moment to understand I was lying on the day bed in the main room, and Mena was waving a small, smoking cloth bag in front of my face.

'*Besmellah rahman rahim*,' she kept repeating. She looked into my eyes and spoke again, and this time I understood the word *jinn*.

And then I saw Aszulay. He came up behind Mena, and spoke to her. She kept her face turned away, pulling her headscarf down so that it completely covered her features, and answered in rapid, short sentences, again picking up my right wrist, her voice rising as she held it tightly.

Aszulay said one sentence, and Mena left. He crouched beside me. 'Mena says a bad woman performed witchcraft on you.'

I tried to smile at the absurdity of it, but it was as though I was floating, as though I was in a painful dream. Was Aszulay really here, or was I just imagining him? 'No. I'm just . . . sick. Maybe food . . .'

He picked up my hand. His fingers felt so cool around mine. My face was burning, my cheek throbbing, and I pressed the back of his hand to it, closing my eyes at the coolness. Then I put my lips on his skin, breathing, trying to smell indigo.

He didn't pull his hand away.

I opened my eyes, and suddenly his features stood clearly, so close, and I realised what I was doing. It wasn't a dream. I let go of his hand.

'Who is the woman you told Mena about?'

'Manon. I went to see if Badou and Falida were all right, earlier today,' I said. 'They weren't there. Manon was.'

'And? What happened to your hand?'

'She wanted to give me a gift. I don't know why. It was an old pen and inkwell. She handed it to me, and the point of the pen stuck in me. That's all.'

Aszulay picked up my hand again, bringing it close to his face and studying it. Now I saw that my palm was even more swollen, the cut already festering. I tried to bend my fingers, but couldn't.

There was a sudden deep sting, and I tried to pull away, but Aszulay held my hand firmly. I moaned as I felt him prodding and digging in my palm with something sharp.

He murmured something in Arabic, something with a soothing sound, as if telling me it would soon be over, or that he was sorry.

I held my breath.

Finally he lifted his head, and I let out a soft cry of relief as the pain stopped. 'I have it,' he said, but I didn't understand what he meant.

My hand burned, and I sucked in my breath and lifted my head to see what was happening. Aszulay was pouring something smelling of disinfectant over my palm. 'It hurts,' I said, and he nodded.

'I know. Soon it will stop.' He wrapped clean gauze around my hand. 'Now drink,' he said, and held a glass to my mouth. The drink was syrupy, but couldn't hide a bitterness. 'It will take away the pain and help the fever.'

I drank it all and lay back again, my hand throbbing terribly. Aszulay sat beside me, silent, and at some point—I had no idea of the time that passed—I realised I was no longer in pain, and a sleepy peacefulness came over me. 'It doesn't hurt any more,' I murmured.

'Good,' Aszulay said, stroking my forehead with his hand.

When I awoke the next morning, I lay for a few minutes, blinking in the dimness, wondering why I wasn't upstairs in my own room.

And then I lifted my hand, seeing the neat gauze wrapping.

Mena came in with a glass of tea, and I struggled to sit up. '*Kayf al-haal?*' she asked, handing me the glass.

I accepted it awkwardly with both hands, mindful of my palm. 'I am good,' I said in Arabic, answering her question. I did feel all right; I was no longer feverish, and my hand felt only a little tender and stiff.

I thought of Aszulay bending over me. 'Aszulay?' I said. 'He is here?'

'*La*,' Mena said, shaking her head.

Within an hour I felt well enough to go up to my room and change my clothes and brush my hair, although I was slightly shaky and my movements were clumsy because of my wrapped hand.

I was sitting in the courtyard shortly after that when Aszulay came in. I was shy as I looked at him; how much of last night had happened, and how much had been in my head?

But he smiled at me, and I smiled back. 'You look much better,' he said, nodding. 'I stayed until early this morning, but when I saw you no longer had a fever and the swelling was less, I left.' He crouched in front of me and took my hand, gently unwrapping the gauze. 'Yes, look. You will be all right now. The poison is gone.'

'Poison?' I said, looking at my upturned hand, resting lightly in Aszulay's. My palm had returned to its normal size, apart from the small sore in the middle.

I suddenly remembered that I had pressed my lips to his hand the night before. But he knew I had been delirious, and couldn't be responsible for my actions.

Aszulay rewound the gauze. 'Leave the wrapping for today, to keep the hand clean,' he said. 'By tomorrow it will be fine.'

'Poison?' I said again. 'What poison?'

'I took out a small shard of something from the wound. Bone. Some older pens had points made of sharpened bone.'

'But why would old bone cause an infection?'

'Old bone alone wouldn't. Perhaps . . . if it had been dipped in some substance . . .' He stopped. 'I don't know with certainty.'

'And if you hadn't taken it out? If Mena hadn't sent for you?'

'In three days I'll take Badou to the country,' he said, not wanting to answer my question. 'Do you still wish to go?'

I nodded, understanding that he wouldn't speak any further about what had happened to my hand. I couldn't ask him if he believed—as I did now—that Manon had tried to harm me. When she knew that I was going off with Aszulay and her son, she wanted to stop me.

I didn't ever want to see her again.

I also didn't want to think about Badou and Falida, alone with a woman capable of such evil.

Chapter Ten

THREE DAYS LATER, Aszulay came to Sharia Soura with Badou. Badou waited in the street while Aszulay came into the courtyard. I was draping my *haik* over my head when Aszulay said, 'Sidonie,' in such a way that I stopped, the cloth partway over my head.

'Yes?' I asked. He looked odd. Perhaps uncomfortable. I had never seen Aszulay uncomfortable.

'You're certain you wish to go?'

I nodded. 'Yes. Why?'

'At Manon's . . .' He stopped, then continued. 'When I went to get Badou—'

'No,' I said, and he fell silent. 'Whatever happened at Manon's, I don't want to know. I want to leave all thoughts of Manon and Sharia Zitoun behind. Just for two days, Aszulay. Please don't tell me anything about her.'

He looked at me for a long moment, as if debating with himself, and then, almost reluctantly, nodded. We went out through the gate, and he and Badou and I walked through narrow medina streets I hadn't yet discovered. I felt completely recovered, and carried a woven bag. Aszulay had two large burlap sacks slung over his shoulder.

We passed through a covered souk and then under a high arch in the medina wall; there was instantly a subtly different atmosphere. The people's dress was slightly altered, and many of the women, although draped in head shawls, weren't covered. The buildings were higher and narrower, the doors more richly ornamented.

'Where are we, Aszulay?' I asked.

'The Mellah,' he said. 'The Jewish Quarter.' He looked at me. 'You know about Morocco's Jews?'

I shook my head. Etienne had never mentioned them.

'*Melh* means salt. After the battles—in ancient times in Marrakesh—the Jews were given the task of salting the enemies' head. The heads were placed on the city walls, as was the custom.'

I thought of the genesis of the name for D'jemma el Fna.

'Now the Jews—especially the Jewesses—are important to the wealthy Moroccan women. They provide many services for those wives unable to leave their homes, bringing them high-quality cloth, making their clothing, showing them samples of jewellery to purchase. They are welcome within the harems. Come this way,' he said, turning sharply into a dark, narrow passage. 'I have my truck parked outside the Mellah's walls.'

Finally we went through another series of gateways, and Aszulay unlocked a wide set of double doors. Inside the enclosure was a vehicle with a boxlike shape. It was dusty and dented; like all the vehicles I had seen in Morocco, it appeared to have been driven hard.

Aszulay unlocked the doors, putting the sacks into the back, which was covered with canvas. I walked around the truck, running my hand over its bumpers.

'What is this vehicle? I don't recognise it,' I said.

Aszulay looked at me over the hood of the car. 'Fiat la Camionnette, 1925.'

'Ah. A Fiat,' I said, nodding. 'We had a . . .' I stopped. I was about to tell him about the Silver Ghost. 'I had a car,' I said.

'Does everyone in America have a car?'

'Oh, no,' I said. 'Not everyone.'

'Come, Badou,' he said now, 'climb in.'

Badou clambered in the driver's side, and, on his knees, grabbed the steering wheel and violently twisted it from side to side. 'Look at me, Sidonie, look! I'm driving,' he said, grinning. I smiled back, setting my bag at my feet. Badou slid beside me on the bench seat as Aszulay got in. He wound the end of his turban over his nose and mouth and turned the key. With a great cough and then a roar, the Fiat came to life.

On the outskirts of Marrakesh we stopped; Aszulay went to a stall and came back with a crate holding four live chickens. He put the crate in the back of the truck, which was separated from the seat by a canvas curtain. The chickens clucked and squawked.

When we were outside of Marrakesh, off the road and onto a *piste*, I asked Aszulay how long it would take to get to his family's home.

'Five hours, if there are no problems,' he said, his voice muffled by his turban. 'We're going southeast, into the Ourika valley. It's less than seventy kilometres from Marrakesh, but the *pistes* are very difficult to drive.' I watched him for a moment, enjoying the spectacle of a Blue Man of the Sahara driving the jolting truck instead of leading a camel. 'My family lives in a small village there.'

The afternoon was blue and red and white: the sky so clear and large overhead, the earth around us its distinctive colour, the snow-capped mountains towering in the distance. Aszulay uncovered his mouth and sang an Arabic song, his voice low and rich, and Badou clapped his hands in time to the rhythm, joining in on the chorus.

What would Etienne think of me if he could see me now? I was no longer the woman he had known in Albany.

Then again, he was not the man I thought I knew, either.

I didn't want to think of Etienne. I joined Badou in the hand-clapping. Jolting along in this truck on the narrow track, I thought I might feel insignificant surrounded by such immenseness. And yet I didn't feel small; instead, the grandness of the sky and mountains filled me with something that was almost, I told myself, the opposite.

'**O**urika valley,' Aszulay said, as we drove through gardens and plots of cultivated land. There were date groves, and intoxicating scents of mint and oleander. I recognised apricot and pomegranate and fig; it was a verdant valley. The sides towered above the masses of fields on the valley floor, and green crops undulated in the gentle breeze. Also on the sides of the hills running down from the High Atlas were hamlets made of the pounded red clay of the earth, mixed with straw: *pise*, Aszulay called them. Everywhere on the meandering *piste* near these small villages were women, trudging with sacks or bundles of sticks on their backs, often balancing babies in slings on one hip or on their chests. I kept swallowing, and my head ached slightly. I put my hand to my forehead, and Aszulay glanced at me.

'It's the height,' he said. 'Drink water.' I took the goatskin of water from behind the seat and drank, giving some to Badou and offering it to Aszulay, but he shook his head.

The valley grew narrower but kept rising gently. And then the *piste* came to an end. As we stepped out of the truck, I heard violently rushing water. Aszulay took the sacks from the back of the truck and slung them over one shoulder, balancing the crate of scolding chickens on the other. He motioned for me to bring my bag. 'You don't need your *haik* or veil here,' he said, and so I left them in the truck, wearing only my kaftan, and followed him, holding Badou's hand, towards the sound of the water. We started our way carefully down the path, worn by hoofs and feet.

Within a moment I knew I wouldn't be able to keep my balance, and picked up a long, firm stick from beside the path. Badou's smooth-soled little red *babouches* were slipping on the pebbly slope, and he stopped, clutching my kaftan for support. Aszulay looked back at us; he'd taken off his own *babouches* and thrown them down ahead of him, and was making the descent in bare feet.

'Wait,' he said, and, at a half-run reached the bottom of the slope. He set the sacks and crate on the ground. Then he stooped, taking a small pinch of the earth, and put it on his tongue. I watched, curious. I didn't know why he tasted the dirt, and yet something moved in me; it signified his connection to this red earth. He came back for us, scooping Badou into the crook of one arm. Badou put his arm around Aszulay's neck. Aszulay held out his hand to me, and I put mine into his, although I still used the stick with my other hand. We went slowly down the rough path. Aszulay's hand was able to close completely around mine; it was warm and dry. I knew mine was damp with nervousness, not only about keeping my balance, but about what was to come when we entered the village.

At the bottom of the slope he dropped my hand and set Badou down and again picked up the sacks and crate.

The village, climbing haphazardly up the side of a sloping hill, was one of the terraced settlements of *pise* houses with flat roofs. Because the hill and the houses were the same reddish-brown earth, and the houses clung to it as if dug out of the very hill itself, there was a chameleon sense about it.

At the foot of the hill was a circle of tents of woven animal hair. I hadn't seen them as we approached; like the village, they were indistinguishable from the earth. Camels sat on their knees in the dust, gazing straight ahead. Donkeys brayed and roosters crowed.

We walked upwards, through the village, and people came from their doorways, calling to Aszulay. He continually set down his burdens, greeting the men by kissing them three times on the cheeks as they hugged, chest to chest. They all stared at me, and I was uncomfortable. The women here wore long, modest dresses, but they resembled flocks of colourful birds; their dresses were embroidered around the hem and sleeves and neckline, sometimes flashing with small bits of silver jewellery. Some of the dresses were hooked on the shoulders with brass or silver clasps, which I knew, from discovering them in the souks, were called *fibulae*. The women, their faces uncovered, wore shawls draped over their heads, but these, while mostly black, were all embroidered with bright designs and flowers. They were all barefoot, and their feet and hands were decorated with henna.

I tried not to stare at them, but they were wonderful to look at. Some had streaks of saffron painted on their faces, or blue patterns tattooed on their chins or in the middle of their foreheads. Many of the forehead tattoos were two diagonal lines crossing each other at the top. Others had a line running straight from their lower lip to the bottom of their chin, with treelike branches radiating from it. Most of the tattoos had a geometric design. I could only assume that as well as being a thing of beauty, they designated a tribal identity.

We continued our gentle upward climb along the winding paths. Aszulay finally stopped in front of a house, setting down the crate and sacks and calling out. An older woman and two younger ones came from inside. While the two younger women wore the same decorated dresses and headscarves as the other village women, their faces were not tattooed, and the older woman wore a simple dark-blue robe and headscarf. Aszulay embraced the older one.

He looked at me and said something to her, but he wasn't speaking Arabic; I recognised nothing he said. Then he looked at me and said, '*Ma maman.*'

I nodded, anxious, unsure of whether to smile. His mother looked at me curiously, speaking in a questioning tone to Aszulay.

He answered, briefly, gesturing at Badou, and whatever he said satisfied his mother, for she just murmured something I took to mean *I see*.

I reached into my bag and pulled out a small bone teapot. I knew enough about Moroccan customs, by now, to bring a gift when visiting. I gave Aszulay's mother the teapot. She took it, turning it over in her hands and nodding seriously.

'And my sisters,' he said, pointing to the two other women, who looked to be in their mid to late twenties. 'Rabia and Zohra.'

I had expected one of them to be his wife.

As his sisters looked at me, I said, '*Ismi* Sidonie,' telling them my name, and then added, respectfully, '*Assalaam alykum*, peace be upon you.' I didn't know whether they would understand the Arabic greeting, but they both replied, in hushed and rather shy tones, *wa alykum assalaam*, and peace be upon you.

I gave each of them a small ceramic painted dish.

Badou stood beside me; the women paid no attention to him.

They all had a similar look: thin, sun-darkened faces with high cheekbones, dark flashing eyes touched with kohl, and strong white teeth. Zohra, the younger sister, had a dimple in her left cheek that gave a certain charm to her smile. In the folds of Rabia's dress a baby with kohl-lined eyes wiggled, peeking its head out. It stared at Badou; its eyes were blue, like Aszulay's.

'A baby, Badou,' I said, as if he didn't recognise what it was. But I was tense, not sure how to behave, and this gave me something to focus on. 'Is it a boy or a girl, do you think?'

He shrugged. I sensed he was experiencing a similar feeling to mine, even though he'd been here before. Aszulay's mother patted his shoulder, saying something to him, and he smiled, a small, tight smile.

'My nephew is Izri,' Aszulay said, answering my question. 'Eight months. Rabia's fourth child. Zohra has two daughters.' He opened the neck of one sack and drew out lengths of cloth and two necklaces of silver and amber, which he handed to his sisters. From the other sack he pulled out a large brass cooking pot for his mother. They all nodded, looking at each other's gifts, smiling their thanks at Aszulay.

Then they looked back at me. Aszulay's mother spoke. 'My mother welcomes you,' Aszulay said. 'The village is preparing a special meal in honour of the other guests, those in the tents below. They're from a distant village, but have travelled to visit members of their families living here now. We came at a good time.'

'*Shukran*,' I said, looking at Aszulay's mother. 'Thank you.'

'The language of the village—the people are Amazigh Berbers—is Tamazight. With my mother I speak our old language of the Sahara, Tamashek, the Tuareg language. The villagers understand only a little Arabic, basic phrases. They're isolated here, not seeing many strangers.'

Standing beside Aszulay, clutching my woven bag, I was very aware that I was not only a stranger, but a foreigner. I shook my head at all he'd just told me.

'It's complicated. But don't worry. I've taught Zohra a small amount of French. She's the scholar of the family.' He smiled at the younger woman and spoke, obviously telling her what he'd said, for she put her hands on her cheeks as if blushing, and then swatted his arm playfully.

Aszulay's mother patted my hand, in much the way she had patted Badou's shoulder, and this time I smiled at her.

A small crowd of children now joined Aszulay, Badou and me as we walked about the village. While the boys ran along beside us, the girls were skittish, stealing glances at me but immediately turning away if I looked back. They eventually left us, scampering off to chase each other, shouting and laughing. At the small river created by the waterfalls, some women washed clothes, pounding them against the rocks, and others filled goatskin water bags.

'Is this where you grew up?' I asked Aszulay.

'No,' he said. 'We didn't live in a village. As Blue Men, we lived on the other side of the High Atlas, across the Tizi-n-Tichka pass, in the southwestern Sahara that borders Mauritania. The women lived in tents while the men traded throughout the Sahara.'

'But why is your family here now?'

'When I was twelve, my father died,' he said. 'It's almost impossible for a nomad woman to live without a husband. As it is all over Morocco, a woman alone is not looked at with respect.'

I knew he wasn't thinking of me, but still, it made me wonder again how I was viewed here.

'So my mother and I and my sisters—they were very young then, babies—came here to live. But it was difficult; I was the man of my family, but still young.' He stopped, as if remembering. 'It took some time for us to be accepted.'

He looked around. 'In spite of that, it was a better place for us than the desert,' he said. 'And later, when I left, I always knew where they were, and could bring them what they needed when it was possible.'

I looked down at Badou, always close at my side. His face did not reflect the light-hearted frolic of these Berber children. He stayed back, obviously wanting to join in, and yet somehow fearful.

Aszulay called out, and one of the older girls—perhaps eight or nine—came to him. She kept her face turned from mine as Aszulay spoke to her. Then she took Badou by the hand and led him towards the other children. Badou walked stiffly at first, reluctant to go with the girl, but she chattered to him and he looked up at her, his eyes wide.

'Can he understand what the other children are saying?' I asked, watching Badou with the girl, and Aszulay shook his head.

'Our visits are too infrequent. But children understand in ways other than language,' he said. 'Children everywhere are children.'

The girl took Badou to the other children, and, as I watched, Badou smiled, a tentative smile, and then joined in the game of tossing pebbles into what looked like concentric circles drawn in the earth.

'He is all right now,' Aszulay said. 'He forgets, between the months we come, how to play with other children.'

Zohra approached us then, and spoke to Aszulay. He looked at me. 'Zohra will decorate you with henna, if you wish,' he said.

I looked down at my own sun-darkened hands.

'It is a gesture of friendliness. Of acceptance,' Aszulay said, and I was ashamed of my hesitancy.

'*Naam*,' I said, looking at Zohra. Yes.

At the foot of the village, in the middle of the circle of tents, was a fire. Over it hung a huge, bubbling black cauldron. A very short old woman stood with one hand on her hip, regularly stirring whatever was in the pot with a stick almost as tall as she.

Other women gathered around us as we sat in the doorway of one of the tents; Aszulay had gone to drink tea with the men. The women all sat gracefully, cross-legged, with their skirts draped over their knees. I couldn't do the same because of the inflexibility of my right leg, and had to sit with it straight out in front of me.

'You take,' Zohra said in French, and I frowned at her, not understanding. She touched the laces of my shoes. 'Take,' she said again, and I realised she meant I should take off my shoes. 'I make feet henna.'

I shook my head. 'I can't walk without my shoe,' I said, and tapped the built-up sole of my right shoe, pulling up my kaftan to the knee and touching my leg, and she nodded. 'You can do my hands,' I said, putting them out in front of me.

She smiled, unwrapping a little roll of cloth, and held up a slender pointed stick. She set the stick in her lap and picked up my hands, turning them over, studying them and murmuring to the other women. By the movements of their heads and the tone of their voices, I knew they were discussing what designs would be best.

Finally Zohra held the wooden stick in the air, and they all fell silent. Someone set down a small earthenware container of green paste, and Zohra dipped the end of the stick into it. Holding my right hand firmly in front of her chest, palm up, she bent over it, dipping and drawing, painstakingly but deftly covering my palm with an intricate pattern of geometric swirls. The tip of the wood touched my skin with the lightest sensation, almost like an insect making its way over my palm; the paste was cool. When she had covered the whole palm and fingers she turned my hand over and created a different pattern on the back. My hand grew tired, holding it so still with the fingers spread, and when it trembled, slightly, one of the other women gently held my wrist in support.

Zohra finished the right hand and took up the left. She reversed the pattern, so that the palm of one hand and the back of the other were the same.

When she had finished, she demonstrated that I was to keep my hands very still; another woman brought over a blackened chafing dish, its coals glowing. Zohra made it clear I was to hold my hands over the heat to help dry the paste.

Then she left me, still sitting on the ground with a few other women. They stayed there, talking and embroidering. My right leg ached from the unaccustomed position. More and more women came to the centre, taking turns stirring the big pot, and setting other pots on the edges of the fire. My hands were warm over the chafing dish. There was the comforting smell of cooking meat, and I realised I was very hungry. I hoped Badou was all right with the other children.

Eventually Zohra returned with a pot of warm water. The paste had turned black, and as Zohra gently washed and peeled it away, the designs, dark reddish-brown and delicate, emerged. I held out my hands, turning them over and admiring them.

'*C'est magnifique*, Zohra,' I said, and she smiled proudly, then gestured for me to come with her and eat, saying, '*Manger, manger*.'

The whole village and their guests were now gathering around the fire. Badou appeared with the older girl, and sat beside me; Zohra and her two daughters sat on my other side. I didn't see Aszulay; surely he was with his wife, I told myself.

One of the older women briskly stirred the pot, and then, with a huge metal lifter, pulled out a large goat's head. I didn't think I would be able to eat it.

Bowls of warm water were passed among us by little girls, and we washed our hands, drying them on the strips of cloth tied around the girls' waists.

I watched the spectacle of more heads being taken from the water and set on large brass trays, and then the stripping of the soft, meaty skulls. At least there were no eyeballs. As the women pulled off steaming, pale-yellow meat, they seasoned it with what looked like salt and crunchy paprika. They passed out smaller, earthen dishes of the meat, accompanied by cooked lentils and rice. I took my plate; I saw that the children ate from their mother's plates, and so I picked up a few shreds of the meat and blew on them, as I noticed the other women doing, and then put them into Badou's mouth. He chewed obediently, then opened his mouth for more, reminding me of a baby bird. I put the plate on my lap and gestured for him to help himself, and then, taking a deep breath, put a small sliver of the meat into my own mouth. It was salty and a bit stringy but surprisingly unobjectionable. Badou and I ate all the meat and lentils and rice on our plate, and then finished off the meal, as everywhere throughout Morocco, with sweet mint tea. The sun suddenly dropped behind the mountains, and, as the sky darkened and the air cooled, the fire grew brighter and higher.

I hadn't noticed when Aszulay returned, but as the women collected the empty plates, I saw him sitting with some other men. Like a few others, he held a long instrument that looked like a flute or fife.

I was glad he was back.

Badou got up and ran to Aszulay, settling beside him. One man beat a steady, slow rhythm on an hourglass-shaped clay drum, its top covered with what looked to be stretched and oiled goatskin, which he held between his legs. Others clapped their hands in a variety of syncopations. And then Aszulay and the other men put their flutes to their mouths and played, the melodic notes a sad lament.

I watched my own hands as I joined in the clapping. They looked beautiful, as if I wore rosy lace gloves. I clapped and clapped, moving my shoulders to the beat, wishing I knew the words to the songs the rest of the village sang.

The music stopped, and women served more tea. There were conversations all around me. Badou left Aszulay and again sat beside me, leaning his head against my arm. Then slowly a drumbeat started, and then another. Others took up their flutes again, but this time the music was not the former rather sonorous tunes, but a lively, rhythmic beat. Some of the men rose; Aszulay did as well, his forehead and lower face covered by the folds of his dark-blue turban.

They danced to the music then, whirling with each other, their robes flying out like dervishes. The women and children watched, clapping and making sounds with their mouths: a clicking and humming from their throats, and a strange high, continuous vibrating with their tongues. The men danced and danced; the fire grew higher, and above the stars pulsed.

Everyone was absorbed in the joy of the night and the music and the dance.

As was I.

And suddenly I saw myself, as if from afar, a woman in Moroccan dress, eating the food of the land, sitting around a fire under the North African sky and clapping my hennaed hands. I understood what it was to love, and to grieve over losing those who meant the most. To feel joy and to feel pain.

I closed my eyes, letting joy wash over me.

When I opened my eyes, a woman I hadn't seen before sat beside Aszulay. He was looking at her tattooed face, speaking intently, nodding, and she answered, and whatever she said made him throw back his head and laugh.

The woman was young and attractive in the bold, nomad way, her hair loosely braided, with a number of silver necklaces against her dark skin, her slender wrists covered in bangles. I watched them across the fire, the heat casting wavering shadows on their faces.

Here she was then: Aszulay's wife.

And suddenly I was overwhelmed, dismayed and confused by my feelings. I couldn't bear to watch them, and yet I couldn't look away.

The sensations of only moments before fled, and somehow, the beautiful evening was now spoiled.

I wanted to be sitting beside Aszulay. I wanted to make him laugh the way his wife did. I had never said anything clever or witty to him. All I had done was force him to be serious, to help me. To look after me, as he looked after Badou.

Like most of the other younger children, Badou had fallen asleep, curled in the cooling dust at my side. Zohra picked up her own sleeping daughter and motioned to me. I got to my feet and lifted Badou; he was limp and surprisingly heavy. I slowly followed Zohra.

As we went towards a tent, Zohra stopped, pointing to a small constellation that looked like a kite with a tail. She said something in Tamazight; I shook my head. She closed her eyes, concentrating, then opened them and said, '*La croix*.'

'The cross?'

She nodded, and I remembered the prediction of Mohammed and his monkey, Hasi. Mohammed had spouted clichés about finding something under the Southern Cross, most likely, I had thought at the time, the same story he told every foreign woman foolish enough to part with a sou or two. And yet, standing beneath the pulsing sky, it was suddenly important that I remember his exact words. *Under the Southern Cross you will understand that what you look for may take a different shape. You may not recognise it* . . . and then something about jinns.

Badou stirred against me, and, still looking at the Southern Cross, I held him tighter. His little body, even in the cool evening air, was so warm, and he smelled like the earth. I thought of Aszulay eating a pinch of red earth.

I looked away from the sky and down at Badou.

His bare feet were covered in dried mud from the river bank—where were his *babouches*?—and his face was content. He turned his head so that his nose pressed against my shoulder.

Zohra pulled aside a tent flap. Here a number of children lay asleep on piles of rugs and skins. A few coughed; the air in the tent was warm from all the bodies. An older woman sat in a corner, a decorated shawl wrapped around her as she watched over the sleeping children. Zohra laid her daughter down, and motioned for me to put Badou beside her. Then she pulled a rug tightly around them both.

I followed Zohra back to the fire. The air was cold now, and I shivered, crossing my arms over my chest. When I sat down, relishing the heat of the fire, I again saw Aszulay, now speaking earnestly to another man. The woman was no longer beside him, and although I knew he would join her later, the fact that he hadn't rushed off to be with her made me feel better.

He had removed his turban, and in the firelight I saw that his forehead and the sides of his face were banded in a shadowy hue; his skin, heated from dancing, had pulled the colour from his turban. Suddenly I wanted to breathe in the scent of his face. He would smell of wood smoke, and indigo.

I understood then that Aszulay would always be thus: a combination of what he had been and who he was now. Whether speaking his lovely, formal French, or Arabic or the complex twist of Tamazight, whether dressed in white, holding a spade in Monsieur Majorelle's garden, or driving a truck along the *piste* in blue, he was both sides of a coin. Distinguishable from each other and yet incapable of splitting.

In a while, Zohra again stood, motioning to me, and I followed her. She carried a small burning torch, but even with the moon and the carnival of stars above us, it was difficult to see. She stopped, looking back at me and holding out her hand. I took it, gratefully, and we walked around the fire. As we passed the men, Aszulay looked up at me.

I looked back at him, and something in his face made me open my mouth as if I couldn't get enough air. It wasn't a quick glance, and it wasn't with the dancing light as when he laughed with his wife. It was something different, something deep and mesmerising, and it made me dizzy, as if the fever of a few days earlier had returned. I stumbled on a root, and Zohra stopped, holding me upright. As I fell back into step with her, the moment had passed, and I didn't have the nerve to look back at Aszulay again.

In a few moments a form loomed in front of me. When Zohra ducked her head, I did the same. We stood inside one of the tents, where what looked, in the wavering light of the torch, like shadowy piles of skins covered with rough blankets were tightly packed together. Some forms lay still, as if deep in sleep. From a corner came girlish whispers and giggles; certainly this was a tent for unmarried women. Zohra led me to one of the piles of skins and left. I took off my shoes and got under the blanket in my kaftan. The young woman beside me pushed closer, her back against my chest. I had seen this type of closeness all over Morocco. Men crushed into each other in the square and the souks; Mena and Nawar and the old servant sat closely together on the roof, their shoulders and hips touching as they worked. Perhaps the closeness and bodily warmth produced a sense of belonging. Even little Badou wanted to be close, constantly climbing into his mother's or Aszulay's or my lap.

The Europeans and Americans in North Africa were the opposite of this. We each kept our polite space; we apologised over an accidental touch.

Lying there in the utter darkness, I tried to still my mind, but it was alive, whirling with what I had experienced under the night sky. With the way Aszulay had looked at me. I thought of him going up the terraced walk into one of the mud houses, lifting a rug or skin and lying beside his wife. Thoughts of her turning to him, of him wrapping his arms around her, came to me, and I put my own arm over my eyes, not wanting to visualise such things.

But, just as unbidden, now visions of Etienne, beside me in my bed on Juniper Road, flooded my head. Etienne. What was I feeling for him now, knowing what I knew? What would my life have been if he'd stayed with me in Albany, and had married me? What would my life have been if I hadn't lost the baby, and had one day been a mother?

What would my life have been if I had never come to Morocco?

But then . . . didn't I still wish that Etienne would marry me? Once he returned to Marrakesh, and I convinced him that his illness wouldn't stop me from loving him, he would surely agree to marry me.

I tried to remember how it felt to make love with Etienne.

But instead, my thoughts went to Aszulay and his wife.

What it would be like to make love with Aszulay. His sensitive mouth. His hands.

I couldn't sleep. I got up and pulled a heavy blanket from the bed. I wrapped it around my shoulders and went out into the night air.

The fire had died down, although it was still glowing. Without its high flames or the flares of torches, it was easier to see in the starlit night. And then I realised that there was a single figure still sitting in front of the fire.

Did I simply want it to be Aszulay, or was it really him? He sat in the place I had last seen Aszulay, but that didn't mean anything. Did I only imagine I recognised the set of his shoulders, the length of his hair? As I watched, the man wrapped himself in a blanket, and lay down by the glowing embers.

I returned to my tent, somehow comforted. It was wrong to feel pleasure at thinking that perhaps Aszulay didn't wish to be with his wife. And yet there it was. I was glad.

I awoke warm and relaxed, when the flap of the rug over the doorway was pulled back and clear morning light flooded in.

Outside the tent, women sat around a large brass kettle and a tin pan, taking turns pouring fresh water into the pan from the kettle, splashing the water over their faces. I did the same; then one of the women produced a tiny mirror and handed it to me. I thanked her with a smile, holding it up and then frowning and shaking my head at my wild reflection. Rabia came up behind me and, on her knees, combed through my hair, then braided it with fingers swift as swallows. She made one long braid, securing it with a twist of goat hair.

Then she came in front of me, again kneeling, and held up a long, thin stick, gesturing towards her eyes, and then mine. Kohl. I had never worn any form of make-up, but I nodded.

She held my chin with her left hand and outlined my eyes with the stick she held in her right. When she was done, she smiled.

I followed her up the footpath to the house where she and her mother and sister and their husbands and children lived. When I entered the one windowless room, the only light coming through the open doorway, it was difficult to see. I smelled something meaty, and there was the sizzle from a pan over heat.

I eventually made out piles of carpets with beautiful Berber designs covering the walls and floor; more were stacked in one corner to be used as beds. I recognised the design on my hands in one of the weavings. In the middle of the floor was a fire enclosed by stones, and a chimney made of pipe led out of an opening in the roof. The men must have left; there was only Aszulay's mother and Zohra, and a number of children of different ages. Aszulay's mother squatted on the floor next to a cluster of pots, stirring one of them.

Badou ran to me; I hadn't discerned him immediately in the tangle of children milling about the small room. His hair stood out at wild angles, and his mouth was smeared with what looked like honey. He again had on his red *babouches*.

'*Bonjour*, Badou. Did you sleep well?' I asked him, and he didn't respond, but held out his open hand.

On his dirty palm was his tooth.

'Badou,' I said, raising my eyebrows, and he grinned at me, showing me the little empty space in his smile.

'Keep it for me, to show Falida,' he said, giving it to me, and I put it into the bottom of my bag.

One of the girls took his hand, and he left the hut with her. He seemed a different child today. I looked at Zohra.

'*Bonjour*,' I said, and she laughed in a delighted way, returning the greeting, gesturing for me to sit down. I sat on one of the beautiful rugs, and she handed me an earthenware plate. I ate a spicy sausage and what appeared to be fried pancakes made from something grainy. It was all delicious.

Just as I had finished, Aszulay spoke my name. I looked behind me, and saw him in the doorway. I was unable to speak. I couldn't let him see, in my face, what I had been thinking about last night.

He didn't smile, and I realised he was studying my kohl-lined eyes. Then he said, 'I'm going to look at some of the crops. I'll take Badou. We'll leave later.'

All I could do was nod.

I spent the next few hours with Zohra and her daughters. We went to the river, Zohra carrying a basket of clothing on her head, and I watched as she and the children pounded the laundry against the rocks. I offered to help, but Zohra shook her head. She chatted with the other women, and I simply sat on a rock, looking around me.

The light was pure, with the sense of a shimmering mirage as I looked at the waving green of the fields. Here and there men moved about; they were too distant to distinguish, but I knew one was Aszulay.

We returned to the house, the wet clothing left behind to dry on the rocks. Aszulay's mother sat in the sun with her back against the wall, sorting olives in a basket. When she saw us she stood and went inside, returning with a beautiful shawl, its edges deeply embroidered with delicate twining vines and multicoloured flowers. She held it out to me.

I looked at it, running my hands over the designs. 'Beautiful,' I said.

She pushed it towards me now.

'*Pour vous*,' Zohra said. For you. '*Cadeau*.'

Refusing the gift would be an insult. I accepted it from the older woman's hands, clasping it against me and smiling at her. Then I draped it over my head and around my shoulders, and she nodded, pleased.

Aszulay came from inside the hut. He stopped, studying me, and then nodded in the same way his mother had, with the beginning of a smile, and that small hint of pleasure playing about his mouth gave me a strange sensation.

'**A**szulay?'

We'd left the village and had been driving, silently, for over an hour. Something had shifted between us since we'd come to the village. The way Aszulay had looked at me at the fire, and at my kohl-lined eyes, as I stood wrapped in the shawl his mother had given me . . . I knew, with certainty, that it wasn't just me feeling the change. I wanted to say something, but didn't know what.

Badou had climbed into the back of the truck, separated from us by the opened curtain of canvas. I had brought more French picture books with me, and had handed them back to Badou. He was slowly turning the pages of one of them.

Aszulay looked over at me when I finally said his name.

I couldn't avoid speaking of her any longer. 'Your wife. I saw her sitting with you around the fire. She's very pretty.'

Something flitted across his face, turning into something odd now, some unreadable expression. His jaw clenched, and suddenly I was afraid that I had, unknowingly, made a mistake with my simple statement.

'I'm sorry, Aszulay. Have I . . . did I say something wrong?'

He took his eyes from the *piste* to look at me. 'The woman—she was just one of the village women. I have known her many years.' I saw his throat move as he swallowed. 'I have no wife,' he said.

My mouth opened. 'But Manon . . . Manon told me you had a wife. She told me . . . when I saw her last.'

He didn't speak for a long time. Then he said, 'Manon was playing with words.' It was an odd statement, and I didn't understand it.

'Oh.' There seemed nothing more to say, and we again drove in silence. Last night, what I had experienced was jealousy. I couldn't deny it. So now, when he dismissed the woman as simply one of the villagers, saying he didn't have a wife, shouldn't I feel something like pleasure? But my reaction was the opposite. Aszulay's response troubled me. His face, his voice, his suddenly stiff hold on the steering wheel all told me there was something more. I had somehow upset him.

He pulled to the side of the *piste* and turned off the engine, and then got out of the truck and unstrapped one of the large metal containers of fuel from the roof. Using a funnel, he poured gas into the tank. When he got back into the truck, the smell of the fuel surrounded him.

'We shouldn't have left so late. The light is going early today; it's the dust,' he said.

I nodded.

'I had children,' he said then. 'Two.'

The word *had* made the air in the truck suddenly too oppressive. It was as if there was no oxygen.

'It was a fever. It killed my children, and my wife. Iliana,' he said, simply. 'Many died of this fever. Rabia's first son also died.'

He tucked the end of his turban over his lower face and started the engine, and we continued along the *piste*.

I thought of Manon, slyly smiling as she told me Aszulay had a wife. I glanced at Aszulay, but he said nothing more.

Within half an hour, the sky had turned a strange pale yellow. There was no more sun, and a wind came up, blowing so strongly that I saw how Aszulay had to grip the steering wheel to keep the truck on the track. Suddenly there was no distinction between earth and sky; it was a solid wall of dust. And yet Aszulay seemed to know where to go. I imagined him in the sandstorms of a desert, and how the knowledge of direction would be part of his nomadic instinct. Perhaps part of his genetic make-up, carried within his ancestors for centuries.

I thought of what Etienne carried from his father.

We had rolled up the windows as soon as the wind started, but still it howled around the cracks, blowing in the sandy dust. Finally Aszulay turned the wheel sharply to one side, and stopped the truck.

Badou kneeled behind us, looking through the windshield. The wind whipped around the vehicle so ferociously that it swayed.

Nothing was visible.

'I don't like it, Oncle Aszulay,' Badou said, and his mouth turned down as his breathing became ragged. 'Is it jinns?' Tears filled his eyes. It was the first time I had seen him cry.

'Of course not, Badou. It's only wind. Only wind,' Aszulay repeated. 'We just have to wait until it stops, so we can see the *piste* again.'

'But . . .' Badou leaned over and whispered into Aszulay's ear.

'He must go outside,' Aszulay said, his hand on the door handle.

'I'll take him,' I said, because I was in the same situation.

'No. The wind is so strong. I'll—'

'Please, Aszulay. Let me take him,' I said, and Aszulay nodded, understanding, while Badou climbed over the seat into my lap.

'Keep one hand on the truck at all times,' Aszulay said, as we pushed open the door and clambered out into the wind.

Badou immediately turned to face the truck, pulling up his jellaba.

'I'm just going around to the back of the truck, Badou,' I said, loudly, into his ear. With one hand on the truck as Aszulay had instructed, I went to the back, where I fought with my kaftan, whipping about me in the wind.

It took only moments, and when I made my way back to the passenger side, Badou wasn't there. I opened the door and climbed in, pushing my hair back and rubbing at my eyes.

'Where is he?' Aszulay said, and I turned to him, blinking.

'What do you mean?' I climbed on my knees, pushing aside the canvas curtain, but Aszulay had already opened his door. 'I left him only for a second . . . I thought he came back. . .'

'Stay inside,' Aszulay shouted, over the wind.

'No, I'll come—'

'I said stay inside,' he yelled again, and slammed the door. I sat as if frozen, staring through the windshield. Surely Badou was just at the front of the truck. He must have been crouching near the tyre. Aszulay would bring him right back.

But Aszulay didn't immediately come back into the truck with Badou. My heart thudded. How could I have left him, even for that moment? I closed my eyes, my fingers laced in front of my face, rocking back and forth, saying, 'Let him find him, let him find him.'

But they didn't come back.

The truck grew darker and darker. I wept, I prayed. Could Badou survive even for a short time in this dust, or would it choke him? And Aszulay. I saw him wandering, calling for Badou. He had just told me he'd lost his own two children. Now . . .

I simply sat there, in the slightly rocking truck, staring at the nothingness beyond the windshield. An hour passed.

And then the driver's door banged open, and Aszulay pushed Badou in, climbed in behind him, and slammed the door.

I grabbed Badou, pulling away Aszulay's turban. It was wrapped completely around Badou's head and torso. I uncovered his little face;

he stared at me. Sand was stuck in dried tracks down his cheeks.

'Sidonie. I was lost. I didn't keep my hand on the truck.'

'I know. But you're safe now. You're safe,' I repeated, 'you're back in the truck.' And then I looked over his head at Aszulay, knowing what a fool he must think me, how angry he would be.

There was nothing but exhaustion on Aszulay's face. His eyes were closed as he leaned his head back. His hair and eyebrows and eyelashes were so coated that they were no longer black, but an odd dusty red. His nostrils were filled with the dust as well.

'Are you . . . you're all right, Aszulay?' I asked, my voice stuttering with tears.

'Give him water,' he said, and I moved Badou so I could lean over the back seat and grab the skin of water. I took out the cork and held it to Badou's mouth. He drank and drank, letting it run down his chin and neck. When he had finished, I held the skin to Aszulay, but his eyes were still closed. I moved closer, putting the mouth of the skin to his lips, and as it touched them he drank, still not opening his eyes.

When he put his hand up to push away the skin, I poured water onto the end of his turban and wiped his eyes, trying to clear away as much grit as I could. He took the wet cloth from me and rubbed his face until he at last opened his eyes.

'I'm sorry,' I whispered.

He didn't answer for a moment. 'I found him not far from the truck. But I couldn't take a chance on not getting back, on wandering in the wrong direction. We took shelter in a small shelf of earth driven up by the wind. I waited, and finally the wind changed direction just enough for me to see the truck.' He looked down at Badou. 'I made you a little Blue Man, yes?'

Badou nodded, and left my lap to push against Aszulay's side. Aszulay put his arm around him.

Time passed. At some point Aszulay began to hum, holding Badou against him with one arm. It was a quiet, sad melody, much like the one he had played on the fife—the *rekka*, I knew now that it was called.

I imagined him holding his own children like this, humming to soothe them. I turned my head, staring at the swirling sand and dust, feeling I was witnessing something too personal.

After a while he stopped humming, and I looked back at him. Badou had fallen asleep, his head on Aszulay's chest.

'Will the wind end soon?'

'I don't know. But we'll spend the night here. Even if the wind stops, it's too dark for me to drive the *piste* safely. Much of it will be covered.'

I nodded. It was almost completely dark in the truck, due to both the dust and the approach of evening. Aszulay reached beneath the seat and pulled out a candle and a box of wooden matches. He lit the candle and wedged it into a small opening on the dashboard.

We sat in the soft light.

'Aszulay,' I said. 'I'm so sorry. I don't know how—'

'It's over,' he interrupted. 'He's all right. He was only frightened.'

'So was I,' I said, my mouth trembling.

'This country can be a fearsome place,' he said. 'I know all of its tricks, because it's my home. I don't expect those not born here to know it in the same way.'

He was telling me he understood, and I was grateful. I took a breath, and then reached my hand to him. 'Thank you,' I said.

He looked down at my hennaed hand, then took it and looked back at me. I thought of the look we had shared the night before, and had to lower my head, staring at our joined hands, unable to look into his face. His thumb traced my palm, gently touching the healed sore.

Finally I raised my head. He was still looking at me. In the flickering candlelight the curve of his high cheekbone was moulded. I wanted to touch it. He leaned closer to me, then looked down at Badou.

'He's asleep,' I whispered, not wanting him to stop because of the child.

But Aszulay sat back, and I felt a deep stab of disappointment. 'Maybe you will tell me a story to pass the time,' he said, softly. His hand closed more tightly around mine. 'A story about America. About an American woman.'

It was difficult to breathe. I shook my head. 'You,' I said. 'Your story, and then mine.'

He stroked Badou's hair with his other hand. 'When I was thirteen years old, Monsieur Duverger bought me, to work for Manon's mother.'

I drew in my breath. 'You were a slave?'

'No. I'm not a slave. I'm a Tuareg. You know this.'

'But . . . *bought* you?'

He shrugged. 'Children often go from the country to work in the city. Children of the *bled* are hard workers.'

'I don't see the difference.'

'There have long been slaves brought in from other parts of Africa. With my father, on our caravans, we sometimes transported salt, sometimes gold, sometimes amber and ostrich feathers. Sometimes black slaves, from Mali and Mauritania. But it's not the same with young Moroccans from the country. The family is given a certain agreed-upon amount, and the children act as servants. They're paid a small sum, and a few times a year, if they know where their family is, they can visit them. Or if a member of the family comes into the city, they're allowed to see each other. When the child servant reaches a certain age, he can leave if he wishes.'

The truck still rocked slightly, back and forth. Back and forth. But now, sitting in the candlelight with Aszulay, my hand in his, Badou asleep between us, it was comforting.

'I told you my father died when we lived as nomads,' he said. 'At twelve I was too young to go on the caravans through the desert by myself, and I didn't wish to join another nomad group. So it was my choice to sell our camels and tell my mother I would work in Marrakesh. She didn't want me to. But I knew that in this way she would get a price for me, and after that I could help provide for her and my sisters. And they would be safe, in the village.'

'But are children sold to the French, or to Moroccans?'

'Both. Monsieur Duverger bought me for Manon's mother, to be the man of the house. He wanted Rachida's life to be better, and so he gave me to her, and I did the heavy work. Manon was a year younger than I, and she became my friend. She was kind to me.'

'Manon? Manon was kind to you?'

The light from the candle wavered across Aszulay's face. 'She taught me to speak French properly. She showed me how to read and write. I don't know how she learned. She was the daughter of an Arab woman; there was no school for her. We became like brother and sister.'

'Brother and sister?'

He nodded. 'We looked out for each other. We were both lonely. I missed my family. She . . . I don't know what she missed. But there was a loneliness about her, always.'

'But . . . you mean . . .' I stopped.

'What?'

I licked my lips. 'All this time, I thought, well, I just assumed, that you and Manon were . . . you were lovers.'

He stared at me. 'Manon? But why did you think this?'

'What else was I to think?' I said. 'How else would I guess at your relationship? And Manon—I saw the way she behaved around you.'

'Manon cannot help herself. If any man is present she acts the same way. But do you believe Manon is the sort of woman I could be with?'

he said, quietly, his eyes fixed on me, and I had to look down, at Badou.

I didn't answer, trying to keep my breathing under control.

'I helped her in the past because of our shared life, but now . . . it's because of this little one. I am attached to Manon only because of Badou.' Aszulay let go of my hand. He took off Badou's *babouches* and closed his hands around the small bare feet.

'And this is how I knew Etienne and Guillaume,' he continued. 'They didn't notice me, as I was of no importance, but I watched them, and knew them through what I observed.'

Suddenly I was embarrassed for Etienne, for how he must have treated—or simply ignored—Aszulay. Etienne with everything, and Aszulay with nothing. And yet now . . . who had more?

'Later, when we all grew older,' Aszulay continued, 'Manon couldn't stop talking about Etienne and Guillaume. She was angry with them because she wanted their lives. When they went to Paris, she begged Monsieur Duverger to send her to a good school too, to study art. But he said no. He told her his sons had one place in his heart, and she another. That she must accept this. But Manon would never accept it.'

Of course.

'It grew even harder for Manon; her mother died and Monsieur Duverger was being consumed by his illness, growing more and more confused. By this time Manon was a young woman; she had to find a job. So she worked as a servant in a French house, like her mother. She was always angry; she was . . . '

'Obsessed?'

'Yes. She was obsessed. She talked about wanting Monsieur Duverger's sons to suffer like she suffered. But what could she do? They now lived in Paris most of the time. Then one summer Guillaume came back, and was drowned, in the sea at Essaouria. Etienne came to Marrakesh for his brother's funeral, but stayed only a few days. The next year he came home again for his mother's funeral; she died suddenly when her heart failed. And the following year Monsieur Duverger died, and that was the last time Etienne came home. Over seven years ago. Manon went to the funeral. She saw Etienne there.'

'And then?'

Aszulay didn't say anything for a few moments. 'Then Etienne went to America,' he said. There was silence but for Badou's soft breathing. '*C'est tout*. That's all,' he said.

But I knew there was something he wasn't telling me.

'Is that when Manon told him that she was his half-sister? There was no reason not to; her mother was dead, and all of Etienne's family. Did she tell him to hurt him, to make him think less well of his father?'

'The rest of that story, the part about Etienne, is Manon's,' Aszulay said. 'I cannot tell it.'

'But you remained friends with Manon all this time,' I said.

'We were apart for some years. When her mother died and Manon went to live with the French family she worked for, I left Morocco.'

'You left? Where did you go?'

'Many places. I was young, and strong. I went first to Algeria, later to Mauritania and Mali. I am a nomad at heart,' he said, and smiled.

I looked at the candle, and its reflection in the windshield.

'And then I went to Spain,' he said.

'Spain?' I turned to him.

He nodded. 'I lived first in Malaga, then Seville, and finally in Barcelona. I learned to speak Spanish easily; it's not so different from French. It was a good time for me. I discovered so much about the world. And about people.'

'How long did you live there?'

He was silent for a long moment. 'I was there five years,' he said.

'That's a long time. Did you think you would stay permanently?'

He reached out and ran his fingers over the tip of the flame. 'I was in the prison in Barcelona for two years.'

I didn't respond.

'I was headstrong. I was in a fight with a group of men. One of the others was hurt very badly,' he said, with no emotion, still watching his hand passing over the flame. 'Prison gives one time to think. When I was there, I could imagine returning only to Morocco. I thought that if I should live to see my homeland, I would go back to the desert, and go on the caravans again, and live in a tent. Life is simple in the desert.'

'And so when you were released . . . that's what you did?'

He nodded. 'First I went to the village. I saw my mother and my sisters and their families. Then I went back to the Sahara, as I had promised myself.'

'But . . .' I said, because I heard it in his voice.

'I had come back from Spain with no money. I couldn't afford to buy my own caravan of camels, and I found it difficult to work under another caravan leader. After one long and unsatisfactory caravan to Timbuktu, I returned to the village. I needed—I wanted—to settle down. I wanted my own family, a permanent home. I married Iliana, and in three years we had two children. A son and a daughter.'

He stopped, suddenly, as though his voice had been cut off.

I waited.

He cleared his throat. 'I loved my wife, and my children, but it was the same as when I had tried to make a new life in the desert; I had been away too long. I had known the life of cities, and had seen too much on my travels. I tried hard to accept the village life, working in the fields with the other men, but I didn't belong to this life. Even though—as you saw—it's beautiful, and the people are friendly, it reminded me, in a strange way, of the prison. I spoke to Iliana about moving into Marrakesh, about raising our children there, but she was frightened at the idea; she had always lived in the Ourika valley. So I resigned myself to my choice, and I tried to make a good life for us for those few years. But after . . .' He stopped again, then continued. 'After I lost Iliana and the children, there seemed no point in staying in the village. There was no happiness for me there any longer.'

We sat in silence for a few moments, listening to the wind.

'I came back to Marrakesh and found work. Of course I saw Manon again, and the life she had chosen. She had left the French family, and lived on the kindness of men. We were both unhappy, but for me it was the sadness of grief. And I knew that grief would, some day, pass, or at least lessen to where it was not a daily and deep pain.'

It was difficult to watch Aszulay speak; I had never before seen his face like this. It was always honest, but now it was vulnerable.

'Manon's unhappiness was different from mine; it was caused by her anger. She held on to an old resentment—that she was not given what she thought she deserved—until it crippled her.'

Aszulay had used the word *crippled* unconsciously; obviously he didn't view me in this way, nor did he know that what he was saying was affecting me, making me think about my own life. My own resentments.

'But when she had Badou—something she hadn't expected or, I believe, ever wanted—she became more desperate. She was not young, and had a fatherless child. She has found it difficult to be a mother. She simply tolerates him, but she doesn't harm him.'

Watching Badou's chest rise and fall as he breathed, softly, in sleep, I thought of Falida and her bruises. 'She ignores him. Sometimes he's hungry, and dirty,' I said, not liking that Aszulay was defending Manon and her treatment of Badou.

'I don't think Manon is capable of the kind of love a woman should have—naturally—for a child,' he said. 'Something is missing inside her.'

The wind changed direction, whispering through the tiny crack at the top of the window, and the candle was extinguished in a sudden whoosh.

'And now you,' Aszulay said.

'Me?' I repeated. I could see nothing in the blackness.

'Your story,' he said. 'I've told you my story. Now you tell yours.'

'But . . . mine has nothing of interest,' I said. 'Nothing at all. Compared to yours. . .'

'What makes you think this?'

'I have lived . . . a small life.'

There was a rustling sound, and the seat between us dipped as he laid Badou down. I gently lifted his head into my lap. I envisioned Aszulay still holding his feet, the child's body a bridge between us. I pulled the blanket on the seat up over Badou.

'No life is small,' Aszulay said, his voice low. 'The life of the bird is as important as the life of the king. Just different.'

And then there was a lift of air, and I felt, rather than saw, Aszulay's face close to mine. I put my hands out, and felt his cheekbones under my fingers, and then his lips were upon mine.

Badou stirred, and we moved apart.

'Tell me your story,' Aszulay whispered in the darkness.

I was silent for a moment, and then began.

Chapter Eleven

I AWOKE SLOWLY, my neck stiff from leaning into the corner. I twisted my head from side to side as I looked through the windshield. The wind had blown itself out, and the morning was still.

Aszulay and Badou crouched around a small fire; a steaming black tin pot sat in a pile of burning twigs.

I got out of the truck, aware of the new intimacy Aszulay and I had shared. It wasn't only our kiss, but even more so the telling each other the details of our lives in the long night.

'We've already had our breakfast,' Aszulay said, watching me as I came to the fire. 'Sit, and eat.' He spoke as always, but the way he looked at me told me something else.

'You had food with you?' I asked, starting to lower myself to the ground, awkwardly because of my leg, but Aszulay gestured to a large stone. He'd folded the blanket over it. I went to it, grateful for his thoughtfulness.

'The people of Morocco never trust the weather,' he said, smiling at me as though we shared a joke. I remembered how Mustapha and Aziz had carried supplies in the trunk of the Citroën. Using the end of his turban, Aszulay lifted the pot from the flames and poured it into a tin can that I could see held crushed mint and sugar. Then, still using his turban, he set the can on the ground in front of me. 'Badou, give Sidonie some bread.'

Badou handed me a thick round he held in his lap. I tore a chunk from it and dipped it into the tea to soften it. I ate it all, suddenly ravenous, and by then the tea was cool enough to drink.

'You look like Maman,' Badou said.

'Really,' I said, trying not to let him see that his statement unnerved me. Manon was earthy, and beautiful.

'*Oui*,' he said, seriously. 'Yes. You look like Maman. Oncle Aszulay!' he called. 'Sidonie looks like Maman now.'

Aszulay had been extinguishing the fire with earth. He glanced at me, but I couldn't tell what he was thinking. 'Come. We're ready to go,' he called back.

As Badou clambered into the cab of the truck, and Aszulay slid in behind the wheel, I stopped, my hand on the passenger door. 'Aszulay,' I said. 'Could I drive the truck back to Marrakesh?'

'But . . . you told me about the accident. With your father. You said. . .'

'I know. But I feel differently today,' I said. 'Today I think it's time for me to drive again.'

'You have forgiven yourself,' he said, and I blinked. Was he right? Did I want to drive because I no longer felt the unbearable weight of what had happened the last time I drove with someone I loved? I thought of my father, and for the first time there was no deep pain. Perhaps Aszulay was right. Perhaps I had found peace.

'A truck is not like driving a car,' Aszulay said, when I didn't respond. 'And as I said last night, the *pistes* will be covered in places. It won't be easy.'

'Probably not. But I can try. I'm sure you'll help me if I have trouble.' I lifted my chin and smiled at him.

He left the driver's side and came to stand beside me. 'Well. It appears I am to be driven through the *bled* by an American woman.' He grinned at me, and ducked his head and looked into the cab. 'I think this will be a good experience. What do you think, eh, Badou? Will you like Sidonie driving us? We can sit back, and let her do the work.'

'*Oui*,' Badou said, seriously. 'Sidonie can do the work.'

I got behind the wheel and placed my feet on the pedals and my hands on the steering wheel. I turned the key, and when the engine roared to life, I looked at Aszulay and smiled. He smiled back.

We were back in Marrakesh just after noon, leaving the truck in the garage on the outskirts of the city. It had definitely been a difficult drive, but I had managed, only once slipping off the *piste*, but immediately redirecting the car and getting back on the narrow track. I let Badou honk the horn in the stillness of the empty *bled*, and he laughed over and over.

We passed through a small, busy souk not far from Sharia Soura. Aszulay and I walked side by side, while Badou was a few feet ahead of us. I was aware of Aszulay's blue sleeve brushing mine occasionally. I glanced up at him. What did I want him to say? I knew he felt what I felt. I knew he wanted me as I wanted him.

'I have three canvases to work on this week,' I finally said, breaking the comfortable silence. 'I took one of my oils to the hotel, and they said they'd take it on consignment, as well as more watercolours.' I smiled up at him, but he was silent, staring straight ahead.

'Aszulay?' I said, and when he didn't turn to me, I followed his gaze.

A dark-haired man, his shoulders gaunt and curved under his linen jacket, turned a corner ahead of us. I had only time to catch a glimpse of his pale profile. But I knew. This time I knew. It wasn't like all the other times I had thought I'd seen Etienne in Marrakesh.

I stopped for one instant, and then, dropping my bag, pushed through the throngs in the square, turning the corner where he had been, but here was a wide street, lined with markets, teeming with people and animals.

'Etienne,' I shouted into the swarming milieu. I snatched my veil from my face so that my voice was clearer. 'Etienne!' I worked my way through the crowds, calling his name, but my voice was lost, blending into the rest of the clamour. Panting, I finally stopped in the middle of the street, staring at the sea of people and animals milling around me.

Aszulay touched my arm. I looked up at him. 'It was Etienne,' I said. 'You saw him. I know you did. He's here, Aszulay. He's in Marrakesh.'

He pulled my arm, leading me away so that we were standing under the shaded overhang of a gate, where the noise wasn't so intense. 'Badou,' he said, reaching into his robe and pulling out a few coins, 'please go and buy bread. From the stall, there,' he said, pointing.

Badou took the money and ran off.

'I must tell you something,' Aszulay said. I absently noticed that he had my bag over his shoulder.

I nodded, thinking only of Etienne. He was here, in Marrakesh.

'When I came to get you, on our way to the countryside . . .' Aszulay hesitated. 'I should have spoken of it, even though you asked me not to. Sidonie. Look at me. Please.'

I was still staring into the street. 'Spoken about what?' I asked, turning towards him.

'At Manon's, when I went to pick up Badou just before I came to you,' he glanced at Badou, waiting for the bread, 'Etienne was there.'

He said the final three words in a rush. I opened my mouth, then closed it.

'I should have told you,' he said. 'Even though you asked me not to speak of Manon, and Sharia Zitoun, I should have told you.'

I leaned against the gate. 'Etienne is at Manon's?' I said.

He nodded. 'And I didn't tell you because. . .'

I waited, watching his mouth.

'Because I wished you to come to the *bled* with us. With me. I knew that if I told you Etienne was here, you wouldn't come. And . . . and something else.'

Still I stood there. When he didn't speak, I said, in a quiet voice, 'What else?'

'I didn't want you to go and face Manon and Etienne by yourself. I didn't want to leave Marrakesh, knowing. . .'

'Knowing . . .?'

But Badou came running back then, the bread under his arm.

I looked down at the boy, who glanced from me to Aszulay.

'Does he know? Does he know I'm here?' I asked Aszulay.

Aszulay nodded.

'But he doesn't know where I am.' I stated it, rather than asked it.

Again Aszulay nodded.

'But . . . if he knew I was here, he must have asked you, or Manon, about me, how I was. Where I was. Wouldn't he have tried to find me, over these past few days?'

Again, Aszulay didn't appear to have an answer. I had never seen him like this.

'Aszulay. Has he been looking for me?'

'I don't know, Sidonie.' He took a deep breath. 'I don't know.'

'Let's go, Oncle Aszulay,' Badou said. 'I have the bread for Maman.'

'You should have told me,' I said to Aszulay, ignoring Badou. 'You let me go off with you, knowing, all along, that this—that Etienne—was the reason I was in Marrakesh. And yet you . . . you betrayed me, Aszulay.' My voice had risen.

'No, Sidonie. I didn't betray you.' Aszulay's voice was low, and his face held something. Perhaps anguish. 'I . . . I wished to protect you.'

I pulled at my bag, and he slid it off his arm. 'Protect me from what?' I said, louder than necessary, then I slung the bag over my shoulder and turned sharply, walking alone back to Sharia Soura.

I went to my room and lay on the bed. Etienne was here; I could be facing him within the hour, if I so wished. But why did I feel more a sense of dread than excitement? As I'd just told Aszulay, this was why I'd come to Marrakesh. This was why I'd waited all this time. Why was I so angry at Aszulay? Was it really anger, or was it something else?

I rose and looked at myself in the mirror.

I saw how I resembled Manon.

Now everything was different. It was so complicated. What had just unfolded between Aszulay and me . . .

I couldn't go to Sharia Zitoun just yet. I needed a little more time, one more night, to prepare myself to see Etienne.

Of course I was unable to sleep at all. My thoughts went from Aszulay's kiss, to Etienne, and what I would say to him. What he would say to me.

I tossed and turned through the endless night, and was glad to finally hear the morning prayer. I bathed in a tub in my room, washing my hair. I pulled my best dress—the green silk with cap sleeves—from my case and put it on. I brushed my damp hair back into its usual style, pinning it firmly, and studied myself in the long mirror.

The dress was all wrong, wrinkled badly and hanging oddly on me. Although I could never appear pale with my darkened skin, there was a drawn look about me, as though I had just recovered from a tiring illness. And with my hair back, my face appeared too severe, too angular.

I sat on my bed. Then I unpinned my hair, feeling the thick waves fall over my shoulders. I took off my dress and put on a kaftan. I took my veil and *haik* and went downstairs. I asked Mena for her kohl, and outlined my eyes. Then I called for Najeeb, and went to Sharia Zitoun.

I stared at the *hamsa* on the saffron gate. I closed my eyes and knocked.

Within a moment Falida called out, asking who it was.

'Mademoiselle O'Shea,' I said, quietly.

She opened the door. I stood there, unable to force my feet forward.

'Mademoiselle?' Falida said. 'You come in?'

I nodded, taking a deep breath, and stepped into the courtyard. There were loud voices from within the house, although I couldn't make out what was said. Badou sat on the bottom step of the outside staircase.

'*Bonjour*, Sidonie,' he said, but he stayed where he was, not running to me as he usually did.

'*Bonjour*, Badou. Falida, is Monsieur Duverger in the house?'

She nodded.

'Please go and tell him Mademoiselle O'Shea is here,' I said.

She went inside, and the voices stopped abruptly.

I stood, trembling slightly, and suddenly there he was. Etienne. My Etienne. My initial reaction was shock at his appearance; he was much thinner than I remembered him. And yet his face was somehow bloated, and very pale. Had he always been this pale, or was it that I was used to a darker face now?

He stared at me.

I tried to remember that I loved him. But seeing him standing there, looking so . . . vacant, I felt nothing like love. I felt hatred. I thought of all I'd gone through, coming here, searching for him, having to deal with Manon. Then waiting for him.

I hadn't thought it would be like this. I had imagined him holding out his arms, and me running to him. Or me weeping, him weeping, both of us weeping. Oh, I'd created so many images.

Instead, we simply stood there, looking at each other.

He took a few steps towards me. He held a glass in one hand; even with the distance between us, I could smell alcohol. 'Sidonie?' he said, frowning, his forehead creasing.

I pulled off my *haik* and veil. 'Yes,' I said. I thought my voice might be shaky, weak, but it wasn't. And my trembling had stopped completely. 'Yes, it's me. Don't you know me?' I asked.

His eyes widened. 'You look . . . you're different.'

'As are you,' I said.

'Manon told me you were in Marrakesh. I couldn't believe it. You came all this way.' His eyes ran down my body, hidden under the loose kaftan. Surely Manon had told him there was no longer a baby. 'But . . . how? And. . .'

He didn't say *why*. But I heard it.

'Yes,' I said again. 'I came all this way. And I lost the baby. In Marseilles. In case Manon hasn't told you. In case you're wondering.' It came out so easily, with so little emotion. I knew that Etienne would be relieved.

He had the grace to shake his head. 'I'm so sorry. It must have been a terrible time for you,' he said. 'I'm sorry I wasn't there with you.'

But he wasn't sorry. I could see it; it was just his usual way of speaking. He always knew what to say. He'd known what to say to me every time he saw me in Albany. And at that, something rough and barbed pushed through me, something that might have been one of the Moroccan jinns, and I ran at him. I slapped his face, hard, on one side and then the other. The glass fell from his hand, crashing onto the tiles and exploding into pieces. 'You're not sorry. Don't say you're sorry, with that simpering look on your face,' I said, my voice loud.

Etienne stepped back, his hand on one cheek. There was blood on his lip. 'I deserved that,' he said, staring at me, blinking. Then he shook his head. 'But Sidonie, you don't know everything.'

'I know that you ran from me, within days of me telling you I was pregnant. You left Albany without even the courtesy of a phone call. A letter. Anything. That's all I need to know.'

'So you came all the way here to tell me that?' Suddenly he listed to one side, but caught himself, and sat down on a stool. 'To slap me?'

'No. I came here looking for you because—'

And then Manon was in the doorway. 'Because she couldn't keep away,' she said. 'And look at your behaviour,' she said to me, shaking her head, but there was something pleased in her expression. 'The woman wronged?' She looked behind me. 'What are you two staring at?' she said then, and I turned to see Badou huddled against Falida, near the gate. She had her arms around him as though to protect him. 'Get out,' Manon said, and Falida took Badou's hand and they ran through the gate, leaving it open behind them.

'I know you're not well,' I said now, breathing heavily. 'Manon told me. What is it? What are the jinns she talked about?'

'I can't practise medicine any more,' he said, lifting one hand and looking at it as if it were his enemy. 'I can't trust myself to be responsible for anyone's life.' Now he looked back at me with a tortured expression. 'All I can do is consult. For a while. My life is over. I saw what happened to my father. Now it will happen to me. It's Huntington's chorea.'

The name meant nothing to me.

'I'm sorry for your illness, Etienne. But you should have told me,' I said. 'You didn't have to leave me like that. I would have understood.'

'I would have understood,' Manon mimicked, her voice high and silly, but with something dark underneath.

'Can we go somewhere?' I said, glancing at her, and then back to Etienne. 'Somewhere where we can speak alone? Don't you have anything to say to me? About us? About our time in Albany?'

'That time is gone, Sidonie,' he said. 'You and me in Albany. Gone.'

I didn't want Manon to hear anything more; I didn't want her witnessing what Etienne and I had to say to each other. 'Manon, please,' I said, harshly. 'Go in the house. Can't you give us a moment alone?'

'Etienne?' she asked. 'Do you wish me to leave?'

He looked at her. 'I think it would be better.'

Why was he treating her with such careful consideration? This had nothing to do with her.

She left, her silk kaftan whispering about her. Once she had disappeared, I went and sat across from Etienne. 'I think I understand, Etienne. I didn't, until Manon told me about an illness that moves from parent to child. The . . . what you called it.'

'Huntington's,' he said, his voice low, staring at his knees. 'Huntington's chorea. It strikes only in adulthood, usually after thirty, so it's often the case that the parent doesn't know of it until he or she has already produced children. There's a fifty per cent chance of it being passed from parent to child.'

We sat in silence.

'Paranoia, depression,' he said then. 'Problems with balance and coordination. Slurred speech. Seizures. Dementia. Eventually . . .' He put his face into his hands.

I stared at the top of his head as I had at Aszulay's, only the day before. A surge of pity went through me.

'I'm sorry, Etienne,' I said. 'But now I know that this is why you left me. Because you didn't want me to have to watch you suffer. But that's what people do. People who love each other. They care for each other, no matter what.'

He lifted his head and looked into my face. His eyes were so dark, flat. I wanted to know what he was thinking. Had his face always been so closed?

'But to leave without a word, Etienne. Not even to have the consideration to try and explain . . . Well, that I don't understand.' My tone was calm, now. Logical.

He looked down. 'It was cowardly,' he said, and I nodded, almost encouragingly. What did I want him to say? 'And so disrespectful to you. I know this, Sidonie. But. . .'

But what? Say you did it to protect me. Say you did it out of love for me. But as these thoughts came to me, I suddenly knew that although a person might be honourable enough to protect someone they loved, it wasn't Etienne. He wasn't honourable. He was a coward.

'I came all the way here, to North Africa, Etienne, to find you. That's how much I believed in you then. In you and me. I needed to find you, to try and understand . . . That's how much I loved you, once,' I said.

I heard the past tense. *Loved*.

'Was it all a game for you?' I asked, surprising myself, thinking of Manon's words. 'Were you only passing time with me, and I . . . I was so naive, so blind, that I believed you cared for me as I cared for you?'

'Sidonie,' he said. 'When I met you . . . I was drawn to you. You let me forget about my trouble. You were good for me. I had known with certainty, shortly before I saw you for the first time, that I hadn't escaped the genetic roulette. I knew what my future held. I didn't want to think about it. I wanted only . . . I needed not to think about it. To. . .' He stopped.

'To be distracted?' I didn't recognise my own voice. Again I was repeating Manon's words.

'Of course. It's as I told you. He never loved you.' It was Manon, in the doorway again. She came towards Etienne. 'Don't you see the obvious?'

I looked at her, then back at Etienne. 'The obvious?'

Etienne turned his face from me. 'Manon, not like this,' he said, then looked back at me. 'If I'd known where you were in Marrakesh, I would have come to you. I didn't know where you were, Sidonie,' he repeated. 'I wanted to speak to you alone. Not . . .' He stopped, and Manon laughed. A hard, brittle laugh.

'Oh, Etienne. For God's sake, speak the simple truth to the woman.' She came to him, putting her hand on his arm. 'She can take it. She may appear fragile, but underneath she's like steel. So tell her the truth. Or I will.'

And then she leaned against him and kissed him. A lingering kiss, on the mouth.

I was too shocked to respond.

Etienne pulled away, pressing trembling fingers against his forehead. Without looking at me again he left the courtyard, through the open gate. I sat where I was, stunned into silence.

'Well,' Manon said. 'Now you know.' She made a tsking sound. 'So weak. And nothing to do with his illness. He's always been that way.'

'Know what? What are you talking about?' Had I imagined the way she'd kissed him?

'He's having such a difficult time trying to come to terms with the truth. He just can't accept the fact that he did what he said he wouldn't.'

I looked at her lips. She had just kissed Etienne. Not as a sister.

'Yes,' she continued. 'He said he would not allow the jinns to pass further. He would not perpetuate his disease,' she said.

Everything was confused, wrong. 'But . . . he knows . . . there's no longer a child . . .' My voice was distant in my own ears.

Manon shrugged as if only mildly interested. 'But there is,' she said.

I shook my head. 'What do you mean?'

'Badou,' she said.

Time passed. I simply stared at her.

'I decided, when I saw him at his father's funeral, that I would punish him as he deserved to be punished. I would make him want me, let him touch and taste me. Of course I made him wait. I made him want me with such ferocity that he lost his mind. And then, finally, I gave in, knowing that he'd be back. He came to me again, and again. He had never known a woman like me. He couldn't get enough of me.'

I tried not to draw a comparison, tried not to think of the way Etienne and I had come together each time. Had there been this fire, the kind of passion Manon spoke of?

'Don't,' I whispered.

'After we became lovers, I had him purchase this house for me, and put it in my name. I had him draw up a legal document that would afford me a generous allowance every month, in perpetuity. Of course that was when I let him think I loved him, that no man could satisfy me like him. He fell for it all. He promised he would stay in Marrakesh, and work as a doctor in La Ville Nouvelle. We agreed there would be no children.

'He did not propose marriage. Of course not. He, the great French doctor, marry a lowly Moroccan servant? Oh no. I would always be his concubine. In his heart I believe he thought no woman worthy to marry. A woman for companionship, for sex, *oui*. For marriage, *non*.'

I had expected him to marry me.

'But when I had the house, and was secure, I told him. "I'm your sister," I said. I had to repeat it. He couldn't understand what I was saying.' Again she smiled, that awful, victorious smile.

I felt ill, imagining the scene. I could see her face, enjoying every moment of it, and I could also see Etienne. The horror and shock.

Etienne, always the one in control, the one with the answers, the right thing to say at the right time.

'That's why he went to America. Because he could no longer be in Marrakesh. He could no longer even be on this side of the ocean, so near to me, but never again able to possess me.'

'Manon,' I breathed, shaking my head. 'Manon.'

'But it was easy to keep track of where he was. Of course I have many influential gentleman friends in the French community. When I realised Etienne had left me pregnant—a complete accident, like you, eh?—I considered getting rid of it. It would have been easy; don't I know enough about these things? I have rid myself of others.' She stared into my eyes. 'But something told me it would be better to keep the child; a further insurance policy. I wrote regularly to Etienne over the years, telling him I was a mother, talking about the child. But I made no accusation. He never replied. And then, last year, my needs grew, Sidonie. So I wrote to him that I was sorry I had used him, that I had changed, and wanted to repent. And that there was a deep secret, something I could only tell him face to face. Of course he suspected, and so because of my urging—and to get away from you—he came back to Morocco.' Then she lowered her chin, looking at me almost coquettishly.

'Did you not wonder why Etienne—a man like Etienne, clever and worldly—wanted a woman like you, Sidonie?'

I blinked. 'What? What are you talking about?'

Manon's face was full of contempt now. 'You idiot. Can you see nothing? Etienne never stopped dreaming of me, wanting me. It's me he loves, not you. Do you not look in the mirror, and see what I see? Do you not recognise that Etienne saw in you something that reminded him of me? Of the one woman he loved? Even the fact that you painted, well . . .' She shrugged. 'Every time he held you, every time he made love to you, Sidonie, he was dreaming of me, closing his eyes and seeing me. You never meant anything to him. Nothing at all.'

I sat on my bed, seeing myself in the mirror across the room. I was exhausted. After all these months of waiting and hoping, it was over.

What Manon had told me was not inconceivable. If I hadn't seen Etienne, seen him with her, witnessed his inability to speak up to her, I might not have believed her. But I had seen it for myself.

The afternoon call to prayer came, and I looked towards the window, picking up the Blue Man's *zellij*. I thought of Aszulay.

He had told me not to wait in Marrakesh for Etienne. After we had been in the *bled* together he told me he hadn't wanted me to be alone when I went to Etienne on Sharia Zitoun. He knew the truth about Etienne and Manon, and thought that I would be devastated, shocked. He worried about me.

I was shocked, yes. But I wasn't devastated. When I had seen Etienne, I had looked at him as though he were a stranger. But had he really changed, or was it me?

I had come to Marrakesh to find Etienne. I had found him. I understood why he had left me. It was simple: he had never loved me.

I was alone again. But not in the way I had been alone before Etienne, before knowing a man, and before the thought of my own child.

I went to the table where my latest canvas—of the jacaranda tree at Sharia Zitoun—was propped against the wall. I thought of Badou opening my paintbox, so proudly and reverently in the courtyard, and at that I put my fist against my chest.

Badou. As Etienne's child, did he carry the monstrous gene in his small, perfect frame? Now I moved my fist against my mouth, thinking of the warmth of his body as I held him. I remembered my unbearable concern when I thought he was lost in the dust storm. The relief and joy when Aszulay brought him back.

The night in the truck with Aszulay, and what I had felt.

I remembered the words of Mohammed, with his monkey, in D'jemma el Fna, telling me I would find what I searched for under the Southern Cross. Mohammed had been right. I had found something.

But I couldn't keep it. Aszulay was a Blue Man of the Sahara. Badou was another woman's child. I had fallen in love with this country, its colours and sounds and smells and tastes. Its people. One tall man, one little boy.

The best I could do would be to go back to Albany and remember it with my paints. But even there, in the cold of winter, I would not paint Morocco with the detached eye of a tourist, a mere observer. I was no longer an observer, but a participant in this life.

I was lying on my bed in the darkness, still in my kaftan, when I heard men's voices in the courtyard. I recognised Mena's husband's voice, and both the sons, and then . . . It was Aszulay's voice. I rose, swiftly, and hurried to the window.

He was there, sitting with them, drinking tea. They were talking as if it were simply a friendly visit. They finished their tea, and the husband and sons stood.

Aszulay said something further, and the husband looked up. I pulled my head back from the window, but in a moment there was a quiet knock on my door.

I opened it. It was Mena. 'Aszulay is here,' she said. 'He asks to see you. Wear your face cover, Sidonie,' she said. 'My husband is home.'

I did as she asked. She went down the back stairs, the staircase the women could use to avoid going through the courtyard if a man was there. I went into the courtyard. Aszulay stood.

'Are you all right?' he said.

'Yes,' I said.

'But you've seen Etienne,' he stated. 'I went to Sharia Zitoun earlier this evening. Manon told me you had been there. She told me . . .' He stopped, and I looked at him. 'Now do you understand why I didn't tell you about Etienne immediately? Do you understand what I meant by wanting to protect you? I knew I couldn't stop you from uncovering the truth—Manon would be certain you knew everything—but I wanted you to have a few more days . . . I wanted. . .'

I sat on a bench. He didn't say anything more, also sitting down again. Finally I said, 'I understand, Aszulay. It didn't go well at all this afternoon.' As I uttered the words, I suddenly thought of Badou. The last thing he'd witnessed was me slapping Etienne, screaming at him. I put my hand over my eyes, imagining the distress and fear on his face as he ran to Falida, both their expressions as they fled the courtyard.

'Sidonie?' Aszulay said, and I lowered my hand.

'I was thinking of Badou,' I said. 'Poor child.'

'It's not been good for him,' he said. 'I have tried to make life a little better for him.'

I nodded. 'I'm glad he has you. I can't bear to think of him growing up with Manon. And what's so heartbreaking,' I said, tearing away my veil, not caring about Mena's husband at that moment, 'is the thought of what he might carry.'

'Carry?'

'You know. The disease. Huntington's chorea.'

'I don't understand,' Aszulay said.

I stared at him. 'What don't you understand?'

'Manon doesn't appear to have it. So why would Badou?'

'But . . . Etienne. Etienne has it.'

'Yes. He's his half-uncle, but it has to come through a parent. Isn't that true? That's what Manon told me.'

I shook my head. 'Aszulay. You don't know? Manon never told you that Badou is Etienne's child?'

'Manon doesn't know with certainty who the father is.'

I swallowed. 'But she does. She told me it was Etienne.'

Aszulay stood and walked quickly, once, around the courtyard, as if trying to contain his anger.

Then he came back and sat across from me again. He shook his head, staring at the wall behind me. I knew him well enough to understand he was composing himself. Finally he looked into my face.

'Manon was with Etienne before he went to America, yes. But she was also with two other men at the same time: a Jew from Fez and a Spaniard from Tangier. And Badou was born ten months after Etienne left for America. His father is either the Jew or the Spaniard.'

'But. . .'

'Sidonie. Manon says what she thinks will achieve her purpose. She's told you other lies, and still you believe her.'

'Her purpose?'

'Her purpose is to hurt you. From the first day I saw you—and saw how Manon treated you—I knew what she was doing. She was initially jealous of you for the main reason, but I've seen her grow more so, because now you have taken not only Badou's attention, but also . . .' He stopped.

'The main reason?' I asked, when he didn't go on.

'She's jealous because she fears that perhaps her brother did love you. Even though she didn't want him once she'd achieved her purpose, she couldn't bear to think of him loving anyone else.' He leaned his back against the wall. 'Manon is like this. Surely you see it.'

I watched his mouth as he spoke.

'She cannot bear to be second-rate; she says it's how she was made to feel, always, as she grew up. She does not want to share anyone with you. Anyone. You have the evidence.' He leaned forward and took my hand, turning it over and running his thumb over the tiny mark in my palm. 'What she did to you, when she knew I chose to spend time with you. How she harmed you.'

I was still concentrating on the fact that Aszulay had said that Manon was afraid Etienne had loved me.

'He was so weak,' I said, trying not to let hostility come into my voice. 'And if he'd actually loved me, as she suspected, he wouldn't have left the way he did.'

I acknowledged the truth of what I had just voiced.

'She told Etienne Badou was his so he would give her money,' I said.

Aszulay nodded. 'She wanted him to provide more for her—in the name of Badou, of course. But I think she meant only to play on his conscience, ask him for money as Badou's uncle. But it was when he spoke of you—I was there—of a woman in America, one who carried his child, that she flew into a rage. He said he didn't know what to do; that he couldn't face it. It was then she told him Badou was his. Like you, he believed Manon; it didn't occur to him she would lie about Badou. He didn't know she had been with other men while she was with him; he didn't know Badou's exact date of birth. For him the circumstances and timing were correct. I heard her, and knew what she was doing. I was so angry with her. I opened my mouth to argue, to tell Etienne the truth, that she lied. But Etienne jumped up; he said his goal was to try and stop it, by not passing on the disease to a future generation. And yet now he had done it not once, but twice; he had already created one child—your child, Sidonie—and now he had just discovered he had created a second. Badou. His face was white as he stood, shaking. I grabbed his arm, telling him, "No, wait, Etienne," but he rushed out into the night.'

I could imagine the scene.

'I argued with Manon, and told her she must tell him the truth. But she said he deserved shame, and humiliation. That maybe now he would know how she had felt, betrayed by their father.' He stopped. 'Manon and Etienne are similar, Sidonie, in their thoughts of themselves. This is their common characteristic.'

I knew he was right.

'Nevertheless, I stayed there all night,' he continued, 'waiting for Etienne to return, in spite of Manon's fury at me. I was going to tell him the truth, that Badou wasn't his.' He gripped his own hands. I saw the corded veins standing on the backs of them. They were hands that could use a shovel with such strength, and could hold a child with such delicacy. 'But he didn't return. He simply didn't come back. He left his clothes, his books, even his glasses. A few weeks later he sent a letter to Manon—the one I first told you about—saying he had had time to think, and would take responsibility for his child. He would come and see him, every few months. He said in this way he would at least make sure the child wanted for nothing.'

I nodded. Manon thought she had won. In this way she could continue asking for anything from Etienne. And he would provide it, out of guilt. We sat in silence, apart from the occasional sound of a dove.

'And so—have you told him?'

Aszulay shook his head. 'When I picked up Badou, before we went to the country, Etienne was there, as I told you. But it wasn't the right time. Badou was present, and Manon hurried us out. And he had said he would stay for some time. I knew I would tell him when we returned from the *bled*. And I went there tonight, to speak of it to him, but he was out, Manon said. But she knows what I wish to do, and will prevent me in any way she can. She's told me I'm not welcome any more; she says I'm not to come back to Sharia Zitoun.'

I thought of how Etienne had left this afternoon, and wondered if he'd run off again, the way he ran to America when he found out the woman he loved was his half-sister. The way he ran back to Morocco when I told him I was pregnant. The way he ran to another city when Manon told him Badou was his. This was how Etienne dealt with what he didn't want to face. By running away.

'All I can do is hope, somehow, to see him again, and tell him the truth. But it will be difficult. Manon will see to that.'

We sat in silence.

'And now, Sidonie?' he asked. 'What will you do?'

'I . . . there's nothing more for me here. In Marrakesh.' I looked at him, waiting for him to say what I wanted him to say. Needed him to say. *Stay, Sidonie. I want you to stay. Stay and be with me.*

He didn't speak for a long time, nor did he look at me. I saw his throat move as he swallowed, and then he said, 'I understand. This is a country so different from what you have known. You need freedom. You would be a prisoner here.'

'A prisoner?'

Finally he looked at me again.

'A woman here . . . it's not the same as America, as Spain, as France. All the countries in the world where a woman like you can do as she wishes. As she pleases.'

I wanted to ask him what he meant by *a woman like you*. I thought of my life in Albany. Had I been free?

'I haven't felt that I've been a prisoner here,' I said. 'Yes, at first it was difficult. I was . . . afraid. But that was partly because I was alone, and came on a mission that perhaps . . . perhaps I wasn't sure about, although I convinced myself that I was. But since I've known . . . since I've been part of Marrakesh, lived here, in the medina, I've still been somewhat unsure of my actions, but not unsure about how I feel. I feel alive. Even my painting is different. It's alive as well, in a way it never was before.'

'But, as you say, the reason you came to Marrakesh no longer matters.'

'Yes. Etienne no longer matters.' I turned from Aszulay's eyes, staring at the tiles on the floor. Didn't he know what I wanted him to say? Hadn't he sought me out, invited me to come to the gardens, to his family in the countryside? Hadn't he shown concern about me when he knew Etienne was in Marrakesh? He'd just said that Manon was jealous because she knew Aszulay cared about me.

Had I completely misread him? But the time we'd spent in the *bled* . . . the way he looked at me. The way we'd told each other about our lives. His mouth on mine.

But he wasn't asking me to stay. Had I been so wrong?

'Maybe . . . maybe I'll just stay to finish the last canvas for the hotel,' I said, forcing myself to look back at him.

He nodded.

I willed him to say something more. But he didn't. He stood, and went towards the gate.

I rose, following him, and put my hand on his arm.

'Is this goodbye, then, Aszulay? Will . . . is this the last time we'll see each other?' I could barely speak the words. I couldn't say goodbye to him. I couldn't.

He looked down at me, his eyes somehow dark, in spite of their light colour. 'Is this what you wish?'

Aszulay! I wanted to shout. Stop being so . . . polite. I shook my head. 'No. It isn't. I don't want to say goodbye.'

He didn't move any closer to me. 'And . . . do you think . . . could you truly live in a place such as this? Live, Sidonie. Raise children.' He stopped. 'And endure the differences between the world you once knew, and this world.'

I couldn't speak. He was asking me too many questions, but not the right one.

'Can you see this life clearly?' he asked then, and again, I was confused by his words, and just looked into his eyes.

And then I opened my mouth. *Yes*, I was about to say. *Yes, yes, I can see it with you*, but he spoke first.

'You don't have the answer,' he stated. 'I understand more than you realise.' He turned from me then, going out of the courtyard, shutting the gate quietly.

I sat on the bench, not sure of what had just happened.

Chapter Twelve

OVER THE NEXT FEW DAYS I did what I had told Aszulay I would do. I completed my final painting, delivering it to Monsieur Henri and collecting my payment for the others that had been sold.

'Your work has become popular in such a short time, mademoiselle,' he said. 'The owner of a gallery on Rue de la Fontaine has mentioned he would like to speak to you.' He gave me a card.

I sat in the coolness of the lobby, looking at the envelope and the printed card. Dare I think that I could sustain myself by my painting in Albany? Would I find the interest for my work there that I had had here?

But I couldn't bear to think of Albany, and Juniper Road.

I walked slowly back into the medina, followed, of course, by Najeeb. As we passed Sharia Zitoun, I instinctively looked, as I always did, at the niche in the wall.

Since that first time, seeing Badou and Falida hiding there with the kittens, I had never seen them there again. But now I made out a shadowy figure.

I went closer. It was Falida, with a small grey kitten on her lap.

'Falida,' I said, and she jumped. She looked up at me, her eyes too big in her thin face. There was something stricken about her. 'What is it? What's wrong, Falida?'

Her eyes glistened. For all I had seen her mistreated by Manon, I hadn't seen her cry. 'I am on the street, mademoiselle,' she said.

'Manon turned you out?'

'They're all gone.'

'All gone? What do you mean?'

'My lady and the man. Gone. And Badou. I don't want to be on the street. It's not good for a girl on the street. Bad things will happen to me. I'm afraid, mademoiselle.' She put the kitten to her face, as if hiding her tears from me. But her narrow shoulders shook.

I leaned down, putting my hand on her forearm. 'Falida. Tell me what happened.'

She lifted her head. Her lips were dry. I wondered when she had last eaten. 'My lady and the men. They fight.'

'Etienne? She fought with Monsieur Duverger?'

'All men, mademoiselle. Monsieur Olivier and Aszulay and Monsieur Etienne. Always fighting. Badou is afraid. He cries and cries.'

'But . . . where did they go? And who? Was it Manon and Etienne and Badou? Did they go somewhere?'

Falida shook her head. 'The other one. Monsieur Olivier. He said he take my lady, but not Badou. He don't want Badou. My lady said she give Badou to Monsieur Etienne. But Aszulay talk to Monsieur Etienne, then Monsieur Etienne fight with my lady and goes away and don't come back. My lady . . . she so angry. Badou and me hide. We afraid. She bad when she angry; she hit us. We hide here, but then night comes, and I don't know what to do. Badou hungry, cries all the time. I take him back to my lady, she give me a paper, and bag with Badou clothes. She tell me take him to Aszulay, and give Aszulay paper.'

'And . . . did you?'

Falida nodded. 'Aszulay not there. I leave Badou with servant. She tell me go away.' Falida put her face against the kitten, and once more tears shone on her cheeks.

'When did this happen?' I asked.

'Two nights I on street,' she said.

'Do you know how long Manon has gone for this time? With Monsieur Olivier?'

Falida shook her head.

'Come with me,' I said, and she put the kitten back into the hole in the wall and stood, and I took her hand.

We went back to Sharia Soura, and I gave her bread and a plate of chicken and couscous, ignoring Nawar's glares. I had the servant heat water, and after Falida had eaten, I let her bathe in my room, giving her one of my kaftans to put on. When I went to check on her, she was asleep, breathing in deep, exhausted sighs. As my room dimmed, I lay beside her on the mattress, and closed my own eyes.

I awoke in the night. Falida was curled against me. I put my arm over her and went back to sleep.

The next morning I combed Falida's hair for her, braided it into two long tails, and gave her breakfast. Although she was so thin, I noticed the kaftan was the right length; she was already almost as tall as me.

When we'd eaten breakfast, I called to Najeeb.

'Can you take me to Aszulay's house?' I asked Falida. I wasn't sure I could find it from Sharia Soura.

She nodded, and with Najeeb following, we went through the medina until I recognised Aszulay's street.

I went to his gate and knocked.

Aszulay opened it, Badou at his side.

'Falida!' Badou said, in a delighted voice, and grinned at me. 'Another tooth is loose, Sidonie,' he said, showing me one on the bottom, rocking it back and forth with his index finger.

Falida kneeled, putting her arms around him. He hugged her quickly, then pulled away, speaking into her face, his words an excited jumble. 'We were looking for you yesterday. Guess what? Oncle Aszulay said the next time we go to the *bled* I can bring back a puppy. And we're going to teach it to fetch a stick, like Ali's dog. And you can help us, Falida. Isn't that right, Oncle Aszulay?'

'Yes,' Aszulay said, looking at me, not the children. He wore a simple dark blue jellaba. He didn't smile. 'Take Falida into the house and give her some of the melon we've prepared for lunch, Badou.'

I watched the children leave the courtyard. My hands trembled slightly. I didn't know if I could look at Aszulay, didn't know what I'd say.

'Poor things,' I said, still in the doorway of the courtyard. 'What's happened? Falida said Manon went away with Olivier.'

'Sidonie,' he said, and by the way he said my name I had to look at him. 'I didn't know if I'd . . .' He stopped, his face so still, so serious. So beautiful. I wanted to touch it.

He glanced at Najeeb, still standing behind me. 'Will you stay for a while? I don't like speaking in this manner, in the doorway.' His face was still unreadable.

When I nodded, a tiny muscle in his cheek twitched. He spoke to Najeeb, and the boy left. Aszulay took my arm and pulled me inside, shutting the gate. I was suddenly weak, and leaned against it.

'I told Etienne the truth,' Aszulay said. 'I went the next morning, after seeing you at Sharia Soura, and told him that Badou wasn't his.'

I waited, watching Aszulay's face.

'He was relieved, of course. He said he would leave the city immediately; even as an uncle, he had no real interest in the boy. He won't be back to Marrakesh.'

Still I said nothing.

'He asked me . . . he wanted me to tell you that he was sorry. Sorry for the pain he caused you. And to wish you well, and to ask that you will some day forgive him.'

I looked down. I didn't know what to feel, didn't want to talk about Etienne with Aszulay. We stood in silence.

'And Manon?' I finally said, when I could again look at him.

'Manon finally has what she always wanted. She left me a letter. She's arranged to have her house sold, and has gone to live in France. With Olivier. I don't know how long he'll be blinded by her; she has the same hold over him she has with all men, at least at the beginning. But if he proves to be like the others, he'll tire of her moods, her demands. Before too long she will lose her appeal.'

'And then she'll return?'

He shrugged. 'Who knows? But there will be nothing here for her any more. Without her house, without her son, without any friends—I cannot call her a friend any longer.'

'But . . . Badou. Manon simply left him?'

He looked over his shoulder, at the house. 'In her letter she wrote that since I was so concerned about the child's future, interfering and destroying her plan to have Etienne take Badou, now I could take responsibility for him. He was of no further use to her. So she discarded him, as she has done to all those who are of no further use.'

He stood in front of me, looking down at me, and then moved closer and put his hand on my cheek, covering the old scar. 'But of course this is not a hardship.' He stopped. 'I love the child.'

I tried to think of something to say, but was too aware of his hand on my cheek, of standing so near to him. I felt the warmth of his fingers, and wondered if when he removed them they would leave a faint blue stain.

'Twice I went to Sharia Soura to speak to you,' he said. 'Both times I was told you weren't there.'

'But Mena didn't tell—'

'They think we are incorrigible. You and I, Sidonie. They don't approve.' He smiled, so slightly, as he said it.

I waited.

'I am an honest man,' he said. 'Tuaregs abide by a code of honesty, and of bravery.'

'I know,' I whispered.

'I was honest with you, the other night, when I said I understand more than you realise. I do understand what you want. That you want to stay. And since the night I came to Sharia Soura when Manon hurt you, and you held my hand against your lips . . . since that night

I couldn't hide my feelings from myself. You are different from any woman I've known, Sidonie.'

I watched his mouth.

'You are willing to be afraid, to accept fear, and move with it. But you also made me afraid, Sidonie. I was afraid that if I asked you to stay with me. . .'

He stopped.

'Afraid of what?' I said, or perhaps whispered.

'I thought it would be easier if you said no. But if you said yes, I was afraid that in time you wouldn't be happy, and would want your former life again. Even with your painting. With Badou and Falida, with . . . with children of our own. That what I have to give you won't be enough. Our lives have been so different, so . . .'

I stepped closer to him. I smelled the sweetness of melon on his lips. 'I can see my life here, with you,' I said.

A bird trilled in the branches overhead.

'You see it? It is enough?' he said softly, his eyes fixed on mine.

I waited until the bird had finished its song. 'Yes,' I said. 'It is enough.'

Inshallah, I thought. *Inshallah*.

Linda Holeman

Can you tell us a little about where you live?

I grew up in Winnipeg, Manitoba, the only city in the central province of Canada that is situated on the prairies, so it's flat and geographically isolated. It reaches bone-chilling temperatures in the winter (down to –30ºC) and can be very hot in the summer (+30ºC). It's a difficult climate, but the people are friendly and warm. I lived in Winnipeg for much of my life—travelling widely from there—but for the last two years I've lived in Toronto. I'm divorced and have three children, all travellers and explorers, all curious and interested in the world, as I am.

You began writing novels for young adults. Is this harder or easier than writing adult fiction?

This is a tricky question to answer. Writing is difficult, period. But when writing for young adults I'm very aware of the audience. I am more conscious of the fact that certain scenes, especially those containing sex or extreme violence or explicit language, should be tempered. The other difference is that I am very aware of ending a novel for young people with hope. It's not that I will necessarily end an adult novel with doom and gloom, but I'm more conscious of making sure young readers are left with the sense that many obstacles can be overcome, and that there truly is goodness in the world.

With adults, it is what it is. So, in effect, I feel more freedom in writing for adults.

How do you begin researching your novels?

For unknown reasons I always want to write about places and peoples I know nothing about: it's the curiosity about the world I mentioned earlier. I start, usually, by reading whatever I can that has been written in the particular era and geographical location I want to write about. I read non-fiction for the facts, and novels for the voice and mindset. I search online and, if possible, I watch films pertinent to my novel and listen to the music of the place and time. I find people to talk to. I love research. What I uncover often changes the actual shape of my story.

Marrakesh was the spark for this novel. What are your most vivid memories of your visit there?

Ah, Marrakesh. I have been there twice and I know I will go back. There is so much to love about Marrakesh: the setting sun like a brilliant red ball as it sinks low over the ramparts of the medina; the calls from the minarets before the birds are stirring; the eyes of the veiled women; the aroma of grilling meat on the streets. And the magic that is D'jemma el Fna, the great square in the middle of the old city. I was, at first, wary, because it's overwhelming on the initial experience. But when I let myself go and opened myself to its charms, I couldn't get enough of it.

Did you travel across the desert?

Yes, I crossed the High Atlas mountains by jeep, driving to the tiny village of Mhamid on the edge of the Sahara. From there I went by a combination of camel and jeep into the desert, ending up at a nomad camp near the Algerian border. It was a magical and spiritual experience. I found it difficult to re-enter the real world when my time there was over.

The novel depicts the restricted life of Muslim women and also the unexpected freedom of 'being invisible'. Do you think you could live this way?

No, I couldn't. Not after having lived in the world the way I have. Sidonie, in 1930, having known only a very small and restricted life, finds an unexpected freedom in her new existence. That said, what I do like is the feeling of anonymity I have in foreign countries. I know I will see nobody I know, and nobody knows me. I have a sense of re-creating myself, if only to myself, if that makes sense. And I like that feeling.

Where will your next adventure be?

Because my next book will be set in nineteenth-century Russia, I intend to return there for research purposes. I want to explore St Petersburg again and then go off on both the Siberian Express and the Mongolian Express. I love trains. That's the plan, but I never know. I'm spontaneous and may suddenly disappear into quite another adventure—if the opportunity arises!

THE QUEEN OF NEW BEGINNINGS. Original full-length edition Copyright © Erica James 2010. Published at £14.99 by Orion Books, an imprint of The Orion Publishing Group Ltd. British condensed edition © The Reader's Digest Association, Inc., 2010.

THE GIRL WHO CHASED THE MOON. Original full-length edition Copyright © Sarah Addison Allen 2010. Published at £12.99 by Hodder & Stoughton, An Hachette UK Company. British condensed edition © The Reader's Digest Association, Inc., 2010.

THE SAFFRON GATE. Original full-length edition Copyright © 2009 Linda Holeman. Published at £12.99 by Headline Review, an imprint of Headline Publishing Group. British condensed edition © The Reader's Digest Association, Inc., 2010.

The right to be identified as authors has been asserted by the following in accordance with sections 77 and 78 of the Copyright, Designs and Patents Act, 1988: Erica James, Sarah Addison Allen, Linda Holeman.

PICTURE CREDITS: COVER: © Imagebank. Erica James's photograph and page 180 © Mikael Mammen. Sarah Addison Allen's photograph and page 300 © courtesy of Random House. Linda Holeman's photograph and page 478 © Andrea Downey-Franchuk. THE QUEEN OF NEW BEGINNINGS: pages 6 & 7: Richard Merritt@The Organisation. THE GIRL WHO CHASED THE MOON: pages 182 & 183: Narrinder Singh@velvet tamarind; image: iStock. THE SAFFRON GATE: pages 302 & 303: Kate Baxter@velvet tamarind; image: Digital Vision.

Printed and bound by GGP Media GmbH, Pössneck, Germany

601-055 UP0000-1